FROM RUSSIA WITH LUST

THE NIKOLAI DANTE OMNIBUS

THE STRANGELOVE GAMBIT • IMPERIAL BLACK • HONOUR BE DAMNED!

It's 2672 AD. In a future where the Russian Revolution never happened, Nikolai Dante is the most wanted man in the Empire. A multi-million rouble price has been put up for his capture, but the Russian rogue always likes to live life on the edge. Swashbuckling, drinking, womanising... it's a tough life being an outlaw!

Nikolai Dante
Created by **Robbie Morrison** and **Simon Fraser**

FROM RUSSIA WITH LUST

THE NIKOLAI DANTE OMNIBUS

David Bishop

A Black Flame Publication
www.blackflame.com
blackflame@games-workshop.co.uk

The Strangelove Gambit and Imperial Black copyright © 2005, Honour Be Damned!
copyright © 2006 Rebellion A/S. All rights reserved.

This omnibus edition published in 2007 by BL Publishing, Games Workshop Ltd.,
Willow Road, Nottingham NG7 2WS, UK

Distributed in the US by Simon & Schuster, 1230 Avenue of the Americas, New York,
NY 10020, USA

Distributed in the UK by Simon & Schuster, Africa House, 64-78 Kingway, London,
WC2B 6AH, UK

10 9 8 7 6 5 4 3 2 1

Cover illustration by Rachel Haupt.

ISBN 13: 978 1 84416 454 7
ISBN 10: 1 84416 454 3

A CIP record for this book is available from the British Library.

Printed in the UK by Bookmarque, Surrey, UK.

CONTENTS

THE STRANGELOVE GAMBIT

ONE

"The wicked flatter to the face, then stab in the back"
– Russian proverb

The scent, smoke and sweat of a casino are nauseating at three in the morning. But the Casino Royale was a different place at three in the afternoon. Its windows and doors were thrown open, allowing fresh air and natural light into the crimson chamber normally designated Members Only. Ashtrays were emptied and polished, carpets cleaned and deodorised, lingering fingerprint smears of desperation removed from the brass fixtures and fittings. The casino interior was being scoured clean with a surgeon's precision.

James Di Grizov watched the preparations and smiled. All his life he had been a grifter in the Vorovskoi Mir, the Thieves' World. Di Grizov had developed and nurtured a reputation as a master escapologist, able to get himself out of almost any situation. But the big score, that single, career-making heist, had eluded him – until now. In a few hours this casino would be choked with the Empire's rich and famous, all gathered for the most talked about event of 2660: an auction. A single item was going under the hammer, but it had generated more interest than any lot in living memory – and Di Grizov planned to steal it.

Satisfied with the results of his final reconnoitre, the silver-haired thief returned to his suite in the adjoining hotel complex. The Casino Royale had trebled its room rates for the week of the auction. The sale was being handled by Sotheby's of Britannia, preventing the casino from claiming any percentage of the final price. But the indirect benefits were plentiful and the casino's management was determined to gouge all they could from them. Di Grizov had spent every kopeck he possessed to cover the deposit on his suite. Fortunately he would be absconding long before the final bill was due for payment. Di Grizov was known in the Vorovskoi Mir as a grifter who had never paid a bill in his life.

A retinal scanner outside the hotel room confirmed his identity and the door slid open with the silky ease of an Imperial courtesan's lingerie coming undone. Inside, the suite was wall-to-wall luxury, its gold and black decor reminiscent of a painted whore. Di Grizov ignored the glitzy interior and strode out on to the balcony. Sprawled below was Monaco, a tiny principality whose sole purpose for hundreds of years had been the pursuit of hedonism. Fewer than fifty thousand people lived in this Mediterranean enclave, but its borders contained many of the Empire's wealthiest individuals. Only the richest and the most beautiful dared venture out on the streets, strolling along the boulevards and nodding to those they deemed worthy of recognition.

The bay was awash with pleasure cruisers, each costing more than the gross national product of minor provinces like Domacha or Rudinshtein. The azure sea stretched out lazily to the horizon, merging seamlessly with the cloudless sky. All was bathed in brilliant sunshine, the resort bronzed and magnificent. If I believed in God, Di Grizov thought, He would come here to relax.

Only one thing spoiled the ambience, a recurrent snoring with all the timbre and tenderness of a chainsaw. Di Grizov sighed and turned to where his teenage assistant was slumbering on a sun lounger. They had first met six months earlier, when Di Grizov caught the upstart trying to pick his pocket at Tsyganov Black Market in St Petersburg. The veteran had almost turned the callow cutpurse in but something had stopped him. Perhaps I recognised a little of myself in him, the grifter thought. But was I ever this stupid?

His protégé had dozed off while reading a book, *Masterpieces from the House of Fabergé*. The hefty tome now rested on the youth's chest, masking a section of skin from the sun. The rest of the recumbent body was now a livid red, except for a triangular area covered by a pair of minuscule black trunks. The most vivid area of crimson was the youth's face. Surrounded by unruly black hair, the features were plain and unremarkable. Age and experience would give his face character but for now it was like an empty page, waiting for a life story.

Di Grizov slapped a hand down hard on his assistant's sunburnt thigh, shocking the sleeper into a sudden consciousness.

"Bojemoi!" Nikolai Dante shouted in pain and surprise, jolting upright.

"Never fall asleep on a job," Di Grizov said sternly. "And certainly never fall asleep in the sun, lest you suffer the consequences."

Dante looked down at his angry pink skin. The neglected book slid out of position, revealing a pale white rectangle where it had been resting. "Fuoco," the teenager muttered. "I always knew I was hot stuff, but this–"

"Is not what I meant by 'Get to know our target'," Di Grizov interjected. "You were supposed to be learning more about the reason we're here, not working on your tan!"

Dante shrugged sheepishly. "Sorry. I couldn't resist."

"That's your problem in a nutshell, boy. You can't resist anything." Di Grizov tried to sound angry but Dante's cherry-red face was too comical. "Take a cold shower and then I'll grill you on what you've learned."

The youth pointed at his sunburn. "Don't you think I've been grilled enough for one day?"

"The auction begins in five hours. We have to be ready. Now go!"

Kurt Brockman raised an eyebrow. "Good afternoon. Tonight on the Bolshoi Arts Channel, we bring you live and exclusive coverage of the bidding for one of the legendary Imperial Easter Eggs, created nearly seven hundred and fifty years ago by fabled jeweller Carl Fabergé. So make sure you tune in to catch all the auction action, live and exclusive, here on the Bolshoi Arts Channel. Don't miss it!" Brockman maintained his pose for five seconds before the red light above the camera filming him blinked off. His sculpted chin, piercing gaze and broad chest all suggested authority, intelligence and an athletic physique worthy of any Adonis. Once the brief transmission was over, Brockman abandoned his masculine on-screen persona and became a simpering bundle of nerves, shoulders slumping forwards, hands flopping about limply in the air. "Yuri, darling. How was it that time? Yuri?"

"Lovely, sweetie. Lovely," a camp voice replied via Brockman's earpiece. "Now we need you to interview the Fabergé expert, Kenworth Snowman. Lots of open-ended questions this time, love – let him do the talking for once, alright?"

"Are you saying I talk too much during interviews, Yuri?"

"Darling, the only time you don't talk too much is when you've got your mouth full," the director snapped back archly. "And try not to stand in front of the bloody egg this time, alright love? We need to see what the expert is talking about, not you trying to hold in your gut."

Brockman muttered an obscenity under his breath.

"What was that, darling?" the director asked.

"Nothing you need to worry about, love," Brockman cooed back. He beckoned to a short, bespectacled man sitting patiently nearby. The bookish expert scuttled over to join Brockman, self consciously brushing specks of dandruff from the shoulders of his tweed jacket. "Now, Mr Snowman–"

"Professor Snowman, actually."

"My apologies, Professor Snowman," Brockman continued, smiling thinly. "Perhaps you could tell our viewers about the fascinating history of this rare and unique objet d'art?" The presenter gestured expansively to the item displayed behind him on a pedestal of black onyx, guarded by a fearsome laser defence grid and a quartet of muscular casino security men.

At the centre of these defences was a steel egg, slightly larger in size than an ostrich egg, with two fine rings of inlaid gold encircling the polished silver surface. Set around the widest part of the circumference were four golden crests, while a small gold replica of an Imperial crown was fixed to its top. The egg sat in the centre of a square formed by four bullet-shaped cylinders, each made of polished silver and ringed with gold. These protruded from a sculpted square of green marble, itself edged with gold. The object was both beautiful and sinister, a work of art made in praise of military might.

"Well, the Steel Military Egg is certainly rare but we cannot say for certain it is unique," Professor Snowman began. Short, wild-eyed and frantic of hair, the expert from Britannia had been flown over especially for the auction coverage. It was a rare opportunity for the crusty academic, his enthusiasm evident in the hushed reverence of his words. "The House of Fabergé jewellers are believed to have constructed more than fifty Imperial eggs between 1885 and the first Russian revolution in 1917. Each was commissioned and given away as an Easter present by the Romanov Tsar of the time to his family and friends. In those days Easter was among the most important dates of celebration for those of the Russian Orthodox religion. Inside each egg was an exquisite surprise, handcrafted wonders that were often automated. Examples of these hidden delights were tiny birds that sang or miniature walking elephants.

"Nearly three-quarters of a millennium have elapsed and it was believed all the fabled Fabergé eggs had been lost or destroyed – until this one came up for auction. It's possible others have also survived and still remain in private hands. So to call the Steel Military Egg unique may be misleading your viewers. Obviously, all the Imperial Easter Eggs were unique in and of themselves, but there may still be other eggs out there. It's a not unimportant distinction, I feel."

"Fascinating, I'm sure." Brockman rolled his eyes before nodding to the camera. The red light on top of it blinked on and the recording began. "Professor Snowman, you've been telling me about the significance of the item up for auction today. Perhaps you could share that knowledge with our viewers?"

The flustered expert peered at the camera in dismay. "I thought I just had. You mean to say that thing wasn't switched on before?"

"Cut!" Brockman shouted, stamping a foot petulantly.

"Did I do something wrong?" Snowman asked ingenuously.

"No, no, professor, nothing at all," the reporter replied, his voice dripping with sarcasm and disdain.

"So that was your fault?"

Brockman resisted the urge to scream. "Yes, professor, that was my fault. Shall we start again?"

Dante stifled a yawn while watching the interview on Channel 88. The expert was droning on and on about the changing styles of late nineteenth century jewellery design, not a subject for which the apprentice thief had much enthusiasm. His interest was stirred when Brockman began asking about a legendary curse that was said to afflict anyone who touched a particular Fabergé egg.

"Superstitious nonsense," Snowman snapped grumpily. "Just because every member of the Tsar's family who touched the egg was dead within a year doesn't mean this item is cursed. As a scientist I cannot endorse such a fanciful and, frankly, implausible notion!"

"But isn't it true that you yourself have refused to lay a hand upon the Steel Military Egg?" Brockman persisted.

"That is simply to preserve the lustre and appearance of the object."

"You might say that, professor, but I'm sure the viewers can reach their own conclusions," the presenter replied smoothly, winking slyly to the camera.

Dante shouted across the suite to his mentor. "You never told me about this egg being cursed, Jim!"

Di Grizov was busy in the luxurious bathroom disguising his appearance with the addition of a false goatee beard and moustache. "It's all in the book, if you'd bothered to read it."

By now the coverage on Channel 88 had switched to outside the casino, showing the arrival of various celebrities and representatives from noble houses. Dante's interest was soon aroused by something on screen. "Fuoco! You could have somebody's eyes out with those," he enthused.

A transformed Di Grizov emerged to find his apprentice staring lustily at a considerable décolletage filling the viewscreen. "Do you ever think of anything besides sex?"

Dante grinned wolfishly. "When you're packing as much manhood as me, you can't help but appreciate those just as well-endowed in other areas."

"The endowment in question belongs to whom?"

"Er, can't say I caught her name…"

Di Grizov sighed wearily. "That's Princess Marie-Anne from the House of Windsor in Britannia. Ambitious, ruthless and utterly amoral. Her father is supposed to be going insane, leaving Marie-Anne free to spend his wealth as she sees fit. We can expect her to be in at the kill when the auction gets going."

"Sounds like my kind of woman," Dante announced. "Think she'll fancy a diamond in the rough?"

"Nikolai, you may be rough, but the princess would be polishing a long time before she transformed you into a diamond of any sort."

"Long as she doesn't give me friction burns, she can rub me up the wrong way anytime."

"Try having a thought that originates above your waist for once in your life, please?" Di Grizov pleaded in exasperation.

Dante held up both hands in mock surrender. "Sorry. I just enjoy making you despair."

"Nevertheless, we are here on a job, so let's concentrate on that. Who's arriving now?" The grifter pointed at the viewscreen where a handsome man with light brown hair was alighting from a hovercar. A double-headed eagle crest was sewn into the fabric on the upper arm of his pristine white jacket.

"That's the symbol of the Romanovs," Dante said. "They're the oldest of the noble houses, the family line dating back to before the creation of the Fabergé eggs. Judging by the beauty of his companion that must be Andreas, the playboy of the Romanovs. He never sleeps with the same woman two nights in a row, according to legend."

"Very good," Di Grizov said. "I'm glad to see you've done some research!"

"He's my role model," Dante admitted sheepishly.

"I should have guessed. No doubt Andreas will be bidding on behalf of his father, Dmitri. Doubtful the Romanovs will stay the course. Most of their resources are tied up in a cold war of attrition with the Tsar. Andreas is here to be seen and to see what everyone else does."

Next on to the red-carpeted steps outside the casino was Mikhail Deriabin, media baron and House of Bolshoi patriarch. His curly brown hair swept back from a pinched face, a monocle held in front of his right eye. He was clad in a finely tailored dinner jacket of black and blue, his head tossed back at a haughty angle. At his side stood a poised, elegant woman in a simple silk gown of red and orange. Brockman appeared from inside the casino and began interviewing his boss, simpering with obsequiousness.

"Arse-licker," Dante sneered. "Who's the woman with Deriabin?"

"The Firebird," Di Grizov replied, his face alive with admiration as he watched her on screen. "She is Ballerina Queen of the Danse Macabre, the greatest dancer of our age. I saw her perform once when I was playing a long con. Such elegance, such finesse."

The last to arrive for the auction was a cruel-faced man with closely cropped black hair. He was alone and refused to be interviewed by Brockman, waving the presenter away with a curt gesture.

"Doctor Fabergé – I wonder what he's doing here?" Di Grizov stroked his chin thoughtfully, watching the final guest disappear inside.

"Fabergé? Like the egg guy?" Dante asked.

"Carl Fabergé was the jeweller who designed the Imperial Easter Eggs. He died hundreds of years ago. The man who just arrived is a scientist called Dr Karl Fabergé. He and Raoul Sequanna co-founded GenetiCo, a genetics research company much favoured by the Tsar. But why come to an event like this? He can't imagine being able to successfully bid for the egg…"

Dante shrugged. "Guess we'll find out tonight. The auction starts soon."

"Hello and welcome back to our live and exclusive coverage of the Auction of the Century! I'm Kurt Brockman, your host for this evening's event here on the House of Bolshoi Arts Channel." The presenter paused and looked over his shoulder at the assembled throng of the rich and famous. "Well, it seems anybody who's anybody is here in this room tonight, waiting for their chance to bid on the fabled Steel Military Egg. The only noble dynasty not represented is that of our beloved Tsar, the House of Makarov. Could the Tsar be the mystery seller of this much-vaunted item? Sotheby's have refused to be drawn on the seller's identity, but speculation remains–" Brockman stopped to hold a finger up to one ear, his face a mask of concentration. "I'm hearing the auction is about to begin, so I'll let the action speak for itself from now on…"

In the auction room a hush descended upon those assembled. All one hundred seats were occupied by some of the best-fed posteriors in the Empire. Ladies fanned themselves with sale programmes as heat from the television lights began to overwhelm the casino's air conditioning system. Those who had arrived too late to claim a seat stood around the walls, Di Grizov and Dante scattered among them, the two men careful to avoid each other.

After an awkward pause a chubby auctioneer appeared from between two curtains of crimson velvet and approached the podium. At his signal the curtains parted to reveal the egg on its pedestal, surrounded by security guards. The audience found their voices again, a babble of excitement passing round the chamber. The auctioneer dabbed a white cotton handkerchief against his sweaty brow and gripped the podium. He clasped a small wooden gavel and rapped it three times against a wooden disc. "Thank you, my lords, ladies and gentlemen. It is now time for the main event of the evening: Lot forty-two, the Steel Military Egg, designed in 1916 by Carl Fabergé." The auctioneer paused, then leaned on the podium. "Ten million roubles I am bid."

A whisper of awe rippled through the room. This opening sum was more than had been bid on the previous forty-one lots, auctioned a day earlier, including some of the most precious artefacts of the millennium. History was being made and everybody knew it.

"Twelve million. Fourteen. Sixteen. Eighteen. Twenty. Twenty million roubles I am bid. And five? Twenty-five million. Thirty. Thirty-five. Forty. Forty-five. Fifty. Fifty million roubles I am bid." The auctioneer paused to let the audience applaud and mopped his brow once more. So far the bids had been almost non-stop, but the world record price was fast approaching and most would blanch at exceeding that psychological barrier. "Do I hear fifty-five million?"

Dante wiped his palms on the legs of his trousers. Fifty million roubles! The sum was astronomical, almost beyond imagining. In his young life Dante had rarely possessed more than a few hundred roubles at once, but as soon as the auction was completed he would be helping Jim steal lot forty-two. Just watching the sale was causing an unpleasant quiver in Dante's lower intestine. How would he cope with being part of the greatest heist in history? If they pulled it off, his reputation as a leading light in the Vorovskoi Mir would be assured. If they failed and were caught, well, he'd be lucky to survive the night. "Live fast, die young, leave a handsome corpse," Dante told himself.

He concentrated on trying to detect who was still in the bidding. Most of the signals to the auctioneer were almost imperceptible, unless the bidder wanted others to know their identity. Andreas Romanov had made no secret of his interest, expansively gesturing with a waft of his catalogue. When the top bid passed forty million he had waved the auctioneer away and smiled broadly to those among him. Honour had been satisfied, it seemed.

Fifty million proved to be the pain barrier for Princess Marie-Anne. She closed her catalogue and rested it on her lap, the merest shake of her head indicating her withdrawal. But who had bid the top price? Dante peered at those present but remained none the wiser. The auctioneer was still calling for fresh bids, hoping to push the price on to the world record and beyond.

"Fifty-five? Do I hear fifty-five? Last chance for this rare and very special lot, going once at fifty million roubles. Going twice. Go–"

"Sixty million!"

All heads turned to see who had called out. In most auctions it was considered bad form to look over your shoulder in search of rival bidders. Calling out your bid was also sneered upon but the figure standing against the back wall did not seem concerned by that.

The auctioneer arched an eyebrow at the newcomer. "We have a fresh bidder – sixty million roubles."

Dante smiled at the audience, all of whom had twisted round to stare at him. He couldn't explain what had happened, even to himself. One moment he was scanning the crowd, the next he was yelping out a bid despite not having two roubles to rub together. Keep a low profile, Jim had reminded him a thousand times; a good grifter never draws attention to himself. Dante did not dare look in his mentor's direction, lest he be struck dead by the venomous glare no doubt being directed at him. Instead he nodded to the auctioneer.

"Sixty million it is," the rotund man with the gravel confirmed. "Do I hear sixty-five? Sixty-five it is."

"Seventy," Dante squeaked, his voice an octave above its normal pitch.

"And seventy, I am bid. Now seventy-five." The auctioneer looked at Dante once more. "The bid is seventy-five million roubles, against you sir."

Dante smiled, shrugged and waved him away. Only when the audience had resumed ignoring him did the youth let out a sigh of relief.

The auctioneer was close to concluding the sale. The world record price of eighty-seven million roubles had been too much to hope for, but lot 42 had gone close. "The bid is seventy-five million roubles. Final chance, selling now at seventy-five million roubles?"

In the audience Deriabin had suddenly begun to smile broadly, unable to quell his pride any longer. Plainly he was the top bidder. His hands clutched the sale catalogue tightly, waiting for the gavel to be struck for the last time.

"Selling now at seventy-five million roubles... Eighty million!"

There was a collective gasp of astonishment. Who was this new bidder? Why had they entered the fray so late on? And who could afford to spend such a sum on anything, even an item this exquisite?

Deriabin's face was a snarl of anger, his knuckles white on the hand clutching the catalogue. The media mogul made no attempt to hide his next bid, visibly twitching his catalogue.

"And eighty-five. Any advance on eighty-five? I'll accept eighty-seven and a half," the auctioneer offered. "No? Then the final bid is eighty-five million roubles. Eighty-five million..." The gavel twitched. "Eighty-seven and a half million roubles! I am bid eighty-seven and a half million roubles!"

The audience began to applaud spontaneously; each of them knowing this would be a story to tell their grandchildren. Only Deriabin refused to take part, his arms folded severely across his chest. When the congratulations had died down he flicked his catalogue once more.

"Ninety million. Ninety-two and a half. Ninety-five. Ninety-seven and a half. One hundred million roubles!" More applause but it quickly died away as the bidding continued in a frenzy. "And five. Ten. Fifteen. Twenty. Twenty-five. Thirty. Thirty-five. Forty! I am bid one hundred and forty million roubles!"

At last Dante had detected who was the other bidder. In a corner of the room Doctor Fabergé was signalling his bids with the faintest of nods. Now Deriabin had the upper hand again. Surely this ludicrous sum could grow no higher? A collective madness seemed to have gripped everyone in the room, Dante included. Where would this insanity end?

"A hundred and forty-five million roubles," the auctioneer said after another tiny nod from Fabergé. In the middle of the room Deriabin sat fuming, all eyes staring at him. The egg had only been expected to fetch fifty million roubles, talk of breaking the world record thought to be merely media hype. Now the bids were close to doubling the old mark. After a long, agonising silence Deriabin stood and stalked from the chamber, flinging his crumpled catalogue to the floor.

"I am bid a hundred and forty-five million roubles. Do I hear any advance on that figure?" The auctioneer paused, then slammed his gavel downward, signalling the end of the sale. "Sold!"

* * *

Di Grizov found his apprentice in the melee that followed and dragged him to one side. "What the hell were you thinking? Why did you start bidding?"

Dante just shrugged. "Sorry. The excitement got to me!"

"Diavolo, do you ever listen? I should have followed my instincts and reported you to the authorities when we first met. You're a menace, Nikolai Dante, and you're in danger of dragging me down with you. It'll be a miracle if you live to see twenty!"

"Calm down, Jim. Nobody will remember me, not after what just happened – the auction smashing the world record, Deriabin storming out."

Di Grizov had to concede the truth of this. "Nevertheless, pull a stunt like that again and you're finished. I'll personally hand you over to the Raven Corps!"

"Yeah, yeah," Dante replied, having heard it all before. "Shouldn't we be getting close to Fabergé? He's the winning bidder."

The senior grifter jerked a thumb over his shoulder. Fabergé was surrounded by a scrum of cameras and reporters, all demanding to know why he had bid so much for the egg and where the money had come from. "Trust me, the good doctor isn't going anywhere for a while. Let's get back to the suite and prepare for tonight. I may have thought of how we can turn your little display of stupidity to our advantage."

"I don't like to talk about money, it's unseemly." Fabergé was surrounded by reporters, all jostling for a chance to question the winning bidder, hoping to catch his eye. The doctor had escaped the auction room but was now holding an impromptu press conference in the corridor outside. Fabergé kept smiling, even if the expression sat oddly on his severe features. "If you must know, yesterday I sold my half-share of GenetiCo to my co-founder, Raoul Sequanna. The dividend from that transaction enabled me to bid with confidence."

"If I may be so bold, why?" The interrogator was Kurt Brockman, determined to keep his face close to the centre of this story. "What possible reason could you have for spending a small fortune on a piece of jewellery?"

"The Fabergé Eggs have great personal significance for me," the scientist replied. "I was raised in an orphanage by nuns and one of the sisters named me after Carl Fabergé, the acclaimed jeweller who fashioned the eggs. Alas, the nun spelled my first name wrongly on the paperwork!"

His joke was a familiar one to the reporters, since he used it in every interview, but they dutifully laughed along with him. For once the weak jest had acquired an extra significance, just as Fabergé was now a man of greater importance than usual thanks to his bidding coup.

"The concept of the eggs with their hidden surprises has inspired a daring and innovative new direction for research I shall be conducting over the coming months and years. It is work of the utmost importance, with the full support of our glorious leader, Tsar Vladimir. This new project means I am no longer able to involve myself in the day-to-day running of GenetiCo – hence the sale. But the company is in safe hands with Raoul and shall go from strength to strength under his leadership. In the meantime it is enough for me to say I shall treasure this day for many years to come and look forward to having the Steel Military Egg as my most prized possession. That is all."

Fabergé forced his way through the melee, waving away any further questions as he struggled towards the lifts. A man distinguished by the characteristic crimson blazer of a Sotheby's official shoved his way through the journalists and took the doctor by an elbow. "Sir, if you'll follow me. I shall escort you safely back to your suite. The egg will be delivered to you there later."

"Thank you," Fabergé said once the two men were safely inside a lift, sliding doors shutting out the media. "The gutter press are tiresome, but one must give them a quote or else they make your life a misery!"

"Indeed. Forty-fourth floor, is it sir?"

"Forty-fifth, actually," Fabergé replied. "Some usurper persuaded the casino management to surrender my usual suite! Probably the red-faced upstart who tried to get himself noticed by bidding against Deriabin earlier. I soon showed that gross pretender!"

The lift sighed to a halt on the forty-fifth floor, its doors parting to reveal a tasteful penthouse suite. A dozen Sotheby's employees were waiting, their faces suffused with obsequious civility.

"Welcome to your suite, Doctor Fabergé!"

"Congratulations on your purchase!"

"A wonderful piece of bidding, if I may say so. Audacious yet assured!"

"You lived up to your famous name in every way today, sir!"

"Silence!" Fabergé bellowed. "I've heard enough questions and false compliments to last me a lifetime. All I want is some peace and quiet. Get out of my suite – NOW!"

The auction house staff scuttled towards the lift, eager to satisfy their most important client. Fabergé stopped them with another barked command. "Wait! Where's the man who rescued me from that unseemly mob downstairs? He can stay. The rest of you – get out!"

Di Grizov emerged from the cluster of cowering staff, one hand stroking his false moustache and beard. "Glad to be of service, sir."

Dante took a deep breath and placed a call to the Casino Royale's concierge. "Yes, I'd like to be put through to Doctor Fabergé. No, I'm not surprised to hear he's not taking any calls, but he'll want to take mine. Why? Tell him I have evidence the Steel Military Egg for which he just paid a world record sum is a fake. If he wants to know more, I will be happy to visit his suite in twenty minutes' time. My name? Dante, Nikolai Dante. He'll know me when he sees me."

Since the age of five Karl Fabergé had known of his own genius. Across the Empire all five year-old children were required to undergo intelligence, aptitude and personality testing. From this the authorities could identify potential soldiers, scientists, athletes, artists, thinkers and troublemakers. Those that could be of use were channelled into the best schools and academies, set on a path to best fulfil their latent talents. Those that posed a danger were watched, detained, and in some cases, exterminated with extreme prejudice. There was no mercy for those who could have been a threat to the Tsar and the glorious Empire.

This reign of terror had been the making of Fabergé. A sickly baby, he had been abandoned on the steps of a convent orphanage. One of the nuns doted on this weakling runt, keeping it alive and secretly suckling the infant on her breasts. She was the sister who misnamed the child, calling him her little jewel. Fabergé could still remember her scent, warm and flowery. By the age of four he had rejected the nun's beliefs as superstitious nonsense, substituting science as his catechism. On his fifth birthday Karl was tested by the local education official and declared a genius, with superior intellect and a brilliant scientific mind. The boy was removed from the orphanage and began his studies at the science academy in St Petersburg.

There he emerged as the leading mind of his generation, revolutionising techniques in several fields and challenging accepted scientific thinking. As Fabergé's fame grew, so did his egotism and self-regard. But being the most acclaimed scientist of the twenty-seventh century was not enough for him. Fabergé wanted to be famous across the Empire. Outbidding the media baron Deriabin for the Steel Military Egg was a bold first step towards that goal. Deriabin's competitors would replay the auction footage over and over again to humiliate their rival, putting the name of Dr Karl Fabergé on everyone's lips. But to now be told the egg might be a fake – it did not bear thinking about.

The man from Sotheby's assured Fabergé these allegations must be spurious. "My firm is utterly scrupulous in checking and rechecking the provenance of every lot it sells, especially one so prestigious as this. What was the name of this individual who claimed to have evidence to the contrary?"

Fabergé was pacing back and forth in front of the penthouse suite's lift doors. "Dante, Nikolai Dante."

Di Grizov shook his head. "Never heard of him. He isn't a known authority on the Fabergé eggs. That can only mean he is either a liar trying to dupe you, or a thief with some knowledge of an elaborate confidence trick involving the egg. In either case, you should trust little of what he has to say."

The scientist nodded hurriedly. "Very well." He strode to the centre of the suite, where the Steel Military Egg glistened behind an elaborate security screen of deadly lasers. That such an exquisite item should be sullied by claims of falsehood and fakery, it made Fabergé's blood boil. Whoever was responsible for this would suffer the consequences.

Di Grizov noted the lift approaching from below. "He's nearly here."

Fabergé whirled round, his features spiked with suppressed rage. "Good."

Dante stepped from the elegant lift straight into a clenched fist. The blow smashed into his nose, cracking the bone and unleashing a gout of blood from both nostrils. The dazed youth staggered backwards, only the closing doors preventing him tumbling into the lift. He cupped a hand up to his chin, trying to stop the blood from staining his tunic. "Why'd you do that?" he demanded.

Di Grizov stood to one side, nursing bruised knuckles. "I recognise this dolt, Doctor Fabergé. He was the upstart who bid for the egg."

"Yeah, so?" Dante demanded, the words thickened by his throbbing nose. "That's no reason to punch me in the face!"

"Should I hit him again?"

Fabergé held up a hand. "That won't be necessary – yet." The doctor approached the new arrival. "Young man, you claim to have information about a potential fraud involving my egg. Speak up or I shall have this gentleman from Sotheby's strike you again. Well?"

"Just give me a chance to explain!" Dante cried out.

"You have one minute." Fabergé retreated to an antique chair and sat bolt upright in it, his fingers forming a steeple in front of his face.

Dante moved away from the lift doors, still trying to stem the blood flowing freely down his face. "There's a conman here at the Casino Royale who plans to steal the egg and replace it with a copy, a forgery. For all I know he's already done it." The red-faced youth pointed his free hand at the laser grid surrounding the bejewelled egg. "All the security in the Empire won't be enough to stop this fiend from stealing your precious objet d'art."

Fabergé smiled. "And the name of this terrifying individual?"

"Di Grizov. He's called Jim Di Grizov. A very slippery thief."

The scientist laughed. "Hardly a name to inspire fear."

"He's the best escapologist in the Empire, able to break into or out of any enclosed space known to man. Master of disguise too, you'd never be able to recognise him." Dante pointed at the man in the Sotheby's uniform. "For all you know this thug could be Di Grizov. He's stolen from kings and queens, even–"

"Enough." Fabergé shook his head. "And why are you telling me all this? Why did you bid on the egg if you had such fears?"

"Because I'm working with Di Grizov, I'm his apprentice. He wanted me to drive the price up so the egg would be worth more on the black market once he'd stolen it. But when I heard about the curse… I got cold feet. Figured you'd offer me a handsome reward for tipping you off."

Fabergé consulted a gold pocket watch. "Your time is up. I must thank you for this fanciful little tale but the entertainment is over. Leave now and I won't have you beaten by the casino's security personnel."

"But what about my reward?" Dante protested.

"Here's your reward!" Di Grizov replied, driving a knee up into the youth's groin. Dante collapsed to the carpet, breath whistling out between his gritted teeth. Di Grizov aimed a vicious kick into his protégé's ribs, sending Dante rolling away towards the lift doors. They slid open and Dante crawled inside, glaring up accusingly at his partner.

"Why?"

Di Grizov smiled. "Got to make it look convincing," he whispered.

"The fabulous Fabergé Steel Military Egg has been stolen!" Kurt Brockman beamed into the camera, unable to believe his good luck at having the lead story on Channel 88's news bulletin for the second day running. "Yesterday the legendary jewelled item attracted a world record price at auction when its creator's namesake, Doctor Karl Fabergé, won the egg with a bid of one hundred and forty-five million roubles. Now it seems lot forty-two has been stolen from inside the doctor's penthouse suite here at the Casino Royale in Monaco. An investigation has been launched but there are no clues and even fewer suspects for what is already being described by some as the crime of the century!"

Dante watched the bulletin with dazed resignation. He knew who had stolen the egg but the knowledge would do him no good. After spending the night in a hospital bed suffering from concussion, broken ribs and other injuries, Dante had hurried back to the hotel after hearing about the audacious theft. The suite he had been sharing with Di Grizov was empty but for a message hastily scrawled on headed notepaper of the Casino Royale: "There is no honour amongst thieves – sorry!"

"Honour be damned," Dante snarled as he tore the note apart.

Heavy fists began hammering against the outer door of the suite. "Hotel security! Open this door or we will be forced to break it down!"

No doubt Fabergé told the authorities what Dante had claimed the night before. With Di Grizov gone and the egg missing, that leaves me to take the blame, the youth thought ruefully. Me and my big mouth. The hammering from outside was getting ever more forceful. Dante cast one last, lingering look around the sumptuous chamber. No way of knowing when he would savour such luxury again.

The doors to the suite began to splinter inwards from a concerted attack. Dante retreated to the balcony, leaning over the railing to see what was below. Another balcony was directly beneath, with its sliding doors open to provide a potential escape route. Even more inviting was the beautiful woman bathing topless on a sun lounger, her voluptuous body bronzed and glistening in the warm sunshine. Behind him Dante could hear the doors giving way. No time like the present to make a new friend...

Dante swung himself over the railing and dropped to the balcony below, landing on the balls of his feet. He almost overbalanced and fell backwards, but succeeded in throwing himself forward instead. The youth landed unceremoniously on top of the sunbathing beauty's chest.

"Sorry, m'lady," he said. "Do you need anyone to rub oil into your back?"

The woman would have screamed but for Dante's groin covering her mouth. Instead she flailed at him with her arms. A shout from above indicated the would-be thief's escape route had been detected.

"I'll take that as a no then, shall I?" Dante got to his feet, glancing round to see security men climbing down from the balcony overhead. "You'll have to excuse me, I have a pressing engagement elsewhere!" He paused to kiss the startled woman before running inside. Behind him he could hear the shrieking sunbather shouting at his pursuers.

"Stop that gentleman! He stole a kiss from me!" she cried.

A gentleman thief, Dante thought. That could be my next career...

ONE

"The thief protests his innocence all the way to the gallows"
– Russian proverb

Di Grizov opened his eyes and winced. Overhead lighting stabbed at his vision, harsh and unrelenting. An acrid mixture of antiseptic and fear assaulted the nostrils, forcing its way into his lungs. But worst of all was the face looming over him; the features cast a sickly yellow by the brutal illuminations. Di Grizov thought a woman was watching him, but couldn't be sure.

Her features were broad and ugly – a bulbous nose with fine white hairs sprouting from both inside and out, two small pink eyes set uncomfortably close together above grinning lips of flaccid skin. Dabs of rouge suggested where cheekbones should be, while double and triple chins wobbled for attention and a single eyebrow stretched across the brow. All of this was punctuated with dozens of warts, some home to clumps of dark hair, others flecked with red veins. As she leaned over Di Grizov, the woman's dank breath, heavy with the odours of sweat and decay, bombarded his senses. Quite simply, this was the most grotesque creature in the world.

"Where am I?" Di Grizov was startled by how thin and weak his voice sounded. He had no memory of how he came to be in this place, or why his throat felt so sore. Beneath his neck he felt nothing, just numb weightlessness. The grifter tried to raise his head but could not summon the strength.

For now he would have to gather information by questions alone.

"Your new home," the woman replied, her voice made thick and guttural by its Siberian accent. She stood upright, resting two meaty fists on the rolls of fat where her waist should be. "Allow me to introduce myself. I am Madame Wartski."

Wartski by name, warty by nature, Di Grizov thought. Best not to say so out loud, I doubt this whale would find it funny. There was a dry, humourless aspect to her face that did little to inspire frivolity. Wide as she was tall, Wartski was clad in a navy blue matron's uniform, fabric bulging across her drooping breasts and rotund hips. Her flabby hands sported as many warts as her face, each finger encrusted with a selection of fleshy growths.

"Di Grizov. James Di Grizov," the grifter replied. "I'd shake your hand but can't seem to feel my fingers at the moment."

"The anaesthetic is still wearing off," Wartski said.

"Anaesthetic? I don't understand – have I been undergoing surgery? Was I in an accident?"

The masculine matron smiled. "Not exactly. The doctor will explain." She moved to the end of his bed and studied a medical chart. "Good, everything's coming along nicely. I'll tell him you're recovering well."

"Recovering? From what?" Di Grizov tried pushing himself into an upright position, fighting against his body's numb inertia. "Tell me what's going on!"

Wartski tutted imperiously. "Getting agitated will not help. I suggest you remain calm and get some rest. You'll need it for what is ahead."

The grifter felt his sphincter contract involuntarily. There was a threat within the matron's words, an unpleasantly sadistic twinkle in her eyes as she spoke. I'm in trouble here, Di Grizov realised, and I don't even know where I am. He decided to keep bluffing, hoping to find a way out of this place.

"You're probably right," he said in a soothing voice, relaxing back into the pillow. "I'll try and get some more rest. Thank you, Madame Wartski."

She smiled and left the room, an automatic door closing behind her more than ample posterior. Once she had gone, Di Grizov hurriedly examined his surroundings, searching for any clue to his location or method of escape. The chamber was small, with a low ceiling and obtrusive strip lighting. No windows punctuated the walls, denying any hint of the world beyond. The room was sparsely furnished, just a bare table and chair in one corner – no cupboards; nothing that might contain his possessions or a potential weapon. Even the bed was a bare hospital cot, utterly utilitarian and without adornment. Everything was a queasy yellow colour, accentuating his feeling of unease.

Di Grizov tried to haul himself into a sitting position, but his arms were still too weak to support any weight. There was a nagging itch below his right knee but he lacked the energy and strength to reach it. If I could remember how I got here, he thought, maybe I'd have a clue about how to escape. The grifter closed his eyes and focussed on pushing aside the blurring in his mind. Last thing he could recall was a New Year's Eve party. The Year of the Tsar 2671 was coming to an end and Di Grizov had purloined an invitation to the richest event in St Petersburg. The Tsar had created three new noble houses as recognition for their help in defeating the Romanovs during the war, and the recipients were celebrating their enhanced status with a joint party.

Di Grizov had arrived early and begun circulating among the guests, acquiring useful gossip about who was going where for their winter holidays, leaving their homes vulnerable. The grifter saw a familiar face during the gathering but couldn't recall where he had known it before. The man appeared just as startled to see Di Grizov at the celebration. Deciding discretion was always the safest option, the grifter decided to make an early exit; in a life of crime without punishment, he had wronged many people. In his experience revenge was best avoided by not staying around long enough to suffer it.

He had arrived home safely, but after stepping through the front door everything was lost in a haze. All he could recall was a male voice, sneering and arch. "I thought it was you. I would congratulate you on possessing such audacity, but since it shall be your undoing, there is little to praise..." After that all was darkness until waking beneath Wartski's repulsive face.

The grifter snapped open his eyes, terror suddenly evident in them. That voice! He remembered where he recognised it from now. "Not him. Please don't let it be him," Di Grizov prayed. "Anyone but him!"

Jena Makarov looked out of her flyer's window as it skimmed over the Black Sea coastline. Below the water gleamed and rippled, flecks of white and silver appearing as gusts of wind created waves or schools of fish broke the surface. A trawler chugged its way into shore, laden down with another day's catch. Soon the fishermen would be unloading their haul, counting their takings and going home to eat, drink, fight and make love to their partners. How Jena longed for such a simple life. The grass is always greener, she knew that. No doubt the fishermen had just as many cares and worries as she – fruitless catches, dilapidated boats, falling prices. What was the old saying? *Expect sorrows from the sea and woe from water*. But their lives could not be any more poisonous than hers, trapped amidst the intrigues of the imperial court.

She had known neither poverty nor hunger; nor wanted for any material object. She had been pampered and privileged beyond all others; yet that was no compensation for a childhood without love or affection. Jena's mother had died long ago, leaving two daughters in the care of their father. But when that father was Tsar Vladimir Makarov, the most feared man in the Empire, happy families were not on the agenda. Any man who bragged about his ability to create ingenious tortures such as the corrosive acid enema was not one to dote on his children. He was a murderous, monstrous creature with ice for a heart. Instead Jena had kept close to her younger sister, Julianna. They argued as many siblings did, fighting over trivial possessions and experiences to distract themselves from the horrors perpetrated in their father's name. All the while he was training them to take his place, to inherit his reign of terror.

The Tsar's long, bitter struggle with the House of Romanov came to a head in 2669, when decades of sabre rattling became a war encompassing the entire Empire. It was Julianna's murder that provoked the bloody conflict, her life stolen by one of the Romanov siblings. At the time Jena thought this event had hardened her father's heart, forced him to take arms against the pretenders to the imperial throne. But the glee with which he had pursued the war soon persuaded her otherwise. The Tsar had wanted his war and done everything in his power to make it happen. Sometimes she suspected he had deliberately sent Julianna into harm's way, turning her into a suitable target for the Romanovs to assassinate and thus create the justification for war. But Jena did not dare investigate these suspicions. She was the Tsar's sole surviving heir, but even that would not be sufficient protection from his wrath.

No, it was not Vladimir Makarov's heart that had been hardened by the death of Julianna – it was Jena who lost a little of her soul that day. At the time she was in love with a key figure from the Romanov side of the conflict. After years of fighting and flirting, the pair had finally consummated their passion for each other. But by the time they decided to tell the world of their union, the war had already begun. Jena would not let herself think of her lover's name, let alone say it out loud. Just remembering his face, the touch of his hands on her body, the look in his eyes as they... No, she would not torture herself with these memories again. Leave the demon behind, lest the mere thought of him conjured his presence into her life again.

The war had been bloody and brutal. Jena fought like a woman possessed: every victory a memorial to her dead sister, every enemy soldier she slaughtered another stain on her heart. Even during the war she found herself face to face with *him* several times, forced to confront her feelings all over again. But the Romanovs eventually lost, betrayed by one of their own, and the Tsar swept aside their forces. The Romanov name became accursed across the Empire, with Jena's former lover a wanted man with a massive bounty on his head. Any sensible, sane individual would get offworld, find a quiet corner of the Empire and disappear. Jena could not help laughing to herself. *Somehow I doubt* he *would follow such advice.*

Since the war ended, her father's regime had been crueller and more tyrannical than ever. Purge squads mercilessly took revenge against anyone suspected of betraying the Tsar. Noble houses that had displayed any loyalty or partiality towards the Romanovs were ruthlessly destroyed and new dynasties built on their ashes, fiercely loyal to the Tsar. Amidst it all Jena did her duty, fulfilled her father's wishes. That was all she had left now.

"Approaching our destination," the flyer's pilot announced, snapping Jena back from her reverie. "Beginning final descent to the island."

"Very good," she replied. "Once we're down begin preparations for our departure. I don't want to be here any longer than is absolutely necessary."

"Yes, ma'am."

Doctor Fabergé could not help laughing. To think this was the brigand who had eluded him for a dozen years. The thief lying on the hospital bed was smaller than he remembered, and older – almost wizened. Time had not been kind to Di

Grizov. His features were lined and careworn, his hair thinning, his body a shadow of its former strength and agility. Most intriguing were his eyes. Once they had shone with intelligence and bravado. Now they showed terror and foreboding. Yes, I'm going to enjoy this immensely, the doctor decided as he chuckled.

"What's so funny?" the patient demanded.

"You are," Fabergé replied, failing to wipe the smile from his face. "In my mind I had built you up into this powerful figure, the only man ever to get the better of me – my nemesis, my hubris, if you will. When I saw you across the room at that tiresome party I struggled to accept that you were the same person. You're just a thief and an old thief at that."

"You don't scare me, Fabergé."

"Your words say one thing but the fear in your eyes says another. Quite right, too. You would do well to be afraid of me. I've spent twelve years planning my revenge. Now the glorious day is finally here, it seems something of an anticlimax. When you stole my Imperial Easter Egg, you stole more than just a priceless piece of jewellery – you stole part of my reputation, my honour. Revenging myself upon you was a matter of principle at first, then a matter of need. Eventually it became an obsession, driving me onward in my work, pushing me to prove I was more than just the victim of this century's most famous theft." The doctor clicked his fingers and Wartski entered the room carrying a silver box. She rested it on the table at the end of Di Grizov's bed.

Fabergé removed the lid with a flourish to reveal the Steel Military Egg, its lustre undimmed. "I must thank you for keeping my egg safe and in such pristine condition for the last twelve years. I feared you might try to break it into pieces for sale or destroy it altogether."

"I'll be happy to see the back of that damned thing," Di Grizov snapped. "It's been the bane of my life since I first set eyes on it."

"Perhaps your assistant was right after all," Fabergé said. "Perhaps the legend of a curse against all who touch the egg is true?"

"We both know you turned that thing into poison," the grifter snarled. "By the time I reached the black market in St Petersburg, word had already been spread that anyone who bought or traded the egg would be hunted down and exterminated, by order of the Tsar himself. How'd you ever swing that, Fabergé?"

"Let's just say our glorious leader and I have a long-standing alliance."

"I couldn't give the egg away, let alone sell it! Nobody would melt it down for me either. I should have just thrown it into the Volga and had done with it."

"Twelve years on the run, a marked man, always looking over your shoulder, never able to relax. That can't have been easy," Wartski interjected.

"Indeed," Fabergé agreed. "But your running days are over now."

Doubts joined fear on Di Grizov's features. "What do you mean?"

"Centuries ago slave labour was used to extract diamonds from mines on the continent of Africa. But the owners had problems with workers trying to escape, taking the precious gems with them to buy a new life. All those who were caught had to be punished and the penalty needed to be so severe it would serve as a warning to others, to dissuade them from fleeing. The process was called hobbling and proved most effective."

"Oh no..."

Fabergé reached down towards the bed covers. "Yes, your running days are definitely over. In fact, to make sure of that," the doctor pulled aside the bedclothes to reveal two bloody and bandaged stumps where Di Grizov's legs had been, "I've amputated both your legs."

• • •

Jena heard a scream, stark and terrifying, as she stepped out of the flyer. It felt unnatural to the ears, almost unworldly. During the war Jena had heard many, many men crying out in agony, begging for their lives, but such screams still cut her to the core. What horrors was Doctor Fabergé perpetrating here in her father's name? She turned back to the pilot. "Remember what I said. We don't want to spend a minute longer here than necessary."

"Planning your departure already?"

"But you've only just arrived!"

Jena spun round to find herself facing the chests of two women. She looked up to their faces, more than a head's height above her own. The pair were identical in appearance, but for the colour of their hair – one red, one black. Otherwise they were exactly the same, with high cheekbones, powerful jawlines and wide, intensely blue eyes. "How's the air up there?" Jena joked.

"My name is Tempest," the red-haired woman replied humourlessly. "This is my sister, Storm. We're the Strangelove twins."

"Of course," Jena said. "Sorry, I've never seen you up close before."

The twins exchanged a look before marching away from the landing pad. "Doctor Fabergé is expecting you," Storm announced.

"Follow us, please," Tempest added, not bothering to look back.

Jena jogged after them, struggling to keep pace with the twins' mighty strides. Both women were said to measure exactly two metres in height, but seemed taller in person. The pair became famous at the last Imperial Games, winning all but one of the seven disciplines they entered. Only the marathon title had eluded them, after the Tsar publicly expressed his opinion that it would be nice to see someone else collect the gold medal. Tempest had finished second, with Storm in third. Despite standing on the rostrum's lower steps, both women had towered over the marathon winner.

After the games had finished, controversy had filled the news media. Where had this pair of goddesses appeared from? What was their background? It was then that Doctor Fabergé stepped back into public life. For ten years, after suffering one of the most famous thefts in recent history, the scientist had remained in seclusion on his private island off the Black Sea coastline. Fabergé said the twins were his students but refused to divulge any more about their personal history. The Strangelove women declined a small fortune in offers to become professional sports stars or advertising icons, instead returning to their mentor's home. Their sudden emergence and subsequent disappearance enhanced the enigma surrounding them, with the media nicknaming them the Furies. All the attention further enhanced the myth of Doctor Fabergé, even if it was one of his own making.

Tempest stopped at a high wooden doorway and gestured for Jena to step inside. Above them towered an old castle, reconstructed on this island stone by stone after being transported from its original location in Britannia. Fabergé had purchased the castle with a fraction of his enormous insurance payout for the stolen Steel Military Egg, along with the island. Gargoyles leaned out from the castle's battlements, their faces curled into grotesque shapes and expressions. Everything about the building hinted at menace. "Lovely place you have here," Jena said with a cheerful smile.

"Inside," Tempest growled, the muscles around her jaw rippling.

"Whatever you say."

"Why? Why did you take my legs?" Di Grizov whimpered, his hands pawing uselessly at the stumps.

"Revenge, that was certainly a motivating factor," Fabergé conceded. "I wanted you to suffer as I have suffered – humiliation, despair, anger. I wanted you to be left scarred, to be hurt, to be transformed by our encounter, just as I was transformed by what you did to me."

"I never touched you!"

"But you crippled my reputation! You turned me into a laughing stock, a cocktail party joke across the Empire! I was forced to hide myself away. But I used that exile as a challenge, an opportunity to further my studies, my research. I emerged stronger, better for the experience – perhaps you will too."

Di Grizov stared at the scientist incredulously. "You're insane!"

Fabergé shook his head. "Passionate, yes. Driven, yes. Even a tad obsessed – that might well be true, too. But insane? No, I think that's little strong in the circumstances." He nodded to Wartski, who strode to the bedside and punched the grifter in the face. Di Grizov's head snapped to one side, the sound of a cheekbone breaking like a rifle shot in the small room. "You would do well to remember I am in charge here, not you."

Di Grizov spat a mouthful of blood and phlegm at Fabergé. The scientist sighed and nodded again to Wartski. She punched the patient again, this time cracking his nose with her meaty fist. The hefty woman drew back her arm, ready to strike again, but Fabergé stilled her with a gesture.

"False bravado will only bring you more suffering," the scientist said to his captive. "Wartski here would happily administer such pain. She's a true sadist, gaining a sexual thrill from each bout of agony she inflicts. Unless you're a true masochist, I suggest you keep your opinions and spittle to yourself. Do we have an agreement?"

Di Grizov nodded weakly, crimson coursing from his broken nose and down his chin, pooling in the hollow in the middle of his collarbone.

"That's better," Fabergé smiled. "You should be honoured. I have chosen you as the guinea pig for an exciting series of experiments to be conducted over the coming days. I have developed a hormone that enhances the body's natural healing abilities. I want to use you as the control subject. Every day at this hour you will be given an injection of the hormone and then be made to suffer the most excruciating agony. Wartski will take notes on how you respond to such treatment and determine how much benefit you are gaining from it. And please, be honest in your replies to her enquiries – this *is* for the advancement of science." The doctor gestured to the matron. She removed a pill from a case in her pocket and pushed it roughly between Di Grizov's teeth.

"Swallow," she hissed. "Swallow!" When the grifter did not obey, Wartski reached down beneath his hospital gown and clenched Di Grizov's testicles in her right hand. One squeeze was enough to open his mouth; another squeeze persuaded him to swallow the pill. "That's better," she said approvingly.

Fabergé nodded his agreement. "Now, what should be the nature of today's agony? Considering what you've already suffered, we don't want to go too much further, lest the results be compromised."

A firm knock from outside the room interrupted the discussion.

"Who is it?" Wartski demanded impatiently.

"Tempest and Storm, ma'am. We've brought Doctor Fabergé's guest."

The scientist's face lit up with pleasure. "Ahh, the beautiful Tsarina! Show her in, please, show her in."

Jena was ushered into a small room where Fabergé was waiting for her. He strode forward and bowed deeply, kissing her hand while mouthing some platitudes. Jena was taken aback to realise the doctor's assistant was a woman, and not an obese and obscenely ugly transvestite in a nurse's uniform. They shared an uncomfortable handshake, Jena all too aware of the clump of warts grasping her own slender fingers. Finally Fabergé waved grandly at an unfortunate soul lying on a hospital bed.

"And this is one of my experimental subjects, a thief known as James Di Grizov. He did me a rather infamous disservice some twelve years ago, but is now making recompense by taking part in one of my studies."

Jena frowned. Di Grizov? Where have I heard that name before? Leaving her subconscious to ponder, she took in the horror lying on the bed. His face was a bloody mess: one cheek swelling up and blood still dribbling from a recently broken nose. Jena noticed the bloody stumps where the patient's legs must have been. Some kind of accident? Jena decided not. The glee in her host's voice told her this double amputation had been utterly unnecessary.

I've seen what shelling and bullets and bio-wire can do to the human body, Jena thought, but that was amidst the atrocities of war. To see such injuries in peacetime made her shudder. What other horrors would she have to bear witness to on her father's behalf during this visit?

"Well, that's enough about this patient," Fabergé continued. "Shall we move to the main laboratory? I've got something that the Tsar has expressed great interest in. With his support, my work here could provide the Empire with a weapon far beyond anything wielded in the last war."

Jena nodded. "Yes, that's why I'm here, to assess your progress. But perhaps I could freshen up first? It's been a long journey…"

Her host smiled placidly. "Of course, of course. Wartski will show you to the nearest facilities, then we may began the full inspection."

Di Grizov waited until he was alone before letting himself cry, the tears mingling with the blood and perspiration on his face. If he had the strength and the opportunity, he'd kill himself soon – maybe one day, maybe two. A lifetime among the Vorovskoi Mir had taught the grifter much about the ways of people, their weaknesses and vulnerabilities. Di Grizov knew he would not be able to endure this torture for long. Better to end it now, put himself out of their clutches. If truth were told, he had contemplated suicide more than once in the last dozen years. The curse of the Steel Military Egg had haunted him beyond reckoning, grinding away at his heart and mind. And now this fate...

To the grifter's surprise, the door slid open and the Tsar's daughter stepped back into the room. "What are you doing here?" Di Grizov asked.

"I have to ask you something," she replied, standing beside the entrance. "Have we met before? I know I've heard your name."

"No. I'd remember encountering a woman as beautiful as you."

Jena frowned. "Perhaps someone else mentioned you?"

Di Grizov shook his head. "Unlikely. My name's been mud in the Thieves' World ever since I stole the egg and left my last apprentice to carry the can."

"The egg?"

"The Steel Military Egg – the auction at Casino Royale in Monaco?"

Jena's eyes widened. "That was you?"

"Yes, with a little help. I got away untouched with the egg, leaving my assistant to find his own escape route. I should have been set for life; instead I've ended up like this... And him! Who ever knew he'd become so famous?"

"Lady Jena? Where are you?" Wartski's approaching voice and heavy footfalls signalled imminent danger. "Lady Jena?"

"Your apprentice – what was his name?"

Di Grizov grimaced. "He was cocky and arrogant even then, seemed to think he was too cool to kill. How he's ever survived this long I'll never know. His name was Dante–"

"Nikolai Dante," Jena said, shaking her head. "I should have known."

"You've met him?"

Jena rolled her eyes. The grifter almost smiled. "That's a yes. Well, if you ever see him again, tell Nikolai that I–"

"Lady Jena!" Wartski was standing in the doorway, scowling at the Imperial visitor. "What are you doing in here?"

"My apologies, Madame Wartski. I heard your patient coughing and thought he might need assistance."

The slab-faced matron narrowed her eyes. "I'll be the judge of that."

"Of course," Jena replied swiftly, letting herself be ushered out of the room. She gave Di Grizov one last compassionate smile before the door shut between them.

The grifter lay back on his pillow. So Dante knew the Tsarina? And from that twinkle in her eye, the rogue knew her in quite an intimate manner. *What I wouldn't give to swap places with him now,* Di Grizov thought bleakly.

It was close to dusk before Jena was back on the landing pad, having finished her inspection of the island's facilities. Doctor Fabergé bowed and kissed her hand in an elaborate show of deference, while flanked by the statuesque menace of the Strangelove twins. "I hope you have been impressed by what you've seen here today, Tsarina."

"An exceptional display," Jena replied. "I've never witnessed anything to rival such scientific... daring."

"Then I can hope for a positive response to my request for your father's personal assistance in the next stage of this project?"

"I will deliver a full and frank assessment of everything I have seen here today. I would not dream of second-guessing his reaction, but I am certain you will have it within twenty-four hours of my return to the Imperial Palace."

Fabergé smiled broadly. "Excellent. Then I shall not delay your return to his side a moment longer, ma'am."

Jena began climbing the steps into her flyer before pausing to ask a final question. "Doctor, what will happen to Di

Grizov? After you have finished the experiments involving him, what shall be his fate?"

"You need not worry, Lady Jena, he will not trouble polite society again with his criminal ways. All those who survive this phase of the trials are being sent to join work details in an Imperial gulag, probably one in Murmansk. Di Grizov is due to be transferred there tomorrow. Should he make it, I doubt he will last long. I understand from Madame Wartski that such places can be quite bleak, apparently. She was born and raised on a gulag, albeit a Siberian one, so she knows them well."

"I don't doubt it," Jena said with a thin smile. "Well, thank you again for the hospitality. A most illuminating visit. Farewell!" The flyer's passenger door closed behind her and the vehicle rose majestically into the sunset.

Fabergé waved goodbye, still smiling as he spoke to the twins. "Well? What did you make of her?"

"Too curious for her own good," Tempest sneered.

"Too good for her own curiosity," Storm countered.

"But still loyal to her father," the doctor replied. "No matter how much her stomach was turned by what she saw here, the Tsarina can still be trusted to give an accurate report on our progress. Indeed, her disgust may be to our advantage." Once the flyer was clear of the island, Fabergé stopped waving and snapped his fingers at the two women. "Come. We have much to do."

Jena wished she could strip off her clothes and burn them, so nauseating was the effect of being around Doctor Fabergé and his experiments. But purging her loathing would have to wait until after seeing her father. Jena knew she had been sent by the Tsar as a test, both of her nerves and her loyalty. Well, two could play at that game. She would give him a full and frank description of every horror, every atrocity she had witnessed inside that castle. Then she would watch his reaction. Any sane man, any man with a scintilla of morality, ought to reject the Fabergé experiments as an abomination against nature. Knowing the Tsar, he would probably embrace them with both arms.

Jena pushed such thoughts aside; they would do her no good for the moment. Better to focus on something else, anything but what she had seen today. As the flyer began the long journey back to St Petersburg, Jena recalled her conversation with Di Grizov. She remembered now where she had first heard the grifter's name mentioned. After the Romanovs had fallen at the end of the war, a quirk of fate had thrown her and Dante together one last time. But instead of lovers they were bitter enemies, Dante her prisoner.

Nikolai had talked about partnering Di Grizov during his thieving days, being taught everything he knew. No prison in the Empire would be able to hold him – a typical Dante boast. Several times during the war the former lovers had been presented with opportunities to kill each other, yet had been unable or unwilling to do so. Rather than deliver Dante for execution, Jena let him escape, urging him to get to safety offworld. "I never want to see you or hear the name Nikolai Dante again," she had said before turning away.

Where was he now, Jena wondered? Despite herself, she combed daily bulletins from across the Empire, looking for his name. The bounty on Dante's head had reached fifty million roubles, with half as much again if anyone should succeed in delivering him alive to the Tsar. Several times Dante had apparently been captured, only to escape again. His apprenticeship with Di Grizov had not been wasted experience, it seemed.

If he had any common sense, Dante would go beyond the reach of the Empire. The ridiculous rogue possessed many qualities, Jena thought, but common sense was not among the strongest. If I know Nikolai, he's probably in trouble right now – up to his neck.

TWO

"Without a ruse the thief won't steal"
– Russian proverb

Dante liked dressing in black. For a start, it hid a multitude of sins and stains, both of which he had considerable experience with. Secondly, it enabled him to disappear into the shadows. Thirdly – and most importantly – it added a hint of danger to what he considered was his already considerable animal magnetism. Few ladies could resist having a kiss stolen from their lips by Dante when he adopted his guise as the Gentleman Thief!

Dante had first pulled on the black mask while staying at the Hotel Yalta, not long after his acceptance to the House of Romanov in 2666. To celebrate his new status, the black-haired brigand had thrown a month-long debauch at the hotel, one of the Empire's most expensive resorts. It was only after the bill arrived that Dante discovered being a Romanov did not also grant him access to the considerable family purse. Ever inventive, he quickly returned to his thieving ways, reviving the skills honed while growing up amongst the Vorovskoi Mir.

He dressed from head to toe in black, pulled on a matching mask and proclaimed himself to be the Gentleman Thief – robbing the rich and then robbing them again. Soon, under-sexed, over-excited ladies were flocking to the Hotel Yalta in the hope of being ravaged by this virile young cutpurse. But all of that was before the war, before Dante's name became a curse upon the lips of millions. A conventional job was beyond his imagination or skills, and laying low for the next fifty years held little appeal. Live fast, have fun and let tomorrow take care of itself was Dante's motto. But you still needed roubles and kopecks to fund such a lifestyle, and so the thief's mask was coming out of retirement.

Dante studied his reflection in a mirror while knotting the mask into place. His eyes sparkled with wit and intelligence, he liked to think – or at least a hint of mischief. A neatly trimmed black moustache and goatee helped enhance his roguish good looks while a lustrous mane of black hair was swept back from his forehead, reaching down almost to collar length. With the mask, few women could resist my considerable charms, he thought.

You're not going out in that I hope, a pious voice said inside Dante's head.

"Why not? It's always been a hit with the ladies."

It does have the advantage of covering half of your face, yes.

"I haven't got time for this, Crest. I've an appointment to keep."

The prim voice sighed heavily. *More petty thievery? If so, you can do it without my help. I wasn't created to enable ease of entry for minor felons.*

"I resent that remark," Dante protested. "I am not a minor felon!"

Really?

"Don't you know what we're going to rob?"

I dread to think.

"The Imperial Mint," Dante announced triumphantly.

The Imperial Mint?

"Yes."

The most heavily guarded, impenetrable and implacable building in all of St Petersburg?

"That's the one." Dante waited but was rewarded with only a lengthy silence. "Well, aren't you impressed?"

Yes.

"I thought you would be."

This must be the stupidest idea you've ever had, Dante, and that is setting it against an already impressive list of stupid ideas.

Dante finished adjusting his mask. "Whine all you want, Crest, but sometimes I think you actually enjoy my little adventures."

Nothing could be further from the truth! I am a Weapons Crest; one of the most advanced battle computers known to mankind, a repository of vast knowledge and wisdom, charged with the task of training my symbiotic host to become a potential ruler of the Empire! I should have been bonded with a pure-born Romanov – instead I got stuck with you, a lust-driven, sewer-spawned, gutter-rat who acts first and thinks last. You have turned me into an accessory for your petty crime sprees and rejoiced in my discomfort!

"Yeah, yeah, yeah," Dante replied. He looked down at the double-headed eagle tattoo on his left arm, the only physical manifestation of the Crest's presence within his body. "Anytime you want to shut up, just let me know."

I wouldn't give you the satisfaction! Our bonding has given you abilities far beyond most men. You have a vastly enhanced healing ability, so you can survive almost any wound. You can extend cyborganic swords from your fists, giving you a significant advantage in hand-to-hand combat. And with the knowledge in my sentient computer brain, you can access and override any computer in the Empire! But what do you use all these gifts for?

Dante sighed. "You nag worse than my first wife, Crest."

You've only been married once – and she's dead.

"Don't remind me."

You still haven't answered my question, Dante.

"You seem to be doing enough talking for both of us."

Lying, cheating, debauching, crime, infamy and indolence!

"And nobody does it better, Crest."

I despair for you.

"Despair all you want, but lower the volume while you do. It's hard to concentrate with an extra voice offering a running commentary in your brain."

Well, at least you've got one intelligent voice inside here, the Crest snapped. *If it wasn't for me, cuckoos could nest in your skull undisturbed.*

Dante clutched the sides of his head. "Diavolo, just shut up!"

Fine!

"Good!"

I will!

"Suits me!"

After a few moments the Crest spoke again. *But you'll be needing me later to break into the Imperial Mint?*

"Yeah, of course."

In that case I'll start hacking the Imperial Net for security logs, alarm codes and other useful information.

"Thanks."

Let me know when I'm needed.

Dante waited a moment; but the prim, haughty voice had gone silent – for now. "Finally, some peace and quiet," he muttered, before emerging from the bathroom into the suite's living room. An unwelcome fug, redolent of death, spoiled fish and horse liniment, hung in the air. Dante's nose crumpled involuntarily as he sought to avoid breathing too deeply. "Bojemoi, did somebody die and leave us their corpse in the will?"

"Worse – tonight is Spatch's turn to cook," an aristocratic voice replied. Dante peered through the fumes to see the speaker. Lord Peter Flintlock was standing by the balcony doors, breathing the night air of St Petersburg in preference to whatever vileness was being concocted inside the suite. Tall and thin, with a carefully coiffed tangle of blond hair, Flintlock acted like a fop and dressed like a dandy. He still wore the scarlet uniform with gold braid from his days as a conscript in the Romanov army. Disgraced and deported from his native Britannia for some unknown depravity, Flintlock had joined the fighting forces rather than be executed. Cowardice kept him alive, as did an unlikely alliance with the other occupant of the hotel suite.

"Fuoco, what he is making? Mustard gas?" Dante approached the corner when Spatchcock was stirring something toxic in a pot on a portable stove.

"A little something of me own invention," the grubby chef replied in a gruff and uncultured voice. "Not as lethal as mustard gas but get one drop on your skin and you'll be retching your guts out for hours. I call it purge juice."

"Charming," Dante said.

"Thought it might come in handy for our raid on the mint."

"*Our* raid? I've already explained – you and Flintlock wait outside while I go in alone. One man might get in and out alive, but never three."

"Still, you never know," Spatchcock maintained. "It might go wrong. We might have to launch a rescue mission for you!"

"If something goes wrong, I know exactly where you two will be headed – straight for the hills, looking after your own asses."

The sly-faced poisoner grinned, displaying a mouthful of decay and broken molars. "Heh. You're probably right." Like Flintlock, Spatchcock had chosen conscription ahead of execution during the war. The pair had met when they were selected to serve under Dante in the Rudinshtein Irregulars, a motley collection of thieves, murderers and human effluent. Flintlock and Spatchcock had fitted in perfectly.

But the grubby little man was unlike his aristocratic comrade in almost every other way. A liar, forger, extortionist and purveyor of filth, Spatchcock had murdered a dozen men with potions, pills and poisons before the war. Fond of eating his own lice, he could make a meal out of anything –

but few would want to consume it. Any clothes he wore seemed to attract grease and stains, and the only baths he took usually involved falling into rivers, lakes or oceans. "Heard you arguing with the Crest again. Surprised you two don't get a divorce."

"I've thought about that more than once," Dante admitted, before leaning forwards to whisper in Spatchcock's left ear. "Secretly I think it enjoys all our misadventures but just can't bring itself to admit that." He straightened up again, not wanting to stay too close in case of catching something unpleasant. "How long before this stuff is ready?"

"Any minute. Just got to let it cool down."

"Good. I want to hit the mint just before midnight, as the security guards are changing shift. While they're busy comparing notes–"

"You'll be nicking the bank notes?" Spatchcock interjected.

"Not exactly. I have something far more valuable in mind."

The Imperial Mint stood to the east of St Petersburg, its imposing stone and marble structure surrounded by cybernetically-enhanced attack dogs, a constantly shifting laser defence grid and a cadre of Berez Enforcers. Recruited from the colony world of Berezova, these fearsome aliens were renowned for the thickness and resiliency of their mottled brown skins. Gravity on Berezova was twice the strength of that on Earth, making the Enforcers vastly more powerful than any human. Anyone who took on an Enforcer without the aid of a large tank was considered foolhardy or insane.

"Should be a piece of cake," Dante said, standing in the shadow of a building opposite the mint's main entrance. Behind him Spatchcock and Flintlock looked less certain, the Englishman hopping nervously from foot to foot while his lice-infested associate scratched at a facial scab.

"You want to take some purge juice, just in case?" Spatchcock asked.

"No thanks," Dante replied. "I'd rather rely on my wits."

"There's a doomsday plan if ever I heard one," Flintlock muttered, earning a baleful glare from his former commander. "Sorry, did I say that out loud?"

"Just stay here and keep the getaway vehicle ready. If I do make it out of there in one piece, I'll probably be running for my life." Dante checked his mask was still in place and then began strolling towards the mint, bold as brass. "Crest, how are those security specs coming along?"

All was silent but for Dante's footsteps.

"Crest, can you hear me?" he hissed under his breath. "This is no time to give me the silent treatment." Dante was close to the mint's security perimeter, but knew retracing his steps now would only attract suspicion. Instead he crouched and began retying the laces on one of his black leather boots. "If this is about what I said earlier, I'm sorry, okay? However I've upset you, I'm sorry!"

By now one of the Enforcers had noticed the stranger lingering just beyond the pulsating laser defence grid. It stumped towards him, carefully choosing its steps across the marble flagstones outside the mint. Dante noticed the guard approaching and continued fiddling with his laces, now retying those on his other boot. Beads of sweat were gathering under the black silk of his mask. He swiftly pulled it off and shoved it into a pocket. Hanging around the mint at midnight wouldn't be easily explained, but wearing a black mask over your face at the same time could complicate matters further.

"Please, Crest, tell me what I've done wrong before that guard realises why I'm *really* here!"

Well, you're tying that lace into a double knot, for a start, the Crest finally replied. *You'll have a terrible time undoing that later.*

"Forget the lace! Tell me how to evade the alarms and get inside!"

Not until you apologise.

"I'm sorry, okay? I'm sorry!"

Now say it like you mean it, the Crest replied with a sniff.

"How can I mean it when I don't even know what I'm apologising for?"

Saying I nag, for a start. Telling me to be quiet. That sort of thing is very hurtful. You should think before you speak.

By now the Enforcer was within earshot of Dante. The would-be intruder stood up and smiled, giving the guard a friendly wave. "Nice night for it!"

The Enforcer glared back, its monolithic features impassive.

"Couldn't sleep!" Dante offered by way of explanation for his presence. "Thought I'd take a stroll, stretch the legs, get some air into the lungs."

Still nothing from the Enforcer.

"Well, guess I'll be moving along. Maybe I'll be see you later!"

Maybe I'll see you later? the Crest spluttered inside Dante's mind.

"Bye!" Dante called to the guard, before turning and slowly walking away, whistling tunelessly. After a few seconds he risked a glance back over his shoulder. The Enforcer was returning to its post outside the mint's entrance. "Okay, I think I fooled him," Dante whispered.

Congratulations, the Crest replied. *You've found someone even stupider than you. That's quite an achievement.*

"Very droll. Now how do I get in?"

Turn and start running towards the laser defence grid. The beams are on a complex rotational system but time it just right and you should be able to pick a way between them.

"And if I don't?"

Even your enhanced healing abilities will have trouble reattaching your head or limbs.

"You're filling me with confidence, Crest."

Makes a nice change. Normally you're just full of sh–

"Shut up!" Dante hissed. He spun round and started running towards the laser defence grid. In front of him red beams danced through the air, appearing and disappearing in a dazzling light show that defied interpretation. "Crest, are you sure about this?"

As sure as I can be. There is one factor I can only guess at.
"What's that?"

Your incompetence. Prepare to jump forwards into a somersault.

"Fuoco," Dante whispered.

Now! the Crest commanded. Dante dived into the air hands first, then tucked his legs up underneath himself as he cleared a red beam that suddenly appeared below him. *Now kick out and tumble into a forward roll when you hit the ground!* The black clad figure followed the Crest's instructions, wincing as his body hit the ground. *Stand up – quickly!* Dante was on his feet in a moment. *Run five paces to your left!* The fleet-footed thief set off in one direction. *Your other left!* Dante twisted round, reversing his direction. *Stop! Stay absolutely still!* Laser beams sliced through the air in a dizzying cycle of movement, each accompanied by a low buzz and flash of heat. One zipped between Dante's legs, searing the fabric just below his crotch.

"Ahhh! Hot, hot, hot!" Dante winced.

Now, run three steps forwards and then go into a cartwheel!
Dante began running again. "What's a cartwheel?" he asked.

Just jump!

"I can't look, I can't look," Flintlock whimpered, peering between his fingers as Dante danced around inside the laser field. "Is he still alive?"

"He's still in one piece," Spatchcock chuckled gleefully, "but I'm guessing he won't need his bikini line waxed anytime soon."

"What are you talking about, Spatch?"

"The lasers have – oh, never mind! He's done it, he's through!"

"Bravo!" Flintlock cheered loudly before realising where he was. "Well done," he continued in a much quieter voice. "I always knew he'd pull it off."

"Hmph! That was the easy part," Spatchcock said. "He's still got to penetrate the building, slip past all the security and unlock the vault."

"Oh dear. And that's more difficult?"

"Put it this way, your lordship – no thief has ever made it out of the Imperial Mint alive."

Dante was thankful for the drop in danger levels once inside the mint. He entered via a side window, its lock picked by a combination of the Crest's sentient computer mind and a cyborganic key extruded from one of Dante's fingernails. Inside there were no lasers to dodge, as the mint did not want its staff sliced and diced as they went about their jobs. Instead security rested with a series of alarms and motion sensors, all swiftly neutralised by the Crest. The Gentleman Thief needed less than ten minutes to reach the centre of the building, the mint's world famous Vault of Doom.

"Bit of a melodramatic name, don't you think?"

The Crest ignored Dante's sarcasm. *Nobody has ever deduced the correct combination for this chamber. It is said anyone hoping to crack the safe could spend a millennia of millennia upon the task and still not succeed.*

"Media hype, just a smokescreen to put off the easily discouraged."

I've scanned through the files for every attempt ever made. This task is almost impossible. I don't know why you persist in setting yourself such unobtainable goals; it's irrational and self-destructive.

"I like a challenge," Dante replied. "Besides, I have an advantage that none of my predecessors ever possessed, Crest. You."

Flattery's the food of fools. Jonathan Swift said that, a thousand years ago.

"Spare me the quotations, Crest. Can you open this vault or not?"

It won't be easy.

"I have every confidence in you."

Stop smirking when you say that, it'll be far more convincing. Dante did his best to comply. The Crest sighed in mild exasperation. *Now place your hands against the vault and cede control of your cyborganics to me.*

"How do I do that?"

Empty your mind of all thoughts – hardly the work of a lifetime.

"Just get on with it, Crest, we haven't got all night." Dante flattened his hands against the vault's door and tried to think of nothing. Tendrils of cyborganic circuitry emerged from his fingertips, a mixture of purple and silver, part flesh and part machine. The tendrils crept between the edges of the vault door and its housing, working their way into the locks.

"Getting anywhere yet?"

Have some patience! I'm trying to concentrate.

"Sorry." Dante pursed his lips and whistled a tune, the notes sliding carelessly from one key to another. The Crest sighed loudly inside Dante's head. "Sorry, sorry. Just passing the time."

Let's hope you never have to make a living with your musical talents.

"My mama said I had a beautiful singing voice as a child!"

Parents frequently lie to protect the feelings of their untalented offspring. Now let me concentrate! The Crest continued its investigation of the vault's locking mechanism. *Nearly got it–*

"So you're saying I don't whistle very well?"

Dante! For once in your life stop prattling and let me do what I do best!

A stony silence followed for the next thirty-seven seconds, until the vault's locks undid themselves one after another, each retracting with a heavy *thunk*. When all were disabled,

Dante removed his hands, the cyborganic circuitry already being absorbed back into his fingers. The massive door swung open to reveal a circular chamber, all burnished brass and gleaming silver. The thief stepped inside the vault and examined the rows of sealed boxes set into the walls. "I can whistle as well as the next man," Dante muttered under his breath.

I estimate you've less than thirty seconds before the central alarm is triggered and the vault flooded with nerve gas. Even I can't override that.

Dante tapped a box with the numbers 027 etched into its front. "This is the one." He opened the container and removed a slim wooden case from inside. "Funny, I didn't think it would be that easy."

Presumably the owners believed their external security system and the vault door were enough to keep that safe, the Crest ventured.

"I guess so." Dante wedged the wooden case inside the waistband of his trousers and shut the door to box 027.

Suddenly sirens and flashing red lights filled the vault. A noxious yellow gas billowed from grilles set into the floor, flooding the confined space.

Dante, get out. Now!

"I know, I know, evasive action," the thief replied, already running for the exit. The door was closing but Dante squeezed through the rapidly diminishing gap, just getting his trailing arm and leg out before the vault was sealed once more. "Phew!"

Phew indeed. Now you've just got to get past all the Berez Enforcers, cybernetically enhanced attack dogs and the laser defence grid again. But this time, they're expecting you.

Dante was already sprinting away from the vault, retracing his earlier steps. "Got any good news for me Crest?"

All this vigorous exercise might help you stave off incipient middle age spread for another day or two.

"Thanks!" Dante replied as he ran round a corner to find three Berez Enforcers blocking his escape route. "I'll bear that in mind!"

Spatchcock shrugged helplessly when the Imperial Mint's alarms started rending the air. "And it was going so well," he said with a heavy sigh.

"What should we do?" Flintlock asked querulously.

"You heard him – stay here and keep the motor running." Spatchcock turned to glance at the vehicle parked nearby. "But it beats me why he wants a limousine as the getaway car. Hardly inconspicuous, is it?"

Dante ducked, dived, dodged and wove his way past more than a dozen Enforcers, outran a pack of attack dogs and somehow eluded everything else the mint's security contingent threw at him, aided and abetted by the Crest's imminent threat warnings and motion sensors. Trapped between two oncoming squads of Enforcers, Dante had taken refuge behind the nearest doorway, ignoring the Crest's protestations.

No, don't go in there, it's–

"Trust me Crest, I know what I'm doing!"

Dante was surrounded by mops, brooms, buckets and shelves laden with cleansers, bleaches and disinfectants. "I'm guessing there's only one way in or out of here?"

Genius, pure genius. With such intelligence it's a wonder you need my help at all.

"Sarcasm is the lowest form of wit, Crest."

Now who's spouting quotations?

"Save it. I need an escape route, not smart-ass remarks!"

You could say you popped in to do a little late night mopping?

"Hmm... I've got a better idea." Dante opened the cupboard door and stepped out, smiling at the seventeen Enforcers crowding the corridor. As one they turned and aimed their pulse rifles at the intruder.

You call coming out of the closet a plan? the Crest spluttered.

"Gentlemen, I believe you've been looking for me," Dante announced grandly. "Congratulations – here I am!"

The Enforcers looked at each other quizzically, nonplussed by this development.

Dante bowed grandly before pulling a rectangle of card from inside his waistband. "Allow me to introduce myself properly. As you can see from my business card, I am Quentin Durward, Imperial Security Consultant."

One of the Enforcers snatched the card and examined it closely.

"All of you have been taking part in an exercise to test the security systems of this building and may I offer my thanks for your part in this. A most able and commendable display by all concerned," Dante continued, smiling broadly at the scowling Enforcers.

I don't think they're swallowing your story, the Crest whispered.

Dante ignored the voice inside his head. "It just remains for me to say something I have always wanted to utter: take me to your leader!"

The alien guard holding the business card dropped it on the floor and ground the card beneath his feet.

Dante's smile faltered slightly. "Is that a refusal?"

The Enforcer pulled back his weapon and swiftly smashed its butt into Dante's forehead. The thief staggered backwards into the broom cupboard, blood coursing from the wound below his hairline, eyelids fluttering weakly.

"That's no way to treat an accredited consultant to the... to the..."

Blackness closed in around Dante and he never finished the sentence.

"Spatch, it's been three hours. Surely he can't expect us to wait here much longer?" Flintlock was standing beside the limousine, his legs crossed, a pained expression on his face.

"How long have we known Dante?"

"Since the war."

"And has he ever let us down?"

"Not yet," Flintlock conceded.

"So we can wait a little longer for him, can't we?"

"I suppose."

Spatchcock noticed the Englishman's unhappy posture. "What's the matter with you? You look like you've been sampling my purge juice."

"If you must know, I need to relieve my bladder."

"You mean you want to take a piss."

"Must you be so crude about it?"

"You want to piss? Then piss. I couldn't care less," Spatchcock said.

"Out here, in the open? That's hardly seemly."

"Bugger that. I pissed my pants an hour ago."

Flintlock's face crumpled with distaste. "I wondered what the smell was."

The hum of an approaching vehicle cut short the exchange. Spatchcock watched intently as a stately silver flyer stopped outside the mint. Two Enforcers used electronic overrides to create a corridor in the laser grid and the flyer moved inside the perimeter. Once parked, a trio of middle-aged men in collar-less jackets emerged and strode into the building.

"I recognise one of them," Flintlock said, the call of his bladder forgotten for the moment. "Eugene Jamieson. He used to run the Bank of Britannia. Refused to extend my credit after an unfortunate flutter at Royal Ascot went awry one year. The arrogant sod!"

"Could be governors of the Imperial Mint. They look like merchant bankers. But what are they doing here, at this time of night?" Spatchcock wondered.

■ ■ ■

Dante opened his eyes to find three concerned men in suits peering at him. "Mr Durward? Are you alright?" one of them asked, his extra chins wobbling slowly.

"I've felt better, I must admit." He tried to stand but the pain stabbing through his skull persuaded him against such movement. Instead Dante sunk back into the plush, upholstered chair. He was sat in the centre of a large, richly furnished office. Portraits of stern-faced men lined the walls, each adorned with a gold plaque noting the past contributions to the Imperial Mint. "What happened exactly?"

The fattest of the three men stepped forward, his hands held open in apology. "I regret to say one of our alien guards was overly enthusiastic in the application of their duties. You received a blow to the head and were rendered unconscious. It was only after the members of the board were contacted about the apparent intrusion at the mint that this mistake was uncovered. I called the number on your business card and was reassured of your bona fides by the President of Imperial Security Consultancy, Lord Spatchcock."

Somebody had been doing some fast-talking, Dante realised. "Very well. In the circumstances, I'm sure my firm shall be willing to set aside any legal action that might otherwise follow from such a violent and painful incident."

"That would be most kind of you," the obese man replied. "Most kind."

Dante held a hand to the throbbing contusion on his forehead. "Forgive my asking, but the blow seems to have clouded my memory a little. What was your name, sir?"

"Sharapov, Sergei Sharapov. I am Governor of the Mint. And these are two of my directors, Boris Onegin and Eugene Jamieson." Sharapov's offsiders nodded at Dante, who acknowledged their presence.

"Well, gentleman, my report on the mint's security systems is mostly positive. Your laser defence grid can be penetrated, by only by an exceptional athlete such as myself," Dante said with a wry smile. "The locking mechanism on your external windows needs improving, but that should not cost you more than half a million roubles. The main area of concern is your so-called Vault of Doom. For such a fabled and supposedly unbreakable safe, it was all too easy for me to gain access to the valuables stored within."

Onegin stepped closer to Dante. "If I might ask, how is it you were able to defeat the vault when so many others have failed?"

"You may ask, but I must decline to reveal my methods. Trade secrets, you understand, must remain secrets, of course. Even when I deliberately triggered the final alarm sensor within the vault–"

Ha!

Dante did his best to ignore this outburst from the Crest. "Even when I deliberately triggered it, I was still able to escape the chamber – removing this with me." He reached into the waistband of his trousers and extracted the slim wooden case taken from box 027. "I doubt you would wish the printing plates for the million rouble note to fall into the wrong hands."

Sharapov's eyes widened with horror. "No, indeed not! Thank the Tsar you were able to uncover these flaws in our security perimeter, Mr Durward!"

"Don't thank me," Dante replied. "All part of the service. Of course, if you felt the urge to add a little extra to my fee as a bonus, I would be most grateful for any such consideration."

"Of course, of course!" Sharapov glanced at his colleagues, who nodded hurriedly. "An extra ten per cent on top of your fee?"

Dante coughed.

"Fifteen per cent, I meant fifteen per cent," Sharapov continued. "Sorry, slip of the tongue there. A fifteen per cent bonus."

Dante smiled. "Most generous. You may be assured of utter discretion. It would not do if the real Gentleman Thief or those of his ilk should learn of the vulnerabilities in your defences."

"I wanted to ask why you wore such curious garb," Onegin said.

"You haven't heard of the Gentleman Thief?" Dante asked. "The most famous cutpurse and cat burglar in all the Empire?"

The three men shook their heads.

"Thank heavens I arrived when I did! He would have robbed you blind. Imagine the consequences if that happened. Imagine facing the Tsar himself and trying to explain such a calamity!"

The trio swallowed simultaneously, their discomfit all too evident. Having had sufficient time to recover, Dante stood. "Well, if you'll just make out a banker's draft to the Imperial Security Consultancy, I'll be on my way. With any luck my limousine will be waiting to collect me outside."

Flintlock pulled the peaked cap down over his eyes, not wanting to be recognised by Jamieson. Fortunately the three men from the Imperial Mint were too busy ushering Dante to his limousine to notice the identity of the uniformed chauffeur holding open the passenger door.

"Well, gentleman, it's been both a privilege and an honour to do business with you. One of my associates will be back sometime in the next year to carry out a spot check, as a way of ensuring the mint undertakes the necessary upgrades and keeping your security forces on their toes."

"Excellent," the Governor replied. "I hope our next intruder is far less successful than you were, Mr Durward!"

"Absolutely. Thank you again for the banker's draft and the bonus. All that remains is for me to bid you farewell." Dante began climbing into the limousine but a concerned whimper from the Governor made him straighten up again.

"Sorry, Mr Durward, but you still have the plates in your possession!"

Dante smiled. "Dear, oh dear, what a forgetful fool I am! You wouldn't want me wandering off with those now, would you? Ha, ha, ha!"

The three men from the mint laughed along with him, their voices cracked with nervous hysteria. Dante produced the slim wooden case and handed it over to the governor.

"Here you are, Make sure it stays safely locked away from now on."

"I will, don't worry about that, I will!"

"Good. Then my work here is done. Good day to you all." Dante entered the vehicle, Flintlock shutting the door politely after him before hurrying round to the driver's side. Within moments the limousine was rolling away, leaving the three directors to heave a relieved sigh.

The Governor looked at his colleagues. "That was too close. My life wouldn't be worth living if the–" He stopped abruptly, colour draining from his face. "I–I–"

"Sergei? What is it? What's wrong?" Onegin asked. He followed the Governor's gaze down to the wooden case. Sharapov had opened the box to find the printing plates were missing. Instead a rectangle of card was nestling on the vermilion velvet lining, a single line of text visible on it: "Congratulations, you have just been robbed by Nikolai Dante, the Gentleman Thief."

"How will I ever report this to the Tsar?" Sharapov spluttered. "I let Nikolai Dante walk out of the Imperial Mint with our most valuable asset?"

Onegin read the card again. "This can't be happening. It can't!"

Jamieson wrung his hands in desperation. "Perhaps we can still get offworld before the loss is discovered?"

Sharapov shook his head helplessly. "It's too late. We're already dead men." He turned and began walking towards the mint's laser defence grid.

"Sergei! What are you doing?" Jamieson shouted.

But the Governor did not reply. He kept walking, never uttering another word, not even when the lasers began slicing his body apart.

"You realise you've condemned those men to death, don't you?" Spatchcock asked. He was sat in the front passenger seat of the limousine, his presence in the vehicle having been hidden by the tinted windows.

"The Tsar will order their executions, not me," Dante replied. "Besides, when you work for that bastard, you deserve what you get. Everyone knows the Tsar's price for failure."

"What about the banker's draft?" Flintlock looked at Dante in the rear-view mirror as he drove. "You can't be planning to cash it?"

That would be both foolish and suicidal, the Crest commented dryly. *Sounds just your style.*

Dante crumpled the draft into a ball and threw it to his accomplices. "You two can keep it as a souvenir. The only thing that piece of paper is useful for now would be wiping your backside."

Spatchcock smiled. "You better have it then, Flintlock, in case you get caught short again."

"You might have a mind permanently residing in the gutter, but some of us still aspire to higher things," the former nobleman said. "Where to now?"

"The black market at Tsyganov," Dante replied, removing two thin sheets of metal from inside his trousers. "I know a counterfeiter there who'll pay well for these. The mint will have changed the million-rouble note by tonight but the old ones will stay in circulation for a few weeks yet. The sooner we can sell these plates, the better the price we'll get."

THREE

"He that is feared cannot be loved"
– Russian proverb

The Imperial flyer re-entered the airspace above St Petersburg shortly before dawn, the majestic city sprawling below like some bejewelled, black velvet gown. But Jena paid the magnificent vista no heed. She had seen it countless times from such a vantage point and her thoughts were elsewhere, still mulling over what she had witnessed in the laboratories on Fabergé Island. The pilot had to clear his throat several times to get her attention.

"Yes, what is it?" she said testily.

"We're making our final approach to the Imperial Palace, ma'am. You asked to be kept informed."

"Very good. Take us in."

"Yes, ma'am." The pilot pressed his controls forward and the flyer surged towards the floating edifice in the sky.

The Imperial Palace was a remarkable melding of technology and aesthetics. Taking its inspiration from the legendary designs of Carl Fabergé, the palace was shaped like a huge white egg. A hundred metres in height, its exterior was divided into a multiplicity of segments. Each was studded with windows, tiny squares set into the vast circumference of the palace. A large circular portal was visible on one side of the structure, open to allow authorised flyers access. Raven Corps troops mounted on flying mechanical steeds encircled the palace, keeping watch for potential attacks.

Once the sun was above the horizon, the palace would cast an imposing shadow across the city, just as the Tsar's will could turn day into night for anyone unfortunate enough to invoke his wrath.

"Imperial Palace to approaching flyer, transmit entry codes."

Jena lent forward and thrust a studded ring on her right hand into a cavity on the flyer's control panel.

"Entry codes accepted. Welcome back, Lady Jena."

The flyer swept through the circular portal and found a docking berth inside. Jena was already disembarking by the time a captain of the Raven Corps ran into view. "Lady Jena! Your father wishes to see you. He's in the Chamber of Judgement. If you'll follow me–"

Jena brushed past the captain, not bothering to acknowledge his salute. "I know the way, thank you very much. Tell my father I'm going to shower and change first. I want to rid myself of Fabergé's taint before I do anything else."

"Er, yes... ma'am," the captain replied fearfully.

Thirty minutes later Jena strode into the Chamber of Judgement, an intimidating and cavernous space near the top of the palace. Ranks of seating were built into the walls, enabling invited guests to witness the Tsar passing sentence on those that had displeased him or broken one of the Empire's many draconian laws. The prisoners' walkway extended out over a sheer drop, while the officers of the court usually loomed overhead on hovering pedestals. For now the chamber was empty, bar the brooding figure sat on a floating throne.

The Tsar glared down at Jena, his arms folded across his chest. Barrel-chested and powerful of build, Vladimir Makarov was a fearsome figure in magisterial robes of silver. Greying hair swept imperiously back from his stern, remorseless features, while a black and grey flecked beard curled outwards from his chin. His face was a permanent snarl, black eyes burning with suppressed rage. "What took you so long?" he demanded. "You were told to come and see me immediately and on your return, yes?"

"I washed and changed first. I wanted to cleanse myself of what I have witnessed," Jena replied. She did a little twirl so her father could see the entire crushed crimson velvet trouser suit she was now wearing. "Perhaps you don't like the outfit? I thought you had no problems with the colour of blood, father."

"Jena, my love," the Tsar growled, "do not try my patience. You flouted my order deliberately! And you know how I dislike being disobeyed." He gestured at the remains of the captain sent to fetch Jena. The body had been flayed alive and now lay in a pool of blood and skin flaps.

"I think the entire Empire knows how you dislike disobedience."

"Then you would do well not to provoke me, child. Now – report!"

Jena outlined all she had seen and heard on Fabergé Island, excluding only her encounter with Di Grizov. That was of little consequence in her opinion and merely mentioning the name Nikolai Dante was likely to send the Tsar into a murderous rage. Instead she offered detailed descriptions of the experiments already completed and the extrapolated outcome of the doctor's ongoing project. Her father listened carefully, nodding as she made mention of the next stage in Fabergé's researches. Only after Jena had finished did the Tsar make any comment.

"Good. You have told me all I wanted to know. But I sense you have more you wish to say about the good doctor and his work, yes?"

Jena nodded, choosing her next words carefully, mindful of the bloody corpse not far from her feet. "I have significant doubts about the sanity of Doctor Fabergé. He is both deranged and potentially dangerous. Certainly he is bloated with his own self-importance, but that in itself is not a crime.

However he appears to be developing unhealthy delusions of grandeur. Fabergé thinks that by playing God he can become like a god himself. I doubt he can be trusted in the medium to long term."

The Tsar nodded at this assessment. "Agreed. That was why I elevated the House of Fabergé to the status of the noble dynasty not long after the war. The doctor has a rampaging ego to rival even my own, but he will remain loyal to me long enough for my uses. After that he shall be expendable. If he dared challenge my rule, Fabergé would soon discover just how expendable he is."

"But what about his next experiment?" Jena asked. "Even you cannot condone such barbarity, an atrocity of that nature – can you?"

"Condone it? It was my idea," the Tsar replied, amusement evident in his deep, booming voice. "If Fabergé can deliver upon his promises, I shall have at my disposal a new weapon that strengthens my grip upon the Empire for decades, even generations to come. Since you are my sole surviving heir, I would have thought the Fabergé experiments were in your best interests too!"

"I could never be a party to such–"

"No one is asking you to be!" the Tsar thundered, his mood suddenly darkening. "For more than a decade the Romanovs held me at bay with their precious Weapons Crest technology. Now they have been swept aside, the survivors no more than a rabble hiding themselves in the corners of the Empire! The Crests they were once so proud of will be the playthings of a child next to the weapon Fabergé is developing. I will become all-powerful! None shall dare oppose me again!"

"None dare oppose you now, father!" Jena shouted back. "You won the war, you crushed all opposition. Why do you need this new weapon? What good can it possibly do?"

The Tsar shook his head sadly. "Weapons are never used to do good, my daughter. Weapons are about getting and retaining power – nothing more, nothing less. If you have not grasped that by now, you never will!"

"But you must see–"

"Enough!" The Tsar piloted his hovering throne down so he could step off it and onto the platform beside Jena. "I have tolerated your insolence and your pious attitude enough for today. You are dismissed!"

"But–"

The Tsar pulled back his left hand, ready to strike Jena across the face, but she did not flinch nor cower. After a moment he lowered his hand again, regarding his daughter thoughtfully. "I am Tsar of all the Russians, my child, and I will do as I see fit. Fabergé's experiments shall continue and by Easter Sunday I shall have my new weapon. Be thankful your involvement with its development ends here." He strode away, leaving Jena alone in the Chamber of Judgement.

She watched him depart, hatred etched on her features. "We'll see about that," Jena whispered under her breath.

At midday Jena was back at her bedchamber inside the Imperial Palace, when one of her ladies-in-waiting knocked on the door. Anastasia was twenty-one, a meek and plain-faced woman who had proven herself completely loyal to the Tsarina. "Lady Jena, I have a report marked for your eyes only."

"Leave it on the bed, I'll read it later."

"Very good, ma'am."

Jena waited until she was alone before hurrying to the bed and tearing open the envelope. She hated herself for the eagerness with which her eyes sped across the words, absorbing the latest information about a man she hated and loved in equal measure. As Tsarina she was allowed a personal staff of ladies-in-waiting, couturiers and maids to attend to her whims and pleasures. The Tsar's daughter was expected to have the finest gowns, always keeping one step ahead of other nobility.

Since the war Jena had been redirecting a fraction of the funding for her private staff to chart the movements of Dante. It was a compulsion, like an itch she couldn't help scratching, but she had to know where he was – even if she didn't allow others to say his name in her presence. Apparently he was back in St Petersburg, the careless fool. He had been spotted near the black market at Tsyganov, involved in a heated transaction with a noted counterfeiter. A considerable sum of roubles had changed hands. Knowing Dante, he was now probably drinking himself into a stupor somewhere.

Nothing surprising there, except for the fool's willingness to put himself in harm's way. Devil may care or too stupid to know better? It was hard to tell with Nikolai. Despite herself, Jena wished she could see him again. The thought of being with him brought a flush to her face and quickened her breath. She shook her head at such folly. Now who was the fool – Dante or the woman who couldn't forget him?

Jena tossed the report to one side. There were more pressing problems than one rascal, no matter how much he invaded her thoughts and feelings. The parting threat from her father had been all too apparent. I'm his only heir, she thought, and that's the only reason I'm still alive today. No one else could challenge him the way I have and expect to survive. But if Fabergé succeeds in what he has planned, if his next experiment should deliver the weapon my father wants...

"He must be stopped," Jena muttered to herself. "But how?" She dared not intervene directly; such an act would sign her death warrant. To achieve her aim, she must move in such a way that Fabergé's failure could never be traced back to her. But the question still remained, how? I need a weapon of my own, a tool – someone I can send to do my dirty work, someone foolish enough to take on such a dangerous mission and yet brave enough to venture in where others would not dare.

"Where am I going to find such a person?" she wondered out loud. Another knock at the door interrupted her thoughts. "Yes?"

Anastasia re-entered, curtsying apologetically. "Sorry, Lady Jena, but you gave me a standing order that I destroy all reports about the whereabouts of you-know-who once you've had a chance to read them. If you have finished with the latest bulletin, I could–"

"Of course!" Jena could not help smiling, the irony of her solution too delicious not to be savoured. She picked up the report and handed it over. "Make sure you destroy all trace of it."

"Yes, ma'am." Anastasia curtsied again before turning to leave.

"Wait, there's something else," Jena added.

"Yes, ma'am?"

"I need you to deliver a message."

Famous Flora's Massage Parlour was among the Empire's most beloved houses of ill repute. While it lacked the House of Sin's legendary status or the breadth of perversity on offer at World of Leather, Famous Flora's was still a five star brothel with something to tickle the fancy of any client. Dante stood outside the parlour's entrance, gazing in disbelief at the doorway surrounded by a neon replica of female genitalia.

"Are you sure this is where you want to spend your cut from the heist?"

"Loathe as I am to admit this, it's been quite some time since I've been able to indulge myself with a lady," Flintlock replied. "Alas, too long spent in the company of Spatch here has rather blunted my appeal with the fairer sex. The finest of colognes can only mask so much."

"Yeah," Spatchcock said, grinning broadly. "They certainly don't cover the stench of dung when you're talking!"

"I resent that remark, and its implications!" Flintlock snapped.

"Resent all you want, I couldn't give a sh–"

"That's enough," Dante interjected. "You two starting a fight outside a cat-house will only attract unwanted attention. Let's get inside."

The trio entered the building, its doors closing with a wet slurp behind them. Ahead a steep staircase led up to the reception area where a bored woman sat watching a soap opera on the ImperialNet. "Six hundred roubles," she announced, not bothering to look at the new arrivals. "Each."

"Six hundred? That's outrageous," Flintlock spluttered. "I'll have you know I'm a personal friend of Flora herself. Ask her to come out here and I'm sure–"

"Six hundred. Each," the receptionist repeated. One of her nostrils twitched as the first waft of Spatchcock's unique personal odour began to insinuate itself into her senses. Dante recognised the signs and quickly handed over two thousand roubles.

"Keep the change," he offered, pushing the still protesting Flintlock onwards. Spatchcock followed happily behind, pausing to leer at the receptionist's cleavage. Dante grabbed the grubby little poisoner and dragged him towards the brothel's inner sanctum. The threesome pushed through a set of double doors and beheld the waiting room.

A vast cathedral devoted to fornication spread itself before them, lushly furnished in gold and crimson. Around the walls hung erotic masterpieces, both painted and photographed, depicting a myriad of human bodies cavorting in daring and unlikely positions. Tall, phallic cabinets of glass held displays of sexual aids and appendages, some of such a size they made the eyes water involuntarily. Dotted around the chamber were dozens of seats occupied by the parlour's customers. Most were men but a few women also waited for the next parade.

"I've heard about this place but I've never been inside it," Spatchcock admitted. "Is it true what they say about the girls here?"

"Yes," Dante admitted, "and the men too – they will do anything you desire, as long as no one dies or is permanently injured."

"Nice," Spatchcock grinned, rubbing his hands together gleefully.

"You should count yourself lucky you even got in here," Flintlock said pompously. "One more whiff of you and I believe that receptionist would have had the lot of us thrown out on our ears."

"Unlikely," Dante commented. "You may have been bluffing about being a personal friend of Flora, but I do know her. I doubt she would have let me be ejected without getting her hands on the contents of my pants first."

"Only if your pants contain an unfeasibly large sum of money," a husky voice replied from behind the trio. The three men turned to find a triple-breasted woman clad in black lingerie regarding them. She was tall, tanned and utterly bald but for a thick black beard.

"Flora!" Dante gasped in surprise. "Since when did you become one of the Devil's Martyrs?" All disciples of that religion were required to sport beards as a sign of devotion, even the women. The Devil's Martyrs were renowned for their wild sexual excesses.

The brothel owner stroked her beard. "Of course, you haven't seen me since before the war. I joined the House of Rasputin once I saw which way the fighting was going. Pledging allegiance to an official Imperial cult gave me protection from the Tsar's pogroms."

"And the extra breast?" Flintlock asked, getting an elbow in the ribs from Dante for his impertinence.

"That's why she's famous," Spatchcock hissed under his breath. "Famous Flora, the only human with three natural breasts!"

Dante smoothed down the bristles of his own goatee. "Hmm, I think the beard suits you. There's not many women that can carry it off, but on you–"

"Enough flattery," Flora said. "Why are you here? I don't know if you should even be allowed in the building."

"My friends would like to partake of your establishment's services."

"I hope your friends have deep pockets. We have a very rich client base and prices to match these days."

Dante smiled. "I'm sure they can meet any tariffs you care to charge."

"Very well," Flora agreed. "The parade is about to begin. You'd better take your seats."

Spatchcock watched the owner depart, licking his lips lasciviously. "Oh, three for the price of two – that's what I call value for money! But I'm not so sure about the beard. Never had it away with a woman whose got a better growth than me, not sure I'd like that."

"You should try it," Dante suggested. "The stubble rash can be a bit painful but there's nothing quite like the feeling of a beard brushing against the insides of your thighs, take my word for it."

"You mean... you and her?"

"No, Flora didn't have the beard when I knew her best. But I did once spend a night with Lady Eudoxia Looshin."

"And?" Flintlock asked excitedly. "Was she as good as her reputation?"

"Let's just say that's one night I won't forget in a hurry," Dante replied. "Now, be quiet, both of you – the parade is starting." The trio found an unoccupied chaise lounge and perched on its plush upholstery. The lights in the room began to dim, half a dozen crystal chandeliers rising into the vaulted ceiling. A catwalk slowly descended, nearly thirty men and women in various costumes and states of undress posing along it. Once the catwalk was locked into position at head height, a set of stairs swung down to the floor, allowing the sex workers to descend.

Flora herself reappeared above the scene, gracefully swinging on a trapeze while picked out by a follow spot. "Good afternoon, ladies and gentlemen. Welcome to my parlour of delights, where you can have whatever you desire – for the right price. Here you will find beauties and beasts, male and female, submissive and dominant, butch and bitch alike. Here you will be teased and taunted, tempted and punished, given pain and pleasure – all in whatever measures you wish. We make no judgements, keep no records and tell no lies at Famous Flora's. We merely wish to fulfil you, in every way possible. Let the fun commence!"

The first person on offer began descending from the catwalk. "We begin today's selection of delights with Hattie," Flora announced, "a former customer from Britannia who so enjoyed her time inside this establishment she decided to remain here permanently." She was a rotund woman in the uniform of a British matron, her mighty bosom hardly held in check by the navy blue latex costume. She strutted among the patrons, one hand smacking against the ample cheeks of her behind. "Hattie loves to punish naughty boys, putting them across her knee and administering six of the best. It's up to you whether you want to receive the spanking with your trousers on or off. Ladies and gentlemen, a big hand for Hattie!"

The customers responded with enthusiastic applause, several already waving large wads of cash in the air, eager to get their hands on her. Flora tutted theatrically from her swinging perch overhead.

"My, my, we do have some eager beavers waiting to be admonished! Don't let your excitement get the better of you, boys, otherwise Hattie will make you clean up the mess personally." That only flushed the faces of those waving their wads further, Flintlock among them.

"Oh, matron!" he cried out. "I've been a naughty boy and I need to be punished!" Flintlock began rising from his seat but a hand pulled him back.

"Restraint," Dante urged. "There's plenty more where she came from."

"Really? I think she brought most of it with her," Spatchcock chipped in.

"You're a fine one to preach," Flintlock told Dante. "You've never practised restraint one day of your life."

"There's a first time for everything."

"Our next offering is Maria," Flora continued, "the youngest of our talents. Just eighteen today, she is looking for a strong authority figure, someone who can teach her how to behave." A pretty, petite woman in a schoolgirl's uniform descended from the catwalk, choosing her steps carefully. "Maria is new here and needs to be taken in hand, if you know what I mean."

"I'll bet she does," Spatchcock leered. "I know just where to put 'em, too."

The parade of sex workers continued – muscled men with gleaming torsos, rampant women in an array of outfits, dwarves, aliens, even robots, all were on offer to anyone with the right number of roubles. Flintlock eventually decided to spend most of his cash on two women – the hefty charms of Hattie and a French maid known as Yvette. Spatchcock left to pursue a tempting young woman called Anya who specialised in naked mud wrestling. "Sounds just my kind of girl," the grubby ex-con announced. "Naked, dirty and ready for a roll in the mud."

But Dante could not get excited by any of the pleasures on offer, instead retiring to a well stocked bar in a corner of the sex cathedral. There he ordered a large bottle of Imperial Blue vodka and began drinking it like water. Once the parade was finished and all the staff occupied with clients, Flora joined him at the bar. "Drinking alone, Nikolai? Not a very healthy pass-time."

"Perhaps I've had my fill of whores," he said, before remembering what Flora did for a living. "Sorry – nothing personal."

"No, that's fine. If you want to drink here at our inflated prices, you'll make my accountant a very happy woman." Flora gestured at the seat beside him. "Mind if I join you?"

Dante shrugged and called for another glass, then poured a generous slug of vodka into it. "Here's to money, the root of all evil." He downed the contents of his glass in a single gulp before pouring another. Flora watched him closely, her face betraying her concern.

"Since when did you hate money, Nikolai? When we were both scraping a living in the back streets of St Petersburg you couldn't get enough roubles to make you happy. Now you're throwing it away like there's no tomorrow."

"Maybe there isn't," Dante replied, his voice beginning to slur a little. "The Tsar's put a bounty on my head that could finance Rudinshtein for a year."

"I know," Flora said. "You should be careful in here, some of my clients might be tempted to try and claim the reward."

"I'm surprised you haven't called the Raven Corps yourself."

"Those bullies would cost me more in damages and lost custom than I would gain by turning you in. Besides, we go back a long way."

Dante pointed a finger at Flora. "You bet your ass!"

She reached out a hand to touch him. "When did you get so bitter? I thought Nikolai Dante was all devil-may-care and honour be damned."

"Maybe I've started to grow up."

"Or maybe you're just feeling sorry for yourself?"

He shrugged in reply. "I never had two roubles to rub together before I became one of the Romanovs. Now I can steal a small fortune in one morning and it still doesn't make me happy. Why not? What's wrong with me?"

"Perhaps you realise there's more to life than just money?"

"Like what?"

"Love? Being happy? Having friends?"

Dante guzzled another tumbler of vodka. "And what would you know about that, Flora?"

The brothel owner smiled. "More than you, I suspect. I may put on the act of a lascivious old whore, but when I get home I know my partner is waiting for me. We can be together, just be, and there's nobody to judge us or trouble us."

"Sounds delightful."

Flora shook her head. "What do you believe in, Dante? What are you for? I followed your progress during the war – you were fighting for something then, something bigger than you, something important. What are you doing now?"

"I'm enjoying myself!"

"So I can see – sat in a whorehouse, pockets bulging with money and trying to drink yourself stupid to blot out whatever you don't want to think about. I'm glad all our customers don't enjoy themselves this much, my staff would be out of work." Flora stood up, leaving a last comment for Dante to contemplate. "You're like a shark, Nikolai. You've got to keep moving forwards, or else you die. It's time to move forwards again."

She strode away, leaving him peering at the last measure of vodka in his bottle. He held it up as a mock salute to the departing woman before draining the contents.

For the owner of a house of ill repute, Famous Flora speaks a lot of sense, the Crest said.

"Oh no, not you too," Dante winced. "I knew you couldn't keep quiet long."

I'm just saying there is more than a little truth in what she observed. You are flailing around, Dante. Why did you rob the Imperial Mint this morning?

"Because it was there."

Bravo! Why not hit yourself on the head with that vodka bottle? It's there too and so is your skull. Why not bring the two together?

"Because that would be stupid."

That's never stopped you before.

"Have you quite finished? I've already had my lecture for the day from Flora, I don't need you joining in."

That's unfortunate, as I have more to say, the Crest replied. *You need a cause, something to get you out of this slough of self-pity and self-regard.*

Dante shook the empty bottle. "I wonder how much vodka I have to drink to incapacitate you, Crest?"

More than your body could sustain. You'll pass out long before I do.

"Pity." Dante threw the bottle over his shoulder, listening with satisfaction as it smashed in the background. "Did I hit anyone?"

No, but there is a woman approaching. She doesn't look happy.

"Flora?"

Not exactly, the Crest replied.

"Excuse me," a soft voice said, "but are you Nikolai Dante?"

"Who wants to know?" Dante asked, rotating round on his bar stool. He found himself facing an unremarkable, plain-faced woman. She was wearing a heavy black cloak and hood that hid her body and even the colour of her hair.

"My name isn't important," she replied nervously.

"Maybe not, but you'll have to display your wares a little better if you want to get any business in this place. Famous Flora's is many things, but subtle is not one of them." Dante was surprised to see her burst into tears. "Sorry – was it something I said?"

Why would she possibly think that? the Crest interjected archly.

"Be quiet," Dante hissed under his breath.

"I'm sorry," the woman said. "I'm trying not to cry too loudly."

"No, not you. I was talking to my..." Dante checked himself. "I was talking to myself. Bit of a one-sided conversation, to be honest."

I'll say, the Crest added.

Dante bit his lip rather than rise to the bait a second time. He stood up and ushered the young woman to a nearby seat. She produced a handkerchief from inside her cloak and dabbed away the tears.

"You must think me very strange, accosting you in this place," she said.

"I've been accosted in worse places."

"It's my Uncle James," the woman continued. "He's dying."

"I'm... sorry to hear that."

"He's dying and I can't get in to see him. I thought maybe you might be able to reach him, or at least get him a message. I know it's dangerous, but I didn't know whom else to turn to. My uncle always said you would attempt the impossible, no matter how foolhardy the venture."

Sounds like he knows you well, the Crest ventured.

Dante grimaced but chose to ignore the telepathic commentary, knowing the Crest would fall silent if he didn't respond to its jibes. "Your Uncle James – could you tell me his full name?"

The woman nodded, tears starting to flow again. "Di Grizov, James Di Grizov. Some people called him Jim."

Dante sat back as if punched in the chest. More than a decade has passed since he last saw his mentor, the lift doors at the Casino Royale closing between them. Di Grizov had beaten him, stolen the Fabergé egg and left him to face the music. But despite all that, Dante found he did not bear his former mentor a grudge – life was too short for that. "You say he's dying? Where is he? I'd like to see him before the end, for old time's sake."

"He's in a gulag, a work camp. I doubt he'll last another week."

"Where?"

"Near the Murmansk Alienation Zone. It's the only gulag in that region. They don't allow visitors and none of the prisoners ever leave the compound alive. I only discovered my uncle was being held there by chance. He bribed one of the guards to carry out a message for me."

Dante smiled. "I'm surprised Jim hasn't escaped. I've never known any cell or jail that could hold him."

"Maybe, when he was younger. Before they took his legs."

"His legs?"

"Amputated, to stop him escaping." The woman was sobbing gently now, unable to hold back her grief any more. "The guard laughed when he told me."

Dante could feel a red mist of anger rising. "Is this guard still in St Petersburg? I'd like to have a word with him."

"No, he's gone back to the gulag. The next shuttle to the Murmansk region leaves at midnight tonight. I was going to catch it, but knew I could never hope to reach my uncle in time. Then I remembered you…"

"Alright," Dante said softly, slipping a comforting arm around the young woman's shoulders. "It's going to be alright. I'll go. I'll find your uncle. If I can, I'll get him out of the gulag. If I can't, then I'll take your message to him. What do you want me to say?"

She turned and looked at Dante intently, the tears gone from her eyes now. "Before he was caught, my uncle had hidden his money in a secret location – said it was his retirement fund. If anything ever happened to him, I was to have it. He had a codename for his hiding place. You need to find out where that money is. Ask him you to tell you about the hiding place."

"You trust me with that knowledge?"

"My uncle said you were among the few men he had ever trusted. I have to show the same faith in you."

Dante nodded. "What's the codename?"

"Ask him to tell you about the Strangelove Gambit." The young woman noticed Spatchcock approaching and rose from her seat. "I have to go now. Remember what I told you, but don't share it with anyone else. Goodbye!" She hurried away, disappearing among the crowd of customers and sex workers mingled in the vast chamber.

Dante started after her. "If I do get a message for you from Jim, how will I contact you? I don't even know your name!"

But the woman was gone, leaving a confused Dante behind. He noticed her discarded handkerchief on the floor and picked it up. A three-letter monogram was sewn into one corner of the fabric: AdG. "Something Di Grizov," Dante speculated. "Alice? Alicia? Anastasia?" None of the names rang any bells in his vodka-muddled mind. "I can't even remember Jim saying he had any family, let alone a niece."

"What are you muttering about?" Spatchcock demanded.

"A mysterious encounter," Dante replied.

"I should be so lucky," the other man said with a scowl. "I couldn't find anyone willing to enjoy a little non-stop erotic action with me, despite offering all my cut."

"Not even Anya, the naked mud wrestler? I'd have thought your down and dirty charms would be right up her alley."

Spatchcock shook his head. "Claimed she was washing her hair tonight. Since when do whores take the night off to wash their hair?"

"Maybe you should have tried washing yours before you came in," Dante offered, trying not to inhale the odours wafting from his partner in crime. "There's a limit to what anyone will do for money."

Spatchcock nodded at the wisdom of this. "You found some company."

"No, I... Oh, that woman? She had a message for me."

"Yeah? How did she know you'd be here?"

"That's a good question," Dante conceded. "How *did* she know?"

More to the point, how many other people know? the Crest asked. *Considering the bounty on your head and the nature of this establishment's clientele, you might be well advised to take your leave. A close encounter with the Raven Corps would not make getting out of St Petersburg any easier.*

"Good advice, Crest. Spatch, where's Flintlock?"

The foul-smelling felon chewed his bottom lip thought-fully. "I think he's either in the schoolroom or the parlour. He paid for a two hour session, so his lordship's still got another twenty minutes left."

"Well, he'll have to finish whatever he's doing in the next two minutes," Dante decided. "You take the parlour, I'll try the school room."

The two men consulted a signpost for directions to each of the massage parlour's pleasure suites before splitting up.

Dante found the schoolroom only after wrongly bursting into the baby's nursery. The sight of three grown men in dia-pers being nursed was enough to remove any lingering effects of his vodka binge. "And you call me a big baby!"

At least I don't have to burp you, the Crest conceded. *The schoolroom is directly ahead. May I suggest discretion as the better part of valour this time?*

"Good idea." Dante knocked circumspectly on the door.

"Yes, who is it?" an imperious female voice inquired.

"I'm looking for a friend of mine, I think he might be in there."

"I'm sorry, young man, but I refuse to carry on a conversation with a door. If you wish to speak with myself or any of the stu-dents, you must ask permission to enter like any other pupil."

"Alright, can I come inside?"

"No, no, not like that! Ask permission properly!"

"Crest?" Dante asked. "Any suggestions?"

You're on your own here. My etiquette training does not extend to the required form of address for a brothel's schoolmistress.

"Thanks, that's a great help."

"Well?" the woman demanded. "Do you wish to come in or not?"

"Er, please miss, may I enter the classroom," Dante ven-tured.

"You may."

Dante twisted the handle and opened the door enough to see inside. It was an exact replica of a schoolroom, complete with desks and chairs for half a dozen pupils, a blackboard on the far wall and a chart detailing the students' recent achievements. Four grown men dressed as school boys were cowering in their seats while a fifth was bent over double in front of the blackboard, his shorts round his ankles. A sour-faced woman of fifty clad in only an academic gown and mortarboard was standing to one side, wielding a prodigious cane.

"Well, young man – is your friend in here?" she demanded.

Dante glanced round the five students but could not see Flintlock among them. Still, he wouldn't put it past the exiled aristocrat to favour such a sexual preference. Dante's few visits to Britannia had convinced him the nation was home to all manner of perversities. Perhaps it had something to do with the weather, being stuck inside all day because of the rain, with nothing better to do than let your imagination run riot.

"No, he's not. Well, sorry to disturb you. I'll just–"

"You'll just what?" the teacher shrieked furiously, several parts of her anatomy wobbling in sympathy with her rage. "You'll just come here and take your punishment for interrupting my class!"

"But I–"

"Now!"

"No, you don't understand," Dante insisted. "I–"

I think you'd better do what she says, the Crest said gleefully. *This is one teacher who doesn't appear likely to take no for an answer.*

"I should have brought her an apple," Dante muttered under his breath.

"What was that, you insolent little boy?" The teacher was advancing towards Dante now, the cane twitching in her right hand. "I'll show you the meaning of discipline!"

• • •

It was Spatchcock who found Flintlock first. The former Lord of Fitzrovia was lying across the ample lap of Hattie the matron, receiving a trousers down spanking on his bare, bony behind. At the same time, Flintlock was being served tea and hot buttered crumpets. She was leaning over to pour another cup, her French maid's uniform riding up to reveal her stocking tops.

"Oh, yes, that's the way to do it," Flintlock purred. In between munches of his crumpet Flintlock gave little yelps of ecstasy as Hattie smacked his buttocks with a wooden hairbrush, the force of each blow wobbling her bosom.

"You've been a very naughty boy, haven't you, Flinty?" she cooed.

"If you say so matron," he replied happily.

"And you know what happens to naughty boys, don't you?"

"They get sent to bed without any supper."

"That's right."

"Will you come to bed with me, matron?" Flintlock began twisting round, trying to catch her eye. "I know a game we can play there. You pull down the top half of your uniform and I put my–"

"Enough!" Dante burst into the room, pushing Spatchcock ahead of him. "I've had quite enough of this place for one day. It's time we were going."

Hattie looked mournfully at the new arrivals. "Oh, do you have to? We were just getting to the good bit." Yvette nodded her agreement eagerly.

Dante held up a hand, not wanting to hear anymore. "Please, ladies, I beg you – share no details with us, lest we learn to think even less of our associate than we already do. All three of us must be leaving, and quickly."

"Why the rush?" Flintlock demanded, trying to pull his trousers up from round his ankles. "I still have at least half an hour of my session to go!"

Dante pointed down the corridor from which he had suddenly appeared. "Maybe you wish to continue your session with her?"

Flintlock followed Dante's gesture and saw the middle-aged schoolteacher approaching at speed, her academic gown billowing outwards as she ran towards them. The sight was neither pleasant nor erotic, and quickly removed any remaining arousal from Flintlock's body. "I see what you mean. Well ladies, please accept my apologies, but it's often better to save something for later."

Dante glanced round the parlour. "Is there another way out of here? I don't fancy taking on the prime of Miss Jean Whiplash."

Yvette pointed at a bookcase set into one wall. "You can leave through the secret tunnel of love," she said. "Just pull out the correct volume and the bookcase will slide aside for you."

Dante strode to the bookcase and began scanning the titles of the dusty tomes: *Another Week in the Private House, Confessions of an Imperial Courtesan, The Wench Isn't Dead* and hundreds of similar volumes. "Which book? Which one operates the mechanism?"

Yvette smiled coquettishly. "I'll only tell you if you make me, master."

Dante rolled his eyes. "I haven't got time for any more slap and tickle. Crest, can you identify which spine opens the bookcase?"

A very appropriate title, in the circumstances, it replied. *The Pervert's Guide to Secret Tunnels and Hidden Crevices.*

Spatchcock had joined Dante at the bookcase. "I see it!" He pulled the thick volume towards him and the shelving slid sideways to reveal a corridor. Dante shoved his pungent companion through the gap and turned back to see what was delaying Flintlock. He was jumping around the room, his trousers still stuck at half-mast, while the semi-naked schoolteacher was whipping him with her cane.

"Diavolo! Haven't you had your money's worth yet?" Dante asked despairingly. He bundled Flintlock into the hidden corridor, before bowing to the three sex workers. "Sorry to leave so soon ladies, but you know what men are like – our priorities always come first. Perhaps another time?" Dante ducked behind the closing bookcase, narrowly avoiding several hurled objects.

Spatchcock winked at his former commander. "You sure know how to show the ladies a good time."

"Just get moving," Dante snapped, pushing his two associates forwards. "We've got a long journey ahead of us and no time to lose."

"Where are we going?" Flintlock asked.

"To see an old friend."

FOUR

"There are many woes, but only one death"
– Russian proverb

Di Grizov had always been proud of his hands. They could crack any safe, disable the trickiest of alarms, and even undo the stays of the most sanctimonious dowager if a job required it. His fingernails were always immaculate, the palms smooth and warm, his grip firm and resolute. The hands of a grifter must never betray his origins or intentions, he had been fond of telling his apprentices over the years; they must reassure and satisfy all those they come into contact with. Di Grizov looked at his hands now and winced. He would have wept, if he'd any tears left to shed.

Just four days in the Murmansk Gulag had broken what little spirit was left in Di Grizov's body. Four days of hell on Earth, tearing at the walls of a mine with his bare hands, trying to claw out seams of glistening ore. With his legs gone, the grifter had been given a low trolley on wheels as his means of transportation, forcing him to propel it around the compound with his hands. Pleas for a pair of gloves were mocked or ignored. The gulag's commander, Josef Shitov, had laughed heartily at Di Grizov's request. A bear of a man, the veins on Shitov's shaven head bulged as he stood over the new prisoner.

"Where do you think you are, a holiday camp?" Shitov lovingly stroked his thick, black moustache while glaring at Di Grizov. "You came here to work! You eat when I say, you sleep when I say and you die when I say – understand?"

"But I need–"

"Need? All you need is to learn your place here, worm. This is my domain, and I shall do with you as I see fit." Shitov looked down and noticed a smudge on the gleaming surface of his boots. "For your first lesson, I want you to clean my boots. With your tongue."

That was four days ago. Four days of torture, ignominy and despair. Di Grizov would have killed himself long before now, if any simple method had been available to him. He even contemplated biting through the veins on his wrists in the hope of bleeding to death, but couldn't face that. Besides, he knew this torment couldn't last much longer. The mines were radioactive, having been used in the past as a storage facility for nuclear waste. Few prisoners lasted more than a month before the tumours and cancers took their lives.

Di Grizov studied his hands. The fingernails were broken and ragged-edged, the skin split open in several places, blisters mingled with each callous on the palms. They looked like a humble worker's hands, with the hardened appearance of a lifetime spent in hard physical labour. Four days of hell had achieved that. What would they be like after four more days? But I'll be dead before that happens, the grifter thought. He welcomed the end. There probably was no life beyond this one, but oblivion had to be better than this place.

His grim contemplations were halted by the sound of sirens wailing outside. Di Grizov pushed his trolley to the nearest window and looked out of the barracks. The sun had long since set but the sky remained a pale blue overhead, thanks to the shortened nights of a northern summer, a full moon adding further illumination. Guards were rushing back and forth across the bleak, snow-strewn compound, shouting to each other and cursing in the local dialect. In centuries past the Murmansk region had been devoted to the sea and naval warfare. Now the remaining local people found work in the gulag, taking out their frustrations on the inmates.

It was good to see a little panic in the dead eyes of these slab-faced sadists, Di Grizov thought. But what could induce such a reaction? Perhaps one of the prisoners was trying to escape. Few had the strength or will to break out of this death camp, and those that did rarely made it past the first fence. The guards were particularly enthusiastic about hunting down would-be escapees, thanks to a generous reward on offer from Shitov. Nobody had ever successfully broken out of the Murmansk Gulag and he was determined to maintain that record, promising a week's extra pay as a bonus for whoever succeeded in bringing down any prisoner trying to escape.

Di Grizov strained forwards and pressed an ear against the frozen glass of the nearest window, trying to catch what was being said outside. Shitov himself appeared to direct operations, trying to bring calm to the panicked ranks. "You fools! Stop and listen – let this enemy come to us. Let them walk between our pincers. Then we shall close in around them and feast on their folly!"

The grifter sat back in his trolley. Let the enemy come to us? If I didn't know better, I'd think somebody was trying to break *into* the gulag. But what kind of idiot would be stupid enough to attempt that?

Dante watched the high security compound sprawled below. A dozen wooden huts were arranged in rows of four, surrounded by guardhouses and a few rudimentary buildings – probably the kitchens and toilet block. At the far end stood several more elaborate structures. Three were large, superior versions of the wooden huts, but with smoke billowing from chimneys and interior lighting visible through the windows. Probably the guards' quarters, Dante reasoned. The elegant, almost palatial home beside them no doubt belonged to the gulag commander. Tall watchtowers stood in all four corners of the compound, the guards inside them sweeping mighty arc lights back and forth.

Beyond the gulag Dante could see a distant orange glow on the horizon. No doubt the light pollution was spilling from the Murmansk Alienation Zone, less than fifty miles away. The zone was an environmental disaster that had started more than five hundred years ago when some long-forgotten regime chose to abandon its fleet of war machines to the Arctic ravages of the Barents Sea. In the intervening centuries this military graveyard had welcomed more relics, its wrecks supposedly haunted by an armada of ghosts from the past. Few visited the alienation zone willingly.

Dante had been there only once, six years earlier, on a journey that changed his life forever. Captured by the Raven Corps, Dante was surprised to be despatched to Murmansk, along with the Tsar's daughter Jena. There they had encountered a two-headed robotic eagle, a Romanov Bird of Prey. The creature decided Dante was genetically suitable and initiated the bonding sequence that fused the Crest to his body.

Only later did Dante discover the Tsar had deliberately sent him to the alienation zone, knowing the thief was a bastard of the Romanov bloodline. The Tsar planned to have him dissected, allowing access to the Crest's secrets and neutering the Romanovs' greatest weapon. But Dante had escaped that fate and joined the house of his father instead. Six years on almost all the other Romanovs were dead. So much for the past.

Kopeck for your thoughts, the Crest said.

"I doubt they're worth that much to you," Dante replied.

Perhaps not, but it's hard to get change on a kopeck.

Dante couldn't help smiling. "I was just remembering when we first bonded. We've come a long way since then, Crest."

And yet you still refuse to listen to reason. Attacking a gulag single-handed is an act of suicide.

"I'm not single-handed. Spatchcock and Flintlock are busy creating a diversion on the far side of the compound."

Why you trust those two knaves I'll never know.

"Sometimes you have to let your heart do the thinking, Crest."

Well, it makes a change from your groin being in charge.

Dante sighed. "Have you finished hacking the gulag's security systems?"

Yes, they were so primitive. I've been triple-checking to see if something more sophisticated was lurking behind them.

"And was there?"

No. As a suitable task for my talents, it was like asking a watchmaker to repair a hammer. The defence grid should collapse right about... now.

In the valley below a cacophony of sirens and alarms suddenly fell silent. The generators maintaining the laser shield clattered to a halt and power drained away from the arc lights in the watchtowers. The gulag was defenceless, but for its cadre of armed guards and their commander.

"Time to stealth 'em up." Dante pulled the hood of his white cloak closer round his face before creeping down the snow-covered slope towards the outer perimeter. "Once we're inside the boundary line I'll need explicit instructions, Crest. I won't have time to search every building for Jim."

Spatchcock was loading sticky green pellets into his sidearm while Flintlock tended the bonfire. The pair had constructed a tower of dead wood from the snowy wasteland around the northern edge of the gulag and lit it on a signal from Dante. The cowardly Flintlock observed the nearest watchtower nervously, ready to scramble for cover at the first sign of danger. "Why do we always end up as the diversion? Why can't Nikolai risk his neck instead of us?"

"You want to swap places with him? Chance your arm breaking into a gulag guarded by two dozen thugs with enough guns to start a small war?"

"No, but I thought..." Flintlock shrugged helplessly. "Isn't there a less dangerous way for us to get their attention?"

"If there is, it's too late," Spatchcock replied, pointing a finger towards the gulag's perimeter. "Here they come!"

A dozen guards were marching towards the bonfire, all bearing pulse rifles and grim expressions. By the time they reached the blaze, the two arsonists had retreated to an abandoned hut nearby. Spatchcock clambered onto the roof and took aim with his sidearm. Flintlock was cowering at ground level, peering round a corner at the confused guards. His hands were shaking so much it was proving difficult to load a green pellet into his weapon.

"Why do I have to use the slingshot?" Flintlock protested.

"Stop whining and start firing," Spatchcock snapped. Ahead of him, half the guards had finished examining the bonfire and were fanning out, in search of the culprits. "They're coming into range... now!" Spatchcock shot first, the green pellet splattering as it hit the chest of the nearest enemy.

The guard looked down at his uniform in dismay, scowling at the viscous emerald substance slowly dribbling down his chest. He dipped a gloved finger into the liquid, peered at it and then brought it close to his nose for a sniff.

"That's it..." Spatchcock urged. "Get a good whiff of that."

The guard inhaled sharply. Disgust crossed his features, rapidly followed by horror. His cheeks billowed outwards for a moment, before projectile vomit spat forth from his mouth and both nostrils. At the same time a splattering sound could be heard from the guard's trousers, their seat suddenly becoming heavier. The unfortunate man crumpled to his knees, one hand trying to stop the spray from his mouth while another clutched at his rear.

"Gotcha!" Spatchcock snarled happily. "Purge juice one, guards nil."

"You mean that vile concoction of yours works?" Flintlock spluttered.

"Course it does – now get firing! We hit enough of those goons, the rest won't want to come any closer."

. . .

Slipping into the gulag proved simplicity itself once the Crest had disabled most of the security systems. The rest of the safeguards had been designed to stop prisoners breaking out, not prevent anyone from breaking in. Dante moved among the shadows, avoiding most of the guards and bluffing his way past the rest. Panic was in charge of the situation for now, but Dante knew that could not last forever. He found Di Grizov at the third attempt, discovering his old mentor inside a frozen wooden hut. Dante found it hard to believe the broken, shrivelled man on the trolley was once the Empire's greatest escapologist.

"Jim? Is that you?"

"Nikolai? What are you doing here?"

Dante closed the door and hurried to the grifter's side. "I've come to get you out of here. Your niece sent me."

"My niece? I don't have a niece. I don't have any family, at least none still alive. I was an only child."

"But then who was...?" Dante frowned. "I met a young woman. She said you bribed a guard to carry a message for her out of the gulag."

Di Grizov laughed bitterly. "Chance would be a fine thing, Nikolai. The bastards in this place wouldn't piss on you if you were burning alive."

"I don't understand – she knew you'd lost your legs. She said they'd been amputated to stop you escaping."

"Yes, but not here. That happened somewhere else."

Dante shook his head. "It doesn't matter how I found you. The important thing is getting you out."

Di Grizov shook his head. "It's too late for me, Nikolai. I'm dying. You could be killed trying to save me and for what? I'll only live a few more days, a week at most. Get away from here, save yourself."

"No! I came here to help you, Jim–"

"You have already," the grifter replied. "You've given me a chance to say something that's been nagging at me for twelve years – I'm sorry."

"I don't–"

"Hush." Di Grizov pressed his broken, battered hands against Dante's mouth, silencing him. "I'm sorry I tricked you at the Casino Royale, how I treated you. You deserved better from me."

"It's okay, Jim. Leaving me there, it taught me a lot. I learned how to get myself out of danger, how to make the most out of an impossible situation. Trust me, they've been useful skills in the last few years."

"I know. I've been following your career. Quite a dash you've cut through the ranks of high society."

Dante smiled. "But I never forgot where I came from, and that's thanks to you. You taught me to always remember my origins, stand on my own two feet."

"Well, that's more than I can do…" Di Grizov rested a hand on the stumps were his legs had been. "Tell me more about this woman who contacted you. Maybe I'll remember her."

Dante quickly outlined his encounter at the bar in Famous Flora's. "She said you had a retirement fund. I'm supposed to mention the codename for it and you'll tell me where to find the money."

The grifter raised an eyebrow. "I don't have a rouble to my name. My life's been one disaster after another, ever since the day I stole that damned egg. I spent all my savings staying out of the gulags – and look where it's got me."

Outside the hut a burly voice was cursing the guards, urging them to begin a thorough search of the buildings. "Friend of yours?" Dante asked.

"Josef Shitov, the barbarous bastard that runs this place."

"We're running out of time, Jim – we should get out while we still can."

"I told you, I'm not leaving," the grifter maintained. "I'll die here. It's as bad a place as any to end my days." His brow furrowed. "I thought I knew who might have sent you here, but the woman you described doesn't match her. You mentioned a codename – what was it?"

"The Strangelove Gambit."

Di Grizov's face hardened. "It's not a codename, Nikolai. It's a warning," he snorted with disgust.

"A warning? About what?"

"My legs were amputated before I was brought here. The man who took them was Karl Fabergé."

"The doctor you stole the egg from?"

Di Grizov nodded. "Fabergé has prospered since our first encounter. He has a private island off the Black Sea coastline, complete with its own castle. The island is home to an exclusive school called by the Fabergé Institute, but that's a front for his real work."

Dante could hear guards stomping around inside the nearest wooden hut, tipping over tables and bunks. In less than a minute the sentries would be searching this barrack. Dante reached one arm under his former mentor's stumps and another round his back.

"Nikolai, what are you doing? I said I don't want to be rescued. I just want to die!" Di Grizov protested.

"Maybe. But I don't like taking no for an answer," Dante replied, lifting the grifter from his trolley. "You of all people should know that about me."

Spatchcock watched with satisfaction as the guards retched their guts out on the snow. Judging by the chorus of wet farts bursting from their trousers, the purge juice had also debilitated them at the other end. "Mission accomplished!" he announced happily, climbing down from the roof.

Flintlock had tied a scarf round the lower half of his face, masking his mouth and nostrils from the vile stench being emitted by the stricken guards.

Spatchcock was checking his pockets. "You got any more pellets left?"

Flintlock held up two unused doses of purge juice. "Take them, please."

"My pleasure." The proud poisoner slotted both pellets into his sidearm, while keeping an eye on the gulag's perimeter. "Hmm, I think it's time we were moving on. Looks like our friends have got company."

Flintlock saw another dozen sentries approaching, hidden behind riot shields. "As Dante often says, discretion is the better part of valour, Spatch." The blond-haired Briton took to his heels.

"Like you'd know anything about valour," Spatchcock muttered.

Josef Shitov strode into the last of the workers' barracks. Most of the prisoners had been in the re-education hall when the attack began, undergoing their nightly indoctrination and loyalty building session. A handful of inmates were excused attendance at these sessions, due to ill health or death – no other reasons were considered acceptable. As a consequence, searching the camp proved straightforward, yet none of the guards had found any evidence of an intruder within the perimeter.

Shitov snapped his fingers, summoning forward the guard assigned to this particular hut. "Kirilenko! How many workers from this barrack were not attending tonight's re-education?"

The heavy-set, slow-spoken sentry saluted briskly before replying. "Just one, Comrade Di Grizov."

"Ah, our most recent arrival. And where is he now?"

Kirilenko looked around helplessly. "I... I do not know, commander."

"Comrade Di Grizov has no legs, is that not true?"

"That is true, commander."

"Then how do you suggest he might have escaped from this building?"

"He has a trolley with wheels, commander. He probably used that."

Shitov turned his head to sneer at the guard. "He probably used a trolley with wheels to cross a compound buried in snow? Was this a magic trolley, Kirilenko? Did it possess the power to levitate, perhaps?"

"No, commander!"

"No, commander," Shitov echoed mockingly. "More to the point, this helpless cripple did not even take his wheels with him!" The commander gestured at the discarded trolley. "Perhaps he has magic of his own. Can Comrade Di Grizov perform magic, Kirilenko?"

"I do not believe so, commander," the sentry replied, his voice trembling.

"Dolt!" Shitov lashed out, his clenched fist smashing into Kirilenko's solar plexus, crumpling the guard as if he were tissue paper. "Search the compound! Find Di Grizov – and find whoever is helping him! Now!"

"You always had a taste for the low life, Nikolai, but this may be going too far. Even for you," Di Grizov said wryly. The two men were crouching inside the gulag's latrine block, hidden behind a row of wooden seats. Icicles of frozen urine hung from the rims. "I'd like to die with some shred of dignity, please?"

"We're not dead yet," Dante replied. "You were telling me about what Fabergé is doing on his private island."

"Secret experiments, fully authorised and funded by the Tsar. I was used as a guinea pig for some of the tests. I heard enough about what Fabergé was planning to scare the hell out of me. He's developing a new weapon, something that will strengthen tenfold the Tsar's stranglehold on the Empire. It's due to be put into effect on Easter Sunday, with the Tsar there to witness it. The Strangelove Gambit: that's what Fabergé is calling his new weapon."

"How many people know about it, Jim?"

"A handful on the island, plus the Tsar and his closest advisors. Beyond that, nobody else, I think. Apparently it's going to be a surprise worthy of the original Fabergé eggs."

Dante shook his head. "So how did the woman claiming to be your niece know of the Strangelove Gambit?"

"Smells like a trap," Di Grizov surmised, "and that's saying something in this block." He studied Dante's expression. "I know that look, Nikolai. You're thinking of taking on Doctor Fabergé."

"Maybe."

"Don't. He spent a dozen years hunting me down because I stole that egg from him. He knows you were my partner at the Casino Royale. If he ever gets his hands on you, I suggest that you commit suicide while you still can." Di Grizov looked down at his ruined hands and the stumps where his legs used to be. "Don't end up like me, Nikolai."

"I won't, I promise you that. I'll make Fabergé pay for what he did."

Dante – I'm detecting a large group of guards closing in on this location, the Crest said. *Now would be a good time to leave.*

"We may have to shoot our way out of here," Dante murmured. He adjusted the rifle slung over his shoulder, then picked up Di Grizov again.

"Since when do you carry a gun?"

"It was a gift. Besides, this is a very special gun." Dante moved to the end of the latrine block and peered through a frost-coated window. "They're almost upon us. I wonder how they knew we were in here?"

Your tracks in the snow. Carrying Di Grizov made you heavier, so you left a clear set of footprints leading right to this building.

Dante looked around the sparse wooden hut. "I'm guessing there's no secret tunnels or hidden trapdoors in this place, right?"

His old mentor smiled weakly. "Sorry."

Commander Shitov kicked in the door of the latrine block, his pistol raised and ready to fire. "Normally I have to wait weeks, even months for fresh workers. You are the first to ever report here voluntarily. Tell me your name before I have my men induct you to the Murmansk Gulag."

"Dante – Nikolai Dante."

Shitov's face could not help betraying his surprise. "*The* Nikolai Dante?"

"In the flesh."

"How wonderful," the commander replied, firing his pistol.

Dante felt something spraying him with liquid, a scarlet aerosol staining the white of his cloak. The body in his arms jerked once, then lay still. "Jim? Jim, are you alright?" He watched the light leave Di Grizov's eyes, the wound caused by Shitov's bullet all too evident. Dante slowly dropped to one knee and laid the body on the floor. "What's your name, commander?"

"Shitov, Josef Shitov." The gulag's ruler sneered at Dante, his pistol aimed at the intruder's head, ready to fire again. "Why do you ask?"

"I want to know whose grave to piss on after they bury what's left of you." Dante reached forward and closed Di Grizov's eyes, resting his hands on the dead man's face. Purple and silver ripples began running along the veins of his arms, hurrying towards the fingertips.

"You're in no position to make threats, fugitive. True, the reward for your delivery to the Tsar while still alive is considerable, but I think it'll be safer if I gun you down in here like a dog and then deliver your corpse instead."

Dante's fingers began to lengthen, biocircuitry extruding itself from his hands, shooting forwards in the shape of blades. "You're welcome to try; but better men than you have failed, commander. What makes you think you'll do any better?"

"Because I have you right where I–" Shitov's words died in his throat, cut short by the bio-blades slicing through his windpipe. Dante flicked his hands in opposite directions, neatly severing the commander's head. It fell to the floor with a dull *thud*, bouncing once on the wooden boards.

Dante, there are still more than thirty armed guards outside. You'll never make it past them all unscathed, the Crest warned.

"I never said I was going to leave them unscathed," Dante snarled. He retracted the biocircuitry into his hands and slung the rifle from his back while walking towards the door. A grim smile crossed his face. Dante kicked Shitov's head out into the snow. "My name is Nikolai Dante and I am the most wanted man in the Empire!" he shouted to the surrounding guards. "I have just murdered your commander. Anyone who doesn't wish to join him in the next life, you have one minute to leave this place!"

A unique strategy, the Crest commented. *I can't think of many cases where a single man in a hopeless position surrounded by dozens of enemies has negotiated the surrender of his adversary.*

"Call it the Dante Manoeuvre. I'm inventing it today."
Let's hope you stay alive long enough to make it work.

Dante peered out of the doorway. The guards were still trying to reach a decision. "Perhaps you need some persuading," Dante yelled. "Let me introduce you to the Huntsman 5000, a rifle designed by the same people who created the Romanov Weapons Crest. This rifle makes its own ammunition and replenishes automatically, so never needs loading. When targeted and fired, the rounds instantaneously adapt into the most effective means of terminating the enemy – whoever or whatever they may be. That probably sounds more like magic than a real weapon to you. But I can assure you it does everything I have just described."

"Prove it!" one of the sentries shouted back.

"I thought you'd never ask." Dante stuck the rifle around the door and began pulling the trigger. A fusillade of bullets flew out, shredding the bodies of those closest to the latrine block. Dante stopped firing, letting the sound of shooting fade in the air, leaving just the whimpers of pain and agony from those still alive. "Any questions?"

Spatchcock and Flintlock were waiting beside their flyer when Dante emerged from the forest, carrying a heavy bundle wrapped in his white cloak. Blood was seeping through the material, but Dante himself appeared unharmed. "We heard shooting," Spatchcock ventured. "You alright?"

"I'm not physically harmed, if that's what you mean." Dante lowered the body to the snow-covered ground. "I thought I saw a laser cutter in the flyer. Flintlock, can you check? I'll need it to dig a grave in this frozen soil."

Spatchcock grimaced. "Your friend didn't make it."

"No. I couldn't leave him in that place, he deserved better."

"And the other prisoners?"

"I told them they were free. It's up to them what they choose to do next. One thing the war taught me well – we can't save everyone, not all the time."

"What about the guards?"

"Most saw sense. As for the others... they'll never see anything again." Dante sighed, looking down at his bloody hands. "Once we've buried Jim, we've another visit to make."

"Where to next?" Flintlock asked as he emerged from the flyer, clutching the laser cutter. Dante took it and began marking out a grave in the snow.

"The Black Sea, to see an old acquaintance."

"If you don't mind my saying so, this visit with one friend didn't go very well," Flintlock ventured. "Why risk another?"

Dante tossed the cutter back to him. "Doctor Karl Fabergé is no friend of mine. We have an old score to settle." He looked down at Di Grizov's corpse. "And a new one as well."

FIVE

"Fear never stormed a citadel"
– Russian proverb

Five days after burying his mentor, Dante sat looking out across the Black Sea. The journey from Murmansk in the north had been long and arduous, thanks to the necessity of avoiding contact with the many Raven Corps checkpoints. Dante and his travelling companions had skirted the edge of St Petersburg, jagged sideways to Kirov and criss-crossed the Volga several times to make sure they were not being followed. Finally they chose a vantage point for watching Fabergé Island and settled down to wait.

Dante had visited this region once before, while staying at the Hotel Yalta, but twenty-seven straight days of partying, drinking and debauchery had left little time for sightseeing. Now, sitting on a high cliff overlooking the Black Sea's glittering waters, Dante could understand why so many of the noble dynasties retained palatial mansions along this coastline. You could watch the sea for hours without getting bored; it also supported hundreds of fishermen alongside swarms of tourists.

But the waters around Fabergé Island were different. Dante had been watching the isle and its environs for hours yet seen almost no activity. No birds flew within a mile of the small rocky outcrop that rose from the water like a fist. Fishing vessels took a wide berth around the island, careful not to steer close to its vicinity. Even the shimmering schools of fish that sometimes broke the water's surface elsewhere avoided Fabergé's private residence, as if afraid of what lurked there.

Two people approaching, the Crest warned, *one from the north, the other from the south – a pincer movement.*

"I hear them," Dante murmured. Bio-blades extended from his hands, forming themselves into the shape of long swords. Dante rolled over backwards and sprang nimbly to his feet, ready for combat. Spatchcock and Flintlock stumbled out of the undergrowth from opposite directions to find razor-sharp blades at their throats.

"I say!" Flintlock protested. "Must you always do that whenever I arrive unannounced? It's dashed disconcerting."

Dante retracted his blades and went back to studying his target. Fabergé Island was some three miles offshore, beyond the range of all but the best swimmers and far enough from land to make any approaching craft obvious. "Well Spatch, what have the locals got to say about the good doctor?"

The foul-smelling forger sat beside Dante and consulted a handful of notes scrawled across the back of his left hand. "Nobody likes Fabergé much, or his staff. All provisions are flown in from outside the region. The island is home to some sort of educational institute but nobody living round here has been allowed to enrol. Apparently the fees for students are astronomical, without exception. The island has its own shuttle that makes one return trip a day to the mainland, collecting supplies, dropping off students, that sort of thing. Security is tighter than a gnat's ass. Nobody gets on or off that rock without Fabergé's express permission." Spatchcock stared out to sea. "It'll be a challenge, that's for sure."

Dante turned to his other partner in crime. "What about the island itself?"

Flintlock shrugged off his jacket. "Apparently the waters around it are empty. No marine life, no nesting birds and no ships. I listened to some of the local fishermen moaning in a tavern by the docks. It could have been the ale talking, but they believe that sea monsters and terrible creatures from the deep surround the island. Nobody I approached was willing to take a boat within a mile of Fabergé Island. You could offer them all the money in the world but I doubt they'd accept it. Everyone is scared of the doctor, and more scared of what happens on that island."

"I am becoming more and more curious," Dante murmured. "Crest, what has your analysis found? Can we launch a covert mission to the island?"

Not a successful one. Fabergé has a state of the art security system built into the rock – motion sensors, laser defence grids, mines set into the grounds outside the castle walls. It's a fortress. The only safe place outside the castle's walls is the landing pad. There's a narrow walkway between the two that is made safe when the daily shuttle leaves and arrives, but that's it.

Dante nodded grimly. He noticed the quizzical expressions on his companions' faces. "Sorry, sometimes I forget you can't hear the Crest talking. It confirms what we already suspected – the only way on or off that island is via the daily shuttle. If we want to pay Fabergé a visit, we have to do it on his terms." In the distance a bulky black and silver shape was rising above the stone turrets of the castle. "Here comes the shuttle now, right on time."

The trio watched as the only viable link to their target swooped over to the mainland, landing neatly on a flattened area below their own vantage point. A dozen locals were carrying heavy crates towards it from a nearby village. The shuttle door opened and a tall figure in a hooded cloak emerged, barking orders. Within moments the supplies were being swiftly loaded into one of the shuttle's compartments. Once their task for the day was completed, the locals retreated to the safety of nearby homes, muttering darkly amongst themselves. But the shuttle remained on the landing pad for several minutes.

"That's unusual," Dante noted. "Normally it doesn't stay a moment longer than necessary. The shuttle must be waiting for something or someone."

After remaining for another four minutes the cloaked figure climbed back into the shuttle and it rose swiftly into the air. The return journey to the island was quickly completed. "Well, whoever or whatever it was, they missed today's flight," Flintlock observed.

"There!" Spatchcock jabbed a grubby finger at the pathway to the landing pad. A lone male figure was hurrying up the track, burdened by kit bags and military paraphernalia. Bushy brown hair framed his scowling features, a clipped military moustache prominent above the mouth. He reached the landing pad and dumped his gear, before cursing at the island in the distance.

"He'll have to wait until tomorrow – they won't send the shuttle back to collect him," Flintlock said with satisfaction. "Nothing like savouring the misfortune of others to make you feel better about yourself."

"Perhaps," Dante pondered. "But his misfortune also offers an opportunity. I think we should offer our condolences to the hapless traveller. I may have crossed swords with his kind before."

Captain Grigori Arbatov was furious. When he had been offered the job with the Fabergé Institute, one thing was stressed to him – there was only one way on or off the island. Miss the daily shuttle and he could expect to spend a cold night outside waiting for it to return the next day. Madame Wartski described the mainland's local residents as a surly lot who would offer little in the way of comfort or aide.

In fact, it was the locals who had conspired to make him late. Most of the road signs leading to the landing pad were defaced to the point of illegibility. When he asked a farmer for directions, they sent him the long way round the village.

Arbatov had seen the shuttle preparing to leave the landing pad, but simply could not reach it in time, weighed down by all his luggage and equipment. Now he was stuck in a hostile environment with little prospect of finding a bed for the night. Hardly the best first impression to make on his new employer. Arbatov snarled another curse, not bothering to keep it under his breath. He was furious and he didn't care who knew about it.

"My, my, captain! What would your commanding officer say if he heard such language?" A sneering voice caught Arbatov's attention. A trio of men was approaching, climbing down the hillside towards him. They reached the scorched surface of the landing pad and moved to surround him, one taking a position on either side while the last remained facing the captain. He must be the leader, judging from his cocky arrogance.

"Who are you? What do you want?" Arbatov demanded.

The leader smiled. "There'll be time for introductions later. You're not going anywhere today, you missed the only shuttle." The leader was wearing an imperial red jacket with gold braid over a creased white dress shirt and skin-tight black trousers. Jet black hair was swept back to reveal a cunning face, his black moustache and goatee beard adding a devilish touch. Alarm bells were ringing at the back of Arbatov's mind, but he couldn't remember why. He sensed this man was dangerous, even if there was no weaponry in evidence.

Arbatov risked a quick glance at the other two. The man to his left was tall and blond, with a faded elegance and stately bearing somewhat at odds with the threadbare nature of his clothing. The creature to Arbatov's right was short, round-shouldered and smirking, a foul face accompanied by an odour of pickled eggs and fresh manure. Yes, there were even lice and ticks visibly moving on the creature's stained clothing. The trio were plainly brigands intent on relieving Arbatov of his valuables. Well, they were in for an unhappy surprise! Nobody got the better of Grigori Arbatov without suffering.

"I demand the satisfaction of your names," he said sternly.

The creature shuffled a little closer, scratching an open sore on its neck. "I'm Spatchcock, but you can call me Spatch if you like. You got any diseases?"

"Certainly not!"

"You want some?" Spatchcock cackled at his own joke, licking his lips to reveal a mouthful of decayed, rotting teeth.

Arbatov took a step back from the rancid creature and bumped into the blond bandit. "My name is Flintlock, Lord Peter Flintlock." The accent was pure Britannia. Arbatov recognised it from an interminable month he had spent stationed on that rain-soaked isle during the war.

"You're a long way from home, Lord Flintlock, and I do not care for the company you keep either."

Flintlock shrugged. "Beggars cannot be choosers."

Arbatov regarded the trio's leader. "And your name?"

The black haired brigand smiled broadly. "Let me hear yours first. I may have encountered your kin in the past and would like to know where I stand before giving you my name."

"Very well." Arbatov drew his sword and held it in front of his face, standing to attention. "I am Grigori Arbatov, one of the finest swords in all the Empire and, until recently, a captain in the Tsar's own Hussars. Now, tell me your name or there will be trouble!"

The trio's leader gave a heavy sigh. "Dante. My name is Nikolai Dante."

Arbatov's nostrils flared angrily. "*The* Nikolai Dante?"

"Why do they always ask that?" Spatchcock enquired.

"Every time," Flintlock agreed. "It's not like there's dozens of people called Nikolai Dante wandering about, causing trouble wherever they go."

"The Nikolai Dante responsible for one of my family being flayed alive on orders from the Tsar?" Arbatov demanded. "The Nikolai Dante who unsportingly beat another member of my family when he demanded the satisfaction of a duel for that first ignominy? The Nikolai Dante who had another of my kin falsely arrested for embezzling at the Hotel Yalta? The Nikolai Dante who has killed, maimed, beaten, emasculated and humiliated more than a dozen of my relatives for no other reason than capriciousness?" He was shaking with fury, such was the rage building within him.

"Don't forget what he did to the Arbatov sisters," Spatchcock chipped in.

"Pink ball in the corner pocket, you might say," Flintlock added. "He snookered three of them during the war. I wouldn't be surprised if they've all given birth to his bastards by now."

"Enough," Dante snapped. "Yes, I'm that Nikolai Dante – bane of the Arbatovs, accursed by your family for all time. Satisfied?"

"Only when I have the pleasure of killing you and dragging your rotting carcass to my family's estate. There we will feast on your sweetmeats and have the skin from your loins made into a ball for dogs to play with. Prepare to die, you festering pustule upon the face of humanity!"

Arbatov drew back his sword, ready to charge at his mortal enemy. But Dante raised his hands in surrender, urging the enraged man to wait.

"Please, captain, I have no quarrel with you or your family, no matter how difficult you may find that to believe. In almost every instance you cited, my brushes with the Arbatovs have been a mixture of bizarre coincidence and an over-developed sense of vengeance on the part of your relatives. Even my, er, encounter with the three sisters, that was purely unintentional. To be honest, they threw themselves at me. I was injured at the time, found it hard to resist."

"That's not all he found that was hard," a rough voice snickered.

"Quiet, Spatch, you're not helping," Dante hissed. "I never meant to be the individual who deflowered those women. It was just a quirk of fate. Sorry."

"Sorry?" Arbatov spluttered. "You're sorry?"

Dante shrugged. "It was beyond my control."

"You say you're sorry and I'm to do what, simply accept that as the truth? Believe the word of one of the Empire's most wanton liars and thieves? Take his feeble apology as adequate compensation for six years of ignominy, humiliation and degradation heaped upon the noble family name of Arbatov?"

"Nikolai, I don't think he's quite on your side," Flintlock said quietly.

"I was getting that impression too," Dante commented.

"Even if I could kill you a thousand times it would not be enough to undo all the ills you have visited upon my family," Arbatov snarled. "Instead I shall kill you once and rejoice in being the man who brought about your destruction!" The captain flung himself at Dante, his sword flashing through the air.

But before he could reach his target, Arbatov's right foot got snagged in the handles of his largest kit bag. The captain threw both hands forwards to break his fall, forgetting one of them still clutched a long and deadly blade. It twisted in his grip, so the point was facing Arbatov as he plunged to the ground. The captain did not even have time to cry out before being run through by his own weapon, the blade puncturing his chest to emerge from his back. Momentum pushed the sword further inwards, all the way down to the hilt.

Dante looked down at the dying man. "What is it with these Arbatovs? Can't they just let sleeping dogs lie?"

The captain spat blood on the ground before replying. "Not where you're involved, fiend! We shall have our vengeance upon you yet, Nikolai Dante. We shall prove ourselves superior. We shall... shall..."

Spatchcock knelt beside the body, checking for life. "He's gone."

"Good. His ranting was proving rather tiresome," Flintlock added.

"Help me shift the body before it bleeds all over the landing pad," Dante said, grabbing one of Arbatov's arms. "Grigori may still be useful to us."

Once the corpse was buried in a shallow grave, Dante and his companions returned to the top of the cliff. The trio sorted through the dead man's possessions, looking for some clue why he wanted to catch the daily shuttle to Fabergé Island. Spatchcock opened a bag and found it full of fencing foils and facemasks. "Those who live by the sword…?"

Flintlock uncovered a cache of personal papers, including travel documents and instructions. "Seems Arbatov was joining the Fabergé Institute as a tutor in self defence, swordplay and two unspecified disciplines. There's a letter from a Madame Wartski, offering the captain a two-week probationary post. If that proves successful, the job becomes permanent."

"Not anymore," Dante noted wryly. "But those papers could give us a legitimate way on to the island."

Spatchcock frowned. "What kind of educational institute offers classes in self defence and swordplay? Who *are* Fabergé's students?"

"Perhaps the contents of this will give us a clue," Dante ventured as he opened the last of the kit bags. A selection of silk and lace lingerie tumbled out. "Or perhaps not. Who carries a bag filled with women's underwear?"

"Maybe the captain fancied himself a ladies man and kept a trophy from each of his conquests?" Flintlock suggested. "They are all different shapes and styles, so they probably come from different women."

"Or maybe he liked dressing up in frilly knickers?" Spatchcock replied with a broad smirk. "Takes all kinds, doesn't it Flintlock?"

"What are you trying to imply, Spatch?"

"I wasn't implying anything."

"I should hope not," Flintlock grumbled.

"I was inferring."

"No, no, no! The speaker implies, the listener infers."

"Whatever you say," Spatchcock said. "Don't get your knickers in a twist."

"There you go again! I will not be subject to these snide little remarks of yours. Just because I come from Britannia, does not mean I am some sort of sexual pervert to be taunted and teased for your pleasure!"

"Well, if it turns you on–"

"Enough!" Dante interjected. "Spatchcock, spare us the details of your sordid fantasies. Flintlock, stop rising to his bait. If you two can't work together you can stay here while I visit the island on my own." He examined the other paperwork. "Spatchcock, how are your forgery skills?"

"A mite rusty, but I can match anything you've got in your hand, given time and the right materials."

"We've got twenty-four hours till the shuttle returns, so you'd better get to work. Flintlock, forage for supplies in the village. We'll be staying here tonight and those look like rain clouds coming round the hills. Beg, steal or borrow food and shelter."

The two men nodded and began their tasks, while Dante continued studying the papers Arbatov had carried. "Crest, forged papers will only get us so far. I'll need credentials listed on the Imperial Net if I'm going to survive more than a few hours on the island."

You're not planning to become Grigori Arbatov, are you? I cannot work miracles, Dante, not without prior notice.

"No need for that. I'm reviving a favourite alias of mine. I need you to hack the Imperial Net and establish a fresh life story for him."

Using what – thin air? the Crest demanded.

Dante produced a slim silver rectangle from among Arbatov's things. Smaller than a cigarette case, it had the Imperial Net logo embossed on both sides. "How about a netski? Will that give you enough access?"

Part credit card, part communications device, and solar powered too. That'll do nicely, the Crest said happily. *Rest your fingers against either side of it and relax. I'll do the rest.*

By noon the next day the trio was ready. Sleep had proved elusive overnight, thanks to a torrential downpour. But strong sunshine in the morning soon helped restore their spirits. A distant, mournful bell chimed twelve. "What day is it?" Dante wondered. "We didn't hear that bell once yesterday."

"Sunday, isn't it?" Flintlock scratched his chest absentmindedly. "The bells must be calling the faithful to worship."

It's Palm Sunday, the Crest told Dante. *Only one week until Fabergé's new weapon becomes active.*

"Religion is wasted on us," Spatchcock smiled. He slapped Flintlock's back. "Something wrong, your lordship? You don't seem comfortable today."

"No, you're right. I can't seem to stop scratching." Realisation dawned on the aristocratic face. "Spatch! What did you do to me in the night?"

"I was cold and wet, so I snuggled against you for warmth."

Flintlock ripped open his shirt to discover a profusion of tiny red bites on his chest, the marks made more livid by scratching. "Fleas! You've given me fleas, you disgusting little worm!"

Spatchcock shrugged, scratching himself under an armpit. "You were sharing your warmth with me. Seemed only fair to give you something back."

"Give it a rest for five minutes," Dante snapped. "I see our ride leaving the island."

In the distance the shuttle rose above the castle and began swooping across the water towards them. Dante led the others down to the landing area, carrying a selection of luggage culled from their own possessions and those of the late Grigori Arbatov. The trio was waiting for the shuttle when it arrived, its afterburners eradicating the last traces of blood from the launching pad.

A burly figure in a hooded cloak emerged from the vehicle. Dante stepped towards him, smiling and offering to shake hands. "Good afternoon, sir. My name is-"

"Address me as either Madame Wartski or simply as Madame, but never as sir!" The hood was pushed back to reveal a wart-strewn face, greying hair scraped back into a bun and a scowling countenance. If this person was not the ugliest woman alive, Dante had no urge to go in search of any alternatives.

"Of course, Madame! Excuse my folly, I could not see your face beneath the hood," Dante continued. "My name is-"

"Why were you not here yesterday, as previously agreed? Why did you not contact us and explain the reason for this unforgivable delay? And why are three of you waiting, instead of one?"

Dante stood his ground before the flurry of interrogation, doing his best to smile ingratiatingly at the horrendous harridan. "Alas, I was only contacted by Captain Arbatov late last night and thus it was impossible for me to be here yesterday."

"So you are not Captain Arbatov?"

"No, Madame Wartski. As I tried to say before, my name is-"

"Your name is of no consequence." Wartski turned back to the vehicle.

Dante grabbed her by the arm, his fingers failing to encompass even half of her fleshy limb's circumference. "Please, Madame Wartski, if you will just let me explain…"

Wartski called to the shuttle's pilot. "How long before we can take off?"

"Fifty-five seconds, Madame!"

She turned back to Dante. "You have that long."

"As I have been trying to say, my name is Quentin Durward and I am a close personal friend of Grigori Arbatov.

Alas, a fencing accident means he could not accept your gracious invitation to join the Fabergé Institute for the final days of this term, so he suggested I offer my services in his stead. Had I been able, I would have called ahead to explain. I wrongly assumed he had already done so and apologise for that error."

Dante produced a sheaf of papers, all of them artfully created by Spatchcock. "I believe you'll find these documents establish my bona fides. As for my travelling companions, they are servants and have been with me since I was a youth." He gestured for them to come forwards. "The shorter, Spatchcock, is a fine cook and would add distinction to your kitchen, while the taller is my factotum, Flintlock. The latter, sadly, is a mute and thus unable to speak." Spatchcock suppressed a snort of laughter.

"Madame Wartski, we're ready to go," the pilot called.

Wartski regarded the trio, her bottom lip curling outwards sourly. "I am not satisfied with these explanations, but your papers appear authentic. You may come to the island, Mr Durward, where I can better establish the truth."

"And my servants?"

"We have little need of their services."

"They work without payment. Mere lodgings and board will satisfy them."

Wartski scowled. "Very well. But be warned of this: should I have any reason to doubt your veracity or that of your servants, all three of you will suffer the consequences equally. Is that clear?"

"As the blue of your eyes," Dante said sweetly.

Wartski leaned into his face, the rank stench of her breath invading his nostrils. "Flattery will get you nowhere with me, Mr Durward. I am interested only in what you can do for the institute."

"Of course, Madame Wartski. I would have it no other way." Dante snapped his fingers at Spatchcock and Flintlock. "You two! Fetch my things!" Ignoring the foul looks they were sending in his direction, Dante followed Wartski into the shuttle. The interior was luxuriously fitted, with four plush chairs for the passengers. But once Wartski had sat down only one of the seats remained, leaving nowhere for Spatchcock and Flintlock. "You'll have to travel in the cargo hold with my bags," he told them, suppressing a smile at their reactions. "And be quick about it! Madame Wartski has waited long enough on our behalf, let's not keep her here any longer!"

The flight to Fabergé Island took only minutes but Flintlock still found time to throw up thanks to airsickness and being confined in the cargo hold with Spatchcock. "A mute? Why did he say I'm a mute?"

"I can think of two reasons," Spatchcock replied. "Either he figured your Britannia accent would attract unwanted attention…"

"Or?"

"Or he didn't want to listen to your whining any longer – and I can't say I blame him. Now put a sock in it!"

"Why should I?" Flintlock protested.

Spatchcock indicated a security camera in the ceiling. "Your lips do a lot of flapping for somebody who's supposed to be mute. Best not to let anyone else see you talking, alright?"

"I– I–" Flintlock sighed in exasperation and clamped his mouth shut.

Spatchcock smiled blissfully. "Ahh, the sound of silence. Could anything be finer?" The sound of violent farting issued from his trousers, closely followed by a noxious stench. Flintlock pinched his nostrils shut and moved to the other side of the cabin, getting as far from the odour as possible.

"I'll take that as a yes," Spatchcock decided.

The shuttle circled Fabergé Island once so Wartski could point out the castle's exterior features to Dante. The imposing square structure covered more than two-thirds of the island's surface area. Each corner was adorned by a tower, standing twice the height of the adjoining building. "This entire complex was reconstructed stone by stone, after the doctor bought it from a Britannia noble family that had fallen on hard times. Most of the building is devoted to the institute's work, but the north tower is reserved for the doctor's private research."

"Sounds fascinating. What is Doctor Fabergé researching, if I may ask?"

"You may not," Wartski replied with a scowl. "The north tower is strictly out of bounds at all times. Anyone caught trespassing there will be dismissed or expelled immediately – without exception."

"I understand, of course. Rules are rules."

"And must be obeyed at all times."

"Precisely," Dante agreed. "I couldn't have put it better myself."

Dante, you've never obeyed a rule in your life!

The shuttle descended towards the island's landing pad. Dante peered out of his window, absorbing as much information as he could about the external facilities. "Well, I must say I am looking forward to working with your pupils," he said. "How many do you have here at present?"

"Most have already returned home early for the Easter holidays, as have many of our regular tutors," Wartski replied. "But the elite class is here for another week. We have a dozen students from around the Empire, most aged between eighteen and twenty-one." The shuttle finished landing procedures and Wartski pulled open the passenger door.

"And what's the split between male and female?"

Wartski stopped and looked at him. "Didn't Captain Arbatov tell you? The Fabergé Institute is a finishing school for young ladies from the richest and most important families in the Empire."

"Really?"

"Yes." Wartski started climbing down the shuttle steps. "I hope that isn't going to be a problem for you."

Dante shook his head slowly. "A finishing school for young ladies aged eighteen to twenty-one? No, I don't think that should present any difficulties."

Except keeping your pants on long enough to take lessons, the Crest said. *This situation will only lead to one thing.*

"No difficulties at all," Dante concluded.

Trouble, trouble and more trouble!

SIX

"Deceit and cunning go together"
– Russian proverb

Wartski marched towards the castle entrance, her chunky legs stomping along the pathway. Dante followed close behind, his eyes roving across the exterior of the stonework. Flintlock and Spatchcock brought up the rear, struggling to carry the luggage between them. "Be careful not to venture off the path," Wartski warned them sternly. "The island may look benign but its external surface is embedded with pressure mines. Your first step off the correct path would also be your last."

"An impressive security system," Dante said. "But is it strictly necessary for a girls' finishing school?"

Wartski stopped outside the entrance and folded her arms. "Firstly, this is an educational institute for young ladies, not girls. Give our students the respect they deserve, Mr Durward. Secondly, there have been instances where predatory males thought they might be able to satisfy their carnal lusts with our pupils. The few who made it to the island alive did not leave it in the same condition. Thirdly, our director believes such security measures are necessary to protect his personal research. You would do well not to question the judgement of Doctor Fabergé."

"Of course. Your comments are noted and will be respected," Dante said.

Chance would be a fine thing.

Wartski pressed her palm against a block of frosted glass in the wall beside the entrance. A beam of light scanned the contours of her hand before the glass turned green. Double doors sighed open, revealing a vast reception chamber inside. "Once your bona fides have been confirmed, your palm print will be recorded and logged into our security system," she explained. "That will enable you to access all areas of the castle necessary to perform your duties. Your servants will also have to undergo such screening."

"Of course," Dante said, nodding vigorously. "We must be on our guard at all times. Heaven forbid anything might impugn the name of Fabergé!"

Wartski raised an eyebrow at this outburst before gesturing for him to enter. "After you, Mr Durward."

Dante bowed deeply, then strolled into the reception chamber, followed by Flintlock and Spatchcock. Wartski was last inside, waving her hand across another palm reader within. The doors slammed shut with a boom of finality. Dante looked around the room, marvelling at its high ceiling and oak-panelled walls. A banner with the Fabergé family crest hung on one wall, close to an honours board marking the achievements of past pupils. The institute had only been open nine years but could already claim several prominent alumni. Top of the list were two names – Strangelove S, and Strangelove T.

Any relation to the Strangelove Gambit?

Wartski noted Dante's interest in the honours board. "Storm and Tempest were our first pupils, the stars of their year. You may remember their success at the Imperial Games?"

"Of course," Dante replied with a smile, the Crest filling his thoughts with facts and statistics from its files. "A remarkable pair!"

"I thought they both had a remarkable pair," Spatchcock muttered, jabbing an elbow into Flintlock's ribs and leering crudely. He wiped the smirk off his face before Wartski could see it.

She opened a side door with a gesture across another palm reader. "If you'll excuse me, I need to report your arrival to Doctor Fabergé and check the identification papers you supplied. Please wait here."

Dante nodded and smiled, watching her depart before turning to his companions. "Now, I want both of you to be on your best behaviour. Do nothing to embarrass the good name of Quentin Durward, is that clear?"

Spatchcock rolled his eyes and grinned. Flintlock began to speak, then stopped, clamping his mouth shut in frustration.

"Very good," Dante continued, his eyes searching the reception area for surveillance devices. "We must be on our guard at all times, to ensure we meet the high standards set by the Fabergé Institute."

Madame Wartski has begun searching the records for your fake identity, the Crest warned. *The false history I created should sustain itself through a routine scrutiny, but if she digs any deeper…*

Dante folded his arms and waited. "I wonder where the pupils are?"

"At mass," Wartski replied, emerging from the side door with his papers clutched in a chubby, wart-ridden hand. "Our director insists all the students observe the main feast days of the church calendar. Why feed the mind if the soul goes unnourished?"

"An admirable sentiment," Dante agreed, reaching for the documents. "I trust everything was in order?"

Wartski smiled broadly, an expression that ill-suited her fearsome face. "We are honoured to have such a distinguished instructor join our faculty. Hopefully we will be able to make your time here a stay of some duration. Perhaps you would like a tour of our facilities?"

"That would be most kind. But I hardly think it appropriate for my servants to join us. If I might be so bold, may I suggest their fate be determined first?"

Wartski acknowledged the wisdom of this. "Very well. You two, take the first door on the right after you leave here. There is a staircase leading down to the kitchen where our resident chef and housekeeper Scullion will find a use for both of you. Once you've been assigned suitable tasks return here and carry your master's luggage to his quarters. I will leave directions. Do you understand?" Spatchcock and Flintlock nodded quickly. "Very good. Off you go and try not to antagonise Scullion. Her temper is short and her tentacles long."

The two men hurried to escape the matron's fearsome gaze. Dante could hear Spatchcock muttering to Flintlock as the pair left the reception chamber. "Her tentacles are long? Who is this Scullion, an octopus?"

Once they were gone Wartski began leading Dante around the castle, explaining the use of each room on their tour. The east tower and nearby rooms were devoted to dormitories and other student facilities, while the south tower and its environs were classrooms and training areas. "We teach all the key subjects our pupils might require for their lives as the leading ladies of the Empire," Wartski explained. "History, business communication, literature, philosophy, organisations behaviour, psychology, ecology, a dozen different languages, economics, etiquette, domestic science, music, ballroom dancing and flower arranging."

"A broad curriculum," Dante replied. "You offer an admirable range of knowledge to the young ladies."

Wartski threw open a door to reveal the top level of the south tower. The entire space was given over to a well-equipped gymnasium, the floor and walls heavily padded to prevent injury. "We expect you to give each of our pupils a strenuous workout, discover their strengths and weaknesses."

"It will be my pleasure," he replied. "Hopefully they will respond well to the personal touch and breadth of experience I can offer."

Take care, the Crest warned. *The matron may have a face to curdle milk, but the woman is no fool.*

"I've been taking the classes myself since your predecessor left," Wartski continued. "Alas, I am not as nimble as I once was. The students are looking forward to having you really stretch them."

Dante merely nodded, not trusting himself to say anything out loud. His tour guide gestured at the west tower, the gymnasium's window. "That area of the castle is given over to the faculty: private quarters, ablution blocks, a study and library area, along with meetings rooms. The junior tutors have left for the term but our senior staff remain on site all year round. You'll meet them at dinner tonight, beginning promptly at seven."

A heavy chiming filled the air, closely followed by the sound of feminine giggling outside. "Ah, mass is over for today, the students are returning to their dormitory. Would you like to see them?" Wartski asked.

Dante looked down at a square courtyard in the centre of the castle. A dozen beautiful young women were hurrying across the cobbles, laughing and teasing each other. All were clad in demure gowns of blue and white, but even the severe cut of the cloth could not disguise their firm buttocks and jutting breasts. The women disappeared into a doorway at the foot of the east tower, the sound of their laughter like music in the air. "They look very fit," Dante said, trying to keep his voice neutral. "You've obviously done a good job of keeping them active."

"I wish I could claim the credit. Your predecessor, Mr Russell, drove the students hard. Sometimes I think he would have been happier teaching a class of young men, such was his passion for the more masculine athletic pursuits , wrestling, boxing and the like."

"I'm all for treating women like women," Dante avowed.

"Good, then you won't mind picking up some of the classes Mr Russell neglected, such as philosophy and litera-ture studies."

Something tells me I'm going to be rather busy, the Crest commented.

"Two of my favourites!" Dante lied. "When do I start?"

"Classes resume tomorrow," Wartski replied. "I'll escort you to your quarters. No doubt you'll wish to freshen up before joining the other staff in the library for a pre-dinner drink?" She began striding from the gymnasium, not noticing Dante lingering at the window. He was studying the north tower opposite, its windows shrouded with black-tinted glass. "Mr Durward?" Wartski called, but got no response.

Dante! She's calling you!

"What? Oh, sorry!" Dante shouted, hurrying after his host. "Just planning my first class for tomorrow. It's always been an ambition of mine to work at a prestigious facility, especially one with such an admirable student body. I do believe I'll fit right in here."

In the kitchen Spatchcock and Flintlock were standing to attention as a green-skinned creature with at least a dozen tentacles studied them with disgust. An entire wall of the kitchen was given over to a pantry, while foul-smelling liquids bubbled away in cast iron vats. A sturdy wooden table filled the centre of the cooking room, lined with chairs on either side. Three doorways led away from the kitchen. One was the staircase down which Spatchcock and Flintlock had descended into Scullion's domain. The other two led to a drainage room and another, as yet unseen destination.

"My name is Scullion," the creature announced, "and no matter what Madame Wartski might think, I am responsible for keeping this institute running. I do this by taking responsibility for all its needs below stairs: the cooking, the cleaning, the laundry and any other ablutions required. Any questions?" Scullion jabbed Flintlock in the stomach with a tentacle, making him wince in pain.

"He's a mute," Spatchcock offered helpfully. "Can't speak a word."

"Thank you, I am aware of what the word mute means."

"Sorry. I just thought, what with you being an off-worlder–" Spatchcock was abruptly silenced as his head was clamped inside another of Scullion's tentacles, moist pink suckers adhering to his face. The squat, emerald-hued alien leaned closer to Spatchcock, its one red eye peering at him intently.

"I've had enough anti-alien abuse to last me a lifetime. On my home planet of Arcneva I was Gourmet Chef of the Cycle twice in a row. I do not need some snivelling weasel of a servant to tell me–" Scullion paused in mid-rant, sniffing the air with disdain. "What is that stench?"

Spatchcock peeled away the tentacle from his face to reply. "Sorry, that's probably me. Most people complain that I smell worse than an alien's arsehole." The words were out of his mouth before he realised what was being said. "I–"

Scullion slapped the tentacle back into place. "Silence! I wasn't talking to you. I was talking to this loathsome creature!" The alien jabbed Flintlock once more. He opened his mouth to protest, remembered his status as a mute and closed his mouth again with a snap. Scullion sniffed at Flintlock's armpits before reeling away, squealing in horror and quickly retracting its tentacles. "Most humans smell like wet pork to me, but you – you carry the foulest of stenches with you! What is your name?"

"He's called Flintlock," Spatchcock chipped in.

"From now on he will be called Faeces," Scullion decided. "He will be addressed only by that name in my presence. Do you understand?"

"Yes, er..."

"You can call me Scullion, or ma'am."

Spatchcock smiled. "Yes, ma'am."

The alien studied him carefully. "Can you cook?"

"I can always rustle something up," he admitted.

"Good. I will tutor you in the ways of Arcnevan cuisine, Spatchcock." Scullion slipped a tentacle round his shoulders and gave them a playful squeeze. "As for your friend Faeces…"

"He could clean out the drains," Spatchcock suggested with a smile.

"A task to match his title and his aroma! Excellent. I couldn't have thought of anything more appropriate myself." The alien pointed at a circular sewer covering in the adjoining drainage room. "You can start over there."

Flintlock hurried to the grille and lifted it up, his head snapping away from the odour of raw sewage wafting upwards. The former aristocrat gave Spatchcock a murderous glare, his fists clenching and unclenching. "I said get started, Faeces!" Scullion snapped. "You brought this on yourself, so don't blame you sweet-smelling colleague. Try following his example in future and I might forgive you. Now get on with your allotted task!"

Dante was less than impressed with his private quarters. The spartan stone chamber contained a wardrobe, stiff-backed chair and single bed as furnishings. Wartski explained that Doctor Fabergé preferred his staff to spend as much time as possible among the other faculty members and students. "Bedrooms are for sleeping in, nothing more," she added with a growl of warning. "Your servants will be permitted to wait upon you here once a day, if their duties are completed, but no other visitors are allowed."

"Perfectly fair and reasonable," Dante replied out loud. How am I supposed to know my students better with this behemoth breathing down my neck, he thought to himself?

You would do better to concentrate on your mission, the Crest suggested. *The Strangelove Gambit, remember?*

"Captain Arbatov told me the institute was soon to be honoured with a visit by the Tsar," Dante said. "Is that true?"

Wartski frowned. "Yes, although I don't know how he can have told you that. It hasn't been announced in the court circular."

"Really? Well, when I see Arbatov next I will remonstrate with him for such a lapse. It does not do to gossip about such matters."

"No, it doesn't," Wartski agreed. "Why do you ask about the Tsar? Have you met him before?"

"Once or twice. We've crossed swords, you might say."

"He is due to visit us a week today. It should be a glorious occasion for the institute, helping promote our efforts to all the Empire. Doctor Fabergé cannot wait to show the Tsar what he has achieved here. Now, if you'll excuse me, I must attend to matters elsewhere in the castle."

Dante listened at his door to ensure Wartski was gone before sitting on the single bed. He bounced up and down on the thin straw mattress, wincing at the lack of give. "Not exactly the lap of luxury."

You can stop talking to yourself, I've finished scanning the room, the Crest interjected. *No obvious listening devices or surveillance cameras. If you are being watched, it's technology beyond my ability to detect. To be safe I've established a low level-jamming signal.*

"What about the palm readers?"

More problematic, the Crest admitted. *I should be able to override the scanning systems but no doubt Fabergé has other methods of securing other parts of his castle.*

"Like the north tower?"

Precisely. His private research is almost certainly the source of this new weapon. The institute's pupils are just a front to distract attention.

Dante smirked. "They're doing a pretty good job so far." He spread himself out on the mattress and closed his eyes. "Keep scanning Crest. The more we know about the castle and its contents, the easier it will be discovering what the Strangelove Gambit is all about."

And what will you be doing?

"Getting some rest. A night under canvas with Spatchcock and Flintlock is no way to get any beauty sleep."

True, but some of us need more than others.

"Call me when it's time for dinner."

I'm not an alarm clock, you know! the Crest protested. *Dante? Dante!* But the only response was the unpleasant grating sound of Dante's snoring.

It was the smell that roused Dante from his slumber. "Diavolo, who killed the cat?" he muttered, sitting up on the thin mattress. "Flintlock? Is that you?"

"Yes, it's bloody me!" A tall figure was standing beside Dante's bed, smeared from head to toe with viscous slime. Whatever colour of clothing he had been wearing was now impossible to tell, replaced by shades of black and brown. The face and hair were just as bad, only the pale blue eyes and white teeth providing any break in the sewage-stained visage. Worst of all was the smell, a rank odour worse than any back street pissotière. Dante waved Flintlock back before standing, eager to keep some distance between them.

"What happened? Did you fall into a septic tank?"

"Not exactly," Flintlock snarled. "That bitch Scullion had me cleaning the drains while Spatchcock, the foulest smelling creature in the Empire, is cooking the soup for tonight's meal!"

Dante clamped his nostrils between the thumb and forefinger of his left hand. "I think your smell might beat Spatchcock's now." He opened the window in the hope of admitting some fresh air. "How come you got sewer duty?"

"Scullion is an alien from Arcneva," Flintlock replied grumpily.

A planet where the indigenous people consider offensive body odour an aphrodisiac, the Crest said. *No doubt Spatchcock's scent seemed like a fine perfume to her.*

Dante did his best to suppress a smile without much success. "I don't see what you've got to smirk at," Flintlock protested.

"No, you're absolutely right," Dante agreed. "What else can you tell me?"

"This mute act – how long do I have to keep it up?"

"A week at the most. Wartski confirmed the Tsar will be here for Easter Sunday, so we've got until then to find and stop this new weapon – whatever it is." Dante stood beneath the window, trying to catch the few wisps of air that crept into the room. "Where have you and Spatch been given access to so far?"

"The drains, the septic tank and the overflow pipes for me," Flintlock said testily. "Spatch hasn't got out of Scullion's clutches in the kitchen yet."

"We need to discover everything we can about what's happening here, especially in the north tower. Tell Spatch to grab every opportunity."

"And what about me?"

"Try not to catch anything fatal." Dante gestured towards the door. "I'm sorry, but you'll have to leave now. I need to get ready for my first faculty dinner."

"So? Perhaps I could help, I am meant to be your servant."

"No disrespect, but the longer you stay in here the worse I'll smell later."

Flintlock turned on his heels and flounced towards the door. "I've never been so insulted in my life," he muttered. "Forced to squeeze down a pipe filled with heaven only knows what then told to–"

"And go quietly, please," Dante called after him. "You're meant to be a mute, remember?"

Flintlock made an obscene finger gesture and departed, but the stench from his visit remained.

It was after seven when Dante found his way to the staff library. Inside the book-lined room five women and an elderly man were talking in hushed voices beneath a towering portrait of Doctor Fabergé. The painting neatly captured the cruel face and dismissive eyes of its subject, but added a haughty grandeur to the driven countenance. The staff gathered beneath the image of their director was not nearly so intimidating.

All of the women were middle-aged; their age reflected in the staid tweeds and checks of their clothing. Sensible shoes and thick woollen stockings, a few strings of second rate pearls, greying hair and crow's feet wrinkles were further evidence of their dry lives and interests. I doubt this lot start many orgies, Dante reflected ruefully.

Dante approached the only other male in the room, a crusty old man in brown corduroy trousers and an ancient blazer with leather patches over the elbows. A pair of half moon spectacles perched on his nose while red, rheumy eyes peered at the volumes on the shelves around him. Dante clapped a hand on the old man's back, sending a small cloud of dust into the air.

"Durward, Quentin Durward – I'm the new self defence instructor!" Dante announced cheerfully. "And what's your name, if I may be so bold?"

The old man coughed and wheezed before answering laboriously. "Mould. Professor Augustus Mould."

Dante suppressed a pun. "Fascinating. And how long have you been here?"

Mould looked at his watch, not noticing the sherry he was pouring over his brown brogues. "About twenty minutes, I think. Yes, twenty minutes."

"Really? I didn't realise the fun started so early here."

"Fun? What fun?"

"I, er…" Dante shrugged helplessly before muttering under his breath. "Crest? A little help here, please?"

Oh no, it replied gleefully. *He's all yours. Enjoy.*

"Wonderful," Dante said to Mould. "Well, a delight to meet you. Perhaps we'll get a chance to talk again later." But before he could move away the elderly professor had grabbed Dante's arm.

"Self defence, you said? Then you must be Russell's replacement."

"Yes, that's right."

"Odd chap, Russell. I think he'd have been happier at a finishing school for young men, if you know what I mean,"

Mould said, conspiratorially tapping the side of his nose. "Played for the other side, you might say."

"Did he? I wouldn't know. I've never met him."

"Never saw the point in that sort of thing."

"Sex?"

"Chasing other men around. Much fonder of the fairer sex, myself."

Dante looked at the crusty professor. "You were? I mean, you are?"

Mould nodded wistfully. "Used to be. Quite the catch I was once. Had to fight the young girls off with a stick. At least I believe that's the expression."

"I thought the Tsar had outlawed corporal punishment," Dante said.

But Mould was no longer listening to him. "I sleep through most of my lessons now. The students here, they're not interested in history or language. They just want fame and fortune, how to catch a husband..."

"Madame Wartski doesn't share your views."

The professor's face darkened. "Beware of her, young Durward. Beware of any woman with that many warts. She has them for a reason, you know."

Dante leaned closer to the professor. "And why is that?"

"Toads. That's all you need to know. Beware of the toads."

"Beware of the toads?"

Mould nodded sagely. "I'll say no more."

"I understand," Dante agreed. "Well, if you'll excuse me..." He turned away and walked face-first into a large pair of firm, proud breasts. "Bojemoi!" Dante stumbled back a step, blinking to clear his vision. He reached out a hand for support and found himself grasping another breast to his right. "Diavolo, I'm surrounded by them!"

"You must be–" a woman's voice began.

"The new self defence instructor," another woman said, completing the first's sentence. "Perhaps you could do with–"

"A refresher course yourself?" the first voice concluded.

Dante looked up to find two Amazons towering over him. Their mighty breasts were level with his eyes, providing a daunting introduction to their physical presence. Their strong, angular features stared down at Dante, a difference in hair colouring the only way of telling them apart. Both were clad in skin-tight bodysuits that left little to the imagination. "Are you offering to give me one?" Dante asked hopefully.

"We already have–" the red-haired woman began.

"A full teaching load," the brunette said.

"Oh," Dante said sadly. "What a shame."

"Mr Durward," a familiar voice called out. Wartski was marching towards the trio, holding two glasses of sherry before her. "I see you've met the Furies." She handed Dante one of the glasses. "Storm and Tempest joined the teaching staff this year and have proved a great success with the students."

The Strangelove twins, Dante realised. He had caught a little of the media hype surrounding these remarkable women. In the flesh they were even more impressive. Dante felt a stirring in his loins at the prospect of finding out how impressive. "Which one's which?"

The red-haired woman offered her right hand to him. "I'm Tempest."

Dante kissed the hand, adding his wickedest of grins. "Enchanted," he whispered before moving on to the other twin. "And you must be Storm. How delightful to make your acquaintance." She did not offer Dante a hand, folding her arms instead. "I'm told you two do everything together."

"Almost," Tempest replied. "We find two heads are better than one."

"Still, three needn't always be a crowd," Dante countered. "Perhaps we could get together and talk about it sometime."

"I doubt that will be possible before the end of term," Storm said brusquely before walking away. "Come along, sister." Dante watched them walk away, admiring the rippling muscles in their thighs and buttocks.

You're out of your depth, the Crest warned. *Those two would eat you for breakfast and leave nothing behind.*

"But what a way to go." Dante murmured. "What a way to go."

"Sorry, did you say something?" Wartski asked.

"Er, I was wondering which way to go – for dinner."

A chime sounded once, silencing the hubbub of voices in the library. Wartski nodded at the others. "Now you will find out, Mr Durward. Dinner is served and Doctor Fabergé is dying to meet you." The hefty harridan strode away, leaving Dante to finish his sherry.

The evening meal was served in an oak-panelled dining hall next to the staff library. A long table ran the length of the room, but most of the seats went unoccupied with only the senior staff in attendance. Wartski stood near the head of the table, motioning for Dante to take the chair opposite her. Mould moved to beside Dante, while the other tutors chose seats nearby. But nobody sat down, all waiting patiently beside their chairs.

Finally a doorway opened and the Strangelove twins emerged from it, Doctor Fabergé following them inside. He moved to the head of the table, fixed the gaze of each staff member and nodded to them individually. Lastly he acknowledged the presence of Dante, then sat down. The staff followed his example, the twins sitting opposite each other but farthest from Fabergé.

Murmurings of small talk began along the table while everyone waited for the first course to be served, giving Dante a chance to cast a furtive eye over Fabergé. Twelve years had passed since their last encounter, enough time for the doctor's hairline to recede further and more lines to appear on his face. But for these changes Fabergé was much as Dante remembered, proud of bearing and inquisitive of eye. He noticed the attentions of the new teacher and addressed them immediately.

"You must be our new self defence tutor, Mr Durward."

"That's correct, Doctor Fabergé," Dante replied.

"And why have you been looking at me so intently?"

A hush fell upon the table, the others waiting for the new-comer's reply.

"I was comparing your true appearance to the portrait I saw in the library."

"Indeed. And how would you rate the quality of that like-ness?"

Dante smiled. "The artist captured your looks, but not your stature."

Fabergé regarded him carefully. "Well chosen words. I wonder how close they are to the truth?"

"As someone versed in the arts of self defence, I know that such skills are as much about brain as they are brawn. You can often talk your way out of trouble with less danger than you can fight your way out."

The doctor stroked his chin thoughtfully. "Have we met somewhere before, Mr Durward? Your face seems familiar, but I cannot recall from where."

Dante shook his head. "I have a common aspect but can say for certain you have never met Quentin Durward before."

"Perhaps I was mistaken." Fabergé was interrupted by the arrival of Scullion, carrying eleven bowls of steaming soup in her many tentacles. "Ah, the starter. Let us eat, drink and be merry."

The meal continued for three hours and twice as many courses, until Dante felt his belly bloating and trousers tight-ening. "I'm not sure I shall be able to lead my classes for long, if you feast like this every night."

Wartski waved away his concerns. "We only eat this well on Sunday evenings. Simpler fare is served during the week."

Fabergé had been watching Dante throughout the meal. "We live by an old proverb here, Mr Durward – eat the honey, but beware the sting."

Dante, be careful! the Crest warned. *He's trying to draw you into a battle of wits – and that's one fight you can never win. Just repeat what I say.*

Dante listened to the voice inside his head and then smiled at the institute's director. "I prefer a different saying: luck is a stick with two ends."

Fabergé laughed out loud at that. "Well said, Mr Durward, well said. Perhaps you've heard another adage: God made two evils, tax collectors and goats. Which one are you, I wonder?"

Dante nodded before replying. "Well, I'm not a god, if that's what you're wondering."

"Few of us are," Fabergé agreed. "But some aspire to match the achievements of the Almighty."

"Is that always wise?" Dante asked, pausing as if choosing his words carefully. "As the proverb has it, the spirit is God's, but the body is the Tsar's."

"Well, the Tsar is expected here in a week's time. You may debate morality and proverbs with him then," Fabergé said. "You have an interesting habit of waiting before you reply, Mr Durward. Why is that?"

I like to think before I speak, the Crest prompted Dante, who repeated the phrase out loud.

"An admirable quality, and one many of our pupils could do with learning. Perhaps you're the man to take them in hand?"

"I'm sure I'll soon have a firm grasp of their strengths and weaknesses."

"I hope so," Fabergé said before standing. Everyone else rose from their chairs, Dante swiftly following their example. "In the meantime I have more work to do if my research is to be complete in time for the Tsar's visit. I bid you all a good night's rest. Tempest, Storm – will you join me in the laboratory? We have a very busy week ahead."

Wartski and the others murmured their good nights, watching as Fabergé and the twins strode from the dining hall. Once the trio had departed everyone returned to the staff library, whether they had finished or not. "Once our master leaves his seat, the meal is over," Mould whispered in Dante's ear. "It always pays to eat as quickly as possible."

"That explains why we were the only ones talking." Dante wanted to ask the old professor a question but Mould was already scuttling towards the sweet sherry decanter, intent on refilling his glass. Instead Wartski gravitated to the new arrival's side, the aroma from her sweaty armpits indicating her presence.

"You'll have to forgive the professor. A brilliant tutor once, but past his prime; now slowly pickling himself to death."

"Why do you keep him on if that's the case?"

Wartski smiled. "Call it user loyalty."

Dante nodded, not wanting to think about what her remark implied. "Well, I think I've imbibed quite enough sherry for a month, let alone one night. I shall be returning to my room for the evening." He walked from the room, nodding a goodnight to the other teachers, but Wartski followed him out.

"Mr Durward, there is something I forgot to mention earlier. I advise locking yourself in each night. Your predecessor was prone to sleepwalking. Indeed, that's what caused his death."

"His death? I thought he went to another place of learning."

Wartski shook her head. "That's what we told the pupils and some of the other tutors. In fact Mr Russell was a frequent sleepwalker. He wandered into the north tower one night and was cut to pieces by the security defence lasers. Not a pleasant sight, not pleasant at all."

"I can imagine," Dante said grimly.

"So, as I said, best if you lock yourself in. We wouldn't want such an unhappy incident to happen to you too, would we?"

"Thank you for the warning. I'll be sure to remain on my guard." Dante walked back to his quarters, seething at the veiled threat. The unfortunate Russell had been murdered to preserve whatever secret Fabergé had locked inside the north tower, just as Di Grizov had been tortured to aid whatever barbaric research the doctor was undertaking.

Just be grateful Fabergé didn't remember you from the Casino Royale, the Crest said. *He would not hesitate to have you killed if he realised you helped Di Grizov steal the Steel Military Egg.*

"Tell me something I don't know," Dante muttered bitterly.

SEVEN

"Temptation is sweet, man weak"
– Russian proverb

"How do I look, Crest?" Dante's luggage had appeared in his quarters while he was at dinner the night before, carried there by Flintlock if the vile smell on the handles was any indication. The next morning Dante took a hearty breakfast, showered and scrubbed in preparation for his first class, and was admiring himself in a mirror borrowed from the late Captain Arbatov.

Like an unshaven monkey, the Crest replied archly.

"I can hardly remove my moustache and goatee, they're keeping my identity secret from Doctor Fabergé."

You asked, I answered. It's not my fault if the truth offends.

Dante sighed. "Let's not start the day by bickering, alright? If I'm going to teach these girls about swordplay and self defence, I'll need your help."

You've had enough women fend off your dubious charms, the Crest said, *I'd have thought you'd have plenty of experiences worth sharing.*

"Yeah, yeah, make all the jibes you want. When the time comes, your programming requires that you help me avoid death or ignominy."

Death, yes. But avoiding ignominy? Even I can't perform miracles.

"Just tell me when I'm going wrong and offer a few helpful hints, okay?"

I'll try.

"Thank you."

But you still look like an unshaven monkey.

"Bojemoi! Give me strength." Dante chose a quilted crimson jacket and matching fencing helmet from among Arbatov's clothes. The jacket was a tight fit across the shoulders, its seams straining to contain Dante's bulkier frame.

May I suggest you avoid the cooked breakfast from now on. I doubt that stitching will last the day if you eat much more.

"You're not my mother and you're not my wife, so stop nagging!"

Fine. Have it your own way.

"I will."

Good.

"Be like that!"

I will!

"Suits me!" Dante snapped.

Unlike that jacket.

Dante resisted the urge to push his fingers into both ears, knowing it would not shut out the insistent, superior voice of the Crest. "Think calm thoughts," he told himself. "Just think calm thoughts".

Natalia Sokorina was not only the youngest pupil at the Fabergé Institute, but also the brightest. Students were not normally accepted before the age of eighteen but Natalia had won her place on merit, having already finished a university degree before her seventeenth birthday. She had never wanted to waste a year in such a place but her ambitious mother insisted. "I let you go to college on the condition you went to a finishing school afterwards. I mean, how can you ever hope to become a young lady if you spend every minute with your nose buried inside text books? How will you ever find a worthy husband? Your sisters all attended finishing schools and now you will do the same."

Natalia knew her older sisters had few ambitions beyond possessing the grandest home, richest husband and most handsome lover in the Empire. But arguing that such things were of little merit carried no weight with her mother, who had followed the same code rigorously and instilled it in most of her daughters. So Natalia had reluctantly agreed to a year's exile at a finishing school, selecting the Fabergé Institute because it at least had some record of academic excellence. True, the Strangelove twins were frightening in person, but not even Natalia could deny their many scientific achievements under Doctor Fabergé's tutelage.

Now the institute's youngest student was a week away from graduating from its mink-lined prison, seven days from escaping the gilded cage. She would be eighteen and free of her mother's authority, free to create a life for herself beyond a stifling world of flower arranging, gossip and business communication lessons – whatever the hell that was supposed to be. For all the attention Natalia had paid in that class, it could have been about how best to catch your boss's roving eye. Now that she came to think about it, that had been the essence of the second term's studies, with particular attention paid to how short skirts should be (the shorter the better for displaying perfectly sculpted thighs), why glossy red lipstick was important (apparently it sent a subliminal signal of sexual availability) and the advantages of wearing the best lingerie (it helped flaunt your assets, allegedly).

Natalia regarded herself in one of the dormitory's full-length mirrors. Plainly, she hadn't been paying much attention in any of those lessons. The other students were women, with fully developed bodies and practiced poise from a lifetime of elocution and deportment classes. Natalia was a late developer, her body still finding its adult shape. She had grown four inches since arriving on the island, this spurt accompanied by a widening of the hips and thickening of the thighs. Her breasts were the most embarrassing change, having swelled to create a pair of attention-seeking balloons. Even ancient Professor Mould had noticed them, making a comment about the baby of the class growing up at last. She'd wanted to climb into a hole and disappear as the others laughed at her embarrassment.

Despite the urgings of tutors to make the best of her looks, Natalia refused to wear make-up unless it was absolutely required. She kept her strawberry blonde hair back from her face in a simple ponytail and did nothing to hide the smattering of freckles across her cheeks. Even her clothes avoided the pouting glamour favoured by the other students, a modest skirt and shapeless top disguising her womanly attributes.

"Oh Natalia! You're not wearing that again, are you?" a voice protested from the doorway. A big-boned and boisterous pupil called Helga was shaking her head in dismay, two plaits of blonde hair pinned to the sides of her head. The oldest daughter from the Germanic House of Hapsburg, Helga occupied the bed next to Natalia's in the senior dormitory and frequently tried to talk the younger woman into more revealing clothing.

"And why not?" Natalia asked.

"Haven't you heard? We've got a new tutor – a man! He's quite a hunk, if you believe Carmen and Tracy. They saw him coming out of the west tower first thing this morning."

"If I believed everything Carmen and Tracy said, I'd be almost as silly as them," Natalia replied dryly. "You shouldn't listen to gossip. The tutor is probably a hundred and covered in cobwebs, like Professor Mould."

"But he's still a man!" Helga enthused, her cheeks flushed red. "I haven't seen a real man in weeks, not since poor Mr Russell left in such a hurry."

"Poor Mr Russell preferred the company of boys, not girls."

"But he was ever so handsome!"

Natalia rolled her eyes. Having a conversation with Helga was like trying to calm the ocean with words during a storm.

"You were barking up the wrong tree then, Helga, and you're no doubt barking up the wrong tree now. Do you honestly think old Wartski would let a virile heterosexual man loose amongst the senior class? The other girls would eat him alive."

Helga began digging through the locker at the end of Natalia's bed, throwing the clothes on to the floor. "I don't care what you say! We're going to find you something decent to wear and make you look pretty, just this once. Thumbelina shall go to the ball!"

"I think you mean Cinderella."

"Whatever," Helga replied. "I never pay attention in literature appreciation class." Her face lit up as she emerged from the locker, clutching the smallest of black silk camisoles. "This is it, this is the one."

Natalia's horror was all too evident. "Forget it! My mother sent me that as a present. I'm not wearing so ridiculous a piece of underwear!"

Helga had an evil glint in her eye. "Who said it would be *under*wear?"

Dante was standing outside the gymnasium, clutching his fencing helmet and trying not to think about the knots his lower intestine was tying itself into. "They're just girls," he told himself. "There's nothing to be afraid of inside there."

They're young women, the Crest replied. *Young women filled with raging hormones who probably haven't set eyes on a virile male for weeks or even months. I hope you brought a whip and chair to keep them at bay.*

"They're just girls," Dante repeated to himself, ignoring the voice in his head. "You've had plenty of experience with them before."

Perhaps. But twelve at once?

"You can do this, nothing to be scared of. You're the man, the boss."

"Psyching yourself up?" a stern voice boomed from behind Dante. He spun round to find Wartski stomping towards him.

"Just preparing myself for the first class," Dante admitted. "I want to make a good impression, announce my presence with authority."

"Then I suggest you do up your fly first," the matron said, her gaze wandering down to his crotch. "What you've got on show there wouldn't intimidate a dormouse."

Dante hurriedly buttoned the front of his trousers. "If you'll excuse me, Madame Wartski, I have a class to attend. Good day!" He pulled open the gymnasium door and strode inside, slamming it shut behind him. What he found inside made Dante's heart skip a beat. "Bojemoi!"

A dozen young women were working on a variety of exercise equipment: climbing ropes, throwing medicine balls around, bouncing on trampolines and limbering up with stretching exercises on the padded floor. All but one were clad in the slightest of clothing, scraps of fabric stretched tautly across rippling thighs, firm buttocks and barely contained breasts. The exception was doing her best to hide at the back of the class, arms folded across herself, a bright red blush colouring her face.

Wartski's boasts about the institute drawing its students from across the Empire were plainly true. The twelve women displayed a variety of ethnic backgrounds, ranging from Latin states and the Orient to those of paler skinned Nordic and European origins. As one the women turned and looked at the new arrival, their gazes filled with an avid hunger and curiosity. Dante had an uncomfortable feeling the pupils were undressing him with their eyes and resisted the urge to protect his crotch with both hands.

"Now I know what a beautiful woman feels like alone in a room full of men," he whispered to himself.

Now you know what any woman feels like alone in a room full of men, the Crest commented.

Dante forced himself to smile and began walking among the students, observing them as they stretched and bounced and displayed themselves. He passed a few appreciative comments and did his best not to ogle the female forms being flaunted. Finally he reached the one pupil straining not to be noticed, a shy girl standing behind a vaulting horse. "And what's your name?"

"Natalia," she replied quietly. "Natalia Sokorina."

"Why aren't you warming up with the others?"

"I, er..." Natalia blushed an even deeper crimson than before. "I wore the wrong clothing for this lesson."

"Let me be the judge of that," Dante said politely and waved her out from behind the vaulting horse. Natalia reluctantly walked around the equipment to reveal her garb: a mini skirt so short it would have been better employed as a cummerbund, and a black silk camisole that was almost transparent beneath the bright lights of the gymnasium. She kept both arms folded across her chest, hiding some of herself from embarrassment.

In the background Dante could hear the other pupils whispering comments and sniggering. "Yes, I'm not sure that's entirely practical for today's lesson. Why don't you go find something more... comfortable... and come back. I'll spend the next few minutes getting to know the rest of the class, so you won't miss anything important. Alright?"

Natalia smiled gratefully and hurried from the room, shooting one of the other pupils a pointed glare on the way past. The big, blonde recipient mouthed an apology but Natalia was already out the door, her exit accompanied by another burst of giggles from the others.

Dante strode to the front of the gymnasium and picked up a foil from a selection. "Everybody gather round please. I'd like to introduce myself. My name is Durward, Quentin Durward." He used the point of the foil to write his name in the air, remembering just in time not to spell out Dante. "You may call me Mr Durward, or sir. I will be your tutor in fencing, self-defence and several other disciplines for the remaining few days of term. If this short stint goes well, I will be invited back to the institute next year, so I will be doing my best for the few days we shall have together. But you also have something at stake here, as my report will influence the marks you receive upon graduation."

A beautiful Oriental student raised her hand.

Dante indicated she should stand. "What is your name?"

"Zhang, from the Black Dragon dynasty, sir."

"And your question?"

"We are the elite class. Surely that indicates we are among the best of the best. What can you add to that in just a few lessons?"

I think she's got you there, the Crest observed.

Dante smiled thinly. "Well, Zhang, our time here together may be limited but I can promise you it will be memorable. I hope to impart a little piece of my experience with each of you–"

I've never heard you call it your experience before, but at least you're being honest about the size.

"–so that you will have something to remember our time together by. I fought in the war and know what it is to stare death in the face. I pray you may never have to make the same choices I did on the battlefield, but I still wish to protect you from any danger that may threaten your lives." Dante raised an eyebrow at the Oriental student. "Does that answer your question?"

Zhang shrugged and sat down again. Another pupil raised her hand, this time an olive-skinned young woman with cherry red lips, fiery eyes and a mass of curling black hair. "Mr Durward, what battles did you fight in?"

"Sorry, I didn't catch your name."

"Carmen, from the House of Andorra."

"Very good. If you must know, I fought in several significant conflicts – on the front line in Tolsburg Province, at Sebastopol, the Battle of Vladigrad, at New Moscow, the Battle of the Baltic Sea, the Battle of Rudinshtein..." Dante's voice trailed away as he recalled the death and destruction he had witnessed, the comrades in arms he had lost.

"And what was it like, fighting for such a glorious cause? To vanquish the Romanov pretenders to the Imperial throne?"

"There are no true winners in such battles," Dante replied sadly. "War is about the taking and using of power to feed ambition. There is no honour in killing. You would do well to remember that."

"Oh." Carmen sank back to the floor, her enthusiasm fading. Silence fell upon the class, as the pupils looked at each other, unsure of themselves. The sombre moment was broken when Natalia returned, now clad in a more suitable leotard and tights. Dante smiled at her and clapped his hands.

"Well, let's see how far you have progressed with your fencing skills. Everybody up on their feet! Show me what you've got." That brought a fresh chorus of giggles from the students. "I meant show me what fencing skills you have got," Dante said with a sigh. "Take a foil and facemask each, put on a padded tunic to protect yourselves, and then pair off, one as the aggressor, the other defending themselves. Begin!"

The pupils were quickly in position, each pairing trying to impress the new tutor as he moved between them. Dante had to be nimble on his feet to avoid getting caught in the action, swaying and ducking to escape the flash of a blade. Each slender, flexible sword was tipped by a button to protect the combatants, but an unwary spectator could still be badly injured if they ventured too close to those duelling. A powerful clash of swords between Carmen and Zhang forced Dante to leap out of their way, sending him hurtling backwards into the blonde who had tried to apologise to Natalia.

She spun round, foil raised and ready to strike, but stopped when Dante threw up his hands in protest. "Sorry, Mr Durward. Sorry!"

He took the sword from her grasp and examined the blade. "You should be more careful, Miss...?"

"Helga." She removed her facemask and brushed an errant strand of hair from her face. "I am Helga, from the House of Hapsburg."

Dante took her right hand and kissed the back of it. "Charmed, I'm sure."

Helga grinned with delight. "I will try to be more careful in future."

"Good. Now, show me how you defend while your partner attacks." Dante stepped aside to watch as Helga tried to fend off her aggressor. The other fighter was smaller and less powerful, but more than made up for that with deft footwork and quickness of hands. Twice she cut through Helga's hapless parries and landed a palpable hit.

"Very good!" Dante applauded the effort, delighted to discover the other combatant was the unfortunate Natalia. He called the rest of the students to a halt and made them watch the pair fight again. Natalia easily outdid Helga, earning the acclaim of the new tutor.

"Let this be a lesson to all of you," Dante said. "Skill and confidence can often undo a physically intimidating opponent."

A chiming bell echoed around the gymnasium. "That's the signal for the end of the lesson," Helga said helpfully.

"Very good. Well, hit the showers and move on to your next lesson. No doubt I'll be seeing you later in the day." Dante smiled and nodded to the pupils as they passed him on their way out, inwardly breathing a sigh of relief. Helga remained behind to ask him a question, peeling off her padded tunic.

"Mr Durward, I have always struggled in these more physical classes. My family, we can be big eaters and I lack the speed of Natalia and the others. I was wondering if you could offer me any further help?" She smiled at him coyly, one finger twirling the plaited braid hanging from one side of her head.

"I suppose that could be possible. I certainly want to be available for all my students," Dante said. "Do you have any free time later today?"

"No, but I could visit your private quarters tonight, after supper." Helga did her best to look coquettish, a twinkle in the corner of her eyes.

Be careful, Dante, the Crest warned. *You've no way of knowing whether this young woman is a spy for Doctor Fabergé, trying to lure you into a trap!*

Dante was suddenly aware of the perspiration forming in the deep valley between her breasts, unable to tear his eyes away from the rise and fall of her breathing. "I'm not sure students are allowed to visit tutors' private quarters."

"Why not?" Helga asked innocently. "When Madame Wartski was filling in after Mr Russell left the institute, she was always trying to persuade one of us girls to visit her room after dark. She said it was to see her collection of toads."

"I hope none of you did."

Helga stifled a giggle at the thought. "Nein! She is covered in warts and she couldn't keep her hands to herself – ugghhh! Repulsive!"

"Nevertheless, I do not believe it would be seemly for us to have a private session in my quarters," Dante maintained, trying to tear his gaze away from Helga's hefty décolletage.

"Then perhaps we could meet here," she suggested. "No harm could come to us having extra tuition in a padded room, could it?"

"I suppose not."

"I mean, there's nothing hard in this room that could hurt me?" Helga whispered, leaning closer to Dante. One of her hands began sliding past the waistband of his trousers.

Dante, don't give in to her! the Crest urged. *Think of something, anything that might quell your desire – Algebra! Madame Wartski naked! The collected works of William Shakespeare!*

Helga's hand swivelled round to encircle his crotch. "Unless you think I could be wrong about that? Maybe there is something hard in here?"

Dante bit his top lip, trying to retain some scintilla of composure. "Perhaps we can continue this discussion later?"

Helga removed her hand. "I'll see you here after nine tonight." She hurried from the gymnasium, her rounded bottom bouncing inside the straining fabric of her leotard. Only when Helga had left did Dante let himself relax, slumping to the padded floor, sweat soaking the armpits of his fencing jacket.

"Fuoco," he muttered. "She knew what she was doing."

You're the one who needs the self defence class, the Crest observed. *She had total control over you, Dante!*

He smiled. "You could say she had me in the palm of her hand."

I was trying to avoid such obvious crudity.

"Yeah? Well, it's my speciality." Dante wiped the sweat from his brow. "Have I got time for a shower before my next lesson?"

No. You should be two flights down by now, beginning a tutorial in the ancient Oriental art of origami.

"I don't suppose that's Japanese for orgasm, by any chance?"

No. It's Japanese for paper folding. And if you're going to continue with the steady stream of smut I'll leave you to lead the class unaided.

"I told you, obvious crudity is my speciality. Besides, how hard can paper folding be – right?"

Having impressed Scullion with his skills as a bottle washer the previous night, Spatchcock had been promoted to cook's assistant after breakfast. So far that had involved cutting, peeling and preparing the less glamorous ingredients for lunch while avoiding a multitude of tentacles the verdant alien was intent upon sliding inside Spatchcock's clothing. He had responded by accidentally slicing one of the fleshy intrusions with his kitchen knife, bringing a howl of pain from the offworlder. "Be careful, you little oaf! These tentacles are precious objects, capable of rendering great culinary joy to many species!"

"Fine, just keep them away from me," Spatchcock muttered under his breath. It was a relief when he was given a break from preparation and escaped Scullion's attentions for a few minutes. A narrow metal walkway ran outside the castle walls across to the servant's quarters in the west tower. For a short section it passed above the waters of the Black Sea. Spatchcock stopped and leaned on the railing, staring out over the gently undulating waves.

The grimy ex-con blew air out through his mouth, his shoulders sagging. The prospect of spending the next week fending off Scullion's amorous advances held little appeal. He was used to being rejected by women, thanks to his repulsive appearance and virulent body odour. It felt strange and unsettling to be on the receiving end, even if the hunter was a green alien with more tentacles than inhibitions. *Maybe I should swap jobs with Flintlock*, Spatchcock thought to himself. *I'm the one who belongs in the sewers, not him.*

A sudden splash nearby caught his attention. Spatchcock leaned over the railing, trying to focus on a shimmering silver shape below the water's surface. It stopped moving and returned his gaze, as if it had a face. But that was impossible, wasn't it? Spatchcock leaned further over the railing, stretching a hand down to touch the water below. If he could reach it, maybe–

"Spatch! What are you doing?"

The foul-smelling felon jerked his hand back, startled. Whatever had been below disappeared into the depths once more. Spatchcock looked up to see the slime-covered Flintlock approaching from the west tower. For the first time in his life Spatchcock felt obliged to pinch his nose shut, lest the smell from his friend overwhelm him. "What've you been doing?"

"Clearing a blockage in the drains beneath Wartski's quarters. I don't know what she's got in there but it gives off this green pus." Flintlock wiped a hand across his chest, pushing the upper layer of slime off his clothing.

"How can you stand the smell?"

Flintlock smiled and tipped back his head to reveal an orange shape wedged inside each nostril. "I kept pieces of carrot from last night's stew, shoved them up my nose. At least they've stopped me from vomiting too often." Flintlock gestured at the waters below. "What were you trying to touch before?"

"Thought I saw something moving down there."

"But nothing swims around this island, unless you believe the fishermen's tales about sea monsters."

Spatchcock shook his head. "Nah, this was something else. It had a face, almost looked human. Thought it was trying to talk to me."

"Spatchcock! Spatchcock, where are you?" Scullion's voice rang out from inside the kitchen. "Come out, my little helper!"

Flintlock's nose crinkled in disgust. "She still trying to get inside your trousers?" Spatchcock nodded disconsolately. "For once you've found someone who considers your unique aroma an aphrodisiac and you're repulsed by her touch! I find that rather ironic, old boy."

"I'm not even sure Scullion is female," Spatchcock admitted. He sized up the green-stained, slime-soaked appearance of his partner. "You want to swap jobs? I'd be more than happy working the sewers."

Flintlock shook his head. "Forget it. I almost smell as bad as you now. Scullion would probably think I was coming on to her. I'm staying put."

"Spatchcock? Get in here this instant!" Scullion shouted. "Doctor Fabergé is calling for his lunch. You'll have to take it to him."

"Lucky you," Flintlock teased. "Another afternoon of close encounters in the kitchens and an audience with the boss. Do give him my regards."

Spatchcock replied with a muttered curse before returning to the kitchen. Flintlock remained for a moment, contemplating the other man's suggestion. "I'm not sure that's physically possible," he decided before heading back to the drains, not noticing the hand breaking the waves below his feet.

In origami class Dante had exhausted his paper-folding repertoire after five minutes, creating an unimpressive hat, a dismal dart and an unrecognisable replica of a boat. Six students stared at their tutor in disbelief, the others being occupied in the next room with one of Professor Mould's tedious history lectures. Dante tried his most winning smile before admitting defeat.

"Okay, let's face it. Origami is not where my true talents lie," he said. "Perhaps we could spend the rest of this lesson on something else?"

"What do you suggest?" Carmen asked tersely. "What are you good at?"

"Have any of your ladies ever played poker?"

Zhang raised her hand to speak. "That is a card game, yes?"

"Yes, but it is much more than that. Poker teaches you life skills. You discover how best to observe others, to notice their strengths and weaknesses. You learn when someone else is bluffing or trying to conceal a winning hand. You develop your own ability to keep a secret, to outwit your opponent. All these talents will be useful in years to come, no matter whether you become the wife of a Tsar or the head of a corporation."

Carmen appeared intrigued by Dante's description. "Sounds interesting, sir. What are the rules for this game?"

Dante smiled broadly. "Well, I can explain the rules as we go along. Does anyone happen to have a deck of cards handy?" One of the pupils, a ravishing redhead from the House of Windsor in Britannia, put up her hand. "Tracy, isn't it? If you don't mind my asking, why carry the cards with you?"

She blushed a little. "I play solitaire during Professor Mould's classes to stop myself falling asleep."

Dante collected the pack from her and began fanning through the cards, ensuring all fifty-two were present. "Hopefully you won't have to resort to such tactics during my lessons. Now, who wants to play first?"

"Why don't we all play?" Helga suggested. "That would make it more interesting, ja?"

"Ja. I mean, yes." Dante began shuffling the cards expertly. "Of course, there is another way of making poker interesting. There's nothing like having something at stake, a slight hint of jeopardy, to increase your excitement and enhance the learning process," he added hurriedly. "Has anyone here ever heard of the forfeit system?"

The pupils all innocently shook their heads.

"If you lose a hand, you are obliged to perform a forfeit," Dante explained. "It can be anything from revealing a secret to removing an item of clothing. How would you all feel about that?"

Tracy nodded vigorously. "I think that would add to the learning experience. Don't you girls agree?"

Dante, are you sure about this? the Crest asked. *You seem to be placing a lot of trust in the word of your students.*

"What could possibly go wrong?"

EIGHT

"Food without salt is like a kiss without love"
– Russian proverb

Spatchcock returned to the kitchen to find Scullion waiting impatiently, a bowl of green soup clasped in one of her tentacles. "You're to take this to the institute's director in the north tower."

"But I thought only authorised personnel were allowed in that area?"

"True. Nevertheless, Doctor Fabergé still has to eat and I cannot risk leaving my soufflé. To make matters worse, that clot Flintlock has somehow succeeded in sabotaging the dumb waiter with his stumbling about in the drains. So you will have to deliver this soup personally."

Spatchcock took the bowl, wondering aloud what the pink lumps floating across the surface were.

"Pea and ham," Scullion snapped irritably. "Now get moving!"

"But how will I get through the security cordon?"

The alien removed a white plastic tag on a chain from round its neck. "Wear this, it will identify you as friend, not foe. Do not remove it, or else the laser grid will remove your head. Now get moving!"

"Which way do I–"

Scullion's only reply was a sternly pointed tentacle.

. . .

Natalia had not been this bored since Professor Mould's lecture series on the development of cold fusion and how it changed twenty-second century history. The ageing tutor had an uncanny ability to drain the life from any and all potentially fascinating subjects, rendering them as dull and inert as his features. Today's lesson was a case in point, sixty minutes of mind-numbing torture supposedly meant to illuminate the Neo Renaissance Movement of 2197 and its relevance to the rise of the Makarov Empire in modern times.

Mould's voice droned on and on, regurgitating whole chapters from set textbooks that Natalia had read whilst at university. Seven more days to go, she told herself over and over. Seven more days. A squeal of delight from the adjoining classroom was followed by wild applause and raucous cheering. That couldn't be right, could it? Surely Mr Durward was meant to be taking an origami class for the less academically gifted members of the elite group.

Natalia leaned back in her chair and sneaked a glance through a glass partition that linked the two rooms. All she could see were the backs of the pupils in the neighbouring class. They were gathered around the teacher's desk, clapping their hands and cheering somebody on. Natalia had opted out of paper folding after the first term, deeming it a topic beneath her contempt. What was raptly holding the attention of those next door? Had Mr Durward introduced some revolutionary techniques?

Suddenly the crowd of students parted to reveal the source of their fascination. Mr Durward was stripped to the waist, attempting a Cossack dance on top of his desk while wearing a brassiere over his head. Judging by the size of the cups, the bra had most recently been worn by the not inconsiderable chest of Helga. Whatever was happening in the next classroom, it had little to do with paper folding.

Natalia realised too late that she had leaned too far back in her chair. Her arms windmilled, trying to maintain a balance, but it was a futile attempt. Natalia's chair flipped over backwards and she was propelled into the desk behind her, crashing her head against its wooden edge with an almighty *thunk*. She slumped to the floor, white dots of light blinking before her eyes.

Mould looked up from his textbook for the first time during the lesson. "Is something wrong?" He studied the faces of his pupils and noticed one was absent. "Miss Sokorina? Where are you?"

Natalia scrambled to her feet, rubbing one hand against the back of her head. "Sorry, Professor Mould. I, er... lost control of my chair." She righted the seat and resumed her place in it. "Sorry."

Mould raised his eyebrows a fraction before returning to his textbook, apparently oblivious to the noise from the next room. "Now, where was I? Ah, yes, the Neo Renaissance Movement of 2197. For many, the highpoint of this cultural revolution was the introduction of direct mind-to-computer terminals, enabling creators to translate imagination into action immediately."

Spatchcock approached the north tower cautiously, a bowl of soup held in one hand, the white plastic tag in the other. While the kitchen held the homely scent of cooking, this part of the castle was filled by the musty smell of neglect – few came through these corridors. At the tower's basement entrance a wall of red light barred entry, its surface crackling menacingly. Spatchcock recalled how Wartski had opened and closed the castle entrance. He swiped the tag across a palm reader beside the energy barrier. After a short, metallic beep the red light faded away, allowing him to walk past. Once he had cleared the doorway, the energy barrier pulsed back into life. Getting out of the north tower was just as hazardous as getting in, it appeared.

The door to a lift stood open ahead. Spatchcock was about to walk in when he realised the security tag was missing from his hand. He eventually found it hidden in a side pocket. He had palmed it, Spatchcock realised – once a thief, always a thief. Retrieving the tag, he waved it in front of the lift doorway. Another energy barrier switched off, this one invisible to the naked eye. Satisfied the lift was safe, Spatchcock entered.

Moments later he was being shot upwards by some unseen force, the walls of the lift shaft sliding down past him. "Diavolo!" he whispered, trying not to soil his trousers. The uplift began to slow, then stopped altogether. Spatchcock stepped out of the lift shaft, sure his stomach must be lodged somewhere below his knees.

A single door of frosted glass stood opposite. Spatchcock could see humanoid shapes moving beyond it, but not enough to make out their identity. After checking it was safe to touch, he rapped firmly on the glass with his knuckles. The door was abruptly pulled open to reveal the Strangelove twins inside, looming over the new arrival.

"Yes? What–"

"–do you want?"

Spatchcock held out the soup for them to see. "I brought Doctor Fabergé's lunch. It's pea and ham – I think."

The doctor was bending over a machine, examining something on a glass slide. "Yes, I ordered lunch more than an hour ago!" The laboratory was awash with shining glass and metallic silver, most of the workspaces choked with machines beyond Spatchcock's knowledge. The doctor gestured angrily at a nearby tabletop cluttered with papers, scribbled notes and data crystals. "Put it over there."

Storm glared at Spatchcock. "You heard the doctor."

He obeyed the instructions, walking uncertainly into the antiseptic air of the laboratory. Spatchcock approached the tabletop indicated by Fabergé and gently nudged some of the clutter aside to create space for the bowl. "Is there anything else I can get you?"

Fabergé did not bother to look up. "Yes – out."

Spatchcock nodded and scuttled from the room, careful to avoid the malevolent gaze of the Furies. Tempest slammed the door shut once he was outside, not noticing the glint of triumph in Spatchcock's eyes. He kept the security tag held up before his face, using it to summon the disconcerting invisible lift. His other hand nestled inside a pocket, clutching the data crystal he had palmed while inside the laboratory. It was tiny, little larger than a fingernail, and felt like a chip of warm glass to the touch.

Hopefully it contained information about what Fabergé was doing in his closely guarded laboratory. Now all Spatchcock need do was find a way of slipping the crystal to Dante so the Crest could analyse it.

I tried to warn you, didn't I? I tried to make you see sense. But no, you knew better. You were sure. You could handle a few innocent girls with limited life experience. What could possibly go wrong?

"Have you quite finished gloating?" Dante replied tensely.

Finished? I've barely begun. Besides, this isn't gloating. I'm attempting to teach you the error of your ways. Since you seem determined to ignore every piece of advice I offer, I've decided to take a fresh approach. Let you make your own mistakes and then try – repeat, try – to see whether you've learned anything from the experience.

"And how's that working for you so far?"

I trust this is not an experience you'll be reliving anytime soon.

Dante nodded his agreement. "That much we can agree on. Now, have you got any advice you'd like to offer at this juncture, Oh Great Oracle?"

Sarcasm does not befit a man who has only an abandoned brassiere between himself and complete nudity.

"I asked for advice, not for you to state the bloody obvious!" Dante shifted one of the cups so it covered his crotch more effectively. The other was clamped across part of his buttocks, while the straps dangled untidily between his legs. "Guess I should be grateful it was Helga who let me keep her bra. Some of the other students aren't so well endowed–"

Look who's talking!

"And I'd be in even more trouble right now." Dante peered round the doorway from the classroom where his poker lesson had gone so awry. The pupils had departed several minutes earlier, taking all his clothes as part of the final forfeit. Before leaving, Carmen revealed that the pupils often indulged in all-night poker parties, using Tracy's marked pack of cards to separate unsuspecting students from other classes of their allowances. At least that quelled Dante's embarrassment at losing twelve hands in succession, if not his shame at being left stark naked and with a hundred metre dash back to the safety of his private quarters. "Those girls are man-eaters," he muttered darkly.

And they had you for dessert.

"Crest, I think that's enough advice for the moment."

Do you think they'll still respect you in the morning?

"I said that's enough!" Dante realised shouting was not going to help and lowered his voice again. "Just tell me whether the coast is clear, alright?"

I sense no imminent danger approaching from any direction–

"Good. Now's my chance!" Dante decided. He started running towards the faculty rooms, looking back over his shoulder to make sure nobody had spotted him.

But there is someone just about to step into your path.

Dante clattered into Natalia as she emerged from the institute infirmary, clutching an ice bag to the back of her head. Teacher and student were both sent sprawling, their respective possessions flying into the air. Dante realised he had lost hold of the bra and made a grab for it as he tumbled over.

Natalia sat up and realised Helga's bra was draped across her own, less voluminous chest. More startling was the sight of the naked teacher holding a bag of ice against his crotch. "Mr Durward! What are you doing?"

Dante stood up, trying to look casual and failing dismally. "I might ask you the same question, young lady."

Natalia pointed at the infirmary door. "I hit my head during history and went to get something for the pain."

"I see."

She gestured towards Dante's crotch. "Could I have my ice bag back?"

"Actually, no."

"Why not?"

Dante shrugged helplessly. "Umm…"

Tell her you have an old war wound, the Crest suggested.

"I have an old war wound," Dante announced, a little too triumphantly.

And you need to pack it with ice once a day…

"And I need to pack it with ice once a day…"

To keep the swelling down, the Crest concluded mischievously.

"To keep the, er…" Dante smiled. "To keep my injury from getting worse."

Natalia was struggling to keep a smirk from her face. "Yes, I understand." She leaned forward and peered at the area Dante was trying to hide with the ice bag. "Well, then, your need is obviously greater than mine. I'd best find Helga and return this item of clothing to her."

"A good idea," Dante agreed hurriedly. "Now, if you'll just excuse me." He began backing away from her.

Natalia peered at one of his arms, her brow furrowing with thought. "Umm, Mr Durward?" she asked.

Dante stopped and raised his eyebrows. "Yes, Natalia?"

The student appeared to be planning another question, but changed her mind. "Nothing. I hope your, er, injury gets better soon." Natalia smiled helpfully. "It must be very painful."

"You have no idea. Good day to you."

• • •

Dante made it through the rest of the teaching day unharmed, except for the blows to his pride whenever students began whispering amongst themselves and giggling during his classes. He found himself looking forward to the evening meal when all the staff were gathered together, as it would offer another chance to assess Fabergé. So far the doctor had shown arrogance not uncommon in those who rate achievement above love or happiness. But how far did Fabergé's ambitions extend? The doctor's comments about the Tsar suggested Fabergé considered himself above the Empire's ruler, a dangerous belief for anyone.

Having lost his first choice of clothing to the unscrupulous poker players, Dante selected a plain black linen suit and shirt for the dinner table. But when he entered the staff library, the collective mood was decidedly more downbeat than the previous evening. Neither Fabergé nor the Strangelove twins were expected at dinner, and Wartski had refused to unlock the drinks cabinet. The female tutors muttered darkly amongst themselves while Mould sat disconsolately in an armchair reading a textbook. Dante approached the five women and tried to strike up a conversation.

"Hi! I'm the new self-defence and swordplay instructor. We didn't get a chance to talk during dinner last night."

The female tutors looked at him with a mixture of disgust and disdain. Dante put on his most winning smile and turned up the charm.

"My first day of teaching here was quite a revelation," he continued.

"So we've heard," one of the women said with a scowl. Dressed in a severe woollen twin-set and a string of pearls, the pinched expression on her face left Dante wondering if she had been sucking lemons between classes.

"I hope the students had good things to say about me, Miss...?"

"Ms Ostrov," she replied coldly. "No, they didn't."

"Oh!" Dante was surprised and rather hurt by this news. "I wonder why?"

"We do not encourage card games at this institution," another of the women interjected. Dante almost thought she might be a disciple from the House of Rasputin, so thick were the black hairs adorning her top lip. "Nor do we favour flirting with the pupils. It's most unseemly."

"This is a finishing school," Dante protested. "Isn't it, Miss...?"

"Ms Zemlya," she said.

"Don't you have a duty to prepare them for life in the real world?" Dante continued. "Flirting and games are part of that life."

"Not at this school," Ms Ostrov snapped. Her four colleagues nodded. "We believe in the power of learning and knowledge. A good education enriches the mind. Your sort of teaching can only harm the reputation of this esteemed establishment."

"Really? I thought I was bringing some fresh air to this place, blowing a few skirts up, injecting some excitement into the lessons."

Ms Ostrov's hands dropped to her own skirt and held it firmly in place, as if worried Dante was going to make good on his notions there and then. "All skirts should remain in their proper positions at all times!"

"I was speaking, you know, um..."

Metaphorically, the Crest prompted.

"Metaphorically," Dante said. "I was speaking metaphorically."

"Nevertheless," Ms Zemlya bristled, "we would prefer if if you kept your distance from us. We don't wish to be contaminated by your errant ideas." The other women all murmured their agreement and turned their backs on Dante. He walked away shaking his head at their attitude.

"I wouldn't contaminate any of you with a ten foot barge pole," he muttered darkly. "Have all the distance you want." Dante approached Mould instead, hoping to have more success with the ageing academic. The professor was examining a textbook about noble families and their lineage through the centuries. "Anything interesting?" Dante asked.

"I've been trying to trace the name Durward in our historical texts," Mould replied. "I can't seem to find any mention of your family in the last two hundred years. Where did you say you came from?"

"I didn't," Dante replied hastily. "Mould is an unusual name. Where does that originate from?"

"It's an Anglo-Saxon name originally. My distant ancestors collected mould for use by apothecaries and alchemists."

"That's fascinating." Dante glanced round the room, searching for a way out of this conversational hell. "I wonder what we're having for dinner?"

A chime sounded and the faculty began moving into the dining hall. The seats normally occupied by Fabergé and Wartski remained empty, leaving Dante alone near the head of the table, with just Mould for company. The prospect of a long and tedious evening was crushing the last of his spirits when a familiar face appeared with the first course. An unusually clean and tidy Spatchcock entered from a side door, carefully balancing half a dozen plates of steaming, green soup on his arms. He served all the female staff first, then gave the final plate to the professor.

By now Dante was more than hungry but had to wait several minutes before Spatchcock returned with the final bowl of soup. The stooped servant put it down before Dante and made a point of engaging him in conversation. "I do hope you'll enjoy the soup, sir."

"I'm sure I will," Dante replied, picking up a spoon.

"It's pea and ham."

"Fascinating, I'm sure."

"I took a bowl to Doctor Fabergé for lunch today."

"Good for you." Dante wanted to make a start but Spatch-cock's thumb remained on the side of the bowl, blocking his access.

"He seemed to enjoy it. The dish was empty when I col-lected it from his laboratory later in the afternoon."

"Yes. Good. Glad to hear it. Now, can I-" Dante tried to push his spoon past Spatchcock without success.

"I hope you'll enjoy it as much," Spatchcock continued, winking at Dante.

"I will if you'll give me the chance!"

"Make sure you go all the way to the bottom of the bowl." Spatchcock's winking continued, becoming ever more exag-gerated.

"Yes, thank you. I get it. Enjoy the soup. Every last drop!"

"Exactly, sir. That's exactly right." Spatchcock nodded at Dante several times, adding a few extra winks for emphasis.

"Is there something wrong with you eye, Spatchcock? You seem to have developed a nervous tick."

"Just finish the soup," the servant hissed.

"I will, given half a chance!" Dante snapped, slapping Spatchcock's hand away from the bowl. "Now let me eat, why don't you?"

"Fine!"

"Fine!"

"Good!"

"Good!"

By now Mould and the other teachers were all staring at this hissing contest, regarding the new arrival and his ser-vant with disbelief. Dante realised he was being watched and offered the others a warm smile. "Please excuse us. My manservant can be a little possessive sometimes."

Spatchcock rolled his eyes heavenwards. "Just eat the damn soup!"

"I will!" Dante snarled. "Haven't you got a kitchen to go to?"

"Fine! Choke on it for all I care!" The servant stomped out of the dining hall, slamming the side door on his way out.

Dante gave an exaggerated sigh. "You just can't get the staff these days." He turned back to his soup and began hurriedly spooning it into his mouth. "Still, this soup is delicious. What flavour did he say it is?"

"Pea and ham," Mould replied. "Don't see what all the fuss is about..."

Dante was slurping his soup eagerly; dribbles of the green liquid covering his chin and lingering in his beard. The female tutors watched his slovenly table manners with horror, but he kept shovelling. Such was his enthusiasm he didn't notice the glint of crystal in the final mouthful. After sucking the spoon dry, Dante slammed it down on the table-cloth and smiled broadly. "Yes, that was quite delicious. I must ask Spatchcock for–"

He stopped abruptly and grabbed at his throat. "Ackkk!"

Dante? What's wrong? the Crest demanded.

"Ackkk! Acckkk-acckkk!"

I don't understand. Are you unwell?

Dante's face was rapidly turning purple, while attempts to clear his throat were proving fruitless. "Mykk throackkkk! Stuckkk ikk myyykkk throackkkk!"

I can't detect any trace of poison in what you've ingested...

"Mykk throackkkk!" Dante gasped, blue replacing the purple in his face. He stood up, knocking his chair over backwards and startling the other staff. "Stuckkk ikk myyykkk throackkkk!"

You've got something stuck in your throat?

"Yekkkk!"

Mould looked up from his soup. "I say, are you quite alright Mr Durward?"

Dante shook his head and pointed at his throat. "I cankkk breaffkkk!"

"Sorry, I can't quite make out what you're saying," the professor replied.

The Heimlich Manoeuvre – tell them to perform the Heimlich Manoeuvre on you, the Crest suggested. Dante just gurgled in response. *Oh, I forgot, you can't talk properly. Sorry. Try miming it!*

Dante began performing an elaborate charade, all the while clutching at his throat and turning ever more blue around the lips. But his gestures for the other staff to help him were misinterpreted when Dante mimed one person thrusting themselves against another person from behind.

"This is too much!" Ms Ostrov protested. "I don't care what your sexual proclivities are, Mr Durward, I will not bear witness to such a display at the dinner table! Kindly cease and desist immediately!"

Dante gave up asking for help and instead began punching himself in the abdomen, trying to dislodge whatever was stuck in his throat. He did succeed in projectile vomiting viscous green bile across the table where it splattered Ms Ostrov's face and chest, but still could not shift the blockage.

Try drinking water. That should force the object down your throat!

Dante grabbed a carafe of water from the table and poured it down his throat, the liquid splashing against his features and soaking the surroundings. After one last swallow the obstruction was washed down his oesophagus. Dante collapsed on to the dining table, gratefully grasping breath into his lungs.

All five women had retreated back against the walls of the dining hall, their faces aghast at this violent spectacle. Mould sipped quietly at his soup. "Hmm, tastes alright to me," he commented.

"I had something lodged in my throat," Dante explained weakly. "Sorry."

Ms Ostrov looked at the hideous bile staining her white top, rendering the fabric transparent. "I've never been so humiliated in my life," she shrieked and ran from the room, the other women following her out.

Mould watched them leave. "Oh well," he shrugged. "All the more for us, eh, Durward?"

"What do you mean you swallowed it?" Spatchcock shook his head in disbelief. "How could you swallow it?"

"Believe me, it wasn't easy," Dante replied. After dinner he had gone down to the kitchens, ostensibly to pass his compliments to the chef. Scullion had already retired for the night, giving Dante a chance to consult with Spatchcock. They stood near the door to the external walkway but insisted Flintlock remain outside, where his stench was less likely to reach them. "What the hell did you put in my soup?"

"It was a data crystal I took from Fabergé's laboratory at lunchtime. I thought you could have the Crest read it. Maybe the information stored inside would give us some clues to this Strangelove Gambit."

"A good idea," Dante agreed.

"But I needed a less than obvious way of smuggling it to you."

"So he put the crystal in your soup," Flintlock chipped in. "I told him not to but Spatch wouldn't listen to me, as usual."

"You could have warned me," Dante said.

"I did warn you," Spatchcock wailed. "What did you think all that winking and nodding in the dining hall was about?"

"Muscle spasms?"

"Muscle spasms!" Spatchcock threw his apron across the kitchen in despair. "I give up, I really do!"

"Can the Crest analyse that crystal while it's still inside?" Flintlock asked.

Unfortunately, no, the Crest said. *The crystal is a sealed data storage unit. I'll need to access its contents via your biocircuitry, Dante, and that can only happen once the crystal is outside your body.*

"Crest says no, not until I've expelled the crystal."

"In that case, may I suggest you keep a close watch on everything coming out of you?" Flintlock said. "I don't fancy having to sort through all the sewerage this place generates to find the crystal again."

"Good idea," Dante conceded. "How long will it take to come out?"

That depends, the Crest replied, *on what you eat for the next day or two. Plenty of roughage is the key that will help drive the crystal through your lower intestine and then out of your bowels.*

"It could take hours or it could take days," Spatchcock complained. "How long before the Tsar arrives?"

"The Imperial Palace is due to arrive on Sunday. That's six days," Flintlock calculated.

"What about some sort of laxative?" Dante asked. "Get things moving more quickly through my system."

"That crystal will take its own time," Spatchcock sighed.

"Maybe some liquorice?" Flintlock said. "Isn't that supposed to give you the runs?"

"I thought it made you more constipated?" Dante countered. "No, we'll just have to wait for nature to take its course. In the meantime, keep your eyes and ears open. Anything you can find out, anything at all could be valuable information. Spatchcock, get closer to Scullion, find out what she knows."

"Thanks a lot," the kitchen hand scowled. "Getting closer won't be any problem. It's keeping her away that's the hard part."

"Flintlock, I want you to investigate Madame Wartski. I've heard a few dark hints about what she does in her private quarters, maybe it's related to this Strangelove Gambit. Get in there and find out, okay?"

"Why don't you do that?" Flintlock asked. "Your quarters are much closer to her."

"I'm not exactly popular with the female faculty at the moment," Dante admitted. "I don't know what the girls have been telling them about me, but none of it has been positive."

"You couldn't keep your pants on for a single day, could you?" Spatchcock asked.

Dante shrugged. "These things always happen to me. I don't know why."

A classic case of denial if ever I heard one.

"What will you be doing in between trips to the toilet?" Flintlock enquired.

Dante smiled. "I think it's high time I paid a little more attention to Tempest and Storm. Since this weapon is called the Strangelove Gambit, it's a fair assumption the twins are involved in its development."

"They *were* working with Fabergé in his laboratory," Spatchcock recalled.

"I wonder if the Furies would be interested in joining me for a little ménage à trois action?" Dante asked.

"A little what?" Spatchcock looked to Flintlock for an explanation.

"In your gutter parlance," the exiled aristocrat replied. "He fancies having a three-in-a-bed sex romp."

"You lucky devil! And with twins, too!"

Dante smiled broadly. "It's a dirty job but someone's gotta do it."

Dante only remembered the rendezvous with Helga after returning to his private quarters. He hurried to the gymnasium, trying to think of some elegant yet subtle way of letting Helga down gently. If he was going to take on both the Strangelove twins, he would need all his energy. But the gymnasium door was firmly locked and Dante could see no sign of Helga through its glass window.

"Looking for someone?" a booming voice demanded. Wartski was stomping towards him, her nightgown flapping in the breeze. He caught a glimpse of what was hidden inside and hurriedly averted his eyes. The sight of that many warts on the human body was more than repulsive – it was obscene.

"No," he replied. "I left a piece of equipment behind when I was teaching in the gymnasium earlier and wanted to retrieve it before morning."

Wartski regarded him suspiciously and then peered in through the window while trying the door handle. Satisfied the gymnasium was both secure and empty, she folded her gown round her voluminous torso. "That area is locked for the night. Whatever is inside will still be there in the morning. I suggest you come back then to collect it. In the meantime, you should return to your room. Doctor Fabergé frowns upon new staff wandering the hallways at night. Better for your future here if you respect that."

"Of course," Dante agreed. "Well, I'll say goodnight then."

Wartski grabbed hold of his arm as he turned to leave. "Unless you wanted to come back to my private quarters for a night-cap? I have an interesting selection of sherry and sweet wines there, Mr Durward."

Dante yawned with great vigour. "Thank you for the kind invitation, but I think I'll follow your sage advice and retire to my room. Some of us need more beauty sleep than others."

Wartski withdrew her hand sharply. "What are you implying?"

"Nothing, nothing at all," he replied quickly. "Well, goodnight!" With that Dante scurried away, counting his blessings at having escaped the matron's attention. He did not envy Flintlock the job of finding out more about her. Dante returned directly to his own room and fled inside, locking and bolting the door after himself. He listened intently for movement outside. A few moments later heavy footsteps approached the door and someone tried the handle. Unable to gain entry, they walked away again.

"That was a close call," Dante muttered to himself.

I don't think it's the only close call you'll have tonight, the Crest said.

"What do you mean?"

You have another visitor waiting for you on this side of the door.

A female voice was next to speak, her soft tones whispering across the room. "Poor Mr Durward. You must be tired. Come to bed."

NINE

"There's a time to chase, a time to run"
– Russian proverb

Dante spun round to see Helga lying in his bed, a single sheet pulled to just above her breasts, modestly covering her more outstanding attributes. "I thought we were supposed to be meeting in the gymnasium?" he asked.

"We were," she purred, "but it was already locked when I arrived for our private tuition. So I decided to see if you had another location in mind. You left the door unlocked, so I slipped inside and waited. I hope you don't mind."

"No," Dante yelped. Realising his voice had climbed an octave, he cleared his throat before speaking again in a considerably deeper tone. "No, that's absolutely fine. Not a problem at all."

"Good," Helga replied coyly. "I wouldn't want to make you angry."

"True. I can be quite fearsome when I'm angry."

"Oh, yes, I can imagine. You might decide to punish me."

"Might I?" Dante was having difficulty in swallowing, suddenly aware that the collar of his shirt was constricting his breathing.

"Yes," Helga said enthusiastically. "I was rather a naughty girl after class, wasn't I? Flirting with you so shamelessly. Madame Wartski wouldn't approve."

"I take it she's against flirting."

Helga shook her head sadly. "She doesn't want us to have any fun at all."

"What a shame," Dante agreed. "Well, I must admit to being rather tired so perhaps we could hold our private session on another occasion."

"You don't want to show me how a real fighter wields his weapon?"

"It's not so much that as–"

"I had so been looking forward to having you put me through my paces. The cut and thrust of a good duel, our bodies glistening with sweat as we strained to outdo each other, the battle of the sexes coming to an almighty climax in our combat," Helga enthused, her eyes alive with excitement. "Doesn't that sound inviting to you, Mr Durward?"

"Very inviting," Dante admitted, "but as I said, it's getting late and we both have classes in the morning."

"What would Madame Wartski say if she found us alone together in your private quarters?"

"I shudder to think."

Helga pursed her lips thoughtfully, pressing a forefinger against them. "It would be a shame if she found out what had been going on in here."

"But nothing is going on," Dante maintained. "Nothing's happened!"

"Nothing yet," Helga replied, letting her forefinger slip between her lips and into her mouth. Her tongue rolled around the sides of the finger, moistening it gently, before Helga withdrew the digit from her mouth with a sigh. "But I might feel obliged to tell her anyway."

"Tell her what?" Dante hurriedly wiped a bead of perspiration from his forehead, all too aware he was not in control of the situation.

"How you invited me back to your room," Helga said hungrily.

"But I didn't," Dante protested.

"How you ordered me to take off all my clothes and fold them across that chair," she replied, pointing at a neat pile nearby.

"But I never–"

"How you commanded me to get into your bed, wearing only a black silk ribbon around my throat," Helga continued.

"But I…"

"And then how you had your wicked way with me, over and over again." Helga suddenly sat up in the bed, the sheet falling away to reveal she was completely naked but for the silk ribbon around her neck.

"But–"

"Of course, I don't have to tell her all that."

Dante smiled weakly. "You don't?"

"Nein," Helga said. "I can be as quiet as you like, Mr Durward."

"That would be best, I feel."

"Or I can scream so loud everyone in this castle will come running." Helga rose from the bed and began walking slowly towards him. "It's up to you."

"Well, I don't think screaming will be necessary," Dante said hopefully.

"No?" Helga smiled and undid the strip of black silk from her neck. "We'll see about that. Now take off your clothes. I know the perfect place to tie this ribbon, somewhere that will keep you up all night if I wish."

You'd better do what she says, the Crest suggested. *Grin and bare it.*

Dante nodded and began tearing at the buttons of his shirt. "You have been a naughty girl, haven't you Helga?"

The House of Hapsburg's eldest daughter gave a tiny squeal of delight. "Yes I have, Mr Durward."

"Call me sir."

"Yes, sir!"

• • •

It was close to dawn before Dante finally got some sleep, having spent much of the night satisfying Helga's needs and wants. He stirred at six to see her hurriedly dressing. "Sorry, I didn't mean to wake you," she whispered. "I have to get back to bed. Madame Wartski checks all the dormitories just before seven, to make sure nothing has happened to us."

"You'll remember our little conversation, won't you?" Dante asked. "Not a word to her about what we did last night."

Helga looked horrified at the mere suggestion. "I'd never tell her anything of the sort! She'd have me expelled immediately."

"Oh," Dante said, realising he had been out-bluffed for the second time in twenty-four hours. "Oh well."

Helga unlocked the door and peered outside carefully. "But I'll certainly tell the rest of the girls! Everybody deserves one of your private lessons." She waved coyly and hurried outside, closing the door behind herself.

Congratulations, the Crest said as Helga's footsteps had faded into the distance.

"Thank you," Dante replied. "I thought it was a remarkable performance on my part too. I didn't realise you were such a connoisseur of lovemaking."

I was congratulating you on becoming Fabergé Island's new gigolo.

"You're exaggerating as usual, Crest. You don't honestly expect little Helga to tell her classmates about what went on last night do you?"

Of course she will, Dante. That woman left here with enough gossip to keep the students whispering for weeks on end. You can expect a steady stream of customers for your talents in the next few nights.

"Well, there are worse things than being a gigolo," Dante maintained. "I always fancied a career between the sheets. I could be the twenty-seventh century Casanova, the greatest lover of them all!"

Most gigolos get paid. All you got was an hour's sleep and a smug grin on your face. Do you honestly think you'll be able to keep that up all week?

"I'll have you know I survived the House of Sin's Hellraiser Gauntlet, a trial of male endurance that only two men in history have completed!"

I know, I was there, the Crest replied wearily. *Not a pretty sight. Anyway, it's time for you to get up.*

"I think I've been up enough for one night."

Maybe. But breakfast is already being served and your first class begins in an hour – self-defence with half a dozen sex-starved young women.

"Bojemoi," Dante muttered, climbing reluctantly from his bed. "How do teachers cope with this sort of schedule?"

They get long summer holidays and sleeping with their students is strictly forbidden.

"Well, that would make it a less strenuous profession, but rather less enjoyable too." Dante pulled on a pair of trousers and headed for the ablutions block. "Wake me if I fall asleep in the shower."

Dante spent much of his day fending off the attentions of his pupils, as word of his exploits spread through the elite class. Carmen from the House of Andorra kept dropping her pencil and asking Dante to pick it up for her, while Tracy from Britannia took every opportunity to pinch his rear as he walked past her desk. Helga was just as happy to see him, winking at the new teacher and giggling whenever she caught his eye.

Dante was examining the bruises on his buttocks after dinner when someone began knocking on the door of his private quarters. "I'm not here!"

"Yes you are," Spatchcock replied from outside. "I can hear your voice."

Dante let the kitchen hand in and then locked his door again.

"Why the extra security?" Spatchcock asked. "Has Fabergé figured out who you are?"

"No, I haven't seen him since Sunday night. I'm trying to keep out any unwanted visitors." Dante pulled down the waistband of his trousers to give Spatchcock a glimpse of the bruising. "See?"

"What have you been up to?"

Better to ask who he's been–, the Crest began.

"Yes, thank you, we get the idea," Dante snapped. "I'll do the smutty innuendoes."

Spatchcock looked askance at him.

"Sorry, just a little side discussion I'm having with the Crest."

"Flintlock wants to know if you've found out anything from the twins yet."

"Why?"

Spatchcock shrugged. "I'm guessing he's terrified of getting caught in Wartski's room. He doesn't want to get too close to her."

"I've seen her in a night-gown. He's got good reason to be scared," Dante agreed. "But he'll have to bite the bullet. Tempest and Storm have been locked away in the laboratory with Fabergé all day, so I haven't made contact."

"I'll pass the message on."

"What about you and Scullion?"

Spatchcock shook his head sadly. "I think she's falling for me, big time."

"Perfectly understandable," Dante said.

"Yeah?"

"Of course. You reek like a rotting corpse. How could she resist that?"

Spatchcock smiled. "I wonder what sex with an alien is like?"

"Just be careful where she puts those tentacles. The suckers on an octopus are strong enough to rip the skin from a human arm once they're properly adhered. Imagine what Scullion could do to you."

"I hadn't thought of that," Spatchcock admitted. "Best be getting back to the kitchen. She wants me to start prep for tomorrow's meals. I'll pass on the message to Flint-lock." Dante unlocked the door and let Spatchcock out. Seconds later an insistent knocking made him reopen the door.

"Spatch, I told you, I can't–"

His words were silenced by a slender female hand clamp-ing itself across his mouth. Carmen appeared in the doorway, pushing Dante back into his room. Once they were inside the Andorran beauty pressed her back against the door, preventing Dante from trying to leave.

"Helga told us all about you, Mr Durward."

"Did she?" Dante smiled thinly. "Good for her."

"But we didn't believe her. No man could do all the things she claimed, as well as she claimed, for as long as she claimed."

"You're probably right. Well, now that we've settled that–"

Carmen suddenly ripped apart her blouse, revealing a red silk brassiere encasing two magnificent, deeply tanned breasts. A waft of perfume filled Dante's nostrils, powerful and intoxicating. "Perhaps such a man could satisfy Helga, for she has never known the fiery temperament of a true Latin lover. But we in Andorra pride ourselves on being the most passionate of people."

"An admirable quality," Dante agreed. "Perhaps we could discuss it further in the morning?"

"You are an animal, aren't you?" Carmen demanded. "You believe actions speak louder than words and now you want to prove it to me!" She clasped hold of her breasts and began to massage them through the brassiere. "Santa Maria, already I can feel my loins burning at the mere thought of your touch. Imagine what love we shall make tonight!"

"Perhaps it's best if we left it to our imagination. Reality can be a disappointment, I often find."

Carmen shook her head. "You're right. Perhaps I should not be imagining such things." Her hand reached for the door, twisting the handle.

Dante smiled, relief flooding his features. "Good. Tomorrow we can–"

Carmen pulled open the door and whistled. The sound of approaching footsteps became audible outside.

"What are you doing?" Dante asked helplessly.

"I do not wish to imagine what love you and I shall make tonight," Carmen replied, licking her lips. "Instead I shall experience an even greater pleasure!"

Don't ask her what pleasure this is, the Crest urged.

But Dante couldn't help himself. "What pleasure is that?"

You had to ask her, didn't you?

Carmen pulled the door open a little wider and another of the pupils slipped inside. Her dark hair was cut in a bob, framing a heart-shaped face with warm hazel eyes. She was wearing a silk robe but it was obvious there was little on underneath it. "This is Mai Lin, a student from the Malaysian Provinces," Carmen explained. "She doesn't speak much English but we've discovered another way of communicating this past year. We talk to each other with our bodies, not with our voices."

Dante swallowed, twice. "I'm not sure you should be telling me this."

Carmen and Mai Lin began to advance on Dante, who was retreating towards the far corner of his room. Soon they had him pinned against the wall, unable to escape. Carmen tore off the last of her clothing and began to remove his, while Mai Lin slipped out of her robe and began to rub her body against Dante. A heady smell of musk filled the air.

"We love you long time," Mai Lin whispered.

Bojemoi, the Crest whispered.

"You can say that again," Dante agreed.

. . .

It was just after breakfast on Wednesday that the data crystal departed Dante's body. After thoroughly washing the offending item, he took it back to his private quarters and locked the door. "Well, Crest, what do we do now?"

After last night I know there's not much you won't do, it replied.

"I meant with the data crystal," he snapped back.

Temper, temper. The Crest analysed the object silently for a few moments before speaking again. *Put your hands next to the crystal, then cede control of your cyborganics to me.*

Dante did as he was told, watching as tendrils of silver and purple biocircuitry began to extend from his fingernails, encircling the crystal. It was a strange sensation to feel your body acting under somebody else's control, a detached helplessness.

It's encrypted, the Crest announced.

"Meaning?"

I've been able to penetrate the outer shell and download everything stored inside the crystal. But the data itself has been run through a very sophisticated form of encryption, far beyond currently known technology.

"Something Fabergé has developed here on the island?"

Perhaps. That's not the important issue. I can break this coding, but it will take time – days at least, perhaps even weeks.

"We don't have weeks! The Tsar will be here on Sunday."

I know, I know. I'll have to devote all my energy and attention to this task until I find and crack the cipher upon which the encryption is based.

"In words I can understand?"

You're on your own.

"Crest? Crest!"

It replied after a long silence. *Yes?*

"Sorry – you just disappeared. I'm so used to having your voice inside my head, it was a little frightening," Dante admitted sheepishly.

Get over it. I'll contact you when I'm done. Understand?

"Yes. Do you still need the data crystal?"

No, I've extracted all relevant data. You'd best hide it for now.

"Okay." Dante waited for another moment, then realised the Crest had gone again. He concealed the crystal in his luggage before leaving for class.

Dante was pleasantly surprised to find Tempest at the faculty library when he went in for pre-dinner drinks that evening. Wednesday's classes had proven even more problematic than the day before, with Mai Lin and Carmen exchanging knowing looks and the other pupils trying to catch his eye. Dante pondered organising an orgy, simply to speed up the process of sleeping his way through the entire class, but decided that would be both risky and impractical. He might be all man but there was a physical limit to how many women even he could satisfy simultaneously. No doubt another of the students would be making a visit to his quarters tonight. If he could find somewhere else to spend the night, he might get some sleep.

"Mr Durward, I wanted to talk with you," Tempest said as Dante entered the library. "There's something we need to discuss."

"Indeed? Well, I'm all ears."

The red-haired woman raised an eyebrow at this statement. "I'm not sure I understand your meaning. I see only two ears and they do not appear any larger or more significant than most."

Dante smiled. "It's an expression. I was saying I'm all yours."

"All mine?"

"Er…" Dante cursed inwardly and realised how much he depended upon the Crest's help in such situations. For once, he'd have to sort this out for himself. "I meant I'm ready to talk with you about whatever you like."

"Good." Tempest nodded, looking down upon him. She noticed Dante rubbing the back of his neck awkwardly. "Is something wrong?"

"You're so tall, it's giving me a stiff neck."

"Then we should sit down." Tempest gestured at two arm-chairs in a corner of the library away from the others. Mould was snoozing in another chair, while Ms Ostrov and her cronies were watching suspiciously from the far side of the room. Once she and Dante were seated, Tempest smiled. "Is that more comfortable for you?"

"Yes, thanks. Now, what did you want to talk about?"

"You must excuse me. Sometimes if I fail to recognise colloquial expressions and vernacular phrasings."

"Now you've lost me," Dante said.

"Slang," Tempest explained. "Storm and I grew up here. The institute and those who pass through it, they comprise much of our life experience."

"You went to the Imperial Games, didn't you? I remember watching the highlights on the House of Bolshoi sports channel."

"True, but Doctor Fabergé insisted we keep ourselves to ourselves during the events. As a result, we do not have your knowledge of the world and its vernacular." Tempest chewed her bottom lip wistfully. "Sometimes I wonder what else we have missed out on."

Dante reached out a friendly hand and patted her on the shoulder. "Trust me, the world outside – it's no better than being here."

Tempest nodded. "That is what Doctor Fabergé always tell us."

"So, what did you want to talk about?"

"Your servant, Spatchcock. He's working in the kitchen, with Scullion."

"Yes. I understand she's quite taken with him."

"Two days ago Spatchcock delivered a bowl of soup to the doctor's laboratory. Soon afterwards we discovered an item was missing from one of the worktops. Storm and I have thoroughly searched the room, but can find no trace of the item. The only feasible explanation we can formulate is that your manservant took the item – either intentionally or otherwise."

Dante nodded, unsure of how to react. "I see."

"The item is of little value, beyond a sentimental attachment for Doctor Fabergé and us – my sister and I. It is a crystal containing a recording of our mother's voice along with her likeness. We would very much like to retrieve it."

"Completely understandable," Dante agreed.

"Do you know anything about this crystal, its whereabouts?" Tempest stared at him intently, her eyes searching his face for a reaction.

"I can't say that I do," he replied carefully, "but I will approach Spatchcock and see if he can shed any light on the matter. It pains me to say it, but my manservant was once a thief. He came into my service during the war as a conscript, just like Flintlock, but both proved themselves worthy of my trust and loyalty. I would be mortified to think Spatchcock had lapsed back into his old, wayward habits." Dante smiled. "Thank you for mentioning this matter to me so discretely. I will ensure it is dealt with this evening."

"All three of us would be most grateful," Tempest said.

"One thing confuses me a little," Dante added. "You said the crystal contained recordings of your mother?"

"Yes."

"If I might ask, what happened to her?"

"She died giving birth to Storm and myself," Tempest said sadly. "It was a great loss for our father."

"And where is he now?"

"In the laboratory, at the top of the north tower."

Dante finally realised the truth. "Doctor Fabergé is your father?"

"Yes, of course." Tempest looked puzzled anyone could think otherwise. "He does not want it widely known, but I thought all the faculty knew."

"Well, I've only been here a few days," Dante said.

Tempest rose from her seat, towering over him. "I must return to the laboratory and tell the doctor what you have shared with me. When do you think you might have any further information?"

"Later tonight, I am certain of that," Dante replied. "Perhaps I could visit your quarters with an update?"

"That would be most kind of you. I share a room with my sister, on the top level of the west tower. Knock twice and I'll know it's you."

"I'll be there before midnight," Dante said.

Tempest nodded, acknowledged the others and then left the library. Dante smiled quietly to himself. *Who says I need the Crest's help with everything? Tonight Quentin Durward will be making a house call.*

After dinner Dante loudly announced he was going down to the kitchen to visit Spatchcock, making sure the other staff knew of his whereabouts. Although Wartski had not attended dinner, no doubt Ms Ostrov or one of her cronies was passing on news of Mr Durward's movements about the castle. It didn't hurt to act out the role he had created for himself as intermediary with the troublesome Spatchcock. Dante found the kitchen hand sulkily scrubbing pots and pans.

"Where's she of the many tentacles?"

"Went to bed early, complaining of a headache. More likely put too much sherry down her gullet instead of into that trifle."

Dante nodded. "It did seem a little lacking in kick. Now, did you steal a data crystal from Doctor Fabergé's laboratory on Monday?"

Spatchcock stared at him as if Dante had grown an extra nose. "Are you off your head? Why are you asking me that?"

"I'm worried that you might have reverted to your old ways."

"What old ways?"

"Don't try to play the innocent with me, Spatch. We both know you used to be a thief and a felon, along with numerous other offences."

"Yeah, so what?"

"Have you embraced that terrible life again?"

"I'm not getting this at all. What are you babbling about?"

Dante abandoned trying to be subtle, since such efforts were proving futile. Instead he explained about the conversation with Tempest, her explanation of the data crystal's contents and the belief the former thief might have accidentally purloined it.

"Oh," Spatchcock said slowly, at least showing signs of understanding. "I see. Well, er, now that you come to mention it, I might have accidentally picked something up – entirely by mistake you understand – when I was delivering the soup to the location you mentioned some two days ago."

"You're not giving evidence in court," Dante hissed.

"Sorry." He sniffed and then wiped a dribble of mucus from the end of his nose on the dishcloth. "So, er, what do we do now?"

"You give me the crystal and I return it to the Strangelove twins later tonight, no questions asked."

"So you get to play the hero–"

"And have a legitimate reason to visit them after dark in their room."

"Kill two birds with one stone," Spatchcock observed.

"Hopefully it won't come to that." Dante folded his arms. "So, where's this crystal then, hmm? Where have you hidden it?"

"Er, I'm not sure I remember."

"I hope you haven't hidden it in my private quarters," Dante hissed through clenched teeth, winking repeatedly at Spatchcock.

"What? Oh! Yes, well, it's funny you should say that."

"Somewhere near the bed? Or amongst my luggage?" Dante accompanied the latter suggestion with another flurry of winking.

"The luggage, it's definitely in amongst your luggage."

"Well, then I shall have to go and recover it." Dante delivered a firm clout to Spatchcock's head for good measure. "Don't you ever dare do something like this again, or I'll have your guts for garters! Got it?"

"Yes."

"Good." Dante began to leave, then stopped and came back. Spatchcock winced, fearful of another blow. "Where's Flintlock?"

"I think he's checking a blockage near Madame Wartski's quarters."

"Excellent. Well, I'd best go and find this data crystal. And remember what I told you, Spatch."

"What's that?" The kitchen hand was swatted with another blow.

"No more thieving!"

Flintlock had scrubbed himself clean before beginning his covert raid on Madame Wartski's quarters. He didn't want to leave any trace of his intrusion, and the lingering aroma of sewerage would not require a detective to identify the culprit. If he was honest, Flintlock would admit the elongated ablutions were merely a method of delaying his attempt at breaking and entering. But the message from Dante had been clear: they had to know what secrets the wart-ridden woman had hidden in her room and Flintlock was the man for the job. Besides, the exiled aristocrat had never been honest in his life, even with himself, and this was no time to start.

Taking what little courage he possessed and forcing himself forwards, the blond-haired burglar knocked on the matron's door. "Madame Wartski? It's Flintlock. I understand there's another blockage in the pipes near your quarters. I was wondering if I could come in and check for any signs of trouble?"

His hopes of being told to come back later proved fruitless, as no reply was made. After knocking and calling out several more times, Flintlock realised he couldn't linger outside the door any longer. He removed a sliver of flexible metal from a concealed pouch inside his trousers and used it to prise open the lock. The door swung open with an ominous creak but no lights were visible inside. "Madame Wartski? Are you in there?"

Flintlock could not hear the matron: neither her voice nor the heavy rasp of breathing that accompanied her everywhere. There was a different noise emanating from inside the room – a faint bubbling accompanied by a low rumble that defied easy identification. Perhaps she had left the Imperial Net on? And what was that smell – like a swamp with a nervous disposition, noxious and nauseating. As Flintlock entered, the stench grew stronger and more cloying. He closed the door and stood still, letting his eyes adjust to the limited lighting.

The room had a green hue, illumination spilling in from another doorway. Wartski's quarters were sparsely furnished, just a bookshelf, wardrobe, dresser and vanity unit. No bed, so that must be in the adjoining room, Flintlock reasoned. He moved to the bookshelf and examined the spines on display: *Toads for Pleasure*, *Toads Across History*, *Tropical Toads*. The matron liked her friends amphibious, that much was certain. But the first room revealed few secrets. It was time to venture deeper into Wartski's privacy.

Flintlock edged closer to the other doorway, peering through the gap. Beyond he could see a double bed, its sheets rumpled and unkempt. A selection of plus size lingerie had been abandoned nearby, apparently cast aside during moments of frenzy or passion. Pity the poor sod who gets caught in here while she's on heat, Flintlock thought, before remembering where he was standing. Best get on with the task in hand.

He ventured into the bedroom, its interior suffused with emerald. The source for this light was an entire wall of glass tanks, each containing a dozen toads of varying shapes, sizes and colours. Even more disturbing were the sexual implements arranged on hooks and handles in front of the tanks – whips, canes, harnesses, handcuffs, chains and a selection of rubber objects with intimidating proportions. Flintlock shuddered, backing away from the display of depravity. His legs collided with the bed and he twisted round in surprise. He noticed there were notches carved into the wooden framework, while chains and fur-lined hand-cuffs were attached to each corner.

That's it, I've seen enough, Flintlock decided. Wartski isn't doing any secret research for Fabergé in here – not unless it involves sexual deviancy and toads. Time to make a tactical withdrawal.

"Is someone out there?" a voice called.

Flintlock stopped, frozen with terror. He urged his legs to move but they seemed to have forgotten their normal func-tions. A door opened in a corner of the bedchamber and Wartski emerged, clad in just a thigh-length white camisole, towelling her hair dry. "I said is someone–" she stopped abruptly, surprised and perplexed by Flintlock's presence.

"Oh! What are you doing in here?" Wartski demanded.

Flintlock shrugged helplessly.

Wartski strode to the doorway between the bedchamber and outer room, waving her hand over the palm reader so the exit was sealed, trapping the intruder. "I said what are you doing here?"

Flintlock opened his mouth to speak and then remem-bered he was supposed to be a mute. Instead he improvised an elaborate mixture of mime and sign lan-guage, trying to communicate that he had wandered in by mistake while looking for a blockage in the drains but plainly there was no blockage here so it was for the best if he left now and–

Wartski stopped his spasmodic movements with a shout. Once Flintlock had abandoned his wordless attempts to communicate, the matron moved closer, an intrigued look on her wart-strewn features. "I can only think of three reasons you would enter my private quarters without permission. Firstly, you have come here on a mission from Scullion to investigate some blockage."

Flintlock nodded hurriedly at that suggestion.

"However," Wartski continued, "I know of no such problem, nor has Scullion mentioned it in our daily briefing. So that cannot be correct. Secondly, you came here to steal from me, hoping to find something of value to sell once the term is finished. Is that why you're here, mute?"

Flintlock shook his head vigorously, denying the charge.

"That just leaves the third reason. No doubt you've heard whispers about what I do here during the little spare time I have from the institute. You're curious. Can she really be the sexual deviant everybody says? Perhaps you have wondered whether you could share in my delight of the obscene, the obscure and the downright disgusting? Perhaps you would like a session in my chamber of delights and debauchery?"

Flintlock shook his head again, his face smeared with dismay.

Wartski reached down between the intruder's legs and grabbed hold of his genitals. "Your head says no but the rest of your body is saying yes. How delightful." She let go, smiling as Flintlock collapsed to the floor with a shriek of pain. "Good. It's a while since I've really enjoyed myself. Best of all, I've got the night off from patrolling the castle's corridors, so you don't have to leave before dawn. Isn't that wonderful?"

Flintlock whimpered helplessly, his eyes clenched shut to stop them seeing the vile woman standing before him. Wartski removed her camisole in a single movement, revealing her repulsive naked body in full. She licked her lips while contemplating the many options waiting in front of the toad tanks. "Let's get started then, shall we? Since you're already kneeling at my feet, you're in the perfect position for your first task of the evening."

TEN

"Trouble appears without prior notice"
– Russian proverb

Dante had drenched himself in cologne, pulled on his cleanest underpants and chosen the best-tailored jacket from among his meagre possessions. He examined his reflection in a mirror, running a hand through the luxurious mane of black hair. "Catnip for the ladies," he murmured, giving himself a wink. "The twins won't know what hit them." An itching sensation on his left arm forced him to pull jacket and shirt aside. The double-headed eagle symbol of the Romanovs was visible below the skin, like a faded tattoo.

"Crest?" Dante whispered. "Crest!"

What is it? I'm close to decrypting the data from that crystal, it replied tersely, *but I'll never finish if you insist on interrupting me.*

"You're becoming visible again," Dante explained. The tattoo was the only visible sign that he bore a Romanov Weapons Crest. The Crest was able to conceal itself when its human host was vulnerable, such as Dante being asleep or unconscious. This skill was more important than ever since the war, since anyone bearing a Crest was liable to execution by the Tsar's forces.

Sorry. The code breaking is taking all my concentration.

"I can't afford to have Tempest and Storm discover my true identity in the middle of a romantic moment, can I?"

You don't seem to understand how much effort is consumed by making myself invisible for such long periods of time. The Crests were not designed to go undercover for days on end.

"Just do your best, okay?" Dante watched as the double-headed eagle disappeared beneath his skin again, merging into the muscle. "Thanks."

Now, if you'll excuse me–

"Since I've already disturbed you," Dante interrupted.

Yes?

"How's the decryption coming along?"

I should have something for you before dawn.

"Good. Well, get on with it."

The Crest muttered a curse into Dante's mind and then fell silent again.

"Don't let your mother hear you talking like that," Dante replied before pulling his shirt and jacket back into place. After one last groom of his hair and stroke of his beard, he departed for the twins' room, whistling tunelessly.

In the kitchen Spatchcock had almost finished preparations for the next day's meals. All that remained was washing down the work surfaces and disposing of the scraps. Tired from a long day's labours, Spatchcock stared sourly at a massive tub laden with leftovers and other swill. Scullion insisted it be pushed through a grinder twice and then poured down a garbage disposal unit, both backbreaking jobs. But Scullion was still in bed.

"There's got to be a quicker way," Spatchcock muttered. "Just this once." He remembered the walkway that stretched over the waters surrounding the island and grinned. Nobody would ever know if he just emptied the scraps into the sea, would they? No sooner had the thought entered his head than Spatchcock was dragging the tub towards the walkway.

Outside a cold wind was slicing through the air, chill and bitter. Spatchcock got the tub halfway across the walkway before his energy and patience were exhausted. He fleetingly contemplated lifting the tub to tip its contents over the side railing, but his small frame could only raise it a few inches off the metal walkway. "Guess we have to do this the old fashioned way." Spatchcock dug both hands into the sloppy mess and scooped out the top layer, hurling it over the rail and into the water. It splattered loudly on contact but soon sank into the inky black depths. Satisfied with his choice, Spatchcock continued lobbing kitchen scraps into the sea. "Much, much easier," he muttered. "Why doesn't Scullion do this all the time?"

His question was answered by a roaring sound from below. A shape burst from the water, vaguely humanoid but unlike anything Spatchcock had seen before. He cowered back in terror, aware of flailing limbs, rows of gnashing teeth and cold, dead eyes staring at him. The little thief fled for his life, screaming and shrieking, the slops bucket abandoned.

Dante bounded up the circular stairway, two steps at a time. At the top of the west tower he paused to catch his breath, then strode purposefully towards a heavy wooden door. It had to be the twins' room, as it was the only opening on this level. Adjusting his jacket one last time, Dante knocked twice. Footsteps could be heard padding towards the entrance and then the door swung open.

Storm was standing inside wearing a revealing black leotard. She mopped sweat from her forehead and chest with a towel while looking disinterestedly at Dante. "Yes, Mr Durward?"

The new arrival turned on the charm, giving her the benefit of his most winning smile. "Your sister asked me to pay a visit this evening."

"Did she?"

"Yes." Dante peered past Storm, not an easy task when the two-metre tall woman nearly filled the doorway. Beyond her he could see Tempest stretched out on a large square of padded matting. Like her sister she was dressed only in a leotard, its fabric stained with sweat from the exertions. "And there she is!"

Storm folded her arms. "Why?"

Dante gave a little wave to Tempest but it went unnoticed. "Sorry?"

"Why are you here?"

"Well, it's a rather delicate matter."

"Could you be more specific?" Storm demanded.

At last Tempest noticed Dante at the door and called to him. "Mr Durward, you're here. Come in, come in."

Dante smiled at Storm again before pushing past her. The twins' quarters were considerably larger than his own, filling almost all of the west tower's top level. Much of the space was given over to a private gymnasium, with a steam room and sauna against one wall. Through an archway Dante could see a double bed in the next room, an inviting prospect.

Tempest continued to stretch and contort her body into new and ever more challenging positions while she talked to Dante. "Did you have any success with the matter we discussed?"

"Yes. Yes I did." Dante reached into his jacket pocket and produced the data crystal. "My servant says he inadvertently picked it up and I tend to believe him. It's been several years since he renounced thieving and he has stuck to that pledge. Nevertheless, I have given him a severe reprimand and you may be assured this sort of incident will not happen again."

"I should hope not," Storm commented acidly from the doorway.

"Could I have the crystal?" Tempest asked from the floor, her legs doing the splits while she bent her torso forwards to touch the mat.

"Of course." Dante handed the crystal to her and watched as she examined its outer casing. He knew there was no visible evidence the Crest had breached the crystal. "I trust everything is in order?"

Tempest smiled. "Perfectly. Well, thank you for all your help."

"Yes, thanks," Storm agreed, opening the door ever wider so the visitor would have no problems departing. Dante frowned inwardly. This was not going according to plan. With most women he could charm his way into their affections a little, but the Strangelove twins appeared utterly immune to him. It was time to try another tactic.

"You obviously both spend a lot of time working out," he ventured.

"Yes," Tempest agreed. "Our athletic careers may have been quite short-lived, but we like to keep in shape. The body is a temple and no temple should be allowed to fall into disrepair."

"I know what you mean," Dante said, sucking in his stomach and puffing out his chest. "I find maintaining a rude health is essential for my teaching."

Storm arched an eyebrow at him. "You do?" she asked, her voice dripping with sarcasm.

"Most definitely. But I do worry about my levels of flexibility. Perhaps you could show me a few techniques for improving that?"

"We really don't have time for–" Storm began, but her sister cut in.

"It would be our pleasure," Tempest replied. "Storm, why don't you come and help me?" Dante thought he caught a look pass between the twins, but wasn't sure of its significance.

"Yes, I will," Storm said, shutting the door and approaching the mat. "This could be most educational for Mr Durward."

Flintlock opened his eyes and resisted the urge to scream. He had already been subjected to more degradation in one evening than he had experienced in a lifetime. Now he found himself stark naked and handcuffed to a bed while

Madame Wartski sat astride his chest, her corpulent body pressing down on him. She was wearing nothing but a black domino mask while her hands caressed a large, brown skinned toad mottled with green spots. The matron stroked the creature tenderly with one hand while smiling down at her sex slave.

"I have a little secret. Would you like to know what it is, Flintlock?"

He shook his head from side to side but she ignored his wishes.

"Everybody knows of my passionate interest in toads, how I like to breed them. They all think that's the reason why I have so many warts on my body. But there's another reason."

Flintlock wished he could tear his hands away from the restraints and shove his fingers into his ears, to block out what was coming next. Wartski leaned forwards, her pendulous breasts brushing against his chest as she held the toad in front of Flintlock's face.

"The toads I breed secrete a powerful hallucinogenic from their sweat glands. Ancient tribes used to partake of it for therapeutic purposes. But via selective breeding I have developed a strain of toad whose secretions are a hundred times more powerful than anything that occurs in nature. All you need do is lick the back of such a toad and you will experience sensations beyond belief. Alas, indulge too often and you become very warty – like me."

Wartski gave her toad a kiss, then ran her tongue along its back, sucking the sweat into her mouth. "The best part about this particular toad is that its glands also secrete a strong sexual stimulant amidst the sweat. Not only do you see visions beyond imagining, you will also reach a state of sexual ecstasy unlike anything before in your life."

Tears began seeping from Flintlock's eyes, running down either side of his face. Wartski smiled benignly at him. "That's right, I also wept with joy when I discovered this delight. Now I am going to share it with you. Ah, Flintlock, if only you could speak and tell me what you are feeling right now."

Wartski turned the toad around so its back was close to her slave's lips. "Lick my beauty's back," she commanded. But Flintlock kept his mouth firmly closed, not wanting any part of the matron's ecstasy. Wartski smiled and reached behind herself to grab hold of his testicles, squeezing them between thumb and fingers. "I said lick!"

Flintlock darted out his tongue and made the tiniest of licks.

"More!" the harridan ordered.

Flintlock licked once more, rolling his tongue back and forth across the toad's back. Wartski released his privates from her grasp. "That's better. Now, we wait. In just a few moments you will begin to see me as the most beautiful creature you have ever encountered. You will do anything I desire, freely and without hesitation, debasing yourself in ways you never thought possible. The best part of it all? Afterwards, you will remember every moment, every wonderful second of pleasure and pain. Let the fun begin!"

Flintlock closed his eyes. Maybe it won't affect me, he hoped. Maybe I'll be immune. Maybe I'll... Then the spots started dancing in front of his eyes.

Dante had stripped off his jacket, shirt and boots, leaving just his trousers to take the strain. Storm and Tempest were already stretched out on the padded mat, bending and twisting their bodies into the unlikeliest of shapes. "Do you know yoga, Mr Durward?" Tempest inquired politely.

"It can be nice with honey," he replied, smiling at his own joke.

"She meant the Hindu system of philosophy aiming at the mystical union of the self with the Supreme Being in a state of complete awareness and tranquillity through certain physical and mental exercises," Storm chided.

"Oh, yoga. Well, I've experienced a few mystical unions in my time, but I wouldn't call my body a supreme being. Yet."

"Let's begin with a basic position, shall we?" Tempest replied.

"Let's. I can certainly handle the basic positions," Dante said.

Five minutes later he was starting to have serious doubts. His body had been twisted, stretched and strained in ways he didn't think possible. Muscles and tendons screamed for relief, while his face tried to maintain a relaxed look. Sweat was pouring down the back of his legs and chest, creating unsightly damp patches on his trousers.

By comparison Tempest and Storm were laughing as Dante's attempts to keep up grew more feeble. Finally he collapsed altogether, arms and legs flailing through the air before his body thudded to the floor. After lying still for half a minute he pulled himself up into a sitting position.

"Well, that wasn't bad for my first attempt, was it?"

"Pathetic," Storm replied.

"Abject, to be perfectly honest," Tempest added.

"Still, practice makes perfect," Dante maintained, wiping the sweat from his eyes. "Shall we hit the showers now or later? I could do with a little steam."

"We prefer to continue our exertions here on the mat," Tempest said, one hand reaching out to stroke her sister's face lovingly.

"Is that a fact?" Dante could feel his energy returning rapidly. "Well, I'm sure I can rise to the occasion."

"After a good workout, we like to keep pushing each other to the limit," Storm continued, her own hands hungrily exploring her sister's body.

"So I can see. Perhaps I can help out?" Dante asked hopefully.

"I don't think…" Tempest said between kisses with Storm, "that will be necessary… Mr Durward… Ohhh."

Storm began peeling off her leotard to reveal the perfect body underneath. "Please close the door on your way out." The twins flung themselves at each other, rolling over and over across the matting. Dante jumped to his feet to get out of their way, retreating to the doorway.

"Well, I can see you've both got your hands full, as it were."

The two women began moaning loudly as they writhed in ecstasy.

"So I'll be off," Dante said, all too aware he was surplus to requirements. He opened the door and stepped outside, looking back wistfully at the spectacle inside. "Try to get *some* rest tonight." He closed the door and began back down the stairs to his own room.

Dante, I've done it, the Crest announced. *I've broken the code.*

"Good, then at least tonight won't be a complete waste of time. What data was stored on the crystal?"

I'm still sorting through it all. The crystal appears to house a virtual reality simulation, made as a dry run for a presentation to the Tsar.

"The Tsar was here?"

No, he must have sent a representative to relay the report.

"What does this presentation say?"

I can do better than tell you, the Crest offered. *I can insert your mind into it, so you can witness what Fabergé wanted the Tsar to see.*

"Do it." Dante opened his door and slipped inside. "Then we can—"

"Then we can do what, Mr Durward?" a female voice asked.

"Oh, no," Dante groaned. "Not another one!"

"Not another what?" his visitor replied. "Don't tell me I'm not the first of your pupils to come inside your private quarters outside school hours?"

Dante found Natalia draped across his bed. Unlike his previous visitors, she was wearing an old fashioned pair of striped pyjamas. As he watched she began undoing the first button of her top, exposing naked skin underneath. "Look, just stop, okay?"

Natalia smiled at him coyly. "Why should I?"

"I don't know what Helga has told you."

"Helga?"

"Or Carmen. Or Mai Lin." Dante thought back, trying to remember if he had bedded any of the other students, but his mind had gone blank. "Or anybody else for that matter. I am not some gigolo willing to provide you with a night of pleasure free of charge!"

"You mean I have to pay?"

"No, of course you don't have to pay!"

"That's good," she replied, rising gracefully from the bed. "I didn't bring any money with me, as you can see from my attire."

"What I'm trying to say is–"

"Yes?" Natalia asked, moving a step closer.

"Is that I am not merely some kind of stud–"

"That's not what I've heard," she continued, her fingers undoing another button on her top to reveal the swell of her breasts.

"What happened before cannot happen again," Dante insisted. "It was a one-off occurrence, that's all!"

"A one-off? I'm told you're capable of more than that – when roused." Natalia stepped nearer to her teacher, close enough to reach out and touch his jacket. "Much more than that."

Dante tried backing away but the closed door prevented that. "Look, Natalia, I'm not sure this is a good idea. How old are you?"

She smiled. "Just seventeen."

"Bojemoi!" he gasped. "It wouldn't be right, wouldn't be proper if I…"

"Who said anything about being proper?" Natalia sighed, pushing Dante's jacket off and stroking her hands across his chest. "I've got a surprise for you, Mr Durward."

"Really? What's that?"

"I've never been with a man – not a real man. You'll be my first." Natalia licked her lips and slipped her hands inside his shirt.

"I'm sorry, but you're just too young," he protested weakly. "The others, they were women, but you're just…"

"Just a girl?"

Dante nodded meekly.

"We'll see about that!" Natalia ripped his shirt apart at the middle, tugging the material away from his shoulders and down the arms. She leaned close to him, pressing her young body against his squirming form.

"Please, don't do this," Dante whispered.

Natalia looked him in the eyes and began to giggle.

"I don't understand," he said in bewilderment.

Natalia was laughing out loud now, staggering away from Dante as her whole body descended into hysterical guffaws.

"Hey! What's so funny?" he demanded.

Natalia collapsed on the bed, still laughing heartily, one finger pointing at Dante. "Your face! If you could have seen your face!" Another fit of hilarity overtook her, making further speech impossible. Dante waited until she had regained her breath before asking another question.

"You mean you didn't come here to seduce me?"

Natalia's face crumpled with disgust. "Euwwww! You're old enough to be my father. Gross!"

"I am not old enough to be your father," Dante protested. "Well, only if I had been a very early developer. Which I was." Natalia was shaking her head so he abandoned that train of thought. "So why are you in my room?"

"I need your help. I know the institute is a finishing school for young ladies of the Empire, but there's something else going on here."

Dante sat beside her on the bed. "Such as?"

"I'm not sure," Natalia admitted. "Fabergé hardly ever comes out of his laboratory, and when he does visit our classes it's more like he's looking at prized exhibits in a science fair instead of students."

"You can't accuse someone because of the way they look at you, otherwise most of the Empire would be in a gulag."

"It's more than that. I think he's conducting secret experiments on us."

Dante, she may be right, the Crest said.

"What sort of experiments?"

"Everyone but me in the elite class has been given a detailed medical examination by Doctor Fabergé."

"That's not so unusual…"

"Under anaesthetic?" Natalia began nervously pacing the room. "I talked to each of the girls when they came back from these medicals. Their memories about what happened were fuzzy, at best – as if they'd been drugged. And the examinations themselves. From what the other girls described, I believe Doctor Fabergé has been removing unfertilised eggs from each of them."

"Why? Why would he do that?"

"I've done some research into his background. Fabergé was a co-founder of GenetiCo, the scientific research company. Have you heard of it?"

Dante nodded. He had visited GenetiCo's orbital headquarters just before the war, with his half-brother Konstantin. The owner, Raoul Sequanna, had committed suicide rather than side with the Romanovs against the Tsar.

"I think Fabergé has been continuing his genetic research on the island ever since, establishing the finishing school as a front for his activities. Whatever he's been working on, it must need unfertilised human eggs as raw material. The doctor has been taking them from his students, using us like white mice in a laboratory!" Natalia burst into tears.

What she has just told you tallies with my findings, the Crest confirmed. *But the Strangelove Gambit is far more terrifying than she could ever imagine.*

Dante went to the seventeen year-old and put a comforting arm round her shoulders. "If what you told me is true, it must be stopped, Natalia. But why choose me as your confidante?"

"That's simple," she replied between sniffles. "I've read all about you, your exploits, the way you battle for lost causes and hopeless cases. You might act first and think last, but you're exactly the right man to stop Doctor Fabergé."

"I don't understand," Dante maintained. "I'm Quentin Durward, a humble teacher. I may be one of the best swordsmen in the Empire but–"

Natalia rested a hand against his lips, silencing him. "Hush. You don't have to pretend for me. I know you're Nikolai Dante."

ELEVEN

"Seeing is easier than foreseeing"
– Russian proverb

"I don't know what you're talking about," Dante maintained. "I'm a substitute teacher here on probation."

"I saw it on your arm," Natalia replied.

"Saw what?"

"The symbol of the Romanovs, the double-headed eagle. It was visible on your left arm that night we met in the corridor, when you were holding my ice bag against your groin."

Oops, the Crest mumbled. *I told you it was problematic trying to maintain stealth status round the clock.*

"That's just an old tattoo," Dante said lamely.

"A tattoo that appears and disappears?" Natalia asked. "Why do you think I ripped your shirt off earlier?"

"I thought you were flinging yourself at me."

"I was searching to see if the symbol was still there." Natalia twisted Dante's left arm round to show the place where his Crest normally was. "It's gone, invisible to the naked eye."

"Maybe I was wearing a temporary tattoo?"

"It was a Romanov Weapons Crest, the kind that can be subsumed beneath the skin when necessary to protect its host from detection."

The colloquial expression for this situation is: 'the jig's up'.

Dante sat back down on his bed. "Have you told anyone else about me?"

Natalia shook her head. "I wouldn't. I had to be sure first."

"Then don't," he pleaded. "You're right, Doctor Fabergé has been continuing his experiments – that's why I'm here. He is unveiling a new weapon for the Tsar on Sunday. I'm trying to stop that."

"I knew it! I knew you coming here couldn't be a coincidence," Natalia said excitedly. Dante beckoned for her to sit beside him on the bed.

"Natalia, it's important nobody else discovers who I am or why I'm here. You must know about the bounty on my head."

"Yes. Don't worry, I wouldn't know what to do with all those roubles."

Dante nodded. "I guess your family is rich enough already to send you to a place like this?"

"No, I got in on a scholarship. The House of Sokorina is almost bankrupt, has been since before the war."

"Oh. Well, anyway, the important thing is–" Dante's words were cut off by the sound of someone screaming in the corridor outside. "Stay here," he hissed at Natalia, hurrying to the door. Biocircuitry was already starting to extrude from his right hand, forming itself into a sabre.

A naked man was running along the corridor towards Dante's quarters, babbling and gibbering wildly. As the figure got closer Dante realised it was Flintlock, the aristocratic face filled with terror and horror in equal measure.

"Flintlock? Flintlock, what's happening?" Dante hissed, as his travelling companion raced past. But the man from Britannia kept running, as if intent on getting back to his homeland before dawn.

"Nikolai? What's happening out there?" Natalia asked.

Dante waved her to be silent. Another figure was running towards him. This one was slower and heavier, judging by the sound of the footfalls. Suddenly Madame Wartski burst round a corner, clad only in a harness of leather straps, much of her body wobbling freely in the night air. She was clutching a black rubber truncheon, but it looked surprisingly flexible. Dante pushed his door shut before she ran past, not wanting to catch her eye.

"Well?" Natalia demanded. "What was it?"

"You mean *who* was it," Dante replied. "In cases like this, I operate a strict policy of 'Don't ask, don't tell', okay?"

"You're not trying to keep secrets from me?"

"No. Look, Natalia, there're two things I have to ask you to do."

"Just name them, Nikolai."

"First of all, don't call me Nikolai or Dante, even when we're alone together. I don't believe this room is under surveillance but we can't take any risks. If Doctor Fabergé discovered who I really am he would not hesitate to have me killed or handed over to the Tsar. You would suffer a similar fate for not having turned me in."

"Alright, I understand."

"The other thing is even more important. Let me investigate what is going on in this castle. You don't have my experience at covert missions and you don't have a Weapons Crest."

"You're saying I'm just a girl and can't be trusted."

"No. I don't want to see you hurt because of me. You've got your life ahead of you. Don't throw it away."

"I suppose you're right."

Dante took her chin in one hand and tilted her face up so she was looking into his eyes. "Promise me you won't do anything to endanger yourself."

"I promise," she agreed reluctantly.

"Good. Now you'd better get back to your dormitory. I don't want to explain why I've got a seventeen year-old pupil in my room this late at night."

"That didn't bother you with Helga. Or Carmen. Or Mai Lin."

"I'm not taking the same chance with you, okay?"

"Okay. Well, goodnight." Natalia bent forward and gave him a quick kiss on the left cheek before hurrying out of the room. Once she had gone Dante locked his door for the night, not wanting any more surprise visitors.

"Do you think she'll listen to me, Crest?"

I hope so, it replied, *for her sake. Are you ready to see Fabergé's report?*

"I guess so," Dante agreed. "What do I have to do?"

Close your eyes and let me interface with your subconscious mind. It'll be like walking into a dream – a very sinister dream.

Dante lay down on the bed and followed the Crest's instructions, emptying his mind of all conscious thought. Blackness soon engulfed him.

"Welcome to Fabergé Island!" Dante was startled to see Doctor Fabergé striding towards him, arm outstretched, ready to shake hands. "You've arrived on a most propitious day. Follow me, follow me!" Fabergé marched away towards the doors of the castle. Dante looked around and found he was outside again, on the island's landing pad.

"Crest! What's happening?" he hissed under his breath.

You're inside the report, it replied. *Don't worry, this isn't the real Doctor Fabergé, just a simulation that will guide you around the castle. I'll skip past the guided tour and take you to the key section of the report.*

Dante's surroundings shimmered out of existence and then reappeared in a new form. The doctor was standing in front of his laboratory, holding the door open for the visitor to enter. Dante walked past Fabergé and into the room, studying its high ceiling, gleaming work surfaces and phalanx of research tools. "Very impressive," Dante said, unwittingly falling into the role of tourist.

"You're too kind," Fabergé simpered in response. "How much do you know about my experiments, codenamed the Strangelove Gambit?"

"Surprisingly little," Dante admitted. "When did you first get the idea for it?"

"The Year of the Tsar 2660. I heard one of the fabulous Imperial Easter Eggs was coming up for auction. I had long been fascinated by those masterpieces of the jeweller's art. When word leaked out the fabled Steel Military Egg was going to be auctioned, I determined to buy it at any cost. That egg inspired me to create an entirely new branch of scientific research, which I call Fabergénetics."

"Tell me more," Dante prompted, taking a seat in the virtual laboratory.

"Each of the Imperial Easter Eggs contained a miniature surprise, some made of clockwork, others exquisite jewels or tiny portraits. I decided to adopt this idea on a genetic level, engineering human embryos so they too would contain a surprise. But my surprises would not be made of clockwork or jewels. No, mine would be far more valuable in years to come."

"Sounds fascinating," Dante said, even though his mind recoiled in horror at the thought of someone like Fabergé playing God.

"I am creating the finest in genetically-enhanced children, each one artificially augmented with weaponry that makes the Romanov Weapons Crest look like a plaything. I won't presume to bore you with the fine details of this research, it can be rather a dry subject for those who have not devoted their lives to the field of genetics."

"A wise decision."

"But suffice it to say the last twelve years of my life have been devoted to this task. There have been many failures – many, many setbacks – but also one glorious success in the earliest days of my research. Now, at long last, I have made the final breakthrough. Unfertilised eggs have been taken from the elite class of pupils here at my finishing school, one from all the most important noble houses. These eggs are being genetically modified to create my little surprises. Once fertilised with sperm from a suitable donor, the eggs will be implanted back into the students before they graduate. The young women will return home to their families, unaware they are pregnant with the next generation of bio-weaponry.

"When their relatives become aware of these unwanted babies, some may attempt to abort the foetus. That cannot be allowed. Your forces must ensure the noble houses remain loyal by letting these pregnancies continue. The babies will be vulnerable until the end of the second trimester. After that the mother can be discarded, her usefulness as a vessel for my Fabergénetics at an end." By the end of this speech the doctor had raised his arms skyward, as if raising himself to the level of a god. Eventually he dropped his hands back to his sides. "Well, are there any questions?"

"How much more of this horror show do I need to watch?" Dante asked.

"I'm sorry," Fabergé replied. "I don't understand the question."

That's enough, the Crest interjected. *Shutting down the presentation.*

Dante's eyes snapped open. He was back on his bed in the castle. "Diavolo! Is what Fabergé has planned feasible, Crest?"

Apparently so. He wouldn't have invited the Tsar here otherwise. That's too great a risk, even for someone with such a bloated view of his own importance.

"I need to find a way into that laboratory," Dante decided. "I don't want to risk a frontal attack, but unless I can get past Fabergé's security system soon..."

Fools rush in where angels fear to tread, Dante.

"Yeah, well, I'm no angel."

That much is certain.

A hammering on the door cut short their debate. "Not another late night visitation," Dante complained. "Even I can only stretch so far." He went to the door and listened intently. The knocking resumed. "Who is it?"

"Spatch," a voice hissed urgently. "Let me in, quick!" Dante unlocked the door and the kitchen hand hurried inside, his face full of fear. "We have got to get out of this madhouse!"

"Why? What have you seen?"

"For a start, Flintlock ran past me on the stairs, screaming blue murder and clutching his privates, closely followed by a nearly naked Madame Wartski. You don't get many of those to the pound, let me tell you."

"They went past here before," Dante agreed. "What else?"

Spatchcock detailed his attempt to throw kitchen scraps into the sea, struggling to describe the creature that reared up at him from the water. "It was half human, half fish – teeth like razors, hundreds of them. And its eyes, dead they were, black as coal and colder than the night. Horrible, it was, horrible." His hands were shaking as he recalled the incident.

Dante retrieved a hip flask from his luggage and let Spatchcock take a drink from it. "Enough, that's enough!" he growled when the former felon tried to steal another sip. "Crest, in his presentation Fabergé talked about having had many failures during his years of research. Do you think Spatch encountered one of them, still alive in the waters round the island?"

The good doctor may be using his failures like guard dogs, letting them scare away curious fishermen and tourists, the Crest speculated.

Dante nodded. "Spatch, I need you to find Flintlock. Try and keep him quiet, he's supposed to be a mute. One of the students has already figured out who I am, we don't need anyone else discovering why we're here."

"Alright," Spatchcock said. "But I ain't going near water again. Ever."

"It's not like you had that close a relationship with washing before, is it? Now, off you go!" Dante urged. He let the kitchen hand out and locked his door once more. "Crest, there's something that's still troubling me."

Only one thing?

"We know where Fabergé keeps some of his failed experiments. But in the presentation he mentioned an early success. Where does he keep that?"

Natalia had lain awake in her bed most of the night, tossing and turning, going over in her mind the conversation with Dante – Mr Durward. She knew she was right about letting him investigate what Doctor Fabergé was doing, that was the sensible course of action. But she had spent her whole life being sensible, doing what others told her, always following the rules. For the first time she was close to something important. She couldn't just lie here and pretend nothing was happening. She had to do something, but what? The answer came to her at dawn.

When the other pupils went for breakfast, Natalia headed directly to the north tower and waited outside the basement entrance. A few minutes later the twins arrived to start work. "What are you doing here?" Storm demanded.

Taking a deep breath, Natalia approached the intimidating women. "Doctor Fabergé sent for me," she said boldly. "I'm overdue for my check-up."

"He never mentioned it to us," Tempest replied.

"Are you sure about this?" Storm demanded.

"Yes," Natalia maintained, trying to keep the fear from her voice. "All the elite class has been given a full medical examination, except me."

The twins exchanged a look before nodding. Storm passed her hand over the palm reader, deactivating the security systems. "Come with us," she said coldly, pushing Natalia towards the lift.

Dante arrived at his first class of the day, a fencing session in the gymnasium. But when the students split into pairs for practice, Helga was left without a partner. "Where's Natalia?"

"She didn't come to breakfast," Helga replied sadly. "Maybe she is sickening for something?"

"Guess she's becoming a woman at last," Carmen said sarcastically, getting a snigger from the other students. "Not before time if you ask me."

Dante turned on her. "Nobody did ask you, so keep your opinions to yourself," he snarled. A chiming sound cut through the air, surprising teacher and class. Dante looked around, perplexed. "The lesson can't be over yet, we've only just started."

Wartski's voice issued from the Tannoy speakers, grating and metallic. "Mr Durward, come to my office immediately. Mr Durward, come to my office immediately. All other teachers and students are to return to their rooms." Another chime signalled the end of the message.

"Who's been a naughty boy then?" Helga whispered on her way out. "The last person called to her office was Mr Russell, and we never saw him again."

Dante escorted all the pupils outside and locked the gymnasium. "You heard the announcement, go back to your dormitories. Hopefully we'll be able to resume this class later in the day." He watched them wander back towards the east tower.

If you're lucky, Wartski is only going to reprimand you for sexual antics with the students, the Crest said.

"She's in no position to preach after what I saw last night."

Could Natalia have betrayed you?

"No," Dante replied firmly. "She believes in me. Natalia would never betray our secret – at least, not willingly."

Doctor Fabergé was already at work in his laboratory when Natalia arrived, escorted by the twins. "What is this girl doing here?"

"She claims you asked her here for a full medical examination, just like the other members of the elite class," Tempest explained.

Fabergé shook his head. "I made no such request."

Natalia smiled nervously, all too aware of the powerful hands gripping both her arms. "Well, I might have, er, exaggerated a little. I was just curious, I guess, about what happened in here. Maybe feeling a little left out, since all the other girls... you know." Realising she was out of her depth, Natalia tried to leave but the twins refused to release her. "Perhaps I should go?"

The doctor regarded her thoughtfully. "No, my dear, you shall have your examination. Tempest, prepare the instruments. Storm, you will sedate young Miss Sokorina, while I perform the procedure." Fabergé approached Natalia, staring intently into her eyes. "You should be careful what you wish for. Now, remove your clothes and get up on to that examining table."

Dante stood before Wartski in her office, a cold room cluttered by administrative paraphernalia. The matron sat behind a broad oak desk, dressed in her usual blue and white uniform. She glared at him for a full minute, arms folded across her more than ample chest. "First things first," she said, "I want to know why you lied about one of your servants, Flintlock."

"Lied? I never lied," Dante replied, determined to maintain his pretence of innocence as long as possible. Better to let Wartski make her accusations than offer any unnecessary admissions of guilt.

"Soon after arriving on the island you told me he was a mute."

"That's correct."

"Yet last night he was shouting and screaming at the top of his lungs – in the accent of a Britannia native. How can you explain that?"

"I can't." Dante shrugged. "May I ask, what were the circumstances of Flintlock regaining his voice?"

"You may not."

"I just wondered if he was undergoing a painful or pleasurable experience at the time. You see, my servant lost his voice as a result of post-traumatic stress disorder suffered during the war. He was trapped for four days alone in no man's land, during the Battle of Vladigrad. When finally rescued by his comrades in arms, Flintlock was no longer able to speak."

"Is that so?"

"Yes. I hate to think what horrors he must have faced, to rob the power of speech from him. That's why I asked about the incident that led to his speaking again, I thought it might be relevant."

"The circumstances are irrelevant. Suffice to say, he has regained his voice, although he is not yet making much sense. I believe your other servant is trying to coax him into forming sentences," Wartski said.

"Well, whatever incident triggered his recovery, it can only be considered a miracle cure. Just a shame we don't know what did the trick, as it could be recommended as a treatment for other sufferers of post-traumatic stress." Dante suppressed a smile, enjoying teasing the matron.

Wartski rose from her chair and began to walk around the office, circling Dante. "After witnessing your servant's sudden recovery, I began to have my doubts about you, Mr Durward. So I instituted further enquiries into your background, with a more thorough check of data on the Imperial Net."

She may be on to you, the Crest warned. *Prepare for evasive action.*

"On the mainland you claimed to be a close personal friend of Grigori Arbatov," Wartski continued, "the man originally appointed to your post. I contacted the Arbatov family, but none could recall such an acquaintance–"

"Well, Grigori and I were–"

"Do not interrupt me!" Wartski bellowed. She was standing to one side of Dante, her face quivering with rage. "You told me Captain Arbatov had suffered a fencing accident that prevented him joining the institute's faculty. I could find no record of any such accident. The captain was last seen in the village near our landing pad on the mainland, asking for directions on the day he was due to catch Doctor Fabergé's shuttle to the island."

Dante waited for a pause in her accusations before speaking again. "I can explain all of this, you see—"

"I did not give you permission to speak," Wartski spat at him, resuming her circling. "Early this morning I sent Tempest and Storm across to the mainland in search of the elusive Captain Arbatov. It did not take them long to discover his body, buried in a shallow grave, along with some of his discarded belongings."

"The Black Sea coastline is notorious for its bandits," Dante offered.

"Meanwhile I was scouring the Imperial Net, delving deeper than I had on my first search. A cursory enquiry would find plenty of evidence to support the claims of Quentin Durward. But something far more interesting came up when I was granted permission to access the files of the Tsar's Raven Corps."

Here it comes, the Crest warned.

Before Wartski could continue, an insistent knocking rattled her office door. "Come!" she commanded. Tempest entered and approached the matron, whispering something into her left ear. Wartski nodded, a cruel smile playing about her lips. "Very well. Thank you for that." Tempest departed again, glaring at Dante on her way out.

Wartski returned to her desk and opened a drawer, withdrawing a sheet of paper from inside. "Quentin Durward does not exist, but the name has been used as an alias by members of the Vorovskoi Mir over the years – among them one of the most wanted men in the Empire." She turned the paper round to show Dante the image on the other side. It was a picture of him, all too familiar from wanted posters erected in the Tsar's name. "Quentin Durward is an alias of this man, Nikolai Dante, and this man… is you!"

Dante smiled, determined to try one last bluff. "You've got me all wrong. I know I look a lot like that rogue, but–"

"Spare me any more of your lies," Wartski replied, reaching into her desk drawer. Before she could pull out the weapon inside Dante kicked at the desk, driving it and Wartski backwards across the office, pinning her to the far wall. She screamed an obscenity at him, struggling to free herself.

"I hope you don't kiss anyone with that mouth," Dante replied, then leapt towards the office door. He tore it open to find Storm and Tempest waiting for him outside, wielding syringes filled with a luminescent liquid. Dante threw both hands up to protect himself, biocircuitry already extending outwards from his fingers to form blades. But the twins stabbed the needles into his palms, ramming the plungers down to inject the syringes' contents.

Dante staggered backwards, a chilling numbness shooting up his arms.

"Crest, what's happening? What was in those needles?

That was, the Crest started to reply, but its voice was fading inside Dante's mind. *That was…*

"Crest? Crest, I can't hear you!" Dante shouted. The twins stepped into the office, standing over their target as he collapsed to his knees. Dante's arms hung uselessly at his side, the numbness spreading across his chest and down his spine. He looked up at Wartski as she approached, a malicious grin on her face. "Help me," he said weakly.

"Help yourself," she replied, slapping him across the face with the back of her hand. The blow twisted Dante sideways and he fell, unable to stop himself. His head thudded into the floor and then blackness closed in.

TWELVE

"He that masters his wrath can master anything"
– Russian proverb

Natalia regained consciousness slowly, as if swimming up from the bottom of a dark river towards the surface. Even when she opened her eyes, the surroundings were at odds with her expectations. The last thing she could remember was shivering on the cold metal examination table in Doctor Fabergé's laboratory, her nostrils filled with the smell of rubber from the gas mask being clamped over her face by Storm. Then all was darkness.

Now she was sitting on the floor of a small stone chamber without windows, just a single wooden door set into one wall. She was shaking, her fingers almost blue at the tips, while her teeth kept chattering together. A heavy metal manacle was clamped around one leg, a chain leading from it to a barred grille in the floor. The smell of seawater and rotting fish hung in the air like a pall. Natalia pulled the thin cotton of her patient's gown closer, trying to keep in some warmth. What was this place? Why had she been put here, it didn't make sense. After the other students were examined by Doctor Fabergé they had spent a night in the infirmary recovering before being allowed to rejoin the elite class. None of them had ever mentioned this place.

"Hello?" she called out. "Can anybody hear me?" No reply came, just the echo of her own voice mingling with the sound of waves beneath the grille in the floor. "Can anyone hear me?

Hello?" Natalia felt a rising note of panic in her voice and told herself to stay calm. A terrible mistake had been made, that was all. Somebody would soon realise and let her go.

As if in answer to her thoughts, the sound of approaching footsteps became audible. A heavy key twisted inside a lock and then the door swung inwards. Storm stood in the entrance, her face as cold as the stone beneath Natalia's legs. "I have bad news and good news," the towering woman said emotionlessly. "Which do you want to hear first?"

"What am I doing in here?" Natalia demanded. "Where am I?"

"The good news or the bad?" Storm repeated impatiently.

"The bad news."

"During your medical examination, Doctor Fabergé removed one of your eggs, but it proved to be infertile – you can never have children."

Natalia was numb to this, still unable to grasp what was happening. "And the good news?"

"You won't have to live with your infertility much longer. Since you are no longer of any use to the doctor, he has decided you can no longer remain as a student at this institute. Your academic career is being terminated."

"Are you expelling me?"

"Not exactly. This chamber is one of the lowest points of the castle. Every time the tide rises, it floods this room with seawater. Within the next few hours you will suffer a tragic drowning – at least, that is what your grieving family will be told. It's the most convenient option for your disposal."

Natalia shook her head in disbelief. "But why? Why are you doing this?"

"Patients often say things as they are being sedated. You kept saying two names over and over, mixing them up."

"Oh no," Natalia gasped.

"The name of our new fencing tutor, Quentin Durward – and the name of a wanted criminal, Nikolai Dante. You confirmed what my sister, Madame Wartski and I had discovered during the night. These men are one and the same. How long have you known that?"

Natalia didn't answer, the reality of her situation becoming too much for her. Tears were welling in her eyes, her hands clasping each other helplessly.

"It doesn't matter," Storm concluded. "You cannot be allowed to leave Fabergé Island alive, but your death must also appear to be accidental."

"Please," Natalia begged. "I wouldn't tell anyone, I promise!"

Storm ignored her, pulling the door closed and locking it again.

"Please, you've got to let me out of here!" Natalia screamed. But she could hear Storm walking away, footsteps fading into the distance. "Help me," Natalia sobbed as water ebbed at the grille in the floor. "Someone, help me."

"Where are they?" Wartski demanded. She was standing in the middle of the kitchen, snarling at Scullion. The alien cook ignored her, continuing to stir a huge saucepan filled with a fragrant stew. "I said where are they?"

"Where are who, matron?"

"Your kitchen hand and his partner in crime – Spatchcock and Flintlock," Wartski replied. "They were here earlier. The blond one was babbling in a corner and your little friend was feeding him vodka."

"I'm not surprised if what he was raving about was true," Scullion said. "He seemed to have hallucinated the most unlikely scenario. It involved you, actually. You, a toad and something about leather and rubber. I didn't get all the details, sounded like nonsense to me."

Wartski made a cursory attempt to search the kitchen but soon abandoned her quest. "If either of those two miscreants come back here, you are to send them to my office. Is that clear?"

"Painfully so," the alien replied dryly. She stopped stirring and turned to face the matron. "Was there anything else, or can I get back to doing my job?"

Wartski didn't bother to reply, storming from the kitchen. Once she had gone Spatchcock emerged from a cupboard in the pantry, unfolding himself from the cramped space. "Has the dragon gone?"

"For now," Scullion said. "What have you and Flintlock been up to?"

"Better you don't know." Spatchcock bit his fingernails hesitantly. "You won't hand us over to her, will you?"

Scullion laughed, a guttural sound full of strange mirth. "Wartski and I have never seen eye to eye. The day I make her life easier is the day I die."

Spatchcock gently stroked one of the cook's tentacles. "Don't let it come to that. I don't want you to suffer because of me or Flintlock." He looked around the kitchen. "Where is he, anyway?"

The alien smiled. "Inside the main drain. I knew that even Wartski wouldn't go looking for him down there."

Dante came to in a room of blazing light, humming machines, cold steel and glass. He was lying on a metal examination table, heavy clamps pinning his wrists beside his head. Antiseptic was the overriding smell in the stonewalled chamber, the air harsh and acrid. More metal clamps encased Dante's torso, which was stripped naked to the waist, but he could raise his head to look round the room. This must be Fabergé's laboratory, he thought, recognising it from the presentation. Not exactly the homeliest of places to visit.

"Crest, I need you to analyse the surroundings, see what you can find out about the security system in here," Dante whispered. But no reply entered his thoughts. "Crest? Crest, can you hear me?" Still nothing. Then Dante remembered the needles stabbing into him, the Crest's voice fading away, the numbness creeping up his arms. "Crest?"

"It can't hear you," a supercilious voice responded. Doctor Fabergé was standing behind him. "Nor can you hear the Crest. All communications between the two of you have been severed. You're on your own, Nikolai."

"We'll see about that," Dante snarled, concentrating his mind to activate the biocircuitry within his hands. Once the bio-blades were extended he could easily cut his way free and take on the gloating Fabergé.

"Your ability to create weapons from your hands is also defunct. Tempest and Storm injected you with a suppressant of my own concoction that nullifies all the gifts bestowed upon you by the Crest. For the next two hours you are just as human as I am. Even your enhanced healing abilities are in remission." Fabergé walked towards the examination table, a gleaming scalpel held in one hand. "Most surgeons use laser cutters these days, believing them to be more precise than metal blades like this. Laser cutters cauterise a wound while they slice. Personally, I prefer the old-fashioned method." The doctor laid the edge of his scalpel against Dante's chest, letting it nestle amidst the coarse black hairs. "Allow me to demonstrate."

Fabergé ripped the scalpel sideways, slicing open skin. Blood began flowing freely from the wound. Dante cried out in pain, cursing repeatedly as he twitched involuntarily against his restraints. "See?" Fabergé asked. "You can bleed like anyone else. If I cut deep enough, you'll bleed to death."

"I get the point," Dante replied. "What do you want?"

"From the likes of you? Nothing. Your precious Crest, the fabled weapon of the Romanovs, is old news. After the war the Tsar let me participate in the vivisection of one of your half-siblings. I used the results of that to develop my suppressant, storing it carefully should I ever encounter another Crest's living host. But now I have developed a process that far surpasses your alien biotechnology, that will beget the next generation of bio-weaponry."

"Spare me the lecture," Dante said. "I saw your show and tell routine on the data crystal Spatchcock stole."

"An unfortunate lapse of security," Fabergé admitted, "and one for which your two associates will be punished. Severely punished."

"One thing you didn't mention in that sick little presentation," Dante said. "Whose sperm are you using to fertilise the students' eggs? Not your own, I hope – that hasn't been a great success so far, has it? Spatchcock saw where you keep your failures, swimming round the island as underwater sentries."

"I unsuccessfully tried using stem cells from marine mammals," the doctor admitted. "But all scientific research is a process of trial and error. I have used my own seed quite successfully, adapting eggs taken from Wartski. She's quite devoted to me, in her own way, and gratefully donated them."

"Better than having sex with her. I'm not sure Flintlock will ever recover."

Fabergé twisted the scalpel in Dante's wound, eliciting another scream from the captive. "No need to be nasty, Nikolai. We all have our flaws."

"Speak for yourself," Dante spat back.

"We also have our successes. You've already met two of mine, Tempest and Storm. I called them the Strangelove twins, for their conception was the product of unusual circumstances – my seed and science, together with Wartski's eggs. The Furies are my genetically-engineered daughters."

"But they're almost thirty. How long have you been working on this?"

"The twins were force-gestated to the age of eighteen, given accelerated growth hormones, along with learning implants and simulated memories of their childhood. The sperm for this stage of my experiments has been provided by the Tsar."

Dante's eyes narrowed as he realised the implications of this. "Your elite class will go home on Sunday carrying his bastard offspring in their wombs."

"Pre-programmed to be loyal only to him once they are born, the perfect soldiers to enforce his regime," Fabergé said. "Sadly, not all the class will be making the journey back to their families. Young Natalia proved infertile when I examined her earlier today. And since she unwittingly revealed knowledge of your true identity, I had no choice but to arrange an accident."

"What have you done to her?" Dante demanded.

"Nothing. The rising tide will cause her drowning, not me."

"You bastard! She's done nothing to you. She's no threat to the madness you've been brewing in here!"

"I beg to differ."

"What about the other students? Won't they notice she's gone missing at the same time as me? Won't that ring any alarm bells?"

"I've had the rest of the class sedated. I need all the time between now and the Tsar's arrival to implant the fertilised eggs back into their wombs."

Dante shook his head, steely resolve in his eyes. "It's taken me this long to figure you out, Fabergé. You're clinically insane. You've been playing God for so long you're starting to believe your own legend."

"I'm not playing God," Fabergé replied. "I *am* a god, or close to becoming one. I can recreate mankind in whatever image I see fit. Soon the children I have engineered in this laboratory will rule the Empire. Is that not the definition of a god?"

"I take it back – you're not mad."

"Thank you."

"You're barking mad!" Dante spat. "Wartski should put you on a leash and take you for a walk. She'd probably enjoy that, too."

Fabergé smiled. "Goad me all you want, it won't change anything. When the Tsar arrives on Sunday he will reward me handsomely for having caught the notorious Nikolai Dante, a task that everyone else has singularly failed. Whether you are still alive when the Imperial Palace arrives is entirely up to you. The reward for your corpse is almost as generous as that for delivering you alive, so I don't mind which bounty I receive." The doctor placed the scalpel on Dante's chest, then walked to the laboratory entrance. "Don't go anywhere, I'll be right back. I've something to show you. A blast from the past, I believe the phrase is." He left the room, the frosted glass door sliding closed behind him.

"Crest? Crest, can you hear me? Crest, respond!" Dante hissed, but no reply came. The suppressant must still be in effect. To escape from this place, he would need to rely on his own skills and talents, instead of letting the Crest save him as usual.

The laboratory door opened again and Fabergé returned, carrying a familiar object – the Steel Military Egg. Dante had not seen it since his painful visit to the doctor's hotel suite, twelve years earlier. "Remember this, Nikolai? I paid a fortune for this at auction and within a few hours it was stolen from me by a grifter and his apprentice. I became a laughing stock, a cocktail party joke across the Empire, and the living embodiment of that old adage that a fool and his money are soon parted. So I vowed to find the two men who duped me and punish them for my ignominy. I never realised the apprentice was the infamous Nikolai Dante, bane of the Empire. You looked very different as a callow youth. At dinner on the first night you arrived, I knew I had seen you before, but couldn't remember where. It's taken me far too long to put the pieces together, far too long."

"I know what you did to Di Grizov," Dante said, disgust in his voice. "I was with him when he died, cursing your name. He's the reason I came here, to avenge his death and to stop you completing this new weapon for the Tsar."

Fabergé began laughing, merely a chuckle at first, then a full-throated roar of hilarity, throwing his head back. "How wonderful! And what a roaring success you've made of that mission! Really, Nikolai, you are priceless."

"Stop calling me Nikolai," Dante warned. "We aren't friends and we aren't lovers. You don't know me, so don't pretend that you do."

"And who's going to stop me, Nikolai? You?"

"Remember this, Fabergé: I'll be there when you die screaming. That egg puts a curse on anyone who touches it and you'll be next to suffer."

The doctor put down the egg and began applauding. "Bravo! Your machismo is almost as admirable as it is pointless. I do hope the Tsar will let me dissect your corpse once he's finished killing you."

Dante cursed Fabergé, who picked up his prized objet d'art and strolled towards the door, still smiling. "Goodbye, Nikolai. One of the twins will be back in a few hours to inject you with a fresh dose of suppressant. We don't want the troublesome Crest helping you make an escape bid, do we?" Fabergé left the laboratory, still chuckling to himself, the door sliding closed behind him.

Dante strained against the restraints binding his arms, but they were too strong for him to break unaided. There must be a way out of here, he thought, there must be. Bojemoi, I trained with the best escapologist in the Vorovskoi Mir, I should be able to–

A broad smile spread across Dante's face as he looked at the scalpel still resting on his bloody chest.

Natalia had given up calling for help. Nobody was coming to rescue her, she knew that. If Doctor Fabergé knew about Dante, he was probably dead already and none of the other pupils would question explanations about her absence. They were products of their upbringing, trained from birth to follow orders, to do what they were told, to conform. If only I'd done the same, she thought ruefully, I wouldn't be waiting to drown in here.

The tide had long since bubbled through the metal grille in the floor and was inching its way up the walls. She was standing in the corner, the cold seawater already lapping around her knees. The chain restraining her movement did not even have enough slack for Natalia to reach the wooden door. She was trapped on the far side of the stone chamber, shivering from the cold. I should just lie down and accept my fate, let the waters wash over me, she thought, but I can't. I have to stay alive as long as possible, even if it is hopeless. I have to give myself every chance.

Dante pushed his chest upwards, arching his spine. This pulled apart the slice on his skin, sending stabs of pain through him, but also dislodged the scalpel from its position. The sliver of metal slid down his chest towards his throat, point first. Time this wrong and he would get a scalpel in his neck. As the blade moved closer Dante shoved his chin down into his chest and opened his mouth. The scalpel picked up speed as it slid, hurrying towards his face.

"Got it!" he hissed after catching the handle between his teeth. Dante twisted his head sideways and passed the scalpel into the grasping fingers of his right hand. They nimbly rotated it so the tip of the blade was facing the locking mechanism that clamped his wrists to the table. Now for the tricky part: picking the lock without knowing anything about its style or manufacture.

Twelve minutes later Fabergé returned to his laboratory, still carrying the Steel Military Egg. He breezed inside, not bothering to seal the door behind himself. "Sorry to bother you again so soon," the doctor said cheerfully, "but I seem to have misplaced my scalpel. And since this was the last place I used it…" His voice trailed off as he noticed the empty examination table, a pool of blood and open clamps telling an eloquent tale.

"Is this what you're looking for?" Dante asked.

A right hook sent Fabergé sprawling. Moments later Dante was on top of the doctor, punching him repeatedly in the face, pummelling him with blow after blow until Fabergé stopped fighting back.

Satisfied the doctor was unconscious, Dante produced the razor-sharp blade so recently used on himself. He kneeled on Fabergé's right forearm and began hacking at the wrist with the scalpel, slicing through skin and flesh, tendon and bone. It was a messy job, with blood spurting from the lacerated limb. Towards the end of the operation Fabergé came to and began screaming for help. Dante rammed his spare knee down on the doctor's throat, threatening to crush the windpipe. "Keep quiet or it won't just be your hand I cut off!" Eventually he succeeded in severing the hand completely, holding it up in the air to admire his efforts.

"Now I can get through any lock or door in this castle," Dante said with grim satisfaction.

"What about me?" Fabergé whimpered, his eyes fixed on the bloody stump where his hand used to be.

"I haven't finished with you yet," Dante replied, a wicked glint in his eye. "Where's Natalia, you bastard?"

The stone chamber was almost completely flooded, only an inch of air remaining below the ceiling. Natalia had let the chill waters float her to the top, treading water despite the chain restricting her movements. It couldn't be long before the tide stole away the last pocket of air and then she would be left holding her breath, hoping and praying. She wished she'd paid more attention during mass on Palm Sunday, maybe there were some words of solace read out that might have been a comfort. But she hadn't planned on drowning less than a week later. I'm only seventeen, I was supposed to have my whole life ahead of me, she thought.

Natalia felt another surge of water rising past her feet, towards the ceiling. She took a final, desperate gulp of air before it was all gone, then let herself drift downwards again. How could she hold her breath for? Thirty seconds? A minute, at most. Not much time, not nearly enough.

Suddenly a dull thudding sounded through the water. Someone was banging on the door outside. Or maybe I'm just imagining it, Natalia thought? She'd read that drowning people who were revived often recalled vivid hallucinations. Maybe the sound was one of those, just an oxygen-starved brain taunting her with a final hope.

Dante slammed his fists helplessly against the door, but the thick wooden beams resisted him. "Natalia? Natalia, can you hear me? Hold on!" Water was pouring out through the ancient lock. Fabergé's severed hand had opened every door between the laboratory and this place, but it could not undo the final barrier. The scalpel, he remembered, I've still got the scalpel. He retrieved the blade from a pocket and stabbed it into the old lock, carefully pushing the tumblers aside one by one. After a final click the lock was undone and Dante began pushing the door, fighting against the weight of water pressing back from within. But once the door had opened more than a crack, the sea found a new space and began rushing outwards.

Dante shoved and shoved against the door, stumbling forwards into the chamber. It was still half-filled with water but that was draining out rapidly now. A forlorn female figure floated face down in the cold liquid, the material of a patient's gown billowing out around her. "Natalia!" Dante cried in anguish.

He rushed to her side and tipped the girl's body over, lifting her out of the water. She appeared lifeless, her skin cold and lips blue, eyes staring sightlessly past him. Dante slapped her face once, twice, but got no response. "No, no, you can't die," he insisted. "Not like this!" Dante dropped into a crouch in the receding water, resting Natalia across his knee. He bent forwards to listen for signs of breathing, but there were none. Dante pinched her nose shut and pressed his mouth over hers, blowing hot air into her lungs. "Come on, breathe! Don't give up on me now. Breathe!"

But there was no response. Natalia was dead.

THIRTEEN

"When the time comes, all will go to their grave"
– Russian proverb

Dante cradled Natalia's body in his arms, rocking her slowly, not caring about the tears on his face or the seawater stinging his chest wound. "I could have saved you if Fabergé hadn't deactivated the Crest," he whispered. "You didn't have to die today, not like this." Then words failed him, leaving him alone with his grief. Another person was dead because of Doctor Fabergé and his insane ambition, another murder to be avenged.

"Nikolai? Are you down here?"

Dante recognised the voice. He wiped his face dry and laid Natalia's body on the cold, wet floor. "I'm in here," he called.

Spatchcock appeared in the doorway, holding a severed hand. "I figured you must be. This looked like something you'd…" His voice trailed away as he saw Natalia's corpse. "What happened?"

"Fabergé had her drowned. I wasn't fast enough to save Natalia, but I can make her murderer pay. I can stop Fabergé's experiment."

"What do you need us to do?"

"Get the other students off the island. I doubt Wartski will let you take the shuttle–"

"We'll convince her," Spatchcock said, a sly grin on his face.

"Try to get the teachers on board too. None of them are involved, except the twins and Wartski."

"Got it. What will you be doing?"

"Stopping this madness, once and for all," Dante vowed. The sound of a siren cut through the air, its wailing echoing along the castle corridors. "I guess Storm and Tempest have found their mentor."

Spatchcock looked at the severed hand he was clutching. "So this is...?"

"A useful way of getting through security doors. Take it with you and go!"

Near the kitchen Scullion was helping Flintlock back out of the drain, where he had been hiding from Wartski. "Are you sure it's safe?"

"Yes, yes," the alien replied, using one of her tentacles to drag him onto the floor. "She was summoned to the north tower, some emergency up there." The wailing of security sirens cut off her voice.

"I decided the twins could deal with that problem," Wartski announced. The massive matron was blocking the only door out of the drainage room, a meat cleaver held in one of her fists. "You'll suffer for hiding this one from me," she promised the cook. "I have plans for Lord Flintlock."

"How do you know my name?" he quailed.

"I know all about you and your master," Wartski sneered. "The Tsar will pay handsomely for the head of Nikolai Dante. But you and Spatchcock – you have no value, except as sport."

"I won't let you touch Spatch," Scullion warned. "He's mine!"

"Don't tell me you're getting attached to the little guttersnipe? Does the appalling odour he gives off excite you that much, freak?"

Scullion pushed Flintlock to one side and threw herself at Wartski, tentacles coiling around the matron's bulky body. Wartski fought back, hacking at Scullion with the meat cleaver. Green blood flew through the air, spattering Flintlock's face. "I say!" he spluttered unhappily.

"Flintlock, over here!" Spatchcock was in the doorway, waving with Fabergé's severed hand for Flintlock to join him. Meanwhile Scullion and Wartski's brawl continued, the two fighting females staggering about the room, battering each other with all their might.

The alien was retreating towards the open drain, Wartski advancing on her rapidly. At the last moment Scullion side-stepped the charging woman, leaving a tentacle behind to trip her up. Wartski tumbled forwards into the hole; face first, screaming in rage. "No! Nooooooo!"

The cry was abruptly cut off when her vast torso became wedged in the circular hole, half in and half out, legs kicking helplessly in the air. Flintlock delivering a kick to her copious buttocks. Wartski howled with rage but remained stuck fast. The former aristocrat savoured the ugly spectacle. "You know what that's called where I come from? Toad in the hole."

But Spatchcock wasn't there to appreciate the joke, having helped Scullion out into the kitchen. He was trying to bandage her wounds, deep slices cut into many of her tentacles, green slime pulsing from the injuries. Flintlock joined them, still enjoying the sounds of Wartski's furious screams. "If the tide keeps rising, so will the levels inside the main sewerage pipe. With any luck that vile woman will drown in effluent."

"Forget about Wartski," Spatchcock urged. "Dante asked me to evacuate the teachers and pupils. He's tackling Doctor Fabergé and the twins by himself, and doesn't want anyone else caught in the crossfire. I'll help Scullion out to the shuttle. Can you fetch the others?"

Flintlock did not look convinced. "What happens if I run into Storm or Tempest? They'll tear me to pieces!"

Spatchcock slapped Flintlock across the face. "Show some backbone for once in your life!"

Dante was surprised to find all the north tower's security systems had been switched off. No doubt the Crest would have warned him to be careful, suggesting it was all part of an obvious trap. Well, so be it. Dante stepped into the lift shaft and let it raise him to the top level. Even there he could see no obvious danger or threats. The frosted glass door to the laboratory stood open, the sound of something dripping audible from inside.

"Please, do come in," a voice beckoned. "I have a surprise for you."

Dante moved cautiously to the door and peered inside. Doctor Fabergé was sitting on the examination table, a strip of leather tightly fastened above the stump on his right arm. Blood was still seeping slowly from the wound, falling into a crimson pool on the metal table beside him. "You needn't worry, I'm quite unarmed." The doctor smiled bleakly at his own pun.

"What's the surprise?" Dante asked, venturing carefully into the laboratory after checking there was nobody hiding in wait for him.

Fabergé gestured at the Steel Military Egg atop a nearby workbench. "When my namesake designed his Easter Eggs, he concealed a surprise within each one. I have done the same with my genetically engineered eggs."

"I've already seen your presentation," Dante replied.

"But did you stop to think why I called this project the Strangelove Gambit? My daughters, Storm and Tempest, were the first successful attempt at this procedure. I have waited more than a decade for the right moment to trigger their transformation." Fabergé spared a glance for his wounded arm. "I think this is the perfect moment, don't you? Girls, why don't you come out and show Dante exactly what you can do."

The twins emerged from behind a workbench, holding each other's hands. They were naked, their statuesque bodies glistening with sweat.

"I've already seen how these two spend their spare time," Dante said.

"This is not about sex, you fool!" Fabergé spat. "This is about life and death – your life and death, to be precise." He turned to the twins and nodded. "Activate the Strangelove Gambit!"

Dante took a step backwards, towards the door. He had no weapons, no Crest and no plan. The hunger for vengeance had driven him to this moment, but now it had arrived he was ill prepared. The Strangelove twins began striding towards him, their eyes glowing angrily. "Fuoco," Dante whispered.

For all her life Tempest felt like she was holding something back, never being true to herself. Childhood had been a blur of memories, growing up with her sister and Doctor Fabergé, blossoming into a woman. Even when she and Storm were allowed to make their public debut at the Imperial Games, their father had forbidden them from revealing more than a fraction of what they could do. Afterwards it was back to the island, back to a life of containment and waiting and stifling claustrophobia. Deep within her there was something squirming and twisting, fighting to break free – no, to escape.

When the doctor gave the command to activate, Tempest's reaction was purely instinctive. She reached down inside herself and let go, let the creature within take hold. It was an orgasmic release, flooding outwards through her body, searing the fingertips and extremities, exploding from the inside out. She shuddered with relief as the last boundaries were broken. The waiting was over. She was becoming her true self at last.

The twins began to glow, their skin radiating pure light. Within seconds Dante could not look directly at them, such was the brilliance of the light. He continued backing away, hands in front of his face to stop himself being blinded. Even then, he could still see the outline of what was happening to the twins.

Tempest and Storm were changing, mutating, their bodies convulsing and warping. As the process accelerated the twins begin screaming, pain and ecstasy given voice, the sound searing into Dante's brain until blood was dripping from both his ears. Stumbling backwards, he found the doorway and retreated through it, unable to tear his gaze from the blazing light in the laboratory.

The twins' screaming grew louder still, its pitch rising note by note until finally passing beyond human hearing. Light flooded the corridor outside the laboratory as Dante flung himself into the lift shaft. It pulled him down towards the basement. As he descended, Dante saw an explosion of light and sound at the top level. Then there was nothing but the air whistling past Dante as he descended.

"WE'RE COMING TO GET YOU," a metallic voice whispered.

"WE'RE COMING TO TEAR YOU APART," another voice echoed.

"RUN, DANTE! RUN, NIKOLAI."

"RUN AS FAST AS YOU CAN!"

"IT WON'T BE FAST ENOUGH."

"YOU CAN NEVER ESCAPE THE FURIES!"

Dante gave one last glance upwards before stepping out of the shaft. Something was moving above him, sleek and silver. Tempest and Storm were coming for him, but what had they become?

Helga was woken by the sound of screaming. She sat up in her dormitory bed, the other students sharing her confusion. "What's happening?" Helga asked Carmen, who was looking out of a window to the north tower.

"I don't know," the Andorran woman admitted. "I was dreaming and then there was some sort of explosion in Doctor Fabergé's laboratory."

"You have to get out of here!" shouted a male voice. Helga pulled the bedclothes up to cover herself as a blond-haired man ran into the dormitory. "You have to evacuate the island," he yelled, gesticulating wildly at the students.

"Why?" Carmen demanded. "What's happening? I saw an explosion–"

"It isn't safe!" the intruder shouted. "Dante said we have to get everyone out while there's still time!"

"Dante?" Helga asked. "Nikolai Dante?" Everyone had heard of him, even if few knew what he looked like. The images taken of him during the war showed a bitter-faced man with a shaven head and angry features.

"I mean Mr Durward," the man said, correcting himself. "Mr Durward is evacuating everyone from the island."

"Mr Durward is Nikolai Dante?" Carmen asked, a sly smile of satisfaction spreading across her face.

The blond man rolled his eyes. "We haven't got time for this," he snapped. "I have to get you out."

Another explosion shook the castle, this time echoing upwards from below. The students screamed in terror, all trace of sleep purged from their systems. Flintlock was almost crushed underfoot as the eleven women stampeded for the doorway.

"Everybody, make for the shuttle!" he shouted after them.

Dante was retreating to the kitchen in the hope of finding a weapon, any weapon. He looked back and glimpsed a blur of silver approaching. The shape threw a fist-sized ball of fire towards him. Dante hurled himself sideways and it flashed past, exploding against the end of the corridor. Electrical energy sparked outwards from the blast, tendrils of high voltage stabbing into everything within twenty feet. Dante was caught in the periphery of this, the shock jolting through his body.

Once the detonation had begun to recede, he continued running, knowing the kitchen was just round the corner. Where the fireball had struck was now a void, a circular hole larger than Dante in the castle floor and walls. Fabergé had been right, the bio-weaponry wielded by the twins made the Romanov Crest look like a child's plaything. I don't even have the Crest to help me, Dante thought ruefully. How long before the suppressant drug wears off, minutes or hours? If it was only minutes, he might have a chance. Otherwise...

A rumbling, scorching noise was rapidly advancing towards Dante as he ran. A glance over his shoulder confirmed the worst. Another of the fireballs was accelerating towards him. He raced into the kitchen, flung the door shut and dived for cover.

Another explosion detonated inside the castle, shaking stone dust from the ceilings. Flintlock was almost grateful to hear the sounds of nearby battle again, as it made convincing the fearful female teachers to flee much easier. He grabbed one of them by the arm as she passed, a hatchet-faced woman with far too many hairs above her top lip. "Is there anybody else left?" Flintlock shouted.

"Professor Mould," Ms Zemlya replied before tearing herself free. "He's in the last room on the left!"

Flintlock hurried to Mould's quarters and barged through the door. But the ancient tutor was already dead, his face twisted in an image of pain and anguish. "Poor chap," Flintlock muttered. "Must have died in his sleep."

A tiny movement in one corner caught his eye. A toad emerged from the shadows, its colouring and shape all too familiar for Flintlock. He looked at Mould again, the horror in the dead man's eyes, the telltale signs of a struggle. No, the professor hadn't died in his sleep. He hadn't been that fortunate.

"Poor sod," Flintlock said and fled from the room.

When the second fireball had finished exploding, Dante risked a glance at what remained of the kitchen doorway. A massive circular hole had been created in its place, the door and surrounding stonework vaporised. Two figures were standing in the space created by the blast, holding hands. They were the same size and shape as the Strangelove Twins, but there the resemblance ended.

Both were encased in what looked like living metal, shimmering with crazed reflections of their surroundings. Blank, featureless surfaces remained where once there had been faces. Each was missing a hand. Instead, the left figure had an arm that ended in a ball of fire, while the right one had a crystalline gauntlet. Ahead of them the kitchen table lay on its side, tipped over to provide cover.

The fire-fisted creature looked at its mate. "SHALL I?" it asked, the metallic voice still recognisable as that of Tempest.

"LET ME," Storm replied, her voice also warped by their transfiguration. She pointed her gauntlet and a ball of ice shot forwards, engulfing the wooden table and freezing it. Storm stepped closer and kicked at the object, shattering the table into thousands of tiny, frozen fragments.

Dante watched from his hiding place in the drainage room. He retreated further into the shadows, almost tumbling backwards into the main sewer. "Bojemoi, who left this open?" he muttered, before silently cursing himself. Maybe the Furies hadn't heard him, maybe his hiding place was still safe.

"WE KNOW YOU'RE IN THERE," Storm snarled. "NOW COME OUT AND FACE YOUR DEATH LIKE A MAN, DANTE."

The fugitive smiled ruefully. So much for playing hide and seek.

Spatchcock was helping Scullion towards the shuttle where the screaming students emerged from the castle, running for their lives. "Flintlock's done his job," the little man observed, straining to keep the badly wounded cook from falling. "Scullion, who normally flies the shuttle?"

"There's a pilot," she replied weakly, "but this is his day off."

"Wonderful." By now the students were running past them, towards the shuttle. The fleeing teachers were also spilling from the castle entrance, searching for a means of escape. "The shuttle! Everybody make for the shuttle," Spatchcock shouted.

"But how...?" Scullion asked.

"Worst comes to worst, Flintlock can get us off this rock. He flew a Sea-Hawk during the war – not very well, but it's better than nothing."

"Only one problem with that idea," the alien said. "Where's Flintlock?"

Spatchcock searched the faces of those outside the castle. "I hope he hasn't gone back to the kitchen looking for us."

"Spatch? Scullion? Are you still down here?" Flintlock strode towards the kitchen. He stopped short of the entrance, startled to find there was no doorway – just a void where it had been. Flintlock walked through the hole into the kitchen, careful not to touch anything with his hands. Sparks of electricity still danced in the air. "What the blazes happened here?"

"WE DID," an ominous voice replied. Two menacing silver creatures emerged from the drainage room to confront the new arrival. "WHERE IS HE?"

"W-where's who?" Flintlock stammered, backing away from them.

"OUR QUARRY."

"OUR PREY."

"NIKOLAI."

"DANTE."

"Looking for me, by any chance?" Dante appeared from behind Flintlock, his face and clothing smeared with sewerage. He dragged the terrified Flintlock away from the advancing Furies by the collar. The two men fled from the kitchen, out onto the external walkway.

"W-where did you come from?" Flintlock gasped.

"Crawled along the drain beneath the kitchen – not elegant, but effective. The Furies need to recharge their weapons between each discharge, that gave me enough time to rescue you. But they'll be–"

Dante! Evasive action!

"Get down!" Dante shouted, throwing himself and Flintlock down on the metal walkway. A frozen blast chilled their backs as it passed overhead, slamming into the far wall of the castle. "Crest – I can hear you again!"

A massive increase in adrenaline levels accelerated your recovery from the suppressant, it replied. *Just in time too, judging by your precarious–*

"Enough pontificating," Dante hissed. "Just find us a way out of here!"

What will you be doing?

Bio-circuitry surged from the ends of Dante's hands, forming itself into two razor-sharp blades. "Turning the tables."

Storm emerged onto the walkway, expecting to see the frozen remains of Dante and Flintlock floating in the water below. But the blond man was alone, standing nervously in the centre of the walkway. "Hello," he said. "Sorry to disappoint you, but I'm still alive."

"NOT FOR LONG," Storm snarled, raising her weapon to fire again.

Dante jumped from his hiding place above the doorway, both bio-blades slicing through her weapon arm. Storm howled in agony, the severed limb spurting metallic liquid into the air.

"Like father, like daughter," Dante quipped.

"YOU! YOU WILL PAY FOR–"

"Yeah, yeah," he replied, bio-blades flashing through the air. One of them cut through Storm's neck, removing her head. The other severed a leg, causing the body to topple sideways so it fell into the water. "Tell it to your relatives!"

• • •

Tempest felt her twin sister's death as if it were her own, the shock too much for her to absorb without warning. She sank to her knees in the kitchen, a chilling numbness spreading through her, dulling the fire in her soul. Storm couldn't be dead, she couldn't be.

Flintlock watched in horror as Storm's torso was torn apart by the creatures guarding the sea around Fabergé Island. Dante used a boot to nudge the dead twin's head and severed leg over the side of the walkway. The face bobbed briefly in the water before it too disappeared, swallowed by hungry mouths. "One down, one to go," Dante said grimly.

Dante, the shock of her sister's death has debilitated Tempest, but I doubt the effect will last for long, the Crest said. *You should attack her now.*

"No," he replied. "The twins were Fabergé's victims, as much as Jim and Natalia. It's the doctor who deserves a taste of his own medicine."

"What about me?" Flintlock asked.

"Get to the shuttle," Dante commanded, already running towards the kitchen doorway. "Fly everyone off the island."

Doctor Fabergé fumed in his laboratory. What was taking them so long? The twins should have despatched Dante by now. He was an inferior being, not worthy of consideration. Even his bond with the Crest was weak, because Dante only had half the Romanov family genes. The fugitive should have been an easy target for Tempest and Storm's first hunt.

Fabergé examined the stump where his hand had been with clinical detachment. The twins would have to assist him implanting the altered eggs back into the pupils, otherwise the process would not be finished before the Tsar's arrival. After that I'll create another hand for myself, the doctor decided, using growth-accelerants to clone a replacement. Shouldn't take more than a few days.

He reached across to the Steel Military Egg and stroked his remaining hand lovingly across its surface. So much he had sacrificed for this beautiful object. Now he would never be parted from the egg again. Ideally, Fabergé would have preferred to kill Dante himself. But the thief was useful sport for the twins. The doctor frowned. What was keeping them?

Another face appeared beside his own reflection in the egg, a man's face. Fabergé slowly turned to find Dante holding a bio-blade at his throat. "Not dead yet?" the doctor asked. "How regrettable."

"I beg to differ," Dante replied. "Your elite class has escaped, the castle is in ruins and one of your precious twins is dead. The experiment is over, doctor. The Strangelove Gambit is a failure."

"Never," Fabergé snapped. "You could never beat one of my creations!"

"A god would never create something fallible, is that it?"

"You are inferior, no match for my beautiful twins."

"One of your beautiful twins is providing a snack for several of your other creations in the sea. They were eating her face, last time I looked."

Dante, be careful! Tempest is approaching from behind Fabergé.

"I don't believe you," the doctor maintained.

"Don't you?" Dante asked. "The twins, they were just guinea pigs, weren't they? A laboratory experiment that succeeded, against your expectations."

"What of it?" Fabergé replied. "They were the first, a happy accident that showed me the way. The next generation is a vast improvement upon them."

"Every child wants to be loved by their parents, don't they?"

Fabergé shook his head. "Those freaks aren't my daughters, they were experiments. Nothing more, nothing less."

"HOW CAN YOU SAY THAT?" Tempest demanded. She had walked silently into the room, observing Dante and her father. "STORM IS DEAD! YOU SHOULD BE MOURNING HER!"

Fabergé whirled round, shocked at her appearance. "If you were truly my daughter, you would have killed Dante by now! He is your inferior – destroy him! Prove yourself to me! Prove yourself worthy of the name Fabergé!"

Tempest looked at Dante, hatred burning in her eyes.

Flintlock ran out of the castle towards the shuttle, where the evacuees where gathered. "Quick, everybody on board! Dante says we've got to get away!"

"Only one problem," Spatchcock whispered when Flintlock reached him. "Somebody else got here before us." He jerked a thumb towards the shuttle door, where a familiar figure sat clutching a pulse pistol.

"Who wants to die first?" Madame Wartski asked.

"I will," Scullion replied, attacking the matron from behind.

Dante backed away from Tempest, bio-blades held up to defend himself from the coming attack. "You heard what he said about you and Storm! He called you freaks, experiments!"

"MAYBE WE ARE," Tempest snarled, the fireball weapon at her wrist growing hotter by the moment.

"Destroy the weakling!" Fabergé shouted. "Embrace your destiny! Show him the power of the Strangelove Gambit!"

Tempest loomed over Dante, her hand drawn back, ready to strike – but she hesitated. "What are you waiting for?" her creator bellowed. "Finish him! Or are you as pathetic as your twin sister?"

The silver creature spun round to face Fabergé. "WHAT DID YOU SAY?"

"I ordered you to kill Dante!"

"WHY SHOULD I TAKE ORDERS FROM YOU?" Tempest asked. "IF ANYONE IS A WEAKLING, IT'S YOU, FATHER. IF ANYONE HERE IS INFERIOR, IT'S YOU – NOT HIM."

"What are you talking about?" Fabergé spluttered. "Do as I say!"

"I DON'T HAVE TO FOLLOW YOUR ORDERS ANYMORE," Tempest replied. "I'VE EVOLVED INTO WHAT YOU ALWAYS WANTED ME TO BE."

"You *must* obey me," he maintained. "I am your father, your creator!"

"BUT STORM AND I WEREN'T YOUR DAUGHTERS. WE WERE JUST FREAKS, EXPERIMENTS GONE RIGHT."

"You misunderstood what I was saying!"

"I UNDERSTOOD YOU PERFECTLY." Tempest drew back her arm, ready to strike. "I'LL GIVE YOU A CHOICE, FATHER. I CAN DESTROY YOU OR I CAN DESTROY YOUR PRECIOUS EGG."

"What?"

Tempest pointed her weapon at the Steel Military Egg. "YOU LOVED THAT MORE THAN YOU EVER LOVED STORM AND ME."

"But–"

"LEAVE NOW AND I'LL LET YOU LIVE – BUT THE EGG STAYS HERE. TRY TO TAKE IT WITH YOU AND I WON'T BE RESPONSIBLE FOR THE CONSEQUENCES."

"I'd do what she says," Dante suggested.

The doctor glared across the laboratory at him, then turned to leave. At the last moment he lunged past Tempest and grabbed the egg. "You won't kill me," he maintained. "I'm your father. I can make you a god like me, giving and taking life as you see fit–"

"YOU ALREADY HAVE," she replied sadly, and fired.

Spatchcock watched as Scullion and Wartski fought each other, grappling for control of the pulse pistol as they rolled across the landing pad. The alien cook had clamped tentacles across the matron's face, stifling her breathing. Wartski's movements grew jerkier and more desperate as the life was crushed from her lungs. There was a last feeble spasm, accompanied by the muffled sound of a weapon firing – then neither of them moved again.

Spatchcock ran to Scullion's side, rolling her away from the matron's corpse. "Scullion? Scullion, talk to me, say something!"

The alien cook opened her single eye and looked at him sadly. "You'll make an Arcnevan a fine husband some day," she said. Her tentacles sagged to the ground as the last breath escaped her lungs.

Dante approached Tempest, who stood over the remains of her creator. "You did the right thing," he said. "I know it wasn't easy, but you did the right thing."

Be careful, the Crest warned. *There's no knowing what she will do now.*

"GET OUT OF HERE WHILE YOU STILL CAN," Tempest said. "YOU DIDN'T KILL ME WHEN YOU COULD HAVE DONE, SO I'M GIVING YOU A CHANCE."

"What are you doing to do?"

"DESTROY THIS PLACE – THE LABORATORY, THE EGGS, ALL OF HIS NOTES. THESE EXPERIMENTS CAN NEVER BE REPEATED."

"And what about you?"

"I SAID GO!"

She's preparing to fire her weapon again. I'd do as she suggests.

Dante paused at the doorway. "Goodbye, Tempest. And... thank you."

Spatchcock was still with Scullion when Flintlock leaned out of the pilot's window. "Spatch, get into the shuttle! Everyone else is on board, we have to go. There's nothing more you can do for her."

"I know," he replied.

Dante emerged from the castle entrance, running as if his life depended upon it. "What are you still doing here?" he shouted. "I told you to get everyone away from this place!"

Spatchcock stood up. "We were just... saying goodbye."

Dante checked his stride as he saw the bodies of Scullion and Wartski. "Are they both...?" Spatchcock nodded. "Then we'll have to leave them here, like Natalia. There isn't time for two trips. Now, come on!" Dante bundled Spatchcock into the crowded shuttle. "Flintlock, take off! Now!"

The shuttle rose creakily into the air, a warning alarm sounding in the cockpit. "We're overloaded," Flintlock shouted. "I can't get any more elevation!"

"Just fly towards the mainland," Dante yelled back. "Skim the top of the waves if you have to, but get us gone!"

The shuttle banked slowly to the left and chugged over the water. A white light ballooned outwards from the north tower, rapidly spreading to engulf the castle and then the entire island. A sonic boom of noise flashed past the shuttle, jerking it forwards through the air.

Dante looked back at what was left. "Crest?"

No signs of life, it replied. *Tempest destroyed everything.*

"Then it's over."

EPILOGUE

"Where there's a beginning, there's an end"
– Russian proverb

The Imperial Palace reached the Black Sea before dawn on Easter Sunday. There had been no contact from Fabergé Island for several days but this was not unusual as the doctor preferred the institute to keep itself to itself. The Tsar was ill-prepared for what he saw when emerging onto his viewing platform at dawn. Instead of a welcoming party standing outside the castle, the island was little more than a smoking crater. Its outer edges remained, but the ground where the castle had stood was gone, utterly destroyed.

A team of Raven Corps flyers was sent down to investigate the ruins while the Tsar raged through his palace. He stormed into his daughter's bedchamber, throwing aside Jena's ladies-in-waiting to confront her. "Who did you tell, daughter? Who?"

"What are you talking about, father?"

"We are above Fabergé Island – what little remains of it. The castle was destroyed by enemy action."

Jena pulled her sheets closer. "And what has that to do with me?"

The Tsar stalked around the side of the bed, moving closer to his daughter. "Only a handful of people knew about today's event. Even fewer knew what Fabergé was doing on that island – you amongst them."

She looked directly into her father's eyes. "I would never betray you," she said, no trace of fear in her voice. "You know I am utterly loyal to the House of Makarov, just as you know I would never dare reveal our secrets."

The Tsar glared at her for fully thirty seconds, searching for any trace of duplicity, before turning away furiously. "Then who...?"

Jena let herself breathe again. "Perhaps there was no enemy attack. You said it yourself, Fabergé had a rampaging ego and questionable loyalty. Either he over-reached, destroying himself and the castle in the process..."

"Or?"

"Or he created the explosion to conceal his treachery."

The Tsar reflected on both of these suggestions until a knock on the door of Jena's bedchamber. "Come!" A member of the Raven Corps entered, gave a note to the Tsar and then hastily departed. Vladimir read the note, his face growing redder by the moment, before crumpling the piece of paper in his fist. "It seems most of the pupils and teachers got out just before the island exploded, thanks to the efforts of one man."

"Who was this man?" Jena asked. But her father strode from the room without answering, leaving the crumpled note on the floor. Jena bent forwards to pick it up, smoothing out the paper on her bed. The final two words caught her eye: Nikolai Dante. "He has his uses, after all," she whispered.

At the bar of Famous Flora's, Dante was sharing a bottle of Imperial Blue with Spatchcock and Flintlock. "We did what we set out to do," the exiled aristocrat offered, his words slurring together. "We stopped the Fabergé experiments, all the genetically engineered eggs were destroyed and the girls are returning to their families, safe and sound."

"Not all of them," Dante replied darkly. "Natalia can never go home."

"Nor can Scullion," Spatchcock said.

Nor can Di Grizov, the Crest added.

Flintlock tipped the last of the vodka into their glasses. "I want to propose a toast, for all those who died – their sacrifice was not in vain."

"You know, we never saw if Tempest died," Spatchcock observed.

"True," Flintlock agreed, downing the contents of his glass. "But she couldn't have survived that blast... could she?"

Dante pushed his drink away. "I've got to go," he muttered.

"Where?" Spatchcock asked.

"To find a church," he replied. "I want to light a candle for Natalia. She deserves to be remembered in a better way than this." Dante staggered away from his companions.

"Will we see you later?"

"I don't know," Dante admitted. "I just don't know."

IMPERIAL
BLACK

PROLOGUE

"The hero does not think of death in battle, but of victory."

– Russian proverb

"2070 AD: The Siege of the Winter Palace and the Battle of Rudinshtein were the final conflicts of the war between Tsar Vladimir Makarov and the House of Romanov. A war begun by a murder ended in atrocities and genocide. Even now, many years later, a visit to either location evokes the horror and suffering endured. You can almost hear the screams, see the clash of troops and smell the blood in the air. After the war, the Winter Palace was left in its ruined state; a mute testament of what happens to all who dare challenge the Tsar's rule, and as lifeless as the nearby Romanov Necropolis. Rudinshtein was not so fortunate.

After the war's momentum had abruptly switched to the Imperial forces, the Romanovs regrouped in Rudinshtein before retreating to their Winter Palace. Only two members of that noble dynasty stayed behind to defend the poorest city in the empire – Andreas Romanov and his illegitimate half-brother, Nikolai Dante. Four years earlier, Dante had rescued Rudinshtein from subjugation and its people proclaimed him a hero. But heroes are not enough against the Imperial Army.

The Tsar's second-in-command, Count Pyre, directed the Battle of Rudinshtein. The 33rd Imperial Artillery Division initiated a relentless bombardment that all but demolished Rudinshtein's ramshackle defences within an hour. In the aftermath of the war, Vladimir the Conqueror denied responsibility for the city's destruction. Tsarist officials claimed it was Pyre's vendetta against Dante – who had killed the count's lover five years earlier – that accounted for the acts of genocide that blackened the Imperial victory. Certainly, it was Pyre who denied the surviving civilians safe passage from the city, but it was General Ivanov who prosecuted that order.

Vassily Ivanov, a brilliant warrior of unequalled savagery, led the Imperial Black, a regiment whose mere mention was enough to void the bowels of most foes. Officially, his thousand-strong force took its name from the jet-black uniform that was proudly worn by the regiment's soldiers. But most believed the sinister sobriquet had been inspired by the horrific conduct of the murderers and rapists that filled the Imperial Black's ranks. The regiment was the hammer that crushed the life from Rudinshtein, both in battle and during the following three years.

Rudinshtein fell upon the third assault. A tide of blood flooded the city as Imperial forces surged forward, cutting a merciless swathe through decimated rebel ranks. A spirited final defence took place around the grounds of the governor's mansion, but even the Hero of Rudinshtein could not save the city he had once ruled.

On the last night of the battle, Dante walked among his men, sharing a final drink with those still alive from his rabble of conscripts known as the Rudinshtein Irregulars."

– Extract from *Tsar Wars*, by Georgi Lucassovich

. . .

Nikolai Dante sat in front of the ruins of the governor's mansion and, with two double vodkas inside him, thought about life and death.

Since the war began, he had killed more men than he could remember. The blood of hundreds, perhaps thousands of enemy soldiers was on his hands. He did not enjoy killing. It gave him no pleasure beyond knowing that the act preserved his own life. At the beginning of the conflict, Dante had entertained the notion that each Imperial soldier he slew brought him one step closer to killing the Tsar. Now he recognised just how fanciful that notion had been. Each death provided carrion for the crows that haunted battlefields across the empire, nothing more.

Around him, the civilians trapped in the ruins did their best to ignore the stench of rotting flesh and burned bodies. In a province all too familiar with poverty, the mansion had once been a building of rare grandeur. Now it was a bombed out wreck. The rubble was useful only as a hiding place for those who had not escaped the doomed land in time.

Tired hands clutched thin clothes around malnourished bodies. Faces smeared with soot and despair stared hopelessly past each other. Some civilians huddled round burning barrels of oil, which provided the sole illumination. Others tried to sleep, their slumbers made fitful by the pounding of Imperial artillery, a barrage so constant it had become merely a dull thudding at the back of each mind. Mothers sought to comfort children or nurse their babies. The few male civilians were cripples and geriatrics, those unfit to fight. Any able-bodied man had long since been sacrificed upon the altar of Romanov ambitions, sent to war against the Tsar, sent to fight and to die. Barring some miracle, their families would be joining them in the hereafter before the next dusk.

A few days ago these people had looked at Dante with hope, believing he would find some way to save them, however unlikely. He had done it before, could he perform another miracle? Their faces no longer registered his presence among them. Such a thin line separated life and death, Dante thought. Tomorrow, they expect to cross that line, he sighed, and so do I.

Rouble for your thoughts, a patrician voice asked inside Dante's mind.

"I'm surprised they're worth that much to you, Crest."

I was being generous, the voice replied archly. *Besides, it's hard to find exact change on a battlefield.*

Dante rolled his eyes. Being bonded with a Romanov Weapons Crest was not without advantages. The sentient battle computer was a repository of vast knowledge and wisdom, and it could access and override any computer in the empire. It massively enhanced Dante's natural healing abilities; and it enabled him to extrude cyborganic swords from his fists, providing formidable weapons in close quarter combat. But living with the Crest in his thoughts at every waking moment was akin to having a supercilious servant occupying your mind day and night – useful when you needed it, an almighty pain in the brain the rest of the time. "If you must know, I was wondering how drunk I have to get to shut you up."

Finish that bottle and you should find out. But I doubt even an inveterate drunkard like you wishes to die with a hangover.

"Good point," Dante conceded. "If I die tomorrow–"

Which seems the most likely outcome.

"If I die tomorrow," Dante persisted, "what happens to you? Do you die too?"

I will cease to function soon afterwards, if that's what you mean. We are symbiotically bonded, so my status is dependent upon yours. It is possible that a gifted surgeon, with the correct tools and expertise, could retrieve some of my mechanism from your corpse, but such talents are rarely found on a battlefield.

"So we die together."

I am a battle computer, Dante. I do not think in terms of life and death, but of success and failure.

"So if I died…"

That would be a failure. I am programmed to mould you into a potential emperor. However hopeless a task, that is my mission. If you perish before that happens, I have failed. I would experience regret, or its machine equivalent. So, if you could find some way to remain alive, that would be preferable.

"Thanks for the encouragement," Dante muttered sourly and swallowed another mouthful of bathtub vodka, the clear liquid searing its way down his throat. He threw the bottle into the darkness, but the expected smashing of glass never came. Instead, a stench like boiling cabbages and day-old pus fouled the air, assaulting Dante's senses and making his eyes water.

"You and the missus arguing again?"

Dante did not need to peer into the shadows to know who had spoken. The man's voice was a lecherous rasp, born of the sewer, raised in the gutter. Such gruff words and revolting smell could mean only one thing: Spatchcock was approaching. Sure enough, a hunched figure emerged from the darkness clutching Dante's discarded vodka bottle, his foul-smelling form clad in the soiled uniform of a Rudinshtein Irregular.

"The Crest might be bonded to me, but we aren't married," Dante replied.

"You argue like you are." Spatchcock drank gratefully from the bottle before offering it to his commanding officer. "Sure you don't want any more, captain?"

Dante shook his head. "It's all yours."

"Cheers." The lice-ridden conscript swallowed the last of the vodka before belching mightily. His face strained for a second, then an explosion of wet noise burst from between his buttocks. "Oh, that's better."

"Diavolo," Dante winced. "We could use your ass as a biological weapon against the Imperials."

"Bit late for that now," Spatchcock said with a shrug. He peered towards the enemy forces encircling the governor's mansion. "D'you think they'll attack again before dawn?"

"Probably not. They'll want to finish us off in daylight, savour the moment."

Spatchcock nodded grimly. He had been a prisoner in a Romanov gulag when the war began, incarcerated for being a pickpocket, poisoner, forger and an all-purpose purveyor of filth. Offered a choice between execution and fighting against the Tsar, he had chosen conscription. He was no soldier, but his murderous skills had been put to good use under Dante's unconventional command. Spatchcock jerked a thumb towards a case of Imperial champagne lying unopened on the ground. "You ready to inspect the men, captain?"

Dante sighed and nodded. Ever since the assault on St Petersburg, he had made a habit of walking among his troops on the eve of battle, sharing a drink and a few tall tales with them. It was his way of saluting their loyalty, a reward for following him to certain death. It would be the last time. Everyone knew that. The end was coming and it was dressed in an Imperial uniform.

Spatchcock threw the empty bottle back into the shadows and was rewarded with a dull thud and a cry of pain. "Oh, I say," an aristocratic voice protested. "You could have had my eye out."

Rai chewed on his fingernails, his teeth gnawing at the corners of each cuticle. It was a nervous, childhood habit that he'd never quite outgrown, despite repeated thrashings from his father. One day you will be this village's leader, the old man had raged – how can they respect anyone who still chews their nails? Since joining the Romanov forces, Rai had bitten his fingernails down to nothing and beyond. He liked to think his father might understand. When you lived on a constant knife-edge, you needed some way of relieving stress. Most of the other soldiers smoked or drank, or went with whores in the long moments of boredom between battles, anything to distract themselves from the inevitability of what lay ahead. Rai chewed his nails; as a vice, it was cheap and harmless. There was little in the war about which you could say the same.

He glanced at the others who were sprawled around him, dozing fitfully in the dark. Most were Russian or from the Balkans, a few came from further away. Like him, most had been released from an Imperial prison that was overrun by the Romanov forces in the early days of the conflict. Offered the chance to join what was the winning side at the time, they had eagerly volunteered. There was no hiding place from war. Besides, most of those in Rai's gulag had been political prisoners of the Tsar's regime, so it was a chance to put their principles into practice. Only a handful of those liberated from the prison remained.

"Deep in thought?"

Rai scrambled to his feet and snapped to attention when he realised who was approaching. "Captain Romanov. Sorry, I was just–"

"Relax, private, relax. This isn't an official inspection. And my name's Dante, not Romanov – not anymore."

Rai studied the face of his superior. The captain was perhaps thirty, but looked older in the light from a fire that was dying nearby. His black hair was cropped close to the skull, while a ragged beard and moustache masked much of his face. There was weariness about the captain's eyes, as if they had seen too much, witnessed more than anyone should.

"I don't understand," Rai admitted.

"I was born a Dante and I'll die a Dante," the captain replied. "Besides, most of my so-called noble family has left us here in the lurch. They can take their damn name with them." He called over his shoulder. "Flintlock, where are you?"

"Here, captain," a harassed voice replied in the cut-glass accent of a Britannia aristocrat. A tall, middle-aged figure with tousled, blond hair and a bruise that was forming under one eye, hurried into view carrying an armful of champagne bottles. He stopped and offered one to Dante. "Here you go."

"They're for the men, not for me," the captain hissed.

"Oh, rightio." Flintlock offered one of the bottles to Rai.

"No, thank you. I don't drink."

"Really? Oh well, all the more for the rest of us." Flintlock smiled and raised the bottle to his lips, but it was snatched from his grasp by the captain.

"You've had plenty already," Dante snarled. "Go help Spatch give out the remaining bottles to anyone who wants it. Soldier or civilian, I don't care which."

"But I-"

"Go!" A swift punt in Flintlock's posterior sent the protesting private away.

Dante smiled at Rai. "There's no need to stand at attention for me, you know. Sit down, relax and take it easy."

Dante sank to the ground, resting his back against the ruins of a stone wall.

"Yes, sir." Rai sat opposite him, resisting the urge to resume chewing his nails. He noticed the captain's fingers were just as careworn.

"What's your name?" Dante asked.

"Rai."

"Where did you join us? You don't look local."

"I'm from the Himalayas. My people live in the mountains, an area we call the roof of the world."

"That explains your appearance. We don't get many people with brown skin and Oriental eyes in Rudinshtein. You're a long way from home. Why?"

"I was arrested shortly before the war began, for protesting against Tsarist oppression in the Himalayas. For centuries one regime or another has been trying to lay claim to the mountains, hoping to exploit them and the native people – my people. I decided something had to be done about it."

"On your own?" Dante asked, a note of disbelief in his voice.

Rai nodded. "I thought I was being brave. My father thought it foolishness."

"You were both right."

"Perhaps." Rai could feel Dante's eyes examining him.

"So you were arrested and...?"

"Brought before the Tsar. I told him to desist any and all incursions into the Himalayas, or else he would suffer the consequences."

"Consequences?"

"My people believe that in the time of greatest peril, our living goddess the Mukari will strike down forces intent upon destroying us, our way of life."

"And you told the Tsar this?"

Rai grimaced. "Once he'd finished laughing, he marked me for execution as a political subversive. But then the war broke out and–"

"The Imperials decided to concentrate their fire upon Romanov forces."

"Yes. We were left to rot in prison, until your men found us."

Recognition crossed Dante's face. Rai could feel the captain staring at him, some inner calculation being made behind those piercing eyes. Finally, Dante spoke again, his voice a low whisper, his face grim and serious.

"Rai, I've been moving among the men tonight, talking to them one by one, looking for someone special. I think you could be that someone."

Rai shifted uncomfortably on the ground. He'd been afraid of this: first the bribe of alcohol, then the proposition. He hadn't expected it from the captain, who was reputed to be a womaniser of great enthusiasm, but war did strange things to men. "Captain, I'm flattered, of course, but I'm not really like that."

Dante gazed at Rai, bewilderment evident on his features. "Sorry?"

"No, I'm sorry, honestly I am. If I shared those sorts of feelings then I'd be more than happy to oblige you, but I don't. If you see what I mean."

"Rai, I'm looking for somebody brave enough and foolish enough to lead a group of civilians out of here at dawn."

"Oh."

"What did you think I meant?"

"I…" Rai couldn't think of how best to explain his mistake and decided not to try. "I'm not really sure, sir. My mistake."

"How do you feel about it?"

"About…?"

"Leading the civilians out."

"Fine. Not a problem. I'm your man. For that job, I mean."

"You sure? This isn't an order. Andreas has said he will take one group of women and children out, but I need more volunteers to take the others. The Imperials have made it clear they'll slaughter anyone who tries to escape, soldier or civilian. In all probability, what I'm asking you to do is a suicide mission."

"We've all got to die sometime," Rai said firmly. "It might as well be for a cause we believe in, right?"

Dante didn't reply. "I'd take the civilians out myself, but the men need me here to lead them. We'll begin a diversionary attack before sunrise. Try and draw the Imperials away from your route. That should give you a chance."

Rai nodded.

In the distance, sounds of a brawl could be heard, two men shouting over a spilt drink. Rai recognised the higher pitched voice as Flintlock, while the other man could only be Spatchcock, judging by the odour souring the air. The scuffle stopped briefly as a bottle broke, before the thud of fist on skin and a muffled sob of pain concluded the conflict.

"If those two spent as much time fighting the Tsar's forces as they do each other, we'd have won the war by now," Dante muttered. He stood and stretched, twisting his neck from side to side. Joints clicked and popped. Overhead, the first glints of light were colouring the early morning sky. "It'll be dawn in an hour. I'd better get the civilians ready."

"Captain?" Rai said, as Dante turned to leave. Dante paused and looked back at him.

"Yes, private?"

"What were you planning to do after the war?"

Dante shrugged. "Hadn't thought about it much, to be honest. I'd like to get back to being me – a rogue and a renegade, the lover not the fighter, always looking for a good time. Why, what were you planning to do?"

"Find my sister. We're twins. I haven't seen her for years, but I know she's still alive somewhere. I can feel it."

"You're lucky. I can't feel anything anymore," Dante said, before going. "I'll call you when it's time."

"Yes, sir," Rai replied. He looked at his fingernails and sighed. I wonder if it's true that they keep growing after you're dead?

General Ivanov watched as the first rays of sunlight stained the clouds red over the Governor's mansion. The battle to seize Rudinshtein from Romanov control had taken far longer than should have been necessary, thanks to the unconventional tactics of the opposing commander, the tenacity of his troops and the stubborn attitude of Ivanov's superior. Count Pyre had left orders that the pleasure of killing Captain Nikolai Dante should be his and his alone. The general argued that Dante should be assassinated, either by a sniper's bullet, or strategic air strike, whatever would do the job best. Once the Rudinshtein Irregulars' charismatic leader was dead, the remaining forces would be smashed within a day and Rudinshtein taken.

But Pyre was adamant that Dante must die by his hand and no other. So Ivanov had pressed his men into service elsewhere along the frontline. The Imperial Black inflicted more damage on the peasant army than all other infantry units combined. The men's uniforms were still glistening hours afterwards, wet with the blood of slain enemies, such was the ferocity of the regiment's attacks. Ivanov smiled to himself, pleasure creasing his cruel-looking features. The pincers were closing around the last stronghold. Soon, the final pocket of resistance would melt like a candle in a firestorm.

Then there would be a reckoning, the general had decided. For every day he had been forced to tarry in the godforsaken province, he would revisit that misery upon Rudinshtein a thousand-fold. For every wound sustained by one of the Imperial Black, a thousand people would be maimed. For every member of Ivanov's regiment that died, a thousand citizens would be executed in front of their families. For every hour the general was forced to remain, he would inflict a thousand hours of torture upon any civilians who survived the coming onslaught. And Ivanov would rejoice in the experience, savouring their suffering and their terror. It gave him a thrill so complete and a joy so satisfying, he wished the war would never end. He was a born warrior and the prospect of peace was like approaching purgatory.

Ivanov removed the black, peaked cap from his bald, polished pate and mopped his scalp with a monogrammed silk handkerchief. Just thinking about the delights that were still to be savoured was arousing him. His thumb stroked the livid scar that ran down the length of his face, a souvenir from the first woman he had ever killed. A hellion from Mongolia, she had sliced his face open like a peach with her fingernails, as Ivanov crushed her windpipe. He was a captain back then, sent into the east to subjugate a minor rebellion. The ringleader proved to be a woman, but Ivanov had not flinched from giving the order for her execution.

That was when she attacked him and he had found the delight of mixing pleasure and pain.

Watching the life slowly fading from her eyes, Vassily discovered just how much he enjoyed inflicting pain. Not satisfied with a single victim, he had personally throttled every adult living in the ringleader's village to make an example of them. His superiors had been appalled by his bloodlust, but it made him a better soldier, propelling him through the ranks in record time. An Imperial psychologist, tasked with assessing Ivanov's mental fitness for command, had once accused him of being a sadist with homicidal tendencies. That diagnosis was confirmed by the time Ivanov finished torturing the psychologist, but the poor man was in no state to file his assessment, having recently choked to death on his own, severed genitalia. When the Tsar heard about the incident, he rewarded Ivanov with command of the Imperial Black.

Approaching footfalls attracted the general's attention. He replaced the moist handkerchief in a pocket and glared at his second-in-command. "Report."

"Sir, our scouts have spotted two sets of movement, one striking out northwards from the governor's mansion, the other heading toward the south-west."

"Excellent. And which one is led by Captain Dante?"

"The strike to the north, sir. The other is mostly made up of civilians."

"No doubt the captain seeks to create a diversion, drawing our focus away from those hoping to elude our wrath. Very well. Inform Count Pyre his quarry is heading directly towards him. Since our glorious leader is so intent on killing Dante personally, he can have that pleasure. Instead, we will gorge ourselves on the civilians. They will bear witness to the fury of the Imperial Black!"

"Yes, sir." The second-in-command saluted crisply before leaving to carry out the general's orders. Ivanov smirked. Already he could feel the excitement coursing through his veins, that familiar thrill of a forthcoming kill bulging the crotch of his black uniform. His fingers twitched for a weapon. Let them come, let them all come, he thought. I shall bring them pain and death as they have never known it. I shall bathe in their blood and be reborn, for I am righteous.

Rai led the cluster of civilians across the wasteland, away from the governor's mansion. Less than a hundred of them were making the journey, the others too frightened or infirm to leave their refuge. Three other Rudinshtein Irregulars were helping him escort the civilians. Judging by their faces, they were almost as scared as him, Rai thought.

Vast tracts of land across Rudinshtein had been sown with a bitter crop of mines and serpent wire so, even if they somehow eluded the Imperial forces, there was little hope of escaping. Of the three possible deaths to encounter, Rai favoured stepping on a mine – at least that would be quick. Being captured by the enemy was worse as they liked to torture prisoners before executing them. But serpent wire was what all soldiers feared most.

A semi-sentient form of barbed wire, the murderous weapon responded to any movement. Touch it and the wire would bind itself round you, digging into skin and flesh. Fight to free yourself and the wire simply cut deeper, slicing through sinew and bone, feeding upon your pain and terror. Serpent wire was banned by all international protocols of war, but such treaties meant little in a conflict so bloody and brutal.

To Rai's left, a woman carrying an infant stifled a cry of pain as her legs gave way. It was not serpent wire, but sheer exhaustion that caused her to stumble. To Rai she looked less than twenty, but her hair was streaked with grey, and black rings encircled her eyes. "Here, let me take the child," he offered. The woman smiled gratefully and handed over her infant.

Rai clutched the bundle, pulling back the blankets to look at the baby within. "Is it a boy or a girl?" he asked. But he noticed the infant's face was still and lifeless, a bullet hole in the centre of its forehead, like a third eye.

"I couldn't leave him behind," the woman said. "I've lost everyone else, I couldn't lose him too."

Rai nodded his understanding. He was crouching down to comfort her when the first bullets strafed the civilians, otherwise he would have died instantly. Metal punched through flesh and bone, killing and maiming. Then came the cries of the attacking soldiers, charging towards them.

Rai pushed the dead baby back into its mother's hands, but she did not notice. She and the baby were both dead. Rai drew his weapon and began shooting as a swarm of soldiers in black uniforms grew closer.

Ivanov was disappointed to find so few of those trying to escape had survived his men's first onslaught. The fugitives had been mostly women and children, but they could have offered something better in the way of sport, couldn't they? I shall miss this war when it's over, the general decided, not for the last time.

"Over here, sir." The familiar voice of Ivanov's second-in-command summoned him across the wasteland to examine the single enemy soldier still alive. Curiously, his skin tone was a deep, warm brown, while hooded eyes that slanted upwards at the edges offset his broad nose. Most of his teeth were missing and crimson spilled from several wounds, but he was definitely still alive. Ivanov smiled at the prospect of what lay ahead.

"What kind of mongrel are you?" he began, spitting into the captive's face.

"Himalayan."

"I swear the Romanovs let any scum fight for them," the general snarled, his men laughing heartily along with him. "Himalayan, eh? You're a long way from home, my little mountain goat. Tell me, do you have any family back there, patiently awaiting your return?"

The prisoner nodded, a movement made harder by his dark shoulder-length hair being clenched tightly in the fist of an Imperial Black sergeant.

"Then tell me your name," Ivanov commanded, "so I may find your family to tell them how you died screaming and cursing their names."

"Rai."

"Is that your first name or your last name?"

"Does it matter?" Rai replied, glaring at the bulky figure leering over him.

"I suppose not," the general agreed. He dropped to one knee in front of the prisoner, taking Rai's chin in his grasp. "Do you enjoy pain, Romanov whelp?"

Rai smiled, then spat a mouthful of blood into the general's face.

Ivanov did not flinch. He waved away the soldiers who were ready to stab the prisoner with their bayonets for inflicting indignity on their commanding officer. "Nobody touches him but me!" Ivanov turned back to his captive. "When I've finished, he'll wish I had let you kill him." The general leaned closer, whispering into Rai's left ear like a lover. "I'm going to spoil your pretty face forever. You're going to beg for mercy and then you'll beg for death. How does that sound?"

The prisoner hissed an obscenity at Ivanov.

"I won't have you hearing such language," the general whispered. He closed his teeth tenderly around Rai's earlobe, then ripped the succulent pendant of flesh and skin away from the captive's head.

Dante was crawling towards the Imperial lines when he heard the sound of a man screaming in agony. The noise was unnatural, both human and animal at the same time. In war such screams were all too common, but Dante had never got used to them. He scanned the horizon for the source. "Crest, where's that coming from?"

Behind and to your left. Your other left, it prompted a moment later.

Dante swivelled round and peered across the battle-scarred landscape littered with broken metal and splintered corpses. "I can't see anything."

Try using the sight on your rifle, the Crest suggested with a supercilious sigh.

Dante brought his Huntsman 5000 upwards, pressing one eye against the sight atop the long barrel. He swept the weapon from left to right, scanning the horizon, until he located a group of men in black uniforms gathered round a single, kneeling figure. From this distance only three things were obvious: the crimson jacket of a Rudinshtein Irregular on the prisoner's chest, the blood pouring from a wound to his head and the colour of his skin. "That's Private Rai," Dante realised. Around the captive lay the bodies of those civilians that had tried to escape.

I sense Imperial forces closing on our position, the Crest warned.

"I can't leave him to die," Dante replied. "He's out there because I asked him."

He volunteered. He knew the risks. You have to withdraw – now.

"No," Dante insisted. "I won't abandon him."

If you don't pull back to the Governor's mansion in the next thirty seconds, you will be killed or captured yourself. Is that what he'd want?

"Fuoco..." Through his rifle's sight Dante could see an imposing, bald figure with the markings of a general standing over Rai. The general gestured to one of his men, who came forward carrying a large metal box. The soldier gingerly placed the container in front of Rai, releasing the catches that held the lid in place before hurriedly retreating.

Already the lid was beginning to open and strands of silver metal crept out from within.

Fifteen seconds until this position is overrun, the Crest insisted.

"They're going to torture him," Dante replied. "I can't leave him to die. You know what serpent wire does. Nobody deserves that, Crest."

Yes, but–

"But nothing! At least this way he'll die quickly." Dante's finger tightened round the trigger mechanism of his rifle. "Forgive me, Rai..."

ONE

"Vice is not bad, it has a bad reputation."
– Russian proverb

"For centuries in Japan, the geisha (literally translated 'a person of the arts') was a female performer skilled in many traditions of that land such as dance, music, flower arranging, poetry and the tea ceremony. It took many years of study for a maiko (trainee) to become a geisha, attaining the high social status that accompanied such a career. But the number of geisha steadily declined after Japan's defeat in the twentieth century's Second World War, until fewer than a thousand remained. The geisha tradition was dying, becoming part of history.

Some seven hundred years later a much-bowdlerised incarnation of this revered profession was to be found at *Okiya*, the Geisha House of the Rising Sun. In essence a Japanese brothel, this establishment had pretensions to something grander and indulged these by staging pornographic versions of the art forms once practised by geisha. Thus clients could have their needs serviced while savouring the delights of ikebana (flower arranging) or listening to singing accompanied by the three-stringed instrument known as the shamisen. The okami (headmistress) of *Okiya* was Kissy Mitsubishi, a woman with the distinction of having worked in both the Empire's most famous brothels: the House of Sin and Famous Flora's Massage Parlour in St Petersburg.

Constructed on a vast pontoon and powered by solar energy, the *Okiya* sailed the Empire, offering a taste of the Orient to all who could afford its exorbitant prices. Alas, the Makarov-Romanov war came close to bankrupting this unique endeavour in the annals of professional sexual services. Within three years it had become a honey-trap, infamous for turning tricks into dupes with customers forced to pay for fake divorces or face public shame and disgrace. The end came in 2673 when the Geisha House of the Rising Sun was all but destroyed by a devastating enemy attack. No group ever claimed responsibility for the surgical strike, but many suspected the paramilitary wing of the puritanical, sex-hating Church of Skoptzy…"

– Extract from *MacCoy's Imperial Sex Guide*,
2677 edition

Waking up with a hangover was an all too familiar sensation for Dante. Since puberty he had been a prodigious consumer of alcohol, his intake increasingly dramatically since bonding with the Crest. Having enhanced healing abilities enabled him to recover far quicker than most from the debilitating effects of inebriation, but even that was not enough to ward off the worst of hangovers. This time, he decided, either his skull had shrunk in the night or his brain had doubled in size, such was the vice-like pain clenching his cranium. Plus someone had replaced his tongue with a furry flap of roadkill and his eyes felt like pinpricks in a frozen potato.

"Bojemoi," he whispered feebly, not daring to look around. Better to stay still and try to get his bearings by other means.

He was lying between silk sheets on what felt like a waterbed, the mattress offering gentle undulations in response to any of his movements. The scent of jasmine and cinnamon mingled in the air like lovers savouring the after-glow of a particularly vigorous bout of lovemaking. The sound of voices murmuring nearby was audible, along with the lapping of water. A curious *plink-plonk* tone in the distance nagged at the senses, at once familiar and foreign. None of that answered the most pressing question in Dante's mind. "What did I drink last night?"

More to the point, what didn't you drink? The Crest's voice was akin to a sudden creeping barrage of explosions in Dante's brain, each syllable a dull detonation across his synapses. *Not only did you sup your way to oblivion, you anaesthetised my systems so completely the last twelve hours are missing from my memory.*

"Please, don't shout," Dante whimpered, nursing his thumping head in both hands. "I'll do anything you ask if you'll just stop shouting."

You'll give up drinking for a week?

"When I said I'd do anything, what I meant was–"

I ASKED IF YOU'D GIVE UP DRINKING FOR A WEEK, the Crest roared.

"Yes, yes. Anything, anything!" Dante cried, his face stricken with agony, desperate to stop the cacophony in his mind.

Very well, the Crest replied, its voice now back to a murmur. *Is that better?*

"Yes, thank you."

Good. May I suggest you find some more suitable clothing while I analyse the surroundings. You could be in imminent danger, and your present attire offers little protection against the slings and arrows of outrageous misfortune.

"What's wrong with what I'm–" Dante's words stopped once he'd opened his eyes and looked downwards. "Interesting. Very interesting."

A more accurate description would be obscene.

Dante was stark naked but for two items of what could charitably be termed clothing. A garter belt of red silk was strapped tightly around his left thigh, while a whisper of cloth covered his crotch. This miniscule triangle of black silk was encrusted with crimson sequins embroidered into the shape of a heart. The legend "GET IT HERE" spelled out by more sequins within the heart. Two tiny straps led away from the crotch and round his hips. Dante could feel them knotted together behind his back, joined by a third strap rising from between the cleft of his buttocks. The size and shape of the g-string suggested it had been designed for female use, as it struggled to encase any of his genitalia. "Perhaps I should have asked for a Brazilian before swapping underwear?"

My sensors are coming back online, the Crest announced. *Beginning analysis of the surroundings.*

"Good." Dante sank back on to the bed. "Let me know if you find something significant. I'll be busy concentrating on lying very still and wishing I was dead."

You should consider yourself fortunate inebriation did not disable my subcutaneous defence mechanism.

"Anytime you want to speak in words I can understand, just let me know."

Subcutaneous – beneath the skin. That's why I'm not currently visible.

Dante checked his left arm. The area below the shoulder was bare; normally the Crest was visible as a circular tattoo resembling the double-headed eagle symbol of the Romanovs. But when Dante was rendered unconscious, an automatic defence mechanism hid the Crest from view.

There's someone approaching this room, it warned. *Be on your guard!*

Dante looked round for an escape route or a weapon. The room was sparsely furnished, just the bed, a small wooden cupboard to one side and a stack of white towels atop that. The only light spilled in from a circular porthole above the bed, while an assortment of oriental paintings and tapestries decorated the white walls. A white door on the far side of the room was the sole exit.

Five seconds...

Dante groped for his Huntsman 5000 rifle under the bed. He habitually hid it there before falling asleep each night, within easy reach. The footsteps were rapidly getting closer as his fingers closed around a heavy cylindrical object on the floor. He snatched it out from under the bed and aimed one end at the door while groping for the trigger with his right hand. But instead of a firing mechanism he found himself pressing a button near the end of a three-foot long rubber phallus. It began vibrating in his grasp, accompanied by a gentle humming.

That's certainly offensive, the Crest observed, *but I doubt it'll make much of a weapon. Perhaps you could use it as a flexible truncheon?*

Dante was still clutching the double-ended dildo when the door swung open to admit an Oriental woman clad in a red, silk kimono that scarcely covered her crotch. She had dark hair, scarlet lipstick to match her kimono and a hungry look about her. Her eyebrows rose at seeing what was clutched in Dante's hands. "You like that, Quentin? I love you long time, but I try anything once if you want."

Realising his actions were being misinterpreted, Dante quickly threw the still-vibrating phallus to one side. "No, no, no, I didn't mean–"

The woman advanced on him, her hands reaching for the sash that kept her kimono closed. "Or maybe little Quentin too tired? For five dollar I wake him, yes?"

"A generous offer, I'm sure, but I've never paid for sex yet," Dante replied, scrambling his way off the bed.

Not with money, the Crest agreed, *but in plenty of other ways you have.*

"You said you'd shut up!" Dante protested.

No, I simply agreed to stop shouting – not the same thing.

The woman looked perplexed, since she was only hearing Dante's half of his conversation. "You want me shut up? I have rubber gag and blindfold in next room, but you pay extra for that, Quentin."

"No, no, I wasn't... I didn't mean–"

"You want me put gag on you instead?"

"No, I was talking to... Look, it doesn't matter." Dante sat down on the bed, all too aware of the g-string strap that seemed intent on garrotting his rectum. He patted the mattress, motioning for the woman to sit down beside him. The bed gently rippled beneath their weight. "Now, could anybody tell me where I am?"

I can, the Crest replied. *My sensors are now fully functional. You are on a floating platform some three hundred nautical miles from the oceanic city-state of Pacifica. I detect close to a hundred people in the surrounding rooms.*

"You on our bed, Quentin," the woman said in broken speech. "You no remember?"

Dante bashfully shook his head. "Sorry, no. I drank too much last night."

That's putting it mildly.

"We celebrate. You too happy," the petite woman agreed.

"In fact," Dante admitted, "I drank so much I seem to have forgotten your name, Miss...?"

"Sang Gen."

"Miss Sang Gen."

I've heard that name before.

"But now I will be called Mrs Durward."

It's all coming back to me now. Oh dear. Dante, I have good news and bad news. Which would you like to hear first?

"Really? Did you get married recently?"

Sang Gen punched Dante playfully on the arm. "Don't you remember, Quentin? It was big wedding. You very generous man."

"Well, I don't like to be a tightwad."

No, you just like getting tight. The good news is this minx believes you are the entirely fictitious Quentin Durward. You must have used that old alias last night while drinking yourself into a stupor. If you'd been using your real name, this little gold digger would have already handed you over for the multi-million rouble bounty on your head.

"And the bad news?" Dante asked.

"Now is time for honeymoon, yes?"

I believe you may have married this woman.

"Honeymoon?" Dante spluttered. Beside him, Sang Gen's smile broadened even further, revealing a mouthful of golden fillings.

"You drink too much last night, you no perform for Mrs Durward. But now you all better, you make me much happiness, yes?"

Dante, better make your excuses and leave, the Crest suggested, urgency apparent in its tone. *Now. While you still can.*

Sang Gen was sliding one hand inside his g-string while her other retrieved a rolled document from within her kimono. She firmly clasped the contents of Dante's underwear while unrolling the sheet of paper to reveal what was written on it. "We husband and wife now, yes? You make me happy." Sang Gen clenched her fist around Dante's testicles, making him gasp in pain and dismay. "Or else you be very unhappy. You understand, little Quentin?"

Five rooms away, Lord Peter Flintlock was having a perfectly dreary time. It was more than twelve hours since Dante had disappeared and, to Flintlock's way of thinking, even the finest houses of ill repute began to pall if you stayed within their walls too long. Savouring the delights of the Orient's finest courtesans was all very well, but eventually you became sated both in body and in spirit, no matter how gargantuan your sexual appetite. You reached a point where you had seen and experienced enough – any more was, quite literally, an anti-climax.

Dante had brought him and Spatchcock to the *Okiya*, the Geisha House of the Rising Sun, after a particularly successful piece of piracy. The freebooting threesome had intercepted an Imperial cruiser bound for St Petersburg that was heavy with wealthy passengers but light on security. Having stripped the Tsar's allies of their possessions, Dante gave his two accomplices the choice of where to celebrate their good fortune. It was Spatchcock who wanted to visit the *Okiya*. "I had a cousin who had such a good time there he ended up in hospital. It took the surgeons three hours just to get the smile off his face."

So Flintlock had spent several tumultuous hours in the arms of a creature calling herself Fragrant Lotus Blossom. But when he emerged from her bedchamber, with a blush on his face and a spring in his step, his two partners in crime were conspicuous by their absence. Dante's vessel, the *Sea Falcon*, was still moored nearby, but the brothel's okami could offer no clue about where Flintlock's friends had gone. Exhausted from his exploits, the man from Britannia hired a private room for the night, paying double for the privilege of sleeping in it alone.

Alas, whoever was responsible for the *Okiya*'s interior decor failed to realise using rice paper for the walls was not a sound idea. It gave the place a veneer of Japanese antiquity, but also meant you could hear everything happening in the adjoining rooms. Flintlock had spent the night trying – and failing – to get some sleep while being aurally assaulted by the comings and goings of innumerable clients, their hostesses screaming with feigned pleasure in a dozen different Oriental tongues. "I'll never eat sushi again," the exiled Brit muttered as he rolled off his unforgiving futon in the morning. He found a washbasin filled with ice-cold water beneath a mirror and splashed the liquid on his face while contemplating his reflection.

There was a haughty, almost arrogant aspect to his features, no doubt a product of his aristocratic origins and severe upbringing. A loveless childhood and fifteen years of schooling with regular thrashings in various boarding institutions – no wonder the upper classes of Britannia favoured

a stiff upper lip. Born a lord of the realm, Flintlock had fled
his native land for certain offences he preferred not to recall.
He still had a full head of hair and all his own teeth, but time
was leaving its mark around the corners of his gimlet-eyed
expression. Flintlock rasped a hand across the greying stubble on his chin and jowls. What I wouldn't give for a straight
razor, some shaving foam and a badger's hairbrush, he
thought wistfully. A female scream from outside the spar-
tanly furnished room got his attention. "I know that voice,"
he muttered and strode to the door.

He looked out in time to see Fragrant Lotus Blossom
sprinting past, a hand towel clasped over her groin, an
expression of pure disgust curdling her pretty face. "You bad
man. You nasty! I hate you. I tell the others. You no joy
here!"

"I say, steady on old girl. What seems to be the matter?"
Flintlock inquired politely, but the woman had already dived
into another room, slamming its door shut behind her.
"Dash it, what could have repulsed a woman of her experience so? I'd have thought there's little she hasn't seen or
done in her time here."

The answer appeared from the opposite end of the corridor: Spatchcock, stark naked, his clothes clutched in
one hand. "Your lordship! You haven't seen a pretty girl
go past, have you? Smelly Local Flower was her name, I
think."

"No, sorry, I haven't." Flintlock averted his eyes hurriedly,
taking care to breathe through his mouth instead of his nose.
Spatchcock might be the closest thing he had to a friend, but
Flintlock would rather have his own scrotum bitten off by a
ravenous rodent than gaze upon the vile little man's repulsive privates. As for the stench... the only times Spatchcock
came close to washing was when he fell into rivers or oceans
by mistake.

The odorous runt cursed loudly, his face scrunching with
frustration as he picked lice from his crusty armpits and

popped them in his mouth. "Shame, I thought we was getting on quite well. She didn't scream once when I undressed."

"A remarkable woman," Flintlock agreed. "Perhaps you should think about putting some clothes on. Don't want you catching your death of cold, do we?"

"Suppose not." Spatchcock began getting dressed again, a cloud of dust escaping each garment as it was pulled on. "You seen the boss this morning?"

"Last time I saw him, he was face-down in a bowl of sake with a cunning little vixen admiring the size of his wallet. Why, do you think he's in trouble?"

Spatchcock shrugged, pausing to scratch his pimple-ridden posterior. "He's always in trouble, isn't he? That's why we stick with him. Life with Dante might be dangerous, but it's never dull."

"Durward. He said we should call him Quentin Durward, remember?" Flintlock hissed, glancing along the corridor to ensure nobody was listening to their conversation. "If the staff here found out there was a fifty million rouble bounty on his head, they'd kill him and claim the reward without blinking."

Spatchcock nodded. "Alright, alright, keep your wig on, your lordship."

"I do not wear a wig."

"Sorry, I meant toupee."

Flintlock's eyes narrowed. He knew Spatchcock took great pleasure in antagonising him, but he refused to let such baseless accusations pass. "I do not wear a wig, a toupee or any other kind of follicle enhancement. My blond hair is all my own, thank you very much."

"You sure? Then why can I see–"

Their bickering was cut short by another scream, which was distinctly male. "That was Dante's voice," Flintlock said, already running in the direction from where the scream had emanated.

"I thought we were supposed to call him Durward," Spatchcock replied, racing after the gangly Brit.

"Shut up, you stupid guttersnipe!"

Sang Gen released Dante's testicles, satisfied she had his attention. "You read!" she snapped, thrusting the marriage certificate into his hands.

Don't bother, the Crest advised. I've already scanned the Imperial Net for data about this woman. Sang Gen is a notorious extortionist who calls the Geisha House of the Rising Sun home. She gets rich young fools drunk, stages a fake wedding ceremony and then demands they pay an exorbitant fee for a quick annulment. I tried to warn you last night, but you were more interested in the contents of her g-string. Perhaps I should have warned her instead. You're certainly a fool, but not so young anymore. And as for riches...

"Will be you be quiet?" Dante hissed. "I'm trying to read."

Sang Gen looked round the bedroom in bewilderment. "Who you talk to? Me? You tell me to shut up?"

"No, I was just talking to my..."

Better half?

"...Talking to myself."

"Time for talk is over, husband. You listen now," Sang Gen said. "Me your wife. You make me rich or you make me happy. You choose."

"Look, for a start, we can't be legally married. I wasn't conscious when the ceremony took place, so how can I be your husband?"

Sang Gen's face folded into a determined scowl. "You no want me wife?"

"I'm sure you'll make a lovely bride for somebody one day."

Only after hell freezes over with this harridan.

"But I'm not the marrying type, okay? This has all been a terrible mistake."

Sang Gen folded her arms. "You want no marriage, yes?"

She has a delightful knack for tautology, doesn't she?

Dante grinned sheepishly. "Well…"

"You want no marriage, you pay for no marriage."

"I would, but I seem to have mislaid my belongings: my jacket, my trousers, my rifle, my money pouch. I don't suppose you'd know where they are?"

"You want them back, you pay for them too."

"But how can I pay for them when I don't have any money?"

Dante's new wife smiled like a barracuda. "You can pay in other ways."

I have a bad feeling about this.

Sang Gen gave a sharp whistle and the door opened to reveal a mountainous man waiting outside. Balding, bearded and barrel-chested, he was wearing nothing but a black leather throng and a crooked smile of lust. "This is Genghis. He like it when boys scream," Sang Gen explained sweetly.

Genghis had to duck his head to step into the bedroom, his massive bulk blocking the exit once he was inside.

I imagine that hangover must seem the least of your worries now.

Dante was already on his feet, careful to keep the bed between himself and Genghis. "I'm open to any brilliant suggestions, Crest."

You could try playing hard to get.

"I don't think that's going to be enough!"

Perhaps not. But use your cyborganic weapons and they'll soon realise your true identity. You need to find another way out of this.

"So you be my husband," Sang Gen asked, "or you be Genghis's wife?"

Dante shook his head. "Decisions, decisions…"

The sleek, silver flyer skimmed, only a few feet above the ocean's surface. Keeping close to the water enabled the aircraft to escape all but the most sophisticated defence systems, slipping unnoticed past Pacifica. In the cockpit the navigator located their quarry. "The *Okiya* is dead ahead. We should be above it in three minutes."

In the flyer's cargo hold the overhead lighting switched from red to amber, a signal that the drop-zone was close. A dozen figures clad head-to-toe in black rose in unison from their seats, checking weapons and making adjustments to equipment. Only their eyes were visible through slits in the black cloth wrappings that shrouded their heads. A single command from the smallest of the twelve brought the others to attention. The leader inspected them briefly before giving a curt nod to the one standing nearest the cargo door. He pulled it open, wind and light flooding into the confined space from outside.

The leader leaned out to look at their fast approaching target. From this distance the Geisha House of the Rising Sun resembled the love child of an aircraft carrier and a jade pagoda. It hovered close to the water's surface, sunlight glinting on the raised corners of its elaborate exterior. A dozen smaller vessels were moored around the *Okiya*, but they did not matter. Few witnesses would be left alive, and those that did survive would not be able to identify their attackers. Get in quick, find and neutralise the target, then get out.

Satisfied, the leader withdrew into the cargo hold and examined the display on a tiny computer strapped to his wrist. All was as expected. "Our target is still on board the *Okiya*," the leader announced, shouting over the roaring wind. "We have a lock on the signal from his Weapons Crest. Remember, the corpse of Nikolai Dante is worth fifty million roubles, but the Tsar will pay considerably more than that if he is captured alive and presented at the Imperial Palace. Make sure we take him alive. Is that understood?"

The men nodded their assent.

"Good. Anybody who gets in the way is collateral damage, nothing more, nothing less. Shoot to kill if necessary. Once we have Dante, the *Okiya* will be destroyed. If you are wounded, we will leave you behind to die. Stand by."

The hold's interior light switched from amber to green. "Green signal! Go, go, go!"

TWO

"The Tsar's wrath is death's emissary."
– Russian proverb

"The aftermath of the war proved more savage and more brutal than many of the atrocities committed during the conflict. The Tsar celebrated his victory over the Romanovs by sending Purge Squads to mercilessly take revenge against those whom he felt had betrayed him. Noble houses guilty of switching loyalties to the Romanovs, when it seemed the Makarov regime was doomed, felt the full force of the Tsar's wrath. Most were destroyed and new ones created from the ashes, their future loyalty assured by the Tsar's limitless tyranny.

Nikolai Dante, the so-called Hero of Rudinshtein, somehow escaped capture and execution by the Imperials. The corpse of Count Pyre was discovered after Rudinshtein fell, apparently murdered by his nemesis. The name of Nikolai Dante became accursed across the Empire, with the Tsar putting a massive bounty on the Romanov renegade's head. But what of the people left behind in Rudinshtein by their former leader?

Despite Dante's apparent desertion, the civilians who survived the war still believed in their hero and hoped he would return to save them. Rudinshtein may have been the poorest city in the Empire, yet its people proved most resistant to the reinstatement of the

Tsar's rule. The job of crushing their rebellion was given to the most feared regiment of all, the Imperial Black, led by General Ivanov. It was during the next three years he earned the name Ivanov the Terrible, a reference to the oppressive regime of Russia's first Tsar, Ivan the Terrible.

Given an entire province as his plaything, Ivanov set to work with relish. He appeared to revel in the pain and suffering of others, personally supervising interrogations, torture sessions and punishment beatings. He authorised his men to use rape and murder as weapons of terror, herding innocent citizens into camps for the most brutal of subjugations. The general announced anyone who dared to say Dante's name out loud was signing their own death warrant, and offered massive rewards to those collaborators who would inform against their family or neighbours. After enjoying one of the most enlightened leaderships before the war, Rudinshtein now suffered beneath the most savage."

> – Extract from *After the Tsar Wars*,
> by Georgi Lucassovich

Jena Makarov hated having to play hostess for butchers like Ivanov. She had willingly fought and killed for her father during his war against the Romanovs, but that didn't give her any liking for the military or its leaders. The generals were men – and they were all men – who made a living from institutionalised murder, yet wished to dress it up as somehow respectable by adopting the notions of duty and honour. Honour be damned, Jena thought to herself before grimacing. Sounds like the sort of thing Nikolai used to... No, I'm not going to think about him today. Just once I'd like to get through a day without wondering where he is or what he's doing.

Three years had passed since the end of the war, when she had let him escape the ruins of Rudinshtein. Since then,

Dante had led his would-be captors a merry dance, eluding all attempts to claim the bounty on his head. Despite herself Jena kept tabs on her former lover's latest escapades. He was an itch she couldn't scratch.

A few months earlier she had rejoiced in using Dante as a pawn to thwart a scheme hatched by one of her father's allies. Now she found herself waiting to welcome a man sworn to destroy Dante.

Jena had encountered Ivanov twice during the final days of the war in Rudinshtein. The bloodlust in his eyes and the sour milk stench of his breath were equally repulsive. She had no wish to ever encounter the general again, but disobeying a direct order from her father was tantamount to treason. So she waited at the Imperial Palace's aerial docking bay, cold arctic air from outside ruffling her auburn curls. In one ear a tiny comms device informed her that Ivanov's flyer was making its final approach from the southeast. "Very well," she replied. "Once the access code is confirmed, lower the energy screen and let him in."

Vassily Ivanov had been waiting for this moment all his life. The personal message from the Tsar, the invitation to step inside the hallowed halls of the Imperial Palace, the fact his contribution to the war and all his efforts since were to be acknowledged and praised by the Tsar himself... These were the moments that made all the sacrifices of the past three years worthwhile.

I must savour every second, the general told himself as he watched his flyer's final approach from behind the pilot's shoulder. I must remember every detail, every element of the experience. I shall want to relive this day many times in years to come.

The flyer sped towards the Imperial Palace, already well under the mighty shadow that the grand structure cast. The Tsar's home resembled a huge, ornate egg hovering about the city of St Petersburg. Fashioned in the style of a Fabergé jewel, the palace was a hundred metres high. Set into one side was a vast entry port, its surface buzzing with luminous energy. As the flyer drew closer the energy faded, a clear window opening to allow access. Ivanov's aircraft swept inside the docking area and automatic systems guided the vessel to its berth.

Satisfied with the nature of his arrival, Ivanov made his way back into the main cabin, surrounded by a phalanx of Imperial Black troops and a single figure that sported the insignia of a major. "Stand easy," Ivanov commanded and his men obeyed in a second. "Sadly, I must ask you to remain here – the Tsar allows only his personal bodyguard to roam the hallways of the Imperial Palace. It seems our reputation has preceded us." The soldiers, except the major who kept his own counsel, responded with an appreciative laugh. "But whatever honour I receive from our leader, I will share it equally with you. We are all brothers under our uniform, bathed in the blood of our enemies, forged in the heat of battle. Where one of us goes, all of us walk. For the glory of the Imperial Black!"

"For the glory of the Imperial Black!" the soldiers responded fervently.

Ivanov smiled at them benevolently. "Very good. Major, if you'd accompany me outside, I believe the Tsarina is waiting for us."

"Yes, sir." Like the other soldiers, the major was clad in the black uniform of his regiment, but his helmet included a full facemask, tinted to hide the features behind its surface. Only the bottom of his jaw line was visible, and that was a horrific mass of scar tissue. The major strode to the flyer's main doorway and activated the ramp. Once that had extended out to the docking bay walkway, the flyer's outer door slid sideways.

Waiting on the walkway was a beautiful woman in a trouser suit of emerald green. Her face was pale and unlined, with perceptive green eyes framed by her auburn hair. A pert, slightly upturned nose gave her an aristocratic look, as did the way she stood.

Ivanov smiled at seeing her again. He strolled along the ramp towards Jena, his right hand reaching forward to grasp hers. "Tsarina. A pleasure, as always, to see you."

"General Ivanov," she replied curtly. There was no warmth in her face.

Ivanov stepped aside to introduce his second-in-command. The major was more than a foot taller than Jena, his imposing physical bulk and ominously blank facemask created an oppressive presence. "And this is my strong right hand, a man known simply as the Enforcer." The major nodded to Jena, who appeared grateful at not having to shake his hand as well.

"My father bids you welcome to the Imperial Palace and says he will see you shortly. I am to escort you to the Map Room."

"So be it," Ivanov replied smoothly, quickly falling into step beside Jena as she strode away. The Enforcer followed, three paces behind. "If I may ask, what occupies the Tsar this morning?"

"You may ask," Jena said icily, "but you should not expect an answer."

The general arched an eyebrow, keeping his rage hidden beneath an otherwise serene face. You snotty-nosed little bitch, he thought. What I wouldn't give for the chance to make you cry. I imagine your face would be almost beautiful when bathed in tears, christened by sorrow, chastened by fear. I could make you fear me, Tsarina. How would that suit you?

Jena led the two men down numerous corridors and through many doors within the palace. Along the way she nodded her head towards the glowering form of the Enforcer. "Is he the strong, silent type, or does he speak for himself?"

Ivanov smiled warmly. "The major only talks when he has something important to say. For most of the time, he lets his actions speak for themselves."

"I've read about your actions in Rudinshtein," Jena said. "I'm not sure they are anything of which to be proud, general."

"We have broken the rebellious spirit of the natives, as your father ordered. To a soldier, there is no greater honour than following orders," Ivanov growled, struggling to keep his temper under control. "I would have thought you of all people should understand that, Tsarina."

She did not reply, but the look of anger and disgust that crossed her face spoke volumes. Yes, I would very much like to make you weep, Ivanov decided.

Jena stopped outside a pair of double doors, their surface covered by an ornate design in gold leaf. She gestured and the doors opened to reveal a vast chamber, the height of three normal rooms. The walls were lined with leather-bound volumes, while a large holographic globe hung above a priceless antique rug on the floor. Reading tables and armchairs were scattered about the chamber, while a musty odour characteristic of libraries hung in the air. "This is the Map Room. It contains a copy of every atlas or cartographic document published in the past thousand years. The globe shows the current status of the Empire's terrestrial endeavours. You are welcome to study any of these items until my father arrives."

Ivanov and the Enforcer watched her leave, before accepting the invitation to enter the Map Room. Its double doors glided shut behind them.

Minutes later, the doors re-opened to admit the Tsar, flanked by four heavily armed guards from the Raven Corps. Ivanov and the major instantly dropped to one knee and bowed their heads, prostrating themselves before their commander-in-chief. The Tsar dismissed his bodyguards, telling them to stand outside and ensure he was not disturbed. Two metres tall, the Tsar was powerfully built with broad shoulders, a formidable face and fierce, flinty eyes. The Ruler of all the Russias was swathed in his crimson and gold Imperial robes.

"Forgive my clothes," he said, after beckoning the two soldiers to stand upright. "Normally I wear a military uniform to meet members of my armed forces, but didn't have time to change after sitting in the Chamber of Judgement."

"There is nothing to forgive, sir," Ivanov said.

"Indeed. Well, general, I have much to thank you for. Rudinshtein's people were a rebellious rabble when I placed you in charge of them three years ago. From all reports they are now a shattered remnant, their spirit crushed beneath the boots of the Imperial Black, their former bravado broken."

"These reports speak true, sir," the general replied, unable to keep the glee from his face. "I have taken much pleasure in enforcing your will. There is not one among the survivors who challenges your rule."

"If only all parts of the Empire were that compliant."

"Indeed, sir. If I may be so bold, I believe that in Rudinshtein we have developed methods of torture equal to any you have at your disposal here. I have tried to emulate your own flair for the creative and the cruel."

"Hmm." The Tsar approached Ivanov's second-in-command. "Major, it is a severe breach of palace protocol for visitors to wear facemasks in my presence without express permission. You would be wise to remove it immediately." The Enforcer leaned forward, slipping the helmet from his head. When he straightened up again, the Tsar blanched at the horrors that had been hidden behind the facemask. "Now I understand," the Tsar eventually said. "What creature did that to you, major?"

"I did," Ivanov interjected. He got a glare of disapproval from the Tsar, but still continued his explanation. "The major once challenged my orders. I was forced to discipline him. Ever since he has been the most loyal of all my men."

"Very well." The Tsar gestured for the Enforcer to put his helmet back on. "Now, I have a new mission for you and the men of the Imperial-"

"Forgive me, sir, but I understood you had summoned us here to reward our efforts in Rudinshtein. I had hoped you might consider appointing me as your second-in-command, bearing in mind–"

A mighty fist smashed against Ivanov's face, cracking his head to one side. The general staggered and coughed blood, but did not lose his footing. The Enforcer took a step forward to intervene, but was waved back by Ivanov. The Tsar moved to within inches of the general's face, his own features red with fury. "You dare interrupt me, your commanding officer? You presume to suggest how I should reward those who fulfil what little I expect of them?"

"Forgive me, sir. I... forgot myself."

The Tsar seethed, sucking in breath between clenched teeth, his chest rising and falling. "Forget yourself again and you will learn exactly how creative and cruel I can be. The acid enema may not be a new innovation in the world of torture, but I think you would find being on the receiving end of such a treatment must instructive in the difference between pleasure and pain!"

Ivanov did not dare meet the Tsar's eyes, keeping his own gaze fixed upon his dazzling black leather boots. "Yes, sir!"

The Tsar turned away after a pause that felt like a lifetime to the general. Vladimir the Conqueror gestured towards the holographic globe floating in the centre of the Map Room. The topographic illusion slowly rotated on its axis. As the raised mountains of Tibet and surrounding areas came into view, the Tsar pointed at that section of the globe. "As I was saying, I have a new mission for you and the men of the Imperial Black, a task of utmost importance. Consider it your reward for the good work done in Rudinshtein. I wish you to find and secure the fortress known as the Forbidden Citadel."

The general almost spluttered in disbelief, but quickly bit back his words of derision. "Yes, sir. And why do we seek this... goal?"

The Tsar smiled, apparently amused at the care with which Ivanov was choosing his words. "For the past three years Imperial interrogators have questioned the Romanov family retainers that were captured during the war. They proved resistant at first, many willing to die rather than betray the confidences they kept, but recently two of them began to weaken. One revealed the Romanovs had a special link with the Forbidden Citadel, and the other confirmed the fact when placed under sufficient... duress. Analysis of flight manifests and pilots' logs captured from the Winter Palace proved the Romanov patriarch Dmitri made several journeys to the Himalayas during the war, one of them at a time when his presence was urgently required elsewhere." The Tsar swivelled round from the globe to glare at Ivanov once more. "I want to know why he went there and you will discover that for me. Use any and all means necessary. My daughter will brief you further. That is all." He abruptly turned away and strode to the double doors. They opened automatically and the Tsar swept out, four of his bodyguards falling into step behind him.

Ivanov only spoke once the Tsar was out of earshot. "That bastard! He's sending us to the ends of the earth, just to satisfy his own curiosity."

The general did not notice Jena appearing in the doorway of the Map Room. "I suggest you speak about my father with a little more respect, general. He does not tolerate insubordination twice in one day, let alone from the same man."

"Forgive me, Tsarina. I did not realise you were there."

"Plainly." She walked into the Map Room, the doors closing silently behind her. "Tell me, general, what do you know about the Forbidden Citadel?"

"Very little," Ivanov admitted. "As far as I am aware, it is a myth, a legend. A supposedly impregnable fortress, hidden in the Himalayas – a fanciful notion."

"Perhaps. But as with many myths, there is a grain of truth hidden within the legend. Our analysis of the Romanov archives suggests the patriarch of that family first discovered the Forbidden Citadel some thirty years ago." Jena strolled across the room towards the holographic globe. "How he found it we do not know. According to legend the citadel may only be seen by those who have been within its walls before. A contradiction, but a useful defence mechanism if true."

"You have a precise location for this fortress?"

"No," she replied. "We know it must be high up in the Himalayas, for the flight logs of Dmitri's personal pilot show several trips to that area. Unfortunately, this is one of the few regions within the Empire that has defied meaningful investigation. The harsh terrain, remote location and lack of strategic value meant there was no reason to waste significant resources on such an investigation."

"But now you want me to lead the Tsar's most feared fighters, the Imperial Black, into this area to find a mythical fortress that may not even exist?" Ivanov asked, unable to keep the exasperation from his voice.

"Precisely." Jena smiled at the general. "If the legends are to be believed, the Forbidden Citadel is home to a religious sect blessed with special abilities, supposedly a mark of their closeness to God. This sect guards the citadel jealously, because it holds a secret so powerful any man who looks upon that secret goes blind."

"A weapon?"

She shrugged. "That is for you to find out. If the Romanovs did have a secret weapon hidden there, your orders are to claim it for the Tsar and bring it back here to the Imperial Palace. If for whatever reason you cannot remove this weapon, you are authorised to destroy it and the citadel. Better it be the property of none than fall into enemy hands." Jena folded her arms. "Any questions?"

Ivanov glared at the holographic representation of the Himalayas as it rotated past him on the globe. "I am a warrior born, I do not believe in myths or fables. Why did the Tsar choose me for this quest?"

"You are an ambitious and dangerous man. Such energies are always welcomed within the Imperial forces, but they can become misdirected if ambition overwhelms reason or judgement. My father says you can be guilty of overstepping your responsibilities, of taking more than is your due."

"I suppose I should be honoured that he takes me so seriously."

Jena laughed. "To my father, you are like the flea that bites an elephant – a minor irritant, but one that can still draw blood. Nothing more, nothing less." She made to leave, but stopped herself. "The Tsar gave me a parting message for you. Take one thousand men as your army. Cost is no object. Succeed in this difficult mission and you will be amply rewarded, Ivanov. Fail in your task and you need never return."

The general contemplated all she had said before nodding in agreement. "Very well. It will be winter soon. No military commander in seven hundred years has been foolish enough to launch an offensive into such hazardous terrain during winter. The major and I will return to Rudinshtein immediately. It will take several days to select and equip my men for the mission, but we will make ready for the mountains with all possible haste. We have but a few weeks to succeed."

"Good luck," Jena offered, before turning away from him. "You'll need it."

THREE

"Rush not at a knife, if you don't want to get cut."
– Russian proverb

"Kabuki is a form of traditional Japanese theatre that dates back more than a thousand years to the early seventeenth century. Early kabuki featured both male and female performers, but the plays became so immodest that women were banned from taking part. Instead, male actors took on the onna-gata (female roles). Over the centuries this style of theatre became increasingly stylised, with elaborate costumers and make-up, the actors speaking in a slow, monotonous tone. Popular plots involve historical events, moral conflicts and love stories. Trap doors and rotating stages were commonplace, enabling rapid changes of set. By the twenty-seventh century, kabuki was forced to diversify to retain an audience, but the use of all-male casts was retained – sometimes with unexpected results…"

– Extract from *Japanese Theatre 1600-2673*,
by Floyd Kermode

"This place is like a rabbit warren," Flintlock complained, pausing to catch his breath. He and Spatchcock had been running from room to room in search of Dante, bursting into bedchambers and startling the *Okiya*'s clientele in the midst of some impressively deviant acts. Twice Flintlock had been forced to drag his libidinous lackey away from those unscheduled peepshows.

"The guests certainly hump like rabbits," Spatchcock agreed. "But we still haven't found Dant... Mr Durward. We still haven't found Mr Durward."

Flintlock rubbed his chin thoughtfully, looking up and down the white-walled corridor. "I was certain his scream came from down here."

His ruminations were cut short by the sound of tearing paper. The body of a naked brute flew horizontally between Flintlock and Spatchcock, before smashing through another rice paper wall. He came to rest, face-down in a bubbling Jacuzzi, a long rubber object protruding from between his buttocks.

Spatchcock studied the unconscious figure with amusement. "Is that what I think it is?" he asked, thumbing at the offending item.

"Brings tears to the eyes just thinking about it," Flintlock agreed. The two men turned to the gaping hole in the wall from which the unfortunate hulk had abruptly appeared. Through the shredded paper they could see Dante standing over an Oriental woman, demanding the return of his belongings.

"You've seen what I did to your friend Genghis," he warned. "Unless you want the same treatment, I suggest you fetch my clothes and rifle. Now!"

"Yes, Mr Durward," the woman replied meekly, bowing deeply as she backed away from Dante towards the door. "Me fetch them now, husband."

"And the honeymoon's off too!" Dante shouted after her. He noticed Flintlock and Spatchcock peering in through the hole in the wall. "You took your time."

"You and her married?" Spatchcock asked.

"Not exactly."

"Just good friends?" Flintlock offered.

"No," Dante said firmly. He stopped speaking, cocking his head to one side like a dog hearing a far-off, high-pitched whistle. Dante's expression darkened, souring into a grimace.

Flintlock recognised the signs – Dante was hearing the crest's voice in his mind. That usually meant only one thing: trouble.

"We're not alone," Dante announced.

"We know," Spatchcock agreed. "There's laughing boy in the jacuzzi, for a start. Once he comes round, I doubt he's going to see the funny side of things."

"He's the least of our worries. The Crest has detected a stealth flyer hovering nearby with twelve new arrivals on board."

Flintlock shrugged. "That doesn't make them a danger to us. Could be high profile people, trying to make a discrete visit to the geisha house."

Dante shook his head. "Somebody has locked on to the Crest's presence here, they're using it to track my movements. That only means one thing – enemy action. The Crest has been forced to shut down temporarily, but we've got to get off this floating cathouse right now." He held out his hands as his skin changed colour, its natural pigment draining away to be replaced by slithers of silver and purple. The shape of each hand mutated as the hilts of cyborganic swords emerged from the discoloured flesh and bone, stretching outwards into metre-long blades. "No need to maintain the pretence of being Quentin Durward anymore. Somebody already knows I'm here!"

The dull thud of an explosion shook the *Okiya*, accompanied by the rattle of gunfire. Dante and his partners in crime sighed. "So much for a quiet night of Oriental culture and copulation," Flintlock observed.

A low rumble of fury got his attention. The trio swivelled round to see the naked brute emerging from the Jacuzzi, his face flushed with rage and agony.

"Meet Genghis," Dante said. "He tried to rub me up the wrong way."

"But you got to him first?" Spatchcock asked. Genghis charged at the three men as another explosion shook the *Okiya*. "I think he's coming back for more!"

The strike team burst through the skylights of the geisha house's roof, dropping to the reception area below, weapons cocked and ready to fire. The *Okiya*'s madam was first to die, cut down by a hail of bullets as she emerged from her office. Two of her personal bodyguards followed within moments, slumping back into the chairs from which they had begun to rise. The strike team's leader studied blueprints and floor plans for the *Okiya*, plotting the best way forward. Four fingers gestured at double doors leading into the eastern section of the structure, sending four black-clad insurgents scurrying forwards to the bedchambers. Four more fingers pointed at the madam's office door, which led into the staff's private quarters, so another group went that way. The remaining three commandos waited as their leader consulted the tiny computer display. Where a blinking light had shown the Crest's location, there was now nothing. It must have detected the signal lock. That didn't matter now the trap was sprung. There would be no escape for Nikolai Dante.

The leader nodded to the other members of the strike team, sending them through the final internal doorway that led to the geisha zone, where traditional Japanese activities like ikebana and kabuki took place. The leader remained in the reception area, guarding the main exit in the unlikely event that Dante had made it that far. Satisfied with these tactics, the black-clad figure dropped into a lotus position on the floor and began to meditate, listening to sounds of battle spilling through the brothel's paper walls.

Spatchcock stuck out a foot and tripped Genghis as the brute charged past, intent on attacking the man who had so humiliated him. But Dante danced around the brute's clumsy lunge, at the same time slicing one of his cyborganic swords across the top of the bed. Genghis tumbled into the mattress, his arrival displacing a cascade of water that drenched the room. A dripping wet Dante admired his hand-iwork. "I didn't know the *Okiya* offered watersports."

"I think his scuba-diving days are behind him," Spatch-cock added.

"Didn't you say we should be leaving?" Flintlock asked.

"Good point. Crest, what's the best way out of...? Crest?"

"You told it to shut down."

Dante grimaced. "Guess we'll have to find our own way off this love boat." He stepped through the hole in the wall cre-ated by Genghis and pointed to his left. "This way, I think."

But Sang Gen was waiting for them at the end of the cor-ridor, wearing Dante's jacket. She was aiming his rifle at the trio, one finger closing around the trigger. "You want no marriage, you pay for no marriage!"

Dante gestured for Sang Gen to lower the long-barrelled weapon. "You can't use that against me. It's a Huntsman 5000, keyed to my DNA. If anybody but me fires that rifle, the bullets will make you their target."

"You lie!" Sang Gen shrieked. "Just like you lie about name. You no Quentin, you Nikolai Dante! Tsar offer big reward for you!"

"Pull that trigger and you'll never turn another trick."

"You lie about name, you lie about gun too!" Sang Gen fired the rifle, a grim look of satisfaction on her features. A second later she was dead, the bullet having entered her forehead and removed the back half of her skull.

Dante walked over to Sang Gen and crouched down, quickly retrieving his jacket and rifle from the dead woman. "I tried to warn you," he said sadly. At that moment half a dozen discs of spinning light flew past Dante's head, slicing through the paper wall beyond him. He glanced up to see four black-clad figures running towards Spatchcock and Flintlock. "Look out! Behind you!"

The two ex-convicts twisted round just in time to see another handful of spinning discs flung at them. Spatchcock dived across the corridor, his shoulder slamming into Flintlock's stomach. The Brit was driven backwards into one of the *Okiya*'s bedchambers, his breath still whistling out from between his teeth.

In the corridor Dante threw his hands in front of his face, the discs deflecting off his swords, taking chunks of flesh and blood with them. Taken by surprise, Dante screamed in pain. His cyborganics were all but invulnerable against most weapons. What the hell were these guys throwing at him? Before he had time to wonder any further, the first of the four was upon him, brandishing a short-bladed weapon in each hand. Dante parried the thrusts of both blades, then flashing his own swords outwards, sliced off the attacker's hands at the wrist. The black-clad figure went down screaming, blood spurting from each wound in a wide arc. Dante dived away from another shower of spinning discs, taking cover behind a corner.

"Flintlock! Spatchcock! Are you alright?"

He pulled on his jacket while waiting for a reply, but none came. "If you can hear me, get back to the boat. I'll meet you at the *Sea Falcon*."

The insurgents' leader studied the team's progress on his wrist computer. One of the twelve lights representing the location of each member stopped blinking, indicating they were dead. Three more were gathering on the spot where their colleague had fallen. The leader activated the comms unit in their ear. "Target has been found in the eastern section. Converge on that area, find and disable the target. Do not, repeat, do not eliminate the target. Aim to wound."

"Have they gone?" Spatchcock peered back over his shoulder, bracing one arm against Flintlock's throat to get leverage. The gangling Brit gasped in protest, his arms flailing weakly at the rancid creature on top of him.

"Get… off of me… you pestilent… oik!"

Spatchcock realised why Flintlock was choking and rolled off. He crawled over to the wall and peered out into the corridor. Dante and his attackers were gone, except for a handless corpse on the floor.

Flintlock was still coughing and complaining from where he had fallen. "What in the name of all that's holy were you playing at?"

"Saving your life, your lordship," Spatchcock replied. "You almost got sliced in two by a fistful of laser shuriken."

"Laser *what*?"

"Old martial arts weapon, new twist. Throwing stars made out of pure light. Can slice through almost anything. Nasty."

"Not as nasty as your body odour," Flintlock whined, his face curdling at the smell on his clothes. "It'll take a week of washing to get your foul stench out of my garments!"

"Stop your bleating for once," Spatchcock snarled. "Dante needs our help."

"You heard him, old boy. 'Get back to the boat!' For once in my life, I intend to do as I'm told. I suggest you do the same." He joined Spatchcock by the wall. "Have those chaps in the black pyjamas gone then?"

"They're called ninja, martial arts warriors. The black clothes help them blend into the shadows. They know more ways to kill you than I've got diseases."

Flintlock smirked. "Impressive. And certainly less offensive than your odour." He stepped out into the corridor. The sound of fighting and death could be heard from the left, where the ninja had gone in pursuit of Dante. The Brit turned to his right. "This way, I think. You coming, Spatch?"

"We shouldn't abandon him. He's saved our necks plenty of times."

"Discretion is the better part of valour, old boy." Flintlock strode away, Spatchcock reluctantly following him.

● ● ●

Dante sprinted round another corner, then slammed himself against the wall, intending to use it as a hiding place from which to surprise his pursuers. The thin white surface gave way behind him and Dante fell backwards into a darkened room. "Fuoco!" he cried out, tumbling head over heels. He came to rest against a row of seats, his head smashing against a wooden support strut. Blackness closed around him for what seemed like a few seconds, but when his eyes opened again three of the hunters had surrounded him. They were only visible in silhouette, the room pitch dark but for the light spilling in from a hole high in one wall created by Dante's arrival.

"Child's play," one of them said in an accent Dante did not recognise. "Why did the Parliament send a dozen of us? Anyone could bring this fool back alive."

"There's more to this fool than meets the eye," Dante replied, slicing his left hand horizontally through the air. His cyborganic blade cut across the knees of the three ninja, neatly disabling the trio with a single blow. They crumpled to the floor in agony, cursing in several languages. Dante scrambled to his feet, one hand rubbing the bump on his head where it had hit the wooden strut. "Now, who's going to tell me about this Parliament? Who is it, and why do they want me captured?" He rested the bloody tip of his left blade against the throat of the attacker who had spoken. "Start talking or start dying, your choice."

"So be it," the ninja replied. He ground his teeth together, creating a faint popping sound. Within seconds white liquid began to seep through the cloth masking his face. The other two men followed his example, their eyes squinting with pain before the pupils rolled back into their skulls.

"Suicide pills," Dante realised. "They killed themselves, rather than be captured or forced to reveal who sent them." He staggered away from the corpses, feeling his way along the row of seats. "Where the hell am I, anyway? Crest? Crest, I need you to reactivate." Dante closed his eyes to concentrate, summoning the battle computer out of its standby status.

You called?

"Finally. I need you to check if there are any more of these goons nearby."

Beginning scanning.

"And could you point me towards the lights?"

There's a switch on the wall to your left, about chest height. Turn that on, it should illuminate your location.

"Thanks." Dante was hitting the switch when the Crest spoke again.

But I'm not sure you're ready for what you're about to see.

The chamber was bathed in light, momentarily blinding Dante. He covered his eyes, squinting to take in his surroundings. Aside from the corpses near his feet, most of the available space was given over to rows of theatre seats, all facing a raised stage. The leading edge of the acting area jutted out into the seating, like the down-stroke of a letter T. Across this, more than a dozen figures in elaborate make-up and the flimsiest of costumes were engaged in numerous sexual couplings and muscular ménage à trois. Men dressed as women were pleasuring other men dressed as women, while their actions were appreciated by yet more men who appeared most intent upon pleasuring themselves.

"Bojemoi!" Dante stared at the stage in disbelief. "What do you call that?"

Oh my, the Crest replied. *Kabuki porn.*

Six ninja dived through the paper wall above Dante's head and landed on the seating in front of him, their weapons already drawn and ready to attack.

Sex and violence, the Crest sighed. *You should feel right at home.*

Dante dived behind the seats to avoid a fresh flurry of laser shuriken. His sprawling hands grasped a familiar shape on the floor. A mischievous smile crossed Dante's face as he pulled the Huntsman 5000 closer. "Diavolo!" he cried. "You bastards, I'm bleeding to death!" Two of the ninja broke cover to check his condition and were quickly dealt with, but the others stayed back. "Seems I've got an advantage over you," Dante announced. "You have to capture me alive, but I can kill as many of you as I want. Kind of evens up the odds, doesn't it?"

He stuck his rifle over the top of the theatre seats and fired a volley of shots towards where his hunters had been lurking. He was rewarded by several cries of pain, but when Dante peered over the top of the seating the ninja were nowhere in sight. However, most of the all-male Kabuki porn cast was advancing towards him, brandishing various sexual implements as weapons. The rest were still on stage, tending the actors wounded by Dante's unfriendly fire.

"Oops."

One thing's for certain, the Crest noted as Dante ran for the nearest exit, pursued by the naked actors. *They know you don't fire blanks.*

Spatchcock and Flintlock burst into the *Okiya's* reception area to find three ninja waiting for them. "Don't hurt us," Flintlock whimpered. "We're innocent."

The tallest of the warriors regarded them with suspicion. "Nobody is innocent in a whorehouse."

"True," Spatchcock agreed, his face curling into an innocuous smile. "But we're more innocent than most of the people in here. If you see what I mean." The warrior glanced at the smallest of his colleagues, looking for guidance. Spatchcock realised the strike team's leader was a woman. All her attention was focused on a device strapped to her left wrist, while her right hand was pressed against one ear.

"Fall back, let him come to you," she hissed. Only her eyes were visible but they displayed her anger eloquently. "Remember, we're to take him alive. I don't care how enraged the porn actors are. If they catch up with him, you'll have to intervene." She noticed the tall warrior trying to get her attention. One glance at Spatchcock and Flintlock was all she needed to decide the pair's fate. "They are of no consequence, let them go."

Spatchcock pushed the quivering Flintlock forwards, but somehow tripped over his own feet and bumped into the nearest ninja. "Sorry, sir, sorry, begging your pardon, sorry," he said, bowing apologetically as he hurried towards the *Okiya*'s front doors. Once outside, Spatchcock scurried to the nearest hover-shuttle and jumped in. Flintlock was still standing on the dock, looking back at the brothel.

"What about Dante?"

"You couldn't wait to leave before, and now you're worried about him? Get in!"

Flintlock did as he was told. "I know Dante can look after himself but... did you see who was in charge of those ninja? A woman."

"I know." Spatchcock twisted the wheel of the hover-shuttle, sending it scudding away from the geisha house dock and towards the nearby *Sea Falcon*.

Flintlock was still watching the *Okiya*. "Nikolai always falls for a woman."

"They've been ordered to take him alive. I doubt even Dante can overcome all of them. So when they leave, we can follow."

"How? We don't know who this lot are or where they're going." Spatchcock retrieved something from his pocket and tossed it to Flintlock. The exile studied it, not comprehending. "What's this? A wristwatch?"

"Dante said they found him by locking on to the Crest. That's one of their tracking devices. I lifted it off that ninja when I bumped into him."

Flintlock smiled appreciatively. "Spatch, old boy, I could almost kiss you!"

"I'll want be wined and dined first, your lordship."

• • •

Dante burst from the kabuki theatre to find the four ninja waiting for him outside. He shot two before they could move, ducked beneath the lunge of another and smashed an elbow into the last one's face as he ran past. By the time his attackers recovered, the enraged and mostly naked porn cast was pouring from the theatre in hot pursuit. The resulting confusion gave Dante enough time to sprint away along the corridor. But the far end was also a dead end, with no doors or windows. Looking over his shoulder, Dante could see the angry mob hurrying towards him. He flung the butt of his rifle against the nearest wall, which ripped apart after a single blow. A sickly sweet, intoxicating scent billowed out from within, dizzying Dante with its alcoholic fumes.

"Fuoco, I remember that smell," he said, choking back the urge to vomit. "Whatever is causing that is how I got this hangover!"

Sake, the Crest observed, *an alcoholic beverage made from fermented rice, and traditionally served at a temperature of between forty and fifty degrees centigrade. Congratulations, you've found the chamber where they warm the liquid in bulk before distributing it throughout the* Okiya.

Dante looked through the torn paper wall. The chamber beyond best resembled a long swimming pool, its liquid contents stretching from wall to wall in all directions. A hatchway at the far end offering his only means of escape. "You're suggesting I swim through a tank of hot sake?"

Either that or take on two deadly ninja and a mob of murderous thespians from an all-male porn troupe.

Dante slung the rifle over his back and dived headfirst into the pool.

The strike team's leader could not understand how a single man had succeeded in escaping her insurgents. She cursed the survivors via her comms earpiece and set off with the two remaining team members to intercept Dante on the far side of the sake tank. "If you want something done properly, do it yourself," she muttered beneath her breath, sprinting through the *Okiya's* corridors.

Dante was halfway when he heard several splashes behind him. *Don't worry*, the Crest reassured him, *that's the kabuki cast after you. The ninja are finding another way round.*

"Easy... for you... to say," Dante gulped, in between mouthfuls of air and warm alcohol. "You're... not the one... being chased... by frustrated sex fiends!"

Now you know how most women feel about you, it fired back. *Try not to swallow so much. You'll be too drunk to open the access hatch.*

Dante spat out a long stream of sake and concentrated on swimming, but his attempt at the breaststroke was rapidly descending into doggy-paddle. When he reached the other side, his hands slipped on the side of the tank, whereby he sank down into the warm liquid. Frantic kicking got him back to the surface, by which time the actors were almost upon him. The nearest dived down and grabbed Dante's waist, fingers clawing at the thin strands holding the borrowed g-string in place.

Powerful arms plunged into the sake and grabbed hold of Dante's flailing limbs, pulling him up and out of the intoxicating liquid. He scrambled through the access hatch and kicked it shut behind him. The lock automatically slotted into place, trapping the actors on the other side.

"I made it," Dante spluttered disbelievingly. "Remind me never to drink again."

Stay alive long enough and I might have the opportunity.

"We have orders to capture you alive," a female voice announced. The smallest of the black-clad figures stepped forward to confront Dante. "However, there is nothing in our instructions about delivering you unhurt. So far you have killed or disabled seven of my colleagues. For that you must pay a price."

"I'd offer you cash," he slurred, suppressing a hiccup, "but I seem to have left my money pouch somewhere. Don't suppose you've seen it, have you?"

The woman lashed out savagely, the back of her hand slapping Dante's face with the power of a whip cracking. He winced and rubbed his cheek.

"I'm guessing I should take that as a no."

The woman slapped him again, first to one side with her palm, then the other way with the back of her hand, repeating the treatment until Dante grabbed hold of her wrist with surprising speed for someone so drunk.

Try not to antagonise her, the Crest warned.

"The last time a woman hurt me that much, we were in love," he hissed.

I despair of you sometimes, I really do.

Dante's attacker glanced down at his crotch, the sake-soaked genitals rapidly shrivelling in the cool, air-conditioned atmosphere. "There's not much of you to love," she said, her lips curling in disgust.

"I've never had any complaints," Dante maintained, ignoring the Crest's protestations in his mind. "I could give you a demonstration, if you like?"

She wrenched her hand free, her dark eyes sparkling with anger. The lithe woman stepped aside and signalled for the others to take over. "Hurt him, but do not kill or cripple. I leave the rest to your imagination."

Dante braced his back against the access hatch, trying to concentrate enough to will his cyborganic swords into place. But the effects of his swim across the sake tank were taking hold, turning his attackers into eight men, then a dozen. "Now boys," he slurred, "you wouldn't fight a man without trousers, would you? Besides, I can't fight all of you at once. Be patient, there's plenty of me to go around, you know..."

. . .

The fight was over in less than a minute.

When the men were satisfied with their work, they stepped aside to let their leader look at Dante's bloody and bruised body. She removed the fabric masking her beautiful face and shook her long, black hair free.

"I should kill you now," she spat at Dante. "It's no more than you deserve."

FOUR

"Know more and speak less."
– Russian proverb

"The Tsar's Purge Squads did much to exterminate any visible opposition to the Makarov dynasty after the war, but undercurrents of resistance remained. Many were those among the Empire's noble houses who spoke of their loyalty to the Tsar in public, while fostering discontent and resentment in private. But few were willing to act upon their feelings while the threat of reprisal hung heavy in the air. One of the rare organised attempts to foment was the short-lived Parliament of Shadows."

– Extract from *After the Tsar Wars*,
by Georgi Lucassovich

Dante woke with another splitting headache and the stench of stale alcohol on his breath. All around him was darkness, the air heavy with dust and neglect. A faint luminescence struggled to illuminate his surroundings. When he tried to move, pain shot through every muscle and tendon in his body. "Bojemoi," Dante gasped. "How many elephants trampled on me?"

You've been beaten bloody, drugged and you nearly drowned in a tank of hot sake, the Crest replied. *But at least you've got some clothes on now.*

Dante peeled back a black, skin-tight top to discover a patchwork of bruises on his skin, the purple and yellow contusions showing he had been unconscious for more than a day. Tight grey trousers covered his lower half, preserving his dignity. "Shame. I was getting rather fond of that g-string. It's always good to feel the sun on your cheeks."

Dante, you wear a g-string on your crotch, not your face.

"I didn't mean those cheeks." Wincing in pain, he sat up. The floor felt smooth and solid, while the air around him was still. Directly overhead a circular glimmer of light offered the only hint of a way out. "So, where am I this time?"

Inside an oubliette.

"That's not some kind of whale, is it?"

Dante, just once I wish you would resist the urge to say or do the first thing that enters your head. Life would be easier if you didn't always act on instinct.

"Yeah, but it'd also be a lot more boring. Besides, you wouldn't get the chance to scold me, or give one of your lectures about things I don't understand."

The Crest snorted derisively. *An oubliette*, it said archly, *is a dungeon with the only exit out of reach overhead. They are frequently circular or oval in shape.*

"Like being stuck inside a gigantic egg?"

Must you always reduce everything to the simplest possible example?

"If I want to piss you off, yes." Dante peered about his confinement. "No sign of my rifle. But they'd have to be pretty stupid to leave me with a weapon."

Like your cyborganic swords, for instance...

"Yeah! I could use those to try and cut my way–" He stopped, realising the Crest was teasing him. "I would have thought of that without your help, you know."

Of course you would.

"I didn't ask to be bonded with you!"

Instead of trying to escape, why don't you argue some more?

"All right, I–" Dante bit his bottom lip, not trusting himself to say anything more. Instead he concentrated on recreating his cyborganic blades. But try as he might, the silver and purple circuitry failed to appear from his hands.

You've obviously been injected with a neural inhibitor that disables your cyborganics, the Crest observed.

"Pity it didn't shut you up too," Dante muttered. Before the Crest could reply, the glimmer of light overhead began changing, becoming first a crescent, and then a complete circle. A metal ladder descended until it stopped in front of Dante's face.

"Climb out," a stern female voice commanded.

"What if I don't want to?" he asked.

"Then you can rot down there."

I suggest you do as you're told – for once.

"Nag, nag, nag." Dante grabbed the lower rungs of the ladder and hauled himself upwards, his arms and shoulders protesting each movement with fresh stabs of pain. "Fuoco, you're worse than my mother." He emerged from the dungeon into the beams of numerous spotlights. The same female voice as before commanded him to push the ladder down into the oubliette and close the entrance. Dante followed her instructions, all the while squinting around, trying to get a grasp of where he was.

He stood in the centre of a large, six-sided chamber. The floor was covered by a pattern of black and white checks that stretched out to the corners. High on the surrounding walls were five platforms that jutted out over the floor. The spotlights were mounted on the edge of these, but Dante could make out two figures standing on each platform. Their shapes were silhouetted in front of open doorways behind them. None of their faces were visible, as each figure was wearing a hood. A familiar scent hung in the air, teasing Dante's senses. What was it? Lavender? Heather? He knew he had smelled it before, but couldn't recall where. His mind was still a drugged muddle.

"Welcome." The voice was male, deep and booming. Dante thought he detected some St Petersburg in the accent, but couldn't be certain.

"Err, hi," he replied, warily.

"Welcome to the Parliament of Shadows," the voice continued. Dante thought it was coming from the middle platform, but the resonant walls bounced sound around in circles, creating echoes upon echoes. "This is our council chamber, where we meet to discuss future strategies and interrogate those who have information useful to our goals.

"Any chance you could turn down the lights?" Dante asked hopefully. "I'm guessing you got me here for a reason, but I won't be much use to you blind."

"These beams help shield our identity. We are a cabal intent on overthrowing the Tsar. Each one of us represents a different noble house, a dynasty that would dearly love to see the Makarov regime swept away and an end to all tyranny. As such, we must protect ourselves from the Tsar's spies and informants. That is why we call ourselves the Parliament of Shadows."

"Uh-huh." Dante scratched the side of his face while smiling broadly up at his captors. "Crest, what's a cabal?" he hissed under his breath.

A secret plot, a conspiracy. Don't you know anything?

"That's your job," Dante muttered.

No, my job is to teach you, mould you into a potential Emperor.

"Good luck!"

"I don't believe we have your full attention," the booming voice interjected. "Perhaps this will enhance your concentration."

There was a clicking sound and Dante felt as if his feet had caught fire. Sparks of electricity were dancing across the surface of the floor and Dante was dancing with them, involuntarily bouncing from foot to foot, trying to keep himself airborne. Whenever his flesh touched the floor another jolt of electricity surged through him, jangling his teeth and wits together.

Another click and it was over, the black and white checks no long alive with the sound of sizzling skin. Dante collapsed to the floor, cursing loudly at the Parliament's leader. He pulled his feet towards his face and blew on them, one hand trying to waft cold air over the scorched soles.

"When you've quite finished feeling sorry for yourself," the voice said, "we will lower the intensity of our lights a little. Consider it a gesture of goodwill."

No sooner were the words spoken than the beams softened slightly, allowing Dante to look at the figures around him without squinting. He stood and folded his arms. "What do you want of me?"

"This is not about you, Dante – this is about the future of the Empire. The noble houses we represent all had covert alliances with the House of Romanov during the war. Like your father, Dmitri, we believe that if anybody has a right to claim leadership of the Empire, it is the Romanovs. Your family can trace its claim to rule over all the Russias back almost a thousand years. We wish to restore the Empire to Romanov rule, and rid ourselves of the Tsar once and for all."

"The Romanovs are all dead, or haven't you been paying attention?" Dante sneered. "They got their asses kicked during the war."

You would do better not to antagonise your captors, the Crest advised.

"I don't give a damn what you or anybody else thinks," Dante continued. "The Romanovs are dead and I want nothing more to do with them. I renounced that name during the Battle of Rudinshtein. End of story."

Another click and a fresh dose of electrocution was the reply. The Parliament's spokesman continued once Dante had recovered. "Yes, most of the Romanovs are dead, but not all of them. Young Arkady is now a ward of the Tsar, kept close beside the Makarov despot. Lulu remains at large, intent on waging her own one-woman war against the Empire. And there are even rumours that Lady Jocasta survived the final onslaught at the Winter Palace, although we have no proof of that, nor knowledge of where she might be."

"I told you, I don't care about my so-called family anymore. They left Rudinshtein to the Imperials, abandoned the civilians while trying to save their own skins. I hope they all rot in hell together!"

"And then there is the bastard offspring of that noble dynasty. The roguish renegade known as Nikolai Dante."

"That's my name, don't wear it out," Dante spat back.

Such sparkling repartee, the Crest groaned. *I've told you before: never engage anyone in a battle of wits, Dante. You're not equipped for such a fight.*

"Your Crest is correct," another voice added from the shadows. "Shut up and listen to its advice, you might get out of here alive."

Dante spun round, trying to deduce who had spoken. He recognised the voice as the woman who had summoned him up from the dungeon, but where else had he heard her? "Hey, how do you know what the Crest is saying? It only talks inside my thoughts. Nobody else can hear it."

"I can read your mind, so I am also privy to what the Crest tells you," the woman snarled. "Now be quiet, for once in your life."

Ooh, I like her, the Crest said admiringly.

"Will you listen to our offer, or must we subject you to more shock treatment?" the Parliament's spokesman enquired, with a hint of menace beneath his calm words.

"You've got an offer? Fine, I'll listen," Dante replied casually.

"Have you heard of the Forbidden Citadel?"

"Can't say I have."

"That is unfortunate."

The Forbidden Citadel is a legendary fortress in the Himalayas, the Crest interjected, *supposedly invisible to the eyes of outsiders.*

Dante smiled. "I once went to a restaurant called the Jade Citadel. Or was it the Forbidden Pagoda? Could have been the Shirley Temple, now I come to think about it. Anyway, that place did a wonderful wonton soup."

"Your flippancy will be your downfall," the Parliament's spokesman warned.

"Yeah, yeah. What's your point?"

"The citadel is home to a secret weapon once jealously guarded by the Romanovs. We believe that weapon will enable us to overthrow the Tsar. Normally only those who have been within the citadel can see it from outside. But we have discovered it can also be found by those bearing a Weapons Crest."

"I should have known," Dante sighed.

"As we speak, the Tsar is sending an army of a thousand men into the Himalayas to find and take the Forbidden Citadel. That mission cannot be allowed to succeed. We want you to lead a small expedition into the mountains. You must reach the citadel first and retrieve the weapon."

"Why should I?"

"Would you rather the Tsar had the use of this device?" the Parliament's spokesman demanded. "We know little about the nature of the weapon, except that your father was keeping it as a last resort in his war against the Tsar. Such was the rapid reversal of fortune against the Romanovs, he never had a chance to deploy the weapon in battle. How would you feel if it was tested on Rudinshtein and its people, for whom you profess such affection?"

"Everything you've said is full of 'ifs' and 'buts'. Admit it, you don't know whether this weapon even works, do you?"

"No, but we do not dare let the weapon fall into the hands of the Tsar!"

"I understand that," Dante shouted back. "I'm not stupid."

All evidence to the contrary.

"Why should I go on this mission? You people don't even have the guts to show your faces, let alone take on the Tsar in the open!"

The woman standing in the shadows near Dante replied to his accusation. "You will go because you know you must. You will go because there is nobody who can go in your place – that's why you were brought here. And you will go because if you do not, I will murder you where you stand." She stepped out into the light to confront Dante. He recognised her as the same women who had supervised his capture on the *Okiya*. She was beautiful, with long, dark hair framing Oriental features and nut-brown skin. Her build was athletic but, to Dante's eyes, it curved outwards against her skin-tight garb in all the right places. Most striking were her eyes, anger overlaid on sadness, a flash of recklessness about their expression. Dante had met a few women like her in his life. She seemed dangerous, passionate and utterly implacable. Every time he'd fallen like a stone for them, and every time it had ended badly. *I'm in trouble here*, he decided.

"Yes, you are," she replied. "I can read your thoughts, remember?"

Dante's face switched from consternation to bafflement in moments, before settling into mischievous. A vicious slap wiped the smile from his features. "Keep your mind off my arse," she warned.

Sound advice, the Crest added.

"Don't you start," Dante muttered.

"You accused us of lacking the courage to show our faces," the parliament's spokesman said. "Very well, then. I shall reveal my face to all those present, so there can be no doubts about my belief in this cause." He deactivated the spotlight that was mounted on his platform and stepped forward so everyone could see him. With slow, deliberate movements, he pulled back his hood. Beneath was a middle-aged man with receding red hair and a prominent nose. "I am Zachariah Zhukov, leader of the House of Zhukov, and I challenge the rule of the tyrant Vladimir Makarov. Who else will step forward and identify themselves, show their courage?"

One by one the other members followed his example. Finally, Zhukov turned to Dante. "Well, we have risen to your challenge, Dante. Will you rise to ours?"

Spatchcock led the way through shattered gravestones and broken memorials, Flintlock hurrying nervously along behind. The ground was frozen by frost, each blade of grass a tiny sliver of ice and green. None of the inscriptions on the masonry were legible, having been systematically vandalised by some previous visitor. "Cheery sort of place, isn't it?" Flintlock whispered, hoping Spatchcock would think the cold was causing the tremors in his voice. He rubbed his hands together for warmth and clouds of steam issued from his nostrils as he breathed.

"Dante's close," Spatchcock muttered, all his attention focused on the stolen tracker strapped to his left wrist. "The signal's strongest over there." He hurried on, clambering over a stone angel whose wings had been shattered.

Flintlock moved more awkwardly, despite his long legs. Spatchcock scuttled like a spider over all kinds of terrain, whereas the exiled aristocrat still felt it beneath him to be furtive. A lifetime of training for greatness did not prepare him for low company and low life. He tripped on the wingless angel, tumbling face first into a freshly dug mound of soil. "I say, I'm most dreadfully sorry," Flintlock spluttered, his mouth full of dirt.

Spatchcock glared back at him. "Will you stop buggering about, your lordship. We're trying to–" He stopped abruptly, noticing the earth beneath Flintlock. "What's that doing there?"

"What's what doing where?" the Brit replied. "Give me a hand, Spatch."

But the little man ignored his fallen comrade, preferring to dig his hands into the dirt. "This shouldn't be here. The ground's frozen, hasn't been touched in months, but somebody's dug this over recently, probably today."

A low rumble of machinery startled them both. They scrambled clear of the dirt mound as it descended into the ground, revealing a concrete staircase hidden below. "That must be the way in," Spatchcock realised.

Flintlock was about to comment when he felt a small, hard circle of metal jab into his back. "Spatch, old boy. I think we've got company…"

"Don't worry, we'll wait until they've gone, then nip down the stairs."

"I don't think that's going to work," Flintlock ventured, peering over his shoulder at the cluster of armed guards standing behind him.

Dante was still arguing with the Parliament of Shadows when Spatchcock and Flintlock appeared from a concealed doorway, striding purposefully into the centre of the chamber. "There he is. What did I tell you, Spatch? My nose for a brigand never fails me. It's that bounder, Nikolai Dante. The Tsar will pay a pretty penny for this rapscallion."

"Who are you two?" Zhukov demanded from his platform, unhappy at the interruption.

"Begging your pardon, sir," Spatchcock replied, bowing grandly. "We are Spatchcock and Flintlock, bounty hunters extraordinaire. We have tracked this fugitive halfway across the Empire and may we thank you all for keeping him detained. Now, we shall relieve you of this burden and take him to face his crimes before the proper authorities."

Dante rolled his eyes. "I hope this isn't your idea of a rescue mission because it doesn't exactly inspire confidence."

Flintlock performed an elaborate mime that suggested there was nothing to worry about, or else he was planning to take up belly dancing; Dante wasn't sure which was the more accurate description. "My learned friend is correct," Flintlock announced, turning back towards Zhukov. "We hereby claim Dante as our captive and will be removing him into our custody."

The woman guarding Dante pulled a weapon from a holster strapped to her thigh and aimed it at the new arrivals. "Lord Zhukov, these men are known accomplices of Dante. They were with him at the *Okiya*." She stepped towards Spatchcock and ripped the tracker off his wrist. "They must have followed him here, after stealing this device from one of my men."

"In that case, they will share Dante's fate, whatever he decides."

"Spatch, old boy, I don't think they're falling for the bounty hunter story," Flintlock muttered quietly.

"We'd have gotten away with it if you'd kept your mouth shut." Spatchcock looked at his former commander. "What's this decision you've got to make?"

Dante smiled, despite himself. "Either all three of us are executed here…"

"Right," Spatchcock said, his face thick with concentration. "No, don't like the sound of that much. What's the second option?"

"…or we can embark on an impossible quest to find a legendary fortress that probably doesn't exist so we can steal a secret weapon of terrifying power."

Flintlock was busy winking lustily at the beautiful, gun-wielding Oriental woman nearby. Spatchcock elbowed him in the ribs. "I say, what were the options again?" Dante repeated them for the Brit. "Well, I think the impossible quest sounds more my cup of tea, don't you?"

Spatchcock nodded his agreement. Dante gave a thumbs-up signal to Zhukov. "I've just got one question. What's the pay like for suicide missions?"

FIVE

"Be a rogue, but be kind."
– Russian proverb

"The so-called Russian rogue is, in fact, a thief, a brigand and a philander for whom the opposite sex is merely a way to provide him with physical pleasure and visual stimuli. Dante's notoriety is well known across the Empire, but the circumstances of his first significant brush with the Imperial authorities are remarkably illustrative of the renegade's salacious behaviour. He was arrested in St Petersburg in 2666, after being found in the bedchamber of Lady Zoya, an Imperial seductress employed by the Tsar's own hussars. Dante made a cowardly attack upon a captain of the hussars, then fled the scene in terror for his life.

Not content with having besmirched the good name of Lady Zoya, he conspired to steal her jewel-encrusted eroticostume as some tawdry souvenir of his sexual exploits. The thief was captured trying to sell the garment at the Tsyganov black market. He was brought before the Tsar on charges of banditry, fraud, deceit, unauthorised duelling and seduction for the purposes of financial gain. The fact that Dante offered no defence for his crimes speaks volumes about his character. It is regrettable the Tsar

did not have this vile creature executed immediately. Such action would have spared the Empire
from Dante's subsequent displays of carnality, law-
lessness and cocksure bravado."

– Extract from *Nikolai Dante: A Character
Assassination*, various contributors

Once they had agreed to undertake the Parliament of Shadows's mission, Dante and his comrades found themselves
being treated like honoured guests. The trio was escorted to
private quarters for their ablutions, before being offered a
hot meal. Spatchcock had little enthusiasm for washing,
heading straight for the food table in the adjoining room. "I
haven't had a square meal for three days," he said. "Anyway,
every time you wash, it invites fresh bacteria on to your
body. I like the bacteria I've already got."

Dante and Flintlock manhandled the odorous ex-felon into
a bath full of hot water and bubbles, holding his head
beneath the surface until Spatchcock agreed to bathe. "If
we're supposed to be racing the Tsar's men to the Forbidden
Citadel, I don't want your lack of personal hygiene giving us
away," Dante said while Spatchcock washed. "One bath a
year won't do you any harm."

The trio emerged to find fresh clothes laid out for them,
form-fitting tops and trousers in stretch fabrics, plus numerous
outer layers for insulation against the mountain cold. Beside
these were a selection of boots and climbing equipment, while
hooded jackets in white and silver hung on the wall.

"White? Not very flattering for somebody with my fair
complexion," Flintlock complained. "I'll look terribly
washed out."

"That's the point. They're camouflage to hide us in the
snow," Dante replied. He was pleased to find his rifle lying
among the equipment, restored to his possession again. The
Huntsman 5000 was made by the same alien technology
responsible for the Romanov Weapons Crests. The rifle

created its own ammunition internally and so never needed reloading, a useful quality in the sort of fire fights Dante encountered all too frequently. He patted the weapon appreciatively, then settled down to dinner with the others. "I could eat a horse."

Flintlock stopped chewing, a forkful of sausage frozen in front of his lips. "You don't think this is horse, do you? I've had some dubious dishes since leaving the old country, but I've no urge to eat equine."

"I don't mind a good haunch of horse," Spatchcock said happily, smacking his lips. "Can be a tasty bit of meat, especially if you marinade it first. Some red wine, a few capers, handful of freshly chopped herbs..."

"Arsenic, cyanide, strychnine," Dante added mischievously.

"I never mix cooking with the concocting of poisons," Spatchcock protested.

"With your cooking it's hard to tell the difference," Flintlock interjected.

"Well, if you lifted a finger to help, your lordship, I wouldn't have to do all the cooking. But you're so high and mighty, I doubt you could boil water."

"The only boils I associate with you, Spatch, are the ones on your arse."

Dante didn't bother trying to referee his two comrades' argument. They bickered worse than him and the Crest. Only a well-matched couple could argue so much and still stay together. He smiled and continued eating, happy at his unholy trinity being back together again. *If only I could escape the nagging feeling I'm being watched, like someone itching the back of my mind,* he thought. Then he remembered the Oriental woman, how she was able to hear the Crest speak inside his thoughts. *She could be watching me through my eyes right now.*

Dante closed his eyes and thought of the most repulsive sexual scenario he could imagine. His mind was flooded with images of the telepathic woman, himself, a bathtub full of jelly and a game of hide the sausage. The presence at the back of his thoughts abruptly vanished. "That's better. Now I can enjoy my meal in peace," Dante announced. His bickering companions looked at him as if he'd suddenly sprouted an extra head. "Don't mind me," Dante replied, happily shovelling another forkful of meat into his mouth.

Lord Zhukov came to bid them farewell in the morning, after the trio had snored through the night in a private dormitory. Dante and the others met Zhukov in the meeting chamber with the black and white checked floor, but now the spotlights were off and the mood much less threatening. On his raised platform Zhukov had seemed powerful, almost magisterial. In person he was small in stature, only a few inches taller than Spatchcock. His eyes flickered around the chamber nervously, as if he expected Imperial troops to burst in at any moment.

"Forgive my unease," Zhukov said. "This is the first time the Parliament of Shadows has taken action against the Tsar."

"We're the ones doing the dirty work," Spatchcock muttered darkly.

"True, but even meeting with the likes of Dante is an offence punishable by death. To conspire against the Makarov regime is to invite severe retribution. Our noble houses would be ruthlessly exterminated if word of this endeavour reached the Imperial Palace." Zhukov explained how the trio would be transported to the foot of the Himalayas in a stolen flyer, before continuing their quest on foot. "We have arranged for a native of that region to act as your guide within the mountains. They will get you close. The rest is up to you, Nikolai."

Dante nodded. It was much as he had expected. "Who's going to be our guide dog then? Some crusty old Sherpa with fewer teeth than wits?"

Look who's talking, the Crest chipped in. *A man with fewer wits than teeth.*

"I will be your guide." The voice was female, the tone severe. Dante didn't need to look round to know who had spoken. It was the same woman who had wished him dead in the Geisha House of the Rising Sun; the same woman who had threatened to execute him in the same room the previous day; the same woman who had been reading his thoughts since he got here. "Correct," she replied.

Flintlock watched Dante and the new arrival glower at each other. "You'd almost think those two used to be lovers," he whispered to Spatchcock.

Dante heard the comment and smiled. He let his eyes wander down over the woman's body, mentally removing her from the skin-tight jumpsuit. She rewarded him with a slap across the face.

Dante cried out, nursing his wounded cheek. "Diavolo! At least take your jewellery off before you hit me like that."

She retaliated with a smile. "I was only using your own emblem against you." She held the ring in front of her face, a smear of blood visible on the metal band. Fixed into the gold was a tiny yellow circle with a double-headed eagle inside – the symbol of the Romanovs.

"Where did you get that?" Dante demanded.

Uncertainty clouded the woman's beautiful features. "I don't know."

"Crest, can you identify the origins of that ring?"

No. I've never seen its like before.

"But that is the Romanov symbol, yes?"

Yes. Beyond that, I can tell you no more.

"You'll have plenty of time to talk about this en route to your destination," Zhukov said. "Your flyer will be ready to leave within the hour. Might I suggest gathering your equipment and then all meet back here? Mai Tsai will escort you back to the dormitory, gentlemen."

The beautiful Oriental strode from the room, Spatchcock and Flintlock hurrying after her, both with their eyes fixed on the bounce of her pert buttocks. Dante followed, still rubbing the side of his face where the Romanov ring had grazed his skin. He waited until they were all in the dormitory before speaking, a wicked glint in his eye. "Forgive me, I missed your name when Lord Zhukov said it before. What did he call you?"

The woman's eyes narrowed as she replied. "Mai Tsai."

Dante couldn't keep the smirk from his face. "Your name is My Sigh?" He winked at Spatchcock and Flintlock. "I'll make her sigh alright."

Another slap resounded against his cheek. "Fuoco, I wish you'd stop doing that!"

"And I wish you'd stop insulting my intelligence and drooling over my body," she snapped back. "At least with your two colleagues I can choose to ignore their lecherous expressions and furtive glances, I don't have to listen to their thoughts as well. I lack that option with you."

Spatchcock frowned. "Hang on... You can read his mind, but not ours?"

"Correct."

"So if I thought of the most disgusting, perverted thing I can imagine..."

"Nothing out of the ordinary then," Flintlock commented, getting a glare from Spatchcock for his interruption.

"...you wouldn't know what I was thinking?"

"I only see into Dante's mind," Mai replied. "Crawling through the sewer of his thoughts is bad enough. I have no wish to sample your cesspit as well."

"Ah, Spatch. You've only just met and already she knows you so well."

Dante and Mai went outside while Flintlock and Spatchcock's argument descended into a frenzy of hair pulling and verbal abuse. Dante closed the door on his comrades. "Ignore those two," he said. "They fight like cats and dogs, but their hearts are in the right place, mostly."

Mai nodded. "They followed you halfway across the continent. That shows great loyalty. It is a useful asset for where we are going."

"How well do you know the Himalayas?"

"I believe I was born there."

"You believe? Don't you know?"

"There are many gaps in my memory, things I do not understand or cannot explain." Mai twisted the gold band on her finger. "The origin of this ring is one such example. My ability to read your thoughts is another fact I cannot explain. I believe this journey may help find answers to these and other questions that trouble me."

Dante nodded and smiled. "Well, it shouldn't take long. I mean, how hard can it be to find the Forbidden Citadel?"

Explorers and treasure hunters have been searching for this lost fortress since before Mount Everest was conquered, more than seven hundred years ago. Nobody has found it. At least, nobody has found it and come back alive to tell the tale.

"Ah, I see."

Nothing's ever easy with you, is it Dante?

He looked at Mai and smirked. "Some things are harder than others, if you know what I mean."

She lashed out at his face, but Dante caught her wrist and held it firmly. "I was goading you deliberately that time, to see how you would react. Unless you learn to control that temper, you're liable to get all of us killed in the mountains. Understand?" Mai nodded and he let go of her arm. "You don't have to like me, but we have to work together, okay?"

"Don't worry," she snarled. "It's my job to keep you alive long enough to find the citadel. But the moment you've outlived your usefulness, I'll take the greatest of pleasure in executing you, you murdering bastard." Mai marched away, leaving Dante utterly perplexed.

"I'd never met this woman until a few days ago and she wants me dead already. I wonder why?"

A good question, the Crest agreed. *Most women need to spend a week in your company before becoming homicidal.*

The door to the private quarters swung open and Flintlock tumbled out, trying to appear relaxed, his bag of climbing equipment being thrown out after him. "I say, is it time to go yet?"

Spatchcock emerged with a smile of satisfaction. He looked around. "Where's her ladyship gone? Don't tell me you've scared her off already."

"Apparently she's planning to kill me once I've outlived my usefulness," Dante replied. "She didn't specify a particular reason."

"Business as usual then," Flintlock said, getting to his feet. "Shall we go?"

General Ivanov savoured the exquisite torment of his cat-o'-nine-tails as it flailed through the air. He had once heard an adage that the first cut was the deepest. Nothing could be further from the truth with the lash. The first taste of leather upon skin, it was the most shocking, yes, but that was only the beginning of a long, seductive process that took place during a whipping. Repeated blows dulled the nerve endings beneath the skin, until the skin split open. As always, that moment brought tears, the pain almost unbearable for whoever was receiving the brutal treatment, as an involuntary cry for mercy would colour the air. The blow after the skin gave way – that was the deepest, when the steel-tipped ends of each leather strand bit into the exposed flesh. Everything after that was an anti-climax; painful, yes, but more akin to a blow upon a bruise. Each successive impact had less effect than the last. To continue was useless.

A rapid knocking took Ivanov's thoughts. He let the lash slip from his grasp to the floor, its leather tails stained crimson with blood. His face was bathed in sweat, such was the effort of his latest thrashing, but it had given him little satisfaction. "Come," he shouted, wincing at the effort.

His second-in-command entered, stood to attention and saluted briskly. "General, the men are ready for your inspection."

"Very well," Ivanov replied. "I've done all I can here."

"Yes, sir."

"Major, I'll need you to administer the final step of the punishment."

"Of course, sir."

The general gestured to a large jar of white crystals beyond his reach. "The salt is over there. I want you to pour it into the wounds. Don't stop until the jar is empty, no matter how much the subject may cry out."

"Yes, sir." The Enforcer strode to the glass jar and removed its lid. He picked up the salt container and approached the general. "Now?"

"Go ahead." Ivanov tensed himself, preparing for the screams that would fill the room.

The Enforcer positioned the jar above the bloody back and began pouring, tipping every grain of salt over his superior officer's writhing body. Ivanov howled with rage and fury, his eyes bulging out in their sockets. Finally, when his self-inflicted punishment was complete, he gave a quiet shudder of delight.

"Very good, major. I will be out to inspect the men once I have finished cleaning myself up. We leave for the mountains at dawn, so I expect to see everyone with all alpine kit and equipment, is that clear?"

"Yes, sir."

"Very well, dismissed." Ivanov watched his second-in-command leave, before rising from the whipping stool. He picked up the cat-o'-nine-tails and held it lovingly against his face, inhaling the pungent, metallic odour of blood and sweat that had soaked into the leather. "You know how to treat me, don't you, my love? You know how I feel about you, your caress upon my skin, your pleasure and my pain. You know it all, don't you, my sweet?" Ivanov kissed the cat-o'-nine-tails, then laid it tenderly inside a specially made box of sandalwood, lined with red velvet and inlaid with his initials in gold lettering. "You rest now," the general whispered, his voice soothing, like that of a lover. "You rest, my beauty."

Spatchcock and Flintlock were first to emerge from the Parliament of Shadows's underground headquarters, finding themselves back in the frozen graveyard. Mai bounded up the steps into the cold air of morning, following them outside. She scanned their surroundings with practiced ease, her sidearm ready to fire, while the two men joked with each other. "Back in the cemetery again," Spatchcock noted. "Hope this doesn't become a habit."

Dante was last to emerge, a hefty backpack laden with climbing equipment slung over his shoulders. As he glanced about for their transport, a chill of recognition crossed his face. "I know this place. Crest, isn't this...?"

The Romanov Necropolis, it confirmed. *It's the final resting place for generation upon generation of your adopted, noble family.*

Dante had been here only once, before the war. The Romanovs had gathered for a hunting party, a tradition among the Russian aristocracy for centuries. It was supposed to be a way for families to get closer, bonding through the butchery of innocent animals. For Dante the experience had been a sobering one. He found himself acting as bodyguard to the Romanov matriarch, Lady Jocasta, when three hired assassins tried to kill her. The hitmen died in the effort, but Dante learned two cold, hard facts that day. All his siblings had been the product of an incestuous relationship between Dmitri and Jocasta, albeit one consummated by science, not between the sheets. Sickening as that was, Dante was more disturbed to discover it was Dmitri who hired the assassins to kill Jocasta. She was a barrier to the ruthless ambition of the Romanovs, as well as its progenitor. From that moment Dante had known he could never truly be part of such a family. That was a few years ago. So much had happened since then. So much pain, so much suffering. He had returned to the graveyard of the Romanovs once again and he felt no different. For the most part he was glad they were dead.

"How can you feel that way?" Mai demanded. "I would give anything to have my family back."

"Do you have to eavesdrop on every thought I have?" Dante demanded angrily. "Bojemoi, it's bad enough having the Crest in my brain all the time–"

Charming!

"I don't need you in my mind as well!"

Mai strode towards him, shaking her head. "You think I want to be inside that slime-infested rat hole you call a brain? Every whim, every notion that passes through your perverted cranium gets transmitted into my mind too."

"Well, try keeping your comments to yourself then," Dante suggested through gritted teeth. "The last thing I need for the rest of this mission is you imposing your morality on me, okay?"

"Morality? You don't know the meaning of the word."

Spatchcock and Flintlock exchanged weary looks of resignation. "I guess we're not leaving just yet," the Brit muttered out the corner of his mouth.

"You think they want to be alone?" the smaller man asked.

"Not yet. They're too busy hating each other at the moment," Flintlock replied. He sat down on a nearby tombstone, Spatchcock following his example.

Dante and Mai were still arguing, their voices getting progressively louder. "Don't lecture me on right and wrong," Dante snarled. "You know why I'm half-Romanov? Because my father raped my mother and I was the result. They called me the bastard of the family, but I couldn't hold a candle to the rest of them."

"Didn't stop you taking their name during the war, did it?" Mai snapped. "Didn't stop you claiming Rudinshtein as your own private fiefdom, did it? Didn't stop you abandoning its people and those who tried to defend them?"

"Were you there?" he hissed. "Did you fight on the front-line? Did you experience one moment of that battle?"

"No," Mai admitted, "but my brother did. And he died because of you, you murdering bastard!" She burst into tears, slumping to the snow-covered ground.

A long, painful silence was eventually broken by the sound of an approaching flyer. Spatchcock stood up and smiled. "Well, I think it's time we were going."

Flintlock nodded. "Absolutely. Nothing like a crying woman and an angry Dante to make any journey fly by." He started towards the flyer, which had landed on a nearby hill-top. "You two coming with us or not?"

Dante looked down at the sobbing woman on her knees in front of him. She's only a girl, he realised. She's eighteen at most. I didn't think–

"You never think," Mai replied, wiping her face dry with one sleeve as she stood. "You blunder in, causing chaos and hurting more people than you help. But when the going gets tough, you run and hide. That's who you are, Dante." She picked up her rucksack and hurried after the others.

A little harsh, but not entirely inaccurate, the Crest added.

"Don't you start," Dante spat. He ran after Mai, Spatchcock and Flintlock, catching up with them as they boarded the sleek, silver flyer. It rose into the crisp air and made a slow circle of the hills surrounding the graveyard. Inside the cabin Spatchcock took the opportunity to do some sightseeing.

"Hey, what's that over there?" He pointed through a window at the remains of a mighty tower. Its structure was torn apart as if ravaged by a ferocious attack in the past.

"The Winter Palace," Dante replied, his words without feeling. "It must have been destroyed during the last days of the war." He looked at Mai, who kept her gaze fixed out of the opposite side of the flyer. "And that wasn't the only thing."

Beneath the graveyard, Lord Zhukov watched the flyer's departure on a screen. Satisfied Dante, Mai and the others were gone, Zhukov ventured out on to his platform over-looking the council chamber. The other members from the Parliament of Shadows were gathered on the black and white floor below, nervous faces betraying their fear. "You will be happy to know Dante and his comrades have left safely for their mission."

One of the members stepped forwards to address him. Lady Nikita was the House of Zabriski's matriarch. She was a stern-faced woman in her fifties who normally shared the leader's platform with Zhukov. "Would you mind telling us what is going on? We were informed you wanted to speak with all of us before we left. Why have we been herded on to the chamber floor like subjects for interrogation?"

Zhukov smiled at her. "Ah, Nikita, I knew I could depend upon you to step forward and confront me. For months you have coveted my position as leader of this assembly. Your ambition for power will be your undoing."

"What are you talking about?"

"All of you are just as guilty," he continued, addressing the other members. "At least she has the courage to challenge me."

"You haven't answered my question," Lady Nikita said, refusing to be ignored. "What is the purpose of this gathering, Zhukov?"

"Why, to make it easier for the Raven Corps to kill you, of course." He smiled at her like a benevolent parent explaining a simple truth to an obtuse child. "The soldiers will be here within minutes. They have orders to execute all of you. The manner and means of your deaths is up to you. Those who co-operate fully, providing the names of other treasonous conspirators against the Tsar, will be slain in as quick and painless a manner as possible. Those who refuse to help will suffer all the torments and agonies we can inflict before their bodies give in."

"The man's gone mad," Lady Nikita muttered. "Come down here this instant and explain yourself."

"I don't think so."

"In that case I will come to you." She strode to the nearest door. As her fingers touched the metal handle, electricity surged through Lady Nikita's body. White sparks danced across her, and her face contorted into a mocking grimace. Lips pulled back from her teeth as if to smile. After several seconds, her fingers let go of the handle and her body fell backwards to the floor, still twitching and jerking. Then she lay still, a wisp of blue smoke rising from her corpse, a pool of urine slowly spreading out from beneath her.

The effect on the other members was all too apparent. Several screamed, others took to praying and sank to their knees, sobbing uncontrollably. Once Lady Nikita was dead, her colleagues turned to face Zhukov one by one, compelled to see his response. Their leader was smiling broadly.

"Simply shocking," he said, a slight giggle of hysteria betraying his words. Zhukov cleared his throat before continuing. "I regret to inform you all that the Parliament of Shadows was a trap, a ruse to flush out dissident elements within the Empire's noble houses. The clue was in the name. You see, this gathering was an elaborate shadow play to lance the boil of petty ambitions and conspiratorial discontent within the aristocracy. Left unchecked, such sentiment could one day have become sufficiently organised to create a significant threat to the Tsar. So he asked me to create the means for such a movement to find its voice and even provided the funding to create this underground headquarters beneath the Romanov Necropolis. Quite appropriate, don't you think? You will all die beneath the graves of those you would resurrect as rulers of the Empire. I can't think of a more fitting epitaph for the last pocket of resistance."

Another of the parliament's members dared to speak up, his face pale and perspiring, his hands nervously rubbing together. "If we co-operate, do you promise to let our families live?"

"No. Why should I? The reprisals against your kin, your noble houses and all you hold dear will be as savage as they are swift. All you can be assured of is that the manner of your own passing will be briefer if you help us. That is all traitors such as you deserve." Zhukov looked down his nose at the man who had spoken. "It will probably be of no comfort for you, but the Tsar had not expected the venture to bear fruit so soon. He was prepared to play the long game and let your trust in me build until you were ready to reveal your identities. It was his idea that the Parliament should meet in secret, so that none of us knew each other's faces. Happily, the arrival of Dante gave me the chance to force events along."

"So, he was part of this conspiracy?"

Zhukov snorted at such a notion. "His hatred of the Tsar is even greater than yours. No, Dante was merely a pawn, a means to an end. His mission to the Himalayas is a fool's quest, an errand that will lead inevitably to his death. Just as his appearance here has led, inevitably, to your deaths."

The sound of marching became audible, heavy footfalls growing louder and louder, echoing around the council chamber.

"Ah, that will be the Raven Corps. Right on time." Zhukov smiled. "I would like to say it's been a pleasure knowing you all, but I consider each member of this so-called Parliament of Shadows a disgrace to the Empire. None shall mourn your passing, nor should they. Goodbye, ladies and gentlemen."

SIX

"The heart hath no window."
– Russian proverb

"Most people have only the slightest knowledge of the Himalayas. Fewer still possess any first hand experience of this remote region of the Empire. Ask any citizen in St Petersburg or New Moscow and they will know it is a mountainous area. To them the Himalayas are a vague concept, a far away place made up of snow-capped peaks and little else. They might have heard of the Sherpa, a people of Mongolian origin who live on the mountain slopes and are much sought after for their climbing prowess. The region in which they live has been fought over for centuries and remains one of the few unspoiled parts of the Empire.

The Himalayas are actually a vast mountain system in South Asia, extending one and a half thousand miles from Kashmir, in the west, to Assam, in the east between the valleys of the Rivers Indus and Brahmaputra. This system covers most of the lands once known as Nepal, Sikkim, Bhutan and the southern edge of Tibet. The Himalayas are the highest mountain range in the world, with several peaks over twenty-five thousand feet."

– Extract from Secret Destinations of the Empire
by Mikhail Palinski

The girl sat alone in her room, listening to the world beyond the windows. She was allowed to leave the temple-residence a few times a year, as part of the key religious festivals observed by the followers of her religion. But even then, she was not permitted to play with other children her own age. She was special. Those who looked after her could not risk her to be injured. Besides, she was forbidden to laugh or even smile in public, as it was believed it would bring great misfortune upon the country. Her family were a distant memory and the laughter of other children in her village barely an echo in her thoughts.

She sat on a throne of exotically carved wood, with clusters of cinnamon-scented candles alight on either side of the raised dais. Lamps burned yak butter for illumination, adding to the heady aromas in the room. Discarded nearby was a plate laden with fresh fruit, while a carved wooden elephant rested alongside, its trunk pointing up to the wooden beams criss-crossing the ceiling. The room was filled with the richest treasures: statues of elephants and lions made of pure gold; glittering gemstones and bejewelled icons; tapestries with the most intricate designs and finely woven fabrics, the most impressive of which, a simple white material interwoven with threads of gossamer-thin silver, hung on the wall behind her throne. The effect of the design was so subtle, it was only apparent when seen from precisely the right angle. Otherwise it was close to invisible – a nagging peripheral vision. The girl knew that design well. She knew its significance better than anyone alive. Such was her burden, one of a thousand she had to bear.

Like the walls around her, the girl was dressed in red and gold. Her long, black hair was held back from her face by a golden tiara. It was merely the frontispiece for a grand headdress, made of the finest plumes and spun gold, encrusted with stones of crimson and black. Painted on her forehead was a vermilion third eye, on a black backdrop of mustard oil and soot. The monks had told her that this was the divine eye that saw everything. She could look through every individual's mind, and fathom things beyond a common person's understanding. This responsibility hung heavy upon her, like the numerous beaded necklaces strung round her neck.

If a stranger walked into her throne room, they would have been struck most of all by the sadness of her countenance. Her eyes were dark and expressive, a gorgeous contrast to the pure whiteness of her teeth. Her skin was unblemished, her hands and bare feet soft and delicate to the touch. But nobody touched her, nobody hugged her, and no strangers were allowed into her throne room: not even the other members of what had once been her family. She was caught in a life of utter seclusion.

Soon it would be time to pray. The monks would return, Khumbu at their head, as always. They would bow as they entered, prostrating themselves at her feet, worshipping her presence, always reverential. Then she would eat. Then she would sleep. Then another day would begin, much the same as before. How much longer would this life continue? But the girl already knew the answer to the question. That was another of her burdens. She pushed it away.

Outside, children were playing, chattering to each other. They were careless and joyful. The girl eased herself forward on the throne until she could put both feet on the floor. As she slid off the high seat, the elaborate headdress, which was fixed to her hair with a dozen tiny pins, tilted and almost fell free. She hurriedly pushed it back into position. It would not do to drop the headdress; Khumbu would disapprove. She heard the distant thunder outside, as if giants were calling from one mountaintop to the next, wistful and angry, searching for their lost loves.

The girl was only seven. She had been living in the crimson chamber for three years. Her old life seemed an eternity ago. It was like an old dream. Back then she was just another child among the many of her village, living high up the mountain slopes, unaware how hard her family fought to survive in such an unforgiving environment. It took a special kind of people to cling on here. They required both resilience and acquiescence to the whims of the mountains. The tall peaks were forces of nature, unbound and unbroken by man. You lived among them, but you never conquered them – she knew that now.

The girl sighed.

Since then the room had become her home. She had known what was to come – it was her talent. She knew that something was almost upon them and still there were no answers, no insight and no wisdom to solve the riddle. She had to go on and play out her part. She had to fulfil her destiny. Whatever comes of that, will come, in darkness or in light, she thought. Beyond that, not even I can see. I must be content with that.

She hitched up her ceremonial garb high enough so she could walk without tripping over the hem. Picking her way carefully over the ancient rugs that covered the black-stained floorboards she walked to the doorway of glass and wood that led out on to the balcony. Her left hand clasped the heavy golden handle and twisted it, pushing against the door. After resisting her temporarily, it opened with a sigh. The girl stepped out of the room, thick with incense and dust, into the cold autumn air.

A riot of aromas filled her nostrils. Meats and spices fought with animal dung and burning wood for precedence. Beneath the balcony was a quadrangle, filled by the monthly market. Merchants and farmers, from villages on the mountain slopes, made the trek up to the citadel, bringing their crops and belongings to sell or exchange. Children ran excitedly between the makeshift stalls and carts, while beasts were fed and watered in a quiet corner of the stone courtyard, straw laid down beside the trough for them. I wonder if my family is among them, the girl thought? Should I even know them if I saw them? Her parents had been present at the ceremony to confirm her as the chosen one, but that was long ago.

The holy men had spent days testing her, asking questions and seeking answers beyond the knowledge of any four year-old. Even when they decided she possessed the required twenty-seven noble virtues, there had been one final trial to undergo.

A dozen buffalo were sacrificed in the courtyard. Their heads were gathered onto a bloody pile. At the urging of the monks, she had walked around the grotesque display, while a man in a hideous mask danced nearby. Somehow, she had not flinched. Perhaps terror kept me still, she thought. It did not matter. Khumbu and his brethren had taken her inside. Their chanting filled the night for hours, calling for the goddess to come down and enter her body.

The next morning she was dressed in the garb befitting her new status and they led her back out into the courtyard. A huge crowd – her family amongst them – watched as she walked across a white cloth, the last rite of passage. From that moment onwards, the monks called her Mukari. But the truth of what was to come had already claimed her. It lived inside her now, a constant companion.

The girl looked down at the quadrangle once more. I see the courtyard as it was, the joyful faces of my proud family, the others applauding and cheering. I see the courtyard as it is now: the running children, the villagers trading goods for grain and bread. I see the courtyard as it will be: blood running along the cracks between the stones, the dead bodies piled like unwanted rags. Beyond that? I see only darkness and sadness and nothing else, nothing more.

She sagged against the wooden rail around the edge of the balcony, her feet nudging a smooth pebble over the side. It fell on the shoulder of a plump man passing below, his arms full of vegetables. Startled, he looked up and smiled, his face coming alive at seeing the girl. "Mukari, Mukari," he called, his voice echoing around the stone walls of the quadrangle. Other merchants and villagers turned towards him. A crowd formed quickly beneath the balcony, dozens of people lifting their hands to the girl in supplication, their sun-bronzed faces creasing into smiles, their narrow eyes sparkling with excitement. Each raised his voice and chanted. "Bless us, Mukari! Bless us!"

The girl waved at them shyly, careful not to let any expression show on her face. You must never smile, Khumbu had told her a thousand times. Never laugh before your people.

Another cry came from inside the chamber of crimson and gold behind her. "Mukari!" It was Khumbu's stern voice. "You should not be out on the balcony. You know it unsettles the people, when you make an unexpected appearance like this. Come back inside please."

The girl sighed and returned to her room, a sudden gust of wind closing the doors once she was inside. Khumbu was on his knees and bent forward to kiss the floor in genuflection. Sunlight filtered through the windows and reflected on his smooth and hairless scalp. The saffron colouring of his monk's robes accentuated his Himalayan tan. He waited until the girl was seated on her throne before looking up. When he did, his sightless eyes stared past her, an admonishing cast about his features. "Please, goddess. You must not look upon your people without protection. These are troubled times. Rumours fly between the villages of Imperial troops that are massing in the valleys below."

The Mukari already knew about the soldiers; how could she not? "Don't worry, Khumbu. I have seen what is to come. I have nothing to fear from my own people. It is the outsiders who bring death to this place. The gates of the Forbidden Citadel will fall–"

"Never! It is impossible!" the monk protested, before realising the temerity of his outburst. "Forgive me, goddess, I lost control of my tongue. You are all seeing and all knowing, if you say something is true, it must be so. But how can outsiders find the citadel? My brethren and I protect these walls day and night. Only those who have been here before can find the way back, and they would never willingly betray us."

"There is another, one who bears the symbol of the Mukari. The gates will open. They will walk inside. When they do, the cataclysm will be almost upon us. The gates of the Forbidden Citadel will fall and there is nothing any of us can do to stop that, Khumbu. I have foreseen it."

The monk slowly rose to his feet, knees clicking. He collected a bowl of broth from outside the doorway and carried it to the Mukari, along with a simple ceramic spoon. "I have brought food to soothe your worries away, goddess. You must eat."

The girl shook her head. "I am not hungry."

Khumbu smiled slyly. "Gylatsen will be disappointed, he made it specially for you. There are shiitake mushrooms at the bottom of the bowl, grown on mahogany wood. Gylatsen said to tell you it's what gives the broth its smoky flavour."

The Mukari looked at Khumbu shyly. "He made it for me?"

"Yes, goddess. Please, you must eat."

She took the bowl from him. Among all the monks that were her constant companions, Gylatsen was her favourite. The others were so serious, but he had mischief in his eyes and joy in his heart. She could not help smiling when Gylatsen was around. He made her burdens lighter. The Mukari dipped her spoon into the steaming broth, careful to scoop some shards of mushroom up with the liquid. She blew over the spoon's rounded bowl, then tipped the contents into her mouth. It tasted just as Gylatsen had said, smoky and warm, comforting to the body as a blazing wood fire on a cold winter's day. Before she knew it, she had finished the broth, eagerly spooning the last morsels into her mouth.

Khumbu smiled as he took the empty bowl away. "I'll be sure to tell Gylatsen how much you enjoyed that, goddess. He will be pleased."

"Thank you, Khumbu."

The monk dropped to his knees and kissed the floor again before leaving, pulling the thick wooden door closed gently behind. Once she was alone, the Mukari leaned back in the throne and closed her eyes, feeling the pleasant warmth of the broth spread through her body. Being so aware, so alive, could be an overwhelming experience. But it was half her lifetime since the Mukari had known any other way of being. It had become natural to her.

The Mukari let her spirit escape its mortal cage of flesh and bone, slipping out through the heavy stone walls to float effortlessly above the market. Even old Khumbu could not stop her going outside like this. No one could see if she was smiling or not. She flew away from the citadel, through the surrounding clouds and then went into a dive, her spirit scudding along invisible zephyrs, passing mountainside villages and ice-covered ravines. Soon the snow on the slopes gave way to the detritus of erosion from many millennia. At last she found them, the killers, the butchers, the bringers of death. To her eye they were no more than human, despite the terrible wrath their gathering would bring upon her people.

I pity you, her spirit whispered, the words becoming a cold breeze from the mountaintops, blowing down to chill the soldiers' bones and put out their fires. The Mukari turned away, the approach of a familiar presence intriguing her. She wanted to get closer, but he was yet beyond her reach. All in good time.

On the throne a frown crossed the girl's face, wrinkling her nose. There was so little time left before the darkness came, and not much of it good.

SEVEN

*"The wheel of fortune spins
faster than a windmill."*
– Russian proverb

"When in residence at the Imperial Palace, Tsar Vladimir Makarov favoured the holding of daily assizes in the Chamber of Judgement. This vast space, with its enormous vaulted ceiling and intimidating architecture, had a seating capacity approaching five thousand people. However, these places were rarely full, except for special events such as the trial of Nikolai Dante in 2668, for allegedly engineering the kidnapping of the Tsar's daughter, Jena. It was this case that helped accelerate the onset of war between the Tsar and the Romanovs. Few trials have had such far-reaching consequences for the Empire at large.

In the Chamber of Judgement criminals ranging from the pettiest thief to the most treasonous of curs were brought before The Ruler of all the *Russias* to have their case heard, make a plea of mitigation and receive sentence. Such phrases as 'due process' and 'innocent until proven guilty' had little currency in a court of law. All were guilty in the Tsar's eyes. The only thing in question was finding a punishment to fit their crimes.

Before the war, Count Pyre often acted as chief accuser. After the war, Lady Jena was sometimes used to fulfil Pyre's former function at proceedings. In cases involving matters sensitive to the security of the Empire, the Tsar chose to hold proceedings behind closed doors. Few accused delivered to the Chamber of Judgement in such circumstances ever left it alive."

           – Extract from *The Law of the Tsar*
           by Johann Grissholm

Zachariah Zhukov was surprised, and not a little disturbed, by the frosty reception he received on returning to the Imperial Palace. Was he not the brains behind the Parliament of Shadows, a covert operation that had successfully accounted for close to a dozen leading dissidents? Had he not masterminded the scheme from the first, persisting with the plan when others had predicted its utter failure? Most importantly, was he not carrying the names of more than a hundred members of the aristocracy, all of them identified as co-conspirators by the parliament's members before they died?

I must not be too proud, or too demanding Zhukov told himself. I must remember my work has been carried out in secret. He doubted there were more than a handful of people at the Imperial Palace who knew what had transpired beneath the Romanov Necropolis. Once the coup against the plotters is made public, then I shall bask in the adulation of my peers, warm myself with the Tsar's gratitude. Until that moment I must be patient.

The red-haired nobleman had endured endless delays, biting back his temper. For two days he was kept waiting on the ground in St Petersburg, denied a place in the authorised airships that made their hourly visits to the great palace, hovering above the city. Twice he had made it to the front of the queue, but was turned away in favour of others with more urgent calls upon the Tsar's time. Finally, when he had almost despaired of being allowed an audience, Zhukov was summoned to a private landing dock on the edge of the city.

Jena Makarov was waiting for him there with a small flyer, a welcoming smile and words full of apology.

"Lord Zhukov, my father wishes me to convey his sincerest regrets that you have been kept waiting so long. He says it was necessary to maintain the deception of your noble house being out of favour, while suspected dissidents were rounded up for interrogation. You understand, of course."

"Of course," he said, allowing a small smile. *Just as well I didn't try to throw my weight around and demand an earlier appointment* he thought. *That would not have gone well with the Tsar.* Vladimir Makarov was many things, but a forgiving soul could not be counted among the many facets of his character.

Jena led Zhukov into her private flyer, motioning for him to take the co-pilot's seat. "Don't worry, I'm fully qualified," she said, laughing at the concern on his face. "When the Tsar needs a special envoy to deliver messages personally, diplomatic immunity ensures the least problems."

Zhukov nodded. *Wait until the Tsar hears all I have achieved, his rewards should be beyond imagining.*

Within the hour Jena led Zhukov into the Chamber of Judgement. He never failed to be intimidated by the vast space, despite it being all but empty. His footsteps echoed up into the high ceiling as he walked to the centre circle where so many had heard their fate pronounced. On either side was a precipitous drop. Nobody knew what lurked in the darkness, as the palace staff were not permitted to speak about it, on pain of death. A handful of Raven Corps soldiers guarded the platform's edges, with long pikes clasped in their gauntlets. Behind them was no railing, just a yawning gap between the platform and the public galleries round the sides of the chamber.

The Tsar floated above the platform on a grand throne, silent thrusters maintaining its magisterial position. He was clad in the Imperial robes of office, a rich mixture of purple and gold fabrics draped round his powerful frame. Zhukov reached the centre circle and dropped to one knee, displaying his obedience. But the Tsar gave no word or signal for the nobleman to rise, so Zhukov was forced to stay on a bended knee.

Jena produced a scroll of vellum and read aloud the text printed in blood red ink. "The court of Vladimir the Conqueror, Tsar of all the Russias, is now in session. Prisoners, do not weep or beg. Undignified signs of weakness or repentance will result only in harsher punishment. Zachariah Zhukov! Prepare to face the judgement of the Tsar."

The nobleman listened to her recitation with growing incredulity. When the Tsarina finished speaking, he could not help but reply. "There must have been some terrible mistake," he protested. "Tsar Vladimir, I came here to-"

"Silence!" the Tsar thundered. "You may speak only when given permission to do so, traitor. Lady Jena, please read the charges against this individual."

She nodded, resuming her recitation from the scroll. "Zachariah Zhukov, you are guilty of conspiring to topple the rightful ruler of the Empire, a treasonable offence. You are similarly charged with promoting anti-Empire ideals, duping others into following your misguided and dangerous notions, and of fomenting insurrection among a dozen noble houses."

"What say you to these charges?" the Tsar demanded.

"Sir, I must confess my confusion at being accused of such crimes," Zhukov began. "I freely admit I am guilty of every charge as stated-"

"Then there is little more to be said," the Tsar snapped.

"But I committed these acts at your behest!" Zhukov said, trying and failing to hide the panic rising in his voice. "I proposed the Parliament of Shadows as a way of luring dissidents out from the protection of their noble houses. You gave me full permission and every assistance to make this covert mission possible."

"Can you prove that?"

"Can I prove it?" Zhukov spluttered.

"Yes."

"I... I have no documents, nothing official to verify these facts."

The Tsar folded his arms. "Then there seems little hope for you."

"But sir, you agreed to let me pretend I was guilty of treason to establish my credibility with the dissidents. Lady Jena was present at the meeting, she is my witness."

"My daughter, do you recall this meeting the prisoner alleges took place?"

Jena shook her head. "I am sorry, father, I do not. You have so many meetings, I must confess they all blur into one after a while."

"No!" Zhukov cried out, standing up. A cluster of Raven Corps troops surrounded him, pointing their pikes at his torso. "Please, Tsar Vladimir, I do not understand why you are doing this to me." Tears of frustration filled his eyes, the nobleman's emotions overwhelming him.

"Consider it a test of your resolve," the Tsar replied. He motioned to the Raven Corps and they returned to their original positions. Jena smiled at Zhukov, her face showing some compassion again.

"You mean... I'm not on trial?" the bewildered Zhukov asked.

"These charges are a formality," the Tsar replied. "Although the Parliament of Shadows's other members are all dead, some may have told friends or relatives about your involvement before the trap was sprung. So you must be seen to stand trial, just as they have been, otherwise your noble house might suffer reprisals from anti-Imperialists."

"I'm not to be punished?"

The Tsar laughed, a rare sound in the Chamber of Judgement. "Zhukov, if what I hear of your exploits is true, you deserve all our congratulations. Come, give me your report and then we shall deal with these charges against you. I'm sure an amicable resolution can be found."

The nobleman let himself breathe again, the tension slowly melting from his shoulders. It had all been a hoax, so the Tsar could maintain culpable deniability. He was merely toying with him, as a cat plays with a mouse it has captured. Zhukov gave a sigh of relief and then outlined his activities of the past week.

The Tsar listened politely until the name Nikolai Dante was mentioned. "What? You had him in your grasp and you let him escape?"

"I didn't let him escape, sir. I sent him on a collision course with your mission into the Himalayas," Zhukov explained, perplexed by the Tsar's sudden, almost volcanic reaction. "One of the other cabal members, Lady Nikita Zabriski, suggested it. She had heard about you sending a contingent to search for the Forbidden Citadel."

The Tsar's eyes narrowed. "How had she heard this? From you?"

Zhukov shrugged. "I had no knowledge of the mission before she brought the matter up. It was her idea we use Dante's Crest to help locate the citadel."

"And why should his Crest be of any use?"

"Forgive me, sir, I thought you knew all this. Lady Zabriski told us anyone bearing a Romanov Weapons Crest could see the Forbidden Citadel. She even provided an electronic means of tracking Dante via his Crest."

"Do you still have these tracking devices?"

"Err, no," Zhukov admitted.

The Tsar looked across at his daughter. "Did you know anything of this?"

Jena shook her head. "We always suspected the House of Zabriski had close links with the Romanovs. One of our spies suggested Lady Nikita shared intelligence with Dmitri Romanov, that the two might even be lovers. But our operative disappeared shortly before the war."

"We've already purged the Zabriski dynasty, thanks to the efforts of Lord Zhukov," the Tsar growled angrily. "Now we may never know what Lady Nikita could have told us and what secrets she took to her grave."

"Sir, I didn't know," Zhukov said weakly. "I couldn't know."

The Tsar ignored the interjection. "Jena, I want you to make contact with Ivanov's expedition. Warn them about Dante's presence in the mountains and make sure the general knows I want the Romanov bastard captured alive." She departed the Chamber of Judgement, leaving Lord Zhukov to face her father's wrath.

The Mukari was meditating, both legs folded into the lotus position beneath her gold and crimson gown, hands held outwards in supplication. The girl's eyelids fluttered as she communed with the mountains, becoming one with the mighty peaks that were worshipped like herself. She could feel every drop of moisture that fell upon them, sense every breeze and zephyr that caressed their sides, touch every soul upon their surface. But already there were those on the mountains whose presence spoke of the darkness to come.

The girl's nose wrinkled in disgust as she smelled the soldiers, their hatred, their cruel spirits and their harsh, guttural laughter. She did not like these men. That would make what was to come easier, but it offered no comfort. The Mukari was moving her mind's eye elsewhere when a sensation like a squall of daggers invaded her thoughts. Dozens of words and images battered her consciousness, seeking a way past, seeking the soldiers. Somebody was trying to communicate with them, warn of approaching danger.

I cannot allow that, the Mukari resolved. What must be will be, but I cannot allow anyone else on to the mountains – in person or as a message. She brought her hands together in prayer, fingertips almost touching her nose. I will hold back the daggers. Let them fall upon deaf ears.

The Tsar glared down at his double agent. "Well, what do you have to say in your defence, Zhukov?"

"Wh... When the Zabriski woman suggested sending Dante into the Himalayas, I... I thought it was a fool's quest, a doomed errand. The renegade has no knowledge or experience of that terrain. It would be remarkable if he survived more than a day in such a hazardous environment."

"Unfortunately, Nikolai Dante seems capable of surviving almost anything anywhere, despite my best efforts to have him exterminated," Vladimir sneered. "He went alone into the mountains, yes?"

"Not exactly. He had two accomplices with him, vile creatures I doubt could be of much use to him. There was also a woman, a native of the mountains. She was the one who found and captured Dante. Curiously, she was able to read his thoughts. She could even hear what the Crest was saying to him."

The Tsar's brow furrowed. "How did she come by this useful talent?"

"I don't know," Zhukov admitted.

"So, not only did you have the notorious renegade in your grasp and let him go, you also had control of an operative able to read the mind of anyone bearing a Romanov Weapons Crest?"

"Well... yes."

"And you didn't think her ability might be of use to your Tsar?"

"I..." Zhukov looked down at his feet. "It never occurred to me." He could see a vein on the Tsar's forehead throbbing and his face was a glowering shade of crimson.

"Lord Zhukov, you may be the greatest fool I have ever had the misfortune to encounter. From all you have told me, it is plain Lady Nikita had access to secret information about the deployment and dispersal of my Imperial forces. She also possessed key facts about the Romanovs and even handed you a means of hunting down the survivors of that accursed family. But you have thrown all of this away in a crude grasp for glory and kudos. What did you call this mission taking Dante into the mountains?"

"A… doomed errand, sir. A fool's quest."

"Precisely. But you were the fool, Lord Zhukov, and now the doom will also be yours." The Tsar snapped his fingers. The Raven Corps on one side of the platform divided, creating a gap in their number. Those on the opposite side advanced on Zhukov, their pikes herding him slowly towards the edge.

"Please, sir, I made a mistake," the terrified nobleman cried out. "Give me a chance to correct that error! I will travel to the Himalayas myself, make amends for my folly."

"The folly was mine, for entertaining your suggestions in the first place. I should have known better," the Tsar snarled. He nodded to the Raven Corps. The scarlet-clad soldiers edged Zhukov ever closer to the precipice.

"Sir, don't do this! I beg of you!" he screamed.

"Never beg," the Tsar replied. At his signal the soldiers sent the still protesting nobleman over the edge of the platform. "If there's one thing I can't abide, it's men who beg."

Zhukov's scream was still audible when Jena re-entered the Chamber of Judgement. The Raven Corps were returning to their positions around the edge of the platform. "Well?" the Tsar demanded.

"I'm sorry, Father, but we are unable to get a message to Ivanov's mission. The mountains block out most conventional forms of communication, but there is something else at work. A deliberate jamming signal has been established, blocking all our attempts to bypass it." Jena smiled. "I imagine the general and Dante will get quite a surprise when they find each other searching for the Forbidden Citadel."

"You sound almost pleased at such a prospect, Jena. Perhaps you are happy Dante still lives?"

"His survival means nothing to me," she replied quickly.

"Rest assured, his survival will not continue much longer," the Tsar promised. "Ivanov will take the greatest of pleasure in murdering the Romanov renegade. They have an old score to settle, and it is written in blood."

EIGHT

"You cannot hide dishonour in your beard."
– Russian proverb

"The Tibetan Plateau is beautiful and bleak. Shielded by the Himalayas from the rains of the monsoon season, the plateau's surface is akin to that of a desert – without the sand. Brown and bare, the vast horizon is littered with glacial rubble from millennia gone by. The forces of nature that created this landscape have, thus far, held back the encroachment of Imperial civilisation. In the most unexpected of places you can still discover ancient scraps of fabric, tattered banners that speak of a religion systematically destroyed in the lower regions by outside oppression. Ropes are secured between cairns and nearby crags. From these, the faithful hung their prayers to the gods, written on coloured flags. The effect is a multi-coloured kaleidoscope of hope and faith, both cheering and mournful. Cheering because these bright colours lift the spirits in an otherwise barren landscape, and mournful because those who wrote the messages have long since fallen victim to the latest invaders of this noble world, close to the clouds.

Despite the best efforts of the Imperials, small communities survive high on the slopes of the Himalayas, eking out an existence on the roof of the world. They lead a simple life, but one that many would envy. Should you ever have the chance to venture into this remote territory, you can expect to be entranced by the ways of these people and envious of their secret happiness."

– Extract from *Secret Destinations of the Empire*,
by Mikhail Palinski

"Bojemoi!" Dante cursed, his teeth chattering a staccato rhythm, while sub-zero blasts of air pushed tears from the corners of his eyes. "How can anyone live in this hellhole?"

Mai glared at him angrily before turning back into the wind, her heels digging into the sides of her yak, urging it onwards.

The four travellers had been left on the Tibetan Plateau the previous morning, their flyer wasting little time before it disappeared over the horizon. Four yaks were waiting for them. Saddling the beasts had proven difficult enough in the finger-numbing cold: riding the creatures was another matter entirely. Dante and Flintlock had come off at least a dozen times, as their bruised buttocks could testify. Mai had whispered to her yak for several minutes before climbing on its back, the beast offering no resistance to her. Most surprising was Spatchcock's steed. The longhaired mountain ox was constantly trying to nuzzle against his legs and trotted along happily with its malodorous master in the saddle.

"I think my yak likes me," he had said with a smile.

"I think she loves you," Mai replied. "And that's a dri, not a yak. Yak is the male of the species. Your mount has udders."

"Must be the aroma of animal dung and dried urine that does it," Flintlock muttered while trying to climb back on to his transportation. "That creature plainly admires anything that smells as bad as it does."

"Are you talking about the dri or Spatchcock?" Dante asked.

"Take your pick."

More than twenty-four hours later and all conversation between the travellers had long since lapsed. Mai hadn't spoken to Dante since they left the Romanov Necropolis, while Spatchcock was more interested in his new best friend than communicating with Flintlock. They continued their slow progress towards the mighty peaks in the distance. At first, the slopes had appeared deceptively close, waiting for them just beyond the next rise. But the brow of each hill always brought another valley beyond it, and then a further rise to climb.

Dante was beginning to wonder if they would ever reach the Himalayas. "Why didn't the flyer take us closer in?" he shouted at Mai, who was ahead of him.

She didn't look back. "When the Imperials couldn't conquer the mountains, they decided to cut this region off from the rest of the Empire." She dug into her pockets and pulled out a smooth, round pebble. "Watch!" She threw the stone into the air. A flash of blue lightning engulfed the pebble. Once it had been vapourised, a fine dust in the air was all that remained of the stone.

"Sonic disruptors," Dante realised.

This area is seeded with them, the Crest added. *Anything moving more than three metres above the ground is targeted and destroyed.*

"That explains why we haven't seen any birds," Flintlock said. "This place is deader than any battlefield I've been on."

"We should reach the foot of the Himalayas tomorrow," Mai announced. "Another hour's ride tonight, then we can rest. In the morning we release the yaks. They will find their own way home."

"Can't we take them with us?" Spatchcock asked sadly. "I've gotten quite attached to my friend here."

"They'll only slow us down," she replied firmly.

"I doubt my spine will ever recover from riding on these monstrous beasts," Flintlock complained. "I haven't been this black and blue since–"

"Your last visit to Famous Flora's Massage Parlour?" Dante suggested. "You always have a spanking good time there."

"My sexual proclivities are my own affair," Flintlock protested haughtily.

"Proclivities? I thought you liked them to be called your meat and two veg." Spatchcock sniggered. "Least, that's what Flora told me."

"Can the three of you talk or think about nothing but sex every minute of the day and night?" Mai demanded. "Does every comment or conversation have to lead straight into the gutter?"

"Are you suggesting we can only converse in innuendo?" Flintlock asked.

"Innuendo and out the other," Spatchcock added with a throaty chuckle.

"Shut up!" she hissed, twisting her yak round to face the trio of men. "We're in one of the most beautiful places in the world. For once in your sordid little lives, try to appreciate your surroundings."

Shame-faced and embarrassed, the three men mumbled their apologies. Mai pointed a finger at Dante sternly. "And when I turn around, I don't want you thinking about anything except our objective, do you understand? Keep your eyes off my arse and your thoughts on the job in hand, okay?"

"Okay," Dante snapped back. "Can we get on, please?"

"Fine."

"Good." Dante was distracted by tittering from nearby. "Now what?"

"Nothing," Flintlock squeaked, struggling to contain his mirth.

"Nothing at all," Spatchcock agreed.

"It's just... she said... on the job." The Brit lost control of his merriment, and Spatchcock was soon laughing out loud. Dante shook his head despairingly and urged his yak onwards. He caught up with Mai and apologised for such gross behaviour.

"Their hearts are in the right place," he offered. "Well, mostly."

"Shame about the rest of them," she sneered.

"I guess," Dante shrugged. He studied her face, noting the pain etched into her expression. "I thought you'd cope better than any of us with the cold."

"It's not the cold." Mai winced. "Or the yak."

"How did you know I was...? Oh yes, you can read my thoughts."

You have my sympathies, the Crest commented. *His is not the prettiest of minds to experience. I suppose I've gotten used to its sordid little nooks and crannies, but they must come as something of a shock to–*

"I'm trying to talk with this woman, Crest. I don't need you butting in with your oh-so-superior observations."

Be like that. See if I care. Before the argument could go any further, Mai slumped forward over her mount. *She's lost consciousness. Get her off that walking carpet, she needs help.*

Dante jumped from his yak and hurried to Mai's beast, lowering her from the saddle to the stone-strewn ground. He stripped off his jacket, folding the garment in half and slipping it beneath Mai's head. Her face was wan, the normally bronze skin blotchy and discoloured. "Crest, what's wrong?"

Rest your palm against her forehead. Direct contact with the skin will enable me to make a more accurate diagnosis.

The others hurried to join them, Flintlock tumbling from his mount in the process. Spatchcock grabbed the reins of both animals so the yaks couldn't wander off in the confusion. "What's the matter with her?"

"That's what I'm trying to find out," Dante hissed. He reached forwards with his left hand, pressing its palm against Mai's skin.

Beginning analysis now, the Crest said tersely. *That's strange. She's...*

Dante waited, but the voice in his head had fallen silent. "Crest? Crest, what's going on? What's wrong with Mai?" Still no reply came. Dante twisted round to look for Spatch-cock, but both his travelling companions had disappeared, along with the yaks. "That's impossible. Crest, what's happened to Flintlock and Spatch? Crest?"

All Dante could hear was the wind whistling from the nearby mountains, then even that died away to nothing, leaving an eerie silence.

"What are you doing here?"

Dante realised he was kneeling on broad wooden panels, his palm resting on the forehead of a beautiful Oriental girl. Surprised, he pulled his hand away. "Sorry," he said quickly. "I was... before, my friend, she was... well, she's not my friend. At least, I doubt she'd call me a friend. Anyway, I was trying to–"

The girl sat and giggled at him. "You're a funny colour!"

"I am?"

"You can't be from the village."

"No, I'm... I'm not sure, to be honest. Where am I?"

"Don't you know?"

Dante shook his head. The girl stood up and gave him a quick kiss on the cheek. "Don't worry. You'll see, in time." She ran away from him, fading into nothing. Dante was still looking for her when a harsh voice cursed at him.

"How much for this one?"

A massive figure loomed nearby, the rancid stench of body odour filling Dante's nostrils. He couldn't make out his face, but somehow knew he must not speak.

"I said how much for this one, old man?"

"Twenty."

"For used goods? Ha! Eight and no more."

"Twelve?"

"I said eight, and that's being generous."

A hand reached down and grabbed Dante by his hair, yanking him to his feet. Fingers probed expertly, feeling his teeth, searching for imperfections. On impulse, Dante bit down, snapping his jaws together. Blood coated the inside of his mouth, the smell of iron in his nostrils and screaming fury in his ears. The blows came quickly, one upon another, snarling and savage. "You'll pay for that."

After another blur, Dante was sitting on a dirt floor, the pounded earth beneath his hands dry and firm. Animal hides lined the walls, insulating the hut from the bitter winds outside. A man clad in black from head to toe walked in and only his hands and eyes were visible. "You will kill for us. You will become us..." Then he, too, faded away, shimmering into nothing like a ghost.

"Dante? What are you doing here?" The voice was Mai's but Dante could not find its source. He twisted round and round, searching his surroundings. The hut melted away to reveal a snow-covered slope, its whiteness tinted mustard yellow by the setting sun.

There you are, a voice said inside Dante's thoughts.

"Crest? Where am I?"

Inside Mai's subconscious. When you put your hand on her forehead, it opened a long dormant pathway into her thoughts. I was drawn inside and your mind must have followed.

"I don't understand."

Hardly surprising. Interpreting the workings of the human subconscious has kept entire professions gainfully employed for more than a millennium.

"Am I inside one of Mai's dreams?"

Not a bad analogy, but these visions are a blend of her past, present and future. A better question is how can she see her future, even at a subconscious level? Perhaps telepathy is only one of Mai's psychic talents?

Dante watched as the mountains changed colour, each vision darker than the last. The sun was almost hidden beneath the distant horizon. As it disappeared, a line of shadow crept up each slope, swallowing the mountain. Above that line the snow turned ever more orange, before its shade reddened. Soon only the tips were catching the sun, the light staining them a sinister hue, as if the peaks were covered with blood red. Dante shuddered.

"Don't touch me!" a girl's voice screamed. She ran past him, terror filling her face. Behind her ran nightmare monsters, their faces devoid of eyes, grabbing hands flailing at the wind, mouths howling in hunger. The creatures ran through Dante, startling him but not touching, wraiths of the mind.

"I've seen enough, Crest. How do I get out of here?"

Silence.

"Crest, can you hear me?"

Dante was colder since the sun had gone down. His hands shivered. He sank to his knees in the snow and hugged both arms round his chest to retain heat. Around him the wind whispered then screamed, its gusts a dozen different voices. Dante could hear words echoing around the mountains, growing louder and louder.

What are you doing here? Don't touch me! You'll pay for that. You'll see... I don't understand. How did I get here? Don't touch me! I don't understand. You'll see... Where am I? How did I get here? Crest...? Crest...?

The voices grew louder, until Dante felt himself being consumed. Another noise began to overtake it, a low rumbling from above. At first it sounded like thunder in the distance. Then the rumble became a roar, forcing him to look up. The night sky was turning white again. It was an avalanche. *Dante, evasive action...*

• • •

Dante yanked his hand away from Mai's forehead, his lungs sucking in air as if he were a drowning man suddenly pulled back to the surface. "What happened?"

You disappeared, the Crest replied. *The moment you placed your hand on Mai's forehead, I lost all contact with you.*

"What do you mean? I talked with you inside her subconscious."

Not to the best of my knowledge.

Dante could see Spatchcock and Flintlock staring at him, their faces confused and afraid. "The Crest says I disappeared."

"Your body didn't go anywhere, but as for the rest of you…" Spatchcock replied.

"You were in some sort of trance," Flintlock added.

"What about Mai?" Dante asked.

"What about me?" She opened her eyes and looked at the three men standing over her. "What's going on?"

"I wish I knew." Dante explained what had happened.

Dante believes we conversed in your mind, the Crest told Mai, *but I have no recollection of such an event.*

She sat up, stroking her temples with one hand. "Last thing I remember was my headache suddenly getting worse. Then my vision blurred and after that… nothing."

"How do you feel now?" Spatchcock asked.

"As if my head wants to split open. It's been pounding like a drum since we landed, but I thought that would pass. Instead the pain keeps getting worse."

Dante recalled the images that had flooded his mind. Mountains were the recurring motif, peaks becoming an ominous blood red. "The closer we get to the foot of the Himalayas, the greater the pain in your head?"

"Yes," Mai agreed. "Why, do you think there's a connection?"

"I wish I knew," Dante said. "It'll be dark soon. We need to find shelter for the night. Spatch, Flintlock – scout ahead for the nearest place we can stop. I need to talk with Mai."

"Gotcha," Spatchcock nodded, climbing deftly into the saddle on his yak.

Flintlock remained standing, his arms folded resolutely. "I refuse to get back on that creature," he pouted.

"Have it your own way," Spatchcock replied. He trotted off on his hairy steed, leaving Flintlock to run behind, dodging the odd spurt of yak manure. Dante waited until both men were out of earshot before speaking.

"How long is it since you've been home, back to these mountains?"

"I can't remember," Mai said sadly. "My childhood is a blur. If I try to focus on it, I start getting a migraine. After a while, I stopped trying to remember. It was less painful."

"So what's the first thing you can recall? Without pain?"

"Waking up inside a bamboo cage, on a dais in a market. Slave traders were selling me. 'Himalayan beauty, never been touched.' Those are the first words I can remember hearing. I was twelve or thirteen at the time."

"How can you be sure?"

Mai gave Dante a withering glare. "A woman knows."

"Oh, right."

"That was six or seven years ago, before the war. I can clearly recall every moment, every experience I've had since then – but nothing before." She faced the mountains, the snow-covered peaks turning yellow in the setting sunlight. "Until now, that is. I'm getting glimpses of growing up in these mountains, of playing with my brother in the snow round our family's hut."

Dante frowned. "If you couldn't remember anything before you were sold, how did you know about your brother?"

"He tried to rescue me from the slave traders." The snow-caps were turning a shade of ochre, then a deeper orange. "My brother was the only link I had back to my childhood. And you killed him."

"Was he fighting for the Tsar?"

"The Tsar?" Mai cursed in a tongue Dante didn't recognise. "My brother would never fight for that bastard." She stood up, refusing Dante's help. "If you'd killed him because he was one of the enemy, I could understand that. But he was one of your own men. You killed one of your own soldiers. That's not an act of war, that's murder." Mai strode off in the direction taken by Spatchcock and Flintlock.

Dante watched her go, the mountains in the distance blood red at the peaks. He realised that it was just like in the vision. That must have been a glimpse of the future. But what else had he seen in Mai's head that had yet to happen? What clues had he witnessed without realising?

He retrieved his jacket and put it back on. "Crest, can you still access the Imperial Net?"

Not without a relay or external power source.

Dante glanced round the barren landscape, darkness rapidly engulfing him. "The sonic disruptors – could you use them as a booster?"

That could work, the Crest decided. *I will try hacking into their control systems, siphoning off a little residual power. What do you need?*

"There's more to Mai than meets the eye. She claims to have no memory of her life before the age of twelve. Check her story, see if it stands up."

Consider it done. Anything else?

"Yes. Why was I sucked into Mai's subconscious when I touched her forehead? Nothing like that happened when I grabbed her wrist at the Parliament of Shadows's HQ. If something important is locked in her mind, we need to know what that is and how to access that knowledge."

I shall investigate further. Of course, many Asian and Oriental faiths believe gods and holy individuals have a divine, third eye set into their forehead, enabling the bearer to see through every individual's mind, and fathom things beyond a common person's understanding.

Dante set off after the others, not wanting to be separated from them for the night. "Get the feeling that you're out of your depth, Crest?"

No.

"Good. So hacking the Imperial Net shouldn't offer a challenge, should it?"

NINE

"What matters is not who you are at birth,
but at death."
– Russian proverb

"The Imperial Net is among the Empire's most remarkable achievements. This vast artificial intelligence is a gestalt entity, collecting every available scrap of data and interrelating this with the ever-shifting zeitgeist of contemporary culture. The net was inspired by a Twenty-first Century phenomenon wiped out in the AI holocaust of 2027. The Imperial Net uses alien technology to achieve similar results, but has liquid media and bioorganic circuitry as its support mechanism. All the user requires is a power source, some access codes and the ability to interpolate the ebb and flow of raw data. What could be simpler?"

– Extract from *The Smirnov Almanac of Fascinating Facts*, 2672 edition

Dante. Dante! The Crest's voice woke its host from sleep before dawn, drawing him out of a dream involving three shape-shifting alien masseurs and a bathtub full of strawberry-scented lubricants.

"Five more minutes. Just five more minutes..." he murmured, sulkily.

DANTE!

"Diavolo!" Dante exclaimed, sitting bolt upright. "Crest, there's no need to shout. I was waking up. I simply wanted to savour the last, lingering delights of my dream." He smirked, one hand rasping through the stubble on his chin. "Some of the things those shape-shifters could do... They ought to be illegal."

Most of them are. You forget that I am privy to your dreams as well as your waking thoughts.

"Yeah," Dante said. He shivered in the cold morning air, briskly pulling on his jacket. The four travellers had found shelter beneath a rocky overhang, using the slumbering yaks as a windbreak. Spatchcock's snoring had kept the others awake for hours, until one by one they drifted off to sleep.

Dante pulled on his boots and crept out of the shelter, stretching and yawning. "So, why did you wake me, Crest?"

While your subconscious has been busy performing indecent acts, I've been scanning the Imperial Net for any mention of Mai Tsai.

"And?"

There is only one.

"One? That's all?"

I was very thorough.

"I know, but... How many times am I mentioned?"

The running tally is fast approaching one point four billion, the Crest replied dryly. *You seem to exert a fascination for young ladies of a certain age. There's an entire sub-genre of romantic fiction about your exploits. Appropriately enough, it is known as Dante slash fiction.*

"Really? Hot stuff, is it? Could you read me some?"

No. Your self-image is already far enough out of proportion with your ability to satisfy any woman. It does not require further inflation. Besides, you asked me for facts about Mai, not an exercise in stroking your ego.

"Yeah, yeah. Spit it out then."

There is no mention of Mai before the war. She does not exist in any Imperial records, or on any census or forms. Nor does she appear to have any documentation issued in her name. Before you ask, I also ran images of her through facial recognition software and image search facilities. Still nothing.

"So what *is* this one mention?"

Eighteen months ago, a clandestine criminal group known only as the Tong of the Red Hand broke cover and issued a rare public statement denouncing Mai. The Tong put her picture on the Imperial Net and said she had turned from the noble ways and traditions of the organisation. Dante, they marked her for death.

The Imperial Black had been advancing on the mountains for three days. A heavy carrier brought all one thousand members of the regiment to the foot of the Himalayas, using an official override code to escape the cordon of sonic disruptors. Once the soldiers were on the ground, they were brought to order by the Enforcer and began their slow ascent. Flight paths recovered from Dmitri Romanov's former pilot had narrowed the search for the Forbidden Citadel to three peaks, but nothing more was known about its location.

Ivanov was proud to lead his men from the front. He couldn't abide armchair officers who preferred to let their men do all the hard work. Ivanov would never ask any soldier to attempt more than he was prepared to do himself. Besides, it was far quicker to make decisions from the front. Then they did not have to be relayed through a dozen intermediaries. Of course, when night fell upon the mountains – and it fell with unusual severity – the general happily retreated to his private tent. This had the benefits of heat pads beneath the ground sheet and a force barrier round its exterior to keep out the cold. Rank must bring some privileges, Ivanov believed.

The regiment had been ascending since dawn of the previous day. There were paths and tracks, but these only allowed three men to walk abreast in many places. That had slowed progress considerably, as did carrying all their equipment. The Imperial Black had a proud tradition of self-reliance that was proving an extra burden in this challenging terrain. With winter so close, the hours of daylight were limited. Continuing at night was beyond question in this unforgiving environment. Ivanov had responded to these difficulties by leading his men at dawn each morning.

Ivanov reached the top of a rise and called for a halt, his order being passed back through the column behind. A snap of the general's fingers and the Enforcer was at his side. "What does that look like to you, major?"

There was a cluster of huts and enclosures ahead, clinging to the mountainside on a narrow plateau. The buildings were simple structures, with thick walls and low ceilings, dug into the side of the slope. Wisps of smoke rose from most of the chimneys and beasts of burden could be seen waiting inside the narrow compounds. Steps led to the settlement, the centre of each stone worn down by centuries of use. The path continued past the village and up the side of the mountain, eventually disappearing into a halo of clouds.

"A village, sir. Little or no defences. No apparent threat to us."

"Exactly. I doubt they get many visitors." The general smiled. "That should make our arrival all the more of a surprise. If this accursed citadel is nearby, the villagers should know where."

"It's doubtful they will willingly surrender such knowledge."

Ivanov's eyes narrowed. "Then we shall have to persuade them."

"When were you planning to tell us about the Tong of the Red Hand?" Dante demanded, glaring at Mai. He returned to the rocky overhang to find the others awake and preparing for the day's trek.

"I wasn't. What I did before joining the Parliament of Shadows is no concern of yours," she said curtly.

"Funny, isn't it?" Dante said to Spatchcock and Flintlock. "She can rant about what I allegedly did to her brother, but we're not allowed to ask what she did during the war."

"I killed for the Tsar," Mai whispered.

"What?"

"I killed for the Tsar," she repeated. "We all did. The Tong of the Red Hand was employed by the Tsar to act as his secret police, hunting and executing dissidents within Imperial ranks."

"You said slave traders sold you–"

"To the Tong. I was inducted into the Red Hand, trained in its ways. I learned a hundred different martial arts. I could kill you a thousand times over, if I wanted, and you wouldn't have a chance. But I promised Lady Nikita you would remain alive until the Forbidden Citadel was found and the weapon secured."

Dante shook his head, hollow laughter catching in his throat. "And you didn't think we should know any of this?"

Mai stepped closer to him, struggling to keep her temper under control. "What difference would it make? I'm not proud of what I did during the war, but I had no choice. I tried to tell myself that by killing the Tsar's men, I was hurting the Imperial war effort. But I knew that was self-delusion, even then. Killing is killing, nothing more, nothing less. All it provided was carrion for the crows that plagued the battlefields during the war."

Dante frowned. Had he not once thought much the same thing? He pushed aside the notion to concentrate on what Mai was telling him. "Once you join the Tong, you join for life. Obey all orders from your sensei or die at his hand. Death is the only way you can ever leave."

"She's right," Spatchcock said quietly. "I had a few dealings with them before the war. Not the most cheerful band of assassins you'll ever meet."

"I dared to desert their ranks when the war was over, so my brothers and sisters in the Red Hand marked me for death."

"Why did you quit?" Dante asked.

"Because of you," she snarled. "The last Imperial I killed worked in counter-intelligence. He was reviewing an Imperial Black report on events from the Battle of Rudinshtein. I had been instructed to make the man's death look like an accident, so I suffocated him. You have to hold the victim's mouth and nostrils shut for ten minutes to make sure of total brain death. While I waited, I read the field reports he was reviewing. One talked about an attempted breakout by a group of civilians from the governor's mansion. I recognised my brother Rai from a description of the soldiers involved. You murdered him."

Dante shook his head. "You don't understand. You weren't there."

"Make me understand! Explain to me how you justified killing my brother!"

"I can't," he admitted.

"You're pathetic," she hissed. "To think I spent months searching for you after the war, searching for vengeance. I fled the Red Hand to hunt you down. I heard a whisper that the House of Zabriski had links with the Romanovs, so I confronted Lady Nikita. She persuaded me to become an operative for the Parliament of Shadows, gave me sanctuary from the Red Hand. I swore to help the cabal overthrow the Tsar and his regime. He's the only living person I hate as much as you. Lady Nikita gave my life a purpose beyond getting my revenge on you. Now I have to make sure you stay alive! I can't decide whether to laugh or cry." Mai spat into Dante's face, then stormed out into the dawn.

That explains why she hates you so vehemently, the Crest observed.

"Thanks," Dante snapped. "I had figured that much out for myself."

. . .

Sonam pushed the bubbling mixture of curds back and forth inside the broad pot, his strong hands using the flat sides of the wooden churn to keep the liquid moving. Beneath the pot burned a fire of yak dung, the year-old manure giving off a steady heat while filling the hut with heady aromas. A bag of cured yak hide hung on the wall, awaiting the hot mixture to be poured inside, but Sonam knew the curds needed another hour before they were close to becoming cheese.

His three youngest children were asleep on the bed, dozing fitfully in their brightly coloured clothes. The two girls were different ages, but the resemblance to Sonam was unmistakeable in their oval-shaped faces and dark hair. The boy took after his mother, chubby around the cheeks and with gentle eyes. She had died giving birth to him, five winters ago, leaving Sonam to raise the children alone.

A distant cry made him pause, his hands faltering at their task. Sonam listened for another scream. Perhaps Dukar was hitting his wife again. She would stay inside her hut for days at a time, eventually emerging with the shadow of a bruise still evident over one eye, or wincing in pain as she bent over a fire. Sonam had warned Dukar about this conduct. It was not fitting, not when they lived so close to the goddess. Dukar always apologised, blaming the barley beer, or some fault of his wife, Namu. "I am headman of this village," Sonam had told him last time. "I say you are lucky to have a wife. Treat her as you would treat the goddess herself." Dukar promised to hold his temper, and he had kept that promise for five months. Was he now lapsing back into the bad ways of old?

The cry came again, more of a scream and it was closer, but Sonam knew Dukar's wife had not made it; the cry came from a man. Sonam lifted the churn from the pot, then shifted it off the flames so the curd would not burn. He pushed aside the heavy curtain from the door of his hut and stepped outside to see who was crying for help. Another scream penetrated the air, drifting up from below the village. Sonam shielded his eyes to see what was happening.

A man was racing up the stone steps that led to the village, one hand nursing a red smear across his face. No, not a smear, Sonam realised, it was a cut. The man was Dukar and he had been sliced across the face with a knife or blade of some sort. Perhaps his long suffering wife had finally suffered enough and fought back, as everyone knew she would one day. If that was the case, why was Dukar running towards the village and not away?

Movement below Dukar caught the headman's eye. A black swarm was surging up the slope, like ants, consuming the hillside. Sonam had lived on this mountain for all his forty-seven years, having next to no contact with the world beyond these slopes, but even he recognised soldiers when he saw them. There was a flash of light from the front of the swarm and it was followed by the sound of a gunshot. The effect upon Dukar was startling. His hands flew out sideways and his face showed surprise, before all life left his eyes. The wife-beater's body slumped forwards.

Sonam ran to the highest point within the village, a stone cairn with a massive bronze bell mounted beside a wooden shrine to the goddess. The headman snatched up a rock and smashed it against the bell, again and again. A deep, booming sound resonated out over the village and then on down the mountain-side, towards the valley far below. "Soldiers!" Sonam bellowed between strikes of the bell. "Soldiers are coming!"

"Why didn't you tell her what happened in Rudinshtein?" Spatchcock was crouching by Dante, trying to talk some sense into him. "Flintlock and I saw the whole thing from the wall of the governor's mansion. You had good reason for doing what you did. She'll understand if you explain to her."

"She won't understand," Dante replied bleakly. "We all know what serpent-wire does to a person, we saw enough of it during the war, but Mai didn't. Besides, maybe I don't want her forgiveness."

Flintlock shook his head. "You want her hating you? Why, as some sort of punishment? Rai volunteered for that mission. He knew the risks, we all did. What happened to him wasn't your fault."

"I pulled the trigger."

"It was a mercy killing!"

"Mai doesn't see it that way."

"Then I'll make her understand," Flintlock said, but a popping noise in the distance stopped him. "What was that?"

"Gunfire!" Dante was already running with his Huntsman 5000 clutched in one hand. Spatchcock and Flintlock followed him. Mai stood in the open, peering at the nearest mountain.

"It came from up there," she said. "Wind can carry sound for miles."

The four of them listened intently, waiting for another gunshot. Instead they heard a bell chiming, each strike low and resonant on the breeze.

The strikes are not in any pattern or rhythm, the Crest noted. *The clustering of chimes suggests panic more than anything else.*

A second shot was heard and the bell stopped ringing. After that nothing was audible beyond the whistling of the wind.

Dante slung his rifle over one shoulder. "We knew the Imperials were ahead of us, but we didn't know how far – until now. If we want to overtake them, we'll have to travel light. Gather any essentials we need from the yaks, then release the animals. From now on we go by foot, at speed. Any questions?" Nobody spoke. "Good. Remember why we're here." He made eye contact with Mai. "Nothing else matters at the moment. We leave in five minutes."

Sonam's hand was a crimson mess from the shot, blood seeping from the cloth he had wrapped around his gaping wound. The bullet had passed through his palm and exited out the other side. The pain was excruciating, but not fatal. Dukar had not been so fortunate. His body lay beside the path to the village, forgotten already and growing cold. Sonam hadn't had time to do anything about his dead neighbour. Indeed, he was still tying a makeshift bandage round his hand when the black-clad soldiers dragged him down the slope to join the other villagers. Hundreds of the invaders surrounded the settlement, their weapons trained on the terrified people. A broad-chested figure was barking orders to the troops, his features hidden behind a black facemask.

Soldiers ran from building to building, searching for anyone who may have been hiding. The wind had died with Dukar, so when the women and children were dragged out into the icy morning, their sobs hung in the air as clouds of steam. Another terse command from the man in the facemask and the villagers were forced into three groups – men, women and young children. Once this was achieved, the soldiers formed themselves into groups of forty, each unit taking a position around the village. The officer, whose voice had commanded them with such authority, turned to a single figure and saluted. "This is all of them, general."

"Very good, major. I want eight units deployed above, and eight units below the village, to make sure we are not disturbed. Anybody else on the mountain will have heard that damned bell, so we may yet have visitors."

"Yes, sir."

Sonam watched the major mustering his well-drilled men. These soldiers looked like professionals: skilled, disciplined, deadly. The ease with which Dukar had been despatched was ample evidence of that, along with the speed of this latest manoeuvre. But it was the glee in the general's eyes that worried Sonam most. He looked at the villagers the same way Sonam's young son looked at his toys. We're playthings to this man, nothing more and nothing less. He will keep us alive as long as we amuse him or have something that he wants. After that, we'll be cast aside. Sonam shuddered at the thought of his son's broken, discarded toys, imagining a similar fate for the village and its people.

"You, the one who was ringing the bell. What's your name?"

The headman realised he was being addressed. "Sonam. My name is Sonam."

The general smiled genially. "Call me 'sir', when you address me."

"Yes... sir."

"That's better. Now, Sonam – you showed remarkable forethought in ringing that bell, alerting the others to our arrival. Are you their leader?"

"I am headman of the village, as my father was before me."

"Sir."

"Sorry, sir."

"Don't forget again, will you?"

"No, sir."

"Very good." The general walked slowly among the villagers, studying their faces, gently patting the heads of the children, nodding to the women. All the while he continued talking to Sonam, as if passing the time of day. "You're probably wondering why we've come to your little corner of the world. Well, I will be completely honest with you, and I hope you'll extend me the same courtesy. We are here on a mission from Tsar Vladimir Makarov, Ruler of all the Russias, and leader of our glorious Empire." The general paused in front of Sonam. "Your people know you are governed by the Empire, don't they?"

"Yes, sir. But it leaves us in peace so..."

"Good." The general strolled to a position up the slope from the villagers, where he could look upon all of them simultaneously. "First of all, I suppose I should introduce myself. I am a general in the Tsar's forces and proud to lead the men around you. They are a regiment known as the Imperial Black, a thousand of the finest warriors ever to walk this planet. My name is Vassily Ivanov, but some of you may know me by another name – Ivanov the Terrible." He smiled. "Any questions so far?"

Nobody spoke. Sonam glanced at the faces of his neighbours. Most were too scared or bewildered to challenge the invaders. A few saw what had happened to Dukar, as everyone had heard the shooting. Guns were not permitted on the mountain, as the monks had labelled them a blasphemy against the goddess.

Ivanov raised an eyebrow, intrigued by the silence. "Very well, I shall get to the reason for our rather abrupt arrival. The Tsar has sent us here to find the Forbidden Citadel, a fortress hidden within the Himalayas. We have good reason to believe it is either on this mountain, or one of the peaks either side. Winter will soon engulf this region, so it is imperative my men and I find the citadel before the weather closes in. You will help us locate it, or suffer the consequences. Do I make myself clear?"

Still nobody spoke. Nobody replied to him. Sonam knew that the mood among the villagers was one of shock and fear. But he also knew his people would never willingly surrender the location of the Forbidden Citadel. Most of them had been within its walls and thus could see it from outside, but they were sworn to protect the goddess – with their lives, if necessary. That vow had never been put to the test until now. Sonam was confident his people would not be found wanting. They owed everything that they were and everything they had to the Mukari. Without her, they would have been swept away by the capricious peaks, their village obliterated by avalanches generations ago. But she protected them from such forces of nature.

They must do the same for her, whatever the cost.

The general's face darkened. "I asked you people a question... Do I make myself clear?" The villagers remained silent, even the youngest child refusing to speak out. Ivanov folded his arms. "I will give you one last chance to spare yourselves. I did not acquire the name Ivanov the Terrible without good reason, and those who helped me earn it paid the cost in blood. Now, who will volunteer the location?"

Sonam took a deep breath and stepped forward. The general smiled at him. "That's better. I was beginning to think none of you had the sense to save yourselves. Where is this legendary fortress to be found, headman?"

"None of us will tell you," Sonam replied. "From birth we are taught to keep this secret close to our hearts, to carry it with us to our graves. You can threaten us, you can torture us, you can murder us – it will make no difference. We shall not tell you, we shall never tell you. Better you leave the mountains now, lest our goddess smite you down."

Ivanov pursed his lips. "Does this goddess have a name?"

"None that I would tell to you."

The general nodded. "I see." He gestured at his second-in-command. "This man is a major in the Tsar's forces but, like me, he has acquired another name during his time with the Imperial Black. He is known as the Enforcer." The major stepped out of formation and snapped to attention. "He is a most observant individual, for whom the tiniest detail can offer a wealth of information. For example, at no time during my latest exchange with your headman, did he address me as 'sir'. I gave him two warnings against failing to show me the proper respect, as dictated by my rank. The Enforcer will have noticed this blatant challenge to my authority. He will also have observed the threat veiled within your headman's suggestion that I leave these slopes." The general smiled at his second-in-command. "What do you suggest I do about that, Enforcer?"

"Give him to me for an hour," the major snarled. "I will teach him respect."

"A capital suggestion," Ivanov agreed. "What is your name again, headman?"

"Sonam."

"And do you have a dwelling of your own here?"

Sonam pointed at his nearby hut.

"Very good. Enforcer, take Sonam into his hut and teach him respect. Sonam, while you are suffering at the hands of the Enforcer, I want you to listen carefully to what is happening outside your hut. My men can be a savage mob when unleashed, prone to take what they want without indulging in social pleasantries. These one thousand men are a gathering of the Empire's worst murderers, rapists and torturers. While you are being given individual attention from the Enforcer, your neighbours will be used and abused by my soldiers. They will start with the men, then move on to the women and, finally, the children. If at any time you wish to stop the screaming you hear from outside your hut, you need only volunteer the location of the Forbidden Citadel. Do I make myself perfectly clear?"

Sonam nodded, his eyes sliding towards the bewildered faces of his three children. Goddess, protect them from the coming storm, he prayed. Take them from this life if you must, but let them come to no other harm.

The general rubbed his hands together, a broad smile spreading over his features. "Good, then that's settled. To make sure nobody else spoils our fun, I will have each man, woman and children partially gagged. They may cry out or scream, but none will be able to speak. That privilege is reserved solely for Sonam. He will take responsibility for the suffering of everyone else in the village and only he can stop that suffering." Ivanov nodded to the Enforcer. "Begin."

The Mukari's body was slumped to one side on her throne. She had known what was coming for the village and its people. She had carried that knowledge since the moment she was crowned as living goddess of the mountains. Again and again, the girl had wished she could warn those who worshipped her and tell them to flee before the black swarm, to surrender the location of the Forbidden Citadel when asked. But that would not change what was to happen, what had to happen. It was inevitable, as inescapable as the darkness that would engulf the citadel; that would lay waste to the heavy gates, and, which would bring doom inside this very chamber.

Carrying such knowledge, hidden deep inside her, had been burden enough. Now that destiny was becoming reality, it was all she could bear. The redeemer was coming, but they needed time to reach the citadel. The death of the village would create that time, however horrific the price to be paid. The Mukari felt herself weeping, but the tears seeping from her eyes were made of blood, the blood of those dying in her honour.

I must help them, she decided, however little good it will do in the end.

The girl's body went into convulsions for a few seconds, then lay still. Her spirit escaped from its earthly domain and floated through the thick walls, out into the early morning air. She did not feel its cold, and her mind was filled instead with the pain and terror of her subjects. A blink of light and she was standing inside Sonam's hut. The headman's body was broken and bleeding, but his eyes lit up at seeing her again. "Goddess, be with me," he whispered.

The Enforcer stood over Sonam, stripped to the waist, his body wet with crimson stains. "Where is the Forbidden Citadel?" he demanded, the same question he had asked dozens of times in the past hour while administering slow, meticulous and brutal torture.

Sonam's head lolled to one side, his tongue hanging uselessly between purple lips, light slowly draining from blackened eyes. "Mukari, have mercy on us."

My mercy shall keep you all of your days, she replied, speaking her thoughts inside Sonam's mind. Be at peace now.

"Thank you, goddess."

The Enforcer grabbed Sonam by the hair and shook his head vigorously. "Nobody dies without my permission, do you hear me? Not until I say you can."

Sonam, there is one more thing you must do for me.

"Yes…"

Listen carefully, and then repeat after me…

"Where is the Forbidden Citadel?" the Enforcer hissed, his facemask almost pressing against Sonam's face. A cloud of doubt passed over the headman's features, before being replaced by understanding.

"I… I will tell you," Sonam gasped. "I will tell you how to find the citadel."

"At last," the Enforcer said triumphantly. "Wait until I get the general–"

"No. She says I must tell you…"

"Who says?"

"The citadel is near the top of this mountain, on a west-facing tor. But you cannot reach it from below," Sonam said slowly, long pauses between his words, his breath was little more than a rasp as it escaped his lips.

"What do you mean?"

"To find the Forbidden Citadel, you must cross an ice bridge over a mighty chasm. That is your only way…"

"What else?" the Enforcer demanded.

"When the time comes, you will see what you seek…" Sonam's voice faded to nothing, the muscles in his face slackening.

The Enforcer shook him again, but the headman did not respond. The torturer tore off his helmet and facemask, then pressed his ear against Sonam's chest, listening for a heartbeat. He could hear nothing beyond the terrified screams and sobbing of those villagers still alive outside the hut. A curse passed the Enforcer's lips, his ugly face contorted further by rage. He retrieved his helmet from the packed earth floor, brushing dirt from the facemask before replacing it on his head. As he did the figure of a girl was momentarily visible in sunlight that seeped into the hut.

"Who are you? What are you doing here?" the Enforcer demanded.

The Mukari stepped back, startled at her spirit form being seen by an outsider. She concentrated and was gone, her essence taking flight back to the citadel.

I lingered too long in his presence, but it was necessary. Sonam's suffering is over and the general will leave the others in peace – those that are still alive. I hope they survive beyond the darkness.

TEN

"War does not cure, but butchers."
– Russian proverb

"The weapon known as the 'White Death' was first used in the early Twentieth Century during a conflict hopefully dubbed, 'the war to end all wars'. The fact that this conflict subsequently became known as the First World War is ample proof that hopes and reality are infrequent comrades in the arena of human conflict. The White Death was among the most feared weapons used in the battle for the Italian Alps. The name referred to thundering avalanches deliberately caused by enemy cannon fire. These massive falls of snow and ice consumed everything in their path, much like the war itself. Subsequent generations have rediscovered this terrible weapon, which turns nature upon the unsuspecting victim."
– Extract from *The Files of the Raven Corps*

Dante and his comrades made speedy progress from the foot of the mountain to its steeper slopes, aided by Mai's expert guidance. They were within sight of Sonam's village only hours after Ivanov and his men had departed. Mai gasped as she crested the same rise where the general had stood that morning, surveying the settlement ahead. "I recognise this place," she said in wonder.

"Why? Is this where you come from?" Dante asked.

"I'm not sure," Mai replied. "But I have been here before, I'm certain of that."

Spatchcock caught up with them, struggling to find his breath. A lifetime of vice and dubious pursuits had not prepared him for such a punishing ascent, nor for the thinness of the air at such a high altitude. "Doesn't look too lively," he said between gasps. "No smoke from the chimneys, no movement round the huts."

"Crest, can you detect whether the Tsar's men are still in the village? Whoever's in charge of the Imperials probably doesn't know we're behind them, but they might have left a rear guard to cover their flank."

There is no obvious Imperial presence. I detect a handful of life signs, several quite weak.

"But I can see dozens of huts," Mai cut in. "A village of that size is normally home to a hundred people."

"The Tsar's men don't leave many witnesses," Spatchcock said bleakly. A wheezing, groaning sound preceded the arrival of Flintlock. The Brit was even less suited to this challenging terrain than the others, thanks to an aristocratic upbringing and a lifetime of indolence. Flintlock's face was crimson and white; his armpits were soaked with sweat and his hands quivered with fatigue. He collapsed at the crest of the rise, flopping listlessly to the ground.

"I don't... think I... can go... much... farther..." he puffed and panted.

"Tough," Dante replied, pointing to the village ahead of them. "We think that's where the gunshots we heard this morning came from. Get your breath back and then join us over there. If the Tsar's men have been through this area, the villagers are going to need our help." He strode purposefully towards the settlement, Mai and Spatchcock close behind.

"I say, Dante," Flintlock protested feebly. "What if any of the Imperials are still lurking round here?"

"Then the sooner you get your bony arse moving, the better."

Spatchcock thought that the village looked like a charnel house. He had witnessed all the horrors of war while fighting with the Rudinshtein Irregulars, but still found himself unprepared for the butchery that had been visited upon the tiny mountain-side settlement. The ground was stained red from the blood shed by those who had lived here until a few hours earlier. A wet carpet of crimson tainted all snow, grass and gravel.

A pyre of corpses had been made in the centre of the village – whether by the invaders or the survivors, Spatchcock could not be sure. The local men had been the first to die, judging from the position of their bodies at the bottom of the pile. Some had been blinded, whilst others were missing fingers or limbs. The women were the next to suffer: hair crudely hacked from their heads, fingernails torn out and their glassy eyes a mute testimony to the other indignities that they had witnessed. Spatchcock felt his stomach turn at the sight of dead children atop the pyre. But at least they were put out of their misery now, he thought.

The survivors were not so fortunate. A dozen people remained: eight children, three women and a man. Not long after Dante and the others arrived, the last man died, coughing blood and sobbing noises of pain. His tongue had been torn out and apparently fed to him by the soldiers, who laughed when their victim nearly choked to death. Two of the women were too traumatised to speak, cowering against a hut and clutching shredded clothes. The children had survived by fleeing when it became clear what was happening. Eight of them escaped the soldiers' wrath, unlike their friends and families. After the soldiers departed, the children had come back to search for loved ones among the dead and dying. The one woman capable of describing what had happened said her name was Namu. "My husband was the first to die. He was shot while trying to warn us the soldiers were coming."

"I'm sorry," Mai said.

"Don't be," Namu replied emotionlessly. "He wasn't much of a husband and he hit me whenever something went wrong. I'm glad he's dead. But as for the others... They didn't deserve what happened to them."

Mai and Spatchcock listened while the woman talked about the villagers' ordeal. Dante and Flintlock gathered the remaining corpses and added them to the pyre, beginning with the remains of Sonam from the headman's hut. Spatchcock called Dante over after hearing Namu's description of the officer leading the soldiers.

"Tell him what you told us," Spatchcock urged.

Namu pushed a strand of hair from her heart-shaped face. Both her eyes were blackened and she had several teeth missing, but Namu had not given in to the soldiers without a fight. Several of them would be walking bow-legged for days, she proudly told the newcomers. "I can't remember the officer's name. He said he was a general. He was fifty, maybe older – he had no hair, so it was hard to tell. He enjoyed watching us suffer, I could see it in his eyes. Dukar looked the same when he used to beat me, but the general didn't join in. He watched; that seemed to give him the most pleasure. He liked it if you screamed. Maybe that's why I'm still alive. I refused to make a sound, even when they took off my gag. I didn't want to give them the satisfaction of knowing they had broken me. The general got bored when I wouldn't cry, so he left me to the soldiers. The general's second-in-command interrogated our headman, Sonam, while we were tortured outside his hut. The Enforcer, that's what the general called his interrogator. He wore a mask on his face."

"What do you think?" Spatchcock said.

"Sounds like the Butcher of Rudinshtein and his flunky," Dante said. "You can't remember his name?"

"No, but I know the name of his regiment," Namu said. "I'll never forget that, because of the colour of their uniforms. The general called his men the Imperial Black."

Dante's face darkened. "Ivanov. Vassily Ivanov."

"Ivanov the Terrible," Spatchcock murmured.

"He told us to call him Ivanov the Terrible," Namu said. She stood, using Mai's shoulder as support to rise. "I'll fetch butter for the fire," Namu said, hobbling away into one of the huts.

Mai watched the beaten and bruised woman go before rounding on Dante. "You know this Ivanov? Friend of yours, is he?"

"Anything but," Dante replied, glaring back at her. He opened his mouth to say more, but walked away instead. When she moved to follow Dante, Spatchcock grabbed her by the arm.

"Let go," she demanded.

"Shut up and listen," Spatchcock snarled.

When she refused, he softened his grip on her wrist. "Please?" Eventually Mai sat down opposite him.

"You think you know what happened to your brother, but you weren't there. You hate Dante, you blame him for Rai's death, but what are you basing that on? An Imperial report? Who do you think wrote that report? Ivanov, or one of his officers. It was propaganda, lies to hide the war crimes his regiment committed. You want the facts? Ask somebody who was there. Ask somebody who saw what happened!"

"How can I? My brother's dead and that's Dante's fault!"

Spatchcock laughed bitterly. "Dante killed your brother to save him."

"What the hell are you talking about?"

"You want the truth? Here it is: yes, your brother got caught in no-man's-land trying to save a group of civilians, but Rai volunteered for that mission. Ivanov and his men were torturing Rai when Dante intervened. The general was using serpent wire on Rai. Have you ever seen what serpent wire does to the human body?" Spatchcock demanded.

Mai nodded numbly.

"We could hear your brother screaming from our position in the governor's mansion. Flintlock and I saw the whole thing from the barricades. Dante had led a diversionary attack against the Imperial forces, in the hope of giving Rai's group a chance to escape. When Dante saw what Ivanov was doing to Rai, the captain did the only decent thing. He shot your brother to save Rai from any more of that torment. I'd have done the same myself, if I wasn't such a coward." Spatchcock shook his head. "That wasn't murder – it was a mercy killing."

"But after the war... why did Dante flee Rudinshtein?"

"You think he had a choice?" Spatchcock gestured at the bodies, the blood strewn around them, the blank-faced children left behind by the Imperial Black. "Look what Ivanov and his men did to this village in a few hours. After the war, that bastard was given Rudinshtein as his private plaything. For three years the Imperial Black have been doing this to the province and its people – murder and rape, looting and pillaging. If someone in Rudinshtein dared say the name Nikolai Dante, they were tortured and publicly executed. Every crop was burned, every treasured possession stolen, every whisper of resistance crushed. The general doesn't soil his own hands, of course. He lets his men do the dirty work. They've got a major, called the Enforcer, who carries out the executions personally. He's almost as sick as his master." Spatchcock locked eyes with Mai's, trying to make sure she realised the importance what he was saying. "Rudinshtein was poor before the war, but its people were happy when Dante was in charge. Now the province is a bankrupt police state, thanks to the general and his underlings. Do you know how many times Flintlock and I have had to stop Dante from going back to Rudinshtein to attack Ivanov?"

"Why? Why did you stop him?"

"Dante is one man – he's larger than life, but still only one man. How can one man hope to stand against an army and hope to win? You've seen how he attacks first and thinks last. Going back to Rudinshtein would be a suicide mission. Dante wouldn't last a day. So, he stays away while thousands suffer because he isn't there to defend them, but knowing that tens of thousands would be summarily executed if he tried to intervene. Have you any idea of the guilt he carries for what's been done to Rudinshtein in his name?"

"I didn't know," Mai murmured, her face coloured by shame. "How could I?"

Spatchcock glared at her sad but beautiful features. "Next time, try getting your facts straight before you start making accusations. Dante's no saint, but his heart's in the right place."

"He said the same thing about you and Flintlock."

"Well, I never said he was a good judge of character." Spatchcock looked across at Dante heaving the last corpse on to the pyre. "Now Ivanov and Dante are on the same mountain, both looking for the Forbidden Citadel. If one of them leaves here alive, it'll be a bloody miracle."

Namu emerged from her hut carrying a large bowl, steam rising from it. She spoke quietly to the cluster of children and they ran to the other buildings. Within a few minutes each of them emerged with similar bowls. The smallest child carried a burning taper, with a flame dancing around its end. Once all of them were ready, the solemn procession approached the pyre, Namu leading the way. She emptied the contents of her bowl over the pile of corpses, then stepped aside and motioned for the children to follow her example. Spatchcock and Mai had joined Dante and Flintlock to one side of the pyre, watching as each child poured viscous liquid over the dead villagers.

"What is that?" Flintlock asked.

"Yak butter," Mai replied quietly. "The animals provide much of the essentials for life here: wood, meat, skins, cheese. But they also provide something essential for death. The butter is fuel for the funeral pyre. We do not bury our dead, we burn them."

"I say, is that wise?" Flintlock worried. "The Imperials are bound to see the smoke rising from the fire. It might warn them that we're coming."

"Let them see," Dante muttered.

The last child threw her taper on top of the pyre and the flames quickly spread, engulfing the corpses and belching black smoke into the sky. Namu beckoned Mai to join the other villagers and handed her a broken tree branch.

"What is it?" Mai asked.

"Juniper. The white smoke from its burning creates a road between the earth and the sky, so the spirits of the dead may find their way."

Mai closed her eyes and whispered to herself before adding the juniper branch to the funeral pyre. She watched intently as pale clouds rose, mingling with the darker fumes from the fire. Around her the children were singing a sad lament.

Further up the slope, the Enforcer noted the plume of smoke and alerted Ivanov to it. The general waved away suggestions of sending a squad down to investigate. "We're close to our quarry, major, and you want to go backwards? That is why you will never attain my rank or status. The bold soldier always goes forwards, no matter what the cost or consequence!" Ivanov continued leading his regiment up the vertiginous slope.

The Enforcer remained where he was, studying the column of black and grey that swayed in the air currents that flowed around the mountain. If what the headman had said was true, they could not be far from the ice bridge. Cross that, and the Forbidden Citadel was within reach. Behind his facemask the major frowned, still perturbed by the vision of that ghostly girl he had seen in the hut. The sooner this mission was behind them all, the better.

It was mid-afternoon by the time the funeral pyre's flames started to die down. Spatchcock had been busy keeping the children entertained with suitably censored tales of his adventures, assisted by a less enthusiastic Flintlock, while Mai helped Namu tend to the other survivors. Dante stayed by the fire, staring into the burning mass of bodies, as if transfixed by it. Even the Crest was unable to tear him away from the grim spectacle.

It was Mai who suggested the time had come to resume their quest for the citadel. Spatchcock and Flintlock agreed with her but Dante remained unmoved. Mai joined him in front of the pyre, watching the reflection of the flames in Dante's eyes. "It doesn't matter how long you stare at those bodies, Nikolai. You can't bring them back. None of us can. What's done is done."

He frowned. "Spatchcock told you what happened to Rai, didn't he?"

"Yes. Why didn't you?"

"Would you have believed me?"

"Probably not," Mai conceded.

"Besides, your hatred made you stronger, drove you on. We needed that anger. We still do."

"Don't worry, I have plenty of anger, more than enough to keep going. And I have a new target for my hatred."

Dante grimaced. "Ivanov."

"Yes. Spatchcock thinks it unlikely you and the general will leave the Himalayas alive."

"Spatch is smarter than he looks."

"Are you going to let your hatred for Ivanov cloud your judgement?" Mai asked. "Spatchcock told me what the general did in Rudinshtein after the war."

"Don't worry," Dante replied. "I know where my priorities lie. We've got to reach the citadel before Ivanov. If that butcher gets holds of the weapon, whatever it is... the consequences don't bear thinking about."

"Then it's past time we moved on. Once we're gone, Namu will lead the other survivors off the mountain. There's another village where they can take refuge. If the Imperials come back this way, the survivors will be safe from them."

"Good."

"Namu says the village headman was tortured for an hour to get the location of the citadel. She overheard the Enforcer telling Ivanov they should climb up this slope, then cross an ice bridge to reach a tor on the western side of the mountain. Namu has never been to the citadel, but she knows that it is located somewhere on that tor."

"Then we know what path to follow–"

"No," Mai cut in. "She says it is quicker to climb down for an hour from here, then take a smaller path that leads up the side of the tor. Namu believes the headman deliberately sent the soldiers by the longest route."

"Why? He couldn't know we were coming."

"Not him – the goddess of the mountain."

Dante raised an eyebrow at Mai. "Excuse me?"

"My people believe each mountain is a goddess, just as they believe each lake is sacred. But this mountain is home to a living goddess. Namu says the goddess knows we are coming, as she knew the soldiers were coming. She knows the past, the present and the future."

"Sounds like a woman after your own heart, Crest," Dante commented.

A living goddess? This will be fascinating.

Mai pointed at the sun dipping towards the distant horizon. "We must get moving if we are to find the new path and suitable shelter before darkness falls."

"Agreed." Dante smiled as she moved away from him. "So I'm not on your list of those marked for death anymore?"

Mai stopped abruptly. "Keep thinking about my body like that and I'll be perfectly happy to castrate you free of charge." She marched away, muttering under her breath darkly.

Mai may not want you dead anymore, the Crest said, *but you would do well not to antagonise her needlessly.*

"I'm keeping some spice in our relationship," Dante replied. "Nothing worse than a love affair that's gone stale."

Love affair? The two of you have never even kissed. That's hardly a relationship, even by your rather limited standards.

"But she's thought about it. Any woman who protests that loudly about my appreciation of her backside must fancy me, right?"

Did you ever think Mai might not want to be seen as a sex object?

"No."

I rest my case.

"Can I help it if my libido overwhelms my better judgement sometimes?"

Sometimes?

"Alright, frequently."

Dante, your libido has gotten you into more trouble than your mouth and fists combined. In matters of the heart, your groin always takes precedence.

"You say that like it's a bad thing."

Spatchcock whistled from the other side of the village. "Dante, time to go!"

The renegade gave the funeral pyre a final look. "You will be avenged," he vowed before hurrying to join the others.

Dusk was approaching by the time Ivanov and his men reached the ice bridge. During their ascent, the soldiers had marvelled at the mighty chasm that opened up between the mountain they were climbing and its secondary peak, to the west. The tor was covered in snow and ice, but its slopes were considerably steeper and more challenging. At the highest point was a jagged stab of snow that resembled a broken tooth against the darkening, blue horizon.

Ivanov studied the terrain with interest, his inner doubts silenced by what he saw. The headman was right to send them this way. The general had harboured suspicions about the directions, but getting so many men up to the tor would have been almost impossible over such terrain. Of course, that was before Ivanov saw the way over the chasm that plunged between the two peaks. Such a crossing gave pause to any sane person.

The ice bridge was two metres wide, at most. It was difficult to tell how deep the accumulation of ice was, perhaps a metre and a half. Certainly, it should be sufficient to sustain the weight of the regiment crossing the precipitous chasm, if not all the soldiers at the same time. Ivanov called for the Enforcer and together they calculated the various factors.

"The men will have to go in two's," the Enforcer surmised. "The chasm is some three hundred metres wide at this point. Allow a metre between each row to spread the weight evenly, and we should be able to cross the divide before nightfall. Those who go first can begin establishing our shelters for the night."

"Very well," the general replied, satisfied with these calculations. "I will lead the first group of two hundred across. When we reach the other side, you may bring the remaining men over."

"Sir, let me go first," the Enforcer suggested. "This ice bridge is an exposed position from which it is impossible to quickly escape – the perfect place for an ambush. If an enemy should choose to strike against us–"

Ivanov waved aside such notions. "You saw how weak those villagers were, no fight in any of them. Are you seriously expecting some secret army to be hidden in these mountains?"

"No, sir, of course not. But I would prefer–"

"Your preferences are not my concern," the general warned. "I have given an order and it is to be obeyed without question. Do I make myself clear?"

"Yes, sir."

"Very well. Assemble the first group by the ice bridge. In the meantime, I will test the crossing on my own." Ivanov marched briskly to the edge of the ice bridge and peered into the looming chasm below. He could see where the snow ended and the rocks began, but one slip would certainly be fatal. Such were the perils of leading from the front, Ivanov reminded himself.

He stepped out on to the ice. Its surface was wet and slippery, but not impassable. The general stamped on the bridge several times, gradually putting more and more weight on the crossing. Satisfied with its solidity, he strode out on to the ice. Ivanov waited until he was halfway across before calling back to his men.

"As you can see, the ice bridge is perfectly safe. However, as a precaution, you will begin crossing in sections of two hundred, with no more than three sections on the bridge at any time. I will see you men on the other side!" He continued his journey and reached the tor's slopes within a minute. The first section of two hundred was already halfway across, with the Enforcer leading a second section on to the ice bridge. Soon there would be nothing to stop the thousand-strong Imperial Black regiment from finding the Forbidden Citadel.

Gylatsen smiled as he entered the Mukari's throne room. He was one of the few monks allowed to visit her on a daily basis. Most of his brethren were serious men, their faces heavy with the burden of responsibility and sacred duty. But Gylatsen had never forgotten the joy of being a child and he always tried to share that joy with their deity. Yes, the Mukari was their living goddess, but she was also a seven year-old – a child who needed to play and have fun. So Gylatsen let his natural exuberance shine through in her presence, never remonstrating with her for smiling or laughing as Khumbu was prone to do.

After completing the ritual bowing that was required of all those who came into the throne room, Gylatsen approached the Mukari's throne. "Goddess, I am preparing the evening meal. I understand you enjoyed the broth I made. Perhaps you want something similar?"

"I'm not hungry," the girl replied. To Gylatsen's surprise she was standing by the windows. Normally the black-haired monk instinctively knew her position in the room, even though he was blind. But his goddess was fond of teasing him by projecting her spirit out of her body. She could be quite the trickster when the mood took her, yet the sombreness of her tone belied any tricks.

"But, Mukari, you must eat," Gylatsen insisted, swivelling to face where her voice had come from. "Going hungry is not good for you."

"I do not want for food," she said quietly.

Gylatsen could hear a gentle sobbing. "Goddess, are you crying? What saddens you?"

"I saw the villagers dying and I could do nothing to protect them. They were beyond my power to help."

"What villagers? Forgive me, Mukari. I do not understand."

"I know, Gylatsen." She walked gently towards him and rested one small hand against his rough, calloused palm. "I shall show you."

And Gylatsen saw what the Mukari had witnessed and the light went from his face too. After he had seen enough, the monk pulled his hand away. "Forgive me, Goddess. I did not know."

"Gylatsen, I need you to stand guard outside the throne room," the girl said, her voice devoid of feeling. "Let none enter, not even Khumbu. I must concentrate, and any distraction will undo that."

"Yes, goddess." He bowed deeply, then withdrew. Though he was blind, the vision of what the soldiers had done repeated itself endlessly in Gylatsen's mind's eye, hammering at his heart.

Inside her room, the Mukari remained still, her breathing becoming increasingly shallow, all her energies concentrated inwards. Finally, when she felt in complete control, the girl clapped her hands together – once, twice, three times. The sound they made grew louder, echoing around the walls of the throne room, building relentlessly. With the final collision of skin upon skin, a mighty rumble joined the sounds, as if the mountain was grinding against itself, harsh and abrasive. Still, the noise got louder, the echoes repeating. The Mukari was oblivious to the cacophony building around her, not noticing the paintings falling from the walls, the candles and small statues toppling over.

In the corridor outside Gylatsen kept his back to the door, both hands clamped over his ears to block the booming sound leaking from inside. Khumbu and several of his brethren appeared, bellowing to be heard above the cacophony, but Gylatsen refused to move from the door. He pushed away any hands that tried to pull him aside. The citadel walls were vibrating: floorboards rippled and shuddered beneath their feet. Whatever was happening, it threatened to tear the fortress apart unless unleashed.

In her room the Mukari smiled, picturing what was about to happen, seeing its effect. She should not rejoice in this, the goddess told herself, but it was no more than they deserved. Content with her choice, she steered the noise to the balcony doors. They were flung open and the noise escaped into the dusk, searching for a target, bouncing from peak to peak in the mighty mountain range. The Mukari nodded and the noise buried itself in the eastern side of the tor. The throne room's balcony doors swung gently shut and the cacophony was audible no more. But its effects were about to reveal themselves with terrifying ferocity.

Ivanov stared into the sky, trying to locate the source of the noises, which were booming overhead. It sounded like a barrage of distant cannon fire. The noise abruptly died away, not even an echo remaining in the air. Ivanov was determined not to be distracted from the task in hand. The first unit of two hundred men had safely crossed the ice bridge, and the Enforcer was already two-thirds of the way across with the next section. Beyond him a third section was resolutely following in their footsteps, while a fourth was stepping on to the ice bridge. Another few minutes and all of the Imperial Black troopers would have crossed the chasm.

It was the Enforcer who first saw what was coming. He gave an order for his men to run across the bridge. The general saw this and demanded an answer from his second-in-command, but the Enforcer did not reply, pointing at the sky instead. Ivanov looked up and staggered back a step. Under the cover of darkness he could see only white and grey, as if the mountain was tumbling towards them. The first wave of ice and snow struck seconds later, punching through the ice bridge like fists, smashing the structure into fragments. Hundreds of soldiers were crushed to death in an instant. More fell to their doom, screaming in pain and fear. Ivanov hugged the side of the mountain, bracing himself for the moment when the avalanche claimed him, too.

Flintlock had been happy to lead the others back down the mountain path, but soon lagged behind when they took the side path that led up the adjoining peak. His whining was alleviated solely by his shortness of breath and the thin air. "Please… Can't we stop… for the night?" he whimpered. Further up the slope, Mai paused at a small plateau in the shadow of an overhanging cliff face.

"Remind me, what talents does Flintlock add to your gang of three?" she asked Dante tersely. "You have the Crest and all it adds to your capabilities. Spatchcock proved himself an adept pickpocket on the *Okiya*, and his body odour is no doubt a useful weapon in unarmed combat. But what does his lordship do?"

Dante smirked. "He makes the rest of us look good."

Not an easy task in any circumstances, the Crest added.

Spatchcock opened his mouth to speak, but was drowned out by a thunderous noise in the sky. He and Dante tried to see what had caused the cacophony, but Flintlock was already running for the concave space beneath the cliff. As the sound died away, he screamed at them to hurry.

"Why?" Dante asked. "There's nothing up there to worry us, it's a clear blue..." His words petered out as he glanced upwards once more. "Hey, the sky's turned white."

That's not the sky, that's an avalanche. Dante, evasive action – now!

"An avalanche? But..." He realised Spatchcock and Mai were hurrying towards the safety of the overhang. "Diavolo!" Dante sprinted after them, the first falls of snow and ice already slamming into the mountainside around him.

ELEVEN

"A caress is better than a fist."
– Russian proverb

"The Dante campaign is perhaps one of the most famous advertising extravaganzas of the pre-war era. Over a period of months the same image of the notorious Romanov renegade was plastered across billboards, airships and almost every other imaginable space. The picture showed Dante stark naked, but for a pair of underpants incongruously positioned atop his head. On either side of him were two curvaceous women, subsequently identified as prostitutes from the infamous House of Sin brothel. Dante was apparently unaware the image of him was being captured, otherwise he might have arranged for his genitals to have appeared larger or in a more flattering arrangement.

Most industry commentators believed that Tsarist sympathisers, who were using Dante to make the House of Romanov look ridiculous by association, funded the relatively harmless campaign. But to this day rumours persist that it was the Tsar's daughter, Jena Makarov, who paid for the campaign from her own allowance. Whatever the source of its funding, the picture of Dante's flaccid groin remains one of the most remembered images from the pre-war era. Despite the amazingly unimpressive genitalia displayed, the notorious rogue continues to exert an attraction for an inordinate number of women who simply should know better."

> – Extract from *Nikolai Dante: A Character Assassination*, various contributors

Dante got within a metre of the cave and dived the rest of the way, throwing the Huntsman 5000 in front of him. He narrowly escaped being crushed by a massive section of the shattered ice bridge as it thundered into the ground where he had been standing moments before. Spatchcock and Flintlock helped Dante to his feet while Mai watched the spectacle outside, both hands over her ears to block out the deafening sound.

The avalanche continued, the area beyond the cliff's overhang resembling a waterfall of snow and ice. The utter whiteness was broken by bodies flying past, the familiar all-black uniforms leaving little doubt of their origins. Most terrifying of all was the noise, as if the mountains were roaring, threatening to crush them alive. Wave upon wave of debris kept hurtling past until, finally, the sound and fury abated.

Dante smiled bleakly. "That was a demonstration of why we keep Flintlock around. He has a particularly strong sense of self-preservation."

"Dante's right," Spatchcock added. "If there's danger nearby, chances are his lordship is already running in the opposite direction."

"I resent that remark," Flintlock protested.

"You resemble that remark, more like."

"Now see here, you vile little guttersnipe. I am a lord of the Britannic realm and I am not to be addressed with such crass insensitivity!"

"Former lord of the realm," Spatchcock reminded him. "What did you do to be deported from your own country, exactly?"

Rolling her eyes in exasperation, Mai pressed a hand against the wall of snow and ice that covered its entrance. Dante joined her, extending a cyborganic sword from his left fist and plunging it as far as he could into the mass of solid white. "Crest, can you analyse how deep this wall of snow and ice is?"

At least twenty metres. Unfortunately, you were near the bottom of the mountain when the avalanche happened.

"I'm not complaining. It gave us enough time to get out of the way. The Imperials weren't so lucky."

True, but the snow and ice stopped when it reached the bottom of the mountain. Everything that fell from above accumulated outside your impromptu shelter. It will be weeks before the debris melts and you will never dig your way out.

"According to the Crest, the good news is we survived the avalanche," Dante told the others.

"And the bad news?" Flintlock asked warily.

"We'll starve to death before a thaw enables us to escape," Mai replied.

Spatchcock picked up the discarded rifle. "Can't you shoot a way out?"

"It's a rifle, not a cannon," Dante said. "The weight of snow would fill any hole the bullets created." He withdrew his cyborganic sword from the white wall. "Maybe those soldiers we saw were lucky. At least they died quickly."

Further up the tor, Ivanov was assessing his losses. More than half his regiment was still crossing the ice bridge when it shattered beneath the avalanche. Fortunately, the Enforcer had reached this side of the chasm before the avalanche hit. But close to seven hundred members of the Imperial Black had been taken in less than a minute, the greatest single loss of life in regimental history.

"Most of the men are in shock," the Enforcer told Ivanov. "They have lost comrades, brothers-in-arms. They need time to mourn."

"They are soldiers in the Imperial Black, they will do their duty," the general retorted. "Don't tell me what my men need!"

"Forgive me, sir. I did not mean to second guess you, I merely–"

"Stop," Ivanov commanded. "There is nothing to forgive, major. You were thinking of the men, as any good second-in-command should." The general rested a hand on his second in command's shoulder. "Night is almost upon us, we can go no further tonight. Tell the men to make camp as best they can. Once that is established, you and I will go among them, giving what comfort we can. If a regiment's officers do not support the rank and file at such a time, we do not deserve their support in battle."

"Yes, sir." The major hesitated before speaking again. "Sir, how do you rate our chances of success after so grievous a loss?"

"We still have over three hundred men. I believe they are more than enough to deal with whatever awaits us."

"I know the men will follow you into hell if they have to," the Enforcer agreed. "But that avalanche… it was almost as if the mountain was guarding its secrets."

Ivanov snorted derisively. "Superstitious nonsense! In the morning we will press on. I do not believe an entire fortress can remain hidden from us, no matter what mystical force may conceal its location. The Imperial Black shall prevail!"

Spatchcock was failing to start a fire, much to Flintlock's chagrin. "What's the point of doing that?" the Brit asked despairingly. "Even if you manage to get that puny pile of twigs and moss to burn, we haven't any fuel to feed the fire. Besides, where is the smoke going to go? Had you thought about that?"

"If you've got a better idea for keeping us warm then spit it out, your lordship," Spatchcock hissed back.

"I didn't say I had a better idea, I was merely–"

"Pissing all over mine!"

"Could the two of you be quiet for more than a minute?" Mai pleaded, her face drained of colour. She was pacing back and forth in the cramped cave, fingertips urgently massaging her temples. "My head feels like it's about to split open and listening to the pair of you is not helping!"

One big, happy family, the Crest observed pithily.

"Don't you start," Mai snarled at Dante.

"Hey, I didn't say anything," he protested.

"Well, try not to think so loud," she replied. "Better yet, try not to think at all. That shouldn't be hard for someone like you."

Charming.

"You said it," Dante agreed. He was sitting with his back against a rock wall. "Strange, it must be dark outside, but it's still light in here."

The rocks are rich with a luminescent ore, the Crest explained.

Mai stopped pacing to glare at Dante. "Have you any idea how annoying it is to be constantly bombarded with the know-it-all comments from your Crest?" The beautiful Himalayan swayed slightly on her feet. "Just shut up, will you? Just–" Mai's eyes rolled back into her head.

"Bojemoi!" Dante dived forward as her legs crumpled, catching her lithe body in his arms as she fell. He eased her gently to the ground.

"Is it the same as before?" Spatchcock asked.

All the symptoms appear the same.

"We need to know what's causing this," Dante said. He pressed one hand against Mai's cold, clammy forehead. "Nothing's happening. I can't–"

Dante blinked, but when he opened his eyes the surroundings were different. Spatchcock, Flintlock and the cave were gone. Mai was still lying in front of him, but now she was a young girl, perhaps five years old, lying on a floor of broad, black-stained wooden beams. Around them wafted scents of cinnamon and hot butter. She opened her eyes and smiled. "Hello. Who are you?"

"My name's Nikolai. Nikolai Dante."

The child giggled. "You're silly."

"Why do you say that?"

"You look so pale," the girl replied. "Don't you ever go out in the sun?"

Dante took his hand away from Mai's forehead. Beneath where his palm had rested was a third eye, red against black. The girl was dressed in a simple white robe that made her bronzed skin tone even more apparent. She was right, the difference in their pigmentation was noticeable – his pale pink, her skin the rich brown typical of those raised in the Himalayas.

Mai gestured at the room around them. "This is my new home. If I pass my last test, the monks will make me the Mukari."

"The Mukari?"

The girl giggled. "Goddess of the mountains. Don't you know anything?"

Apparently not.

"Crest?" Dante glanced around the red and gold chamber. "Is that you?"

I am a Crest, but not the one with which you are bonded.

"I don't understand. What is this place? Where am I?"

"In my room," Mai replied, playfully punching him in the arm. But her face was changing: cheekbones became more prominent, while the rest of her body blossomed into that of a young woman. "Nikolai, what's happening to me?"

"You're getting older," he realised. "You're becoming a woman."

The girl screamed, clutching at her abdomen, face contorting with pain. "It hurts," she gasped through gritted teeth. "Make it stop – please!"

"I can't. It's called growing pains."

Mai grabbed his hand, her fingernails digging into the skin. "Don't let them take me. Don't let them touch me!" A pool of blood appeared on the floor, seeping out from beneath her.

A door was shoved open behind Dante, and three men in saffron robes burst into the room. All were blind, their eye sockets hollow, yet they stared accusingly at Mai on the floor.

"She is bleeding," one of the monks announced.

"The goddess has left this earthly vessel," another intoned.

The monk who had opened the door regarded the girl coldly. "Her time is passed. She is nothing to us now – less than nothing. Her mind must be emptied. She must be cast out forever. She must be purified before the next Mukari can be chosen."

"Purified," the other monks echoed.

The three monks advanced on Mai. "Let the cleansing begin," their leader said. The trio walked through Dante as if he was a phantom.

"Don't let them do this Nikolai," Mai pleaded. "Not again."

Dante flailed at the holy men without effect. The monks surrounded Mai, trapping her in the centre of the room, their lips muttering a language Dante could not recognise. As the trio touched the screaming Mai, she faded to nothing.

So it was for her. So it is for all the Mukari and has ever been thus.

"What did they do to her?" Dante demanded.

What they believed was necessary.

"Who are you? Show yourself!"

"Show yourself!" Dante shouted, his hands bunched into fists. Spatchcock was holding him back from attacking the wall of ice and snow. He stopped fighting and let his anger subside.

"Who were you shouting at?" Spatchcock asked. "You were ranting and raving at thin air. His lordship got in the way and you nearly knocked him out cold."

Dante saw the blond Brit sprawled on the rocky floor of the cave, one hand clasped over a bloody nose. "Flintlock, I'm sorry. I didn't realise…"

The supine figure acknowledged the apology. "I'll survive – just."

Mai stirred on the ground, her eyes fluttering open. Dante crouched beside her, resting one of his hands atop hers. "Don't worry. You passed out again."

She winced. "The closer we get to the citadel, the closer my headaches appear too."

"I saw inside your mind again," Dante said.

"I know," Mai nodded. "I saw what you did this time, as if I was watching everything through your eyes. Thank you for trying to defend me."

"For all the good it did."

"But you tried." She stroked the side of Dante's face. "That means more than you know."

He noticed the others watching them, so Dante recounted what he had witnessed. Afterwards Spatchcock looked at Mai with a new respect. "You were some sort of living goddess?"

"The Mukari, yes. It's a religious tradition that stretches back many, many centuries in this part of Asia."

Dante had been thinking about the vision's implications. "Crest, the gaps in Mai's memory – could they be man-made?"

Psychic blocks to stop her recalling her time as this goddess? It's possible. But that would require telepaths of unusual strength and ability, to say the least.

"That might also explain the headaches," Flintlock observed after the Crest's words had been relayed. "They could be a defence mechanism, to stop Mai from returning to the citadel or even from trying to remember her childhood."

The others looked at Flintlock, all equally surprised.

He folded his arms sulkily. "I'm not a complete moron, you know."

"There's still one thing I don't get," Spatchcock said. "If that wasn't your Crest in the vision, whose was it?"

"One of the other Romanov Crest's, I guess, but what would they be doing here?" Dante shrugged. "Crest, can you identify others like you?"

Of course. Each of my kind has a specific signature, like a fingerprint. I know all the other Romanov Crests as you would know your own siblings.

"So, which one of my noble family is nearby?"

The Crest in Mai's vision was not one I recognised. It was distinctly different from all the Romanov Crests, and much more powerful. Whoever is bonded with it possesses a weapon of formidable force.

"That must be the secret hidden inside the citadel," Mai realised. "The Mukari must be bonded with a Crest – that's what makes her a living goddess."

"But how is it transferred from one Mukari to the next?" Spatchcock asked.

"Good question," Dante agreed. "The Romanov Crests bond with their host for life. When the host dies, the Crest does too. This Crest must be different."

"There's only one problem with all of this," Flintlock pointed out testily. "We may know what the citadel's secret weapon is, but we're still trapped in this bloody cave, aren't we?"

Dante blew between his hands before rubbing them together. "We're exhausted too, we need to get some sleep."

"How?" Flintlock protested. "We'll freeze."

"Then we'll have to sleep together, share our body warmth." Dante regarded his three companions in the cave. "I'll bunk down with Mai. Flintlock, you can snuggle up with–"

"Never!" the Brit protested. "I'd rather freeze to death than spend a night in the arms of this vile, repugnant and malodorous streak of urine!"

Spatchcock smiled. "Is he talking about me?"

"Yes, and not even behind your back," Dante replied. "Fine, if you two want to become human ice blocks, be my guest. Mai, you're welcome to choose another sleeping partner if you want."

She looked at the three men in turn before pointing at a grinning Dante. "But remember," she warned, "if I feel your hands wandering anywhere they shouldn't in the night, you'll lose all sense of touch before morning. Permanently."

"Fine by me," he agreed hurriedly, already unrolling the bedding from their few possessions. Dante let Mai get between the blankets first, then clambered in behind her, pressing against her back. He wrapped one arm around her in a hug, trying to still the sudden warmth in his groin. After much grumbling and griping from both men, Flintlock and Spatchcock agreed to share bedding for the night. They settled down together, the Brit insisting he face away from Spatchcock to avoid death by suffocation.

Dante closed his eyes and left himself drift off, trying not to inhale the sweet scent of the woman pressing against him. Within minutes he could hear snoring from the other side of the cave, and Mai's breathing settled into a deep, steady rhythm. Despite his best intentions, Dante could not help wondering what it would be like to know her better. Perhaps when this mission was over...

"I suggest you put that rifle to one side," Mai whispered, surprising him.

"I thought you were asleep."

"I was, until you started digging that thing into my back. I'll never get any rest while that's in here with us."

"The Huntsman 5000 is over there," Dante said sheepishly, pointing at the nearby weapon.

Mai sighed. "Then what's sticking into my–" Her words stopped abruptly. Dante could feel her squirming away, but the bedding kept them locked together. "It's no good, we'll have to turn over. That's safer for both of us."

Dante reluctantly did as he was told. Soon Mai was curled into his back, her thighs pressing against the back of his legs, her breath warming his neck, her pouting breasts creating two circles of warmth either side of his spine. Fuoco, this is going to be a long night, he thought.

Concentrate on the sound of Flintlock snoring instead, the Crest suggested. *You often say his voice could put anyone into a coma. Perhaps his snoring will have the same effect?*

Dante gasped as a hand closed around his groin. "Tell your Crest I'm trying to get some sleep too," Mai whispered. "If he doesn't shut up, I'll squeeze what I'm holding until your eyes pop out. Is that clear?"

"Understood," Dante squeaked quietly.

Dante snapped awake to find the hairs on the back of his neck standing up. His eyes searched the cave, but could see no obvious cause. Spatchcock and Flintlock were engaged in a mutual snoring contest nearby, while Mai was lying beside him, her face serene and beautiful in sleep. I must have turned over during the night, Dante realised. Temptation got the better of him and he leaned closer to steal a kiss. To Dante's surprise Mai responded warmly, her lips moving against his, her tongue sliding into his mouth. One of her hands slid across his body. Slowly her eyes opened and she smiled.

"I thought you hated me," Dante whispered. "You wanted to murder me."

"I changed my mind," she responded with a mischievous glint in her eyes. Mai kissed him again, her hand now slid down his chest.

"You should always give someone a second chance," Dante agreed, his hands slowly, deliciously exploring her body. "I like to think that–" He stopped abruptly.

Mai paused, her face displaying confusion. "What's wrong, Nikolai?"

He hushed her with a finger over the lips, before craning his head to look at Spatchcock and Flintlock. The two men were watching them intently, lascivious expressions on their faces.

"I say, don't stop on our account," Flintlock exclaimed.

"That's right," Spatchcock urged. "Nothing I like better than a good peep show. Warm the cockles of my heart, and the heart of my–"

Dante, I'm detecting a presence nearby, the Crest interjected.

"I'm aware of that. It's two presences and both of them are in trouble."

I wasn't talking about your disreputable travelling companions, I was–

Suddenly the cave was ablaze with brilliant white light. A girl was floating in the centre of it, her legs and arms folded into the lotus position. She was wearing a rich gown of red and gold, while long black hair spilled from beneath an elaborate headdress. In the centre of her forehead was a third eye, vermillion against a black background. She smiled at the surprised group benevolently.

I was trying to tell you about her, the Crest concluded.

When the girl spoke, her voice was audible in their minds, not their ears. *Your Crest is correct: you are not alone here. You are never alone on this mountain, not while the Mukari sits on the holy throne. But a day is upon us all when the reign of the living goddess ends forever – unless you intercede. A blackness is coming, when the snows of this peak will run red with blood.*

TWELVE

"Winds erode mountains, words rouse people."
– Russian proverb

"In the ranks of the Imperial Black, many crimes and misdemeanours, which would never be permitted within other regiments bearing the Tsar's emblem, are tolerated. Rape, murder, looting – all are perfectly acceptable behaviour for these troops, once the commanding officer has given his men leave to indulge their baser instincts. However, there is one crime that even the worst elements within the Imperial Black consider beyond redemption: cowardice. General Vassily Ivanov makes it known to all new recruits that any soldier who runs from the enemy can expect to be executed by their own brothers-in-arms. Such ferocity of will has created an army that never turns away, never backs down and never surrenders, no matter how overwhelming the foe or how uneven the odds in any conflict."

– Extract from *The Files of the Raven Corps*

Dante used a hand to shield his eyes from the Mukari's blinding apparition, squinting at her through a gap in his fingers. The ghostly girl floating inside the snow-bound cave looked similar to Mai, but her features were sharper and her eyes less hooded. This must be the current Mukari, Dante decided, projecting her spirit into here from the Forbidden Citadel.

I am doing all I can to hold back the darkness engulfing my realm, the Mukari told Dante and the others. *But I cannot contain the forces sent against me much longer. You must reach the citadel soon, or else all is lost.*

"How can we?" Mai asked. "The avalanche entombed us in this cave."

There is another way, faster than climbing the side of this mountain. The girl clapped her hands three times, and a cracking sound tore the air. Flintlock and Spatchcock scrambled to safety as the rock wall behind them split apart, releasing a cloud of dust into the air. When this dissipated a stairway was revealed, its steps winding upwards into the heart of the mountain. *Climb the stairs,* the Mukari said, *but hurry. Even I cannot sustain them indefinitely.*

Dante was first to his feet, hastily gathering his possessions. "Get your things together," he told the others. "Now!"

You will not need bedding or spare clothes where you are going. All will be provided for you. Bring only your wits and your weapons.

"Flintlock'll be travelling light then," Spatchcock cackled and received a clout round the ears.

Dante shoved his two comrades towards the staircase, then stood aside for Mai to go next. "After you?"

"Better if you're in front," she replied. "That way you'll focus on the job in hand and not on my arse."

"But it's such a nice ass," Dante said, smirking.

The Mukari cleared her throat, glaring at him pointedly.

"Sorry, force of habit," he replied before taking to the stairs.

Mai lingered in the cave briefly, staring at the girl's apparition. "You look like me – when I was your age." She strode to the staircase and began climbing upwards, taking two steps at a time. The doorway in the cave closed behind her.

． ． ．

Khumbu pounded his fists on the throne room door. The Mukari had sealed herself inside the chamber for hours, not allowing anyone to enter since the previous sunset. Back then, the citadel had trembled at the noises emanating from behind this door, noises that triggered a massive avalanche outside. Gylatsen had refused to allow anyone into the throne room, enraging the head monk. In retaliation Khumbu had banished Gylatsen to guard duty at the citadel gates. The young monk was too familiar with the Mukari, in Khumbu's opinion. A living goddess should be treated with reverence, not as a friend.

Despite sending Gylatsen away, Khumbu had still been unable to get into the throne room. The door remained sealed shut and the Mukari did not respond to the voices of her disciples. At midnight Khumbu had retreated to his cell for prayer and meditation, hoping these might offer him solace and guidance. But calm proved elusive and sleep as hard to find.

It was dawn – long past time for the goddess to eat. Khumbu had warmed a bowl of Gylatsen's broth and brought it to the doorway. He called to his goddess, but she did not respond. "Mukari, why do you keep us out? Have we offended you in some way? Tell us how to deserve your forgiveness. We will do whatever you ask. Please, Mukari – let us in!" He tried the handle once more, but it remained resolutely still.

Khumbu leaned his back against the door and let his old, weary legs fold together, sliding slowly down to the floor. Tears of frustration were pricking at his eyes, anger knotting his chest. Why was she treating him this way? Had he not devoted his life to her worship, kept alive the customs and traditions held sacred by the monks for generation upon generation? What more could she ask of him? I'm a fool, Khumbu realised. It is not for mortals to question the ways of the goddess. I am a disciple of her will – nothing more.

A thick clunk sounded behind Khumbu and the throne room door swung slowly open. The old monk got to his knees, bowing at the entrance before moving inside. He could hear the Mukari. She was sitting on the throne, her breathing shallow but steady. "Goddess, forgive this intrusion. Are you hungry?"

"No," she replied quietly. But after she stopped talking to him, Khumbu's keen ears could hear her lips and tongue still forming words. He had witnessed this phenomenon once before, when a previous Mukari had taken to projecting her spirit beyond its mortal shell.

"My apologies, goddess. I shall leave the chamber and stand guard outside, to make sure you are not disturbed again. Forgive my intrusion, my goddess."

"Thank you, Khumbu," she replied.

Ivanov had tasked the Enforcer with rousing the men at dawn. A roll call of the survivors found their number to be three hundred and twenty-seven, not counting the general or his second-in-command. Ivanov inspected the troops as best he could on the difficult terrain, before addressing them from a rocky outcrop a few metres up the mountainside. His breath formed into vapour in the cold air, each phrase becoming another small cloud in the still atmosphere.

"I know the events of yesterday were a shock to you all, as they were to me. Losing so many comrades so quickly was a blow, but one from which we must recover quickly. Do you want their loss to stand for nothing, their sacrifice to have been in vain?"

"No, sir!" the soldiers shouted back in unison.

"Will you still follow me, even if our mission should lead into hell itself?"

"Yes, sir!"

The general nodded, a grim satisfaction evident on his face. "Very well. Today will be an end to our endeavour, for better or for worse. The top of this peak is not far above us, and the Forbidden Citadel must be close by. We shall make a systematic search of the mountain. If this legendary fortress is here, we will find it, and we will take it!"

The troops responded with a roar of approval, brandishing their weapons.

Ivanov waited until the noise subsided before speaking once more. "When the Enforcer and I received our briefing for this mission, we were told the citadel is guarded by a religious sect blessed with special abilities. These holy men possess a secret weapon so powerful any man who looks upon it goes blind. Are you afraid?"

"No, sir!" the soldiers shouted back.

"You are the Imperial Black, the most feared, the most notorious, the most dangerous regiment in the Tsar's forces. If anyone should be afraid, it is these monks, for they know what terror we bring. Are you with me?"

"Yes, sir!"

"I said are you with me?"

"YES, SIR!"

The general nodded, satisfied with their response. "Before another sunset, we shall hold the Forbidden Citadel in our grasp, we shall take this mighty weapon for our own. And then every army, ever regiment in the Empire will tremble at our name. We are the Imperial Black and we shall be victorious!"

"Did you hear something?" Spatchcock asked. He and the others had been climbing the stairs inside the mountain for more than an hour, their backs aching from the effort.

"Only my stomach rumbling," Flintlock replied sourly.

"No, it was more like shouting – hundreds of men shouting." Dante leaned against the curved wall that encircled the staircase. "Crest, can you detect any unusual sounds through the mountain?"

Nothing distinct, it replied. *The last noises audible from the rocks did sound man-made, but I could find no pattern or rhythm to them.*

"The Mukari said she could not hold back the forces sent against her much longer," Mai recalled. She paused below the others on the staircase "We know that the avalanche killed many of Ivanov's men, but the survivors cannot be far from the citadel. We must press on."

"How do you know the soldiers are close to the fortress?" Flintlock asked. "How do we even know this citadel is near the top of the mountain?"

"Why else would the Mukari be helping us up the mountain, except to defend her?" Spatchcock replied, shaking his head. "What did you think she was inviting us for? Tea and bloody crumpets?"

"Don't mention food," Flintlock protested. "I feel like I haven't eaten in days." The former aristocrat yelped in pain, jumping up two steps at once. He spun round to find a grinning Dante wielding one of his cyborganic blades. "You stabbed me in the arse!"

"Anything to get you moving," Dante said with a smile. "Now get climbing again or else I'll carve my name into your backside!" Flintlock scurried up the steps, pushing his way past Spatchcock to take the lead.

Ivanov's men searched every square metre of the tor above where the ice bridge had been, but could not find any evidence of the Forbidden Citadel. The general reacted angrily, raging at his second-in-command, at the mountains around them, even the sky. When his fury had passed its peak, Ivanov demanded the major repeat every word uttered by the village headman. "There must be some clue among what he told you, some hint to where we shall find this fortress!"

But the Enforcer was looking past Ivanov, pointing into the sky. "General, look..."

Ivanov twisted round to see what was so important. The surviving soldiers were all doing the same, staring dumbstruck at what was looming over them. It was a massive, translucent skull floating in the air, thirty metres tall. Scraps of flesh and skin hung from its bleached white bones. An eyeball floated within each socket, but they had no lids or lashes. The mouth of the skull opened and shut soundlessly, its words spoken directly into the mind of each man on the mountain. *Why have you come to this place, outsiders? Speak now or I shall send another avalanche to smite you from my holy mountain!*

Ivanov stepped forwards, puffing out his chest and clasping his hands together behind his back. "My name is Vassily Ivanov and I am a general in–"

I know who you are, fool. I asked why you came here!

"We were sent by the Ruler of all the Russias, Tsar Vladimir Makarov, on a peaceful mission to find the Forbidden Citadel. Our leader wishes to open a dialogue with those who live inside the citadel."

You lie, the skull retorted coldly. *You wish to steal and you would kill my people to get what you want. That is the truth.*

"You are mistaken. Since you can speak into our minds, you can probably read our thoughts too. Look deep into mine and witness the truth there!"

I know your truth all too well, Ivanov the Terrible, Butcher of Rudinshtein. You have killed women and children, murdered and tortured thousands for your own pleasure. Even here, in my sacred mountains, you have spilled the blood of dozens solely to make one man speak. You are the worst of creatures and I will not weep at your death later today!

That last remark caused a stir among the soldiers, the general could hear them muttering to each other. "You are mistaken, whoever you are! I will not die today, nor will any of my men," he shouted at the ghostly skull.

You do not believe me?

"Why should any of us believe the lies of a creature that hides behind this elaborate illusion, a creature that lacks the courage to face me in person, a creature so weak and feeble it dare not even reveal its name?"

My name is death and this mission will be yours, Ivanov. I shall let all of your men see their own deaths. Close your eyes and bear witness, mortals!

Ivanov felt his eyes closing, despite trying to keep them open. Then his mind was filled with a vision of his body bleeding to death on a black floor, his throat run through by an unseen blade, his legs brutally severed at the knees. Ivanov shuddered at the vision that replayed itself over and over in his head, the same few seconds, the same excruciating pain lancing through his body in sympathy with the injuries.

Perhaps I can't stop myself seeing this, Ivanov decided, but that will not still my voice.

"No, this is a lie," he bellowed. "I deny this future, it is a falsehood designed to frighten the weak and feeble. I deny this future and say it is a lie!" The general shouted to his men. "Imperial Black, repeat after me: 'I deny this future and say it is a lie.' Say it!"

"I deny this future and say it is a lie," the nearest soldiers repeated.

"Louder!" Ivanov shouted. "I want to hear every man, every voice!"

"I deny this future and say it is a lie," the soldiers shouted, more of them joining in, the chant becoming stronger and more powerful.

"Again!"

"I deny this future and say it is a lie!"

Ivanov forced open his eyes and glared in triumph at the apparition. "Listen to my men. They reject your falsehoods! We shall find you and we shall destroy you, pretender! Ivanov the Terrible will rule this mountain!"

Not yet, butcher. And not all your men agree with you. See for yourself. The general realised dozens of his soldiers were fleeing down the mountain, scrambling over the snow-covered rocks, terror etched on their faces.

"Cowardly scum!" Ivanov snarled. "No soldier ever disgraced the uniform of the Imperial Black by fleeing a battle or an enemy. Enforcer!"

"Yes, sir!" the major responded, snapping to attention.

"You know what we do to deserters in this unit."

"Yes, sir." The Enforcer produced a weapon and began executing those fleeing, a single bullet exploding the head of each soldier. His shots rang out, one after another, until close to a hundred men lay dead on the slope below. The blood from their wounds drained into the snow, staining it crimson. Once the slaughter was concluded, Ivanov folded his arms and glared at the ghostly skull.

"I brook no opposition, be it the running coward, or the supernatural spectre. This fortress will be found and it will be mine!"

In her throne room the Mukari cried out, her concentration broken by the deaths of so many terrified men. She collapsed to the floor, hands struggling to keep her elaborate headdress in place. "Forgive me," the girl whispered. "I have failed."

Outside, the translucent skull glowed brightly for a second, then disappeared. Ivanov heard a gasp from one of his soldiers. "General, look!" Above them, a white fortress appeared, clinging to the side of the mountain. Its outer walls were ten metres high, with a pair of mighty gates built into them. Inside the wall were wide white buildings and windows dotted across their upper levels, each structure topped by a golden pagoda roof. The Forbidden Citadel was visible, at last.

"We searched that area, I know we did," the Enforcer hissed.

"Our eyes were deceived," Ivanov said quietly. As he spoke the citadel faded away once more, leaving no trace of its presence. "Our eyes are deceived once more, but our brains know the truth. The fortress of our enemy is but a hundred metres above this position. Enforcer, I believe the time is right for you to don the exo-skeleton. Forward, men! Destiny awaits us."

THIRTEEN

"Amens alone won't ward off evil."
– Russian proverb

"The exo-skeleton is among the more formidable weapons available to members of the Tsar's armed forces. It is a lightweight suit of body armour panels that can be worn over any uniform, without impeding the user's movements. Indeed, the exo-skeleton significantly enhances the physical power of whoever wears it. Activated by a hidden control button on the chest plate, the suit generates a force field around the user, simultaneously protecting him from harm and enhancing his strength by a factor of ten. A single blow from a normal soldier's fist can break bones and glass. A single blow from anyone wearing the exo-skeleton can smash through walls with ease."
– Extract from *The Files of the Raven Corps*

Dante's legs ached, his muscles weak and giddy. He and the others had been climbing the steps within the mountain for what felt like an eternity. At long last, there was a glimmer of daylight above them. Flintlock saw it first and gave a feeble hurrah of relief, before quickening his pace. Spatchcock followed suit and Dante hurried to keep up with them, Mai close behind. Finally, all four stood at the top of the stone staircase, where a landing broadened out into a hollow space. Sunlight poured into the cave's mouth, dazzling the four after so long in the near dark.

"Let's give ourselves a minute to rest," Dante said. "We don't know who or what is waiting for us out there, or how close we are to the Forbidden Citadel. We need to be ready for anything."

Flintlock pulled a sidearm from the holster beneath his left armpit and a dagger from the inside of his right boot. Spatchcock produced a vial of purge juice – a pernicious concoction of his own making that reduced its victims to violently vomiting, diarrhoea-stricken wrecks. "This should make the Imperials sorry they came to the mountains," he muttered happily. His other hand dug inside his trousers and removed a tiny pistol.

Flintlock arched an eyebrow at this revelation. "Since when did you have a gun concealed beside your crotch?"

"I've always had this," Spatchcock replied. "It only fires six shots, so I've kept it for emergencies. Nobody ever searches my groin thoroughly enough to find it."

"I wonder why," Dante said dryly. He removed the Huntsman 5000 from its usual position, slung across his back, and went through the ritual of checking the long-barrelled rifle. Beside him, Mai unwrapped a cloth bundle to reveal two short-bladed swords and a bandolier laden with dozens of throwing stars. She secured the bandolier diagonally across her chest, slotting one sword into a sheath that hung down over her left hip. The other sword she clasped in her right hand.

Dante admired her weaponry. "Sure you've got enough there?"

"I don't have the luxury of cyborganic swords," she replied testily.

"Hey, I was only saying…" Dante began, but then saw Mai swaying slightly. "Bojemoi!" He caught hold of her as she swooned, gently lowering her to the cave floor. Before passing out, Mai grabbed his hand and pressed it to her forehead.

■ ■ ■

An old, bald monk was looming over Dante, his eye sockets hollow and empty. "We must empty her mind, brothers, tear out every memory of her time here. She must never recall this place, never return here. When that is done, I will take her down the mountain." There was a murmur of assent from unseen voices. The monk leaned closer to Dante, his orange robe falling forwards, his breath thick with yeast and honey. "Forgive me, but what must be, must be done." Dante felt hands touching his body, fingernails clawing at his mind. He screamed in pain and terror, but the voice he heard cry out was that of a girl – Mai's voice. Then he knew only blackness, swallowing him like a cold ocean.

When his senses returned, Dante shivered. He was sitting cross-legged inside a cage, clad in a simple white robe. Hard bamboo canes dug into his legs and he felt hungry, prying eyes staring at him. "How much for this one?"

A massive figure loomed over him, the rancid stench of body odour filling Dante's nostrils. He couldn't make out its face, but somehow knew he must not speak. They would kill anyone who spoke out of turn.

"I said how much for this one, holy man?"

"Twenty." Dante twisted round in the cage to see who had responded. It was the same monk as before, but now he wore heavy winter clothing over his robes. The monk was bartering with Dante's life, selling him like a yak or a goat.

"For used goods? Ha! Eight and no more."

"Twelve?"

"I said eight, and that's being generous!"

Another blur and Dante saw a face he recognised staring at him. It was a man, a Himalayan with the familiar brown skin and dark hair. Something about the features reminded him of another face – but whose? "Farewell, daughter. We are so proud of you. This is the greatest honour any of us can imagine."

"Please, don't leave me here," Dante pleaded, but this time the voice was that of a child, young and afraid.

The man smiled benevolently. "Nothing bad will ever befall you here, daughter. Besides, we will see you for feasts and holy days. We love you, all of us. Never forget that, will you?"

"No Father, I will never forget," Dante whispered. He opened his eyes to find Spatchcock and Flintlock staring at him quizzically.

On the cave floor Mai sighed and looked up, her face free of all pain. "My headaches. They're gone," she said. "I can remember what happened. I remember everything."

The last psychic block in her mind has collapsed, the Crest said. *They must have been what caused Mai such pain. Her subconscious has been fighting them all these years, battering against the walls somebody else built in her mind.*

"How do you feel?" Dante asked.

"Better than I have in years," Mai replied. She got back to her feet, retrieving the short-bladed sword that had fallen from her grasp. "Let's go." Mai led the way out of the cave, followed by Dante and Spatchcock, with Flintlock nervously bringing up the rear. The four emerged into blazing sunshine, the sky a vast canopy of brilliant blue. The tor's snow-covered peak was visible a few hundred metres above them. The Mukari's staircase had brought them out on to a plateau within striking distance of the summit.

"So where's this bloody fortress?" Spatchcock asked. "After all we've been through to get here, I thought it would be right outside."

Flintlock's shoulders sagged. "We climbed all those stairs for nothing?"

Dante stared at his travelling companions, amazed. "Can't you see it?"

In front of them stood the Forbidden Citadel, its whitewashed walls rising from the snow as if hewn from the mountain. Beyond the wall stood the citadel buildings, wide structures with golden roofs and dozens of rectangular windows studding their sides. The fortress had an unearthly quality, as if it had been standing on this mountain for centuries beyond measure. Barring the entrance were two massive wooden gates, each inlaid with panels of gold.

"It's incredible," Mai whispered, her voice awestruck.

"You see it too?" Dante asked.

"Yes," she smiled. "It's like coming home."

"Do let us know when you've finished pulling our legs," Flintlock said petulantly, folding his arms. "I don't think it's clever, trying to make fools of us."

"We've got bigger problems than that," Spatchcock warned, pointing down the mountainside. "Look!" Soldiers were swarming below them, ascending the mountain like an incoming, inexorable tide. One of the Imperials saw the foursome and shouted, his voice alerting others.

"I take it all back," Flintlock said hurriedly. "If you two can see a citadel round here, now would be a good time to get all of us inside it."

Ivanov was leading his men to where the fortress had briefly appeared when an advance scout spotted four figures emerging from a concealed cave in the mountainside. "Sir, there's somebody else up there, ahead of us!"

The general pulled a pair of binoculars from a pouch on the side of his uniform. When he saw who was leading the new arrivals, Ivanov spat out a curse. Of all the people that should suddenly appear, here and now... "Send for the Enforcer!" he barked. Within a minute his second-in-command was at the general's side, standing to attention. The black regimental uniform was partially hidden by blue body armour, while matching gauntlets encased his hefty fists. "Major, if I believed in fate, I would say it was playing a trick on us. Look at the four people on that plateau and tell me who you see."

The Enforcer focused his attention on the area Ivanov was pointing at. "Nikolai Dante! What in the Tsar's name is he doing here?"

"No doubt he, too, is trying to secure the weapon inside that fortress," the general snarled. "But I very much doubt he is doing it in the Tsar's name."

The Enforcer had already drawn his weapon and was taking aim at the Romanov renegade. "Do you want me to kill him, sir?"

"No," Ivanov said, his lips forming a cruel smile. "That's one pleasure I shall reserve for myself. Tell the men that the three people with Dante are fair game, but the so-called Hero of Rudinshtein is mine."

"Yes, sir!"

Dante pushed against the citadel gates, but they did not move. He shoved his shoulder into the wood and strained with all his might, but still could not shift them. "Open up!" he demanded. "In the name of the Mukari, open these gates!"

Mai was observing the advancing soldiers below. "Hurry, Dante! The Imperials are almost within firing range."

"Hey, I'm doing my best. I don't notice anybody else offering to help," he snarled. Spatchcock and Flintlock looked on with bemused expressions.

"It's like one of those things you see in parks, where they don't talk," Spatchcock said, scratching his stubble.

"A memorial garden?" Flintlock offered.

"No. You know, the actors who don't say anything."

"Oh, mimes!"

"That's the one," Spatchcock agreed, pointing at Dante. "He looks like one of those mimes, pretending to push against an invisible wall."

Dante swore at them. "It's not invisible, you fools. *You* just can't see it!"

"Sounds like an invisible wall to me," Flintlock decided.

Dante swore again, before another thought occurred to him. "Crest, can you do anything to open these gates?"

If they were controlled by some computer or electronic circuitry, yes. But these gates are simply blocks of wood, albeit of a density and size so great you have no hope of ever moving them.

"In other words?"

For once, I'm of absolutely no use to you.

"Fuoco," Dante muttered. Bullets flew past his face and thudded into the gates, several ricocheting off the golden panels. Mai hastily retreated from the edge of the plateau, Spatchcock and Flintlock following her example. "I guess we're now in firing range," Dante noted sardonically.

Mai stepped back from the gates and shouted something in a tongue Dante did not recognise. She repeated the phrase with added urgency in her voice. Moments later the mighty gates began to open inwards, a gap appearing between them. Spatchcock stared at the gates, openmouthed.

"Where did those come from?" he spluttered. Flintlock shared his bemusement, momentarily forgetting the bullets flying past both of them.

"How did you...? Where were those...? I don't..."

Dante rolled his eyes. "At least we're all on the same page now. Don't just stand there, get inside!" He shoved the two men through the gap between the gates, while aiming his rifle towards the advancing soldiers. Mai took position beside him, extracting a handful of throwing stars from her bandolier.

"Ready?" she asked.

"I guess. What was that language you spoke?"

"Nepalese, I think. It was the common tongue in these mountains for centuries. The people inside the citadel must still recognise it."

"When did you learn Nepalese?" Dante asked, his finger tightening round the Huntsman's trigger.

"I must have always known it, but the blocks in my mind suppressed that knowledge."

The first line of the Imperial Black reached the edge of the plateau. Mai's left arm cut an arc through the air, flinging throwing stars at the soldiers. Each went down screaming, slices of metal embedded in their faces or throats, blood spurting from the wounds. "Makes me wonder what else I'll recall."

Dante took out the next wave of troops with a dozen shots from his rifle. "You go inside. I'll keep them back."

"We both go in," Mai replied. "The Mukari brought us here to protect the citadel, not to die outside its gates."

"Ladies first," Dante replied, taking out a trio of soldiers.

"Age before beauty," Mai said, hurling another handful of throwing stars.

"Tell you what, let's go in at the same time," he suggested. "On the count of three. Ready? One... Two... Three!" The duo retreated backwards through the gap before bumping into Spatchcock and Flintlock, both of whom were standing with their hands in the air.

"Out of the frying pan..." Spatchcock hissed.

"...and into the bloody fire," Flintlock added.

A phalanx of blind monks in saffron robes blocked the way, their empty eye sockets crackling with purple electricity. All too aware of the Imperials rapidly approaching the citadel, Dante stepped towards the monks and smiled broadly.

"Hi! My name's Nikolai Dante," he began.

Oh yes, that always wins people over, the Crest sighed.

Dante maintained his smile. "Perhaps you've heard of me? Hero of Rudinshtein, bastard offspring of a noble dynasty..."

The monks said nothing, their silence a stark contrast to the sounds of gunfire and boots crunching on rock and snow outside the gates.

"Anyway," Dante continued, "we've been sent here to save you from a regiment of the Tsar's most vicious soldiers, who plan to storm the citadel and probably slaughter you all. The good news is we got here before the soldiers, thanks to your Mukari's intervention. The bad news is, well…"

"The citadel is ours for the taking, men," a voice bellowed from outside the gates. "Prepare yourselves for glory!"

Dante shrugged. "You can probably guess the bad news for yourselves. My point is that now would be a good time to close the gates again, yes?"

As one the monks raised their hands and pointed at Dante. Purple energy shot from their fingertips to engulf him, sending his body into spasms so that he danced like a rag doll in the hands of an angry child. Mai cried out in Nepalese, gesturing for the monks to stop. The holy men lowered their hands and Dante collapsed on the cobbled path, his limbs still twitching.

Another monk emerged from a side door in the nearest building, his face kinder and friendlier than the others. "Forgive my brethren. They were told to defend the gates with their lives!" The new arrival crouched beside Dante, who was almost unconscious, his hands rummaging inside Dante's clothing for injuries. "He will quickly recover, his…" The monk's words stopped when his fingers reached Dante's left arm. "Can this be true?"

Spatchcock peeked out through the gap in the citadel gates. Dozens of Imperial Black soldiers had formed a line on the plateau outside. They were waiting for something or someone, their weapons aimed and ready to fire. "Whatever you're doing, I'd make it snappy," he advised.

The monk peeled back Dante's top, exposing the upper left arm to reveal the double-headed eagle symbol of the Romanovs, the mark of the Crest. "Brothers, this man bears the sign of the Mukari! He is one of us!" The other monks murmured amongst themselves.

Mai knelt on the other side of Dante. "You should tell them to shut the gates. If the soldiers get inside, the citadel will fall within minutes." The monk nodded. He sent eight monks out to face the Imperial Black and told the other four to close the gates once their brethren were outside. "They'll be slaughtered," Mai protested.

The monk smiled sadly. "I know. But all of us vowed to die for our goddess. We live to serve her, should we not perish in the same cause?"

By the time Ivanov and the Enforcer reached the plateau, the fortress gates had closed and more than three-dozen soldiers lay dead or dying in the snow. But the Forbidden Citadel was no longer hidden from them. It stood directly ahead with eight elderly men guarding the entrance. Their frail bodies were clad in saffron robes, their eye sockets hollow.

"Stand aside or suffer the consequences," the general shouted, but the monks did not move. "Suffering it is, then. Major?"

The Enforcer called forward three ranks of men, twenty in each row. Those at the front lay on the ground, the middle row dropped to one knee and the rear rank remained standing. "Take aim!" the major bellowed, and all sixty soldiers choose a target from among those blocking the gates. The monks raised their hands, purple electricity crackling at their fingertips. "Front rank – fire!"

A volley of shots rang out, but none reached their targets. Instead the rounds slowed to a halt in mid-air, then fell to the ground.

The Enforcer's face darkened. "Middle rank – fire!" Another fusillade of gunfire, but the result proved the same. "Rear rank – fire!" By now the monks were slowly moving towards the soldiers, still untouched by the invaders' weapons. With each step they took, a bolt of purple lightning would leap out and electrocute several troopers. The Enforcer drew his own sidearm. "Independent firing – fire at will!" In an instant all the soldiers were shooting.

Such was the volume of ammunition being fired at the monks that it was forming a wall in the air where each bullet met the psychic force-field. "Keep firing," the Enforcer bellowed to his men. "They can't keep this up forever!" He shot at the holy men and was surprised to see the bullet pass through the barrier, although it missed his intended target. "It's working, they're tiring," he shouted triumphantly. "Keep firing!"

More bullets began punching through the faltering force-field. One hit a monk in the shoulder, jerking him sideways. Another passed through a hand before embedding in the same monk's chest.

As he sank to one knee, the barrier weakened further and the deadly blasts of psychic energy from it ceased. Another bullet among the many penetrated the barrier, then another, the latter wounding a second monk. After that it took less than a minute for the force field to collapse completely and the eight monks to be left bleeding to death on the plateau, soldiers still pumping bullets into the crimson-stained corpses.

"Cease firing!" Ivanov shouted, taking charge from his second-in-command. A thick cloud of cordite filled the air, mingling with the dying moans of the last monk. The general drew his sidearm and silenced the final defender with a bullet to the brain. "So much for their much vaunted special abilities," he sneered. "Major?"

The Enforcer snapped to attention. "Sir!"

"I want those gates open. Now."

Dante regained his senses as the sound of gunfire died outside the gates. "Wh... What happened? Wh... Where am I?"

"The Forbidden Citadel," Flintlock said. "We made it."

"Now we have to save it from Ivanov and his bastards," Spatchcock added.

"I wish I hadn't asked," Dante admitted, sitting up with help from Mai. He noticed the friendly-faced monk at his side. "I don't think we've been introduced. My name's Dante, Nikolai Dante."

"Gylatsen," the monk replied with a smile. "I shall take you to Khumbu, he will want to see you. It is too long since a Romanov visited us."

"I'm not a–" Dante began, then checked himself. "Sure, take me to your leader. But Mai comes with us."

Gylatsen shrugged. "If you wish that, Master Nikolai."

"Call me Dante, okay? I'm nobody's master."

The monk pointed at Spatchcock and Flintlock. "What about the smelly one and his lover? Are they not your servants?"

"Servants?" Spatchcock laughed.

"His lover?" Flintlock protested simultaneously.

"Not exactly," Dante said, getting to his feet. "We are travelling companions." He approached Spatchcock and Flintlock, who were arguing with each other about Gylatsen's descriptions of them. "Will you two stop bickering? I need you to stay here, help the monks keep Ivanov and his men out for as long as possible."

Spatchcock jerked a thumb over his shoulder. "Those gates won't last long against an Imperial assault. It sounds like the monks outside have already been finished off."

"Do your best, okay?" Dante pleaded. "I'm not asking you to commit suicide, just slow them down. Every minute gained gives me and Mai the chance to find this weapon. Then we can use it on Ivanov."

Flintlock clutched his sidearm in one hand and his dagger in the other. "Alright, but the second those gates start going, so do we."

"Master Nikolai, we must go!" Gylatsen called. The monk was already leading Mai into the nearest building, one hand waving for Dante to follow.

Khumbu felt the last of his brethren die in the snow beyond the citadel wall. The old monk lit a yak-butter candle for the fallen soul, the eighth such flame that he had created in the last few minutes. How many more must die to keep our secret, he wondered? Could the outsiders be stopped, or would this day be the last time a living goddess resided upon the sacred mountain? The sound of hurried footsteps was getting closer. Khumbu rocked back from his knees on to his feet, then rose to a standing position, his joints creaking at the effort.

Knocking resounded at the door of his cell. "Brother Khumbu, it's Gylatsen. There is someone here to see you. He is one of the Romanovs and he bears the sign of the Mukari."

"Praise be to the goddess!" Khumbu whispered thankfully. "Bring him to me, Gylatsen. Bring him in." Khumbu heard the young monk usher in one person, then another, before entering the small stone chamber himself. "I hear three sets of footsteps. Who is my other visitor?" Khumbu was shocked when he heard a female voice, and even more shocked by what she had to say.

"I am known as Mai Tsai, but you called me by another name, didn't you?" she said quietly. "Once you called me goddess."

The Imperial Black had tried everything within their power to open the citadel gates. The brute force of two-dozen men had made no difference. Shooting at the gates was no more effective, every bullet bouncing back at them. Even explosives made little difference, beyond charring the wood and blackening the gold panels. Finally, Ivanov nodded to his second-in-command. The Enforcer punched the concealed control button on his chest, powering up the exo-skeleton. Artificial energy surged through his body, tendons of power creating junctures between the adjoining plates of body armour. Satisfied the equipment was working, even in such cold conditions, the major charged head first at the gates.

The effect was remarkable. A single blow knocked the two huge slabs of wood out of shape. His second blow destroyed whatever mechanism was locking the gates together. A third blow shattered them completely, reducing most of the wood to kindling. From within came a volley of gunfire and bolts of purple electricity, but both sides knew this battle was nearly over.

The Enforcer stood aside and bowed to his commanding officer. Ivanov smiled gratefully, then commanded his troops to return fire against those within. "The citadel is ours, men. Forward to glory! Forward to victory!"

"This is impossible," Khumbu protested. "What is she doing here? It is forbidden for one of her kind to return to this place!"

"I do not understand," Gylatsen said, looking to Dante for guidance.

"Mai used to be the Mukari, your living goddess," he replied.

"How can this be?" Gylatsen wondered. "Brother Khumbu?"

The old monk pointed at Mai with a wavering, bony finger. "She must leave, now! She will bring doom upon us all!"

"If it's doom you're expecting, it has already arrived," Dante said. "There are three hundred Imperials smashing their way into the citadel right now, led by the cruellest, most sadistic man on the planet – excluding the Tsar."

"Khumbu probably runs both of them a close third," Mai spat angrily. She glared at Gylatsen. "Do you know what your leader did to me, him and his brethren? Once they'd decided I was no longer fit to be the Mukari, they cast me out of your little paradise. But that wasn't enough for them. No, they invaded my thoughts, tore every memory they could from my brain. Khumbu and his holy men raped my mind, over and over and over. It wasn't enough to steal away the experience of having been a living goddess – they also gouged out memories of my family, my parents. Then, once they had finished with me, the noble Khumbu took me down the mountain and sold me to a slave trader for eight roubles. I was worth less to him than a pound of salt. That's how your precious leader treats his goddess, Gylatsen!"

"Brother Khumbu, is this true?"

The old man shook his head. "I did what I did for the good of us all."

"What about my good? What about my rights?" Mai demanded furiously. "Is that how you reward someone who was your living goddess for eight years – by ravaging her mind, by filling it with such pain and torment she cannot bear to come back here, so she can never discover the truth? Tell me I'm wrong, Khumbu! Tell your brethren I'm wrong!"

"You are not wrong, sister," another voice replied. "Khumbu cast you out of this hallowed place, as he casts out all Mukari once they reach the age of womanhood. As he would have cast me out, in time." A young girl walked into the crowded chamber, one hand holding up the hem of her red and gold robes to stop from tripping over them. As she spoke, Khumbu and Gylatsen dropped to their knees, bowing before her, their hands clasped together in supplication.

"Goddess, you should not be away from the throne room," Khumbu urged.

"Perhaps not, but I wanted to see more of the citadel, while I still could. The end is upon us, but we all have our parts to play."

"Does she always speak in riddles?" Dante wondered out loud.

That girl has the power of a goddess, the Crest interjected. *You would do well not to anger her.*

"You must be Dante," the Mukari said. "Your Crest is as bossy as mine."

"You can hear it too?"

I also bear a Crest, the girl said inside Dante's thoughts, *but mine has a different purpose than yours. A purpose that will become clear all too soon.*

A series of thunderous noises boomed through the citadel – once, twice, then a third time. The Mukari listened to them, her face filled with sadness. "The gates have given way before the Imperial onslaught. The blackness is upon us, and death follows close behind. It is time I went back to the throne room. Khumbu, you choose to come with me."

"I choose, goddess?"

The girl hitched up her robes again, preparing to leave the stone cell. "This is what will happen. You can stay here if you wish, or go with the others to launch a counter-attack against the invaders."

"No, I will guard you in the throne room," Khumbu decided.

"The choice is made, as it always was," the Mukari said. She smiled at the others. "I will see you soon enough." Then she was gone, Khumbu hurrying after her.

"Weird," Dante commented. "It's like she knows what is going to happen, before it happens."

"She has always known," Gylatsen said. "That is her burden as the Mukari, to know the future as you know the past. To her the past, present and future are one and the same. What must be, will be – it is inevitable."

"So what do we do now?"

Mai pulled a fresh handful of throwing stars from her bandolier and strode to the doorway. "We launch a counter-attack, of course. Coming?"

FOURTEEN

"War loves blood."
– Russian proverb

"A typical Himalayan monastery or holy palace is divided into three levels. The ground floor is devoted to places of worship and functional rooms such as kitchens. The middle level is given over to individual cells for each of the monks or priests that reside within the structure. Finally, the top floor is reserved for the holiest individual of all, with various adjoining antechambers and places of meditation."
– Extract from *Secret Destinations of the Empire*,
by Mikhail Palinski

Spatchcock ran as fast as his stubby legs could carry him. He had become separated from Flintlock in the chaos caused by the sudden implosion of the citadel gates. Both men had decided that staying alive was more important than trying to hold back the Imperial Black's inevitable advance. Spatchcock shouted at the four monks guarding the entrance to follow his example, but they remained in place, their psychic energy keeping the soldiers at bay temporarily. "Well, we tried," he called over his shoulder to Flintlock. But the blond Brit had already fled inside, so Spatchcock did the same.

He sprinted through a room filled with burning candles and religious icons, resisting the urge to pocket what looked like a gold statue. There was a time for looting and a time for saving your own skin. Spatchcock was not a religious man, but decided displeasing whatever deities looked after this place probably wasn't the best of ideas.

The next room he entered was a dining hall, with long wooden tables and benches neatly lined up for the next meal. He dodged round these and ducked through a darkened doorway. Beyond was the kitchen, if the smell of cooking oils and spices were to be trusted. Spatchcock squinted to see better, his eyes still adjusting from having been outside in the blazing sunshine. A haunch of cooked meat sat atop a bench, steam rising slowly from it. Can't remember the last time I ate, Spatchcock thought. He searched his surroundings for a knife or any kind of blade. Finding nothing of use, he tore at the flesh with his grubby fingernails instead, saliva dribbling down his jowls. Finally he freed a hunk of meat from the joint and shoved it into his mouth.

"Ahh, that's good," he enthused while masticating furiously, his mouth hanging open. "I haven't tasted anything that good since–"

Out in the dining hall, the wooden legs of a bench scraped across the stone floor. Spatchcock froze, half-chewed flesh hanging from his lips. It could be one of the monks – or it could be one of the Imperials. They'll have finished off the old guys in orange by now, he thought. They could already be searching the building.

Spatchcock saw a shadow in the doorway and threw himself to the floor, retrieving the tiny pistol from inside his trousers. He scrambled across the floor, his eyes watching the doorway. Another bench scraped across the dining room floor and someone cursed. They were close. Any second, any second now.

"Spatch? I say, old boy. Are you in there?"

"Flintlock!" Spatchcock exclaimed, standing up. He walked over to the doorway, pocketing his pistol. "I almost fired, you stupid bastard! I thought you were one of the Imperials."

The Brit stepped into view with another figure behind him, holding a gun to Flintlock's head. Before Spatchcock could react, a second soldier appeared, his weapon aimed and ready to fire. "Sorry, old boy," Flintlock said apologetically. "These chaps got the drop on me. Said they'd blow my brains out if I didn't help them. Haven't seen Dante, have you?"

"No," Spatchcock scowled. A third Imperial emerged from the darkness behind Spatchcock and nudged him in the back with a gun barrel.

"Outside," the soldier commanded, reaching into Spatchcock's pocket to remove his small pistol. "Our commander will want to interrogate you personally."

"Your commander?"

"General Vassily Ivanov."

"Ivanov the Terrible," Flintlock said nervously.

"So the avalanche didn't get him?" Spatchcock enquired. "Shame." He got a rifle butt in the back of his head that sent him staggering into Flintlock.

"I say," the former aristocrat protested. "There's no need for that!"

The soldier advanced on him, rifle butt raised and ready to strike the Brit too. "We decide what is needed, not you. Move!"

Dante found a window on the second level overlooking the broken gates where soldiers were still marching into the citadel. "Time to even the odds a little," Dante muttered, taking aim with his Huntsman 5000. He began firing rapidly, knowing his weapon would correct any flaws in his aim. By the time the Imperials began returning fire, Dante had downed three-dozen of their number and dived out of view. He scuttled along the corridor, keeping below the windows, before popping up at the other end and opening fire again. The soldiers reacted more quickly this time, his element of surprise lessened, but Dante had still killed another twenty before he

was forced out of harm's way. Two more attempts netted a
dozen more men in total, by which time the remaining soldiers
had made it safely inside the citadel. From now on the fighting would have to be hand-to-hand, Dante decided. He hid his
rifle behind a small shrine, then ran to the nearest staircase,
his cyborganic swords extruding themselves from each fist.

Mai was waiting at the bottom of the steps. Between her
and the nearest doorway was an uneven pile of Imperial
Black corpses, which had all been killed by throwing stars.
Mai was holding a short-bladed sword in each hand, the
razor-sharp edges of each weapon not yet sullied by blood.
She smiled at Dante. "What took you so long?"

"You know how it is – places to see, Imperials to shoot.
You've been busy in my absence. Where's Gylatsen?"

The monk came through the outer doorway at speed, leaping over the pile of dead invaders with ease. "They're
coming!" he shouted as he ran past. "I delayed them as long
as I could. I'm going to the throne room."

"How many are coming?" Dante called after him.

"Plenty," Mai replied, pointing out the door. At least a hundred Imperial troopers were storming towards them,
weapons drawn and ready to fire.

"Good, I've got a score to settle with these bastards,"
Dante muttered. "For Rudinshtein!" he roared, charging at
the oncoming soldiers. Mai was one step behind him, her
blades flashing through the air, hungry for blood.

Khumbu paced back and forth inside the throne room, the
sounds of death drifting up from below. The Mukari sat on
the floor, playing with a wooden elephant, talking to it softly
under her breath. At last the monk could stand the tension
no longer. "How can you do that now, of all times, goddess?"

The Mukari looked at him with sad eyes. "You always forget, Khumbu. I may be your goddess, but I'm also a child. I
like to play with my toys. Besides, this is what I am doing
when the soldiers break down that door."

"You've seen that?"

"Of course, how could I not? Did I not prophesy all of this to you? "It is the outsiders who bring death to this place. 'The gates of the Forbidden Citadel will fall and there is nothing any of us can do to stop that.' I said those words to you in this room, not so many days ago. Now the darkness is here." The Mukari went back to playing with her wooden elephant. "Beyond that I see no further."

"General, we have captured two of the outsiders from the plateau!"

Ivanov heard the soldier's voice and smiled. Excellent. Killing Dante would the culmination of three years' endeavour in that tiresome backwater Rudinshtein, he thought. But before the Romanov whelp dies I plan to extract the maximum amount of pleasure from torturing him. When he is beaten and broken and utterly spent, only then shall I take off his head. Perhaps I shall impale his rotting skull on the tip of a spike and have it paraded through the streets of Rudinshtein, one final indignity to crush any rebellion in the hearts of that lice-ridden rabble.

The general pivoted on his heels to discover his moment of pleasure was not yet at hand. His soldiers proudly clutched the collars of two men, one with an odour to equal any battlefield latrine, the other displaying a haughty, upturned nose that cried out to be punched. "What are these... dregs?"

"They were with Dante when he entered the citadel, sir," one of the soldiers said, his face crestfallen. "We thought you might wish to interrogate them."

"You thought? You thought?" Ivanov raged. "Since when did I encourage my men to think? If I wanted a regiment of philosophers, I would not have recruited a thousand of the Empire's worst scum to fill my ranks, would I?"

"No, sir."

"I wouldn't sully the heel of my boot on these pieces of excrement! Get them out of my sight. Now!"

"Yes, sir!" The soldiers snapped to attention, then bundled the prisoners away, eager to put as much distance between them and the general as quickly as possible. "You made us look bad," one of the soldiers hissed at Spatchcock and Flintlock. "You'll pay for that."

"What a shame," the Brit replied cheerily. "And I was so looking forward to having a chat with the mighty Ivanov the Terrible."

"Me too," Spatchcock agreed. "I was going to tell him about that bag of gold coins I hid down the front of your trousers."

Flintlock looked at his companion as if he were insane. "Spatch, old boy, what are you talking about? There's nothing down the front of my trousers."

"You can say that again."

"Shut up and keep moving," a soldier warned, shoving his rifle butt into Spatchcock's back.

Dante cut a swathe through the first five Imperials that crossed his path, his cyborganic blades severing hands, arms and even the head of one unfortunate soldier. Mai was just as effective, the shorter blades of her weapons enabling the Oriental assassin to stab as well as slice her targets. Together the duo fought the Imperial onslaught to a standstill, using the soldiers' own numbers against them. The battle was taking place in a narrow corridor, so only three or four men were able to take on the duo at once. Those in front blocked anyone behind them from shooting at Dante or Mai, while the close quarters combat made rifles all but useless.

Realising the folly of their frontal assault, a veteran soldier shouted to his comrades to use bayonets and other blades against the enemy. Dante smiled at the order. That's right, he thought. Fight us on our own terms. He leapt atop the corpses of the fallen Imperials, using their bodies to gain superior height over the next wave of soldiers. Several troopers charged at him, bayonets fixed to their rifles, a war cry on their lips. *Dante, evasive action!*

"Don't worry. Mai and I can handle this," he told the Crest.

Dante jumped nimbly over the thrust of the bayonets, but landed awkwardly on top of the soldiers. "Fuoco!" he cried out, before plunging to the corridor floor in a tangle of Imperial arms and legs.

You were saying?

"Mai! A little help here!" Dante shouted, elbowing one of the soldiers in the face while kneeling on the crotch of another.

The Himalayan woman came flying over the pile of corpses, her leading leg smashing into the chest of an onrushing soldier. He tumbled backwards, knocking over several of his colleagues. Mai landed neatly on the floor, using her left blade to decapitate an Imperial before he could stab Dante. Her right sword plunged into another soldier on the floor, severing his spinal column in one devastating movement.

Mai helped Dante back to his feet while delivering a swift kick to the head of the nearest trooper. "We're getting bogged down here," she said. "We need to fall back, before they outflank us."

Dante flashed his blade through the air, disabling another four Imperials with a single movement. He could see soldiers running past the end of the corridor, looking for another way up into the heart of the citadel. "You're right," he conceded. "Head for the throne room. I'll see you there."

Mai nodded and flung herself over the pile of corpses in a compact somersault. Dante dodged a stabbing bayonet that was aimed at his head, then drove the point of his right sword through the hand of his attacker. "You should be more careful," Dante said, cheerfully twisting his blade. "You could have somebody's eye out with that."

The soldier spat blood at him. "You'll die here, Romanov scum!"

"The name's Dante – Nikolai Dante. Remember that!" Dante ripped his sword out of the soldier's hand, slicing off four fingers in the process. He smiled at the remaining Imperials. "Sorry to loathe you and leave you, but I'm required elsewhere." Dante dived over the corpse pile and rolled into a somersault as he hit the floor on the other side and came up running.

Mai was racing up a stone staircase to the citadel's top level when she heard a voice sneering at her from above. "Quite the little hellion, aren't you? The Imperial Black has a fearsome reputation, but such strength is borne of numbers, not skill. How would you cope with an adversary worthy of your talents?"

She slowed her advance, creeping to the top of the steps, tensed for the inevitable attack. "I've killed more men than I can remember," Mai hissed. "Another one will make little difference to me."

"Brave words, but such bravado is wasted on me."

Mai searched the landing around the top of the staircase. It was a wide corridor, with half a dozen doors leading away, all of them ajar. The source of the taunts was not obvious, hidden amidst echoes and stone walls. She dropped into a crouch, a short-bladed sword in each hand, ready for action. "If you're so invincible, stop hiding in the shadows and show yourself."

"Very well." The mighty figure of the Enforcer emerged from the nearest doorway, his black uniform glistening wet and crimson, blood splashes staining the blue plates of his exo-skeleton. His face remained hidden behind the blankness of his mask, Mai seeing only her own reflection on its burnished surface. "How much do you want to die?"

"Yours will be the death here," she said evenly.

The Enforcer folded his arms. "I ask because there is no need for me to kill you. Surrender or run, either will keep you safe. Engage me in combat and there can be only one outcome. In this exo-skeleton I am invulnerable, whereas all you have to defend yourself are two puny blades and those clothes."

"Before my brother was killed on the orders of your master, I was an assassin for the Tong of the Red Hand," Mai snarled. "I know more than a hundred ways to kill and I will need only one to finish you."

"Then we fight to the death, warrior against warrior. So be it." The Enforcer bowed gracefully to her, his shoulders higher than the top of her head. "Begin."

Dante was fighting a running battle through the citadel's lower levels. Every time he reached a staircase, half a dozen Imperials had already occupied the way up. He sliced them apart, his superior agility and speed enabling him to escape each skirmish unhurt. But another half dozen would be waiting beyond the first, forcing him into a tactical retreat. Sheer weight of numbers was driving Dante sideways, stymieing his progress.

"Crest, I need to find another way to the top level," he whispered, pausing to catch his breath behind a stone pillar. "I don't suppose they've got an elevator in this place by any chance?"

Dante, this is an ancient stone citadel dating back hundreds, if not thousands, of years, built on the side of a mountain in one of the world's most remote regions.

"You're telling me no, aren't you?"

Your knack of stating the obvious does you credit – even if little else does.

"Any other easier methods of reaching the throne room?"

None, unless you plan on climbing the citadel's exterior.

"Thanks for the help," Dante sighed. He ran along a stone corridor and found one last set of steps leading upwards. Curiously, there were no Imperials blocking his path. "Call me old fashioned, but this looks too inviting."

Plainly, this is a trap. You must find another way, the Crest insisted.

"There are no other ways," Dante replied.

Nevertheless, you cannot–

The Crest's words were drowned out by a mocking voice, its words drifting down the stone steps. "That pipsqueak I hear talking to itself below – I wonder who it can be? Perhaps a rat has wandered into the fabled Forbidden Citadel, searching for cheese. Run away, vermin, there's nothing for you here."

"Ivanov," Dante snarled.

"Why, the vermin recognises my voice. Perhaps it is not a rat after all. Is somebody else down there? The so-called Hero of Rudinshtein, perhaps?"

"What do you want, scumbag?"

"A little respect will do for a start," Ivanov replied. "Call me general."

Dante spat an obscenity at the taunting voice.

"Such language! And I thought the Romanov family was taught proper manners, like every other noble house. But then, there's nothing noble about you, is there? Nikolai Dante, bastard offspring of a disgraced dynasty and a sea-hag, who murdered women and children to line her purse!"

"That's rich, coming from a butcher who's raped and murdered most of a province," Dante retorted. "During the war there was a rumour you could only achieve sexual climax by violence. What's the problem, Vassily? Can't get it up unless somebody's bleeding in front of you?"

"Sticks and stones may break my bones," Ivanov snapped back.

"But at least they'll give you a hard-on."

"The Hero of Rudinshtein reveals his true colours: a foul-mouthed guttersnipe excreted by some ocean-going whore too lazy to have an abortion. Of course, what could I expect from a coward who fled his own kingdom, who left his people to die while he went adventuring across the Empire? What kind of hero does that? You could have come back to save your precious province, tried to rescue the scum you claim to love. But you didn't have the balls."

Dante's face twisted with anger and fury as he moved closer to the stone steps. *Don't do it*, the Crest warned. *Ivanov is trying to goad you into making a mistake.*

"I don't need his goading to make those," Dante said bitterly.

Perhaps not, Nikolai, but even you must see sacrificing yourself to silence him will achieve nothing.

Dante paused. "Did you call me Nikolai? You never call me that."

Anything to get your attention, the Crest said. *Or save you from yourself.*

"Sorry to interrupt your schizophrenic small-talk," Ivanov called down. "Are you coming up or do I have to send down my men to fetch you?"

Dante smiled. "Come and get me, general."

Ivanov had sent down a dozen soldiers to capture the Romanov renegade, but they had not returned. He waited three more minutes with the rest of his men, listening to the sounds of fighting, then the sounds of pain, then the sounds of dying. After that, all was silent below. "How tiresome," the general said to himself. From the fifty soldiers still at his disposal, he sent another twenty down to pursue Dante while taking the rest up to the citadel's top level. It was time to secure the secret weapon, whatever it was. If must be here, otherwise why would Dante fight so hard for this place?

Mai flung herself sideways, avoiding another killing blow from the Enforcer. He was surprisingly fast, despite his bulk. She knew it would only take one direct hit from those hyper-powered gauntlets to finish her. Blue energy rippled between the joints of his body armour, maintaining a force shield around him that was almost impossible to penetrate. Mai had danced around him for more than ten minutes, somer-saulting gymnastically from one point to another, flailing at him with her swords. But each thrust bounced away harm-lessly. If there was a weak spot in the Enforcer's exo-skeleton, she would not find it from this distance.

I'll have to get inside his guard, she realised, and turn his size against him. Yet in the moment it took her to grasp this, he was already upon her. A mighty fist clutched at the air where her head had been. The Enforcer missed, but caught her long black hair, yanking Mai back in mid-air. She stabbed one of her swords into his chest with all her strength, but the blade broke off at the hilt and flew to the wooden floor beams. Mai tried to cut through his fingers with the other sword. However, he snapped the steel blade in two and tossed it aside as if it was a child's toy.

The Enforcer gripped her throat below her jaw, and held her up in the air at arm's length, examining Mai's pretty fea-tures. "You fight with great courage and skill," he said. "But you are no match for my power."

"You triumph without honour, letting your exo-skeleton fight for you. A true warrior would not need its power against me."

"Perhaps you are right," he conceded. "But I am not so foolish as to switch it off now." The Enforcer held up his free hand before Mai's face. "Such is the power of this suit, a sin-gle jab of my fingers would push your eyes out through the back of your skull. Does a quick death meet your wish for honour?"

"There is no honour in murder," Mai retorted.

"Of course, I could slap your face like this," the Enforcer said, his free hand swiping across her face like a thunderclap of pain. "To me that felt like the lightest of touches, but it almost took off your head. How much punishment can you take before the brain damage becomes permanent? Before it claims your life?"

A trickle of blood spilled from Mai's mouth, running down her chin on to the gauntlet round her neck. She lashed out with her feet, kicking desperately at his chest, trying to inflict some pain, however hopeless the attempt. This brought a laugh from the Enforcer, the futility of her actions amusing him. "And still this vixen fights back! You have a spirit that does you credit, but it will not save you. I shall close my gauntlet around your neck and crush the bones within. It will not be the quickest of deaths, but your pain will soon be over. Goodbye."

Dante, this is foolhardy at best and potentially fatal if you fall from this height, the Crest warned. *The odds against an unskilled, inexperienced individual like you successfully free-climbing a structure like this are–*

"Never tell me the odds," Dante hissed under his breath. He was hanging from the outside of the citadel's second level, his fingertips clinging to the slightest of handholds. Above him, a wooden balcony protruded, its base supported by thick struts that dug into the side of the building. "You said it yourself, this is the only way to get to the top floor without fighting my way through all of Ivanov's men."

Yes, I know what I said, but I didn't expect you to take it as a suggestion. I could count the number of times you've done that on one hand. If I had a hand, that is.

"For once in your precious existence, could you let me concentrate?"

Fine. But on your own head be it.

"That's exactly what I'll land on if you don't shut up!"

Charming. Kill yourself. See if I care.

"Thank you." Dante closed his eyes, preparing himself mentally for the leap to grab at the nearest support strut. On the count of three, he told himself. One... Two... Th–

Which I don't, by the way.

"Diavolo!" Dante cursed, almost losing his handholds on the citadel wall. "Must you always have the last word?"

Not always.

"Good, then shut the hell up!"

I simply prefer to offer the occasional observation in the hope these comments of mine might guide you towards a wiser course of action.

Dante screamed obscenities at the sky, then hurled his body towards the wooden support before his Crest could make another comment. His fingers scrabbled at the strut, clawing, grasping, then finally taking hold of it. He reached up to the balcony and dragged himself over to its edge. Straining mightily, he lifted his head high enough to see past the wooden banisters and through a pair of glass doors. Beyond them Dante could make out Khumbu, pacing back and forth, and the Mukari seated on the floor. This must be her room, he realised.

"Crest," he said, but no response came. "Crest?"

I thought you didn't want me to speak.

"Stop sulking and scan that room. The Mukari said she was bonded with a Crest. Can you detect it inside that room?"

Yes. It is bonded with the Mukari's mind.

"Like you are with mine?"

I cannot be more specific. Her Crest is far more powerful than any other I have encountered before, preventing me from discovering its secrets undetected.

"Then there's no need for subtlety, is there?" Dante asked, clambering up and over the balcony's railings.

You were being subtle?

Khumbu heard the balcony door's opening and swung round to confront the intruder. "Who are you? What are you doing here?"

"It's me, Nikolai Dante," the new arrival announced. "I see Ivanov hasn't got here yet, there's still hope." He crouched beside the girl. She was still playing with her toy elephant, sadness in her eyes.

"Ivanov is looking for a weapon. Is it nearby?"

"Yes," she said evenly.

"Can we use it against the Imperials?"

"Not directly, no."

"But you created the avalanche that swept most of Ivanov's men away."

Khumbu intervened, grasping Dante's arm and pulling the unbeliever back from the goddess. "Show the Mukari the respect she deserves, outsider!"

Dante wrenched his arm free. "Don't you get it, old man? The general will kill everyone and everything in this place to get that weapon. Without it we have no defence against him. Your precious citadel will be levelled and your goddess murdered in front of you."

"I cannot act against the darkness directly," the Mukari said. "That is why I brought you and Mai here, and the others. You are my champions. If you fail, all is lost. But no victory comes without a cost."

Khumbu could hear shouting in the corridor outside the throne room. "That voice, I know that voice."

"Poor Gylatsen," the girl said, a single tear rolling down her sad face.

Gylatsen had heard the soldiers coming long before they arrived outside the throne room. He pressed his back against the wooden door, preparing himself for what was to come. The Mukari had told him about this moment long ago, how the end would engulf the citadel, how his life would be sacrificed to save hers. To know he would die in such a worthy cause had been a comfort before today. But now the moment was almost upon him, it was no comfort. Gylatsen pressed his palms together, letting all the energy stored within his thin frame gather between them.

Along the corridor he heard the general talking with another man. Ivanov told him to kill the woman and be quick about it. He must mean Mai, Gylatsen realised. She might still be alive – but not for long.

Now the soldiers were marching towards Gylatsen, boots stomping in time with each other on the wooden beams, bringing death with them.

Forgive me, goddess, but I am scared, he prayed. I don't want to die.

Everything dies, the Mukari whispered into his mind. *I am with you, now and forever. I always will be.*

"Thank you," he whispered, swallowing hard.

A phalanx of soldiers surrounded the monk, their weapons aimed at his chest. From nearby a voice commanded them into action. "What are you waiting for? He's one man. Strike him down!"

As the soldiers opened fire Gylatsen opened his hands and let the purple energy escape, electrocuting all those within reach of him. He died, but more than twenty of the Imperials perished with him, screaming in agony.

The Enforcer waited until Ivanov and the other soldiers had passed before turning his attention back to Mai. His fingers tightened their grasp round her neck, until Mai could feel the blood pounding inside her forehead, blackness closing over her vision. A voice entered her head, childlike and soothing, urging her to keep fighting, to lash out with all her might. Mai kicked one last time and felt something give way under her foot, as if she had connected with a small button. The gentle hum of energy from the Enforcer's exo-skeleton faded and then was gone, his grip on her throat slackening at the same time. "N... No!" he stammered. "You couldn't have known how to do that!"

Mai kicked at him again, this time aiming her blow higher so it caught him under the chin. The Enforcer's head snapped backward and he let go of her, both hands clawing at his throat, choking and gasping for breath.

Mai dropped to the floor, one hand closing over the broken blade of her sword. Before the Enforcer could react, she was slicing it across his body, hacking at the gaps between his body armour, blood spurting from the wounds.

He went down before her savage attack, crumpling to one knee, his gauntlets held up to ward off further blows. Mai stabbed the broken blade through one of his hands, pulled it free and impaled his other hand with it. She stepped back, satisfied with the amount of blood the Enforcer was losing. But something about his response disturbed her. Most men would be begging for mercy by now, or weeping in agony. But the Enforcer remained where he was, staring at his pierced hands. Finally, he started laughing.

"What the hell is wrong with you?" Mai demanded.

"Even if you kill me, I won't feel it," he said quietly. "My master had all my nerve centres surgically shut down, to turn me into an unbeatable fighting machine. 'The man who feels no pain almost feels no fear', that's what he told me after the operation." The Enforcer pressed the gauntlet impaled by the broken blade against the floor, gradually forcing the slice of metal through his hand until it fell free.

Mai spun round on the spot, one foot arcing through the air to smash into his head. The impact cracked his helmet apart and the facemask fell free, revealing the ruptured features underneath. They were a mass of scar tissue and ancient wounds, a road map of pain. A chill of recognition ran through Mai. No, it couldn't be, it wasn't possible. She knelt before him, one hand reaching for the broken face. "Rai? Is it you?"

FIFTEEN

"Freedom for the free,
and heaven for the survivors."
– Russian proverb

"Samovar is part of the Romanov dynasty and widely considered to be the harshest prison colony in the Empire. Nicknamed the Gulag Apocalyptic, it was said no one ever returns from Samovar. I was despatched to this distant outpost in the Starship *Andrei Tarkovsky*, as bodyguard to a distinguished visitor [name deleted]. I subsequently discovered the prisoners were being used as raw material for [remainder of text deleted by an unknown hand]."
– Extract from Nikolai Dante's report on the
Samovar Incident, 2667 AD

Dante recognised the smell of burning flesh and the screams of pain coming from outside the throne room door. He had seen what the citadel's monks could do, but Ivanov had too many men to be held back for long. Dante extended the cyborganic swords from each of his hands, stepping between the doorway and the Mukari. He glanced over his shoulder at Khumbu standing by the windows. "If you've got any tricks, old man, now's the time to use them!"

The door smashed inwards, soldiers brandishing their weapons. Dante killed five of them before he was overwhelmed. A soldier gripped each of his arms and held them in check, pistols levelled against Dante's head. Khumbu offered no resistance, his quivering hands hanging at his sides. Once the throne room was declared safe, the general strode in, a broad smile on his cruel face. "Ah, the redoubtable Romanov renegade! I might have known you'd get here first – but it will do you no good. Your partners in crime are being held captive by my men, while your slant-eyed sidekick is having her neck crushed by the Enforcer. Whatever you came here to do, you have failed."

"Spare me the gloating, Vassily," Dante replied.

"I don't recall saying you were permitted to address me by my first name," the general snapped. "Such impertinence will be your undoing." Dante did not speak, preferring to make an obscene finger gesture. "And such crudity too. You should be honoured to stand in the presence of such a fine soldier!"

"Honour be damned."

"Rai, what happened to you? I thought you were dead," Mai whispered to her brother. The Enforcer knelt in front of her, his hands dripping blood on the black floorboards.

"I thought I was dead, too," Rai replied, his scarred lips struggling to form the words. "Ivanov and his men captured me outside the Governor's mansion in Rudinshtein. The civilians I was leading to safety, they–"

"Were all slaughtered, I know. Dante said you volunteered to take them."

Rai nodded. "I was young and idealistic, a fool. The general taught me the error of my ways, tutored me in the reality of the world. The reality of war."

"I read a battlefield report about your death, signed by Ivanov himself. He said Dante shot you to prevent his interrogators getting any information about Romanov troop movements."

"Dante fired because the general was going to use serpent-wire on me. He thought the bullet killed me, but it hit the

canister of serpent-wire instead." Rai touched a bloody hand
to his horrific face, caressing the scars as though they were
old friends. "When the serpent wire exploded, I caught most
of it in the face, tiny fragments all fighting to slice through
me. Ivanov's own surgeon worked for eighteen hours to get
them out before they reached my brain. Dante did this to me,
but the general saved my life."

Mai shook her head. "That's a warped version of reality,
Rai. Ivanov's twisted the facts, turned you into his slave, his
pet torturer."

Rai glared at her. "The general said you wouldn't understand. He knew how it would be if we ever met, face to face.
He's a great man, Mai. He's been like a father to me."

"What about our real father? Did you ever wonder what
happened to him?"

"I don't need to wonder," Rai said, smiling bitterly. "I
already know. He was headman of the village we attacked. I
killed him myself."

Mai stared at her brother, disbelieving. "You couldn't...
You wouldn't!"

"The Imperial Black is all the family I need," Rai smiled.
His hands shot forwards, grabbing his sister by the throat.
"That's why I have to kill you, Mai."

Spatchcock and Flintlock were held captive in a latrine block
at the eastern end of the citadel's lowest level, guarded by
four Imperials. When Flintlock complained at the smell of
stale urine, the soldiers laughed bitterly. One removed his
helmet to sneer at the Brit, the insignia of a sergeant evident
on his black uniform. "This place doesn't stink half as bad
as you two."

"My associate may have the odour of a dung heap while
possessing none of its charm," Flintlock replied, "but I pride
myself on–"

"Shut your mouth," the sergeant retorted. "I don't care if
you smell sweeter than the Tsarina's purse. You made us

lose face in front of the general. That's gonna cost you both. Now, how do you intend to pay?"

"I'm not sure I understand your meaning," Flintlock said.

"It's simple. You fill our money pouches with roubles or else we have to find another way of getting our money's worth out of you two." The sergeant grabbed his own crotch and shook it, to the amusement of his comrades.

"Sorry to be obtuse, but I'm still not quite with you," the Brit bumbled.

Spatchcock sighed. "It's simple, your lordship. Either we pay up or else they turn us into their whores."

"Oh," Flintlock said, his mind processing the information. He caught the lecherous glint in the eyes of their captors. "Oh!"

"Don't worry your lily-white ass," Spatchcock continued. "We can pay these boys off with that bag of gold I hid down your trousers."

"Bag of gold?" Flintlock glanced down at his crotch in bewilderment.

"I heard you mention that before," the sergeant said. "Let's see the proof."

"Certainly," Spatchcock smiled, plunging a hand inside his partner's pants.

"I say!"

Spatchcock leaned closer to Flintlock. "Whatever you do next, don't breathe in," he whispered, his hand clasping a small object in the Brit's breeches.

"Whatever you do next, don't squeeze," Flintlock replied.

"Oh... Sorry," Spatchcock said apologetically. He resumed rummaging.

By now the soldiers were growing impatient. "What's taking so damned long? If this bag of gold is going to satisfy all of us, it'll need to be impressive!"

Spatchcock smiled and winked at Flintlock as his search located its target. "Don't worry, boys... I'm sure this will make a big impression on you." He pulled his hand free and flung its contents at the Imperials in a single movement. Glass shattered on the stone floor by their feet and green gas billowed outwards, rapidly engulfing the surprised soldiers. Spatchcock was already running for the door, pulling Flintlock along with him. Behind them were moans of pain mixed with the sounds of vomiting and bowels being evacuated.

"What the devil was that?" Flintlock shouted.

"I hid my supply of purge juice in your pants when the Imperials took us captive," Spatchcock called back, fleeing for his life.

"But what if the vial had broken inside my trousers?"

Shot flew past the two fugitives as the stricken soldiers opened fire.

Spatchcock smiled. "Then you wouldn't be quite so full of sh–"

"Shut up and run!" Flintlock snapped, overtaking him.

Ivanov lashed out, his right fist plunging into Dante's midriff. The prisoner doubled over in pain, air whistling out from between his teeth. The general stepped closer and thrust a knee up into Dante's groin, the impact so hard it lifted him off the floor. Once the captive had finished coughing and retching, Ivanov lifted Dante's head by the hair and spat phlegm into his eyes. "It's time somebody taught you some manners, whelp. A little respect for your elders and betters."

"You might be older than me, but you're no better," Dante replied. That earned him a slap across the face. "Getting warmed up yet? In the crotch area, I mean." Another slap, then another, and another. "I'll take that as a yes, shall I?"

"You'll take it and you'll like it," the general hissed, his breath coming in short, excited gasps. He straightened up, letting go of Dante's hair. "But I have more pressing matters than teaching you how to behave. The Tsar sent me here on a specific mission and it is time for that mission to be accomplished." Ivanov strode across the room to Khumbu. "Where is the weapon?"

"I do not know of what you speak," the old monk replied.

"This citadel houses a powerful weapon, a weapon the Romanovs had planned to use against the Tsar during the war. The Ruler of all the Russias has sent me and my men–"

"What's left of them," Dante interjected.

"–to take possession of this weapon for the good of the Empire," Ivanov continued. "You will give the weapon to me or suffer the consequences."

"We have no weapon," Khumbu insisted. "We are holy men, disciples of the Mukari, living goddess of our people."

The general looked around the room. "Do you mean this girl?" he laughed.

The monk nodded gravely. "She is our deity, made flesh on this earth."

Ivanov snapped his fingers and one of the soldiers produced a knife, its hilt inlaid with the symbol of the Tsar. "You claim to have no weapon, yet your monks used some form of psychic energy to kill dozens of my men."

"The goddess gives us such ability for her defence, nothing else."

"I was told the weapon you keep here is so powerful, its secret so great, that anyone who looked upon it would be blinded." Ivanov rested the point of his knife against one of the empty sockets in Khumbu's head. "Is that what happened to you and the other monks?"

"No, we blinded ourselves, out of respect for the Mukari's greatness."

"You blinded yourselves?"

"Yes."

The general nodded in admiration. "Your fervour does you credit, no matter how misdirected it might be. Plainly, you and your men are willing to die in the service of your goddess. Threatening your life would be of little use." Ivanov took his knife away from Khumbu's face. He went to the Mukari and snatched her up, lifting the girl from the floor, his foot kicking aside the wooden elephant she had been playing with.

The general examined her face. "Remarkable. She is quite flawless. Not a blemish, not a mark."

"That is one of the criteria for choosing our goddess," Khumbu said.

Ivanov studied the Mukari closely. "And what are the other criteria?"

"She must be born on the nearby mountain. She must never have shed blood. She must never laugh or smile in the presence of anyone but her disciples. She must–"

"Enough." The general smiled at Khumbu. "I'm sorry to say you may struggle to find a replacement. The nearest village suffered a tragedy recently."

"You mean you had its people tortured and murdered for your amusement," Dante snarled.

"Tragedy or torture, the consequences are the same." Ivanov held his knife close to the Mukari's throat. "So, if I were to slip and accidentally slay this child, you would be without a goddess, yes?"

"If what you say is true, then the holy line would be broken," Khumbu said fearfully, "and everything we have preserved will be undone."

"Then you have a simple choice," Ivanov replied. "Hand over possession of the weapon or else I gut your goddess like a fish. I will do it too, won't I Nikolai?"

"Yes," Dante admitted.

"I cannot give you what we do not have," Khumbu maintained.

"Then your living goddess will live no longer," Ivanov vowed, his hand drawing back the knife in the air.

The Enforcer squeezed his hands together, pressing both thumbs against Mai's windpipe, slowly crushing the life from his sister's slender neck. He was surprised how quickly she died, her body falling limp in less than a minute. After satisfying himself she was dead, the major tossed her corpse to one side and marched towards the throne room. Ivanov will need me by now, he thought. I have wasted enough time on the past.

"Killing me will not be necessary," the Mukari said, before Ivanov could plunge his knife into her. "If you want the secret of the Forbidden Citadel, you need only ask. I am the keeper of this legacy, as have been all the Mukari who came before me."

The general relaxed, letting the knife drop back to his side again. "Show me this mighty weapon, so I may look upon its wonder for myself." As Ivanov spoke, the Enforcer strode into the room. "Where is your facemask?"

"The woman knocked it free before she died."

"Mai's dead?" Dante twisted round to see the new arrival. "I know that voice…" His eyes studied the Enforcer's exposed face, realisation slowly dawning on him. "Private Rai? But I saw you die in Rudinshtein. I killed you!"

"Not quite," Ivanov snarled. "Guards, if Dante speaks again, you have my permission to cut out his tongue. If he tries to resist, you have my permission to kill him. I had hoped to keep that pleasure for myself, but I will not be interrupted again." The general smiled at the Mukari, his eyes glinting with excitement. "Well, goddess – unveil this secret so we can all see it."

The girl brought her hands together as if praying, closing her eyes. The air temperature within the throne room dropped dramatically and the balcony doors were flung open for a moment before slamming shut again. The exotically carved wooden throne flew across the room, narrowly missing the Mukari's head before crashing against a wall. Swirling winds whipped at the white tapestry that hung behind the raised dais where the throne had stood. Silver threads in the centre of the tapestry glowed and pulsated with energy, the subtle design woven into the fabric becoming obvious to all those watching it.

Dante, I'm detecting something else besides another Crest in this chamber – a massive power source. There's something familiar about it.

"The double-headed eagle of the Romanovs," Ivanov said, pointing at the tapestry. "But what is the significance of this?"

The Mukari smiled, blinking once. As she did the glowing white tapestry shimmered out of existence, the wall on which it had hung also disappeared. In their place was a walkway leading towards a swirling globe of alien energy, a vortex some two metres wide. Khumbu dropped to his knees, bowing before the holiest of holies in the citadel.

Dante looked deep into the vortex and shuddered. He knew where it led, the power it represented, and what its existence in this place could mean if the Tsar harnessed that power for himself. Until now this mission had been merely another adventure in a life full of such adventures. Suddenly, the stakes were much higher than he could possibly have imagined. The future of the Empire was up for grabs in this room.

Ivanov stepped closer to the vortex, the Enforcer joining him. "What is it?" the general asked, his eyes filled with wonder.

"A doorway to another world, a bridge to another universe," Khumbu said reverentially. "It is the source of our power. It is the source of all that we are."

"I tire of your riddles and religious babblings," Ivanov snarled. "How do we control this weapon? How do we use it? Tell me!"

Khumbu shrugged helplessly. "I do not tell you because I do not know. My brethren and I are merely the humble disciples of the Mukari. She alone controls the power of the vortex."

"So why am I wasting time talking with you?" The general kicked the old monk in the head, sending him backwards across the floor. Khumbu thudded into the far wall, his bones snapping at the point of impact. Ivanov nodded to the Enforcer, who grabbed hold of the Mukari. Ivanov rested his knife against the girl's left cheek, letting the tip nudge into the soft skin. "Tell me how to use this weapon or else."

The girl did not flinch, did not turn away from the general's maniacal gaze. "What must be, will be," she said quietly.

"She isn't afraid of you," Dante called out.

Anger flushed Ivanov's face. "Guards, I said I did not wish to hear the prisoner's voice again. Cut out his tongue. Now!"

Dante struggled against the Imperials but with his arms pinned, there was little he could do to resist. One of the soldiers forced a knife between Dante's clamped teeth, trying to slice at what was beyond them.

"Hold!" the Enforcer screamed, stilling the soldier's movements.

Ivanov rounded on his second-in-command. "You dare countermand one of my orders, major? You know the penalty for flouting my authority!"

"And I will suffer that punishment gladly, sir, but hear me out. That tapestry had the symbol of the Romanovs woven into it, just as Dante has the same symbol on his left arm: the mark of the Weapons Crest. The girl does not fear death, she will not tell us how to use this vortex's power. But Dante will, as long as he still has a tongue with which to speak."

"And why should he tell us?" the general demanded.

"Because if he doesn't, you cut the girl's throat in front of him." The Enforcer glanced at Dante. "Women and children are his weakness, he never wants to see them hurt. I know – I almost died for his pathetic compassion."

Ivanov smiled, patting the major's shoulder. "You are right. Forgive me for doubting you. There will be no punishment for your timely intervention."

"Thank you, sir."

The general turned his attention back to the Mukari, sliding the edge of the blade down her face to rest against the girl's neck. He signalled for the guards to remove the knife from Dante's mouth so the prisoner could speak. "Well, will you tell me what you know about this vortex, or shall I cut this child's throat?"

Spatchcock and Flintlock ducked into a darkened doorway, eluding another squad of Imperials still searching the citadel's ground level for them. The pair waited until the soldiers' footsteps faded out of earshot. "It's all clear," Spatchcock decided. Flintlock was already creeping towards the battered gateway. "Where the hell are you going?"

"Away from here," Flintlock replied. "We've done all we can. We're out of our depth here, Spatch."

"Saving your own skin and never mind about the consequences, is that it?"

"If you say so – are you coming?"

Spatchcock grabbed the Brit's collar and hauled him back to the doorway. "What about Dante?"

"What about him?"

"He's saved our worthless hides more times than I can remember. Don't you think we should do the same for him?"

"With what? We haven't got any weapons. He's got the Crest and Mai."

"We can use this," Spatchcock insisted, tapping the side of his head.

"Dandruff? Lice?"

"Our brains, you fool! We've outwitted some of the richest and most important people in the Empire before now, we can outsmart Ivanov too."

"Ivanov the Terrible? The Butcher of Rudinshtein? I don't think so," Flintlock muttered, pulling his collar free of Spatchcock's grasp. A moment later he gasped in dismay as a grubby hand closed around his crotch. "I say, there's no need for that, old boy. I was simply expressing an opinion."

"Good," Spatchcock replied grimly, squeezing a little tighter. "Then you'll be volunteering to help me rescue Dante?"

"Yes, of course," Flintlock squeaked.

"That's better." Spatchcock released his grip. "After you, your lordship."

The blond Brit muttered curses under his breath as he led the way towards the nearest staircase.

"I'm not a patient man," Ivanov warned. "What do you know about the vortex, Dante? Is it why your father, Dmitri Romanov, visited the citadel during the war?"

The general is a borderline psychotic with sadomasochistic tendencies, the Crest observed. *He will carry out his threat to murder the Mukari unless you say what he wants to hear, and he will enjoy the experience.*

"I never knew about this place during the war," Dante replied quietly. "Sorry to disappoint you, but I was a minor part of the Romanov campaign at best: cannon fodder for the Tsar's forces. Why else do you think my so-called family abandoned me in Rudinshtein at the end?"

"If you never knew about the citadel, what are you doing here now?" Ivanov pressed his knife closer to the Mukari's neck, his eyes blazing with hatred.

"I was sent here by an anti-Tsar organisation to secure the citadel and its secret. Like you, they thought it was a weapon, but they knew no more than that."

"Why should I believe you?" the general demanded.

"I would not risk that child's life by lying," Dante said.

Ivanov gestured at the vortex. "What about this doorway to another universe? What is its significance?"

"I have seen something similar once before, on the Romanov gulag at Samovar, before the war. Prisoners were sent to that planet as slave labour. When they were too weak to work, the inmates were sent through the gateway as raw genetic material for those on the other side."

"Raw material... for what?"

Dante hesitated fleetingly and the general pulled back the knife, ready to kill the Mukari with his next movement.

"Raw material for what?"

"Beyond that vortex is another universe where technology like my Crest is commonplace. It was introduced to improve evolution, but instead the technology began transforming the people into creatures more cybernetic than organic. Their society split into two factions, one siding with the technology, one against it. The Romanovs discovered these gateways and forged an alliance with the anti-technology faction. Dmitri sent untainted genetic material to help them preserve their humanity, they gave him Crest technology." Dante's head sagged forward listlessly. "That's it. That's everything I know," he admitted.

Ivanov looked at the vortex with renewed interest. "Your father must have been coming here in the hope of obtaining more Crests with which to arm his troops. Now I control this gateway, I can acquire a Weapons Crest of my own. My men could become the ultimate warriors, unbeatable in any battle. The Imperial Black would soon rival the Tsar himself as the most powerful force in the Empire!"

You humans never fail to disappoint, the Crest sighed. *One sniff of power and it goes directly to your heads.*

"Ivanov was well on his way to madness before this," Dante muttered.

The general smiled at his captive. "Thank you, young Nikolai, a most informative little speech. For once, I believe you were telling the truth."

"I was," Dante insisted. "Now let the girl go, she's no threat to you."

"If only I could believe that," Ivanov replied. "Alas, I cannot suffer a goddess to live, lest her disciples rise up and try to reclaim this weapon as their own." His knife whipped through the air, a flash of blood accompanying the movement. The general stepped back and admired his handiwork.

A red line crossed the Mukari's throat where Ivanov's blade had been. For a second Dante thought it was merely a flesh wound, until he saw the distress on the girl's face. The Enforcer released her body and she sank to the floor, her elaborate headdress falling off.

Ivanov held up his knife, smiling joyfully at its crimson edge. "The goddess is dead! Long live the new god of the Forbidden Citadel!"

SIXTEEN

"A multitude of hounds signals death for the hare."
– Russian proverb

"Asphyxiation is when oxygen is stopped from reaching the human brain. If asphyxia is not treated or prevented within a few minutes, it leads to loss of consciousness, irreversible brain damage and, subsequently, to death. The shorter the period of oxygen deprivation, the better the prognosis for recovery."
– Extract from *The Imperial Heath Guide*,
2671 edition

Mai opened her eyes to find Spatchcock crouching over her, his cheeks flushed red and his expression filled with concern. "I think she's coming round," he told Flintlock, who was standing nearby.

"I don't see why you got to give her the kiss of life," the Brit protested. "I've got as much wind-power in my lungs as you, Spatch."

"You gave me the kiss of life?" Mai asked, horrified.

"Don't worry, I didn't slip you the tongue," Spatchcock replied. "Much." He patted Mai on the shoulder. "You've some nasty marks on your neck, but you're lucky whoever was strangling you didn't finish the job."

"It was my brother," she gasped.

"Your brother. You mean…"

"Rai. He's alive," Mai said weakly. "He's the Enforcer."

"Crikey," Flintlock exclaimed.

Spatchcock helped Mai to her feet. "We can't stay here long," he said. "Imperials are everywhere, most of the monks are dead and we can't find Dante."

"The throne room," she whispered. "He'll be in the throne room. That's where Ivanov was going, that's where Nikolai will be."

"She's probably right," Flintlock agreed. "He's got a nose for danger."

"Then it's up to us to get him out of trouble," Spatchcock vowed.

Dante shook himself free of the guards and crossed the throne room to crouch by the Mukari, cradling the dying girl in his arms. Ivanov shook his head, telling the Enforcer to stand guard over them. Then the general summoned the other soldiers to his side. "I want this building secured and a command post set up in the next room. Find and execute any civilians still alive on the premises. Nobody is to get in or out of the citadel without my express permission."

"Yes, sir!" the soldiers saluted in unison. All but one of them hurried from the throne room. The Imperial who remained behind bore a sergeant's insignia on his uniform. "Sir, when will you be contacting the Tsar?"

"Contacting the Tsar?"

"Yes, to tell him what we've discovered here."

Ivanov smiled thinly. "Sergeant, what makes you think I have any intention of contacting the Tsar? The fate of what I have discovered here is for me to decide, not some armchair general sitting in his palace above Saint Petersburg."

"But, sir, you must see that—"

A single thrust of the dagger Ivanov was holding silenced the sergeant. The Imperial sank to his knees, then toppled sideways, quite dead.

Ivanov looked down at the corpse dispassionately, discarding his dagger. "Enforcer, have someone remove this carcass. I don't want the blood of that fool staining the floorboards of my throne room."

"Yes, sir!"

The general cast a withering glance at Dante. "Keep an eye on the prisoner. He's not as weak and pitiful as he looks. I am going to review the situation elsewhere within the citadel."

"Yes, sir," the Enforcer replied, calling for a soldier to remove the sergeant's body. Ivanov strode out into the corridor, not noticing Khumbu's broken body stirring in the corner. The old monk groaned in pain, his weak sounds attracting the Enforcer's attention.

Dante leaned closer to the Mukari, hugging the girl to his chest, rocking her gently back and forth. "It's alright, everything's going to be alright," he whispered tenderly.

"Do not grieve for me," she said. "Everything happened as I had foreseen it. But now I see beyond the darkness. There will come another, Nikolai."

"Who? Who is it?" But the Mukari had died, her pupils rolling back into her head. Dante shut both eyes, then kissed her forehead. "She's gone."

I am detecting a sudden surge of energy from the gateway, the Crest said urgently. *Whatever was holding it in check is gone. The vortex is unravelling.*

Dante twisted his head to look at the unearthly shape where the tapestry had been. Flashes of energy sparked around the globe, snaking out to the edge of the bridge. "The Mukari must have been controlling it with her Crest. Now she's dead, her Crest is dying too, and the vortex is destabilising."

Perhaps, but the Mukari's Crest is still fully active.

"How is that possible?" Dante wondered. "You've told me before that when I die, you'll cease to function too."

Yes, but I also told you the Mukari's Crest has significant differences to the way I function. It must be able to maintain an existence without her as host.

Dante's eyes narrowed. "But that's impossible, unless…" He glanced at the Enforcer, but Rai was still focused on Khumbu in the corner. Dante eased up the dead girl's left sleeve to expose her upper arm – there was no Crest symbol visible on the skin. He checked the other arm, but it was also unmarked.

Her death could have triggered the subcutaneous defence mechanism.

"Maybe," Dante agreed. "But I think she was never bonded with the Crest. At least, not in the same way as you and me." He noticed the Mukari's fallen headdress lying on the floor nearby, forgotten amidst the violence. "Maybe her Crest was housed within something she wore as the living goddess."

Pain coursed through Khumbu's frail body as consciousness replaced the dark. *One of my legs and both arms are broken,* the old monk realised. *Something is making it hard for me to breathe.* He tried to sit up and fresh stabs of pain made him cry out in agony. It felt as if knives were shifting inside his chest, their edges gnawing at his core. *No, not knives,* he decided. *They must be broken ribs, the jagged ends piercing my internal organs. Death could not be far away.* Already he could feel a cold numbness consuming his legs.

"Still with us, old man?" a voice asked.

"Who are you?" Khumbu rasped weakly.

"I was once a native of these mountains. I believed in goddesses and sacred things like you, until the general taught me to honour only that which you can touch and see and feel."

"What a hollow, empty life you must lead," the monk said. He could feel movement on the other side of the throne room, but was doing his best to distract the figure crouched beside him. *If I keep my tormentor busy, perhaps the others can still escape,* he thought. "Have you no faith, nothing to believe in?"

"I believe in the general, his words, his orders. He knows best."

Khumbu smiled. "Too much belief can be as bad as having too little. You must not blind yourself to the wrongs you do. I know that better than anyone." The monk felt a hand closing around his neck. "I am dying already. Killing me will make no difference, except to stain your soul with another life stolen away."

"I have no soul to stain."

"Then you are truly lost," Khumbu whispered with his last breath.

The Enforcer straightened up again, having crushed the life from the old monk. "See what happens to all those who challenge the general, Dante?" But when he swung round to confront the prisoner, only the Mukari's lifeless body remained. It began to glow from within, a blazing white light that flooded the throne room. When that faded, the Mukari's body was gone. Beyond her, the vortex bubbled angrily, errant strands of energy escaping from its slowly expanding outer shell. The Enforcer cursed under his breath and called for help. But it was the person he least expected who entered the throne room.

"You should have killed me when you had the chance," Mai snarled.

Spatchcock watched a unit of Imperials race past, then closed the door. Flintlock was already dragging a piece of furniture across to blockade the entrance. Spatchcock helped him finish the job. Dante stood nearby, staring at the Mukari's headdress in his hands, the girl's blood a red smear across his top.

"You did all you could," Spatchcock said.

"I wish that was true," he replied, "but my gut tells me otherwise. Crest, have you finished analysing this?"

You were correct. It houses the other Crest I detected. That's how each Mukari was able to pass on her abilities to her successor. That's how she controlled the vortex, kept all that power in check.

"What's going to happen now she's dead?"

Left unattended, the vortex will continue to expand, consuming everything in its path. Its hunger will grow exponentially – the more the vortex swallows, the more it wants. In less than an hour it will have consumed the throne room, this floor of the building and then the entire citadel. By sunset most of the mountain will be gone. Unless we find a way to stop it, the vortex will continue expanding until it devours the entire planet: all within a matter of days. When it tries to swallow the sun, that will create a black hole, a cannibal star sucking in solar systems as a child swallows soup.

"What does the Crest have to say?" Flintlock inquired.

Dante smiled grimly. "We're up to our asses in trouble."

"Business as usual, then."

"Not quite." Dante quickly relayed the Crest's doom-laden assessment of events.

The Brit scratched his head thoughtfully. "This is probably a stupid idea," he began, "but why doesn't your Crest bond with the Mukari's Crest? Between them they should be capable of finding a way out of this mess, right?" Dante and Spatchcock looked at Flintlock, then at each other, then back at the exiled aristocrat. "I said it was probably a stupid idea," he protested.

"Flintlock, you're a genius!" Dante said warmly.

"I am?"

"Maybe not a genius," Spatchcock hastily interjected, "but you have your moments, your lordship." Flintlock smiled, a quiet pride evident on his features.

The Enforcer lumbered across the throne room towards Mai, shouting for reinforcements. She somersaulted over him, delivering a swift kick to back of his neck as he passed underneath, sending the bulky figure sprawling to the floor. By the time he was back on his feet, Mai had grabbed up

Ivanov's dagger from the floor. A handful of Imperials appeared in the door but the Enforcer sent them to search for Dante. "This bitch is mine," he snarled.

Mai danced inside another clumsy lunge, rapidly stabbing her brother three times in the chest plate, before escaping from his grasping gauntlets once more. "That exo-skeleton is slowing you down," she said. "You would do better without it."

"This exo-skeleton will be your downfall," Rai promised. "It deflects your blows with ease, even when not switched on. Now, when I activate it..." He pushed the hidden control button, but the suit did not respond. He glanced down at the button and noticed three stabs marks in the mechanism, disabling the controls. Mai leapt at him with a flying drop kick, the impact sending him stumbling backwards.

"I wasn't stabbing you," she smiled. "I was disabling the exo-skeleton."

"Very well," Rai muttered, tearing off the body armour panel by panel. "Throw aside your weapon and we shall see who is the superior warrior, sister."

Mai embedded the knife in the floor, then adopted a martial arts stance, ready to parry his next attack. "Take your best shot, brother."

"Crest, what's the best way to establish a link between you and the Mukari's Crest?" Dante asked, still holding the dead girl's headdress in his hands.

It was in close proximity to her brain, so I suggest you do the same.

"Put this on my head?" Dante looked doubtfully at the tiara, with its attached headdress encrusted with stones of crimson and black. "I doubt it'll fit."

All Crests adjust to suit whomever they bond with. I certainly had to.

Dante shrugged. "Maybe, but I'll look ridiculous."

This from a man recently chased through a floating brothel by a dozen enraged Kabuki porn actors while wearing little more than a prostitute's sequinned g-string bearing the leg-end "Get it here".

"Good point," Dante conceded. He turned to Spatchcock and Flintlock. "Do either of you two want to give me a hand putting this on?"

"If you insist," Flintlock sighed, taking hold of the head-dress. He eased the elaborate collection of fabrics, gemstones and finery on to Dante's head. "There you go – pretty as a picture."

Spatchcock whispered for them to be quiet. The heavy footfalls of Imperials could be heard passing outside the room. Dante held the headdress as close as possible to his skull. "Crest, are you ready to make contact?"

Initiating inter-Crest communications... now.

Dante screamed in agony before collapsing to the floor, his hands clamping the headdress in place. Flintlock crouched beside him, while Spatchcock hurried to the door, straining to hear if the sudden scream had attracted atten-tion. Within moments soldiers were shouting for the door to be opened, their fists hammering the thick wood. Spatchcock shoved back against the barricade, trying to keep it in place. "Bloody hell, that's torn it," he cursed. "How's the boss?"

Flintlock leaned closer so he could listen to Dante's chest. He sat back on his haunches, his pale face drained of colour. "Spatch, I think he's copped it."

"What the hell are you talking about?"

"I can't find a pulse. He isn't breathing and I can't hear a heartbeat either," Flintlock explained. "Dante's dead."

Rai lunged at his sister, but she easily eluded his attack, dart-ing her slender frame sideways out of his reach. As he passed Mai stabbed her bent fingers into his side beneath the armpit, eliciting a grunt. Rai swung round with a straight arm, but she ducked under it, delivering a firm blow to the solar plexus. Mai jabbed upwards with the side of her hand, intending to chop into his throat, but was surprised to be caught in his grasp.

Rai pulled her closer, his breath hot in her face. "You can dance around all day, but sooner or later I'll wear you down. When I do, this is over."

She responded by ramming a knee into his crotch, followed by a straight arm shove in the chest. Her brother staggered backwards, sucking air in urgently. Mai dropped to the floor and swung one leg round in a sweep kick, taking Rai's legs out from under him. He tumbled over, his head cracking against the broad wooden beams. A dull cry shot from his lips, then he did not move.

Mai moved in to finish the job and was felled by a fist punching in the back of her knee. As she sank to the floor, Rai leapt at her, moving with great agility for someone so big. He closed his hands around her throat and pinned her to the floor, straddling her torso with his legs. "I should have stayed to finish the job the first time," he said. "I won't make the same mistake again."

She flailed at him with her arms, fingernails gouging at his face, her legs kicking uselessly at his back. With her last reserves of strength, Mai sent a spasm of movement up her body, propelling Rai over her head. She rolled away to one side, coughing and choking, gasping for breath. Before she had time to recover, Rai was standing over her again. The knife she had embedded in the floor was now held loosely in his left hand.

The Enforcer grabbed Mai by the hair and lifted her up with his right hand, the blade balanced lightly in his left. "Goodbye, sister." He rammed the knife into her stomach, then gave the hilt a vicious twist inside the wound. Rai let go of her hair and Mai fell back to the floor, blood quickly pooling around her, her hands feebly clutching at the blade.

The Imperials burst through the door, kicking aside the blockade to get in. Spatchcock and Flintlock were crouching beside Dante's corpse, the Mukari's headdress still stuck on his head. One of the soldiers hurried away to fetch Ivanov, returning with him less than a minute later.

The general studied Dante's body, his face a mask of hatred. "Shame, I was looking forward to killing him myself. Still, you can't expect to get everything you desire in a single day." Ivanov kicked the corpse, but the body merely shuddered in response. "Have these two carry this piece of offal into the throne room. I want them to witness all the indignities I shall inflict upon their master's corpse before I have them slain."

Ivanov marched from the room, smiling to himself. The Imperials saluted crisply as he passed, then turned back to Spatchcock and Flintlock. "You heard the general," one of the soldiers snarled. "Pick up this carcass and take it into the throne room. Now, maggots!"

SEVENTEEN

"Even a bear cowers when taken by surprise."
– Russian proverb

"The out-of-body experience is a post-death phenomenon that has been talked about, debated and discussed for most of a millennium. While there are still those who would have you believe that there is nothing beyond the world you can see, touch, taste, hear or smell, the fact remains that near-death events are both common place and well documented. Are they merely the hallucinations of oxygen-starved brains, or is something more fundamental happening? Does the human spirit leave the body at the moment of death in search of the next life? And, if so, what would happen if this spirit did not return when its body was revived?"

– Extract from *The Little Book of Imperial Spirituality*, 2669 edition

Dante opened his eyes and knew something was awry. Around him dozens of smiling Himalayans were clapping and cheering, their eyes alight with joy, their faces beaming at each other. I know some of these people, he thought. They were among the bodies we burned on the funeral pyre yesterday. This must be the past I'm seeing, or a vision of something that never happened. It certainly can't be the future.

Dante was standing in a familiar stone courtyard, surrounded by brown-skinned revellers. They were chanting a name, over and over: "Mukari! Mukari!" Suddenly the chant became a cheer of joy, people pointing into the sky. Dante followed their fingers and realised they were gesturing at the balcony outside the throne room. A small girl was emerging from inside, clad in the red and gold of the living goddess, the Mukari's elaborate headdress on her young head. Khumbu was standing to one side of the child, Gylatsen on the other. The old monk motioned for the people for silence.

"The new Mukari has been chosen," he announced. "Bow before her and she shall bless you all!" As one the people dropped to their knees, clasping their hands together in silent prayer, backs bent forward so their noses almost touched the stone cobbles beneath them. Dante watched as the little girl, the same girl he watched being murdered by Ivanov, waved to the crowd.

"Be happy," she said, "and savour your life while you can."

There were a few confused murmurings from the people in the square, but they accepted her cryptic blessing nonetheless. Gylatsen clapped his hands three times. "Now, let the celebrations begin!"

In an instant the people were up and cheering again. But they faded away before Dante's eyes, becoming wraiths in the wind before disappearing altogether. He stared at the Mukari, who was bleeding profusely from her neck wound – the same cut that had killed her. She also faded away, but her headdress remained, falling down from the balcony into Dante's hands. A voice welled up inside his mind.

So began the reign of the last living goddess, the voice told Dante.

"Crest? Is that you?" he asked.

I am a Crest, but not your Crest. I serve as servant of the Mukari, holding in check the power of the gods.

"You're talking about the vortex. But I thought the Romanovs were the first to have Weapons Crests in the empire."

Not all Crests are weapons, Dante. Just as not all warriors are brave.

He looked round the citadel's courtyard. "What will happen to this place?"

That depends with you. You hold the future in your hands. Without a Mukari to bear the Crest, all shall be lost.

"So where do I find another living goddess?"

By tradition the living goddess was selected from young, untainted girls of a nearby village. They were taken from their families and made to act as the conduit for the power of the Crest. Over time this process became shrouded in myths and legends, much like the citadel itself. The monks believed their goddess lost her purity when she came into womanhood, so they cast the girl aside and choose a new Mukari.

"But Ivanov's men butchered the villagers," Dante said. "The few survivors – I doubt any are untainted, not after what the Imperials did to their families."

The Mukari must be born of the mountain, but that is all. The rest is dogma, imposed by Khumbu and those like him, who sought to control the power of the living goddess. Strange how so many faiths of this world denigrate and oppress women, even when putting them on the pedestal of godhood.

"I need solutions, not a lecture on religious sexual equality," Dante replied.

You have already been told the solution. The question is whether you have the wit to identify it in time. With that the voice was gone, leaving Dante alone in the courtyard. Above him shards of energy exploded outwards from the throne room windows, showering Dante with broken glass. The vortex was consuming the citadel from the inside out.

Spatchcock and Flintlock carried Dante's corpse into the throne room, his body still wearing the Mukari's headdress.

They placed him carefully on the floor next to Mai, who lay in a pool of her own blood. Her face was ashen, while her hands clasped the knife buried in her abdomen.

Ivanov dismissed his guards, then glared with satisfaction at his four prisoners.

"So this is the mighty army sent by the Tsar's enemies to storm the citadel? A Romanov reject, two festering sores from the rectum of humanity, and a slant-eyed whore too stupid to know when she is outmatched. Not what I'd call a fighting force to inspire fear!"

Mai spat an obscenity at the general.

Ivanov moved closer, unable to keep his gloating sneer from his face. "My dear, you're in no position to call anyone names. I expect you to bleed to death within the hour, barring some kind of miracle. Since your goddess is already dead, I believe this place is fresh out of miracles, don't you?" He shifted his focus to Dante's corpse. "Why on earth is he still wearing that ridiculous headdress? Enforcer, I want that thing removed and destroyed! No trace of the Mukari or her disciples is to be left here. I plan to make the citadel an impregnable fortress for the new Imperial Black regiment I shall build here."

Rai knelt by Dante's head and tore the headdress free. As he did Dante's eyes flicked open. The general stared in disbelief. "But that's impossible! He was dead a minute ago!"

"Appearances can be deceiving," Dante replied with a smile. He braced his arms on the floor, then kicked his legs up and over his head into the Enforcer's face. Rai tumbled over backwards, his head thudding heavily into the wooden doorframe by the balcony. He slumped to the floor and lay still.

"Enforcer, I command you to get up!" Ivanov yelled, but Rai did not move.

"Guess it's just you and me," Dante hissed at the general, who was climbing to his feet. "No regiment to cover your back, no soldiers to hold your victims down while you torture them. How's that, Vassily – exciting enough for you?"

He launched himself at Ivanov, not giving his target time to draw a weapon. The two men slammed into the nearest wall, the impact winding the general. Dante punching a fist into Ivanov's groin, then snapped a knee into his chin. "Spatchcock! Flintlock! Barricade the door!"

"Got it!" Spatchcock replied, already dragging the discarded throne towards the entrance. Flintlock hurried to help him. Together they shoved the heavy wooden chair against the door, wedging it beneath the handle. Within seconds fists were hammering from the other side, but the door remained closed.

Ivanov spat a mouthful of teeth and blood onto the floor. "I don't need my men to beat you, Dante. Any soldier in the Tsar's army could outfight street-scum like you, but they would consider it beneath their honour."

"Honour be damned," Dante snarled. "Where was the honour in murdering innocent civilians during the war? Where was the honour when you herded the women into rape camps? Where was the honour when you tortured anyone who dared speak my name after the war? Where was the honour when you slaughtered a village of people yesterday, simply to get directions?" Dante grabbed Ivanov by the throat and lifted him off the floor, slamming the general's head against the nearest wall. "Don't you dare talk to me about honour, you bastard!"

A burst of blue light oscillated around the room, exploding outwards from the ever-exploding vortex. It had expanded to twice its original size and was engulfing the bridge that led into its ravenous core. Spatchcock pointed at the menacing spectacle, the light bursting from its centre casting strange shadows across his features. "Is that thing meant to be getting bigger like that?"

"Not exactly, no," Dante called back over the noise of soldiers trying to break into the throne room. He noticed movement on the other side of the chamber. "Mai, your brother is coming round. Can you deal with him?"

"I'll try…" She grimaced and wrenched the knife from her abdomen, screaming in agony as more blood spurted out. Clutching the wound with one hand and the blade in her other, Mai crawled towards the Enforcer. Rai's eyelids were fluttering and blood dripped from his nostrils. One of his hands opened and closed spasmodically, but he showed few other signs of life.

Mai rolled him over on to his back, pressing the knife against Rai's throat. "Don't move," she warned. "Don't even think about moving."

With Dante distracted, Ivanov used the opportunity to let his hand drop to the sidearm holstered at his waist. He tilted it backwards so the barrel was aimed at Dante, then the general slid his fingers inside the trigger. "You know what I liked most about Rudinshtein?" Ivanov whispered.

Dante, be careful, the Crest warned. *This sadist didn't becoming a general without learning a few tricks.*

"I can handle this sick bastard's taunts," Dante retorted.

"It was the children," Ivanov smiled before pulling the trigger. "The sweet way the children screamed just before they died. It got me so… over-excited." The bullet punched clean through Dante's ribcage, bone, flesh and blood exploding out of a fist-sized hole in his back, creating a fine, pink aerosol.

Dante staggered backwards, blood bubbling from his lips. Ivanov fired again, this shot tearing a hunk of flesh from Dante's right shoulder. He toppled to one knee, gasping for air, one hand feebly trying to stop his internal organs leaking out through the hole in his front.

"Dante!" Flintlock shouted, stepping forward to intervene. But he was driven back by the gun in Ivanov's hand, retreating to Spatchcock's side.

"I know a coward when I see one," the general snarled. "You two lack the foolhardy courage of your master. Stay back or share his slow, painful death." Ivanov lashed out with one of his legs, the black boot kicking Dante in the face, knocking him to the floor. "Nikolai, tell your Oriental bitch to unhand my Enforcer."

"Mai does not answer to me," Dante replied through gritted teeth. Mai kept her knife pressed to the Enforcer's throat, holding him down on the floor.

Ivanov stepped on Dante's torso, grinding his heel into the entry wound, winning a scream of pain from the stricken man. "Don't make me repeat myself, boy. Tell her to release my second-in-command or I'll shove this boot through your spine. I doubt even your enhanced healing abilities will recover from that."

"You're welcome to try..." Dante said, his hands coming alive with purple and silver cyborganics, "...but you might find that difficult without any legs!" He ripped a cyborganic sword through the air, slicing clean through both of Ivanov's knees. The general tumbled to the floor, screaming with agony.

Dante rolled over on top of Ivanov, pinning the Imperial Black's leader to the wooden beams. "Now, tell me again how you got off watching children being butchered!"

Ivanov shook his head, refusing to give in. "Damn you to hell, Dante!"

"You first!" Dante stabbed his blade through the general's throat and down into the black floorboards beneath. Dante pulled the sword free and rolled off Ivanov's body. "At least you'll never touch Rudinshtein again, you bastard."

Flintlock and Spatchcock rushed over to him, the shorter man peeling off his jacket and pressing it against Dante's back. "This doesn't look good."

Dante, you've lost a lot of blood, the Crest said. *Ivanov may have been right. I don't think your enhanced healing abilities can repair the damage in time.*

"What about Mai?" Dante gurgled, blood stains visible on his teeth. "Has she finished off the Enforcer?"

"I can't," she admitted. "I know what he has done, but Ivanov brainwashed him. Rai is still my brother, I can't murder him in cold blood."

Mai's bleeding to death, the Crest said. *She's almost as badly injured as you, but she doesn't have a Crest's enhanced healing abilities.*

"She bonded with one before, she can do it again," Dante said.

"What are you talking about?" Flintlock asked, but it was Mai who answered.

"I used to be the Mukari," she said. "I'm too old now."

"You're wrong," Dante whispered. "The Mukari must be a woman born of these mountains, but her age doesn't matter. Khumbu and his brethren made sure only young girls became the Mukari–"

"So they could control them," Mai realised.

Spatchcock was glancing nervously over his shoulder at the vortex. It had swallowed the bridge and was eating into the floorboards of the throne room. At one edge the glowing globe was consuming the doorway, expanding outwards to attack the soldiers in the corridor. "Whatever you two are planning, you'd better do it quickly. That thing's getting bigger by the second!"

"Put it on," Dante urged Mai, pointing at the discarded headdress. "Once you wear that, you are bonded with the Mukari's Crest."

Mai shook her head. "You don't know what it's like, having the past, present and future all happening simultaneously in your head – coping with knowing all there is to know, being responsible for holding everything together."

"Think what you could achieve with that knowledge," Dante pleaded. "I put on the headdress and it almost killed me, Mai. You're the only one who can do this."

Finally, she nodded. "One of you will have to watch Rai," she said. Flintlock took the pistol from Ivanov's corpse and aimed it at the Enforcer. Mai moved over to the headdress, which was lying dangerously close to the edge of the ever-expanding vortex. Closing her eyes, Mai pulled the headdress into position. Pain stabbed through her features, then she relaxed.

"Is it working?" Spatchcock asked.

Mai nodded. "I can hear the Crest in my head, welcoming me back." She stood, one hand still held over the wound to her abdomen. "The Crest's healing ability, it's repairing my injuries." Mai took her hand away and the gaping hole in her skin sealed itself, leaving just a bloodstained hole in her clothes.

"What about the vortex," Dante cried. "Can you stop the vortex?"

"I'll try," she said, closing her eyes to concentrate.

Suddenly Rai leapt forwards from his position slumped against the wall. He smashed the pistol from Flintlock's grasp, grabbing the startled Brit by the throat. "I'm getting out of here," Rai announced. "If anybody tries to stop me, I'll snap this fool's neck like a twig!"

"Go ahead and snap it. We don't care," Spatchcock replied.

"Spatch!" Flintlock cried in horror.

"I was trying to trick him, you idiot!"

"No more tricks," Rai warned, backing towards the doorway. But the throne room's internal exit had already been consumed by the swirling vortex.

"Don't go any further," Dante said. "You can't get out that way."

"I said no more tricks!"

"This isn't a trick," Spatchcock shouted back. "Look behind you!"

"How stupid do you think I am?" Rai demanded.

"You'll soon find out, but I'd prefer it if you didn't take Flintlock to his doom as well," Dante replied. "He may be annoying, prissy and a royal pain in the arse, but he does have some redeeming features."

"Just don't ask us for a quick list," Spatchcock added.

"Spatch!" Flintlock cried out.

"Only joking."

Dante, the vortex – it hasn't stopped. If anything, it is expanding faster than before.

"Mai, what's happening?"

She was shaking her head, teeth biting her bottom lip. "I can't do it, the vortex. It's already too strong for me!" Her legs gave way beneath her and Mai crumpled to the floor, both hands struggling to keep her headdress in place.

A scream burst from the other side of the throne room. Rai and Flintlock were being sucked into the periphery of the vortex, a crackling tentacle of blue and white energy wrapped around Rai's left leg, hauling both men towards it.

"Crest! Any brilliant suggestions?" Dante asked in desperation.

If the vortex is already too strong for a single Crest to control, perhaps two Crests can achieve that task, it replied.

Dante pushed himself up on to one knee. "Spatch, help me over to Mai."

"You're the boss," the rumpled runt replied, dipping his shoulder under one of Dante's arms. Together they staggered over to Mai, where Dante sunk back to the floor. He pulled her closer and pressed his lips against hers.

Beginning bonding process...

Spatchcock glanced over to Rai and Flintlock. Both men were moments from being swallowed by the vortex, half a dozen tentacles dragging their writhing bodies into its edge. "Whatever you're going to do," he urged Dante, "do it now!"

The vortex retracted for a second, like a wave about to crash upon a beach, then white light filled the room in an explosion of light and sound. After that was nothing. A blank and empty nothing.

EPILOGUE

"Great talkers are great liars."
– Russian proverb

"The blackout of 2673 remains one of the enduring mysteries from the years immediately after the war. Across the Empire every power supply, every light, every candle, every source of energy ceased to function for forty-seven seconds. The cause is still unknown, as is the reason for its abrupt end. It was as if the entire universe blinked and then held its breath, waiting for some great cataclysm to occur. But the cataclysm never came and the universe breathed out again. Some reports suggest the blackout began in a remote region of the Himalayas, an area cut off from civilisation by freakish weather conditions ever since. But that same isolation makes it impossible to prove or disprove those reports."

– Extract from *Unsolved Mysteries of the Empire*, by Danilov Mulderski

Nikolai Dante, with two wounds slowly healing inside him, sat in front of the Forbidden Citadel and thought about life and death.

He could remember little about what happened after he kissed Mai in the throne room. There was a skittering of alien minds within his own thoughts as the two Crests had bonded before attempting to regain control of the vortex. The inter-dimensional gateway had been like a wild animal inside Dante's head, gnawing, hungry, almost feral. It sensed the Crests coming and launched a pre-emptive attack. Everything after that was a blur of light and fury.

Dante had come to in what was left of the throne room, most of his clothes seared from his body, with Mai's unconscious and equally naked form nuzzled into his. He kissed her and she woke, a quiet joy on her face. Things may have become even more interesting, but for a polite cough from nearby. Spatchcock and Flintlock had been sitting in a corner of the throne room, a few rags hanging from their bodies, observing Dante and Mai's embrace. Spatchcock looked particularly disappointed at being denied a free floorshow, while Flintlock smiled sheepishly.

The cough had come from another corner, where a fresh-faced Himalayan youth was standing. It was Rai, but as Dante had first known him, in the dying days of the war. The horrific scars on his face were gone, and so were all the wounds and injuries he had acquired since.

Lastly Dante had turned to look at the vortex. It too was restored to the way it had been, a glowing ball of energy under firm control. A huge section of the throne room was missing, a gaping void showing how close the vortex had come to consuming them all. But the crisis had been averted – just.

All of that was three days in the past. Since then Spatchcock and Flintlock had busied themselves organising a funeral pyre for the monks killed by Ivanov's men. Mai used the immense power of her Crest to send the few survivors from the Imperial Black back to the Tsar with a warning never to invade or attack the Himalayas again. To underline her threat, she sent every Imperial corpse too, including the remains of General Ivanov.

Dante had spent the three days recovering in Gylatsen's cell, letting his enhanced healing abilities do their job. He emerged much the better for his rest, but still experiencing stabs of pain from where Ivanov had shot him. "Guess I'm not rid of that bastard yet," Dante muttered to himself.

I hope you're not talking about me, the Crest said.

"No, the late, unlamented general. But where have you been hiding the past three days? I expected an endless lecture series on what I should have done differently, but you haven't said a word to me."

I was... preoccupied. The Mukari's Crest required my aid to bring the situation completely under control. Besides, you needed peace and quiet to heal.

"Well, I'm feeling strong enough to leave now," Dante said. "I'm waiting for Spatch and Flintlock to find my rifle, then we can go."

You aren't staying for the funeral?

"I've seen enough death to last me a lifetime."

Mai emerged from the citadel, sitting beside Dante in the autumnal sunshine. "A beautiful day, isn't it?"

"Yes. Spatch, Flintlock and I should make good time down the mountain."

"So you're definitely leaving today?"

Dante nodded. "You're not wearing the headdress. Is that wise? You don't want the vortex–"

Mai rested a finger against his lips, silencing him. Her other hand opened the front of her top to reveal a small, double-headed eagle symbol in the nape of her neck. "I couldn't stand the idea of having to wear that hat for the rest of my days, so your Crest and mine arranged for a more physical manifestation. I can always transfer it back, when the time comes."

"Interesting," Dante said. "Crest, that does mean I can shift you to–"

No.

"But if Mai can do it, why can't I–"

Her Crest is different from yours. Very different.

"We could at least try–"

No.

Mai smiled at their exchange. "Sorry. But at least you can go where you want. I have to stay here on the mountain."

Dante noticed Rai walking past. "Your brother... How much does he remember of his time as the Enforcer?"

"A little." Mai frowned. "I know it was selfish of me, using the vortex to change Rai back to how I remembered him before the war. But I'll need someone to keep me company here in the citadel. Unless I can change your mind."

Dante shook his head. "Sorry. Your place is here, but I don't belong anywhere – not since the war."

"You could always come back for a visit," Mai offered, smiling impishly. "We never did get to finish what we started in that cave."

Dante was still kissing Mai when Spatchcock and Flintlock appeared, the latter carrying the Huntsman 5000. "Well, we finally found your precious rifle," he said. "Why you decided to hide it behind a shrine I'll never–" A sharp elbow from Spatchcock abruptly silenced the Brit, as Dante and Mai hastily separated.

"Ready to go?" Spatchcock asked, grinning broadly.

"Yes," Dante replied, standing up. He smiled fondly at Mai. "Say goodbye to your brother for us. Tell him... tell him not to worry about the past. The future is more important now."

"I'll do that."

The three men strolled out of the citadel and onto the snow-covered plateau beyond the repaired gates. The trio paused as they surveyed the Himalayas, the majestic peaks spread out around them as far as the horizon.

"You know, I can't help thinking we should get some sort of reward for saving the Empire," Spatchcock commented. "Hell, for saving the whole universe."

"Getting away from you would be reward enough for me," Flintlock muttered under his breath. "What about you, Dante? Do you reckon we should get a reward? Or maybe you think getting vengeance on Ivanov was enough."

"It was a hollow victory," Dante replied. "I can't bring back the tens of thousands he had murdered, or undo the horrors he did in Rudinshtein and other places. All I did was murder a murderer. Where's the honour in that?"

Honour be damned, the Crest said. *There is more to life than honour. You of all people should know that, Dante.*

The three men turned back to see Mai and Rai waving from inside the citadel gates. Beyond them, a column of smoke drifted from the burning funeral pyre, creating a road to the heavens. Dante waved to the siblings, then set off down the mountainside, his travelling companions following him.

"It's strange," Dante commented. "My Crest has been surprisingly busy these past three days, ever since it bonded with the Mukari's Crest."

"What's strange about that?" Flintlock asked.

"When I put on the headdress, I heard the voice of the Mukari's Crest, and it was distinctly female." Dante paused, waiting for a reply from his Crest. "I was wondering if somebody not too far from me has been playing away recently."

A long silence followed.

"Well?" Spatchcock asked eagerly. "What did your Crest say?"

Dante smirked. "Nothing I could repeat in polite company."

"Since when have we been polite company?" Spatchcock asked Flintlock.

"Just shut up and walk," the Brit replied grumpily.

"I dare say Flintlock is right." Dante pulled his coat closer around himself, shivering in a cold wind that blew from the north. "Bojemoi. It's a long hike back to civilisation from here."

HONOUR
BE DAMNED!

ONE

"Laws are not written for the lawless."
– Russian proverb

"2673 AD: King Henry Windsor McKray continues to enjoy his status as ruler of Britannia, despite openly supporting the Romanovs during their doomed revolt against Tsar Vladimir Makarov. It is the first time in Imperial history a monarch has retained powered by pleading insanity. King Henry remains popular among the majority of his people, but the ruling upper class consider his eccentric behaviour a grave embarrassment. They would much rather his daughter Princess Marie-Anne Britannia took charge, but she is still a prisoner in the Tower of London after being found guilty of conspiring against her father.

The princess has sworn to avenge herself against Russian rogue Nikolai Dante, who supplied the evidence leading to her incarceration. Meanwhile Britannia remains a nation divided, its parliament stuck in a mire of political manoeuvring, scandal, sleaze and corruption. Some would say it was ever thus. The most popular member of the royal family was the Queen Mother, Barbara 'Babs' Windsor McKray. Her title stemmed from the fact she had been queen before Henry was born, but also acknowledged that she was mother of the current monarch. To

confuse matters further, she looked younger than her son, thanks to the remarkable effects of ingesting royal jelly..."
– Editorial commentary from *The Imperial Times*

It was one of those days when it seemed to Nikolai Dante that all life, as someone put it, was nothing but a heap of six to four against.

Dante prided himself on being a gambling man. He was prone to taking on impossible odds and winning through, escaping almost certain death to emerge smiling from the other side of any adventure fate might throw in his path. But diving from a stained glass window on the Palace of London's tenth floor without bothering to look first was pushing even his legendary good luck to its limits and beyond. If he had any doubts about this, the disapprovingly patrician voice inside his mind had little hesitation in confirming it.

Dante, when I said evasive action, I did not think even you would be so foolish as to jump to your own death to avoid an assassin's bullet!

"I was improvising," Dante replied as he plummeted towards the stone courtyard below.

That much was obvious. The voice belonged to the Weapons Crest, a sentient battle-computer bonded to Dante's DNA. This remarkable piece of alien technology was created to train its genetic host as a potential ruler of the Empire. *My presence may significantly enhance your body's natural healing abilities,* the Crest observed, *but even I cannot resurrect the dead. Seven seconds to impact, by the way.*

"At least I'm still alive!"

Only for another five seconds.

"Shut up, I'm trying to concentrate." Dante could see a row of flagpoles that protruded from the building below. The palace whistled past his face as he twisted in the air, trying to get close enough to grab one of the poles. Miss these and he would be a red smear in–

Three seconds.

"I said shut up!" His flailing hands missed the nearest pole, but got hold of the rectangular flag hanging beneath it. Dante's body jerked to a halt, the sudden deceleration nearly wrenching his arms from their sockets. "Gahhhh!" He hung grimly to the royal standard, his breath coming in short, ragged gasps as the bitter taste of adrenaline filled his mouth.

Gahhh? Not quite what I'd call famous last words, the Crest commented dryly.

"Why... W-Why should they be... famous last words?"

The flag to which you're so gratefully clinging was not designed for such violent use. I estimate the fabric will tear itself free at any moment...

Dante looked up in time to see the material ripping apart. He tried to grab hold of the flagpole, but that only accelerated the disintegration.

...now, the Crest concluded as Dante resumed his rapid descent.

"Bojemoi!"

Mildred Barnstaple despised tourists. For thirty-seven years she had been a guide at the Palace of London, welcoming visitors to its grand halls and galleries, politely answering questions, aiding the helpless, the hopeless and the hapless. But never once in all that time had one of these ungrateful wretches thought to say thank you. An only child, both of Mildred's parents had died in a freak zeppelin accident over Walthamstow when she was twenty. The resulting inheritance had ensured she never need work, but left the young woman with a lifetime to occupy. A quiet passion for the beauties of the past led Mildred to the Britannia Heritage Society, a voluntary organisation striving to preserve the country's finest historic buildings. Since then she had more than done her bit – baking cakes, organising whist drives and running raffles. To her eternal shame, Mildred had even agreed to pose for a nude calendar. The results had proved an underwhelming failure and so Mildred had returned to her post by the green velvet canopy outside the Palace of London's entrance, wishing something exciting would happen.

"Look out below!" a voice screamed from the heavens. A man was plummeting towards the canopy, his arms and legs flailing violently as if he were trying to fly. Mildred took an involuntary step back and tumbled over, her eyes still fixed on the bizarre descent. The man fell on the taut green canopy, which bounced him towards Mildred. The man landed with a heavy thump, his face burying itself into Mildred's crotch.

"Oh my word!" she shrieked, suddenly aware of hot, masculine breath warming her in a way she hadn't experienced for at least a decade. At first she was shocked, then affronted and soon rather excited.

Mildred craned her neck forward to study the manly windfall positioned between her legs. He was around thirty in age, with a taut, athletic figure and shapely buttocks. Skintight grey trousers clung to his thighs before disappearing inside a pair of supple brown leather riding boots, while a crimson jacket with gold braid hugged his back. He had a thick mane of black hair, but his face remained hidden. Mildred felt her inner thighs being tickled by his beard. "I say," she sighed happily and clenched her legs together.

It took Dante more than a minute to prise apart the thighs holding his head captive. When he succeeded, a soft moan of disappointment issued from the middle-aged woman who had cushioned his impact. Dante scrambled to his feet, grinning sheepishly at her. "Normally I don't like to leave a lady unsatisfied, but my presence is required elsewhere – sorry!" He noticed a line of hover-taxis waiting on a nearby rank and waved at the first one.

"Take me with you!" the woman pleaded.

"Not today." Dante made a run for it, diving into the black cab. "But thanks for the soft landing!"

The taxi sped into the sky. "Can you take me to Nelson's Column?" he asked the driver.

"No problem, guv," a surly voice replied. "They've just finished rebuilding it after what happened during the war. Bloody disgrace it was."

"That's where the assassin fired from," Dante muttered darkly. "Take me there!"

Are you sure this is wise? the Crest enquired. *If the sniper was trying to kill you, getting closer only makes you a bigger target.*

"I don't think they were shooting at me."

"You talking to me?" the driver asked.

"King Henry suspected someone was planning to kill him," Dante continued, ignoring the cabbie. "Princess Marie-Anne can't wait to take his place on the throne. She must have hired an assassin to speed up the process."

"What you muttering about back there?" the driver demanded. "You got something to do with what happened at the palace? They was talking about it on the news – some kind of shooting."

"I was with the king when he was hurt," Dante admitted.

"Why'd you do it?"

"I didn't do anything!"

"What? You stood by and let somebody murder him? That's worse, you bloody coward!" The cabbie twisted round to glare at Dante, not bothering to watch where his hover-taxi was headed. Nelson's Column was looming ahead of them.

"There were three shots, moments apart," Dante protested. "By the time I reacted, the king was already down, blood everywhere. I saw what direction the shots came from, so I decided to go after the shooter. Now, will you watch where you're going, please?"

The cabbie lunged over the back of his seat to grab hold of Dante's jacket. "Don't you tell me how to do my job, you bloody foreigner! Look at you, in your fancy clothes! Come over here, telling us how to live our lives. There used to be a British Empire, you know, long before you bloody Russians started sticking your noses in–"

Dante, this cab is on a collision course with–

"I know, I know!" he said.

"I don't care what you know," the driver snarled. "I'm going to teach you a lesson!"

Dante–

The assassin was so intent on watching the palace he didn't notice the hover-taxi careering across the sky. The assassin clung to the statue on top of Nelson's Column, one eye closed while the other peered through a high-powered sniper's sight. It was only when a dark shape blurred across his field of vision that he belatedly realised how imminent danger was. "Bloody hell!" The assassin reached back to pull the ignition toggle on his jetpack but he was too late.

The hover-taxi smashed nose-first into the column, neatly severing the replica of Nelson from its base. The sundered statue fell on top of the taxi, impaling the vehicle on the specially reinforced column below. The assassin clung on to the statue, but his weapon tumbled to the ground far below. The shooter cursed in frustration; this had not been part of the plan. His client had been quite specific: a single shot, two at most – kill the king and get out of sight without attracting any attention. *I doubt this qualifies,* the assassin thought ruefully. But when he reached back to fire up his jetpack's twin engines, another hand was already resting on the ignition toggle. "Going somewhere?" a Russian-accented voice asked.

Not for the first time today, Dante was grateful for the augmentations he had gained from being bonded with a Romanov Weapons Crest. Enhanced healing abilities had protected him from a brutal concussion when the hover-cab collided with Nelson's Column. The Crest also gave Dante the ability to extend razor-sharp swords of bio-organic circuitry from his fists. One swipe of these cut a path out of the crushed cab, enabling him to intercept the escaping assassin.

The two grappled on Nelson's toppled statue, the violence of their struggle threatening to send the golden effigy tumbling from its precarious perch. The assassin was wearing a slate–grey bodysuit and mask that hid everything but their eyes. "Who are you?" Dante demanded to know. "Why did you try to kill the king? Who sent you?"

The assassin tried to wriggle free, but Dante kept one hand clasped on the jetpack. "I won't let go until you tell me!" he warned. A lithe foot kicked Dante's groin with a sickening thud. He doubled over in pain, his grip loosening involuntarily. The assassin broke free and ran to the other end of the horizontal statue, one hand activating his jetpack. Still wincing, Dante flung himself at the killer as they lifted off. His clasping fingers caught hold of the assassin's flat-soled shoes and clung on. Then the two men were flying across London's twilight sky, the setting sun colouring the horizon in hues of orange and pink.

A magnificent vista, even if it is probably a localised side effect of air pollution levels.

"Crest, this is no time to be admiring the view!" Dante snapped. By now the assassin was kicking and thrashing his legs, trying to dislodge his unwanted passenger.

I fail to see what else I can do. You seem determined to kill yourself today, so I thought it best if I savoured my remaining moments. Sightseeing was the obvious option at this height.

"Diavolo!" Dante snarled as a knee connected sharply with the side of his head. "You could suggest some ways of bringing this bastard down to earth!"

I don't think that will be an issue for much longer, the Crest replied.

"Why not?"

In your earlier struggle you dislodged the jetpack's fuel line. It's been venting ever since. I doubt there's enough left in the tanks to keep both of you airborne for more than a minute.

Dante looked down and realised they were several hundred metres above the ground. If the jetpack cut out now, both of them would fall to an exceedingly unnatural death. He crawled up the assassin's still thrashing legs and yanked the jetpack sideways, sending them into a rapid, spiralling descent. Below, the Thames grew larger as it got nearer. Most of London's greatest attractions had been relocated to a cluster on the river's north bank, making it easier for visitors to savour the best of Britannia. As a result the Houses of Parliament, the Tower of London, Big Ben and New Covent Garden all stood cheek by jowl with each other, competing for tourist roubles.

The assassin flailed at Dante with both fists, pummelling him repeatedly until his tenacious grip began to loosen. When Dante thought he could hold on no longer, the jetpack's engines began to splutter and cough. Fortunately, they were now less than ten metres above the flower stalls of New Covent Garden. Beneath them a trader was trying to shift a cartload of yellow roses. "Five big bunches for a rouble, guaranteed thorn-free!" she cried out in a gravelly voice. "Get your roses. Show your good lady wife how much you love her!"

The jetpack died completely, sending Dante and the assassin tumbling towards the flower stall. They hit the rose pile with an almighty thump, Dante crying out as his trousers were sliced to ribbons by the foliage. By the time he had extricated himself the assassin was already fleeing on foot. The flower seller stared at her devastated stock. "Where the hell did you come from?"

"St Petersburg," Dante replied tersely, removing a sharp triangle of green from his posterior. "I thought you said these roses were thorn-free?"

"*Caveat emptor,*" the stallholder said, folding her arms imperiously.

That means buyer beware.

"I know what it means, Crest!" Dante snapped, clambering from the cart to pursue the fleeing assassin.

"What about my bloody roses?" the flower seller protested as Dante ran off.

"Try making potpourri!"

The assassin could feel his energy draining away as the chase wore on. No matter how fast he ran, no matter what obstacles he left, the man chasing him kept coming – sprinting through the darkening streets as night closed in, implacable and utterly relentless. Doesn't this bastard ever get tired? Who the hell is he? There was no choice but to keep running. If I can reach the rendezvous in time, I'll be fine. Otherwise... No, there was no otherwise, the killer thought. I have to make it. He sprinted round the corner of an old sandstone building.

Dante ran round the same corner, straight into the waiting assassin. A fist punched Dante's throat, choking him. As he staggered back, a hand smashed into his nose, snapping his head backwards. A knee slammed into Dante's stomach and he crumpled to the ground, gasping for air. The assassin moved in for the kill but the sound of approaching sirens rent the twilight. The sniper ran off, leaving Dante spitting blood.

Britannia's law enforcers are closing in on this location.

"About time. Where were they when the shooting started?"

I also sense a skimmer circling nearby – it could be the assassin's getaway vehicle.

"Where?"

A few hundred metres ahead, at a river crossing known as Westminster Bridge.

■ ■ ■

The assassin ran onto the bridge, searching the sky intently. Fog was rising from the sluggish river below, casting a shroud across the city centre. Night had claimed the sky but a few foreign visitors still strolled over the bridge. Those close enough to see the assassin's curious garb and wounded leg hurried on, not wanting to get involved. Despite the rising mist, the illuminated dial of Big Ben was still clearly visible, its larger hand creeping towards apogee. Within a minute the mighty bell would chime seven times.

"You left in such a hurry we never got introduced," a voice slurred from behind the assassin. He twisted round to see one of Dante's bloody, bruised fists hurtling towards him. It smacked into the killer's facemask, sending him sprawling to the footpath. "My name's Dante, Nikolai Dante. What's yours?" Dante kicked the assassin hard in the groin, then flung himself on top of him, pinning his arms to the ground with his knees. "What's the matter? Cat got your tongue?" Dante punched the crumpled sniper once, twice, then a third time. He grunted in pain but still said nothing, gave no reply.

Dante–

"Not now, Crest!"

But you need to–

"I said not now!" Dante snarled. Then there was a sharp pain at the back of his head, followed by darkness and nothing more.

Dante was shocked back to consciousness when his body tumbled into the Thames. "Bojemoi!" he gasped, swallowing a mouthful of river water. He spluttered and sank beneath the surface, arms flailing uselessly. Someone had hit him from behind. Icy water was numbing Dante's arms and legs, cramping his already exhausted muscles. A glimmer of light danced overhead, pale and inviting. Dante willed his limbs into action, but the Thames seemed determined to hold him with its chilling embrace, extracting the maximum of effort for every stroke.

Dante could hear the blood pumping through his ears, while his lungs were screaming for air. He gave another kick and broke the surface, gratefully breathing in something other than water. To his surprise Westminster Bridge was some distance away. The Thames obviously had a powerful undertow beneath its slow moving surface. Rising mist made it hard to see the faces of anyone on the bridge, but Dante could make out a male silhouette watching him. He was talking with another, unseen figure, occasional words and phrases audible across the water. "I'll see you soon... Yes, the old man... Hoy..."

A low-flying skimmer dropped to the bridge, catching the man in its headlights. He was quite bald, with a solemn face and curling goatee beard. Then the vehicle's lights swung left and he was gone, lost in the thickening mist. Dante realised the current was dragging him further away. Treading water, he looked for the nearest riverbank but could not see either edge.

"Which side is closer, Crest? I can't tell in this accursed fog." Dante waited but got no reply. "Crest, this is no time to be sulking!" Still nothing. He sighed with exasperation. The Crest was the product of a superior alien intelligence, but it was not above extracting petty revenge for having its feelings hurt. "All right, look – I'm sorry I snapped at you before, okay? I realise you were simply alerting me to danger. I promise to pay more attention to your warnings in future."

The Crest laughed hollowly in Dante's head.

"How about if I promise to try?"

That would be more realistic.

"So – which side is closer?"

Swim to your left, the Crest advised. *Your other left,* it added a few moments later.

By the time Dante reached the nearest bank the river had swept down to the next bridge. He tried climbing out but his cold, stiffening fingers could not get a purchase on the slippery surface. "Fuoco, is nothing ever easy in this country?" Dante cursed. As if in reply, a red and white life preserver splashed into the water beside him. It was tied to a rope which disappeared up into the fog-shrouded bridge. Dante grabbed the preserver and was dragged from the water. As he rose, Dante could see flashing red and blue lights tinting the air. Britannia's law enforcement agencies had arrived at last – but were they in time to catch the assassin?

Once the life preserver was level with the bridge's parapet he scrambled over the edge, shivering in the cold early evening air. "Thanks for getting me out of there," he said. "If you're quick there's still a chance you can get the shooter. They were on Westminster–"

The sound of a dozen weapons being cocked silenced Dante. He glanced at the surly faces of the policemen surrounding him and realised something was badly amiss. "What's wrong? You look like you're ready to kill someone!"

Dante, you might have been better off staying in the river.

"You don't think I had anything to do with shooting the king, do you?"

A trench-coated man emerged from the throng. "We don't think anything of the sort." The speaker struck a match, its flame briefly illuminating his middle-aged face and receding ginger hair. He was lighting a pipe, its rich, pungent tobacco smoke adding to the mist in the air. "We *know* you tried to murder him."

"That's ridiculous," Dante protested. "I've chased the sniper halfway across London!"

"An interesting interpretation of reality," the pipe-smoker replied. "I was told you were fleeing the scene of the crime, trying to make good your escape. Happily, you failed. Another triumph for Rucka of the Yard." He gestured to the surrounding policemen. "Take him into custody. If he resists, subdue him. Use force if necessary, but he's to be brought in alive."

Dante fought like a wounded animal but even with his bio-blades fully extended he could not hold off all twelve of them. The last sounds he heard were his own screams of pain and the thud of boots into his already bruised and battered torso. Then merciful darkness took him. It was hard to believe it was less than twelve hours since his arrival in Britannia.

TWO

"Any scrap of paper will please a bureaucrat."
– Russian proverb

"For the world-weary tourist, travelling by airship may be the slowest method of reaching Britannia but it is also the most delightfully decadent. It is well worth the exorbitant price simply for the stately way you approach this green and pleasant land. As the ubiquitous fog parts you get your first view of Dover's legendary white cliffs. These iconic surfaces are repainted every summer to ensure they retain that peculiarly lustrous hue, but don't allow that to spoil your appreciation. When the cliffs hove into view, your journey is almost at an end. Only one chore remains: clearing customs. Other parts of the Empire may favour free movement from one state to the next, but Britannia retains many of its sovereign rights despite being a Tsarist territory. As a consequence, gaining entry can take longer than the three-day journey from Paris."

– Extract from *Around the Empire in Eighty Ways*,
Mikhail Palinski

"The queue is a great British tradition," Lord Peter Flintlock said to his travelling companion with a wan smile. "Almost from birth we are trained to form into long lines and wait patiently for anything and everything. You become inured to the process, you almost welcome it after a while. Getting into a queue gives you a feeling of security, of comfort – you know you're home when you join the back of your first queue."

"Is that a fact?" Spatchcock scowled while scratching at his lice-infested pubic hair. The two men were startlingly different in appearance. Where Flintlock was thin and aristocratic, Spatchcock was short and dishevelled. The Britannia nobleman was blond and blue-eyed, but his associate was foul smelling and even fouler looking. Spatchcock removed the scratching hand from inside his stain-ridden underpants and examined his fingertips with professional disinterest. A tiny white insect jumped from one finger to the next. Spatchcock popped it into his mouth. He munched happily on the crunchy creature, before belching noisily. "Do you usually have to strip half naked first?"

The unlikely duo had kept company with Dante occasionally since serving under him in the war. More recently the three men had helped foil a dangerous genetic experiment to create a terrifying new weapon for the Tsar and saved an ancient monastery from an army of murderous Imperial soldiers. Now Spatchcock and Flintlock were together again, stripped of everything but their underclothes, waiting for Dante in a featureless holding cell. It was something of a comedown after their luxurious journey on the Paris-to-Britannia airship.

Normally the threesome was forced to travel incognito, thanks to the hundred million rouble bounty the Tsar had placed on Dante's head. But this trip had been different, thanks to a communiqué from King Henry to Dante, offering the Romanov rogue full diplomatic immunity and a first class passage for this trip to Britannia. "What's the catch?" Spatchcock had asked when the letter arrived. "Nobody gives you something for nothing in this life, I know that for a fact."

Dante re-read the communiqué but could find no obvious danger. "The king requests my presence and says I am welcome to bring an entourage as large as I see fit."

"Perhaps he's set a date for the royal wedding?" Spatchcock suggested. Britannia's monarch rejoiced in numerous eccentricities – wearing a fruit bowl as his crown, trying to outlaw baldness and urging the creation of a welfare state for the underprivileged. Among his stranger quirks was a long-standing proposal of marriage to Dante, whom he insisted upon calling Nicola instead of Nikolai. Spatchcock smiled, his crooked teeth a greasy mix of black, yellow and green hues. "I can just see your face next to his on a commemorative tea towel."

Flintlock remained stubbornly opposed to the invitation. He had been born and raised in Britannia, but left the country under a cloud. The exact reason for his abrupt departure remained unclear, but rumours spoke of a crime so vile all detail of it had been suppressed to save the nation's embarrassment. Whatever the cause of his leaving, the exiled aristocrat had been back to Britannia only once in the past twenty years. That was a flying visit during the war, when the country was in chaos and his presence could pass unnoticed. It had taken all of Dante's powers of persuasion to talk Flintlock round. Now the wisdom of that was looking more dubious by the minute.

A door opened and Dante was propelled into the holding cell, like the others clad only in his underwear. In Dante's case, it was less than dignified: a black silk g-string he had acquired from a duplicitous prostitute at the Geisha House of the Rising Sun, the legend "GET IT HERE" embroidered in sequins within a Valentine's heart logo. Spatchcock raised an eyebrow at the unconventional apparel. "My mother always told me to wear clean pants when travelling," Dante said, by way of explanation, "in case you have an accident."

I doubt she had that sort of undergarment in mind, the Crest said despairingly.

"We should never have come back here," Flintlock fretted, an embarrassed hand hovering in front of his plaid boxer shorts. "I told you this was a mistake."

"There's been some kind of mix-up with our travel documents," Dante sighed. "The head of customs should be here any minute to sort it out, okay? Don't get your knickers in a twist!"

"That's good advice from a man wearing a whore's drawers," Spatchcock commented.

Fortunately, the doorway reopened and a sour-faced woman in a uniform strode into the holding cell. The navy blue jacket and skirt did little to forgive her rotund figure, while the greying hair pulled back into a tight bun gave her face a stretched, arched quality. An identity tag pinned over her left breast identified the new arrival as STAINES, MURIEL. She waited until the door closed, then sternly addressed the trio. "I am Officer Staines, of His Majesty's Royal Customs Department. Which of you is Nicola Dante?"

"Nikolai," Dante said, correcting her. "My first name is Nikolai."

Officer Staines glared at him. "You were travelling under the name Nicola."

Spatchcock shrugged, grinning ruefully. "That'll be the king's fault. He insists on calling Dante here Nicola – even wants to marry him."

"Indeed?" Officer Staines's gaze shifted to the small, squat man. "And what is your name?"

"Spatchcock. Like the chicken."

"Like the chicken."

"That's right."

"A curious name." the customs official said, noting it down.

"Not as bad as yours, though," Spatchcock replied cheerfully, failing to notice the frenzied gesticulations to be silent from his travelling companions. "I mean, I wouldn't want to be called Staines all my life! I can only imagine how the other kids teased you at school–"

"Yes, thank you for that," she snapped back.

"Dirty Staines, they probably called you," Spatchcock continued. "Grubby Staines. Maybe even Semen–"

"That's enough!" the woman shrieked at the top of her voice, the words echoing round the bleak cell. She paused to regain her composure, then moved on to the last member of the trio. "And your name is?"

"Flintlock," he mumbled in reply.

"A little louder please!"

"Flintlock. Lord Peter Flintlock."

"Lord... Peter..." she repeated, scribbling down his reply. Her writing tool snapped in two as Staines reached the last word. "Flintlock?"

"Yes."

"*The* Lord Peter Flintlock?"

"Yes," he agreed, nodding his head sadly.

"The one who... Who did *that* with... and then..."

"Yes!" Flintlock shouted. "It was me, okay? I did it, I bloody did it!"

All hint of colour drained from the customs official's pallid features. She gazed at Flintlock with undisguised disgust while slowly shaking her head, as if he was the vilest piece of excrement ever to sully the underside of her shoes.

Spatchcock took a step nearer to Staines.

"What did he do, exactly? I keep trying to find out but the old bugger won't say."

"Get away from me," she snarled, sending the little man scurrying away. Once he was standing alongside Dante and Flintlock again, Officer Staines glared at them in turn. "Never in all my years as a customs official have I had the misfortune to encounter such a vile, repulsive, ungodly trio of unwanted arrivals here at Dover – a cross-dresser, a vile and vulgar ferret of a man and..." Words escaped her when she looked at Flintlock. "It pains me more than I can express to say what I now must."

"Here it comes," Spatchcock whispered out of the side of his mouth.

Officer Staines swallowed hard before concluding her speech: "Welcome to Britannia." She snapped her fingers and three more officials entered, each carrying a pile of clothing. "We found nothing untoward in any of your clothing, although health and safety regulations forced us to have Mr Spatchcock's garments destroyed for fear of allowing an unknown number of bacteria into the country – replacements have been provided for him. The Palace of London confirmed your right to enter Britannia and a royal skimmer has been despatched to ferry you directly to his majesty's presence. It should be here within the hour. In the meantime, I am obliged to ask if there is anything else I can do to make your stay more pleasant?"

Spatchcock was about to speak, a lascivious grin spreading across his grimy features, but a sharp elbow in the ribs from Dante stopped him.

Flintlock replied instead. "Any chance of a nice cup of tea?"

It was nine in the morning when the royal skimmer carrying Dante, Flintlock and Spatchcock arrived at the Palace of London. The ornate gold and green vehicle had flown low over the city, giving the new arrivals a glorious tour of the sights, before approaching the royal residence. The palace was a perfect cube of stone and glass, a formidable gothic tower at each corner. In the middle of the structure was the former dome of St Paul's Cathedral, now used as the palace's centrepiece. Above that was a golden statue of Britannia herself, a flagpole bearing the Union Jack clutched in one hand whilst her other held a mighty shield bearing the royal crest. Beside her stood a golden lion, proud and regal. As the skimmer got closer the statue sank into the vast dome, its place taken by a circular landing pad.

Inside the palace, Dante and his travelling companions were greeted by two soldiers in full ceremonial dress, complete with black bearskin hats and sabres. "If you'll follow us, we have orders to escort you to his majesty," they said in unison.

"Lead on!" Dante said grandly, waving for Spatchcock and Flintlock to follow. Within minutes they were outside the royal bedchamber.

Dante told his associates to wait by the double doors. "Best you stay here while I assess the king's mood," he said. "Henry may be pants-on-his-head-mad, but he's no fool. I want to make sure this isn't some kind of trap after all."

The others were happy to stay put while Dante ventured inside. The first thing he saw was a vast four-poster bed standing in the centre of the room, surrounded by courtiers and attendants in various states of undress, all standing to attention. Rich tapestries lined the walls, while naked soldiers stood in front of the windows, facing the glass exterior. Of King Henry, there was no sign. His bed was unmade but empty. "Er, your majesty?" Dante said nervously.

"Hello! I know those dulcet tones anywhere," a voice called from beneath the bed. "It can only be the lovely Nicola, come to rescue me again!"

Dante raised an eyebrow at the nearest member of the household staff. The attendant sighed wearily and shrugged. Dante stepped closer to the four-poster. "Where are you, your majesty?"

"Under the bed, of course! Safest place to be – come and join me!"

"Well, I don't know if that's wise."

"I said *join* me," the king insisted. "Otherwise I'll be forced to give you a smacked bottom, you saucy little minx!"

Perhaps you'd best do as he says, the Crest suggested. *I doubt even you would enjoy receiving a spanking from an elderly man.*

Dante dropped to his knees and crawled towards the bed. A single candle lit the scene beneath the mattress, where the king was cowering in a blue and white striped nightshirt, clutching a white porcelain chamber pot to his chest. Henry had aged since Dante saw him last. The king's hair was snow white where once it had been greying, and heavy bags underlined his eyes. The ruler of all Britannia had lost weight too, his short but rotund figure a shadow of its former opulence. "There you are!" Henry said, a hint of desperation audible at the edge of his rich, rasping voice. "Hurry along, Nicola, we haven't got all night you know."

"Actually, it's morning outside," Dante replied, joining the king in his refuge.

"Already? My, how time crawls." Henry offered the contents of his chamber pot to the new arrival. "Care for a drink?"

"No thank you, your majesty."

"Oh well, all the more for us!" The king supped greedily from the yellow liquid in the bowl.

"Us, your majesty?"

"Yes, of course! Haven't you ever heard of the royal wee?"

Dante decided to ignore Henry's latest flight of fancy. "You sent for me, sire."

"That's right, I did, Nicola!"

"Nikolai, sir."

"That's what I said, Nicola – don't contradict me, damn you!"

Be careful what you say, the Crest warned. *It seems his majesty is more unstable and paranoid than the last time you met here. Remember, he could have you executed on a whim.*

"Of course, sire. You were going to explain why you sent for me?"

"I was?"

"Yes, your majesty."

"Isn't it obvious?" Henry asked, gesturing at the naked legs of his attendants and courtiers standing around the bed. "They're trying to kill me!"

"Who is trying to kill you, sire?"

"Everyone, obviously. That's why I don't let anyone remain fully dressed in my presence, as a way of ensuring they don't have any concealed weapons about them."

"I see." Dante replied cautiously. "Have specific threats been made against you?"

"Not since my daughter tried to have me beheaded in Trafalgar Square, but you and your valiant troopers saved me on that occasion. What I wouldn't give for a squad of such soldiers!"

"That was during the war, sire. The Rudinshtein Irregulars were disbanded after the Tsar won, but I have brought two of my men with me."

The king smiled gratefully. "Good, Nicola, good. Besides Babs, you're the only person I can trust anymore. I knew you wouldn't let me down."

"Never, sire."

"There'll be knighthoods in this for all of you, if you can ferret out the conspirators."

"Well, we'll do our best," Dante promised.

"That's the ticket!" Henry enthused, shaking his chamber pot enthusiastically and slopping the remaining contents all over the floor.

"Coo-eee!" a female voice called out. "Anybody in here?"

"We're under the bed, my dear," the king replied cheerfully.

"Who's we?" the woman asked.

"Henry and Nicola – Nicola's come all the way from the continent to see us!"

"I don't think I've met her. Send her out so we can be introduced."

"Yes, dear," Henry said. "It's high time you met Babs, Nicola. She's been a boon to me these past few months. Well, off you go!"

Dante twisted round to see the new arrival. Most of her was obscured by the vast bed overhead but he could make out a pair of dainty feet leading to two slim, shapely legs. "Who is it? You never told me you had a lover, your majesty."

"A lover? Don't be disgusting!" The king's face crumpled disdainfully. "As if I'd do anything so unsavoury with a member of my family!"

That confused Dante still further. Princess Marie-Anne was still being held captive in the Tower of London. "I thought you only had one daughter?"

"I do," Henry insisted, pushing his guest out from under the bed. "Now go and talk to Babs. Don't worry, she won't bite – the dear lady should have had her breakfast by now."

Dante reluctantly emerged from beneath the royal bed, not at all sure what he would find waiting for him. Amidst all the semi-naked staff stood a beautiful young blonde woman, wearing a translucent black baby doll nightie. She was petite in height, the top of her head level with Dante's shoulders, but possessed a gently heaving bosom of remarkable proportions. She smiled at Dante with gleaming white teeth, a twinkle of mischief at the corner of her warm, friendly eyes. "Hello? I thought Henry said your name was Nicola? You don't look like a Nicola to me, duckie!"

Dante shook his head politely and smiled. "My name's Dante, Nikolai Dante." He leaned forward and kissed the back of Babs's left hand. "Delighted to make your acquaintance."

She gave a raucous giggle in response, her considerable décolletage bouncing in time with her laughter. "Ooh, ain't you a charmer? I bet you're a real smoothie with the young ladies!"

"They don't come much younger than you, Miss...?"

"Miss! You hear that, Henry? He called me Miss!" Babs giggled again, flapping her hands in the air. "You'll make me blush, you will!"

Dante, I'm searching all Imperial records for any mention of a Babs Windsor McKray. There's only one such name listed in my database.

But Dante was not listening to the warning voice in his head. "Perhaps we could get better acquainted, once my assignment for the king is completed," he said smoothly.

"Ooh, that would be nice," Babs enthused. "Normally young men run a mile when I try to persuade them to be my special friend." She winked heavily at Dante, then broke into another raucous round of tittering and hand flapping.

Babs Windsor McKray is better known as Queen Barbara Windsor McKray, the Queen Mother. This woman is a hundred and three years old!

Dante froze, his gaze still fixed on Babs's bouncing bosoms. "I…"

The king emerged from beneath his bed, still clutching the chamber pot. "Well, how are you two getting along?"

"I think this young man is coming on to me," Babs confided.

"I… I…" Dante repeated helplessly.

"Nonsense, mother!" Henry said brusquely. "Eating all that royal jelly may make you look younger than my daughter, but we all know what happens when the effect wears off – don't we?"

Babs nodded unhappily.

"Besides," the king continued, "young Nicola is already betrothed to me!" He illustrated the point by slapping Dante's buttocks and waggling his eyebrows suggestively.

Spatchcock and Flintlock stood outside the royal bedchamber, their arms folded, backs leaning against the gilt-edged doorframe. A slow smile of satisfaction crossed the smaller man's face, closely followed by a look of disgust on Flintlock's features. "I say, where is that vile smell coming from?" He caught the mischievous glint in his companion's eye. "Must you break wind in every building we ever enter?"

"I like to leave something behind everywhere I go," Spatchcock said, grinning broadly.

"You could at least give me fair warning!"

"The element of surprise is half the fun."

Before Flintlock could reply Dante hurriedly emerged from the bedchamber, leaving behind two giggling members of the royal family. "Well, what's the story?" Spatchcock asked.

"The king thinks he is going to be assassinated soon."

"Not an unlikely event, considering the bloodline," Flintlock observed. Britannia's royal household had survived its last crisis through intermarriage with London's most infamous crime family. The result had secured the future of the monarchy but doomed its descendents to a lifetime of bloodletting and backstabbing worthy of the Borgias. Princess Marie-Anne's many attempts to usurp her father were notable for their lack of subtlety. The McKray blood was obviously more dominant in her genetic make-up. "But why should it happen sooner rather than later? And what does he want with you?"

Dante shrugged. "Apparently Britannia Intelligence intercepted a coded transmission of an assassin being hired to kill the king. They didn't get all the message, so we don't know who is behind it, but the hit is due to take place any day now. The king believes I'm the only one he can trust and it's our job to keep him alive." Dante tugged thoughtfully on the bristles of his beard. "I want you two to stay here and keep watch over Henry. He's madder than a three-pound note, but I believe he's genuinely afraid for his life. Whatever insanity he drags you into, play along – just make sure he stays safe until I return, okay?"

"Where are you going?" Flintlock asked.

"To see the person with the most to gain from Henry dying." Dante sighed. "Get one of the courtiers to call ahead to the Tower of London. Tell them Nikolai Dante requests a private interview with Princess Marie-Anne."

THREE

"Better free than in a gilt cage."
– Russian proverb

"The Tower of London's history dates back almost 1600 years when William the Conqueror had a wooden fortress built beside the Thames to keep locals from rebelling against the Normans. A stone keep known as the White Tower was constructed on top of old Roman fortifications and soon grew into a full-scale castle. The Tower was best known as a prison for many centuries, holding such celebrity inmates as Queen Elizabeth I, the explorer Sir Walter Raleigh and Twentieth century German war criminal Rudolf Hess. The famous structure later became a tourist attraction and home to the fabled Crown Jewels. Fifty years ago the historic structure was disassembled, moved a mile west along the Thames and reconstructed as part of the new look London tourist zone. Lately the Tower has resumed its role as a place of incarceration for out of favour royalty."

– Extract from *The Smirnoff Almanac of Fascinating Facts*, 2673 edition

Dante emerged from the king's private skimmer to find twenty-five yeoman warders waiting for him. Each was clad in full ceremonial uniform, their red knee-length tunics resplendent with gold piping. The midday sun gleamed on each warder's black patent leather shoes and glinted from the blades of their ceremonial swords. A dozen guards stood on either side of the grey cobbled path that led into the Tower of London.

"Bojemoi," Dante muttered under his breath. "Does this entire country like nothing better than getting in a queue?"

The yeomen are forming an honour guard for your visit, the Crest sighed.

"Oh!" Dante smiled. "I usually see the inside of a prison when I'm under arrest or trying to break somebody else out."

One of the warders marched towards Dante and saluted briskly. "Yeoman First Class Marcus Reynolds at your service, sir! Please accept our apologies for the paucity of this reception party, but we were only informed of your imminent inspection ten minutes ago, sir!"

Dante did his best to return the salute. "No need to apologise, er, yeoman – this is not an official state visit. I've come to speak with her royal highness, Princess Marie-Anne."

"So I understand, sir. If you don't mind my asking, is that wise?"

"Wise?"

Reynolds looked abashed. "It's simply that... Well, her royal highness is not the easiest prisoner we have kept in our custody here. She is prone to unhappiness and... outbursts."

Dante's eyes strayed to the other warders. Almost all of them bore bruises, livid scars or broken noses. Reynolds himself had a badly blackened eye, the surrounding skin purple and blotchy, while a savage cut extended through both lips. "So I can see. I trust you have a safe enclosure in which to keep her during my visit?"

The warder nodded grimly. "We've recently transferred her to our maximum security wing in the basement, as much for our safety as anything else, sir. Her royal highness may have all the airs and graces of a princess, but you should never forget what she is."

"What is that?"

"Oh, she's a monster," another voice interjected. "Pure sociopath. It's so rare to have one in captivity – normally they occupy positions of power within the political system."

The person speaking was a tall, elegant man who had appeared from within the tower. He advanced towards Dante, hand outstretched in welcome. "Forgive me, I'm Doctor Eric Malvern, the Tower of London's resident psychiatrist. I've been counselling the warders in how best to deal with her royal highness – or the people's princess, as she likes to be called."

Dante shook the offered hand, struggling to mask his distaste at Malvern's moist, clammy grip. "She's always been prone to delusions of grandeur, in my limited experience of her."

The doctor's eyebrows shot up. "You've met her before?"

"Twice. I proved she had used the drug Psykd: Range 27 to drive her father insane. That led to her being imprisoned. I also stopped her having the king executed during the war."

Malvern could not disguise his delight. "You're Nikolai Dante!"

"In the flesh."

"This will be fascinating! To see her royal highness brought face to face with the man responsible for her downfall – psychiatrists wait years to witness such confrontations! Of course, she hates all of us, thinks I'm her nemesis."

Dante, you will get nowhere with the princess if Doctor Malvern insists on observing your meeting with her. He shows a level of fascination far beyond professional interest, to the point where it verges on sexual arousal. You need to dissuade his attendance, the Crest suggested.

"Indeed," Dante replied, "I couldn't agree more. Perhaps you could show me the way to her royal highness's cell?"

Malvern beamed happily and led Dante into the tower through a foreboding wooden doorway. They strode along ancient corridors, then descended a narrow stone staircase to an underground chamber where more warders were waiting. As they walked, the psychiatrist did his best to warn Dante how dangerous the princess could be. "I fought in the bloodiest battles of the Tsar Wars. I doubt I have much to fear from a single woman."

The doctor's eyes narrowed against Dante's sarcasm. "Good, then you should be able to remember the rules. Do not touch the glass. Do not approach the glass. Give her nothing. If she attempts to pass you anything through the food carrier, do not accept it. Do you understand me?"

Dante nodded. "If you are her nemesis, perhaps it would be best if I went in on my own?"

"But I-"

"That would be the sensible approach from a psychological standpoint, wouldn't it?" Dante added, prompted by the Crest. "What do you think?"

Malvern's face fell as he acknowledged the truth of Dante's suggestion.

"Very well," the doctor said huffily. He nodded to Reynolds, who had followed them down from the entrance. "When our guest has finished, bring him out." Malvern stomped back up the stairs, his fussy, leather-soled shoes squeaking with each step.

The chief warder smiled sympathetically at Dante, then unlocked an old but sturdy metal gateway leading to a holding chamber. "She's past the others, the last cell. Keep to the left."

Once Dante was inside the holding chamber, he could see a long corridor beyond another metal gateway. The walls were made of the same cold bricks as the rest of the tower, crumbling mortar visible between the stones. Intermittent sections of glass and iron bars marked the presence of cells on the right hand side of the corridor. Light spilled in from a metal walkway overhead, but it could not remove the dank, dismal feeling that hung in the air. Dante had been in more than his fair share of prison cells but the tower was as bad as any of them. This place was despair made real. A folding chair was already positioned outside the most distant cell, facing the glass-fronted enclosure. Dante nodded his readiness to Reynolds.

"I'll be watching you," the warder said kindly, gesturing at a selection of security screens set into the stone wall behind him. Reynolds signalled another yeoman and the inner gateway between Dante and the underground cells swung open. "You'll do fine."

Dante stepped into the corridor, unable to stop himself being startled when the gate closed again, even though he knew it would happen. The sound of prison doors closing was never comfortable for someone so familiar with the wrong side of the law. Willing himself to be calm, he strolled along the corridor towards Princess Marie-Anne's cell. Dante could smell her before he could see her, the sickening aroma of expensive perfumes cloying his nostrils. When he did reach the cell she was waiting for him, clad in an elaborate gown of silk and brocade, her blonde hair delicately coiffured, her make-up immaculate. She saw him and grimaced.

"Nikolai Dante," she sighed. "Why hasn't someone had the good sense to end your worthless, pathetic life once and for all?"

"Do you think anybody would mind terribly if I murdered the king?" Flintlock asked loudly as he strode into the servants' dining hall at the Palace of London. "I mean, if I accidentally stabbed him to death with one of those blasted paint brushes, or arranged for him to be impaled on something large and fatal – do you think anyone would raise a finger to object? I doubt it, I bloody doubt it!"

Spatchcock was next into the room and dismayed to discover half the palace staff had heard his associate's petulant outburst. "He's joking, he's joking."

"I bloody well am not," Flintlock replied. "Henry may be king, but he is madder than a badger in a hot air balloon.

We could pay an assassin to finish the king off – call it a mercy killing. How much money have you got?" The former aristocrat plunged his hands inside Spatchcock's pockets to search for cash but quickly withdrew them again. "My word, what is in there? Are you keeping worms now?"

"Just the one," Spatchcock replied with a smirk. "He's my best friend."

Flintlock shuddered with revulsion. "Don't tell me anymore, I don't want to know." He spun round to find dozens of staff glaring at him with ill-disguised disgust. "I say, what's the matter?"

A pageboy folded his arms, a sour expression on his face. "You are! Since you two arrived with your lord and master, the whole palace has been in uproar – routines disrupted, the king doing whatever he pleases, the Queen Mother amok amongst the pages – it's a nightmare!"

"What's your name, boy?" Flintlock demanded.

"Fitzwilliam. Darcy Fitzwilliam."

"Well, Master Fitzwilliam, our arrival may have upset the rhythm of your working day but that's as nothing to the indignities I've been subjected to! Your royal highness has required me to pose nude as a subject for him to paint in watercolours."

"Is that what he was trying to paint?" Spatchcock asked. "I wasn't too sure."

Flintlock ignored this comment. "When I got a glimpse of the painting in question, it transpired King Henry had me posing like a fool for nothing – he choose to paint a banana!"

"Are you sure it was a banana?"

"Look, you vile little man, I think I know a banana when I see one!"

Spatchcock shrugged. "I thought it looked more like a painting of your pen–"

"Don't be ridiculous. The thing in the portrait was shaped like a banana!"

"So's your–"

"It was covered in little black spots!"

"Still sounds like–"

"And it was yellow from one end to the other!" Flintlock concluded, glaring at Spatchcock. "And before you say another word, no, my willy is not yellow and it does not look like a banana!"

Spatchcock nodded gravely, waiting for his friend to calm down. Only when Flintlock's nostrils finished flaring did Spatchcock speak again. "Not a full-sized banana, anyway."

The two men were still fighting on the dining hall floor when a footman came in, saying the Queen Mother requested their presence. "Any idea why she needs us?" Spatchcock asked.

"Something to do with a corset, a crowbar and a pot of lubricant," the footman replied, struggling to keep the grin from his features. "And a feather duster, too."

Flintlock wailed bleakly. "Why did I ever let Dante talk me into coming home again? And where is that Russian rapscallion in our hour of need?"

Dante smiled blandly as the princess cursed his name, questioned his parentage and mocked the size of his reproductive organs. "It's a pleasure to see you again, too, Your Highness," he replied once her rant had come to an end. "Yes, I am a bastard. No, I don't mind you taking my name in vain. And as for the contents of my pants…" Dante paused to look down appreciatively at his groin, then grinned broadly. "I haven't had many complaints in that department lately."

"Because no woman is fool enough to sleep with you, most likely!" the princess replied.

"You've been behind bars too long," Dante observed. "Prison has coarsened you."

Marie-Anne hurled another mouthful of abuse and obscenities at him. "See what I mean?"

"Why are you here?" she demanded.

"Your beloved father invited me to Britannia."

"My beloved father is a simpering dolt who doesn't know one day from the next. He isn't fit to lead a dog, let alone rule a country!"

"King Henry is a delightful eccentric," Dante countered.

"King Henry is a doddering lunatic. The sooner he's dead the better."

"When have you scheduled the assassination?"

"What?" The princess glared at her visitor as if he was the madman.

"Your father believes there is a plot to have him murdered, something that would conveniently clear the way for you as heir to the throne." Dante folded his arms. "The king summoned me to Britannia to prevent that from happening."

Marie-Anne stared at him in disbelief, then a grin slowly spread across her pert, pretty face before she dissolved into a fit of giggles. "Y-You?" she spluttered between gasps for air. "P-Protect my father?"

"I've done it before," Dante protested. "I can do it again!"

The princess sniggered with quiet satisfaction. "The sole reason you saved his life last time was thanks to the intervention of an entire platoon of airborne Romanov troops. But for them I would now be in my rightful place as ruler of Britannia."

This bickering is getting you nowhere, the Crest pointed out. *If there is a plot to kill the king, you need details.*

"When will the assassination take place?" Dante demanded.

"I don't know," Marie-Anne replied smugly. "Not precisely."

"But you admit there will be an attempt on the king's life?"

She shrugged. "I certainly hope so. He's an embarrassment to the entire country."

"Answer the question!" Dante bellowed.

"Why should I?" the princess spat back at him. "I've been in this place for six years now, Dante. I know they'll never

ever let me out while my father is still alive. What possible reason would I have for preventing his murder, assuming I even knew anything about this alleged plot?"

Game, set and match to her royal highness. New balls, anyone?

"Shut up," Dante said.

"Make your mind up," Marie-Anne replied, not realising his comment had not been directed at her. "Either you want me to talk or you don't."

"What I want doesn't seem to matter, does it?"

"Perhaps not, but I'm going to give you a piece of advice anyway," she said. "I may be a captive but I still have friends in high places. A whisper of conspiracy has reached my ears, no doubt the same whisper that has penetrated the befuddled mind of my dear, soon to be departed, father. In the next twenty-four hours I expect to be released, due to the untimely death of a royal personage not too far from this godforsaken prison. Is that what you wanted to know? Has that made your task any easier, you repulsive piece of Russian excrement?"

"No, but it should make your trial much shorter if I fail to stop the assassination," Dante replied. "You've admitted to complicity in planning a murder."

No, she hasn't, the Crest interjected. *The princess is no fool. She gave you hints without foundation, a glimpse of the truth but nothing more.*

"We'll see," was all Marie-Anne said, but her smile spoke volumes.

"If an attempt is made on the king's life in the next twenty-four hours, I'll make sure your neck ends up on an executioner's block," Dante vowed.

"If the king dies in the next twenty-four hours," she replied, "my first royal proclamation will be to have you hunted down like the dog you are. All the armies in the Empire will not be able to protect you from my wrath!"

"I've been hunted by the best," he said. "The idle threats of a disgraced royal jailbird don't frighten me, princess. You want to see me dead? Get in line. I'm Nikolai Dante and I'm too cool to kill! Or hadn't I told you?" He strolled away from her cell, ignoring the torrent of abuse that followed him along the corridor. Within minutes he was back inside the royal skimmer as it returned to the Palace of London.

Well, that was pleasant, the Crest commented. *It's safe to say her royal highness could swear for Britannia if she took it up professionally.*

"How did she seem to you?" Dante asked.

You're asking my opinion?

"Yes, how did she seem?" Dante waited but the voice in his head did not reply. "Crest?"

Sorry, I was calculating how many days had elapsed since we were first bonded together.

"Why?"

To see how long it has taken you to ask for my view on something, anything.

Dante sighed. "Sarcasm is the lowest form of wit."

Better to have some wits than only possess half of one.

"Crest!"

Sorry. What was the original question?

"The princess – how did she seem to you?"

Dr Malvern's diagnosis was partially accurate. She may be a sociopath, but her narcissistic personality disorder is a greater problem. As for her hatred of you, well, obviously, that's quite understandable in the circumstances. The remarkable thing there is how quickly she reached such a fever pitch of antagonism – most women need to meet you four times before their dislike reaches murderous levels.

Dante gritted his teeth. "Putting to one side her feelings towards me, I wanted to know what you thought of her general demeanour."

I would have to say calm. Yes, cool, calm and collected.

"That's what I thought too. Her raging at me was a smoke-screen, a sideshow to distract from her real feelings. She fully expects to be Queen of Britannia before noon tomorrow."

I'm glad to discover all the years I've spent grooming you are finally beginning to pay off. You are, at last, showing some hints of perceptiveness and intelligence.

"Of course," Dante added with a smile, "it might just have been her sexual frustration at never having slept with me that fuelled all that rage and anger."

I take it all back, the Crest muttered despairingly.

As the skimmer approached the royal residence, Dante noticed black smoke rising from one of the windows on the palace's northern face. "Pilot, do you know what's inside that room?"

"It's one of the royal apartments, sir, where King Henry and the Queen Mother live."

"Bojemoi," Dante gasped. "We're too late. The assassins have already attacked!"

Dante sprinted through the palace, shouting for the nearest pageboys and footmen to follow him. By the time he reached the royal apartments smoke was billowing from beneath the doors. Dante kicked them open and threw himself inside, bio-blades already extended in anticipation of a battle to the death. Instead he found King Henry dancing naked around a pyre of burning furniture and paintings in the middle of the carpet. An equally undressed and somewhat sheepish Spatchcock was flinging more fuel on to the flames.

"Nicola, there you are!" the king proclaimed happily. "Come and join us, we're performing a rain dance to summon Cumulonimbus, the god of torrential downpours!"

Dante retracted his bio-blades. "If you don't mind my asking, sire – why?"

"Why? Well, why not? The more the merrier, eh, Cocksplutch?"

"Yes, your majesty," Spatchcock replied, throwing another painting onto the roaring fire before joining in the king's gyrations with gleeful abandon.

Dante folded his arms. "No, sire, I was asking why you were doing a rain dance indoors. Isn't it more traditional to perform such rituals outside?"

"I can hardly venture out with assassins lurking behind every corner, can I?"

"I suppose not," Dante agreed. "Then perhaps you could have foregone the fire?"

"I've never heard such arrant nonsense," the king spluttered, coming to an abrupt halt. Spatchcock blundered into the back of the monarch, unable to stop his forward momentum in time. Henry gasped in surprise before looking over his shoulder unhappily. "I say, old chap, careful where you're sticking that thing – I don't mind a bit of sport but there's a time and place for buggering about, Cockscratch, and this isn't it!"

"Sorry, your majesty," Spatchcock said apologetically, retracting the rolled up canvas he had accidentally jabbed into Henry's back.

"I should think so too!" The king turned back to Dante. "I was hoping to watch the annual cheddar cheese chasing championships from Cheshire, but the Britannia Broadcasting Corporation will insist on covering the real tennis tournament at Wombledin."

"Wimbledon?"

"That's the chappy! So I decided to summon some rain clouds to wash out play for the day." Henry peered through the smoke to the view outside. "No sign of success yet, alas!"

"And the broken window?" Dante asked.

"That was me," Spatchcock admitted. "The room started filling up with smoke, so I decided to create some ventilation. Smashing the glass seemed the only sensible option."

"I'm surprised you didn't set off every smoke alarm in the palace."

"Disabled the ones in here before we started, old chap," the king replied, absentmindedly scratching his dangling scrotum. "We're not madmen, you know!"

"Of course not, your majesty," Dante sighed. "But there are smoke detectors in other rooms besides this one." No sooner had the words left his mouth than an alarm started ringing nearby. A monsoon of cold water gushed from the apartment's overhead sprinklers.

"By Jove, it worked!" The king resumed his rain dance, waving his arms in triumph. "I told you, Cocksnitch! Dull old Nicola didn't believe us, but we proved her wrong, eh?"

"Yes, your majesty!" Spatchcock replied, shouting to be heard above the deluge. Pageboys and footmen were racing round the apartment, trying to rescue antique furniture and artworks from the indoor rainstorm. Dante remained by the doorway, slowly shaking his head.

"Twenty-four hours," he told himself. "Just keep this lunatic alive another twenty-four hours and then we can get out of this madhouse."

Congratulations Dante, the Crest said. *For once in your adult life you are the most sensible person in the room. I suggest you savour the sensation while it lasts.*

Dante waited until Spatchcock danced within reach and then pulled him to one side. "I doubt the answer to this question will make me happy, but I don't suppose you know where Flintlock is?"

The grubby-faced runt shrugged. "Last time I saw his lordship, he was trying to escape the amorous advances of the Queen Mother."

A terrified scream from out in the corridor got Dante's attention. He looked out in time to see a naked Flintlock race past with what looked like a feather duster protruding from between his buttocks. Moments later Babs appeared clad in black stockings and a crimson corset, her not inconsiderable bosom bouncing playfully as she scuttled by, a crowbar in one hand and a large pot of lubricant in the other. "Come here, you little tease!" she shouted after the fleeing Flintlock. "You know you love it!"

. . .

Four hours later Dante had finally got the rampant royals back under some sort of control. King Henry grudgingly agreed to resume wearing trousers and stop setting fire to priceless Britannia heirlooms, while the Queen Mother was given a fresh dose of royal jelly to calm her down. The Crest had analysed the viscous purple foodstuff and marvelled at its restorative qualities. *One spoonful of this is enough to halt the ageing process – temporarily, of course. Two spoonfuls actually reverses the process. How much is the Queen Mother consuming?*

Dante had already checked with the royal chef Ramsey. "Two litres a day, every day, for the past twenty years apparently."

No wonder her behaviour is somewhat erratic. This jelly contains trace elements of mind-altering chemicals. After eating so much for so long it's astounding she can still form sentences.

"Try telling that to Flintlock." The beleaguered Brit had spent three hours hiding in a broom cupboard and was only coaxed out with the promise that Babs would be suitably restrained. Now Flintlock, Spatchcock and Dante were all gathered in the palace's opulent drawing room on the tenth floor, watching the king and his mother bickering on a chaise longue.

"I keep telling you to cut down on that blasted jelly, Babs! It's sending you doolally."

"That's rich coming from a man who wears a gorilla suit to the opening of Parliament!"

"At least the only lovers I chase were born in the same century as me–"

"Enough!" Dante bellowed, his patience utterly exhausted. "I've listened to you two fight, squabble and rant long enough! Bojemoi, you're meant to be mother and son, not competitors in a constant contest to outdo each other in acts of lust-addled lunacy!"

The abashed pair stared at the rich oriental rug on the floor in front of them.

"Well?" Dante demanded. "What have you got to say for yourselves?"

Henry and his mother mumbled something inaudible under their breath.

"I can't hear you!"

"We're sorry," the royals admitted.

"That's better," Dante agreed. "Now, if the urge should take either of you to start a fire in the middle of a room, what should you do?"

"Ask for help from one of the servants?" Henry asked sweetly.

"No! You never start fires in the middle of a room!" Dante thundered, his fists shaking.

"Oh," the king replied sulkily.

"And what about sexually molesting the royal staff? And before anyone mentions penises, by staff I mean the household retainers – chambermaids, pageboys and footmen."

Babs stuck out her bottom lip. "We shouldn't exploit our status for our own gratification."

"Exactly."

The Queen Mother folded her arms. "But what's the point of having all this power and status if we can't exploit it?"

"Dash it, you're right, Babs!" Henry agreed. He jumped to his feet and began pacing back and forth in front of a large picture window that offered a glorious view of central London. In the late afternoon sun the city gleamed like a trophy, light glinting off the towers and spires. "I won't be told what to do in my own kingdom, not even by you, Nicola. We may be betrothed but King Henry Windsor McKray takes orders from no woman!"

"Oh, do sit down and shut up," his mother sighed.

"Yes, dear," the king said meekly, returning to the chaise longue. Dante's attention was caught by a flash of light outside the window.

"What was that? It almost looked like a–"

Suddenly the pane of glass exploded inwards, showering the drawing room with razor-sharp shards. Dante screamed a warning as he dived towards the king. "Everybody, get down!"

Spatchcock and Flintlock had not needed telling, having already taken cover at the first sign of trouble. Their time with the Rudinshtein Irregulars had drummed into them the need for speed when in danger, but both also possessed an unusually strong sense of self-preservation. The king and his mother lacked such killer instincts, which was why they both suffered mortal wounds in the next few seconds. The first bullet was sent askew when it shattered the window, flying sideways into a wall to emerge in an adjoining room, where it startled several servants.

The second projectile had no such problems. But for Dante's diving tackle the round would have exploded the king's head like a hammer smashing a ripe watermelon. Instead it entered Henry's left shoulder blade, punctured a lung and departed through his chest, a few centimetres above his heart. The exit wound removed a clump of flesh the size of a child's fist, along with a shower of blood and bone fragments. The third bullet missed the king altogether as he tumbled to the floor beneath Dante, but the Queen Mother was not so fortunate. Babs was standing up to see what all the fuss was about when the window exploded. She had time to gasp in shock before the third bullet shot inside her open mouth and removed the back half of her skull, taking much of her brain stem with it. The elderly nymphomaniac was dead before her body had slumped back on to the chaise longue.

Dante rolled off the king, glancing at Babs long enough to know she was beyond help. His right hand reached instinctively for his Huntsman 5000 rifle, but palace protocol had required he surrender it before entering the building. Dante cursed himself for giving in to such stupidity and twisted round to see if any more attacks were imminent. When no more bullets were forthcoming, he ripped a strip of fabric from the Queen Mother's gown and used it as an impromptu bandage on her son. "Crest, can you analyse the trajectory of those bullets, calculate where the assassin is firing from?"

Completing my calculations now, the voice in his head responded tersely. *All three rounds began from a position of not more than sixty-two metres above the ground.*

"Search your database – what's that high on the city sky-line, within range of here?"

Two structures, but only one has a clear line of sight – Nelson's Column.

"Then that's where I'll find the bastard who did this," Dante snarled. "Spatch! Flintlock! Are you okay?" The two men nodded from their hiding places. "Good, then get over here and look after the king before he bleeds to death."

Spatchcock was immediately crawling across the glass-strewn floor. "What about Babs?"

Dante shook his head grimly. The Queen Mother had been a sex-crazed centenarian, but she never meant anybody any harm. Her murder deserved to be avenged as much as the attack upon the king. "Crest, how long does the fastest route to the palace landing pad take from here?"

Three minutes and seventeen seconds.

"Too long. I'll have to take a short-cut to our killer!" Dante pulled himself into a crouch, then ran to the shattered window and dived through the hole, falling towards almost certain death.

In the drawing room Spatchcock ignored Dante's daredevil departure and concentrated on tending to the king. Blood was coursing from Henry's wounds faster than it could be staunched. "Flintlock, get out from behind that chair and go for help!"

"Do I have to?" the inveterate coward asked feebly.

Spatchcock spat a curse at him and Flintlock scuttled to the drawing room door, calling for the royal staff. Within seconds a phalanx of footmen and pageboys was pouring into the room, Darcy Fitzwilliam among them, his young face shocked by the violence he found. "My God – they've butchered the royal family!"

"Don't be an ass," Spatchcock snarled. "We didn't do this – we're trying to save them!"

Fitzwilliam searched the faces of the others. "You heard them in the dining hall! They were shouting about killing the king! Now they've done it!"

Flintlock shook his head, pointing at the shattered picture window. "The shots came from outside. We were lucky not to get hit ourselves!"

The pageboy jabbed a finger into Flintlock's face. "Murderer!" he screamed.

Agent Penelope Goodnight was making love to a beautiful woman when the emergency signal came through. For six months Britannia Intelligence's finest female operative had been working on the French ambassador, breaking down her barriers. The ambassador was as careful as she was beautiful, a full bodied woman who kept herself in shape despite having been a widow for ten years. It had required all of Goodnight's cunning, feminine charm and guile to persuade the ambassador into having an affair that would make her susceptible to coercion and blackmail. Now, after all that delicate preparation, all those subtle romantic overtures, the Marquise de Rosemonde had finally given in to lust – Goodnight's mission objective was about to be consummated. But, just as the secret agent's fingers invaded the Marquise's lingerie, a voice of authority spoke in Goodnight's concealed earpiece.

"All agents, respond immediately!"

Startled by the harsh, patrician voice, Goodnight pulled away involuntarily pushing her long hair away from her face.

"No, *mon cherie*, don't stop now," the ambassador pleaded. "I resisted you for so long, don't torture me like this. I have surrendered myself to you. I can't live unless I make you happy. I promise – no more refusals, and no more regrets."

"All agents, respond immediately!" the earpiece said again.

Goodnight knew ignoring the message was impossible. It would keep repeating itself, louder and louder, until it got a response. Better to find out why the emergency channel had been activated, then return to the job in hand. "Forgive me, I am not sure I can go through with this."

"No, do not torment me," the French woman pleaded, her fingers grasping imploringly at thin air as Goodnight climbed off the silk sheets.

"Give me a moment to think – please?"

"Only if you promise to return and... fulfil me."

Goodnight smiled. "I promise." The secret agent retreated to the doorway, blew a lust-filled kiss to the Marquise, then slipped from the room. Once out of earshot, Goodnight activated the earpiece microphone. "What the hell is so important that you pull me from between the French ambassador's thighs?"

"The king is dying or possibly dead by now, the victim of an assassination plot. The Queen Mother's corpse is getting cold, and the government is in uproar. All operatives are being recalled to headquarters immediately for a full briefing."

"But my mission–"

"Can wait! F is allowing no exemptions from this, and you know what a bitch she can be if anybody challenges her orders."

"Don't remind me." Goodnight's department had undergone a brutal purge, courtesy of Britannia Intelligence's new commander. "So how do I placate the French ambassador?"

"You're creative – make something up. I'm sure her thighs will be just as warm and welcoming once this little emergency has past."

"I wouldn't count on that. It's taken me half a year to melt this ice queen."

"Nevertheless, F's command stands. Put your trousers on and get back here!"

FOUR

"Wrath is a poor adviser."
– Russian proverb

"Scotland Yard has served as London's police headquarters for close to a millennium. The original building was sited near a courtyard supposedly used by a Caledonian king, a myth that gave the area its name. In the many centuries since, the capital's police force has shifted headquarters more than a dozen times as a consequence of overcrowding, terrorist attacks or structural problems. Following the second relocation the building became known as New Scotland Yard. After that it was decided that adding further prefixes would verge on the ludicrous and all subsequent headquarters have been known simply as Scotland Yard. The current police HQ is a gross, intimidating cube of concrete and steel less than a kilometre from the Palace of London. What few windows it has are restricted to the top floor. Only the most dangerous suspects are ever taken to Scotland Yard for interrogation, usually for matters that threaten national security. Fewer still ever emerge alive."

– Extract from *Places to Avoid in Britannia,*
first edition

Dante came round in a dark, dank cell. The air was thick with the stench of stale piss and fear, while a cluster of flies feasted on a clump of faeces in one corner. The walls were coarse, grey cement, as was the floor beneath Dante's battered and bruised body. The sole source of light was a small opening high above the blank metal door. Dante uncurled himself from a foetal position to find his hands were cuffed together behind his back. Manacles also bound his ankles, a few links of chain between them. His jacket and boots were gone, as was his leather belt. He shivered in his white linen shirt and thin trousers.

How long had he been held prisoner here? More to the point, where was this place? Dante rasped a hand across his neck below the line where his beard usually stopped. Not more than a night's growth, so that made it Wednesday morning. As for his location, he could hear murmuring voices outside the cell, gruff London accents clearly audible even if their words were not. So, he was almost certainly still in Britannia. The last thing he could recall was being pulled from the Thames and accused of trying to murder the king. Everything after that was a jumble of memories from the previous days.

The sound of approaching footsteps snapped Dante back to the present.

He heard a beeping noise, then the door swung inwards, flooding the narrow chamber with light. Once his eyes had adjusted, Dante could see three men standing in the corridor, staring at him. The one in the centre he recognised from the previous night – an inspector of some sort. The man certainly displayed all the dull arrogance of a policeman, his stance redolent of self importance. The inspector nodded to the other two, a burly pair whose uniforms marked them out as guards. "He should be ready," the inspector said. "Take him to interrogation room two. Don't give him any water. If he soils himself, he can stay that way until we get some answers."

The two men produced truncheons and moved inside the cell, grinning from ear to ear. Before the still dazed Dante had time to react blows rained down upon his head, beating all resistance from him. Blackness closed in, a blessed relief from the dull thuds of pain.

The second time he came round, Dante was strapped to a chair in a white room, his arms pinned behind him with both wrists clamped to the back of the seat. When he extended his bio-blades they were unable to find anything to cut. Someone had obviously done their research and found a way to negate the abilities given him by the Crest. "Crest, where am I?" But no reply came. "Crest?"

"Good, it can't hear you," a crisp, slightly nasal male voice replied. Dante twisted round to see the police inspector leaning against one of the clean, bare walls.

"Why not? Have you drugged me?"

The inspector smiled thinly. "The Tsar may possess the chemicals to overcome a Romanov Weapons Crest, but we are not so fortunate here in Britannia." He gestured at their surroundings: a perfectly square chamber, its walls, floor and ceiling all gleaming white. There were no light fixtures visible anywhere. Instead all the surfaces gave off a faint glow. "We call this the White Room. All the surfaces have a luminescent coating that also debilitates psychic abilities. This has the side effect of breaking the link between you and your Weapons Crest."

"Who are you?" Dante demanded.

"I told you my name last night, when I arrested you for the assassination of King Henry."

"He's dead?"

"Not yet, but it's a matter of time. His wounds are severe. The surgeons and doctors doubt he will survive another day." The inspector extracted a wooden pipe from his grey jacket and tapped the bowl against the side of Dante's chair. Next he produced a slim packet of tobacco from another pocket and began filling his pipe. Finally, he struck a match and used its flame to light up. "My name is Rucka – Inspector Rucka, of the Yard."

"Rucka?" Dante snorted derisively. "That rhymes so nicely with fu–"

The inspector lashed out with a fist, the vicious blow snapping Dante's head sideways. Rucka waited until his captive had recovered before replying. "Spare me any juvenile attempts at humour. Trust me, I have heard them all over the years and I do not intend to be insulted by a murdering misanthrope like you."

Dante spat a mouthful of blood on the floor. "Hope that doesn't ruin your interior design."

Rucka ignored the comment, preferring to suck on his pipe. "You may be interested to know both your accomplices were captured at the scene of the crime."

"Spatchcock and Flintlock? They aren't my accomplices – none of us had anything to do with the attempt on King Henry's life."

"You simply happened to be in the room when he was shot, is that it?"

"He invited us to Britannia," Dante insisted. "The king believed someone was planning to assassinate him."

"So he wasn't quite the lunatic everyone thought, eh?" Rucka said thoughtfully. "But his judgement of character still leaves a lot to be desired."

"Henry wanted me to protect him!"

"Poacher turned gamekeeper, is that your story?"

"Sorry?"

"You claim to have been acting as his majesty's personal bodyguard, is that it?"

"Yes," Dante agreed vehemently.

"Then why did you flee the scene of the crime?"

"I didn't flee. I was doing your job for you – hunting down the assassin!"

"I see. Well, can you give a description of this person you claim to have been hunting?"

"The shooter was wearing a mask so I didn't see his face."

"But you're certain it was a man – why?"

"I…" Dante thought back to the previous night, trying to remember past the beatings. "I got a glimpse of him, after I was thrown into the river. He was bald, with a goatee beard and an unhappy face. His accent, it wasn't local. I heard him arranging a meeting with someone – I think he called him 'the old man'."

Rucka arched an eyebrow at his prisoner. "Bald, a goatee beard, an unhappy face – not exactly a description likely to make finding this alleged suspect any easier, is it?"

"It's not my job to make your job easy," Dante snarled.

"Quite the reverse, I would have thought." The inspector smiled thinly. "All of this is irrelevant. Every piece of evidence points to you as the assassin. Your partners in crime were heard by royal household staff loudly proclaiming how much they wanted to see the king dead. You fled the scene when your plan went awry and resisted arrest when my men intervened. You even told Princess Marie-Anne of your plans to murder her father! Hardly the actions of an innocent man, wouldn't you agree?"

"The princess hates me, she'd say anything to incriminate me. Diavolo, she probably hired the assassin. Can't you see I'm being framed? How stupid are you?"

"Stupid enough to have caught Nikolai Dante, supposedly the most dangerous man in the Empire. Stupid enough to have him banged to rights for murdering our beloved Queen Mother. Stupid enough to have found more than sufficient evidence to prove complicity in King Henry's slaying – assuming his royal highness does not survive."

"What about the shattered window? That broke when the first bullet hit it. You must have noticed the window was smashed in from outside – how did I manage that while I was still inside the room, inspector? Answer that!"

Rucka smiled. "Quite simple. You had an accomplice shoot the window from outside, in an effort to provide you with an alibi. For all I know your accomplice is this bald man with the goatee and unhappy face to whom you seem intent upon shifting all the blame."

"This is ludicrous!" Dante snapped. "I demand to see a lawyer. You do still have lawyers in Britannia, don't you?"

"There's no need to be insolent," the inspector warned. "Of course we still have lawyers. Some of the finest legal minds in the Empire reside in Britannia. Alas, they will be of little use in this case, since you have already been found guilty of murder."

"I haven't even been tried! What about due process, the letter of the law?"

"Overruled, in view of the national crisis precipitated by your heinous actions." Rucka smiled. "The people of Britannia are demanding justice and that is what we shall give them. Your accomplices are already en route to the Tower of London where they will await execution. Once we have concluded our little chat, you will be taken to join them."

"This isn't justice, it's a farce! No one has the authority to overrule an entire legal system!"

"I do," a woman's voice replied. A doorway appeared in the seamless white walls and Princess Marie-Anne entered, smiling broadly. She was wearing a pristine white gown, a diamond tiara perched atop her blonde tresses. Once she was inside the door vanished, leaving no chance for escape. "With my father so close to death, the government felt obliged to release me from the Tower – I am the heir apparent, after all."

"You're a figurehead," Dante insisted. "The monarchy has no real power in Britannia."

"Not as such, but I contacted the Tsar. Vladimir was most amused to hear of your travails and only too happy to vouchsafe me sufficient authority to overrule our tiresome legal process. He's hoping to clear a window in his schedule for an Imperial visit to Britannia, simply so he can attend your public execution – he must hate you almost as passionately as I do. Isn't that sweet?" The princess nodded to Rucka, who produced a document and read aloud from it.

"Nikolai Dante, by the power vested in the nation of Britannia by Vladimir Makarov, Tsar of All the Russias, you are hereby found guilty of murder and sentenced to death. You are to be taken from this place to await execution, whereupon your lifeless body shall be transported to Saint Petersburg for verification and vivisection. Has the convicted felon anything to say?"

Dante spat a fresh mouthful of blood at the princess, spattering her gown with crimson phlegm. Her mouth remained fixed in a smile but her eyes glared at him with murderous intensity. "For that little indignity I shall ensure your execution is as slow and painful as humanly possible. I look forward to seeing you die, Dante – you have been a thorn in my side for far too long." She snapped her fingers and the doorway reappeared. "Get this filth out of my sight," she commanded. "Tell the warders at the Tower of London to put him in my former cell. He should find the accommodations less than satisfactory."

Agent Goodnight strode north across Westminster Bridge towards the most famous clock in the Empire, Big Ben. The covert operative moved unnoticed among the tourists crowding the bridge, the visitors battling for the best position to have themselves pictured in front of the legendary landmark. None had a clue the secret HQ of Britannia Intelligence was a few metres away, the agent thought, but then it would hardly have been a secret if they did. Goodnight nonchalantly descended a stone staircase on the bridge's eastern side, close to the Houses of Parliament.

The staircase passed an inconspicuous green metal door in one of the bridge's support columns. Goodnight rested a hand lightly against the door for five seconds, letting hidden circuitry identify and compare the palm-print, heat signature and DNA likeness with that held on file. Once the computer-controlled system was satisfied, the secret agent had permission to enter, the door slid open with a sigh and Goodnight slipped inside. Moments later the door was closed, nearby tourists still blissfully unaware of what they had missed.

There was a tiny elevator on the other side of the doors, no bigger than a broom cupboard. It plunged thirty metres into the ground, far below the level of the Thames and the old Underground train tunnels. The elevator shuddered to a halt and a new door opened, allowing Goodnight access to Britannia Intelligence's headquarters. The secret agent strolled along the corridors, nodding to other staff members and saluting whenever a senior officer strode past. In less than a minute Goodnight slipped into the main briefing room, where the lights had been dimmed in anticipation of F's arrival. Dozens of other operatives and HQ staff were gathered in the musty chamber, most seated in rows of stiff-backed chairs. Those who had arrived late lined the walls, all facing the small podium at the front of the briefing room.

Agent Golightly noticed her colleague's arrival and sidled over. "Cutting it fine?"

"I made it, didn't I?" Goodnight said with a smile. "Where's the ice queen?"

"Due any second now. How's the ambassador?"

"I had to pull out at the last minute." Goodnight slid a hand across the other agent's buttocks, gently massaging them. "And we both know how frustrating that can be."

Golightly shook her pretty head, a rueful smile on her pursed lips. "Tease! Always leave them wanting more, that should be your motto."

"I'll try to remember that when I commission my epitaph," Goodnight replied. The low murmur of voices around them died away as their commander approached the podium.

■ ■ ■

When Dante came round for the third time, he was lying on a cold metal floor, chains and manacles binding his wrists and ankles together once more. The first thing to enter his mind was an after-image of the last thing he could recall. Rucka had arranged for Dante to be beaten unconscious again once the princess had left the White Room. "It's the only way to make certain you can't escape before we get you to the Tower," the inspector explained as truncheons pummelled Dante. "After that, you cease to be my responsibility. You will be what one of our greatest authors called an SEP – Somebody Else's Problem."

Dante made a mental note to kick the crap out of Rucka if they should ever meet again. The inspector was the worst kind of bully, one who gets other people to do his dirty work, the sort who rarely sullies his own hands. But dealing with Rucka would have to wait. Dante had more pressing problems now, such as finding a way out of his situation.

Whatever you do, don't speak. Don't do anything to let the guards know you're conscious – they'll only beat you senseless again and your enhanced healing abilities are still struggling to mend a fractured skull and severe concussion. So, for once, keep silent and listen to me.

Dante nodded his head imperceptibly to let the Crest know its words were understood.

Good. You're in the cargo hold of a police hover-van called a Black Maria. *By my estimation the vehicle should arrive at the Tower of London within minutes, so there isn't much time. There are three guards in here with you, and three more in the front. All except the driver are armed. Relax your mental defences and cede control of your bio-blades to me.*

Dante willed himself to relax but involuntarily tensed as the Crest flexed inside his mind.

I said relax! If you don't escape before this van reaches the Tower, you may not get another chance. Empty your mind of all intelligent thoughts – an easy task for you, of all people.

Dante ignored the jibe and concentrated on thinking about nothing. Gradually the Crest claimed control of his nervous system, an uneasy sensation akin to having a dozen spiders running back and forth across his brain.

That's better, the Crest said. *Extruding bio-circuitry... now.*

Dante watched as ripples of purple and silver danced below the skin of his hands. His fingernails slowly stretched themselves out into elongated talons, before curling round to infiltrate the locks on his manacles. Within moments each binding was undone. Dante tried to move but the Crest told him to wait.

Your limbs are stiff and sore. Allow thirty seconds for your restored circulation to revive them, it urged. *All the guards are wearing body armour, but it only extends down to their thighs – they don't expect to be attacked at floor level. There are two men directly behind you within striking distance, and a third beyond them. He's the most dangerous target as you can't reach him straight away.* Dante gave another nod to show his understanding. *Good. Your arms and legs should have recovered. I'm releasing control of the bio-circuitry. Do your worst.*

Dante allowed himself a grim smile, extended his bio-blades to their full length, and then went on the attack. He swiped his swords across the floor, neatly severing the feet of the two guards within reach. They went down screaming, their blood spraying the air. The third man was still drawing his weapon when Dante dived full-length at him, bio-blades pinning the guard to the back door. When Dante ripped his blade free, the dead man slid mutely to the floor. "Three down, three to go," he muttered. "Crest, how far are we off the ground?"

About a hundred metres. Diving out the back door is not an option.

"Guess I'll have to land this thing instead." Dante strode to the front end of the cargo hold and flattened his hands against the wall. "How far am I from the other guards in the front seat?"

Half an arm's length. Why?

● ● ●

The woman known as F would never be described as beautiful. True, a mischievous sparkle sometimes appeared in the corner of her eyes and her bosom had a comely aspect to its sway, but her looks were no aphrodisiac. She knew her face was haughty and arrogant, with its high cheekbones and prominent, almost Grecian nose. Her mouth was unusually wide but it rarely had a chance to smile, such was her stern demeanour. She kept her body hidden behind an armoury of tweed skirts and polo neck jumpers, her hair clipped into a curt bob. Everything about her outward appearance indicated she meant business. Only the stiletto heels of her black, knee-length leather boots hinted at anything out of ordinary – sensible shoes were not F's style.

Power turned her on; the getting of power, the wielding of it, the delicious delight of having dominance over another human being. She savoured it as a gourmet enjoys fine cuisine. Her rise to prominence within Britannia's intelligence community had not simply been a matter of career fulfilment or proving she was the best of her generation. No, for F the acquisition of authority was a way of sating her most rapacious desires. Every order she gave, every memo she drafted, every underling she disciplined or humiliated – each of these acts was a dirty little thrill. Addressing a gathering of every available operative in Britannia, commanding their attention, holding them in her thrall... that was a multiple orgasm for F. But none of her staff would ever know that from her expression.

She glared at those assembled, hands clasped together behind her back. "By now you will all have heard about the tragic events at the Palace of London last night. The king remains in a critical condition, with surgeons offering little hope of recovery. The Queen Mother's body is being worked on by the finest undertakers. Once fit to be seen by the public, it will lie in state at Westminster Abbey before a full state funeral is held. With the king incapacitated, her royal highness Princess Marie-Anne has been released from the Tower of London and is already assuming responsibility for many of her father's day-to-day duties."

There was a murmur among the agents but it was silenced when F cleared her throat. "I do not recall asking for anyone's opinion," she snapped, a shiver of delight running down her spine. "Questions will be asked with regards to how the assassin got through our defences, why we did not anticipate this attack and what we could or should have done to prevent it. No doubt heads will roll, but not from within this department, you may be assured of that. However, we must remain vigilant, keeping one step ahead of the police investigation, to ensure the intelligence community does not take the blame for this lamentable incident. Your individual controllers have specific assignments for each of you. All other investigations and assignments are temporarily suspended until this matter is resolved. This is a black day in the history of Britannia – let our conduct show that we can respond to the situation with the verve and skill required! That is all."

F nodded curtly, then stepped down from the podium, moving among the operatives and headquarters staff as they filed out. Her eyes lit upon a particular agent who had been at the back of the room. "Goodnight!"

"Yes, ma'am?"

"Wait here, please – I have a special assignment for you."

"Yes, ma'am."

Once the room had emptied, F gestured for Goodnight to sit down. But the head of intelligence remained standing, to reinforce her position of dominance. "First of all, I must remind you of our policy regarding sexual harassment – groping fellow agents like young Golightly may help pass the time in staff meetings, but it is strictly prohibited under Britannia Intelligence's rules and regulations. Do I make myself clear?"

"Yes, ma'am," Goodnight said meekly, eyes not meeting F's gaze.

"You may be our finest seducer, but that does not give you leave to practice on my staff."

"No, ma'am."

"Very well," F said, moderating her tone slightly. "Now, this special assignment – you have been requested by Princess Marie-Anne for an unspecified task to be undertaken on her behalf. No matter what she asks of you or offers you as a reward, remember where your true loyalties lie. An unmarked hover-car will transport you to the palace. In the meantime, I suggest you have a shower and change into something suitable."

The agent frowned. "How can I know what's suitable if I don't know what this task is?"

F smiled. "Use your imagination. I'm told it's one of your strong suits."

Constable Jackson Shaw loved to fly. He loved to fly in planes, in hover-vehicles, even in airships. All his life he had been obsessed with flying, but his limited intellect had prevented him becoming a professional pilot. Shaw was big, he was burly and he was thicker than concrete, all of which left one career opportunity to him: Shaw became a policeman in the Britannia Royal Constabulary. His passion for flying soon shone through and he was given the job of ferrying prisoners in a Black Maria hover-van. It was poorly paid, often mind-numbingly dull work, but when Shaw took to the sky he felt a little closer to heaven.

Today's trip to the Tower of London was unusual, but not unheard of. The government was not afraid of locking away political prisoners in the ancient dungeons there. The poor sod in the back was supposedly the most dangerous man in the Empire, or so Shaw's boss had told him. That must be why the prisoner had been beaten unconscious for the journey, but it didn't sit well with Shaw. He didn't have the stomach for handing out punishment beatings. He preferred being behind the wheel of a hover-van, zooming across the sky.

The two men beside him in the front seat had resisted all attempts at conversation. The *Black Maria* started its final approach to the Tower and the driver gave up trying to talk with them. Surly buggers, he decided. Let 'em rot. Shaw didn't notice when a pair of purple and silver blades stabbed through the metal wall behind his passengers, neatly slicing their spinal chords. Both men slumped backwards in their seats, as if dozing off. They'll get a right rollicking if they're still asleep when we land, the driver thought.

Moments later the passenger side door was ripped open and one of the guards fell out. "What the hell–?" Before Shaw could finish his thought, a hand reached in and extracted the second passenger. The *Black Maria* swerved across the sky as Shaw struggled to control his amazement and terror. Then the prisoner climbed in from outside, slamming the door behind him.

"Who are–? How did you–? I mean, that's– T-That's impossible!" Shaw spluttered.

The prisoner smiled. "I always try to do six impossible things before breakfast."

"But it's nearly midday."

"I haven't had breakfast yet." The prisoner pointed a hand at Shaw and the driver felt a razor-sharp blade press against his neck. "Now, either you land this thing or I throw you out and try to land it myself – you choose."

Shaw loved to fly, but he didn't fancy trying it unassisted.

Dante waited until the *Black Maria* had landed before disabling its systems with his bio-blades. The driver was quaking in his seat, a wet stain round his crotch ample evidence of the man's terror. "Look, I haven't done anything to you, okay?" the policeman pleaded. "I'm not even armed. You go and I promise not to raise the alarm for at least ten minutes. Better still, knock me out and then I can't raise the alarm, can I?"

Dante aimed a bio-blade at the driver's throat. "I could just kill you."

"All the others had guns, you had to kill them to escape. I'm letting you go. Kill me and it's murder. Do you want that on your conscience?"

He's right. Killing him will only confirm you're a murderer doing anything to flee Britannia.

"I don't need your advice," Dante said.

"I know," the driver said, closing his eyes. "But if you're going to kill me, at least make it quick – like you did with the others, okay?"

Dante drew back his bio-blade, then punched the driver in the head, smashing him sideways against the van door.

Dante slid out of the passenger door, looking round in search of a landmark. "Where am I, Crest?"

Two minutes from the Tower, but if you're planning a rescue mission for Spatchcock and Flintlock, you'll need help. The cells are in the most heavily guarded and fortified section.

"Which way is the Tower?"

To your left.

Dante retracted his bio-blades and strode briskly away to his right.

Your other left, the Crest sighed.

"I'm not going to the Tower," Dante replied curtly, "and I'm not planning a rescue mission."

Why not?

"Why should I?"

Spatchcock and Flintlock are your friends.

"Spatchcock and Flintlock are two good-for-nothing para-sites who latched on to me after the war. The only thing they care about is themselves."

Mr Kettle, allow me to introduce you to this black pot.

"Spare me the riddles, Crest. Where's the nearest heliport or international train terminus?"

I was alluding to the fact you are frequently just as guilty as Spatchcock or Flintlock of the charges you accuse them of.

Aren't you even going to try and save them? Flee the country and that will be taken as final, irrevocable proof of your guilt. Those two parasites, as you disingenuously describe them, will be executed in your stead for a crime they didn't commit.

"I never asked them to tag along after me."

No, but you never told them to go away, either. You were their commander during the war, you kept them alive when others could not care less. They respect you, consider themselves your friends and they would not abandon you like this.

Dante laughed bitterly as he quickened his pace. "Flintlock is a craven coward and Spatchcock thinks only of himself. There's been plenty of times when they've left me to die!"

True, but there have also been occasions when they risked their own lives to save yours. What about on Fabergé Island, when they helped you stop that madman's experiments? Or at the Forbidden Citadel – they could have fled when the Imperial Black troops attacked.

"Diavolo, I was there, I know what happened!"

Yet now you choose to ignore it. What kind of man are you?

"You said it yourself, I can't break them out of the Tower single-handed."

Then prove their innocence – and your own – before it is too late.

Dante rounded a corner and saw the London International Train Terminal ahead. "At last!"

Running away won't solve anything, the Crest insisted.

"Spare me the sermon," Dante replied as he approached the train station. "I gave up praying long before I reached puberty."

Perhaps. But I doubt getting out of Britannia will be as simple as you surmise.

Goodnight was escorted into Princess Marie-Anne's private office after passing numerous security checks. The princess gestured grandly to a chair, motioning for the secret agent to sit down. Marie-Anne remained behind an antique black desk lavishly decorated with gold leaf and elaborate carved motifs. Spread out across its surface were swatches of fabrics, dozens of vibrant colours fighting with each other for attention. To Goodnight's eyes it seemed the whole office had been decorated to match the desk, a sinister opulence about the black walls and golden ceiling. The high-ceilinged chamber was thick with the scent of expensive perfume. "Excuse the vile decor in here," the princess said, waving blithely at her surroundings. "My father had it done to irritate my late mother, who hated this desk. I intend this room to be my new seat of power so, of course, I'm having it remodelled immediately."

Goodnight decided against pointing out the king was still alive.

The princess sighed, then swept everything from her desk on to the floor. "None of this will do, none of it. I want something that makes a bold statement about who I am – pinks and pastels are never going to achieve that!" Having finished her display of petulance, Marie-Anne sank into a high-backed leather chair and stared at the new arrival. "So, I'm given to understand you've never failed an assignment."

"Yes, your majesty."

"Give me examples of your latest endeavours – and don't worry, I have full security clearance for anything you might mention."

The secret agent outlined three recent missions: the ongoing seduction of the French ambassador, five months spent undercover as a croupier in the Casino Royale at Monte Carlo, and a torrid weekend spent in bed with the Tsar's senior financial minister that ensured a constant flow of information about the state of the Makarov fortunes.

"Very well. Your credentials are impeccable, so I am going to trust you with a difficult but not unimportant assignment. During his interrogation, the king's assassin alluded to having an accomplice, a bald man with a goatee beard and an unhappy face. He claimed to have last seen this person on

Westminster Bridge, less than an hour after my father was shot. Assuming this individual exists, I want you to find him and bring him before me so I may determine his part in these tragic events. Is that clear?"

"Quite clear, Your Highness."

"I have one stipulation to add. You must not–" But the princess's words were cut off by an abrupt knock at the door. "Come!"

A footman entered and approached Marie-Anne. He whispered a message in her ear, then withdrew. Goodnight was startled by the effect this had on the princess. She became tense and agitated, her shoulders hunching around her neck. "Your majesty, is something wrong? Has the king passed away?"

"It's Dante. He's escaped." The princess rose from her chair and went to look out of a window, her face hidden from Goodnight's view. "This changes everything."

"Perhaps you wish me to leave?"

"No, stay. I meant this changes the nature of your mission. No doubt the police will blunder about in search of this fugitive, along with fools from every other law enforcement agency in Britannia. I want you to find Dante first and bring him to me."

"Is that wise? If he shot your father–"

"I do not recall asking for your advice!"

Goodnight blushed, angry at having overstepped good sense. "My apologies, ma'am."

"You will find Dante and bring him to me. He is not to be captured by anyone else. If he is, I shall hold you personally responsible."

"Yes, your majesty."

"He must be brought to me alive. I want to look into his eyes as the death sentence is carried out." Marie-Anne looked over her shoulder. "Are you a creature of ambition?"

The secret agent frowned. "Yes. Yes, I suppose I am, ma'am."

"Good. Succeed and I shall make you commander of all Britannia Intelligence agencies. Fail and you shall know my wrath like no other person ever has. Do you understand?"

Goodnight nodded. F must have known the assignment would be something of this nature, it explained her reminder about loyalty.

The princess smiled. "I must ask you to reveal nothing of what we have said here today – not to your colleagues, your commander, your family or friends. Betray my trust and the consequences will be ruinous to you and all who know you. Good hunting!"

Goodnight realised the interview was at an end. But a thought occurred that had to be spoken aloud. "Excuse me, Your Highness, but I've seen official briefing papers on this Nikolai Dante before. His Weapons Crest makes him a dangerous, elusive quarry. I've little doubt I can find and catch him, but how do I hold him?"

Marie-Anne returned to the vast, imposing desk. "I was wondering if you would have the wit to ask that. F chose wisely when she sent you." The princess opened a drawer, removed a pair of black handcuffs and tossed them to Goodnight. "When the Tsar heard of Dante's presence here, he sent these bindings by overnight courier. The connecting chain is all but unbreakable, it requires a diamond cutter to sever any of the links. The cuffs themselves incorporate an experimental substance developed by the Tsar's scientists that should disable most Weapons Crest capabilities, such as Dante's bio-blades. While wearing those he will be no more dangerous than any other criminal. Find him, Agent Goodnight. Find him, catch him and deliver him to me – I will make certain justice follows swiftly afterwards."

FIVE

"A thief knows a thief even in the darkest night."
— Russian proverb

"Trains bearing the name *Flying Scotsman* have journeyed up and down Britannia for hundreds of years. The first such vehicle was a steam engine that travelled between London and Edinburgh in the Nineteenth century. The service was discontinued but the name remained alive and was applied to other trains. Most recently the soubriquet has taken on a literal meaning with the introduction of the *Flying Scotsman* hover-train. Predominantly a tourist service, this airborne locomotive and its passenger carriages offer a gentle return to the luxurious train travel of centuries past. It may be most popular with foreign visitors to Britannia, but the *Flying Scotsman* remains one of the most romantic ways of seeing the nation."

— Extract from *Around the Empire in Eighty Ways*,
Mikhail Palinski

The London International Train Terminal's concourse was awash with people, luggage and misery. Every face around Dante was tired or unhappy, the wan features of waiting passengers bleached yellow by harsh overhead lighting. The station was a vast space stretched out beneath a grime-coated glass roof. Three of the four walls were given over to overpriced traders with surly faces. Never in all his days had

Dante seen such a depressing, dispiriting place. It stank of body odour and hopelessness.

"Fuoco," he muttered. "I've been to funerals with better atmospheres. What happened?"

You did, the Crest replied. *Look at the departure boards.*

Above the gate of each platform floated a holographic display unit showing when the next train was due to leave, the stations it would visit and a final destination. All but one of the boards was bright red with the words "TRAIN CANCELLED DUE TO NATIONAL SECURITY ALERT" flashing on and off in large, unfriendly letters. "What's that got to do with me?" Dante asked.

News of your escape has obviously reached the authorities. They have cancelled all international train services out of Britannia. I will hack into the Imperial Net to see if there is another option still open to you.

Dante sighed. As usual, the Crest had been right. Getting out of the country would be all but impossible now. He needed to find a place to lie low, to plan his next move. So far he had been operating on pure instinct and it wasn't enough.

It's the same everywhere: no international flights, no ships are being allowed to leave port, nothing. For all intents and purposes the borders of Britannia have been sealed. It won't be long before they–

The Crest suddenly fell silent, leaving Dante waiting. "Crest? It won't be long before what happens?"

You need to get out of here, it replied. *While you still can.*

"Why?"

Because of what's about to be broadcast on every holographic display in the country.

Dante heard a crisp, slightly nasal voice speaking via the station's public address system. "Is this thing on? Good. People of Britannia, my name is Inspector Rucka of Scotland Yard. I have an important message for each and every one of you." Like everyone else in the station, Dante felt his gaze shift to the departure boards. Each display was filled by Rucka's unsympathetic face. "As you know, our king lies close to death following a cowardly attempt on his life. The same craven attack claimed our beloved Queen Mother Barbara. But you will be overjoyed to hear the Britannia Royal Constabulary has wasted little time in capturing the fiends responsible for this sickening act of terrorism. Two of the culprits await execution. Regretfully I must tell you their ringleader escaped during transportation to the Tower of London, killing five good men in the process. The driver responsible for allowing this fugitive to flee has been executed for his folly."

Dante began walking towards the nearest exit. So much for sparing the driver's life, he thought – my escape still got him killed. The station's outer doors opened to admit a phalanx of policemen, all carrying sidearms and murder in their eyes. Dante quickly retreated the way he had come. The only hiding place on the concourse was a row of antique red phone boxes in the central area, so Dante ducked inside the first empty booth. Even inside, there was no escape from Rucka's relentless broadcast. The Imperial Net screen inside the booth was also showing the inspector's stern speech.

"Every way out of the country has been sealed to prevent the fugitive escaping justice. I gave that order and I hereby apologise to all those innocent, trustworthy citizens whom it has inconvenienced. However, I feel certain you willingly make this sacrifice to help us capture the monster who murdered Queen Babs and mortally wounded our monarch!" Behind Dante all the passengers on the concourse simultaneously applauded, nodding their approval at Rucka's draconian actions.

Bojemoi, Dante fretted, they actually believe these lies.

Rucka's message continued over the clapping. "I show you now the face of the fiend we seek. As I speak policemen are entering all major train stations, airports and transportation centres in search of him. If you have seen this vile killer, approach a constable. With your help, this cowardly assassin cannot remain at large for long. The murderer's name is Nikolai Dante and this is what he looks like." Rucka's face was replaced with a particularly unflattering image of Dante, his face puffy and bruised from one of the many beatings he had taken recently.

"Is that the best photo they've got of me?" Dante protested. "I look terrible!"

It's not your most flattering likeness, the Crest conceded, *but you should be grateful.*

"Why? For making me look fat?"

The less accurate the image, the less likely you are to be identified.

Dante scratched his chin thoughtfully. "There is that, I suppose."

He noticed the line of policemen was getting steadily closer, checking the identity of each and every person on the concourse – man, woman or child. Rucka was back on the holographic displays, a smug smile smeared across his face like excrement on poor quality toilet paper.

"To encourage everyone in Britannia to do the right thing, a reward of ten million roubles is being offered to whomever supplies information leading to Dante's capture. If you see him, contact the number listed below, and apply for your reward. Thank you for your time and patience. Rule Britannia!" The displays dissolved to static, then resumed showing their messages.

Once again Dante cursed himself for accepting King Henry's invitation. "For that reward every scumbag and bounty hunter in Britannia will make it their business to hunt me down."

Not to mention every law enforcement officer and intelligence agency operative, the Crest added. *In other parts of the Empire your notoriety keeps you safe, despite the Tsar's bounty on your head. Here you are fair game. Rucka has declared open season on Nikolai Dante.*

The fugitive was still cursing his bad luck when movement nearby caught his eye. Among the travellers being questioned by the police was a balding man clutching a heavy suitcase and a timetable. He was facing away from Dante, but once the police were done with him the man turned towards the phone booths. Dante was startled to recognise the traveller's goatee beard and sad face. "That's him! That's the man I saw on Westminster Bridge!" The traveller walked past the booth towards a nearby gate, not noticing Dante staring at him. He went on to the platform with a cluster of other passengers.

"Crest, what train leaves from that platform, number thirteen?"

The Flying Scotsman. *It's a leisurely tourist service, stopping at various scenic destinations en route to Orkney before returning to London in several days time.*

"When is the next one leaving?"

Any minute. But that train won't get you out of Britannia.

"I've decided to take your advice and clear my name. If I hunt down the real assassin and bring him in, Rucka will have to let Spatchcock and Flintlock go free."

Why the change of heart? Has your little used conscience got the better of you?

"I'm certain one of the assassins just got on the *Flying Scotsman*. I'd guess he's planning to blend in with the other tourists, then slip out of the country with them when the train trip ends."

Quite a coincidence, him catching a train from this station. Dante, it has all the makings of an ambush.

"Why would the authorities bother with an ambush?"

Not everybody will want you found alive, the Crest pointed out.

"It doesn't matter – I have to get on that train!"

Then get moving, the police are almost on top of you.

Dante turned his jacket collar up to conceal his face, then slipped out of the booth and walked slowly towards Platform thirteen. "Excuse me, sir, could you stay where you are," a constable called, but Dante kept walking. "Sir? I must ask you to stop immediately!"

Faster, the Crest urged as Dante quickened his pace.

"Stop now or else I will be forced to intercede," the constable shouted.

"Not the most threatening phrase I've ever heard," Dante commented, breaking into a jog. Around him others on the concourse were looking round to see what was happening. Several pointed at Dante, calling out his name. "Britannia's police must be the most polite in the Empire. All the others are usually shooting at me by now!"

Dante–

"Let me guess, evasive action?"

Evasive action, the Crest agreed. *Now!*

The first shot was a warning blast that skimmed over Dante's shoulder. The other officers felt no need to offer such a warning. Within seconds the concourse was a shooting gallery as dozens of constables opened fire.

"Diavolo!" Dante cried out, flinging himself towards the closing gateway. He slid beneath the metal gates just before they slammed down from above. Bullets thudded noisily against the reinforced steel barriers, but Dante was safely on the other side. Ahead of him the *Flying Scotsman* hissed clouds of steam as the final few passengers climbed on board the last carriage, among them a beautiful woman in a figure-hugging navy blue catsuit. She was struggling with several hat boxes and an antique trunk, shoulder-length strawberry blonde hair falling over her pretty, delicate face. "Crest, how long before the train leaves?"

Less than a minute, but the police will be through the barrier before then.

"I'll have to risk that." Dante sprinted to the last carriage. The young woman had got all her hat boxes inside, but was still trying to manhandle her trunk on board. Admiring the curve of her taut buttocks, Dante grabbed the other end of her awkward luggage. "May I help?" The woman nodded gratefully and climbed into the carriage. Dante spared a glance back at the gates, where the police were shouting for the barrier to be re-opened. The woman followed his gaze, before raising an intrigued eyebrow at Dante. "Overdue parking tickets," he smiled. "You can never find a space when you need one."

"I know exactly what you mean," she said, her voice betraying a private education but with a hint of mischief behind the precise vowels and phrasings. "Thank you for helping me, Mr...?"

"Durward," Dante replied, reverting to his usual alter ego when in need of an impromptu alias. "Quentin Durward, at your service." He bowed his head to her, but let his eyes hungrily examine the contents of her catsuit. The woman could not yet be thirty, her breasts still proudly straining against their confinement, while narrow hips led to slender, athletic legs. As Dante straightened up again, he was struck by the sardonic arch of her eyebrows and pert, upturned nose. Everything about this woman said she knew how to enjoy herself and anyone invited to the party would have the time of their life.

Dante, try to concentrate on the matter in hand, not on the commands of your groin.

"You can call me Penelope," the woman said. "My car broke down on the way to the station and by the time I reached the platform all the porters had vanished."

"It's my pleasure to be of service," Dante smiled, all too aware of heavy footfalls rapidly approaching the train. His eyes lit upon a doorway behind Penelope. "If you'll forgive me, I have an urgent call of nature." He clambered over the trunk, then squeezed past Penelope to gain access to the toilets. As he passed her a waft of exquisite perfume filled his nostrils, causing a stirring in his loins. Dante slipped inside the bathroom and locked the door as pursuing policemen reached the carriage.

"Madam, an escaped murderer just got on this train – dark hair, beard, a scruffy looking creature by the name of Nikolai Dante – did you see which way he went?"

Dante held his breath, willing the woman not to give him away. But his heart sank at hearing her next words.

"Yes, I did see him actually!"

Dante extended his bio-blades and got ready to fight his way out of the cubicle.

"He ran to the far end of this carriage and jumped on to the tracks on the other side. I thought he must be crazed, he had a wild look in his eye. You say he's an escaped murderer; who on earth did he kill?"

"The Queen Mother. You're certain he got off the train?"

"Absolutely, and thank heavens he did! I mean, a murderer on board the *Flying Scotsman*, it doesn't bear thinking about!"

"No, madam, you're right. Thanks for your time."

Dante strained forward, trying to hear whether the policeman had disembarked yet. A whistle sounded shrilly in the background, along with a gruff voice from nearby on the platform. "Stand away, please, stand away – this train is leaving the station! Stand away!" A warning beep announced the doors were closing, then came the sound of someone jumping back down to the platform as the doors slid shut. The train slowly rolled forward, picking up speed. Dante retracted his bio-blades, listening carefully for any hint of a trap outside. Once he was certain the police had left the train, Dante emerged from his hiding place.

Penelope was waiting for him in the narrow space between her trunk and the door, lips playfully pursed. "Overdue parking tickets, eh?"

Dante offered his most winning smile. "I didn't kill the Queen Mother. Honestly."

"Would you tell me if you had?"

"That would depend."

"On what?"

"Whether you would pull the emergency cord and stop the train."

Penelope smiled. "I'm more likely to applaud you. To me the royal family is a wildly outdated anachronism that should have been abandoned centuries ago."

"Really? I thought someone with your accent would be all for Henry and his kind."

"Heavens, no! The Windsor McKrays are dreadful, they give old money a bad name."

"Well, I didn't try to kill the king."

"What a shame," Penelope teased. "Here was I hoping to dine out on stories of how I helped a cold-blooded killer escape justice."

"However," Dante added quickly, "I am considered quite the scoundrel in some parts of the Empire." He gave a gasp of surprise as Penelope rested her left hand against his groin, gently sliding the palm up and down in time with the rhythm of the train.

"And which parts would they be?" she asked coyly.

Before Dante could devise a suitable response the train's public address system crackled into life. "All passengers, please take your seats. The *Flying Scotsman* is about to leave the tracks and take to the skies."

"Sounds like we should be getting to our respective berths," Dante said, as the sound of the train's wheels on the tracks faded. It was replaced by the wind whistling past as the train rose with stately grace into the early evening sky.

"Do you have a ticket?" Penelope enquired with a wicked smile.

"Not as such," he admitted.

"Well, I have a luxury sleeper compartment to myself and nobody to share it with. It's one of the perils of being a beautiful, rich heiress, I suppose – when you have everything money can buy, it's so hard to find something you actually… desire." She closed her hand firmly around his groin. "Perhaps you would like to join me? We could see the sights together."

Dante felt his eyes bulging. They weren't the only things. "I... I might well take you up on that offer," he said, struggling to keep his voice from climbing an octave. "But first I have to locate another passenger on board. He has something of value to me. Once I've retrieved that, perhaps we could meet for dinner?"

Penelope stepped away from Dante, a shadow of disappointment evident in her eyes. "Fine. Well, don't let me delay you any longer."

"I'll be back before you know it," Dante promised, but the moment had passed.

"Don't hurry back on my behalf," Penelope snapped, sitting down on the edge of her trunk. "If you find a steward on your travels, could you send him back here? I still need to get my luggage stowed away."

Dante nodded, then started working his way forward through the train's many carriages and compartments, still bemused by how quickly Penelope's passions rose and fell. "Women," he muttered. "I'll never figure them out."

That much seems certain, the Crest agreed.

Sergeant Jones never enjoyed the company of bounty hunters. For the most part they were criminals, with a history of violence and few moral scruples. To them a target was merely a way of making money. Some enjoyed the chase, the thrill of hunting another human being while living on the edge of the law. Others needed the rewards to feed insidious vices, be they gambling, drugs or women. True, bounty hunters were sometimes able to find and catch fugitives the law could not touch, but that didn't make their existence any less repugnant to the veteran policeman. After twenty years with the Britannia Royal Constabulary, Jones still felt his skin crawl when a bounty hunter came into Scotland Yard. Now there were a dozen of the scum standing in front of his duty desk, waiting for Inspector Rucka to come down from the top floor.

The bounty hunters were a mixture of humans and aliens, most bearing scars from their bloody trade. Among them were two Enforcers from the colony world of Berezova, creatures with squat torsos and mottled brown hides, said to possess incredible strength and power. Cyborgs of varying shapes and sizes scowled at each other as best they were able, not easy for those who no longer possessed a face. The rest stayed near the fringes of the gathering, not getting in anyone else's way. They were parasites, hoping to pick up a few crumbs when the action started. Jones was grateful for one thing about this gathering – at least Dobie and Boyle were not present. That pair was the last thing he needed today. But no sooner had this thought crossed the sergeant's mind than he heard the screech of protesting rubber from outside. "Cover me!" a burly, masculine voice shouted. The entrance doors burst open as a man dived into the foyer, his sidearm drawn and ready to fire. Moments later another figure flung itself inside, performing an entirely gratuitous forward roll in the process.

The pair went through a series of elaborate poses while still crouch on the floor, nominally checking the large, airless room was secure. Both men swept their weapons round the others present, before nodding to each other with knowing smiles. The pair stood and sauntered cockily towards the duty desk, sliding their pistols into shoulder holsters with practiced ease. Boyle was first to speak, a mass of brown curls framing his sensitive blue eyes and bruised cheekbones. He was wearing a loud plaid jacket of red, white and black over a taupe knit shirt and faded denim jeans at least one size too small. "Sergeant Jones! Still propping up the front desk at the Yard, I see. How's the BRC treating you these days?"

"Fine, Ray. Still hanging around with this mercenary?"

Boyle scratched the side of his head, not looking at his nearby partner. "Don't call him a mercenary, it only gives him delusions of grandeur."

"That's rich coming from you," Dobie interjected. He was dressed in tan slacks and a brown blazer over a cream shirt. His short brown locks were brushed forward over his scalp to mask a receding hairline. "An ex-copper who decided he was worth more than a badge!"

"At least I know which side of the law is the right one," Boyle remarked.

"I didn't know there was a right side," Dobie said with a smirk. He leaned nonchalantly against the front desk and surveyed the other bounty hunters already gathered. "Well, it seems the gang's all here. Bad news, boys – now Ray and I have arrived the hunt is already as good as over. We need a new spoiler for the back of the hover-car, so this reward is ours, got it?" The others did not dignify his comment with a reply. Dobie smiled broadly at his partner. "I think they understand."

"Oh yeah, you definitely convinced them," Boyle agreed, rolling his eyes.

An inner door swung open and Rucka stepped into the room like a visiting dignitary, with a constable following him. The inspector moved along the bounty hunters, studying each one with disdain. The constable joined Jones behind the duty desk. The sergeant could not resist whispering a comment out of the side of his mouth to the younger policeman. "Bounty hunters. We don't need their scum."

"Yes, sir," the constable agreed quietly.

"The fugitive won't escape us," Jones added.

Rucka began addressing the gathering in his clipped, nasal voice. "There will be a substantial reward for the person who finds Nikolai Dante. You are free to use any methods necessary but I want him brought in alive." The inspector noticed two men slouching by the front desk and pointed a finger at them. "No executions!"

Dobie and Boyle gave Rucka a mock salute. "As you wish," they replied in unison.

The inspector waved for the bounty hunters to leave, then approached the duty sergeant. "Well Jones, what news from our bobbies on the beat?"

"A squad of constables saw Dante at London International Train Terminal a few minutes ago. He tried to throw them off his trail by boarding the *Flying Scotsman*, but a witness saw him run away across the tracks. The pursuit is continuing, sir."

"Very good," Rucka replied patronisingly. "I know the presence of bounty hunters is repugnant to most policemen, but such mercenaries have a proven track record in flushing out this type of fugitive. Think of them as a little insurance if your men don't catch Dante."

"Yes, inspector," Jones agreed, seething as the inspector went back upstairs. The sergeant muttered an Oedipal curse that neatly rhymed with Rucka's name, then got back to co-ordinating the search for Dante.

Outside Scotland Yard, Dobie and Boyle were slouching in the bucket seats of their tan Phord Capri hover-car, each man listening to the surveillance device they had hidden by the duty desk. The pair laughed out loud at Jones's turn of phrase. "Sounds like your old mate isn't too fond of the inspector," Dobie observed.

"Can't say I blame him. Rucka was always good at grabbing the headlines but he needed real coppers to catch the villains for him."

"Real coppers like you, you mean?"

Boyle made an obscene finger gesture to his partner, then started the Capri. "Let's go," he said, gunning the engine needlessly.

"Where?"

"King's Cross. It's a good place to pick up a few tips."

"It's a good place to pick up a few diseases," Dobie observed. "Still, it's not far from the train terminal. Our target might be trying to lie low near there until the heat cools off."

Boyle smiled wryly. "My thoughts exactly." He released the handbrake and the Capri roared along the road before leaping into the sky, tyres squealing in protest as usual.

Half an hour later Dante had reached the front carriage of the *Flying Scotsman* without finding his quarry. Ahead lay only cargo carriages and the locomotive. "I don't understand how I could have missed him," he fretted. "I searched all the seated passengers."

But not the sleeper compartments, the Crest pointed out. *Your target must be inside one of the first class berths. The only time he's obliged to come out is during the sight-seeing stops, when the staff clean and re-supply all the individual compartments.*

Dante saw a steward approaching, clutching a handful of timetables. Like all male staff on the train, he was wearing full Highland costume including a kilt, sporran, white ruffled shirt and shiny black patent leather shoes. Dante gestured for attention. "I say, could you tell me, when is our first sight-seeing excursion off the train?" he asked, affecting a Britannia accent.

The steward smiled indulgently. "We pause above the Watford Gap so passengers can take pictures, but the first time we land will be tomorrow at Nottingham. There's a choice of day-trips on offer there: the castle, Sherwood Forest or the historic country estate of the Fforbes-Lamington family. You may have already selected one when you bought your ticket. Perhaps if I could see it?"

Dante made a great show of patting all his pockets. "Ahh, I think my wife has both our tickets. She's at the other end of the train. We were among the last to get on and our luggage is rather cluttering the gangway. Penny could do with some help getting things stowed away."

The steward nodded understandingly. "Of course, sir. Perhaps you'd like to take a drink in the lounge while I placate your wife?"

"Capital idea, capital! I shall do just that. Make sure you get a generous tip from her, by way of compensation for all your efforts on our behalf – they're most appreciated." Dante clapped the steward on the back and strode back to the first class lounge he had passed earlier.

Penelope was still sitting on top of her luggage when a rotund man in a kilt approached her with a menu for dinner. "Excuse me, madam, is your name Penny?"

"Penelope, if you don't mind. And you are?"

"Gordonstoun, head steward for this excursion," he replied, bowing slightly. "Your husband sent me along to get your luggage squared away, said you were having some trouble."

"My husband...?" Penelope said, her mind racing. "Oh, him!" She permitted herself the slightest of blushes. "Well, as you've probably surmised, we aren't actually married."

Gordonstoun clasped his chubby hands together and smiled benignly. "Here on the *Flying Scotsman* we pride ourselves at being the souls of tact and discretion. Your secrets are safe with us, madam, even if your, er, travelling companion is rather less discreet."

Penelope sighed theatrically. "Yes, he can be rather a bore but he means a lot to me. Once this luggage is out of the way, perhaps you could show me to my sleeping quarters?"

"Of course, madam. It would be my pleasure." Gordonstoun bowed again, then activated a staff intercom and summoned other attendants to fetch the hatboxes and trunk.

Once they had arrived, the head steward escorted Penelope to her quarters. He opened the gold and green door, then politely stood aside to let her enter first. The compartment was surprisingly large and lavishly furnished, with a four-poster bed at one end and matching chaise longue at the other. A tall mirror was mounted directly behind the bed, making the sound-proofed chamber appear even bigger than it was. A thick sheepskin rug covered most of the floor, complementing the plush, decadent decor.

Once Penelope was inside, Gordonstoun pointed to the berth's many features – a separate dressing room with ample storage for clothes, shoes and other accoutrements, a bathroom equal in size to the bedroom with both a freestanding tub and walk-in shower, plus a heavily stocked private bar concealed in an oak cabinet. All the wood in the compartment was oak with gold leaf ornamentation, whilst small crystal chandeliers concealed the light fittings on the walls. Gordonstoun gestured at a control panel skilfully hidden behind a tapestry on one wall. "This provides you with an encrypted communications environment. Like all our first class compartments, this berth is sealed to prevent any noise from outside disturbing you or any sounds you make being audible when the door to the corridor is closed. Your discretion and privacy are paramount at all times while you are a passenger on board the *Flying Scotsman*."

Penelope gave the steward an outrageously generous tip. His eyes flashed hungrily for a moment until his calm, collected demeanour reasserted itself. "If there is anything you require madam, do not hesitate to summon me – day or night. I am happy to be of service. Ask for me by name: Gordonstoun."

"I'll be certain to remember that," Penelope replied with a small smile. Her brow furrowed as a thought occurred. "There is one thing. Where did you see my... husband... last?"

"The far end of the train, madam. He was going to the first class lounge for a drink."

"Could you give him a message for me?"

Gordonstoun listened, then repeated the message to Penelope for her confirmation. "I shall ensure he does as you ask, madam."

Penelope waited until the steward had gone before throwing herself on the vast bed, letting herself sink into its down-filled quilts. This was the life, she decided. A discreet knock summoned her back to the main doorway. Two more stewards staggered inside, bringing her trunk and hatboxes. "Put them in the dressing room, please," Penelope said. She made sure to tip them generously as they left.

An insistent beeping from one of her hatboxes soon demanded Penelope's attention. She retrieved a tiny, circular disc hidden within the brim of a hat and inserted it into her left ear. "Receiving loud and clear." Penelope returned to the main room, adjusting the position of the translucent device until it was firmly lodged inside her ear. "Yes, I have seen and locked on to my target." She went to the nearest mirror and twisted her head sideways, checking to make sure the disc was all but invisible. "No, the target does not suspect me, I'm certain of that. He thinks I want him sexually. You know what some men are like – all the world revolves around their groin."

Penelope paused, listening to the voice inside her ear. "No, I will not be able to get him off the train tonight. That will have to wait until we reach Nottingham in the morning." Another pause as a stream of words transmitted themselves to her. "I'm about to have a meal with him. After that I'll invite him back to my sleeping compartment – I'm sure you can imagine the rest." Penelope nodded, and then laughed. "No, Your Highness, I don't think you need fear for my virtue. If anyone should be afraid, it's Nikolai Dante. The fool doesn't seem to realise the danger he is in." She listened to one last comment from her caller. "Thank you, ma'am. I'll deliver him to you before dusk tomorrow. Agent Goodnight, signing off."

The first class lounge was packed with people, most of them talking in foreign accents . Despairing of his quest, Dante ordered the largest drink available and settled in for the evening. The barman set about mixing an elaborate cocktail involving almost every kind of alcohol known to man, while Dante passed the time examining the faces of his fellow passengers. Foreign tourists were obvious from their gaudy clothes and propensity for ugly facial hair, while those from Britannia tended to be ruddy-cheeked and uptight in appearance.

Do any of these people look familiar to you?

The Crest's question puzzled Dante. "No," he whispered back. "Why, should they?"

There's something nagging me about several of these passengers. I feel as if I have seen them before, but I cannot remember where or when.

"But they still look familiar?"

Yes. I cannot explain it.

Dante's eyes swept round the room, searching for anything that jogged his memory – a profile, a family resemblance, anything. It was only when his gaze reached the far end that he recognised anyone. "It's him, he's right here!"

Who?

"The assassin – he's here in the lounge!" Dante said, trying to push his way through the throng. Ahead, the sad faced man with the goatee was sitting at the bar, finishing a drink. He drained the glass and left the lounge, a rectangle of paper falling from his pocket. By the time Dante had struggled past his sixth party of Scandinavian revellers the assassin was long gone. Dante cursed his own incompetence, until he noticed the discarded document. It was a timetable for the *Flying Scotsman*'s journey north, like those the steward had been carrying earlier.

Dante picked it up and studied the list of destinations. Three names were circled several times – Nottingham, Peebles and Orkney.

If this timetable was dropped by the assassin, it suggests he is staying on the train all the way to the north of Scotland. That gives you until Saturday to find and confront him.

"Three days," Dante calculated. "Plenty of time to get the truth from this bastard."

A chime sounded. The portly steward appeared beside Dante in the doorway. "Ladies and gentlemen, that is the first bell for dinner. Would those staying in the sleeping compartments at the far end of the train like to make their way back? You'll find the evening meal awaits you there."

Dante became aware of his empty stomach rumbling and realised a day had passed since his last meal. The rotund steward whispered politely in Dante's left ear. "Your wife is waiting for you in that dining car, sir. I suggest you do not delay in joining her – she seemed less than pleased you left her to cope with all the luggage."

"Ahh! Yes, indeed, I have been rather remiss," Dante agreed. "I'd better pop along and soothe the old girl's furrowed brow, eh?" Dante set off, eager to re-establish his acquaintance with the delectable Penelope. I wonder what her last name is, he thought idly.

Are you forgetting something?

"Like what?" Dante replied under his breath.

Your manhunt for the assassin? The quest to clear your name of murder, saving Spatchcock and Flintlock from the executioner?

"You said it yourself, Crest – I've got three days to find this sniper and make him confess. One night of pleasure with Penelope won't prevent that."

Your friends could be executed at any time.

"They can look after themselves," Dante insisted. "Besides, I have my honour as a ladies' man to uphold, and you know how I feel about the importance of my honour."

This from the man whose personal motto is 'Honour be damned!'

"No, Your Highness, I don't think you need fear for my virtue. If anyone should be afraid, it's Nikolai Dante. The fool doesn't seem to realise the danger he is in." F listened to the intercepted transmission, her stern face evidence of a growing anger. "Thank you, ma'am, I'll deliver him to you before dusk tomorrow. Agent Goodnight, signing off." The recording clicked to a halt. F sat back in the high-backed swivel chair behind her desk of pine and glass, glaring at the meek messenger standing opposite.

"Why am I only hearing this now?" F demanded.

"Ma'am, the transmission was intercepted a few minutes ago. It took our cryptographers time to decode the scrambler signal on the line," Agent Golightly replied quietly.

"Not good enough! From now on I expect all of Goodnight's communications with that bitch princess to be relayed to me in real time – is that understood?"

"I'm not sure that will be possible–"

"Is that understood?" F repeated.

"Yes, ma'am. I'll pass that on to the code breakers." Golightly turned to leave.

"Wait!" F rose from her chair, strolling round the desk towards the trembling, terrified agent. "Tell me, what do you think is the significance of this communication?"

"M-Me?" Golightly stammered. "You want my opinion?"

"Obviously, otherwise I would not have asked for it, would I?" F stopped behind the young woman. "Give me your assessment – dazzle me with your acumen."

"It seems clear that Agent Goodnight–"

"Traitorous bitch!" F snapped.

"She has been suborned into reporting directly to Princess Marie-Anne. Her royal highness has assigned Goodnight to find and bring back the fugitive Dante – alive, by the sound of it. This message was transmitted from aboard the *Flying Scotsman*, so it's clear Dante remained on board. Someone – possibly Goodnight herself – lied to the police about seeing him flee the train."

"Yes, yes, all that is obvious," F said. "What I wanted to know is your interpretation of this betrayal's significance. Does the heir to our monarch intend claiming control of my intelligence service for herself? Perhaps the royal bitch has plans to install Goodnight as her puppet in my place." F stepped nearer Golightly, close enough for the beautiful young agent to feel the commander's breath on the back of her neck. "Would that be your interpretation?"

"It would fit with the ambitious behaviour patterns the princess has previously shown."

"Quite," F agreed, allowing herself a cruel smile of anticipation before activating the intercom on her desk. "I want a squad of Rippers despatched immediately."

"Yes, ma'am," a voice responded. "Target?"

"The *Flying Scotsman*. It should be over the Watford Gap in the next hour or two. The Rippers should find Nikolai Dante – his DNA records are still on our system from his last visit to Britannia. He is to be executed on sight."

"Yes, ma'am."

"Agent Penelope Goodnight may well be with Dante when the Rippers kill him. I do not want her eliminated – yet. Is that clear?"

"Yes, ma'am."

"Very good. I am not to be disturbed for the next hour. After that I will leave for my house in the country. You may contact me en route or at my home when I get there." F switched off the intercom and glared at Golightly. "I'm sorry to say I'm disappointed in your performance in this matter. You will have to be disciplined." F undid the leather belt from the waist of her tweed skirt. "Bend over and touch your toes."

SIX

"Eat the honey but beware the sting."
– Russian proverb

"The Rippers are covert assassins attached to Britannia's secret service, often used in a death squad capacity. They are genetically engineered for maximum stealth and sadism, with olfactory nerves designed to literally smell the DNA of their intended victims. Rippers always maintain a particular look: black cloaks lined with red silk; black stovepipe hats; black suits and ties; white shirts and pallid faces. This sinister appearance is carefully choreographed to strike fear into the underclass of Britannia, tapping into hereditary memories of the original Ripper murders that terrorised London almost nine hundred years ago. For this same reason they are armed with viciously sharp blades as their weapons. Rippers usually fly into action on single-seat aerial mounts fashioned like black hornets with bulbous red eyes."
– Extract from *The Files of the Raven Corps*

"Well, this is cosy, isn't it?" Flintlock remarked, his voice dripping with irony. "Only yesterday I was thinking to myself I never get to spend enough quality time with my good friend Spatch – and now look at us. All the time in the world, just the two of us, as close as close can be."

"Shut your mouth," Spatchcock urged. The two men were manacled together in a dungeon at the Tower of London, their hands clamped to each other's ankles. The cell was cold, damp and dank, the stench of rat droppings and fear apparently impregnated into its ancient walls. They had been shoved into this hovel within hours of the king being shot. The only facilities provided were a bowl of brackish water, a single straw-filled mattress and a metal bucket for urine and faeces. Forced to huddle together for warmth overnight, Flintlock had spent most of the following day complaining to the sentries about the lice Spatchcock had given him. After several hours of listening to this persistent whining, a guard came in and manacled the prisoners together. When Flintlock protested this would make the lice infestation worse, not better, the guard replied the shackles were a punishment, not a treatment.

"I will not shut my mouth, as you crudely put it!" Flintlock snapped indignantly. "I reserve the right to say what I please whenever I please and there's nothing you can do to stop me!" His words came to an abrupt halt as a sulphurous stench filled the air. "My word, what is that? It's as if the very bowels of Hell have opened to release their noxious gases."

"Close enough," Spatchcock smirked.

"That vile stench emitted from your posterior?"

"I told you to shut your mouth."

"Like most civilised people, I sense smells through my nostrils, not my mouth."

"Oh, stop whining for once in your bloody life. Nothing's ever good enough for high and mighty Lord Peter Flintlock, is it? You're no different from me or Dante – just another scoundrel, trying to stay one step ahead of trouble. You stink as bad as the rest of us at the end of the day."

"Only when I've been shackled to a foul-smelling wretch and denied decent facilities in which to carry out my daily ablutions. It must be twenty-four hours since I've had anything to eat. I feel weaker than a kitten," Flintlock said.

"You *are* weaker than a kitten."

"You know what I mean. We are being denied our basic human rights."

Spatchcock shrugged. "Since they've got us down for murdering the Queen Mother, I don't think the powers that be are much bothered about our rights – basic, human or otherwise."

"I fear your summation is accurate."

"Come again?"

"I think you're right," Flintlock replied. "Don't you understand the King's English?"

"Of course I do," Spatchcock smiled. "I wanted to hear you say I was right again, that's all."

"You are the most tiresome of creatures."

"Here he goes again," the ruddy-faced runt snarled, before twisting round to shout at the narrow metal grille in the cell door. "Guard! Guard!" A sour-faced sentry appeared on the other side of the bars. "When's our execution planned for?"

"The date hasn't been finalised yet."

"When are they thinking of having it, then?"

"A week from today, give more people the opportunity to watch."

Spatchcock grimaced. "Any chance they could bring it forward? I can't stand seven more days being manacled to this whining turd, listening to all his pissing and moaning."

"Shut your mouth!" the guard said before walking away.

Flintlock aimed a kick at his fellow prisoner, eliciting a yelp of pain. "You might be in a hurry to die, but I've no wish to meet my maker yet, so don't speak for me in such matters."

"I wasn't," Spatchcock explained. "I was trying to find out how long we've got to wait before Dante comes to rescue us."

The Britannia native laughed bitterly. "We're in a basement cell inside the Tower of London, one of the world's most infamous prisons. There hasn't been a successful escape from this place for centuries and it is guarded by a small army. Dante will not be coming to rescue us. If he does try, he'll be dead long before he reaches our cell door."

"He'll come for us," Spatchcock insisted.

"Your faith in our former commander is touching, old boy, but I fear it is also misplaced. If Dante has any sense he'll have managed to get out of the country before the borders were sealed."

"Shut your mouth!"

"I'm telling you the truth," Flintlock insisted. "We're doomed, quite doomed, both of us."

"I meant shut your nostrils," Spatchcock replied, as another waft of vile air escaped from his anus.

"What? Why– Oh no, not again!"

"Well, this is cosy, isn't it?" Dante said as he sat down opposite Penelope in the first class dining car. Around them a selection of wealthy, well-dressed passengers were studying the *Flying Scotsman*'s extensive menu and lengthy wine list. Like the rest of the hover-train, the dining car was sumptuously furnished and decorated. Gentle, sympathetic lighting cast a gold glow over everything, turning each table into a noasis of dining splendour. Penelope was already waiting for Dante when he came in, seated at an intimate table for two in a corner of the carriage, her back to the wall. She had smiled and waved, beckoning him towards the vacant chair across from her.

"You'll be happy to know I have taken possession of a rather grand compartment near this end of the train, where the steward has promised I will not be disturbed," Penelope said, smiling playfully at Dante. "There's a wonderful dressing room and I even had time to change before dinner." She held out her hands to display the plunging neckline of a black velvet gown that struggled to contain her jutting breasts. "Sadly, the magnificent bed looks far too large for me to fill on my own. I was wondering if you had any suggestions how I could resolve that problem?"

"Let me think... Were you expecting to be joined by another traveller later on the journey north? Your partner, or a lover?"

Penelope sighed theatrically. "I have no husband, nor a long-term companion to help fill the lonely evening hours. I am quite alone at present."

"Then I think you should take a lover," Dante said. "Being alone at night is most unhealthy. What if you should take ill and need someone to soothe your troubles away?"

"Are you suggesting I organise an infidelity?"

"Certainly."

"With someone on board the train, perhaps?"

"With me, for example."

Penelope appeared almost shocked at Dante's boldness. "Why, sir, I hardly know you."

"You seemed to have a firm grasp of my particulars earlier."

She smiled at the memory. "That's true. I have always favoured the hands-on approach."

"I'm much the same myself," Dante agreed.

"Yet you left me to fend for myself with all that luggage."

"I apologise. Sometimes my manners leave a little to be desired, but what I lack in sophistication I more than make up for with... enthusiasm."

Penelope smirked. "I always applaud enthusiasm, as long as it is well directed."

"I aim to please." The cut and thrust of their flirtation was interrupted by the arrival of an obsequious waiter with the menu. Dante rashly chose a dozen Caledonian oysters, followed by a braised haunch of Aberdeen Angus beef, to be washed down by a rich red wine. Penelope was more circumspect, preferring the risotto with truffle shavings and a cheese soufflé. "Are you a vegetarian?" Dante asked once the waiter had left.

"In all places but the bedroom," Penelope replied.

"How interesting," Dante said, rearranging the linen napkin over his bulging crotch.

Try thinking with your brain instead of your genitals, the Crest interjected. *You don't even know this woman's last name, yet you are behaving like a lust-crazed animal. Find out something about her so I can check it against the Imperial Net.*

"Yes, indeed," Dante said. "After I got your invitation to dine from the steward, it struck me that I don't even know your last name. You know who I am, therefore you have me at a disadvantage. Perhaps you would care to even the balance?"

"Perhaps," Penelope teased. "To be honest, I find my family name something of an embarrassment. People always take it the wrong way."

"Well, I promise to keep an open mind."

"Very well. My name is Goodnight – Penelope Goodnight."

"Really?" Dante asked, trying to keep a straight face. He was aware of movement between his legs and glanced down to see his napkin being expertly moved aside by a probing female foot clad in a black silk stocking. The foot began massaging his groin, toes working their way into the folds of his ever tightening trousers. Dante realised the waiter was returning with their first course and hastily rearranged the napkin to conceal his embarrassment. "I can't imagine why your name would give anyone the wrong idea."

Penelope smiled at him, licking her lips hungrily as their food was placed in front of them. "You'd be surprised. Some people are apt to misinterpret anything as a sexual overture."

A second foot joined the first between Dante's legs, coaxing and cajoling the contents of his trousers. He struggled to keep a straight face, both eyebrows popping upwards in surprise and delight at the movements beneath his napkin. "I pride myself being able to... recognise and appreciate the difference between innocent flirting and the more intense cut and... thrust... of a genuine invitation to act."

"I do hope so," she replied, putting a spoonful of creamy risotto into her mouth and savouring every morsel. "Misinterpretations of one's motives can be so... disappointing."

"Absolutely. But I always try to... rise... to the occasion." By now beads of perspiration were forming on Dante's forehead, but he did not dare remove the napkin to mop his brow.

Penelope gestured to the neglected plate of oysters. "You've hardly touched your starter. Has your appetite deserted you?"

"Quite the opposite," he said. "I feel rather ravenous, but these aren't what I had in mind."

She nodded at his glass. "What about the wine? Does that not excite your palate?"

Dante's eye bulged slightly as a wave of pleasure surged through him. "I prefer something with a bit more... body."

"I know what you mean," Penelope agreed. "There's a fully stocked drinks cabinet in my compartment. We could retire there and see if there's anything that's more to your taste."

"That would be... delightful," Dante gasped. He stood up abruptly, using the napkin to hide his groin. "If you'll excuse me for a minute, I need a few moments to... compose myself."

"Of course. I'll be waiting right here."

"Good. Don't go away." Dante strode from the dining car, not meeting the eye of any other passengers. He brushed past their waiter, ignoring inquiries about the quality of the meal. Only when Dante was out in the corridor did he breathe again, panting excitedly as pleasure flushed his features. "Bojemoi, that woman has toes that could out-crush a boa constrictor!" he gasped.

She may be dangerous in other ways, the Crest observed dryly. *I can find no trace of a Penelope Goodnight on the Imperial Net. The name she gave you is an alias or else her identity has been deleted from all public records. Either way, this woman is not to be trusted.*

"I gave her a false name when I got on the train," Dante countered.

Yes, but you're accused of trying to assassinate the king. What is she hiding?

"A husband, or maybe an entire family. I don't know and, to be honest, I don't care," Dante insisted. "She is willing to give me a place to spend the night–"

Between her thighs.

"–and I need a place to lie low."

I could not have put that better myself.

"Thank you."

That wasn't a compliment. Dante, how many times must I warn you against tumbling into bed with strange women?

"I'll take a wild guess and say two hundred." The Russian renegade grinned. "Am I close?"

As always, you are your own worst enemy.

"I know what I'm doing Crest, so leave me in peace, okay?"

Fine.

"Good."

But don't say I didn't warn you.

"Whatever."

Agent Goodnight smiled as she studied her reflection in the dining car window. With her strawberry blonde hair pulled back from her face in a delicate arrangement, she bore a striking resemblance to her mother. Mary Goodnight had been a top operative for Britannia Intelligence, also specialising in the age-old art of the honey trap. That was how Penelope's parents had met, when Mary lured an unsuspecting spy from the Imperial court into bed. Danilov defected to be with the woman he loved, but a Makarov assassin had killed him before Penelope was born. The daughter of two spies, Agent Goodnight often felt her career had been all but inevitable, a hereditary legacy. Unlike her mother, Penelope was determined to remain aloof, unaffected by any feelings for the men and women to whose seduction she was assigned.

Maintaining that professional detachment would not be a problem in this case, Agent Goodnight decided. Yes, Dante had a certain boyish charm and he was closer to her own age than most subjects she lured into bed and betrayed. But he had the subtlety of a sledgehammer and almost as little wit. He had been putty in her hands thus far, if somewhat harder when placed between her toes. Nevertheless, he clearly did not suspect her motives, believing himself to be worthy of her undivided attention and lust. The arrogance of the man! No, arrogance was the wrong word, she thought. Cockiness – yes, that best described Nikolai Dante: cocky.

A whisper of static through the train's public address system got her attention. "If those passengers on the eastern side of our carriages care to look out of their windows, below us they will see the physical anomaly known as the Watford Gap. Decades ago a devastating and utterly unexpected earthquake tore a hole out of this area of Britannia. Within minutes a bustling metropolitan conurbation was gone, swallowed by the ground. All that remains is the hole where once the city of Watford stood – hence its name, the Watford Gap. According to legend, if you look closely enough you can see the ghosts of all those who perished in that tragedy."

Penelope had seen the gap before but never from this height nor at night. She peered through the window and was struck by how beautiful even a scene of such devastation could look at night. The jagged edge of the chasm was well lit but the yawning absence where a city had once stood was nothing but blackness, like a ragged mouth in the night. No, wait, there was something moving across the darkness – several somethings. Penelope looked closer and realised the shapes were between the train and the topographical anomaly below. They almost resembled insects, a swarm of them buzzing through the air, moving ever closer to the *Flying*

Scotsman. But no insect should be large enough for her to notice at this distance, should it?

Within seconds Penelope was out of her seat and striding briskly from the dining car. She had to find Dante and find him fast. A death squad of Rippers was surrounding the train in mid-air and there could be little doubt who they were looking for. She had scant minutes to conceal their quarry before the Rippers boarded the *Flying Scotsman* and hunted Dante down.

Her mind raced with questions. How had they traced him here? Yes, their genetically engineered senses were remarkably effective tools, but even they could not detect a single person's DNA on a sealed train without having been directed to this location. Either someone had spotted Dante on board and called in the Rippers, or else her last communication to the princess had been intercepted. Either way, somebody wanted Dante dead by any means necessary. Unleashing the Rippers meant whoever gave the order did not care who got hurt in the process.

Penelope spotted Dante walking along the corridor towards her, still adjusting his bulging trousers. "I was coming to fetch you," he said warmly.

"No need. Come and see my cabin," she replied, grabbing his left hand and dragging him along after her. "I promise you an experience you'll never forget."

"Sounds intriguing," he said, jogging to keep up with her. "Why the rush?"

"I've had my fill of flirting for one night," Penelope said. "Appetisers are all very well, but eventually you want to savour a nice piece of flesh."

"I couldn't agree more."

"Good," she said hurriedly as they reached the door to her compartment. Penelope unlocked it and shoved Dante inside, then followed him in and relocked the door. "Strip!"

"Sorry?"

"Get your clothes off!"

Dante's face split into a broad grin, then he tore off his jacket. "I was wondering how long you'd be able to resist getting your hands on me. Not that I'm complaining about your use of feet," he added, as he removed his leather boots, tossing one over each shoulder. "Your toes are remarkably skilful. But I find fingers have a lightness of touch that few other parts of the anatomy can match, don't you?" In the time it had taken him to finish his speech, Dante had peeled his shirt off over his head and stepped out of his trousers. He was standing in the centre of the compartment, both hands doing their best to hide the borrowed g-string that singularly failed to conceal his rising excitement. "Now what?"

Penelope studied the words "GET IT HERE" emblazoned across Dante's underwear. "You seem like a broad-minded individual. How do you feel about trying a little bondage?"

For the last time, listen to me, the Crest insisted. *This woman—*

"I like to think of myself as tri-sexual," Dante replied. "I'll try anything once."

"Good," Penelope said, gathering the rest of his clothes. "Give me your underwear and then lie face-up on the mattress." She watched him comply, resisting the urge to laugh as he clambered willingly onto the luxurious, four-poster bed. Penelope made a neat pile of Dante's clothes by the compartment door, then reached for a small case resting on a nearby side-table. She extracted a pair of black handcuffs and held them aloft. "I'm going to give you a night you'll never forget."

As head steward on board the *Flying Scotsman*, it was Gordonstoun's job to ensure nothing disturbed or upset his passengers. A panicked call from the front of the train had brought him running, forcing the portly attendant to abandon his usual station during the dinner service. When he saw the sinister squad of hollow-cheeked hunters sniffing their way along a corridor, his heart fluttered with terror. A dozen knife-wielding maniacs in black cloaks, suits and stovepipe hates certainly qualified as disturbing in Gordonstoun's estimation. Despite his inner fears, the steward stood his ground outside the dining car, refusing to let the Rippers pass.

"I don't care whose authority you claim to have for your dreadful intrusion, I am responsible for the care and welfare of all those on board this train. I will not have you frightening the passengers or staff with your bully-boy tactics," Gordonstoun maintained.

The Rippers' leader sneered at the steward, a grey moustache quivering with repressed rage. "You shouldn't be takin' liberties with us, guv'nor – we slice and dice the likes of you for breakfast without thinkin' twice." He held the point of his left dagger close to Gordonstoun's throat while the right dagger reached underneath the steward's kilt. The blade scratched its way up one of Gordonstoun's legs, edging ever closer to his unprotected groin. "One slip of my knife and you'll be singing with the boy sopranos for a long, long time, if you catch my drift. Now, get out of my way, you officious nonce!"

The head steward stepped aside, his bottom lip wobbling as tears filled his eyes. Gordonstoun stared at the floor as the Rippers shoved past, too ashamed to meet their gaze. Dear god, he prayed, let them find whichever poor soul they're searching for quickly. Maybe they'll leave us in peace after that.

Penelope secured one end of the black handcuffs around Dante's left wrist, pulling his arm up over his head to the hefty wooden post at one corner of the bed. She stretched forward over Dante to feed the other end of the cuffs behind the post, her velvet-covered breasts brushing across his eager face. "Now give me your other arm," she commanded.

"Do I have to?" Dante asked. He was busy using his free hand to caress Penelope's firm but well rounded buttocks.

"It's having quite a good time where it is." His fingers slipped sideways to explore between the top of her supple thighs.

Penelope sighed, reaching back to extract Dante's groping hand and yanking it up to meet the other end of the cuffs. "That's better," she said, clamping his wrists together.

"Ouch!" he protested. "Do those have to be so tight? I'm not big on pain."

"A typical male," she sneered, climbing off the bed. "Happy to savour the pleasures of sex, but you never stick around to face the consequences." Penelope stood back to admire her handiwork. Dante was lying naked on the mattress, his wrists clamped together above his head while each ankle was secured to the resolute wooden posts at the other end of the bed by carefully knotted silk scarves.

"So, what do we do now?" he grinned, waggling his eyebrows suggestively.

"I noticed earlier you were wearing a pair of women's underwear."

"Like I said, I'll try anything once."

"Good." Penelope disappeared into her dressing room for a few moments, then returned with several pairs of delicate lace panties. She held them up for Dante to see. "Which of these do you prefer? The black or the red?"

"They'd both look good on you," he replied. "Come to think of it, aren't you a little overdressed? Feel free to strip off and join the party."

"Oh, these aren't for me," Penelope laughed. "They're for you."

"You'll need to untie my legs first to get them on me."

"True," she agreed, approaching the bed. "But I had something else in mind." Penelope pulled down the front of her gown and let her breasts spill out in front of Dante's mouth. He stretched forwards and opened his lips wide, eager to put them around her aroused nipples. Instead he found both pairs of panties shoved into his mouth. Confusion crowded his face and he started to gag against the fabric. "Breathe through your nose," Penelope urged, "otherwise you're likely to drown in your own vomit."

Dante struggled to follow her instructions, puzzlement evident in his eyes as Penelope hoisted her gown back into place. "I haven't got time to explain," she said, "but this is for your own good." After that she ignored her captive, instead searching through a small case containing bottles of scent and eau de toilettes. "Yes, this should do the trick," Penelope decided, choosing one particular bottle of perfume from among the many. She removed the lid and tipped most of the contents over Dante's writhing, thrashing body. An overpowering odour of sandalwood and musk filled the compartment, eradicating every other smell. "This is called Bitch, it's the new fragrance from the House of Klein. In small doses it stinks like a tart's boudoir at low tide, so it should mask your natural body odour quite effectively."

Dante yelled and howled in protest but his cries were muffled most effectively by the mouthful of lingerie. Penelope looked at his crotch and smirked. "Not quite so cocky now, are you?" She strode to the outer door and pulled it open, then tossed Dante's clothes and boots out into the corridor. She emptied the last of the perfume over the spot where his garments had been lying. "There, that should do it. Now to lay a scent." Penelope went out into the corridor and closed the door, gently waving to her prisoner as she departed. Dante heard the door being locked, then the sound of something being dragged along the corridor towards the rear of the hover-train.

I tried to warn you, the Crest sighed.

Dante attempted to reply but his words were all but unintelligible thanks to the improvised gag in his mouth.

What was that?

Dante tried again.

The handcuffs? They must be made of a special compound that suppresses your cyborganics. Dante spoke again, another garbled collection of grunts and noises.

If I had to guess, I'd say Ms Goodnight is an operative for one of the local intelligence agencies. She seems remarkably resourceful and well equipped.

Another outburst came from Dante.

I was referring to the handcuffs, not her décolletage, the Crest replied. *Even tied up your libido is more active than your brain, isn't it?*

Dante simply shrugged.

Penelope hurried towards the back of the *Flying Scotsman*, dragging Dante's clothes behind her. As she approached the final carriage the translucent disc in her ear began to vibrate. She pressed a finger against the device, activating its two-way communications link. "Agent Goodnight responding."

"This is her royal highness, Princess Marie-Anne. Have you located the fugitive Dante?"

"You know bloody well I've located him! Why have you sent in the Rippers? I had the situation under control, now you've forced me to compromise my cover!"

"What are you talking about? I didn't send the–" A scream of static cut through the transmission, forcing Penelope to pluck the tiny device out of her ear. It bounced against a window, then fell to the carpet. Seconds later the static was gone, no sound issuing from the comms disc. Penelope retrieved the small circle but could get no response from it. Someone was jamming the signal, cutting off the outside world. The Rippers must be closing in.

After checking the final carriage was unoccupied, Penelope threw Dante's clothes and boots inside it and locked the connecting door... Next she smeared her make-up and rubbed her eyes, forcing them to look red and weepy. Lastly she tore the top of her dress, letting it hang limply from one shoulder, and removed one of her shoes. The sound of heavy footfalls running towards her became audible. Penelope burst into tears and staggered slowly away from the final carriage. The Rippers appeared, knives drawn, the lust for blood all too obvious.

"Please, you've got to help me!" Penelope whimpered. "This man, I think his name was Dante – he attacked me! He dragged me into the final carriage and tried to have his way with me. I managed to fight him off and lock him inside. He was bleeding, I don't know if he's dead or alive!" She broke down in tears, her ordeal apparently too much to bear.

"Don't you worry, miss," the Rippers' leader vowed in a broad Cockney accent. "If that scum ain't dead already, he will be by the time we've finished with 'im!" The other Rippers leered their approval, light glinting off their blades.

Penelope pointed with a shaking hand. "H-He's through there…"

The twelve Rippers moved as one, storming along the corridor to the final carriage. The locked door was quickly dealt with and the death squad rushed inside. Their leader picked up the discarded clothes and boots, sniffing them suspiciously. "I smell his stench on these rags, boys! The Russian bastard must be in one of these compartments! Spread out and start searching."

Penelope waited until all twelve were busy with their manhunt before returning to the connecting doorway. She closed and locked it again, then smashed the glass on a small box marked with the words "EMERGENCY CARRIAGE RELEASE – WARNING! DO NOT ACTIVATE WHEN TRAIN IS IN FLIGHT". Penelope shoved her fist into the large red button. A warning klaxon sounded and a stern male voice announced carriage separation would commence within ten seconds. The leader of the Rippers reappeared in the corridor opposite Penelope, uncertain what was happening. His confusion turned to anger as the automated countdown began. He ran to the adjoining door but could not undo the lock in time. Penelope waved as the countdown reached zero, ignoring the Rippers' threats.

With a hiss of hydraulics, the *Flying Scotsman*'s final carriage uncoupled itself and tumbled away, turning end over end as it fell from the sky, plummeting into the black emptiness of the Watford Gap. Penelope watched as the Rippers' flying mounts raced after the descending carriage, but they could not catch up with it in time. In less than a minute the detached section of train had disappeared from view, along with its unscheduled cargo of DNA-sniffing psychopathic killers. "Secret agents one, Rippers nil," Penelope said with quiet satisfaction.

SEVEN

"However the devil is clad, he's still the devil."
– Russian proverb

"Traditional Highland dress for men has changed little over the centuries. Scotland may have been renamed Caledonia and transformed into a tartan tourist trap, but the kilt, sporran and Sgian Dhub remain much as they always have. A true kilt is made of eleven ounce quality pure worsted tartan, with a three buckle fastening and double fringed apron edge. Over the crotch any decent wearer will rest their sporran, a large pouch made of leather and fur that hangs from the belt. Below the knee is the kilt hose, usually an off-white sock or stocking often worn with flashes on adjustable garters.

Slotted into this on one leg is the Sgian Dhub, a small dagger held in an ornamental sheath. For the feet it is still traditional to wear ghillie brogues, the black leather shoes that have served Scotsmen for over a millennium. Above the waist a white shirt is most common, sometimes laced together across the chest. Last but not least is the Prince Charlie, a cut-off black wool jacket with gleaming silver buttons. Only the most crass of kilt wearers also sports a tam-o'-shanter, the brimless wool cap with a bobble in the centre. If you must indulge in this act of millinery madness, at least match the tartan of your hat with the tartan of your kilt. But whatever else you do, a true Highlander never wears underpants beneath his kilt. Your sporran will protect your modesty, so let everything else hang free as nature intended."

– Extract from *What's Scot to Wear*,
2670 edition

A polite knock at the compartment door woke Penelope shortly before dawn. With Dante handcuffed to the bed and snoring loudly, she had spent a fitful night on the chaise longue. The stench of *Bitch* still lingered in the room, like flatulence under a duvet, but with more acrid intensity. The knocking persisted so Penelope pulled a robe over her crimson silk pyjamas and approached the door. "Who is it?" she asked meekly.

"Gordonstoun, your steward," a familiar voice replied worriedly.

Penelope opened the door a fraction and peered out. The portly attendant was wringing his hands in the corridor, nervously shifting his weight from foot to foot. "Yes?" she asked, her voice becoming more forceful. "Surely breakfast is not for at least another hour?"

"You are correct, madam. This regards another matter entirely," Gordonstoun said apologetically. "It seems there was an incident late last night. We were boarded by Britannia Intelligence agents. They refused to explain their presence and began searching each carriage. Shortly afterwards the last section of the train fell into the Watford Gap, apparently with all the intelligence operatives on board. Our head office has asked me to take a full inventory of passengers, to ensure none were lost in this unfortunate incident."

Penelope smiled. "As you can see, I'm fit and well."

"What about your... husband?"

"Him? Well, his snoring remains as intolerable as ever, but he is otherwise well."

Gordonstoun nodded, his face still full of apologies. "I am glad to hear that, madam. Alas, I must ask to see him in person. My superiors have made it clear I must personally lay eyes upon all our passengers, to ascertain for myself nothing untoward has befallen any of them."

"Well, if you insist…" Penelope replied and opened the door wider, allowing the steward an eyeful of Dante's naked and bound body. A gust of *Bitch* escaped into the corridor. "Satisfied?"

"Yes, madam," Gordonstoun said with a blush, choking as the florid, cloying perfume flooded the air around him. "I see you have been busy."

"We've been tied up all night, you might say."

"Indeed. There has been quite a lot of that on board," he replied, shaking his head gently. "Well, I will delay you no longer. Breakfast will be served from seven onwards and we are due to stop at Nottingham a little after nine. Good day to you both." Penelope closed the door and returned to the chaise longue. What had the steward meant?

"It doesn't matter," Penelope told herself. Nottingham would be where they got off.

The Phord Capri screeched to a halt outside the Tower of London, back tyres protesting as the car spun through a hundred and eighty degrees before neatly inserting itself between two other vehicles. "Now that's what I call a piece of parking," Dobie announced smugly from the driver's seat. "What do you think, Ray?"

Boyle was too busy adjusting his mass of brown curls with the aid of an afro comb and a small, hand-held mirror. "Are we there yet?"

"Are we there yet?" Dobie replied in mock indignation. "I cross London in record time and you ask if we're there yet? I swear, my talents are wasted on you, they really are."

"I'd agree, if you had any talents to waste."

"Hark at him! So busy preening, I'm surprised you had time to think up a witty one-liner."

"Some of us are better than others at multi-tasking."

Dobie rolled his eyes. "Can we go and question those idiots? With you being so multi-talented, it shouldn't be a great challenge."

The two men sauntered towards the Tower's main gates, each trying to appear more causal than the other. Dobie bashed his fist against the wooden gates.

Boyle couldn't resist having the last word. "Obviously, I *am* multi-talented, but that wasn't what I said."

The gates swung open to reveal a man mountain of a sentry inside. Dobie flashed some credentials and pushed his way past. "I'm Dobie, he's Ray Boyle. We're bounty hunters, here on official business. We want to see Flatcock and Spatchlint."

"Spatchcock and Flintlock?" the sentry asked.

"Them," Boyle agreed, following Dobie inside. "Hey, do you think Flintlock is any relation to Lord Peter Flintlock, the one who got deported for–"

"Nah, he couldn't be," Dobie replied, shaking his head dismissively. "I doubt he'd ever have the nerve to show his face in the country again."

Dante opened his eyes and groaned. It had not been a bad dream after all, nor some kind of nightmare. He was naked, handcuffed and tied down on a four-poster bed. There was no sign of his captor and no way of calling for help thanks to the panties stuffed into his mouth. His nostrils felt as if they had been scoured with floral acid, thanks to the perfume Penelope had splashed all over his body. Dante's jaws ached from being gagged all night and his bladder was full to bursting. Unsympathetic comments from the Crest were doing little to improve his mood. *Perhaps now you'll listen when I try to warn you about the dangers of dubious women.*

The compartment's outer door opened and a member of the train's staff entered. His eyes widened at what he found inside. "Jings! Where's ye trews?"

Dante tried to answer but could make no more than muffled yelps. The steward ventured closer, sniffing the air suspiciously while stroking his ginger beard. "What a smell? Have ye been torturing a skunk in here?" Another muffled cry from Dante. "Did ye ken you have a pair of lassie's pants in your mouth?"

Penelope entered the compartment in a black version of her habitual catsuit, clutching a small pistol. The steward pulled the lingerie from Dante's mouth, staring at each garment in disbelief. "I was wrong – ye had two pairs of pants in there! Are ye some kind of bampot?" Before Dante could answer, Penelope smashed her pistol down on the steward's head, knocking him unconscious. He fell forward on top of Dante, who groaned at the added pressure on his bladder.

Penelope began stripping off the steward's Highland dress uniform. "You should be grateful. I searched the whole train to find anyone with the same build as you."

"Please," Dante pleaded. "I need the toilet. Now."

"Well, I'm not stopping you."

"No, but these are," Dante said, rattling the handcuffs. "Either you let me free or else I soak the sheets, the mattress and possibly the ceiling. It's your choice."

Penelope paused after removing the steward's kilt. "I see this one's a true Scotsman." She bit her bottom lip while studying her prisoner. "Very well. But one false move and I'll call the Rippers myself to deal with you."

"The Rippers? They've been here?" Dante asked while Penelope untied his numb legs.

"Last night. I used your clothes as a diversion to get them off the train."

"They'll be back."

"Yes, but we'll already be heading for London by then." She undid the cuff from Dante's left wrist, pulled it round the post and then reattached it to his arm. "The bathroom's through there, but leave the door open. I don't want you trying anything stupid."

"I'm stark naked and my legs are stiff from being tied up all night," he protested. "What am I going to do, fly out of here?" He staggered across to the bathroom, both legs weak and wobbly.

"You'd have to, we're still in the air." Penelope finished undressing the steward, then used her discarded silk scarves to tie up the attendant.

She shoved both pairs of saliva-soaked pants into his mouth and rolled him under the bed. The sound of splashing water made her check Dante's progress in the bathroom. "Haven't you finished in there yet?" Penelope found him struggling to throw water at himself while still in handcuffs.

"I'm trying to wash some of this perfume off," he scowled. "I stink like a bitch on heat."

"Get dressed," Penelope said, indicating the clothes she had stolen from the steward.

"What if I refuse?" Dante challenged.

"My orders are to deliver you alive," she replied, aiming her small pistol at his genitals. "That doesn't mean I have to take you back to London unharmed."

Dante arranged his hands across his groin. "Watch where you're pointing that thing!"

"Don't worry, I'd have to be a sharpshooter to hit something that small."

I like her, the Crest announced cheerfully.

"Well, don't get used to having her around," Dante replied.

Penelope glared at him. "What did you say?"

"Nothing – a private conversation."

She smiled. "That's right, the Crest communicates with you telepathically – I read about that in a briefing paper. A remarkable piece of kit."

"It has some uses," Dante conceded.

Like keeping you alive more times than I care to remember.

"Don't let it go to your head," Dante snapped.

Penelope sighed. "Being with you is like sitting next to a surly husband arguing on the phone with his ex-wife about their divorce settlement."

"You should try being inside my head!"

I doubt she'd enjoy the experience, the Crest commented.

"I doubt I'd enjoy the experience," Penelope unwittingly agreed.

"Bojemoi, the two of you even talk alike," Dante lamented. He finished wiping himself with a hand towel and returned to the main cabin. He surveyed the steward's clothes unhappily. "I haven't worn a kilt since visiting the Victoria Falls in Africa. It's not the most reassuring outfit." His eyes lit up after spotting the Sgian Dhub among the accessories. Dante crouched beside the clothes to retrieve the dagger in its elaborately carved sheath.

"I hope you're not planning to stab me with that blade."

"The thought never entered my head," Dante replied. In a single movement he pulled the dagger from the sheath and flung it across the room at Penelope. The blade hit her between the breasts, then bounced away to the floor. She smiled and picked up the ceremonial dagger, bending its blade between her fingers.

"Purely ornamental. This one's made of rubber, it wouldn't hurt a midge."

"I knew that," Dante maintained. "I was simply testing your reflexes."

Penelope rolled her eyes. "Your lying is worse than your snoring. Now, get dressed if you want to eat before we get off the train."

Flintlock's constant complaining had won him a reprieve from being manacled to Spatchcock, but the captives were still sharing a cell. The malodorous runt had retreated to one corner while his aristocratic companion kept to the other, near the door. "We've got visitors," Flintlock announced.

"Female?" Spatchcock asked hopefully. "I was going to ask for a roll in the hay as my final request, before the execution."

"I'm not sure they'll let you have a goat in here, old boy." Flintlock retreated from the door as it was unlocked. A burly sentry let two men into the dank, dismal dungeon, then shut and locked the door once more. The visitors' faces curdled at the stench.

"That guard wasn't kidding about the smell, was he?" one of the newcomers gasped. "I've been to slaughterhouses that weren't this bad."

The other man pinched his nose shut and breathed through his mouth. "Which one of you is Lord Peter Flintlock?"

"He is!" the prisoners replied in unison, pointing at each other.

"Very droll." The curly-haired visitor introduced himself as Ray Boyle, then jerked a thumb towards his nose-pinching associate. "Forgive Dobie's appearance, but he always looks like that."

Dobie looked down at his clothes, a plethora of brown and taupe. "What's wrong with the way I dress?"

"I was talking about your face," Boyle replied with a smirk. He studied the two prisoners before pointing a finger at Flintlock. "You must be his lordship, judging by the white hair and haughty discomfort. I'd have thought the most disgraced man in Britannia would be used to hovels like this by now. You've been in exile long enough – what made you come back?"

"I'd rather not talk about it," Flintlock said primly, folding his arms.

"Have it your own way." Boyle drove a fist into Flintlock's midriff. The prisoner crumpled like a paper bag, gasping for air as he sagged to the stone floor. Spatchcock took a step closer to defend his friend but was stopped by a punch in the head from Dobie. The small man went sprawling, his skull smacking against the nearest wall. He too slumped to the cold floor, blood streaming from a gash on the side of his face. Boyle crouched in front of Flintlock, his cold blue eyes staring into the prisoner's trembling face. "Or you can have it my way. So, which do you prefer? Pain or more pain?"

"What do you want?" Spatchcock asked sourly.

"That's better," Dobie smiled. "See how much easier life can be if you co-operate?"

"Just ask your questions," Spatchcock said.

"All right," Boyle agreed, straightening up again. "Nikolai Dante – where is he?"

"How should we know?" Spatchcock replied. "The last we saw of him was when he jumped out a window at the Palace of London, after the king was shot."

"You haven't seen him since?"

"We were arrested within minutes and brought here. That was at least a day ago, if not longer." Spatchcock gestured at their surroundings. "Not having my social secretary handy, it's a little difficult to be precise about dates."

Boyle used his left knee to give Flintlock a nudge. "What about you? What have you got to say for yourself?"

"Spatch is right," Flintlock whispered between strained breaths. "We don't know where Dante is. He doesn't confide in us."

"So he left you behind to take the rap while he flees London, is that it?" Dobie sneered.

Spatchcock glared at the bounty hunters. "He's left the city?"

"He's betrayed you – both of you."

Spatchcock shook his head. "Not after everything we've been through together. I know Dante, his conscience will get the better of him, sooner or later. He'll come back for us, he'll find a way of getting us out of this place."

Boyle laughed. "I wouldn't count on it." He kicked at Flintlock. "What about it, your lordship? Do you share your foul-smelling friend's faith in Dante?"

"No. If I knew anything useful, I'd tell you," Flintlock said. "I'm no hero."

"But Dante is," Spatchcock maintained. "By now he's busy planning how to free us while sleeping with anything in knickers. You'll see!"

Penelope slapped Dante hard across the face. "Put your hands on me again and I'll chop them off!" They were returning from breakfast in the dining car, where she had kept Dante under control by having her pistol constantly aimed at him beneath the table. But when Penelope tried to unlock her compartment, Dante had been unable to resist fondling her firm buttocks.

"I was checking to see if you have any more concealed weapons," he said.

"Your feeble attempts at seduction couldn't arouse a nymphomaniac." Penelope shoved him into the cabin. "We're due to land at Nottingham within the hour. When we get off, I don't want any trouble. Keep your hands to yourself and you'll keep your hands. Otherwise I'll be forced to disable you – permanently."

"I've been tortured by the best," Dante boasted. "There's nothing you can do to me that hasn't been tried and failed."

"Is that a fact?" Penelope asked, moving closer to him. She ran a hand across Dante's chest, then let it slide down between his legs.

"Absolutely," he affirmed.

"What if I was to seduce you, would that change things?"

Dante shook his head, trying to ignore the sensations her hands were creating. "I possess total self control," he said as Penelope's fingernails dug into his muscular buttocks.

"Total self control?" she asked huskily.

Dante nodded, not trusting himself to speak. Penelope's hands slid up and down, gripping, teasing, taunting him. Her tongue slid between his lips, exploring him hungrily, her body forcing him back until he slammed into a wall.

Penelope pulled her lips away from his. "You don't think I could have you whenever I wanted?"

"Not at all," he whispered, willing her to undo the zip that ran down between her breasts to the catsuit's crotch

"We'll see," Penelope said, smiling broadly. Her hand suddenly clenched around Dante's crown jewels, squeezing with the grip of a vice. He screamed in agony and she kissed him again, momentarily relaxing her hold on his scrotum, then clenching again, harder than before. Dante's face showed every paroxysm of pain stabbing through his body. Just as suddenly she released her iron grip and stepped backwards, letting him sink to the floor, hands nursing his bruised body parts. "So much for total self control. I'll never understand why people call women the weaker sex. One squeeze in the right place and you men keel over like a broken bicycle."

"Urgh," Dante replied weakly.

Penelope retrieved a tiny key from between her breasts and used it to unlock the cuff around Dante's right wrist. She clamped the empty binding around her left wrist and locked it into place, tugging hard at the metal to make sure it was securely fastened. Satisfied with the results, she slapped Dante's face to get his attention. "I am now going to swallow the key for these unique bindings. It is the sole method of opening them. Even if you managed to overpower me, you cannot escape me. Better you know that now and save both of us any further trouble. Penelope stuck the key on her tongue and then swallowed. "By the way, as long as any part of the handcuffs remains in contact with you, neither of your bio-blades will function. You and I are stuck with each other until that key flushes through my body."

You certainly know how to pick them, don't you?

"Oh, shut up," Dante winced.

Dobie and Boyle emerged from the Tower of London to find Rucka sitting on the bonnet of their hover-car. "What a pleasant surprise!" Dobie said sarcastically. "Inspector, that's twice in two days you've been seen with us – people will talk. To what do we owe this dishonour?"

"Spatchcock and Flintlock have no idea where Dante is," Rucka replied.

"That much we found out for ourselves," Boyle remarked.

"But I know where he is," the inspector continued, producing a slip of paper. "On here is written the location where Dante can be found today – if you hurry."

The two bounty hunters exchanged a quizzical look. "Why give that to us?"

"For a start, I'm not giving it to you," Rucka said, standing upright. "I will pass useful facts to you in exchange for a percentage of the reward you claim by finding and killing Dante."

"What kind of percentage?" Bole asked.

"Fifty."

Dobie snorted derisively. "You're joking! The only people we share anything with is eachother. How do we even know your information is accurate?"

"You'll have to trust me," Rucka said. "But if you can't trust a policeman, who can you trust?"

"We don't trust anybody," Boyle sneered.

The inspector shrugged and started strolling away. "Have it your own way."

The two bounty hunters watched him go, trying to call his bluff. After a few seconds they caved in, calling him back. Rucka's smile was smugger than ever when he turned round. "Fifty per cent."

"If we don't catch him, that'll be fifty per cent of nothing," Boyle observed.

"Then don't fail. Have we got an agreement?"

The partners nodded reluctantly. The inspector handed Dobie the slip of paper. "Your quarry is on the *Flying Scotsman*, It should be arriving in Nottingham any minute. He's almost certainly in the custody of a Britannia Intelligence operative called Penelope Goodnight. Your job is to find and kill him, then bring the body back to claim the reward. Don't underestimate Agent Goodnight. She's the best."

Dobie laughed. "With a name like that, how dangerous can she be?"

"Goodnight has lured more men and women to their doom than you've had hot dinners."

"Her feminine charms won't work on us," Boyle said, shaking his head dismissively.

"Why not?" Rucka asked.

"We prefer our lovers a little more butch," Dobie replied. "Don't we, Ray?"

Boyle blew a kiss at his partner.

The inspector sighed. "Nevertheless, Agent Goodnight is a resourceful woman, she could get the better of you two. Kill her and you'll have the entire secret service hunting you to the ends of the earth. But Dante cannot be permitted to return to London alive. He's too dangerous."

"You're the boss," Boyle agreed. "One last question – why us? Why not send your own men after this fugitive?"

"You two may be the scum of the earth, but you're the best," Rucka said. "I've read your files – you've never failed a contract. Don't start now." He consulted his watch. "If I were you, I'd already be en route to Nottingham. Every minute you spend talking with me is a minute wasted, and you don't have time for that. Good day, gentlemen."

Gordonstoun breathed a sigh of relief as the *Flying Scotsman* landed on the tracks outside Nottingham. He had been a crew member for ten years, working his way up from the lowliest position to become head steward. In all that time he had never experienced as many incidents as he had since leaving London on this journey. The shenanigans involving Ms Goodnight and her 'husband' were nothing unusual – aristocrats and the rich were perpetually using the train as their love-nest for adulterous interludes. Even the use of handcuffs and other bondage paraphernalia were not unknown among certain passengers. But to have the train boarded by a dozen Rippers, that was exceptional. Gordonstoun did not relish the prospect of preparing a report for head office when the train finally got back to London. Perhaps I can delegate it to one of my assistants, he thought as the *Flying Scotsman* braked to a halt at Nottingham Station.

The head steward banished such musings to concentrate on ensuring the large group of travellers leaving at this station took all their belongings. A typical passenger was a foreign visitor who wished to see Britannia in style, and the *Flying Scotsman* provided that style: sedate, luxurious, old fashioned and yet simultaneously ultra-modern with its innovative use of hover-technology. But this particular party had come from all over Britannia simply to ride the train between London and Nottingham. There were far cheaper and quicker options available to them, but they had willingly paid full price for one night aboard the train. Ours is not to reason why, Gordonstoun reminded himself. Life on board would be a lot less hectic once they were gone.

He moved through each compartment, checking closets and drawers and under the beds for any forgotten possessions. Besides the usual selection of discarded stockings and lonely shoes he also uncovered five sets of handcuffs, several rubber masks and what looked suspiciously like a metre-long double-ended black dildo. "Perverts," Gordonstoun muttered while locking the items away in his personal locker. If nothing else they should make for amusing presents at the crew's Christmas party. Gordonstoun was so busy he missed the news flash broadcast in Nottingham Station as the passengers finished disembarking.

Penelope tugged her left arm, jerking Dante down the stairs on to the platform. The fugitive was still bitterly nursing his testicles and almost lost his footing. "Diavolo, what's your rush? Some of us are still recovering," he protested.

"The only thing I hurt was your pride," she snapped. "Stop touching your groin, it makes you look like a pervert."

"I doubt the handcuffs are making that image any better."

Penelope's face lit up as she spotted an information board beneath a huge holographic display. She dragged Dante towards it, passing three junior stewards in strange garb. Each was acting as a gathering point for the *Flying Scotsman*'s day trips.

"This way all those passengers who want to visit Nottingham's castle!" the first steward shouted, ushering a handful of people towards a waiting bus. He was wearing a jerkin of simulated chainmail and clasping an unwieldy pikestaff.

"Everybody who wants to savour the Robin Hood experience by having lunch in Sherwood Forest, come with me!" cried another steward, clad in ungainly green medieval clothes. Like the first option, this was drawing only a handful of passengers.

"All those bound for the historic country estate of the Fforbes-Lamington family, gather here for transportation," the third steward called out. She was dressed in a pink hunting jacket, light brown jodhpurs and black leather riding boots. An enthusiastic crowd quickly gathered around her, all demanding to be taken to the country estate. "Golly!" she said, somewhat overwhelmed. "I didn't know we would get so many of you today! I'll have to go and arrange for a larger coach to transport everybody." She made urgent signals to another staff member for help.

Dante observed all this with little interest until he saw a familiar figure among the passengers lining up to visit the castle. When the man looked around, Dante could clearly see a goatee beard and mournful expression. "That's him! He's one of people who tried to kill the king," Dante said excitedly, jerking his manacled arm to get Penelope's attention. But by the time she turned to follow his gaze, the man had vanished among the crowds on the platform.

"What is it?" she asked.

"One of the other passengers on the train, he was an accomplice to the assassination attempt on King Henry. That's why I got on the *Flying Scotsman*, I was following him!"

"You're claiming to be innocent?"

"Of trying to kill the king? Yes, of course!"

Penelope did not look impressed. "You would say anything to escape execution."

"Of course, but for once in my life, I'm telling the truth," Dante insisted. "You're not giving me a chance to clear my name!"

"Why should I believe you?"

"Help me catch the real killer and I'll show you."

Penelope shook her head. "This is a ruse to distract me – and not a very good one."

"What have you got to lose by trusting me?"

"My job, my reputation, my chance of promotion – almost everything, in fact."

"Why won't you listen?"

"Because you're a liar, a thief, a conman, a rogue, a brigand and one of the most wanted men in the Empire. If our positions were reversed, would you believe me in such circumstances?"

"No," Dante admitted.

"There, you see–"

"But I'd still give you a chance to prove your innocence."

Penelope shook her head. "Then you would be a sentimental fool."

"Better that than a cold, heartless bitch more interested in furthering her career than discovering the truth. Don't you believe in justice?"

"I believe in what I can see, hear, taste, touch and smell," she snarled. "Everything else is irrelevant. Now, let's get moving." Penelope shoved Dante towards the exit, but they had only gone a few steps when a woman's voice boomed through the station's public address system.

"We interrupt your regular programming to broadcast this news flash. According to sources within the intelligence community, one of Britannia's own secret service operatives may be a co-conspirator in the attempted assassination of King Henry. A leaked document suggests Agent Penelope Goodnight has links with the fugitive Nikolai Dante, who has already been found guilty of his involvement. It is believed she may be attempting to smuggle Dante out of the country. Police and other law enforcement agencies have already been placed on high alert in the search for Dante. No picture of Agent Goodnight is currently available, but the authorities hope to publish such an image within the next few hours. Thank you for your attention."

"It seems we're partners in crime," Dante observed. "Welcome to my world."

"This isn't right," she protested. "I've done nothing wrong!"

"Now you know how I feel." Dante held open his arms. "Group hug?"

Penelope slapped his face instead. "You did this! Somehow you've dragged me down to your level. I need to find a policeman, tell them they've got it wrong."

"Oh yeah, that works every time," he said. The smirk on his lips was wiped away when she started waving frantically at a policeman who had wandered on to the platform. Dante grabbed her arm and pulled it back down. "Fuoco, what are you doing?"

"Trying to get his attention."

"You'll get both of us arrested or executed where we stand! Your boss may have wanted me captured alive, but the police have shoot to kill orders – and they know what I look like!"

"You're right. We need to find a place to hide, give ourselves a chance to think." The people waiting to visit the Fforbes-Lamington estate were now being loaded onto coaches nearby. "We'll join the back of that group lose ourselves amongst them for the rest of the day while I figure out what's gone wrong." She strode towards the queue, dragging Dante along behind.

He pulled the tam-o'-shanter forwards to hide his face as they passed the policeman. "You've changed your tune all of a sudden," Dante commented once they had joined the queue.

"What are you talking about?"

"Five minutes ago I was a liar, a thief, a conman, a rogue and one of the most wanted men in the Empire. You couldn't care less what happened to me, as long as you got the credit for bringing me to justice. Now 'we' need to find a place to hide and figure out what's gone wrong. Since when did we become a team?"

"Since somebody in Britannia Intelligence turned me into a fugitive like you," Penelope said angrily. "Don't make the mistake of thinking I'm happy about this. But you're right – as far as the authorities are concerned, we're partners in crime now." Their queue was diminishing rapidly as the last passengers clambered on to the coach. Dante couldn't help smiling. "What's so funny?" Penelope demanded.

Dante held up his right wrist, the one handcuffed to her left arm. "Bet you're wishing you hadn't swallowed that key now, right?"

"Don't remind me!"

EIGHT

"Many words, little truth."
– Russian proverb

"The Fforbes-Lamington estate is one of Britannia's last remaining examples of a country seat still owned by the landed gentry. Over the past nine hundred years financial strife and mismanagement have bankrupted most of the families that once held feudal rights to vast sections of the countryside. Historic estates were broken up, parcels of land sold off piecemeal to developers and turned into soulless housing dormitories. Happily, the Fforbes-Lamington estate outside Nottingham did not suffer this ignominious fate.

The family has kept hold of its assets and even added to them in recent decades, thanks to adroit acquisitions by the head of the household, Audrey Fforbes-Lamington.

A formidable woman in every sense of the word, her first husband died of a heart condition. She temporarily lost possession of the estate for four years, then married immigrant businessman Dick Revere, who had bought it at auction. He died within a year and Ms Fforbes-Lamington reverted to her maiden name. Few visitors are allowed on the estate, which is said to be guarded by an extensive network of security droids. Once a year Ms Fforbes-Lamington holds a weekend of

events for a few select friends. Invitations for this event are among the sought after items on Britannia's social calendar – gatecrashers are certainly *not* welcome."
    – Extract from *The Smirnoff Almanac of Fascinating Facts*, 2673 edition

Dante and Penelope were still arguing as they tried to find a seat on the last coach. The hover-bus was filled with passengers Dante recognised from his brief visit to the train's first class lounge the previous night. One of them, a slender man with silver-grey hair and a bushy moustache, stopped the duo as they came down the aisle. He grabbed hold of the handcuffs for a closer look. "I say, what an unusual pair of handcuffs! Wherever did you get them?"

"They were a gift from her royal highness," Penelope said archly. "Now, if you'll excuse–"

"You see, I was wondering where I could get a pair," the man persisted. "Mine are almost worn out from years of abuse, so I'm always searching for a good replacement."

"They're a one-off, specially commissioned by the Tsar himself," Penelope snapped.

"Is that a fact? Fascinating!" the passenger enthused. "Well, I'll let you go get changed." He shifted his attention to a leather bag on the seat next to him. "Now, where did I put my cuffs?"

Dante noticed that the back row of the hover-bus was empty and led a bemused Penelope to the vacant seats. The two fugitives took shelter in one corner, away from the prying eyes of the other passengers. "I thought you wanted to find a place to hide so we could plan our next move?"

"That wasn't my fault," Penelope said. "I can't help it if some old pervert wants to know where I got these handcuffs, can I?"

"No, but telling him they were a gift from the princess is not what I call keeping a low profile," Dante snapped back. "Diavolo! You've got a lot to learn about being a fugitive."

"And you'd be an expert in that, having been on the run most of your life!"

"Can I help being popular?"

"I didn't realise shoot-to-kill orders were a sign of popularity," Penelope sneered.

Dante, I–

"Not now, Crest! I'm pointing out a few facts to Agent Know-It-All here."

But I've recalled where–

"I said not now!" Dante said, before switching his attention back to Penelope. "I've been the most wanted, most hated, most hunted man on the planet, but few have caught me and nobody has kept me. I trained with James Di Grizov, the greatest escapologist in the *Vorovskoi Mir*, the Thieves' World. You might have lured me into bed, but I would have got away again long before you ever got me back to London. Nobody keeps Nikolai Dante under lock and key for long!"

Penelope applauded him with slow handclaps. "Congratulations."

"Why?"

"Never have I met a man more full of his own self importance than you."

I've remembered where I recognised all those–

Dante smirked. "Crest, I think the lady protests too much."

"What?" Penelope demanded.

"Almost every time a woman says she hates me, it's usually because she hates herself for wanting me. The Tsar's daughter Jena was just the same. She couldn't decide which she wanted most: seeing me dead, or getting me in bed."

"Trust me," Penelope vowed. "My hatred for you is strictly personal."

Dante reached for the hem of his kilt. "Sure you don't want another peek at the goods, see if they change your mind?"

She slapped his hand away. "Please, it's not long since I ate breakfast – don't make me throw it all back up again."

Will you listen to me for once in your miserable, misbegotten life, the Crest raged.

Dante winced in pain from the shouting in his mind. "Fuoco! All right, all right, I'm listening! What's so important I should stop flirting with Penelope here?"

"Flirting?" she spluttered. "You call this flirting?"

"You love it," he replied with a lecherous wink. "Well, Crest?"

I've been trying to tell you I remember where I recognised the other passengers.

"Go on, then, don't keep me in suspense."

Before the war, you went to Venice with one of your Romanov half-sisters, Lulu.

"She's a member of the Cadre Infernale – she wanted me to join," Dante recalled.

Penelope frowned, struggling to make sense of the conversation from only Dante's words. "I've heard of the Cadre. It's a secret society for aristocrats and politicians from across the Empire, allowing them to indulge in decadence and vice without fear of scandal."

The people on the train, the Crest continued, *are all members of the Cadre Infernale.*

"Are you sure?" Dante asked.

Absolutely. It took me this long to identify them because almost everyone you saw at Venice was naked except for their masks.

"So how were you able to recognise them now?" Dante became aware of Penelope tapping him on the shoulder. "Not now, the Crest is trying to tell me something important!

"So am I," she replied. "Look!"

Dante twisted his head round to find the other passengers on the hover-bus gathered around them. All were dressed in rubber and leather bondage garb. Most of their faces were covered by black, studded masks, while male genitals fought to escape from obscene posing pouches and women's breasts dangled from cup-less chain brassieres. Each of the passengers was clutching a whip or handcuffs, several also had riding crops and cattle prods in their hands. Dante's face fell as he surveyed the perverts clustered around him and Penelope. "Would it be stating the obvious to say I have a bad feeling about this?"

Boyle was piloting the Phord Capri as it approached the outskirts of Nottingham. He tipped the sleek hover-car over into a banking manoeuvre. Dobie cursed from the passenger seat. "Watch it, Ray! Some of us are trying to pluck our eyebrows."

"You mean clear a path through the undergrowth of your mono-brow?"

"Jealously will get you nowhere. I simply have an excess of testosterone in my system that requires a little more care and attention when it comes to grooming."

"Dobie, you spend so long looking in a mirror, it's a wonder you don't go blind."

"I like looking at beautiful things. Can I help it if I'm one of them?"

Boyle rolled his eyes, but couldn't help smiling too. "Where's this train station then?"

His partner pointed through a gap in the clouds. "At a guess, I'd say where those train tracks all converge."

"From what I hear Dante's a slippery customer – you ready for this?"

Dobie pulled a ludicrously hefty handgun from a holster in his left armpit. "You know me, Ray – I was born ready."

Dante and Penelope were rigorously searched by the other passengers during their journey to the Fforbes-Lamington estate. Dante had nothing to lose since he was already in borrowed clothes, but an unhappy Penelope was forced to surrender a small pistol, her boots and her wristwatch as the coach landed outside a pair of ornate, wrought iron gates. Silver security droids took custody of the two unwanted guests. Dante and Penelope were frog-marched from the vehicle by the two-metre tall mechanoids. Once the bus had entered the estate, the droids shoved their prisoners inside before the gates slid shut. A sky-sled appeared overhead, slicing through the air like a metallic magic carpet. The sole augmentation to its utilitarian design was a handrail above the outer edge at waist height. The sled dropped from the sky and the mute droids stepped up, dragging Dante and Penelope behind them. The words 'HOLD ON' flashed on the floor twice.

"Is that telling us to wait?" Dante asked.

The message is probably more literal, the Crest replied. *The sled's hover-engines are preparing for take-off. I'd advise you to get a grip on something solid.*

Penelope had already grabbed the nearest handrail, but Dante was not so quick. Suddenly the sled flung itself back into the sky, throwing him off his feet. Only the handcuffs binding him to Penelope saved Dante from flying off the sled and tumbling to his death. One of the droids pushed Dante across to the nearest handrail, which he gratefully gasped. "Bojemoi!" he gasped after finding his footing again. "You don't get much warning on this thing, do you?"

Penelope glared at him. "It's a wonder you've stayed alive as long as you have, considering how little intelligence you display."

If only she knew how right she is, the Crest sighed.

"I like to lull my enemies into a false sense of security," Dante replied.

"Try not to lose yourself in the role," Penelope advised.

The sky-sled skimmed over a glorious patchwork of fields and hedgerows, streams and thickets. It was still mid-morning, but the sun was already baking the countryside below. A stately home appeared in the distance, rapidly getting closer.

That must be Fforbes-Lamington House, the Crest observed. *A most remarkable building, the last great example of rococo architecture in Britannia. The marble interiors were imported from Italy, while each pane of glass was ground by hand to match the prescription of the Fforbes-Lamington patriarch, so he wouldn't have to wear glasses indoors. The entire structure was relocated here seven hundred years ago to avoid demolition work for a bypass. The task took a thousand craftsmen more than twenty-seven months.*

Dante frowned as the sky-sled landed outside the front entrance on the gravel courtyard. "Looks like the world's ugliest wedding cake to me."

Must you always act the philistine?

"Who said I was acting?"

Penelope sighed theatrically to the security droids. "You see what I have to put up with? This fool talks to himself constantly. He took me captive, forced me on board that coach."

Dante arched an eyebrow at her. "What are you doing?"

"Don't listen to a word he says," she continued. "He claims I'm his accomplice, but I had never seen him before he abducted me yesterday." The mechanoids stepped off the sky-sled, dragging Penelope and Dante with them towards the stately home's huge double doors.

"They're not buying your little Miss Innocent act," Dante commented. "I guess your powers of seduction only work on creatures of flesh and blood."

"Actually, no," another voice replied. "Ms Goodnight has had some success with robots that possess emotion circuits. Alas, my security droids do not, so her charms are lost on them."

Penelope looked at the woman who had emerged from the double doors. "You! *You're* Audrey Fforbes-Lamington?"

The mistress of the estate laughed. "But of course! Who were you expecting?" The middle-aged woman was dressed in a dowdy tweed skirt and cream woollen top. Her face was haughty and severe, framed by sandy brown hair cut in an unforgiving bob. Everything about her screamed asexual harridan to Dante.

"I'm guessing you two know each other," he quipped, trying to lighten the mood.

"Quite so," Fforbes-Lamington replied. "But young Penelope here knows me by another name. Within Britannia Intelligence I am simply called F. I am Agent Goodnight's commander."

"That explains the perverts!" Dante exclaimed.

"Sorry?" Penelope and F said in unison.

"It's traditional for the head of Britannia Intelligence also to be leader of the Cadre's Britannia chapter. That's why you had a coach-load of sex freaks coming to visit. You're holding the annual Sabbat here."

F applauded his powers of deduction. "Precisely. Now, since you've so kindly presented yourselves at my door, why don't you come inside – if you'll pardon the expression."

After they parked the Capri, Dobie and Boyle sauntered into Nottingham's train station. All looked normal except the entrance to Platform Five. A dozen men in black cloaks and top hats were guarding the gate, while the sound of frenzied activity was audible beyond them. "Do you see what I see?" Boyle asked his partner quietly.

Dobie nodded. "Rippers. The *Flying Scotsman* must be on that platform. Sounds like they're going over it with a fine tooth comb."

"Being Rippers, they're probably using a stiletto – but the principle's the same. Know what I like most about the Rippers?"

"Not their fashion sense. Don't they know black is out this season?"

"No," Boyle said impatiently. "Their lack of imagination. Somebody told them Dante is on that train, so they'll keep searching 'til they find him."

"But if he isn't on the train?"

"He must be nearby."

Dobie smiled. "Time to find some answers. Meet you back here in ten minutes?"

His partner nodded. "See you soon." The pair strolled away in opposite directions.

F escorted Penelope and Dante through her stately home to a huge, empty room facing the back of the estate. The floor was a checkerboard of black and white marble, while tall picture windows afforded a magnificent view of sculpted gardens outside. The other walls were given over to row upon row of bookshelves, all of them barren of volumes. There were only three pieces of furniture in the cavernous space – an elaborate throne of silver and blue, and a pair of old dentist's chairs. Each of these was augmented with several leather restraint straps and both stood on a dais of thick, black rubber.

"This was the library for several centuries," F said grandly, "but I sold all the old books to the Britannia National Library. Nobody ever read the bloody things, they were a nightmare to dust and the money paid to restore the house to its former glory after my second husband's timely demise." She gestured towards the dentist chairs. "Would you like to take a seat?"

"I prefer to stand," Penelope replied tersely.

"Perhaps I did not make myself clear," F said. She gestured to the four corners of the ceiling, where small laser cannons appeared among the rococo ornamentation, their terse snouts taking aim at her guests. "Take a seat, both of you, or else my interior security system will incinerate you. It's a simple choice."

"Well, since you put it like that," Dante smiled and jumped into the nearest chair. "Penelope, come and join me."

"First, use the leather restraints to tie him down," F commanded. "I want to avoid any unpleasantness. Young Nikolai does have quite a reputation for causing mayhem and chaos."

"Vastly exaggerated," he said as Penelope bound him in place, strapping his arms and legs into position. She sat in the other dentist's chair, securing both her legs and an arm in place.

"That will do," F said, easing herself into the imposing throne opposite them. "I think we can trust the laser cannons to dissuade you from taking any direct action. Unlike Dante, you do not have the advantage of enhanced healing abilities." F smiled at her guests. "I must say it's quite a coincidence, you two appearing at my door! If I believed in such nonsense, I might call it fate."

"Bad luck would be a better description," Penelope said sourly.

"Whichever makes you feel better, my dear. Tell me, how did you evade the Rippers?"

"You sent them! I should have known... Why?"

"My code breakers intercepted a transmission between you and Princess Marie-Anne. It was obvious she had turned you in, no doubt with some lofty promise to appeal to your vanity and ambition. Did she offer you my job, perhaps?" Penelope did not answer, but her silence was eloquent enough. F nodded. "I thought as much. Beware her royal highness, Agent Goodnight – she cares for nobody but herself, as I'm sure Dante here can confirm."

"That bitch and I have had our moments," he conceded.

"Twice you've succeeded in thwarting her plans and having the princess confined to a cell inside the Tower of London. I'm surprised you're still alive, frankly."

"I'm too cool to kill."

"Take care," F warned him. "One day that could become your epitaph."

"Not if I can help it," he replied. "My half-sister Lulu is leader of the Cadre Infernale. That makes you her underling. Shouldn't you check with her first before engineering my execution?"

"I've always hated that bitch," F snapped. "She uses our members for her own twisted ends, to further her crusade against the Tsar. She abuses her rank and its privileges!"

"I thought that was the whole point of your little perverts' club: twisting members and acting the bitch. You're like the Freemasons, but with more ball gags and fewer aprons."

"The Cadre Infernale is a sexual release for its membership, not a political powerbase. Yes, if one of us needs help when in trouble, we do what we can for them. The acquisition and retention of power is not what drives the Cadre, what puts fire in our bellies or a thrill in our loins. We value perversity, in all forms, above everything else. Nothing is more important to us."

"So, you're just a bunch of sick, sex-obsessed losers trying to get your rocks off?" Dante asked. "In that case I'm glad I never accepted Lulu's offer to join – I get all the action I want without having to dress in rubber or beg for a spanking."

"You're not a begging man?" F asked. When Dante nodded, she pressed a button built into the left arm of her throne. The effect was startling. Electricity surged through the two dentist chairs, passing back and forth across the prisoners' bodies, making them jerk and thrash like rag dolls in the grip of an angry child. Dante and Penelope screamed in agony, blue sparks escaping from their chattering teeth. After a full five seconds of this treatment, F removed her finger from the button and the electrocution ceased. She waited until they had recovered before speaking. "Now, what were you saying?"

A few bribes, some vague threats and careful questions soon secured Boyle and Dobie all the facts they needed. Dante and Penelope were last seen boarding a hover-bus bound for the Forbes-Lamington estate on the outskirts of Nottingham, with a bus full of sexual deviants. Dobie smiled to himself. "Sounds like our kind of party, Ray."

"That's what I was thinking." Boyle looked down at his taut jeans, knit shirt and plaid bomber jacket. "But I feel overdressed for a weekend of bondage and discipline."

"Well, let's find something more suitable for the occasion. I'm sure we can whip ourselves into shape in no time."

The Capri was gone in sixty seconds, a puff of blue smoke and rubber burn marks on the roadside the only signs it had even been there.

F took her finger off the button, having administered a third, brutal dose of shock treatment to her prisoners. Dante gasped for air while Penelope spat a mouthful of abuse at her commander. "Such language!" F replied haughtily. "Not very ladylike, I must say – not very ladylike at all." She gave both of them another jolt, letting her finger linger on the button slightly longer this time. When she had finished, Dante gave a low, throaty chuckle. "May I ask what is so amusing?"

"You are."

"Please elucidate," F prompted but got no reply.

She wants you to explain, the Crest told Dante.

"Oh. Right. I knew that," he muttered. "I was laughing because I've met your kind before. You get your kicks by hurting and tormenting others – not from their actual pain, but from wielding the sort of power you have over us at present."

"Is that a fact?"

"He's right," Penelope agreed. "I've seen how you operate at headquarters, the way you deliberately humiliate the operatives – your hands start to quiver with excitement. You start sweating too, the skin between your nose and your top lip gets all moist. It's disgusting."

"It's probably not the only area getting moist," Dante added.

Another stab at the button, and a fresh jolt of electricity shot across the prisoners' torsos. F let them dance about inside their restraints for a full minute before stopping the torture.

"I'll bet every time you touch that button, we're not the only ones getting the juice," Dante snarled, his lips pulled back from his teeth in an animal grimace of pain. F sent another jolt of power through them, then another and another. When she finally sat back in her chair, the head of Britannia Intelligence could not disguise her lustful panting.

"You sick, twisted bitch," Penelope said, shaking her head.

"Yes, I am," F agreed, "but you don't become mistress of the Cadre Infernale without having a few kinks in your system. Now that I've enjoyed myself, it's time for you to answer a few questions. Dante, why did you try to assassinate the king? Before this visit you were his greatest supporter. Why turn on him when he needed you most?"

"Bojemoi, when will somebody believe me?" Dante protested. "I had nothing to do with the attack on the king, nor the murder of his mother. Henry brought me here to protect him from an assassination attempt. All I feel guilty about is failing to stop the hit happening."

F pondered this. "That would fit with your previous pattern of behaviour."

"At last! Somebody who can see the truth!" he rejoiced.

"But your reputation as a liar and a scoundrel makes anything you say difficult to trust," F concluded with a small smile. "Convince me. If you weren't responsible, who was?"

"I don't know," Dante conceded. "Why? Could you intervene on my behalf?"

"I could, but I'm not going to," she said. "You make a convenient scapegoat. The attack on the king's life is a useful catalyst for change. Had someone else not perpetrated this crime, I might have been forced to commission it myself."

"How can you play god with people's lives like this?" Penelope demanded.

"Please, don't lecture me on morality, Agent Goodnight. You've destroyed plenty of lives with your bedroom antics for Britannia. I've never noticed any qualms from you in the past."

"That was different. I was doing my job."

"Just following orders, is that your defence?" Penelope spat more curses at her commander. "You've been spending too long with Dante," F said, "judging by your vocabulary's rapid descent into the gutter. I'd expect such obscenities from a low-born wretch like him, but not a cultured, highly trained agent of Britannia Intelligence."

"Who are you calling a wretch?" Dante protested, but F ignored him.

"I know Princess Marie-Anne wanted young Nikolai delivered to her alive but, alas, I cannot permit that to happen. Far better for him to die a guilty man than survive and prove his innocence – assuming, of course, he is innocent. As for your duplicity, Agent Goodnight, I'm afraid there can be but one punishment for such a blatant show of insubordination to my direct orders."

"Let me guess," Dante interjected. "You're giving her a severe reprimand and a bare bottom spanking. I'd be happy to administer the second half of that punishment if you'd like."

"Silence!" F snapped, her voice echoing around the empty library. "Since my Rippers singularly failed to do their job, I've decided to let my associates in the Cadre Infernale have that rare pleasure instead. You will be taken from this place by my security droids and released in the grounds of the estate. Ten minutes later my all too eager members will be let loose with orders to hunt both of you down like dogs. Whoever catches you first has permission to perform whatever acts of depravity upon you he sees fit. Afterwards, when you are begging to be released from this purgatory of punishment and perversity, I may deign to grant your wish. I advise against attempting to leave the estate – my automated security system is quite ruthless. Any questions?"

"Are you sure we can't go with Dante's suggestion?" Penelope asked.

F gave them a last dose of shock treatment as retaliation for that comment. When both prisoners had lost consciousness completely, she released the button and summoned her security droids. "Put homing beacons on them," she commanded brusquely. "We don't want the hunt dragging on all day, do we?"

NINE

"What is born a wolf cannot become a fox."
                                        – Russian proverb

"Blood sports such as hunting have been a country-side tradition in Britannia for more than a millennium. An attempt was made to outlaw hunting with hounds in the early Twenty-First century on the grounds of animal cruelty, but ultimately this failed due to the royal family's continued support of the sport. To this day gangs of aristocrats can be seen racing across the countryside in hunting pink jackets – a curious name since the garment in question is actually warm red in colour. In the past such events were held on horse-back, but the equine plague of 2626 put paid to that."
                    – Extract from *The Smirnoff Almanac of*
                              Fascinating Facts, 2673 edition

Having been incarcerated, manacled and interrogated, Spatchcock and Flintlock were beginning to give up hope. Shortly after midday the two prisoners were marched from their basement cell to the open courtyard in the centre of the Tower of London. Flintlock was convinced their execution had been brought forward, a fear that grew worse when he and Spatchcock were shoved against a wall, facing a line of armed guards. The prisoners' hands were tied behind their backs and both men were offered blindfolds, which they refused.

"Spatch, old boy, I think this is it for us," Flintlock whispered.

"So much for waiting until next week," the rancid runt complained. "What about our final requests? Even a last meal for the condemned men would have been nice. I don't want to die on an empty stomach, I'll be all grumpy when I get to the next life."

"You believe there *is* a life after this one?"

"I bloody hope so," Spatchcock grumbled. "I'd have made more of an effort otherwise."

Flintlock wept quietly, his bottom lip wobbling as tears spilled down his face. "I never believed in anything, except looking out for myself. Now I wish I'd paid attention in chapel Eton. I don't even know any prayers I can say."

"What happened to people from Britannia having a stiff upper lip?"

Flintlock managed a smile. "I prefer to save stiffness for another part of my anatomy."

"You dirty dog," Spatchcock said approvingly. Still the guards remained opposite them, keeping watch but making no attempt to carry out the execution. Eventually the foul-smelling thief lost patience with the situation. "Well, are you going to shoot us or not?" He demanded. But the guards gave no reply, continuing to stare resolutely at the prisoners. "Perhaps they think we'll die of starvation soon, save them the cost of a few bullets?"

"At least we got to feel the sun on our faces one last time," Flintlock replied wistfully, tilting his head up towards the blue, cloudless sky.

"Since we've got a few minutes to spare, your lordship, tell me what it was you did that got you deported. What could be so bad, so depraved, it got you kicked out of your own country?"

But Flintlock ignored his associate's question, preferring to keep his attention on the sky overhead. "I say, is that a skimmer coming in to land?"

Spatchcock followed his friend's gaze. "Looks like it. Quick, while we've still got time, tell me what you did. I'm dying to know!"

"Rather a poor choice of words in the circumstances, don't you think?"

"Yeah, but–"

"Attention!" The scream of a military voice cut off Spatchcock. Another sentry marched into the courtyard, three strips on his epaulets indicating he held the rank of sergeant. A single bellow from him dismissed the line of men that had guarded the two prisoners. Three new sentries replaced them, two unreeling a fire hose while the third carried a toy bucket and spade.

"Now what?" Flintlock wondered. "Are we going to make a sand castle?"

"Strip!" the sergeant bellowed.

"Do you think he means us?" Spatchcock asked blithely. "But we hardly know you."

"I said strip!"

"Rather difficult in the circumstances," Flintlock said, twisting sideways to show his hands were bound behind his back. One of the guards hurried forward and undid the shackles.

"I won't ask again," the sergeant warned. The prisoners quickly stripped, creating two untidy piles of discarded clothes at their feet. "Kick those away from you!" Spatchcock and Flintlock did as they were told. "Commence hosing – now!" The two guards holding the hose unleashed a torrent of ice cold water over the prisoners, pinning both of them against the stone wall. "Cease hosing!" The deluge stopped abruptly, giving the captives a chance to gasp for air and dry their eyes. "Administer delousing powder – now!" The third guard marched across to Spatchcock and Flintlock, then used his plastic spade to coat them with grey powder from inside the bucket. It stung their skin and burned their eyes, the stench violating their nostrils. "Prisoners – turn around!"

The unhappy duo did as they were told, receiving another heavy dusting across their backs, buttocks and legs. Then the hosing resumed, blasting the powder off the bodies of the weeping, choking captives. By the time this scouring procedure was complete, both men were close to collapse. The sergeant dismissed his men, calling for replacement clothes to be brought out. Spatchcock and Flintlock were handed silver boiler suits and told to put them on. Once dressed, the prisoners were led to a ground floor room that faced out on the courtyard. Another guard passed them, wielding a lit flamethrower. They watched with bemusement as he burned their discarded clothes.

The sergeant noticed his prisoners dawdling and raced across the courtyard towards them. "Move, you worthless maggots! Her royal highness Princess Marie-Anne is due any minute!" He shoved both of them into the small, featureless room, his nostrils flaring like bellows. A metal ring was set into one wall, two manacles at either end of a chain suspended from the ring.

The sergeant locked Spatchcock and Flintlock into the manacles, then pocketed the key. "The princess has said she wants to meet you vile worms. But say one word out of turn, make one obscene remark to her royal highness, and I will make certain your few remaining days, hours and minutes on this earth are filled with pain, misery and anguish. Do I make myself clear?"

"Not quite," Flintlock replied, tipping his head over to one side and shaking it. "I think I've still got water in my ears. Could you shout a bit louder?"

"Silence!" the sergeant bellowed. "You will speak only when spoken to and maintain a respectful decorum at all times!"

"You mean brown nose her like you do?" Spatchcock smirked. "Talk about changing your tune – a few days ago she was your prisoner, now you're treating her like..."

"Royalty?" Flintlock chipped in.

"Oh yeah," Spatchcock conceded. "I guess it does make some sort of sense." He smirked. "Well, bring the prissy cow in here, I'll show her a good time."

"Why, you–" But the sergeant's response was cut short by the royal skimmer landing in the courtyard. Once its engine noise had died away, he leaned closer to Spatchcock. "You'll pay for what you've done, you little shit," he snarled before storming out of the room.

"I think you've made a friend there, Spatch," Flintlock observed dryly. The prisoners watched from their limited vantage point as a door appeared in the side of the skimmer and a set of stairs unfolded, disgorging a dozen security guards into the courtyard. Princess Marie-Anne emerged from inside the skimmer, sniffing the air disdainfully. "Oh good. The bitch is back."

"If you tell me what you're looking for, I'd be more than happy to help find it," Dante offered. He had regained his senses in the middle of a small, flat field, surrounded by tall grass baked yellow by the sun. The warm, pleasant smell of hay-making hung in the air. Penelope crouched beside him with her hand buried deep inside his sporran, groping and grasping at the small pouch's lining. Eventually her face lit up with a smile of triumph. Dante noticed she had a smattering of freckles across her nose and cheeks. He had always found freckles curiously attractive, so he leaned closer to kiss her sensuous mouth. Penelope responded by slapping him hard across the cheek. "Diavolo!" he protested. "What was that for?"

"Why were you trying to kiss me?"

"I thought you wanted me to! You were feeling around my groin and smiling, so I–"

"You thought I had finally fallen for your roguish charms?"

"Well... yes."

Penelope removed her hand from inside his sporran to reveal a tiny pistol. "I hid this earlier, in case of emergencies.

I knew you'd never have the wit to look inside and I doubted anyone else would want to search the area near your genitals too closely."

"I'm famous as a great lover across most of the Empire," Dante replied.

A great liar, more like.

"Crest, keep quiet if you haven't got anything useful to add!"

I wanted to get your attention and uncomfortable truths usually have that effect. There's rather a large group of people coming this way.

"How many?" Dante asked, getting to his knees to peer over the tall grass.

More than thirty, approaching from the east. Most are on foot but a few seem to be mounted. They are being led by a pack of hounds. As the Crest finished speaking the distant barking of dogs became audible over the cries of black crows in nearby trees. *I estimate you have three minutes before your hunters reach this location.*

Penelope was already crawling away in the opposite direction, but the black handcuffs held her back. "Come on," she said, jerking her left arm to pull Dante after her. "We need to get under cover." The two fugitives got to their feet and ran towards a nearby thicket, crouching low to avoid being seen. They reached the trees, sweat already dripping down their faces. The sun was directly overhead, its scorching heat offering little respite, even in the shade.

Dante scanned the horizon for a sight of their hunters. "I can't see them yet."

"There they are!" Penelope whispered, pointing at the far side of the field. A crowd of nearly naked people was spilling through a wooden gate, their pale white skin almost aglow in the blazing sunshine. Black lines were visible across their bodies and many faces were hidden behind black masks. A few were clad in shiny PVC bodysuits fashioned in the style of hunting garb. Most bizarre in appearance were the horses several of the men were riding. "Those sick perverts," Penelope muttered. "They're using pony girls."

"Pony girls?" Dante asked, unfamiliar with this jargon. "Crest?"

One of the more unlikely sexual fetishes is the urge to be treated like a horse. Men and women are stripped naked, then strapped into custom-made replicas of a horse's bridle and riding tackle – buckled leather restraints around the head and body, a mouthpiece, even reins, so the beast can be controlled. For added verisimilitude the equine imitator will sometimes have a probe inserted so a horse-hair tail protrudes from between their buttocks. In extreme cases, these steeds are ridden as if they are real horses, with one rider mounted on two horses simultaneously. When younger women submit to this treatment, they are known as "pony girls". The things you humans do to get your thrills never ceases to amaze.

"And people do this willingly – for pleasure?"

They have done for centuries, particularly here in Britannia.

Dante shook his head. "Well, if we can't outrun them we deserve to be caught."

"Sunstroke and exhaustion will eventually eliminate most of our hunters," Penelope agreed. "But the hounds are bred to run for hours without tiring. They're our biggest problem. Come on!" She dragged Dante through a thicket and out into a neighbouring field of ploughed earth. He lost both his borrowed brogues within a few minutes, each shoe buried in a clump of glutinous, rapidly drying mud. The two fugitives were still crossing the open ground when the first hounds emerged from the thicket behind them, yelping excitedly.

"Diavolo, they've spotted us!" Dante said, putting on a burst of speed.

Princess Marie-Anne was enjoying her visit to the Tower of London. Having been held prisoner there for far too long, she was savouring the chance to torment her former captors, making the guards run ludicrous errands and perform endless drills in the courtyard beneath the blistering midday sun. For once the familiar aroma of raven droppings and brass polish did not turn her stomach as it had done every day she was kept incarcerated here. Eventually she tired of watching the sentries wilt and summoned their leader to her side. He was a big, blustering man with a bristling brown moustache and a knack for shouting. "Sergeant Barnes, isn't it?"

"Yes, Your Highness," he snapped, unable to keep the military training from his voice.

"I think I've seen enough of the guards' precision for now."

"Very good, ma'am," Barnes agreed. "It is quite hot, the men will be glad of a rest."

"You misunderstand me," she responded with a sadistic smile. "I merely said I had seen enough. Your men can keep at it until I am ready to depart."

"Oh, right. If you say so, ma'am."

"I do. In fact, why don't you go and join them in a few minutes? I always feel those in positions of power – however humble, like yours – should lead by example. Don't you?"

"Yes, ma'am. Absolutely."

"Very good. But first I'd like to see the prisoners."

Barnes nodded his assent. "This way, ma'am, if you please." He led her to the room where Spatchcock and Flintlock were chained to the wall. The princess paled at the powerful body odours emanating from the two men. "My apologies for the smell, your royal highness. We did have both prisoners deloused before your arrival, but even that could not counteract their stench."

She nodded hurriedly, clutching a white linen handkerchief over her nose and mouth as a shield from the noxious vapours filing the room. "Stand to attention!" Barnes bellowed.

"Shove it up your arse," Spatchcock replied cheerfully.

"I can have them thrashed for that display of impudence," the sergeant offered, but the princess waved him away. She waited until he had left before approaching the prisoners.

"Enjoying the accommodation?" she asked icily.

"We've had worse," Flintlock replied lightly.

Spatchcock nodded. "After you've been held prisoner by the Imperial Black, a few days in the Tower of London is more like a holiday resort."

"How distressing," the princess agreed. "I'll ask the sergeant to institute a regime of hourly punishments for you, perhaps some extra torture sessions too. We don't want you thinking the people of Britannia are soft on crime, do we?"

"Heaven forefend," Flintlock said, rolling his eyes.

"Did you have a reason for asking to see us? Or was this purely a social call – a spot of gloating before returning to the palace?" Spatchcock asked.

"A little of both," she replied happily. "I have good news and bad news. Which would you prefer to hear first?"

"The good news," both men said simultaneously.

"Very well – although our definitions of good and bad may differ," she warned. "The good news is your trouble-some friend Nikolai Dante remains stubbornly alive." Spatchcock began to give a small cheer but an icy glare from the princess made it die in his throat. "The bad news for you is that my father's condition is improving, however slightly."

"Why is that bad news?" Flintlock asked.

"If he survives, the king may decide to send her back here," Spatchcock said.

"Precisely," she agreed, "and I can't allow that to happen. Too much of my life has already been wasted in this hell-hole. I do not intend to spend another day here! So, once the excitement from your execution has died down, my father will suffer a terrible relapse and pass away."

"Why tell us any of this?" Spatchcock asked.

"To see the reaction on your repellent, smug faces. Since my agent has failed to bring Dante to me as I wished, I've decided to use you two as bait for a trap. I've arranged for your executions to be brought forward to this Saturday."

"But that's only two days away," Flintlock protested. "I'm not ready to die yet!"

"That matters little to me," she said with a broad smile. "Dante will not be able to resist an attempt to rescue you from the executioner's blade or the hangman's noose – to be honest, I haven't yet decided which way you should die. Regardless of that, your foolhardy friend cannot turn down the chance to save his accomplices while humiliating me. That will costing his life."

"And ours," Spatchcock noted. "The agent you sent to catch Dante – male or female?"

"Her name is Penelope Goodnight, not that it's any of your business. Why?"

"Knowing Nikolai, he's probably making love to her right now," Flintlock replied.

"Shagging her senseless, you mean," Spatchcock corrected. "They'll be too busy having a good time to even notice we're being executed."

"You know how to show a girl a good time, don't you?" Penelope asked accusingly. She and Dante were crouching on the bank of a small lake, hiding from the hunting party of perverts. The hounds had temporarily lost the fugitives' scent after Dante and Penelope had run through a lavender field, but the dogs would soon be closing in on them again.

"It wasn't my idea to come here," he said. "We need to find a place to hide, you said, give ourselves a chance to think – we can lose ourselves here for the rest of the day."

"How was I to know the hover-bus would be full of sexual deviants?"

"I'd have thought you could spot them in seconds, considering your line of work," Dante said. "We should get going.

The longer we stay in one spot, the more likely they are to find us. Trust me, I've spent most of my life on the run, one way or another."

"Then it's amazing you're still alive," Penelope observed. "Trapping you was one of the easiest assignments I've ever had."

"That's been bugging me," Dante admitted. "How did you know I'd go to that train station? I could have decided to hide anywhere in London."

"Fugitives run," she said. "There was a better than average chance you'd try to get out of the city. Once I knew the location of your Black Maria, I headed for the nearest major terminus. Luckily for me, the *Flying Scotsman* was the only train still running, so I put on my best damsel in distress act and let your rampant libido do the rest. It was child's play." An excited yelp from a nearby hound signalled the fugitives' scent had been sniffed out again.

"I don't understand how they keep finding us," Penelope muttered under her breath. "Unless..." She leaned closer to Dante and inhaled deeply from his body. "You stink of *Bitch*!"

"Charming! You're not exactly covered in rose petal aromas either, you know!"

"No, I meant *Bitch* – the perfume I sprayed over you last night to throw the Rippers off your scent. You obviously didn't wash it all off. The perfume must be attracting the hounds – they don't call it *Bitch* without good reason." She dived into the lake, pulling Dante in with her. Together they swam underwater as far as they could, before surfacing halfway across the lake. The duo took shelter beneath a selection of lily pads, watching the water's edge where they had been hiding. A stream of hunters appeared along the bank, searching the shallows for their quarry.

An obese pervert spotted the swimmers and pointed at them, his breasts wobbling above an obscenely large belly, his puny genitals dangling limply in the shadow of his massive stomach. "There they are!" he cried, the sun glinting off his bald, sunburnt scalp. "All you riders, take your pony girls round to the left! Everybody else, follow me!"

Dante and Penelope were already swimming towards the far side of the lake, their movements hampered by the handcuffs. "Our hunters don't seem to have any weapons except the dogs," Dante observed, between strokes. "How many shots have you got in that pistol?"

"Six – not nearly enough to deal with all of them," Penelope said between gasps as they reached the water's edge. "I'm saving those for F, if we make it back to the house." She scrambled up the muddy bank, dragging Dante out of the water. "Come on, move it!"

He stumbled after her, the sodden kilt slowing him down. "I'm doing my best!" he shouted.

F watched the twin homing beacon signals on a holographic display screen in her private office. As head of Britannia Intelligence she was expected to have a state of the art communications centre at her private residence, to ensure she was never out of touch with events. Happily, the cost of this equipment and its installation was borne by Britannia's taxpayers, so F had arranged for the conversion of a small space adjoining the library into her comms centre. In centuries past the chamber had been a panic room for Fforbes-Lamington family members paranoid about home security. Before that it had been a priest hole, a hiding place for clerics on the run from religious oppression. Now the room gave F an armchair view of the world.

An entire wall was devoted to a hundred holographic displays set in a ten-by-ten grid that reached up to the ceiling. In front of them was a control desk and black leather swivel chair. F sat forward in her chair, manipulating the security cameras carefully placed around the grounds. Alas, having such a sprawling estate made total coverage impossible. Dante and Agent Goodnight had fled into an area that defied

F's eager gaze, but she could still monitor their progress thanks to the homing beacons hidden on their bodies.

F activated the microphone on the control desk and barked an order to the hunt leader, an ageing cabinet minister fond of wearing women's lingerie and being sexually misused while sucking a satsuma. "McClory! Your targets are headed due west, away from the lake. They have half a mile head start, but you should be able to see them once you clear the next hedgerow."

"Understood, ma'am," a wheezing, groaning voice responded.

F sat back in her chair and smiled. She would dearly love to be leading the hunt personally, but her status as queen bitch of the Cadre Infernale in Britannia forbade her from mingling with members of a lesser rank. She must appear imperious and aloof at all times, otherwise her air of mystique would be forever tainted. F let her fingers wander between her legs, searching for a distraction. Vicarious enjoyment was all very well, but hands-on action was better.

They ran away from the lake, crossed a field of golden grass and scrambled through a hedgerow of box and hawthorn. The duo emerged from the other side, their skin and clothes covered in tiny rips and tears from the thorn-laden hedge. The sound of yapping hounds still rang loud in their ears, so Dante and Penelope kept running. They reached the far side of a cornfield and took shelter in a hedgerow before their stalkers came into view. Despite the fact both fugitives were well hidden, the perverts continued to unerringly follow their path, as if they already knew what direction to take. "So much for your *Bitch* theory," Dante observed.

Penelope frowned. "I was sure they must be..." Her words trailed off, realisation lighting up her features. "Stupid, stupid!" Penelope began patting herself down, examining her body through the catsuit's torn and tattered fabric.

"I like to watch a woman enjoying herself if you know what I mean," Dante commented, "but I'm not sure this is the time or the place."

Penelope's fingers paused over her belly button. "There!" she said excitedly and tore down the zipper holding her catsuit together. paying no attention as her breasts spilled out.

"I see you've got freckles in all sorts of places," Dante said appreciatively.

Penelope extracted a small silver disc from her belly button, then did the catsuit back up. "If I've got one, you probably have as well," she said.

"Got one what?" Dante wondered.

Penelope tore his shirt apart and pointed at a silver disc hidden inside Dante's belly button. She plucked it out, removing several black, curly hairs at the same time. "Bojemoi," he protested. "Watch what you're doing!"

She showed him the identical discs. "Homing beacons. No doubt F had them put on us before we were released out. She's been helping the hunters track us."

"And you said I stank of *Bitch*?"

"Not as bad as her," Penelope conceded. She drew back her arm, ready to fling the beacons away, but Dante stopped her.

"I have a better destination in mind for those."

I'm getting too old to be a pony girl, Muriel told herself. Getting dressed in the beastly equipment had been exciting once upon a time, while letting herself be groomed by several breathless young women was joy unconfined. Even galloping around courtyards or acting as willing steed for some burly, sweaty man had been acceptable, no matter how foolish it made her feel, because she could look forward to a treat at the end of the day. Perhaps some frolicking with the other pony girls amongst the hay bales in the stables, or being pleasured with the specially tailored end of a riding crop. Pain and humiliation, they went hand in hand with pleasure and desire for Muriel.

But today's hunting, it was hard work and nothing more. Chasing some unseen quarry across fields and streams, that was all very well for the riders – but what about the pony girls? Muriel was used to carrying someone on her back for a few minutes, not a few hours. It was when they reached the first fence after skirting the lake that Muriel refused to go any further. Her rider, an ugly brute from the Inland Revenue with a fondness for the whip, was unceremoniously unseated and Muriel couldn't have cared less. Good riddance to bad rubbish. He was no kind of master for a fine mount like me, she told herself. Besides, I'm pink with sunburn, my knees and hands are rubbed raw and my back hurts. Enough is enough!

So, while the rest of the hunters hurried onwards, Muriel sat down under a tree to peel off her pony girl harness and bridle. She heard a twig snap behind her and found a pistol pointing at her face. Beyond it were the two fugitives, a woman in a battered black catsuit and a bare-chested man in a kilt. He looked at her thoughtfully, making Muriel blush with embarrassment.

"I've seen you somewhere before," the man said, then cocked his head slightly to one side, as if someone was whispering in his ear. "Of course – the customs official at Dover!"

At that moment Muriel wished the ground would swallow her whole. "Yes," she whispered. "Please don't tell anyone you saw me like this, they'd never understand."

The female fugitive produced a pair of small, silver discs. "We won't talk if you'll do us a favour or two in return. First of all, what's the quickest route from here back to the main house?" Muriel pointed north, her upper arm wobbling slightly. "Very good. The second favour is of a more... intimate nature. Turn around." Muriel did as she was commanded. "Touch your toes." Again, she followed the woman's orders, straining to reach past her knees. "That'll do," the fugitive commanded. "Now, brace yourself, while I find a suitable repository for these homing beacons."

● ● ●

Boyle brought the Capri in low over the boundary wall of the Fforbes-Lamington estate. He was too busy admiring the leather posing pouch, PVC corset and black peaked cap worn by his partner to notice the laser cannon emplacements in the wall's ancient stonework. "You should wear that sort of thing more often," he said. "Think of the work we could pick up around Brighton."

"That's not all we'd pick up," Dobie agreed, gesturing towards Boyle's black rubber body stocking. "Think of all the tight young–"

Suddenly a beam of light lanced through the vehicle's bonnet, slicing the engine in two and turning the rest of the flying car into a hunk of tumbling metal and glass. Boyle had time to scream before the remains of the Capri plunged into the ground, gouging a mighty divot from the earth before the vehicle flung itself end over end over end. On and on it rolled, before finally coming to rest upside down by a scarecrow in a field of brutalised corn.

Four dull thuds were audible inside the car as both bounty hunters used their handguns to deflate the Capri's airbags. They smashed out the side windows and crawled from the wreckage, each leaving a trail of blood on the ground. Neither had got more than a few metres when the car exploded in a fireball, setting ablaze the surrounding corn.

"What the hell was that?" Dante wondered. He and Penelope watched a fireball curling into the sky from several fields away, followed by a mushroom cloud of black smoke.

"I don't know and I don't care," she said, tugging at his arm. "I need to find F. She can clear my name, tell the authorities I had nothing to do with the assassination attempt."

"How do you know she wasn't the person who implicated you?"

"She probably was, the vindictive old cow," Penelope conceded, pausing to check her small pistol was ready. "I'm going to convince her that was a mistake."

Muriel was running from the hounds when she saw the car fall out of the sky. The rest of the Cadre Infernale had been unwittingly hunting her across field after field of head-high grass and corn, ravenous dogs leading the pack of perverts ever closer. Muriel considered stopping to explain her predicament, but the savage barking of the hounds terrified her too much. Now, as her last reserves of energy were close to exhaustion, she saw a Phord Capri tumbling from the sky at her. Muriel dived amidst the corn and prayed for mercy as the metal meteor shrieked by.

Dobie and Boyle found each other ten minutes after their vehicle exploded. Both men were singed, but otherwise unhurt. The aroma of barbequed corn on the cob mixed with scorched rubber and gasoline in the air. The bruised and bloody bounty hunters surveyed the charred wreckage of their Capri with fond sadness. "We've been through a lot in that car," Dobie said wistfully. "Killed our first target in the back seat."

"Had our first kiss in the front seat," Boyle recalled.

Dobie smiled at the memory, before frowning again. "What the hell hit us?"

"The estate must have the mother of all security systems round its perimeter. We're lucky to have got out of that alive." He brushed broken glass out of his curly hair, then adjusted Dobie's peaked cap to a jauntier angle. "Our normal clothes were in the boot, you know."

"Yeah, and all our other guns. I've got this pistol and five clips of ammo."

Boyle checked his handgun. "I've only got this, but I'm nearly out of bullets. You'd better give me two of your clips."

"Get your own ammunition, you lazy sod!"

"From where? In case you hadn't noticed, we're in the middle of a burning cornfield on a country estate. I doubt there're many dum-dum stockists around here."

"Moan, moan, moan – that's all you ever do, Raymond."

"I've told you before, don't call me Raymond. My father called me Raymond and I bloody hated him for it, amongst other things."

"You know I only do it to wind you up," Dobie said.

"Well, don't, okay?"

"Okay, Raymond."

"That's it!" Boyle exploded. "I have had a gut full of your sly innuendoes and little digs."

"Well, you know my policy – innuendo and out the other," Dobie quipped.

"Hey, you there!" An aristocratic voice interrupted the bounty hunters' bickering. They quickly concealed their weapons, then swivelled round to see a cluster of perverts in leather and rubber marching towards them. "What the dickens do you think you're doing on this estate? This is a Sabbat of the Cadre Infernale, not a come-as-you-are party for any passing rough trade!"

"Rough trade?" Dobie snorted derisively. "Look who's talking!"

"Come as you are?" Boyle added. "You think we dress like this normally?"

"I don't care how you dress," the leader of the pack replied sternly. He was over sixty, flat-chested and wearing a selection of frilly pink lingerie. His right hand was clenched around the butt of a black leather whip, tapping it against his stocking-clad thigh. "Clear off, or else we'll be forced to give both of you a short, sharp shock – the more shocking the better!"

The bounty hunters exchanged a glance. "Oh, piss off, grandad," Boyle warned.

The old man's face quivered with rage. "Why, you little swine! Right, you asked for it – now you're going to get it.

Brothers! Sisters! Let's show these gatecrashers they're not welcome!"

The perverts advanced as one towards Dobie and Boyle, pushing their way through the blackened heads of corn. Boyle looked at his partner. "Do you want to sort this, or shall I?"

"Let's do it together," Dobie suggested with a smile. The bounty hunters opened fire.

F was surprised to hear gunfire drifting in through the library doors from outside. "Oh, for heaven's sake! I specifically forbade anyone from taking sidearms on the hunt to avoid exactly this sort of incident," she muttered. The head of Britannia Intelligence wandered outside onto the balcony to see if she could spot the culprit and remonstrate with them. Instead she felt the barrel of a small pistol pressing against one side of her head.

"I guess somebody didn't get the memo," Penelope commented. "Call for help and I redecorate these doors with your brains. Nod if you understand." F quickly indicated her obedience. "Good. Let's go back inside – you first."

F returned indoors, followed by Penelope and Dante. "You'll never get off this estate alive," the mistress of the house said in a matter of fact voice. "My droids conduct a random sweep of the building every few minutes, so they're bound to discover you sooner or later."

"Not if you disable the security system," Dante pointed out.

"I can't, it's controlled from another location," F insisted.

"Liar!" Penelope snapped.

"Can you be sure of that?" her boss replied. The sound of mechanoids moving nearby was audible and getting louder. "As you can hear, my droids are close by – they could come in here any minute. You have me at gunpoint, but you're the ones trapped – we are at an impasse."

"Crest, can you hack the security system, take it out of action?" Dante asked.

Not while you wear those cuffs. Most of my functionality is disabled by their influence.

"Well?" Penelope asked hopefully, but Dante simply shook his head.

F smiled. "Let me offer you a solution. I must insist upon Dante's execution going ahead as planned, but there's no need for you to suffer the same fate, Agent Goodnight."

"That's not what I call a solution," Dante said.

"Keep talking," Penelope told her commander.

"Hey!" Dante protested. "I thought you were on my side!"

"Since when?" she replied tersely. "Just because we're hand-cuffed together, that doesn't mean I believe a word you've told me. We've been forced to work together to stay alive, but that's as far as my loyalty to you stretches, Dante. I couldn't care less whether you live or die, and I have no interest in ever knowing you better. Get that through your thick skull!"

Oh yes, you're definitely winning her over, the Crest observed tactfully.

"What's your solution?" Penelope asked F.

"It seems her royal highness is getting impatient. She's brought forward the execution of Dante's two accomplices to Saturday afternoon. No doubt she is hoping this Russian renegade will be foolish enough to attempt a rescue mission."

"I wouldn't put it past him," Penelope said. "So?"

"As I said, Dante must die. But your fate need not be so... fatal." F took a step closer to her operative, one hand reaching forwards to stroke the side of Penelope's face. "Submit yourself to me for a year and I will quash all suggestions that you were in any way associated with the assassination attempt. I can guarantee you a handsome promotion, your pick of future assignments at Britannia Intelligence and a lifestyle any sane woman would envy."

"What do you mean by the word 'submission'?"

"Exactly what I say. You will become my slave for the next twelve months, giving yourself over to my will, doing whatever I command without question. At the end of that time you will be a free woman, considerably richer and with a much broader experience of all life can offer." As F spoke she let her hand slide down from Penelope's face, passing over the secret agent's right breast and abdomen, before coming to rest between her legs. "Give yourself to me and I promise a sexual education that will make your hair curl."

"Don't do it," Dante urged. "You said it yourself, this bitch can't be trusted!"

"If I ever break my word to you," F told Penelope, "you have my permission to shoot me."

"All right," the secret agent replied, pressing herself against F's hand. "I'll do it."

"How delightful!" F said, giving a tiny squeak of pleasure. "I can't wait to get started."

Penelope shook her head. "You misunderstand me." She aimed her pistol between F's lips, a finger reaching for the trigger.

"No, don't, I—"

But F never finished her sentence, the words ripped away along with the back of her skull and much of her brain. The middle-aged woman's body tipped over backwards, the remains of her head hitting the marble floor like a wet flannel. Penelope spat on the corpse.

"I'm nobody's slave, bitch!" she snarled at the dead commander.

Dante rubbed the back of his neck. "You could have told me you were going to do that! You really had me going with all those lies about not caring if I lived or died."

Penelope's eyes narrowed. "What makes you think I was lying?"

"Oh. Right." He looked round the empty library. "So, how do we get out of here without setting off the security system? We outwitted the perverts, but I doubt the droids are that gullible."

Penelope crouched beside F's corpse. "When she escorted us through the house, I noticed F was using an old fashioned retinal scanner to confirm her identity. So, all we need do is borrow a little something from her and then we can walk out of here unscathed." She glanced at Dante. "Which eye should I pluck out? The left or the right?"

TEN

"The day is over and death is nearer."
– Russian proverb

"It goes without saying that Dante became a far more formidable opponent after he was bonded with his Romanov Weapons Crest. But an examination of his earlier career as a thief, adventurer and brigand proves he was no slouch in unarmed combat before his unexpected augmentation. For example, Dante's first encounter with the Tsar came after the renegade was charged with fighting and besting an entire squad of the highly trained hussars. His skills as a fighter should never be doubted or downgraded. Nikolai Dante is a worthy adversary for any man."

– Extract from *Nikolai Dante: Hellraiser Extraordinaire*, Maria Beria

Penelope and Dante used their grisly acquisition to contrive a way through the stately home's internal security system, flashing the eyeball at anything that questioned their presence. Within minutes they were out on the gravel courtyard in front of the house. "Now what?" Dante asked

"I don't know," Penelope admitted. "I probably shouldn't have killed F, but she was going too far. Bad enough to be labelled as your accomplice, but I won't be anybody's sex toy."

"Crest, what time is the *Flying Scotsman* due to leave for its next destination?"

Shortly after six. You've less than two hours.

"We can't go back to the train," Penelope insisted.

"Why not?"

"When we arrived here F was complaining the Rippers hadn't killed you. She must have sent another squad to the train after the first team failed. They've probably spent the day tearing it apart, looking for you. Plus we left a naked steward underneath my bed. The other staff will have found him by now. I doubt they'll welcome us back on board with open arms."

"I'm sure you can talk them round, since you're such a great seducer," Dante countered. "We have to get back on that train before it leaves. The real assassin is going to Peebles on the *Flying Scotsman*. He's the only person who can prove our innocence, especially now you've killed the one woman who could have cleared your name!" He folded his arms and glared at Penelope.

She blinked at this accusation. "God, you're right. What have I done?"

"Nothing anybody else in the same position wouldn't do."

"I've murdered my boss. Even if I can prove I had nothing to do with the attack on the king, I'm still guilty of slaughtering the head of Britannia Intelligence!"

Dante waved her concerns away. "You were defending yourself against a sexual predator. She's probably groped every woman who ever worked under her at the secret service."

"And a few others besides," Penelope agreed.

"Then you don't need to shed any tears for her." Dante studied their surroundings. "Crest, how far are we from the nearest estate boundary?"

More than twenty kilometres.

"Then we haven't time to get out of here on foot. We need a hover-car of some sort."

Penelope pointed to her right. "Or something larger?" The end of the bus that had brought them from Nottingham

Station was visible beyond the house's eastern wing. "That must have pre-programmed safety clearance, otherwise it would never have got through the gates."

Dante smiled. "Do you want to drive, or shall I?"

Boyle and Dobie reached the rear of the stately home sixty seconds later, having slaughtered most of the Cadre Infernale's hapless members and sent the rest fleeing into the undergrowth. The bounty hunters found a trail through the long grass that led directly to the imposing house. The duo heard the roaring noise of a hover-bus taking off nearby and took cover beside the doors to the library. They relaxed as the sound faded into the distance, removing any threat to them.

Dobie sniffed the air. "You smell what I smell?"

Boyle's nose wrinkled disdainfully. "Cordite and faeces. That means one thing..."

"Somebody's been shot and killed," Dobie agreed. "I'm going in – cover me!" He burst through the double doors, throwing himself into a forward roll and coming up with his gun drawn, ready to fire. Moments later Boyle followed him in, pistol ready, eyes scanning the empty shelves and empty corners for any sign of movement. Once they had confirmed the room was devoid of life, the pair straightened up again, letting themselves relax. Dobie sauntered over to the female body on the floor. A crimson pool had spread out around her head, while a puddle of yellow and brown had spilled from between her legs. "That's something I'll never get used to, Ray."

"What?" His partner looked around the room for anything that might identify the corpse.

"The way a human body purges itself after death."

Boyle shrugged. "The muscles naturally relax. It's not purging, more like spillage."

"Yeah, well, remind me to get an enema before I die. Or wear rubber underpants."

"You better not get killed in that posing pouch then. Not much dignity to be had in there."

Dobie nodded, still studying what remained of the corpse's face. "I've seen her before somewhere. The state opening of Parliament, maybe?"

Boyle joined him, crouching down for a closer look at the body. "Hard to tell with one eye and the back of her head missing... But you're right. We've met her before somewhere."

"Not a target or else we'd have killed her, not somebody else."

"A client?"

"Of course!" Dobie said, snapping his fingers. "Ray Boyle, allow me to introduce you to F – the head of Britannia Intelligence. Or what's left of her."

"You're right! She hired us to finish the career of that cabinet minister who wanted to cut her budget. A very dangerous lady, I seem to recall." Boyle studied her remains with fresh interest. "Maybe we've underestimated Nikolai Dante. He must be pretty resourceful to take out a woman like F. Single shot, as well – up close and personal. This guy is not to be taken lightly."

"But why did he take her eyeball? Some kind of trophy?" Before Boyle could reply, two security droids burst into the library, their weapons raised and ready for action. The bounty hunters dived in opposite directions, emptying their handguns at the menacing mechanoids.

The hover-bus swerved drunkenly around a clock tower above central Nottingham, narrowly avoiding a mid-air collision. As Dante piloted his way past the erection, Penelope pointed out the time on display. "It's nearly six! We'll miss the train if you don't land soon."

"I'm trying, I'm trying," he protested.

"You said you could fly this thing!"

"I said I'd give it a try. Here!" Dante let go of the steering wheel and the bus plunged towards a crowded pedestrian plaza. "You think you can do better, you take over!"

"Just get us down near the station, okay?" she pleaded.

"Okay!" Dante took hold of the controls again but they did not respond. If anything, the bus accelerated its rapid descent. "Ahh – Nottingham, we have a problem."

"What kind of problem?" Penelope asked angrily.

"The kind of problem that involves crashing, burning and large amounts of pain," he replied. "I mean, I'm guessing, but it's an educated guess."

"Look out!" she screamed as the pedestrian zone filled the hover-bus's windscreen, residents diving out of the way. At the last possible moment the vehicle wrenched itself sideways, then straightened out until it was running parallel to the ground. Penelope opened her eyes again. "You did it!" she cried happily. "I can't believe you did it!"

"Neither can I," Dante said, pointing at the steering wheel. The bus was moving of its own volition, the wheel twisting from side to side as it drove along the city streets. Signs for the railway station became increasingly frequent. "Guess this thing has some sort of automatic pilot for the last part of its programmed journey. Look, the station's up ahead."

The bus glided to a halt by the entrance, front doors sliding back gracefully. Penelope and Dante hurled themselves out of the vehicle and sprinted into the station. "How long, Crest?"

Thirty seconds and counting.

"Bojemoi, why do I always cut things so fine?"

You crave excitement, deliberately creating situations that push you to your limits and beyond, probably in an attempt to distract yourself from the ultimate futility of your life.

"I wasn't actually asking for your opinion!" Dante shouted as he and Penelope ran to the platform where the *Flying Scotsman* had been that morning. But the tracks were empty. "Diavolo, we're too late!"

Penelope pointed at another platform close by where their train was waiting. "No, look – it's over there! They must have shifted platforms during the day. I don't see any sign of the Rippers. They must have been and gone."

The station tannoy crackled into life. "The train now leaving from Platform eleven is the *Flying Scotsman* tourist service, calling at Peebles, Edinburgh and Orkney. Stand away from the doors now, please, this train is ready to depart. Stand away from the doors!"

Penelope raced towards Platform eleven, dragging Dante after her. As they reached it the train was already rolling away from them, gathering acceleration in preparation for take-off. "Come on!" Penelope screamed, quickening her speed. She reached the back door and pulled it open, Dante running as fast as he could to keep up with her. Penelope pulled herself into the rear carriage, then reached back to help Dante on board. The train gave a sideways lurch as it left the tracks and rose into the air, tipping Penelope towards the open doorway. She fell over, Dante's weight dragging her back outside. Penelope jammed her legs against the door frame, wedging herself in place. "Hold on!" she screamed at him.

"I'm holding, I'm holding!" he shouted back, dangling in the air beneath the train.

Dante, evasive action!

He looked round in time to see the same clock tower the bus had narrowly avoided earlier looming towards him. Dante swung his legs up in the air and the tower scraped beneath him, ripping through the fabric of his kilt. The tartan fabric was wrenched from his body, wrapping itself around the weather vane on top of the clock tower. The cool evening air whistled past Dante's naked body as he hung from Penelope's grasp, only the handcuffs keeping the two of them together. "I can't hold on much longer!" she warned. "My legs are giving way!"

Dante nodded, painfully aware of the precariousness of their situation and the ever increasing strain upon both their bodies. "I'm going to try and swing myself upwards," he shouted, raising his voice to be heard above the whistling wind.

"Whatever you're going to do, make it quick!" she called back.

Dante kicked both his legs back, then swung them forwards, repeating the motion over and over until the tendons in his shoulder were screaming in pain. Finally, keeping time with the pendulum swing of his body, Dante flung himself into a backwards somersault up into the air. His upside-down body smacked into the side of the carriage, but he managed to grab hold of the door frame. As his battered and bruised back slid down the woodwork, Dante pulled himself into the open door and collapsed. The two of them lay there for more than a minute, gasping for breath and moaning in pain, Dante's naked body splayed out on top of Penelope.

A polite cough from the corridor eventually got their attention. "While I applaud your obvious gymnastic abilities," Gordonstoun said icily, "may I suggest that in future you leave sufficient time for your return journey from any of our scheduled day trips?"

"Whatever you say," Penelope whispered.

"Also, I must ask you to refrain from involving my staff in your sexual shenanigans. The man you left bound and gagged under the bed is still in Nottingham, receiving counselling." The head steward stepped past them and closed the back door of the carriage. "Dinner will be served in the dining car from seven," he said brusquely. "While evening dress is usually considered optional, we do ask our guests to show some measure of decorum."

"Don't worry, I'll make sure she changes out of her catsuit," Dante replied cheerfully.

"I was referring to your current attire, sir – or lack of it." Gordonstoun's withering gaze lingered on Dante's groin. "My, there must be quite a chilling wind out this evening." He strode away along the corridor, muttering under his breath.

Penelope got up with a groan, rubbing her left shoulder. "I swear, this arm is going to be half a metre longer than the other before this is over."

Dante grimaced. "At least you've still got your own clothes. I've just given half of Nottingham a worm's eye view of my genitals!"

"At least the other half didn't miss much," she replied. "Let's go back to my compartment, see if we can't find you something to wear. Then I need to eat."

"Food can wait," he said as they strode along the corridor. "Since the attempt on the king's life I've been arrested, beaten, interrogated, stripped naked – twice! – and hunted by a pack of sexual deviants. All I want now is some answers. I vote we search every cabin and carriage on this train until we find the real assassin."

"Assuming he's still on the train."

"He has to be," Dante insisted. "Otherwise…"

Penelope paused outside the door to her compartment. "Otherwise what?"

He shrugged. "I don't know. I'm out of my depth and the Crest is next to useless while I've still got these damned handcuffs on."

Don't blame me for your current predicament!

"I wasn't," Dante said. "I guess I've come to depend upon the Crest, it gets me out of so many tight spots. It's only now I haven't got that help that I'm learning to appreciate it."

I hope you'll remember that in future.

"Look, this is all very touching," Penelope said, "but I've seen enough of your genitals to last me a lifetime. I need a change of clothes and some food. After that I'll be more than happy to help you find this elusive mystery man, okay?"

"Okay."

"Besides, I've only got five shots left in my pistol," Penelope said, producing the tiny handgun from inside her catsuit. "If this person is part of a conspiracy to kill the king, we'll need more firepower than I'm carrying at the moment."

"I said okay," Dante replied, opening the compartment door. Inside were four expectant Rippers, all of them clutching a stiletto in each hand, malevolent grins spread across each face. Dante slammed the door shut again and smiled. "However, a slight change of plan might be wise."

Dobie and Boyle disabled the first pair of security droids with ease and despatched the next set of mechanoids to approach the library, but both men knew their limited ammunition supply would not be sufficient to see off any further attacks. It was Boyle who first grasped the significance of the missing eyeball. "Of course! This place must use retina scanning as a security override. Dobie, keep watch at the door while I get her other eyeball out."

"Why I do always get guard duty?" his partner said.

"Because you're a better shot than me."

"You're saying that to butter me up."

Boyle grinned. "Save that idea for later, lover boy." Unable to prise the eyeball free from the front, he tipped the corpse over and shoved his fingers through the exit wound. Within moments the eyeball popped out and rolled across the floor like a marble.

"We've got company, Ray – time to get moving!" Dobie spun away from the door and inadvertently stood on the eyeball. It squashed beneath his weight with a wet popping sound.

"Brilliant! That's brilliant! Our one chance of getting out of here alive and you stand on it!" Boyle raged, getting to his feet. "What are we supposed to do now?"

His partner glanced back at the cluster of security droids gathering outside. "Run!"

The duo raced to the external doors but another group of mechanoids was also blocking that exit. "We're trapped!" Boyle said.

Dobie pointed to a corner of the library. "What's that?" One of the bookshelves jutted out slightly from the wall, a glimmer of light spilling out through the gap.

690 FROM RUSSIA WITH LUST: THE NIKOLAI DANTE OMNIBUS

The duo sprinted across to the corner and tugged at the bookshelf, until it moved far enough for both of them to squeeze through. Once they were on the other side, a mechanical warning sounded and a solid steel barrier slammed down to block the only exit. Dobie spun round, his eyes urgently scanning their surroundings. "If we weren't trapped before, we are now!"

"Not exactly," Boyle said. They were standing inside a cube-shaped room. An entire wall was covered in holographic display screens showing a hundred different scenes. Most were images from security cameras around the estate, but there were also feeds from the main news channels, communications channels and entertainment networks. "This must be the dead woman's private office. From here we can contact anyone in the world."

"So we're safe?"

"Yeah."

"But we can't get out?"

"Not until we call in a favour or two." Boyle sat in the swivel chair facing the display units, studying the range of switches and controls in front of him. "If our hostess was head of Britannia Intelligence, she'll have a direct line to Scotland Yard. Ahh, here we go: the police." He smiled over his shoulder at Dobie. "I think it's time we gave a progress report to Inspector Rucka, don't you? No doubt he's been wondering how we're getting on."

Penelope killed the first Ripper to open the compartment door, blowing the back of his head clean off. Her second shot only wounded the next in line and her third shot jammed inside the pistol. "Misfire!" she shouted to Dante, shaking the tiny pistol in frustration. "Run!" The pair bolted along the corridor, only to find two more Rippers waiting for them at the far end.

Dante – evasive action!

"No kidding!" he replied, ducking beneath a stiletto as it sliced through the air. Dante thrust his knee into the Ripper's gut so the black-cloaked figure folded forwards, then smashed the base of his left hand into the Ripper's nose. Bone was punched backwards into the Ripper's brain and the murderous invader was dead within moments, crimson spraying from his face.

"You don't get rid of us that easily, sunshine!" the second Ripper in the corridor boasted, climbing over the crumpled body of his colleague.

"We'll see about that," Penelope snarled, cracking him across the face with the butt of her pistol. The weapon fired, its bullet ricocheting off a brass fitting before lodging in the Ripper's brain. He collapsed on top of Dante, who was crouching on the floor, searching for a knife.

"Lucky shot," Dante said, finding a discarded stiletto among the corpses.

"I'll take any luck I can get," Penelope replied. "I've only got two shots left."

"Then you'd better make them count – here come the others!" The rest of the Rippers were pushing past their dead brother to get out of Penelope's compartment. Dante charged at them, roaring at the top of his voice, but was abruptly jerked back again by the handcuffs. His feet flew up into the air, a look of comical bewilderment crossing his face before he fell to the floor with a heavy thud. "Bojemoi," he gasped. "I forgot."

The Ripper with the gunshot wound sneered at Dante's naked body. "Well, well, well. What 'ave we 'ere? Looks like this one's been a naughty boy!"

"He needs to be punished," the next Ripper agreed.

"We'll cut out his lights and giblets," the Ripper cackled. "We'll feast on his sweetmeats for our dinner, eh lads?" A flying stiletto impaled itself in his left eyeball, the tip stabbing deep into the Ripper's brain. He was dead before his body hit the floor.

"I don't share my sweetmeats with any man," Dante said smugly, smiling at the accuracy of his knife-throwing skills. "Now, if you were female, things might be rather different."

The remaining two Rippers launched themselves at Dante, lunging at him with blades in both hands. "Look out behind!" Dante shouted, pulling his feet up to propel the first Ripper over his head. Penelope dropped to one knee and shot the Ripper as he flew past her in the air. When the murderous creature hit the floor, already twisting round for another attack, she used her final shot to remove his lower jaw. He stayed down after that. But the last Ripper landed right on top of Dante, twin stilettos gouging into the floor on either side of his face. Dante responded with a head butt, smacking his forehead into the Ripper's nose. Both of them screamed in agony, blood streaming down their faces. "Diavolo, that hurts!" Dante cried out.

"Not as much as this will, my pretty," the Ripper promised, ripping a dagger out of the floor and pulling it back into the air, ready to plunge the blade through his enemy's heart. Dante yanked the other stiletto free and stabbed it into the Ripper's chest. He twisted the knife, making the blade squirm around in the wound. The Ripper vomited blood into Dante's face before collapsing on top of him, the knife falling safely to one side.

Penelope rolled the Ripper away, moving closer to look at Dante. "Nikolai! Nikolai, are you all right? Speak to me, damn you!"

His face split into a smile. "That's the first time you've ever called me Nikolai."

"I thought you were–"

"Dead?" Dante coughed up a mouthful of blood, spitting it onto the Ripper's corpse. "Not yet. It takes worse than that to kill me, even without my enhanced healing abilities." He sat up, crimson-flecked phlegm dripping from his face. "Is that all of them?"

"Probably," Penelope said. "Rippers travel in squads of six or twelve. Count yourself lucky there were only half a dozen this time." She helped him up, wiping the scarlet mucus from his face. "Let's get you clean and find some fresh clothes. Then I must eat, or else *I'll* kill someone."

Dante nodded at the corpses in the corridor. "What about this lot?"

"Okay, I need to eat before I kill someone else."

"No, I meant – shouldn't we dispose of them first?"

Penelope sighed heavily. "I suppose you're right. The train will be spending the night over the Lake District. We'll put these carcasses into an empty compartment for now, then throw them out when we're above Lake Windermere."

"You know," Dante said as they dragged the Rippers out of sight, "fighting these freaks would have been easier if we weren't cuffed together. Are you any closer to passing that key?"

"Not yet," Penelope admitted. "That's another reason for eating soon. A little extra roughage in my system would help speed the key's progress." She pushed one Ripper into a vacant berth, then went back to collect another corpse. Right now I'm so hungry I'll eat anything they put in front of me." Her gaze caught sight of Dante's exposed genitals as the duo continued their grisly task. "Anything except sausages."

ELEVEN

"Women's tears are nets, not water."
– Russian proverb

"Traditional games of strength and agility have been practised in the Highlands for many, many centuries. These annual gatherings became formalised around 1820 as part of a national revival of tartan culture. With Caledonia principally a tourist destination, the Highland Games are more popular than ever. Travellers from across the Empire come to witness such arcane sports as putting the shot, tossing the caber and throwing the weight. Highland dancing is an essential part of any Games, as is the inevitable skirl of the bagpipes. So, put on your kilt, strap down your sporran and get ready for a sporting event unlike any other!"

– Extract from *The Duffer's Guide to Britannia*, 2670 edition

Dante and Penelope spent an uncomfortable night on her bed, thanks to Penelope's insistence on keeping a row of pillows between them as a divider. "We may be handcuffed together, but that doesn't give you any claim over my body," she warned.

"Don't flatter yourself," Dante replied. "Besides, I've seen how you treat uninvited sexual overtures. I'd like to keep my brains intact."

Despite that, the two of them still ended up in each other's arms the next morning. Dante opend his eyes on Friday to find Penelope snuggling into his back. "I knew you couldn't resist me forever," he whispered huskily. Her scream of dismay when she woke quickly shattered that illusion. Both of them bounded off the bed in opposite directions, then were jerked back together by their handcuffs. A string of obscenities filled the air as their heads collided with a crack.

Early morning ablutions proved just as problematic, Dante leaning out the bathroom door whistling loudly while Penelope emptied her bladder. She was considerably less squeamish, offering a stream of unwelcome observations as he tried to urinate. "We haven't got all day, you know. They stop serving breakfast in half an hour."

"I am trying to concentrate," he replied through gritted teeth.

"Well, it doesn't seem to be working."

"Look, I find this difficult with anyone watching, let alone offering a running commentary!"

"What about having the Crest in your head?" Penelope asked. "How does that work?"

"We have an understanding. It allows me a little privacy when I need it most – like now."

"How about when you're making love?" Penelope asked. "I imagine having an alien battle computer offering advice on your technique must be quite distracting."

"Please," he said quietly. "Could you give me a minute's peace, okay? Just give me one minute of silence and then we can go and have breakfast, all right?"

"One minute?"

"Yes!"

"Fine by me," Penelope said. Seven seconds of agonising silence followed, unbroken by the sound of any liquid splashing into the toilet bowl. "I mean, I have absolutely no problems with keeping quiet for that long. I–"

"Oh, forget it!" Dante snapped, flushing the toilet and stomping out of the bathroom. "We'll go and eat. With any luck breakfast will shift the key from your vice-like bowels, putting an end to this nightmare for both of us. Then I might be able take a piss in peace and quiet!"

Henry Windsor McKray blinked. "I think he's coming round," a voice whispered. The king breathed deeply, the smell of frying bacon drifting into his nostrils and awakening his taste buds. He opened his eyes to find himself in a small, pale green room filled with doctors, nurses, a camera crew and a chef. The last of these was clutching a sizzling skillet with seven rashers of bacon cooking on it, each slice cheerfully spitting pork fat into the air.

"I say," the king murmured sleepily. "Is it breakfast already?" The doctors and nurses burst into spontaneous applause, laughing profusely at his first words in three days. "That bacon smells wonderful. Any chance of someone slapping it inside a roll with brown sauce for me?"

"King Henry!" shouted a rat-faced reporter in a suit and tie, waving from behind the cameraman. "King Henry, how do you feel?"

"Quite hungry," he replied, smiling weakly. "Positively ravenous in fact." A shrieking female voice became audible, getting louder by the moment. "Has someone let a banshee loose in here?"

"Where is he?" the woman demanded from outside Henry's room, her aristocratic voice akin to hawk talons clawing a blackboard. "He's my bloody father! You will let me see him and you will let me see him right bloody now!"

"Oh dear," the king lamented. "I thought my daughter was still in prison."

Princess Marie-Anne burst into the hospital room, ruthlessly shoving doctors and nurses out of the way to reach the king. Seeing his frail body on the bed, she began sobbing theatrically and collapsed beside him. "Father, my dear papa! Speak to me! Say something – if you're able!"

"Hello. What are you doing here?"

The princess looked up abruptly, surprise etched into her features. "You're conscious!"

"Yes, that's right," Henry said brightly.

"You're talking!"

"Right again, daughter."

"But… the doctors… they didn't think you'd make it!"

"Well, here I am, on the mend."

She glared at the doctors, her voice a venomous hiss. "You said he wouldn't make it!"

The nearest surgeon shrugged, hands buried in the pockets of her white coat. "The king apparently possesses remarkable powers of recovery, your royal highness."

"What's your name?"

"Bhamra, ma'am. Doctor Parminder Bhamra."

"You told me he had a one in ten chance of surviving his wounds – at best."

"What can I say? He beat the odds."

"He beat the odds," the princess repeated slowly, her gaze slowly taking in the camera crew filming everything in the room. "He beat the odds! What a blessing for us all!" The princess removed herself from the floor, adjusting her clothes and trying to recover some dignity. "Tell me, what was it that brought him back from the brink of apparently not so certain death?"

Doctor Bhamra pointed out the trembling cook in the corner. "Your royal chef, Ramsey, told us the king could never resist the aroma of frying bacon. We had tried everything else, so we decided to make an appeal to his sense of smell – and it worked! Quite remarkable."

Marie-Anne raised an eyebrow at the chef. "I couldn't have put it better myself. Ramsey, remind me to give you a special reward for the service you have done us all by reviving my father."

"Y-Yes, y-your royal highness," the chef stammered fearfully.

The king raised his left hand, trying to get some attention.

"Yes, your majesty?" a nurse asked.

"So, do I get a bacon sandwich or not?"

Everyone in the room burst out laughing again, the princess laughing louder and harder than the others at her father's unwitting jest. "Oh, papa, what a joy it is to see you alive and on the way to recovery. Some days I think you'll out last us all!"

"Well, you never know," he agreed.

Marie-Anne leaned down to hiss in his ear. "I wouldn't count on it, you old goat!"

Henry pinched her cheek, an affectionate gesture but for the force of his grasp. "You'll rot in hell before you sit on my throne, you poisonous little harridan," he whispered back at her.

The princess dug her fingernails into his wrist, forcing him to let go, then stood upright again. "Well, I'll come back this afternoon to update you on all the important matters of state," she announced for the camera crew's benefit. "Two of the men responsible for your wounds and for murdering the Queen Mother are awaiting execution, while a third is being hunted down."

"Babs is dead? I didn't know. That is sad news." The king's face fell, but he quickly rallied. "Still, she had a good innings, the old girl, you can't deny that."

Marie-Anne rested a consoling hand on her father's arm. "Yes, the Queen Mother was an example to us all, with her youthful exuberance and playful attitude to life, Sadly, she was slain by three cowardly assassins. The worst part is you invited them into the palace."

"Did I?"

"Don't you remember, Father? The man who murdered my beloved grandmamma was that vicious Russian renegade, Nikolai Dante."

"Nicola? She would never–" Henry protested, but his daughter hushed him to silence.

"Poor father, you're still confused by what's happened. I said Nikolai, not Nicola." Marie-Anne glared into the camera lens. "If you're watching, Nikolai Dante, I want you to know I will never rest until you pay for what you've done to my family!" In an instant her expression switched to a gracious smile as she addressed the doctors and nurses. "Would you all be kind enough to leave the room? I'd like to say a prayer of thanks at my father's bedside before I leave."

Doctor Bhamra nodded hurriedly. "Of course, your royal highness." She ushered all the others out, then bowed low before leaving, shutting the door after her.

Once father and daughter were alone, they dropped any pretence of liking each other. "You old fool!" Marie-Anne snarled. "Why couldn't you die like grandmamma?"

"Some of us are made of sterner stuff," he snapped. "I have few illusions about your feelings for me, but having your own grandmother killed – isn't that beneath even you, dear?"

"I didn't hire the assassins!" the princess protested. "If I had you wouldn't still be here."

"Nicola will discover the truth," Henry insisted. "My betrothed never lets me down."

"You really are madder than a gift box of badgers, aren't you? His name is Nikolai, not Nicola, and he fled London like the coward he is, leaving his two accomplices to die for him. Every policeman, every secret service operative and every bounty hunter in the country is stalking that pernicious piece of filth."

The king smiled. "Most of our constables couldn't find their way out of a wet paper bag with a sharp pencil. Lovely uniforms but not a brain between them. As for the secret service – if you didn't hire the assassins, they probably did. I doubt they'll find young Nicola. Besides, she is a wonderfully resourceful woman. I've seen her get out of all manner of scrapes."

"*Nikolai* Dante is as good as dead," the princess snarled. "That's if he isn't dead already!"

. . .

"I wouldn't be seen dead eating some of this," Dante said, disdainfully studying the breakfast menu in the *Flying Scotsman*'s dining car.

"Take this one: porridge. What is porridge?"

A traditional Scottish delicacy, made of oats stewed in milk or water. It is usually served with salt or sugar and milk, the Crest replied. *According to legend, families would store it inside a drawer, cutting off a slice whenever they were hungry.*

"Sounds disgusting!"

If you think that sounds disgusting, I won't tell you what is used to make a haggis.

"Good." Dante lowered his breakfast menu to look at Penelope. "What are you having?"

She smiled. "Definitely porridge, and possibly kippers to follow."

"Kippers?"

"Yes, a pair of kippers would be lovely. I haven't had kippers in years."

"Crest?"

A kipper is a fish which has been split from tail to head, eviscerated–

"Enough, enough, I've heard enough," Dante replied hastily. "I'll stick with what I know. Last time I was in this country the hotel served something called a full Britannia breakfast. It included this delicious thing called a black pudding. It was round and had been–"

Made out of suet, breadcrumbs, oatmeal and pig's blood.

Dante swallowed hard. "Pig's blood? I ate a sausage made out of pig's blood?"

Plus suet, bread crumbs and oatmeal, the Crest confirmed. *You said it was delicious.*

"That was before I knew what was in it." He glared at Penelope. "I thought this was a cultured country, but you people eat the most obscene... Words fail me."

If only.

"I'll stick to toast," Dante decided. "You don't do anything strange to that, do you?"

Penelope smiled. "Not unless you count spreading marmalade all over it."

One of the stewards approached them, doing his best not to stare at Dante's clothes.

Gordonstoun could only produce a spare kilt, so Dante was forced to wear that with a frilly white blouse borrowed from Penelope. The two passengers gave their breakfast orders and handed back the menus. They were sitting at a corner table with Dante facing the dining car.

"I can't see the assassin," he admitted after carefully studying the other travellers.

"Maybe he didn't get back on at Nottingham. The train is much emptier today."

"Because all the Cadre Infernale members stayed behind at your boss's estate." Dante bit his fingernails nervously. "No, I'm sure he's still on board. His timetable had the stops at Peebles and Orkney circled. Why would he get off before then?"

Penelope shrugged. "Let's hope you're right, otherwise both of us are in trouble."

The steward returned with their food, giving Dante a fully laden toast rack and putting two steaming plates of food in front of Penelope.

"How long before we reach Peebles?" she asked.

"An hour," the steward replied. "Can I get either of you anything else?"

Penelope shook her head, while Dante kept his gaze fixed on the vast repast opposite him. "Are you sure you've got enough there?"

She smiled. "Breakfast is the most important meal of the day – didn't your mother ever teach you that?"

"My mother was a pirate queen who kicked me off her ship before I reached puberty. All she taught me was how to fight and how to hate." Dante fell silent, deep in thought while Penelope munched her way through a meal fit for someone twice her size.

Sixty minutes later the *Flying Scotsman* was coming in to land at Peebles, a charming lowland settlement next to the River Tweed. Penelope was still belching from her breakfast as the train settled smoothly on to the tracks at the edge of town. It rolled into the station and halted, the tannoy inviting everyone aboard to enjoy the Highland Games nearby. Dante stood quietly beside Penelope in the compartment, looking out of the window at the stone houses of Peebles in the distance.

"Spatchcock and Flintlock will be executed tomorrow unless I clear my name, but I don't feel any closer to a solution than I did when the king was shot three days ago."

"You believe this man on the train is the assassin?"

Dante shrugged. "I'm not sure anymore. The more I think about it, the more I wonder if this whole trip has been a fool's errand."

Penelope frowned. "You told me the man you've seen on board was one of the shooters."

"I said he must be involved–"

"Involved? You convinced me he pulled the trigger!"

"I might have exaggerated," Dante said. "He was definitely standing on Westminster Bridge close to the spot where I confronted the assassin. After I was thrown into the Thames, rising mist made it hard to see, but I definitely heard him talking with someone else. He had an accent I didn't recognise, but it wasn't a dialect from Britannia. He told the other person he would see them soon and there was something about an old man with a short name – Troy? Malloy?"

Penelope shook her head, plainly unable to believe what she was hearing. "You're telling me all of this could have been a wild goose chase?"

"I guess," Dante admitted. "I did see this guy's face, when a skimmer dropped towards the bridge and caught him in its headlights. I'm certain it's the same man I saw at the train station where I met you, the same man who dropped the timetable in the dining car, the same man who was in the other queue at Nottingham – it must be him. It must be."

"You sound like you're trying to convince yourself," Penelope said.

"I know. Sorry."

Dante!

"Not now, Crest."

"Look, we'll find this guy and interrogate him," Penelope decided. "We'll soon discover what he does know. Maybe you're right, maybe he doesn't have anything directly to do with the assassins – but if he was on that bridge, he probably saw what the assassins looked like, yes?"

Dante, you need to–

"Later, Crest, okay? We're trying to come up with a plan of action. You're the one who always nags me for acting first and thinking second. Well, let me think first for once, all right?"

But the man you are hunting just walked past the corridor outside this compartment.

"He did?"

Yes!

"Well, why didn't you say something before?"

I did, I– Oh, I give up, the Crest sighed wearily.

Dante hurried to the compartment door, dragging Penelope after him. "Which way did he go, Crest? Left or right?"

Left, towards the rear of the train.

Dante tried to run in the same direction, but Penelope was slowing him down. "Come on! He's getting away from us!"

"I can't run," she said, belching heavily as they got off the train. Dante was craning his neck, trying to spot their quarry among the other passengers on the platform.

"Why not?" he asked.

"That second plate of kippers was definitely a mistake. I can feel them churning round inside me." Penelope belched again, clamping a hand over her mouth. "I need a toilet. Fast."

"Can't it wait?" Dante protested. His eyes lit up as a bald man with a goatee appeared for a moment among the crowds marching towards a sign bearing the words 'PEE-BLES SHOW GROUND'. "There he is! Come on!" Dante hurried after the man, pulling Penelope along behind.

"You're not listening to me! I need a toilet – right now!" Penelope stopped, refusing to take another step. "Trust me, this is in both our interests."

Dante looked at the handcuffs connecting them, then at her pale, perspiring face. "Oh. Right." He glanced about, spotting a set of public toilets nearby. "Over there?"

"Over there," Penelope agreed, already striding towards the conveniences. She barged in through the door marked 'LADIES', dragging Dante after her. Within were three cubicles, each with a wooden door. Two were occupied but the last was mercifully empty. Penelope shoved her way in and Dante was forced to follow, locking the door behind him. By the time he turned round she had already peeled her catsuit down past her thighs and was sitting on the toilet.

"Bojemoi! You're not going to do that while I'm watching, are you?"

"Right now, I couldn't care less what you do!"

Dante closed his eyes and willed himself not to listen.

Jean Brown loved the Highland Games. Every year Peebles came alive for this event, playing host to thousands of new faces and welcoming as many old friends. Jean might have been eighty but she never missed the Games, no matter what

the weather did. Seeing the old traditions kept alive was important to her. Besides, she always hoped for a strong gust of wind
when men in kilts were tossing the caber. Alas, old age had
played havoc with her bladder control, so Jean kept close to the
nearest public toilets. She was still on her way into the show
ground when the call of nature forced her to turn aside in
search of relief. Into the conveniences she bustled, relieved to
find the middle cubicle was free. Jean arranged herself on the
seat and let nature take its course, sighing contentedly. Then
she heard a most unexpected sound from the cubicle on her left
– a man's voice. What on earth was he doing in here?

"Well, is it out yet?" he asked.

"Not… yet!" a woman replied, strain and pain evident in
her tone of voice. Jean forgot her own troubles and leaned
closer to the adjoining wall, trying to overhear what was
going on.

"If it won't come out voluntarily, maybe we need a way of
inducing it," the man said.

"I can do this!" the woman snarled back. "Give me
another minute, you impatient sod!"

Jean blanched at such language. What in heaven's name
was happening? It sounded like the poor woman was having
a baby. Of all the times and places she could have chosen!

"I know you can," the man said soothingly. "Relax and it'll
come out naturally."

"Get away from me, you bastard. This is all your fault!"

"You're the one who put the handcuffs on us, not me."

Handcuffs? It was a long time since Jean had experienced
childbirth, but she didn't recall handcuffs being an intrinsic
part of the process.

"Ahhh – it's moving, I can feel it moving!" the woman
cried out. "Here it comes."

"I can't look!" the man said. "I think… I think I'm going
to pass out!"

"Don't you dare!" his companion snarled. "We're in this
together, remember?"

"I can't go through with it!"

"You haven't got a choice – we're stuck with eachother until this thing comes out of me!" A fist banged against the adjoining wall, surprising Jean so much she almost fell off her seat. "Here it comes…" the woman screamed. "Here… it… comes!"

Jean had heard enough. She pulled up her bloomers, flushed her toilet and scuttled out of the cubicle, not daring to look back. Outside she bumped into two men wearing ambulance crew uniforms. "I think you should get inside there – quickly!" she urged.

"Why is that, madam?"

"Some poor woman is having a baby in one of the cubicles. I don't know if that's her boyfriend or her husband in there too, but he's no use at all – she needs your help!"

Penelope finished rinsing the key, then wiped it dry. She held the small sliver of metal up for Dante to see. "Who'd have thought such a little thing could cause so much trouble."

He grimaced. "Let's not dwell on the past. Just undo the handcuffs, okay?"

She removed the metal manacles from her own wrist first, then took the other end off Dante's arm. He threw the handcuff into the rubbish chute. "There, you're a free man again," Penelope said happily. "It'll probably take a few minutes for the disabling effects to wear off, but you should have full use of your bio-blades soon enough."

"Good," he replied, rubbing the raw red mark round his wrist where the cuff had been secured. "Now, let's go and search for this assassin. The sooner we discover the truth, the better." But as they moved towards the exit, Dante and Penelope found their path blocked by two men in fluorescent green overalls, both holding pistols.

"You must be the elusive Nikolai Dante," the man on the left said, smiling cruelly. "I'm Dobie and this is Boyle; we've been looking for you everywhere."

His partner took aim at Penelope's heart. "And you must be Agent Goodnight, Britannia Intelligence's most accomplished seductress." Boyle looked Dante up and down, mentally undressing him. "Have you added this one to your long list of conquests? He's not much to look at, I'll grant you that, but I'm sure you must have enjoyed full use of his facilities by now."

"Who the hell are you?" Dante demanded.

"He told you," Boyle replied. "We're Dobie and Boyle."

"Are those names supposed to mean something to me?"

"They're bounty hunters," Penelope said. "Parasitic scum, taking on the cases the Britannia Royal Constabulary can't – or won't – handle. We've got a file on these two at HQ, filled with reports of their illegal exploits. Dobie was a mercenary who travelled the Empire, fighting in petty border squabbles for whichever side paid better. Boyle was a policeman, until his partner died in mysterious circumstances. They've got a reputation for killing without mercy or compunction."

"We're the best there is at what we do," Dobie said proudly.

"Top of the turds, in other words?" Dante asked.

"Kings of the shit hill," Penelope agreed. "Or should I say queens?"

"Our sexuality is irrelevant to our effectiveness," Boyle replied.

"I'll say. How long has it taken you to find us?"

"Shut up!" Dobie yelled, smacking his pistol across Penelope's face. Dante moved to retaliate but Boyle already had his pistol aimed and ready to fire.

"I don't need an excuse to kill you," he sneered. "Our employer made it perfectly clear he doesn't want you coming back to London. At least, not alive."

"How's it going in here?" an elderly voice asked from behind the bounty hunters. An old lady with snow white hair came into the public bathroom, shoving her way past Dobie and Boyle. They hastily concealed their weapons inside their overalls while glaring at Dante and Penelope. The old lady looked around, confused by what she found. "So, where's this baby then?"

"Baby?" Dante asked.

"I heard some poor lass in here, screaming in agony as she tried to give birth. It sounded like she was having the most terrible time of it, so I sent these ambulance men in to help."

"It was all a misunderstanding," Dobie said loudly at the old woman. "You must have been confused, dear."

She shot a stern look at him. "Don't tell me what I did and didn't hear, young man! I may have snow on the chimney, but there's still fire in my belly, let me tell you!"

"Of course there is," Dobie replied, trying to placate her.

"Don't patronise me, you two-faced so-and-so! There's a terrible stramash outside, with so many people waiting to see you bring out the young woman and her baby. So, where is it?"

"Yes, where is it?" Penelope asked, still nursing the cheek Dobie had pistol-whipped. "You'll have some explaining to do if there's no baby to be seen." She took Dante by the hand and tried to lead him out of the toilets. "Come along, darling, let's go see what's happening outside. I think we've been in here long enough."

"Er... yes!" Dante said, slowly catching her drift. The pair attempted to push past the bounty hunters but Boyle was too quick for them. He pushed the barrel of his pistol into Penelope's ribs, out of sight of the old woman.

"I'll come with you. I need to fetch the ambulance for this baby. Dobie, why don't you stay here and show this delightful old lady what we found in the cubicle?"

"Good idea," Dobie agreed. "Off you go. I'll be out in a minute."

Boyle gave Dante and Penelope a shove towards the exit, then followed them out. As the old woman had promised, a crowd had gathered, waiting for news. Boyle told them his partner was still inside, looking after the baby. "Please, let us past," he called out, nudging his captives through the ring of expectant people. Once they were clear of the crowd Boyle pulled a silencer from inside his overalls and began screwing it on to the end of his weapon. "Keep walking and smiling," he urged. "The ambulance is parked inside the show ground. When we get there, you'll climb in the back. Try anything stupid and I'll kill you both in a second."

"Crest," Dante whispered under his breath. "Have the effects of the handcuffs worn off?"

Not enough for you to survive a mortal wound, it said. *But your bio-blades should be available again any minute now.*

"What are you whispering about?" Boyle demanded.

"He was talking to himself," Penelope replied. "He does that all the time. It's been driving me crazy. You taking him off my hands will be a relief, to be honest."

"Nobody asked your opinion," the bounty hunter said as they entered the show ground. The smell of sweat and exertion filled the air, along with sweeter scents like lavender and cherry blossom from nearby fields. The show ground was a vast field with dozens of events underway and hundreds of people in traditional Highland dress moving from one activity to the next. Kilts were the norm among all the men, with twenty different tartans on display. Boyle pushed his prisoners towards the ambulance, parked in a corner of the show ground. "Keep moving!"

A group of men was standing in front of the ambulance, arguing amongst themselves. A big, bearded man with flaming red hair loudly berated those around him. "This is a disgrace! For three hundred years our forefathers and their forefathers before them have competed at these games and won more trophies than they had rooms in which to keep them. Now look at us – a clan with not enough men to enter the competitions, let alone win anything!"

The others shuffled their feet and stared at the grass, too ashamed to reply. Their leader glared at them one by one, his nostrils flaring and his cheeks flushed crimson with indignation. "One more man – that's all we need! One more man who can legitimately wear the tartan of the Douglas clan and then we're in business! Can we not find one more man anywhere?"

The youngest of the Douglas clan noticed the trio approaching the ambulance. He pointed at Dante's legs and laughed. "What about that Jessie in the blouse? Will he do, Tam?"

The clan's leader spun round to see where the lad was pointing. "Aye, he'll do, Alistair, he'll do!" Tam marched across to Dante, followed by all the others. "Welcome, brother! I don't know your face but you're a bonny sight for all of us, right enough!"

"Sorry?" Dante asked.

Tam pointed at Dante's kilt. "You're wearing the Douglas tartan, man!"

Say "Aye!", the Crest prompted.

"Aye!" Dante ventured.

"That makes you one of us, doesn't it lads?"

"Aye!" the Douglas clan members roared in response.

Tam wrapped his arm around Dante's shoulders. "What events are your best, laddie? Throwing the weight? Putting the shot? How about tossing the caber, we could always do with another good tosser, couldn't we lads?"

"Aye!" the others shouted back happily.

"Tossing... That's a public event here?" Dante asked fearfully.

"Of course! Once you've had your hands wrapped round a huge piece of wood, you'll be a changed man," Tam promised.

Dante looked over his shoulder at Boyle. "Perhaps you want my colleague, he's more used to wood handling than me."

Tam snorted derisively. "Don't talk pish! You're the one in the kilt, laddie!" He started dragging Dante away, but Boyle intervened.

"I'm sorry, but this man is unwell. I was taking him and his girlfriend to the ambulance for treatment. I can't let him out of my sight."

"Nonsense! Look at him – he's as right as rain!" Tam nodded towards Penelope. "That lassie's got a nasty cut on her face, that needs seeing to all right, but our man is fighting fit!"

"You go, Nikolai," she said. "I'll be fine."

Boyle searched the crowd in vain for Dobie, then stepped closer to Dante. "I'll send my partner to bring you back. Don't try to escape or else your girlfriend dies – painfully."

"Why should I care what happens to her?" Dante replied.

Boyle stared at Dante. "You care. I can see it in your eyes."

The other Douglas men had already marched towards the registration desk and Tam was tugging at Dante's arm. "Come on, man, we have to get you entered or we'll be disqualified!" Dante reluctantly let himself be led away, his eyes still fixed on Boyle and Penelope. The bounty hunter was forcing her into the back of the ambulance, a murderous look on his face.

Tam rubbed his fingers against the fabric of Dante's borrowed blouse. "Once you're signed up, we need to find you a better shirt. I hope you don't mind my saying, but this one makes you look soft! Now, what's your name? I missed what your girlfriend called you before."

"Nikolai D–"

"Och, you've no need to tell me your last name, I can see it on your kilt, man!" Tam slapped his meaty hand hard against Dante's back. "Welcome to the clan, Nikolai Douglas!"

TWELVE

"Luck is a stick with two ends."
– Russian proverb

"The Tower of London has been the site of only a small number of executions, contrary to popular belief. Six prisoners were beheaded on Tower Green, among them three wives of the much married monarch Henry VIII. Another sixteen were shot dead, mostly in the Tower's East Casemates Rifle Range. These included three Black Watch mutineers in 1743, eleven spies during the First World War and a German parachutist during the Second World War. The vast majority of condemned prisoners were taken from their cells to other places in London to be beheaded or hung, drawn and quartered."

– Extract from *The Smirnoff Almanac of Fascinating Facts*, 2673 edition

Dobie opened the back of the ambulance, expecting to see two corpses inside: Dante and Agent Goodnight. Instead he found his scowling partner pointing a gun at the secret service agent. "Don't even ask," Boyle snarled. He jerked a thumb towards the Highland Games going on outside the front window of the ambulance. "Dante's out there somewhere, competing for the Douglas clan. You'll have to find him and bring him back here while I guard this one."

"Why not kill her, then help me look for Dante?" Dobie asked.

"Remember what Rucka said in London? We'll have the entire secret service hunting us to the ends of the earth if we kill her. Dante is our target, not her."

"Inspector Rucka?" Penelope smiled. "Of Scotland Yard? So he hired you two idiots."

Boyle lashed out with his pistol, cracking it against her face. "Shut your mouth, bitch! It may be in our best interests not to kill you, but that doesn't mean you get away unscathed."

She glared at him from the floor of the ambulance. "Keep hitting me like that and you'll be the one getting scathed," she promised.

Dobie stepped in to stop Boyle attacking Penelope. "Leave her, Ray, she's not worth it!"

"I'm worth more than both of you put together," she snapped.

Boyle silenced her with a kick to the stomach, then sent Dobie out in search of Dante. "Beg, steal or borrow a kilt and get yourself entered into the games. If you can't extract Dante, arrange for him to meet an unfortunate accident. I'll bring the ambulance over and we can get the hell out of this place. Got it? Good, then go!"

Dante marvelled at the games' bizarre range of sporting contests. An area at one end of the vast field was devoted to conventional track and field events like the sprints, long jump and the hop, step and jump. But the rest of the show ground was devoted to more arcane pursuits. Wrestling was a popular spectator sport, with a crowd of excited women watching men in kilts grapple with each other, their kilts frequently flying above the waist to great cheers of approval. Nearby burly men were attempting to toss a mighty weight over a bar that was being raised progressively higher and higher. Others were throwing a hammer, trying to get it the greatest distance. But the most spectacular of the heavy events was tossing the caber. Each man was given a length of wood that resembled a tree trunk and was expected to throw it through the air.

Now the Douglas men had found sufficient numbers to enter themselves as a group, Tam was quickly showing why he was their leader. His hammer throwing easily won first prize, while he proved a demon at wrestling. But the red-haired hurler overdid it tossing the weight over the bar and came away nursing his back. The other Douglas men winced in sympathy, but none were willing to take his place in the caber tossing. "It's a crying shame," Tam said through gritted teeth. "That's my speciality too!"

Dante turned away from him. "Crest, are all my enhanced abilities back at full strength?"

Yes, but that doesn't mean–

"I'll toss the caber!" Dante shouted.

The others looked at him as if he were mad, but Tam smiled and nodded. "I knew you were something special laddie, the first time I saw you!"

When he says special, do you think he means mentally impaired?

Dante strode into the open space where the caber was being tossed. So far, few competitors had managed to lift the six-metre-long wooden pole, let along throw it any distance. A judge asked for his name. "Nikolai Dan– Douglas! Nikolai Douglas!"

"Next to toss the caber is Nikolai Douglas," a loudspeaker announced to the rest of the show ground. "This year the caber weighs more than sixty kilograms, a record for these games!"

Fortunately for Dante, the caber was already standing on one end, held in place by several organisers. He crouched beside the tall length of wood, making a great show of preparatory puffing and panting to mask a conversation with the Crest. "How do I actually toss this thing?"

You volunteered for this and you don't even know how to take part?

"I didn't want to let the Douglas clan down," Dante said with a shrug.

Of course not. Very well. First, you lift the pole with a swift movement into a vertical position. Dante dug his fingers underneath the caber. *Try not to open your legs too wide while crouching,* the Crest suggested. *You may be dressed like a true Scotsman beneath the kilt, but you haven't got a sporran to protect your modesty.*

Dante glanced across the field and noticed a cluster of young women pointing at him and laughing. "Bojemoi!" he muttered. "As if I haven't got enough to think about." With a mighty grunt he pushed up from the ground, lifting the caber into the air.

Good. Now you start running forwards.

"You've got to be kidding me."

You volunteered for this, remember? You start running forwards.

Dante did as the Crest urged, slowly putting one foot in front of the other until he gradually picked up speed. "Okay, now what?" he gasped between gulps of air.

Evasive action!

"What do you mean, evasive action?" Dante snapped, still running with one end of the caber balanced in his hands, the other end pointing into the sky. "Is that part of the event?"

One of the bounty hunters is on the other side of the field, aiming a gun at you!

By this point Dante was close to the far side of the area cleared for the caber tossing. "Crest, I'm running out of room! When do I toss this bloody tree trunk?"

Sorry, it said apologetically. *I was distracted by the imminent threat to your life. Pardon me for trying to keep you from being shot.*

"Crest!" Dante bellowed. Ahead of him he could see Dobie standing apart from the rest of the laughing spectators, taking aim with a silenced pistol.

You're meant to stop dead and hurl the caber upwards.

Dante did as he was told, launching the mighty pole into the air. It turned over three times before plummeting back down towards the spot where Dobie was standing. The rest of the crowd had already dived out of the way, but the bounty hunter was slow to realise his danger. He dived out of the way with moments to spare, his weapon falling to the ground. The caber slammed into the earth, crushing the pistol beneath it. The judges ran forward with a measuring tape to see how far Dante had tossed, while Dobie melted away into the crowds. Within a minute the show ground's public address system crackled into life. "Ladies and gentlemen, we have a new games record! Nikolai Douglas has tossed the caber twelve metres further than anyone ever before! Can we have a big round of applause for Nikolai Douglas of Clan Douglas!"

Having impressed the crowds with his record-breaking efforts with the caber, Dante found himself in demand for all manner of events. Every time he tried to make his way back to the ambulance, another group would grab his hand and drag him away to a different area of the show ground. He was a useful addition to the Douglas men in the tug of war, helping them reach the semi-final before they were eliminated, but was worse than useless when dragged into dancing a reel with three sprightly youths. Dante staggered off the raised dais where the dancing events were taking place and walked straight into Dobie. The bounty hunter was dressed in a red tartan kilt and was clutching a long sword in each hand. "Going native, are you?"

"You may have buried my gun but I don't need it to finish you off," Dobie snarled. "These ceremonial sabres will do the job just as well!"

Dante smiled as the purple and silver cyborganics extruded bio-blades from his fists. He crossed them in front of his face, raising an eyebrow at the bounty hunter. "You were saying?" The two men circled round each other, searching for an opening.

But before either of them could strike, an adjudicator on the dancing stage saw what they were doing and commandeered the public address system. "Ladies and gentlemen, it seems we have a treat in store. Two of our male competitors are volunteering to perform a Gillie Chaluim!" The crowd gave a collective gasp, everyone nearby looking round to see who the announcer was talking about. "That's right, a Gillie Chaluim! And unless I'm much mistaken, it looks like one of our volunteers is Nikolai Douglas!" Dante and Dobie stopped circling each other and looked up at the dais. The adjudicator gestured for them to come up on stage. "Come on, now, don't be shy!" she called out. "Everybody, give these brave boys a round of applause!"

People left nearby events to join the crowd around the dais, all of them clapping wildly and shouting their approval. In less than a minute more than a hundred spectators gathered to watch. Dante could see Tam among those joining the throng. "Good on you, son!" the red-haired man shouted over the cacophony. "But you be careful, you hear?"

The adjudicator waved for Dobie and Dante to join her on stage. "Come on," she urged. Trapped by the surging crowd around them, the pair had little choice but to do as she said.

"Try to escape and I promise you a long, slow, painful death," Dobie said into Dante's ear as they climbed up on to the dais. Meanwhile the crowd was shouting, clapping and stomping their approval of this new development.

"Crest," Dante whispered. "What the hell is a jilly charloom?"

I was wondering when you'd ask. A Gillie Chaluim is the oldest of the Highland dances, said to date back to the time of King Malcolm Canmore in the Eleventh Century. After defeating an enemy in battle, the king would lay his sword over that of his adversary in the sign of the cross and execute a dance of victory. The Gillie Chaluim was an exclusively male dance at first, but later it was kept alive by women and particularly young girls. The object was to dance with the feet as close as possible to the swords without ever touching the blades.

"That doesn't sound too bad," Dante said. "From the way it was announced, you'd think we had to dance each other to death."

Funny you should say that. The Gillie Chaluim was outlawed thirty years ago after the name became associated with an altogether more dangerous form of dancing. Men reclaimed the name and used it for a duelling dance where each combatant wields a pair of swords.

"Let me guess – it was made illegal because so many people got hurt?"

Because so many people died, Dante. The winner is usually declared when one of the dancers draws the blood of his adversary. But at its most savage, the Gillie Chaluim is a dance to the death where neither opponent puts down his sword until the other man falls.

The adjudicator called for silence from the hundreds gathered around the stage. "Ladies and gentlemen, quiet, please! If there are any children present, they must be taken away now – the Gillie Chaluim is not to be witnessed by anyone under eighteen." There were disappointed cries from children clustered at the front of the crowd as parents dragged them away. Meanwhile the adjudicator approached Dante and Dobie. "Well, how far are you gentlemen willing to go? Will first blood be enough to satisfy honour?"

"That sounds good to–" Dante began.

"To the death!" Dobie interjected. "We fight to the death!"

"You dance to the death," the adjudicator corrected him.

"I dance," the bounty hunter spat, then pointed at Dante. "He dies!"

The crowd overheard this interchange, shocked whispers passing through the throng. "Did you hear that, hen? They're dancing to the death!"

The adjudicator looked both men in the eye. "Are you both agreed on this? Your decision must be unanimous or else the Gillie Chaluim cannot go ahead."

"Well?" Dobie asked his target. "Have you got the guts for this?"

Dante sighed and nodded. "We dance to the death."

"Very well," the adjudicator agreed, then announced their decision to the crowd. A thrill of excitement passed through the people thronged around the stage. The adjudicator made the sign of the cross, then rested a hand on both men's shoulders. "May God have mercy on your souls." She climbed down from the dais, leaving the two enemies surrounded by a thousand people.

"How do I get myself into these situations?" Dante wondered out loud.

Stupidity and stubbornness usually do the trick, the Crest replied.

Inside the ambulance Boyle was getting restless. "What's taking Dobie so long?"

"Finding Dante will not be easy," Penelope said. "He's a master of disguise, able to blend into any crowd and simply disappear. If he is still here, your partner could walk right past him and never even notice. But Dante's got no reason to stick around. Best guess? He'll be a hundred kilometres away from here by now. You'll never find him." She paused, savouring the pained expression on her captor's face. "I'm sorry, was that a rhetorical question?"

Boyle grabbed the front of her catsuit and wrenched Penelope towards him until their faces were almost touching. "Shut your mouth, or else I'll take great pleasure in smashing your teeth down your throat, one by one," he snarled.

"You have the most amazing eyes," she said softly. "A shade of a blue like I haven't seen outside the Mediterranean, flecked with white like shards of ice. A person could lose themselves in those eyes, Ray." She stroked the side of his face tenderly, softly caressing the bruised cheekbones and taut, angry mouth. "Someone hurt you once, I can see in your eyes, the set of your mouth. Someone hurt you and you swore you'd never be hurt again. I could take the pain away, I could kiss it all better." She moved closer, her lips hovering over his, her eyes staring into his, her breasts pressing against his chest. "Let me make it better, Ray."

He reached a hand up to Penelope's face and shoved her backwards across the ambulance, so her skull smacked against the wall. "Get away from me, you bitch!"

She shrugged while rubbing the back of her head. "Well, you can't blame a girl for trying."

"I can," Boyle warned, aiming his pistol at Penelope's face. "I don't care what Rucka says. Try one more stunt like that and I'll bury your corpse where they can never find it. You won't be dead, just missing in action – one more secret agent who disappeared in the line of duty."

Dobie attacked first, a crude lunge with the sword in his left hand that Dante easily eluded. But the bounty hunter's attempt was merely a feint, drawing his opponent off balance. While his left sword was still in motion, Dobie pivoted on one heel and whipped his other sword through the air. The blade cut through shirt fabric and sliced to the bone, the metal edge gouging into two ribs. Dante cried out in pain, a crimson stain spreading down his left side.

"First blood to me," Dobie crowed. He took a step back and licked the blade clean with his tongue. "It's said the first cut is the deepest – but I promise my last cut will hurt the most."

"Come and have a go if you think you're hard enough," Dante replied. When Dobie stepped in for another attack Dante's bio-blades cut his opponent's shirt into rags, leaving two livid cuts in opposite directions across Dobie's chest. "X marks the spot," Dante said. "That's where I'll bury my blade when I kill you."

"Promises, promises," Dobie smiled. He bowed to Dante, then struck a pose with his two swords. "Enough of the preliminaries. Let battle commence!" Dobie hurled himself at Dante, who danced aside, spinning through the air in a graceful pirouette. The bounty hunter went high with both his blades, but Dante ducked under them. When Dobie went low, his opponent jumped over the top of both swords. "Stand still, damn you!"

"This is meant to be a sword dance, not a sword fight," Dante smirked. "Can I help it if you're not much of a dancer?" He attempted a few dance steps of his own and tripped over his own feet, landing clumsily on his behind.

The bounty hunter laughed, his blades drawn back for the kill. "You were saying?" But when he attacked, Dante rolled aside. Another attack and Dante rolled the other way, narrowly avoiding being impaled. On the third time his luck ran out and Dobie stabbed a sword clean through Dante's stomach so the tip was buried in the wooden dais. The crowd gasped in horror, their new found favourite pinned to the stage, his blood forming a scarlet pool underneath him.

Dobie took a step back, savouring his triumph. "And now, for my next trick," he announced, turning in a slow circle to look at the audience round the stage, ten-deep in places.

Suddenly Dante rammed his left bio-blade through Dobie's back so far the front half emerged from the bounty hunter's chest. "How do you like your wounds?" Dante asked, his teeth flecked with blood. "Straight up?" He wrenched the blade round through ninety degrees, bringing a scream of pain from his opponent. "Or with a twist?" Dante ripped his bio-blade back out of Dobie's back and walked round so the bounty hunter could see his sword was still wedged through Dante's body. The bounty hunter collapsed to his knees, disbelief clouding his eyes. He tried to swipe his remaining blade at Dante but it fell uselessly to the floor, along with Dobie's neatly severed right hand. The crowd was chanting, baying for blood.

Dante slowly, painfully pulled the sword out of his stomach then let it drop to stage. The dais was awash with blood spilling from his wounds, and from Dobie's. The bounty hunter's face was ashen, the knowledge that death was upon him all too obvious. "Please," he gasped, his breath a series of short, wet wheezing sounds. "Don't let me bleed to death."

Dante drew back one of his bio-blades, ready to finish Dobie off, urged on by the crowd around him. Instead he paused and looked up at the sky, studying the clouds as they floated lazily overhead. "Enough," he murmured to himself and turned away.

The crowd booed and jeered, but Dante paid them no heed as he stumbled down the steps to the grass, his knees almost buckling beneath him. Tam was waiting for him, the burly redhead slipping Dante's right arm over his shoulders. "Come on, laddie! You've done the Douglas tartan proud today. I'll see you to that ambulance, get you cleaned up."

On the dais Dobie fell face first into his own blood, splashing those nearest. He gasped a few more times, then made no further sound, his eyes staring lifelessly at nothing.

Flintlock woke to find a dozen guards standing over him. "Spatch, old boy, I think we've got company." The two prisoners were still being kept in the ground floor room looking out on the Tower of London's courtyard, where Princess Marie-Anne had visited them the previous day. By now the air was ripe with the stench of Spatchcock's all-pervasive body odour.

"I had nothing to do with it," Spatchcock mumbled as his eyes opened.

"You say that every time you wake up," Flintlock sighed.

"It's a defence mechanism." He stretched and yawned, then counted the heavily armed sentries filling the room. "All twelve of you to look after the two of us? Isn't that overkill?"

"I'd prefer if you refrained from using words like that," Flintlock whispered.

Spatchcock shrugged, then shifted his attention back to the guards. "I was beginning to think you had forgotten all about us." The sentries remained silent, their faces impassive, weapons aimed at the two prisoners. "Talkative bunch, aren't they?"

"You'll have to forgive them their silence," a man replied from the doorway. He paused to light a pipe, its pungent smoke quickly spreading through the confined space, then made his way through the armed guards. The new arrival had a thoughtful face with piercing eyes, and receding ginger hair. He sucked on his pipe, smiling contentedly. "They are trained not to speak unless given permission by a superior officer or authority figure."

"I'm guessing we don't qualify," Flintlock ventured.

"You guess correctly," the man said. "My name is Rucka, Rucka of Scotland Yard."

Spatchcock grinned wolfishly. "Rucka? That rhymes with mother–"

"Thank you," the inspector cut in. "I'm quite aware of what my name rhymes with."

"Some people have got no sense of humour," Spatchcock complained.

"And other people struggle to elevate their sense of humour from the gutter," Rucka replied. "I can see why Dante chose you two as his accomplices. Both of you are as vile and base as him, a pair of repellent creatures without moral fibre or character."

"I must object," Flintlock spluttered angrily. "This guttersnipe is in no way my equal!"

"You can say that again," Spatchcock agreed. "I've got much more class than you."

"Both of you are as bad as each other," the inspector sneered. "The Raven Corps was kind enough to send me its files on your criminal careers. Spatchcock, your past is littered with sufficient convictions to have you incarcerated for a thousand years – forgery, poisoning and all manner of other felonies."

"Well, I don't like to brag," Spatchcock said with a smile.

"Then there's Lord Peter Flintlock, a man whose youthful exploits were so disgusting, so repulsive, the government of Britannia had no choice but to deport him." Rucka shuddered. "It makes my flesh crawl merely thinking of what you did."

"Both Spatchcock and I have paid for our past crimes," Flintlock replied primly. "Our trespasses were forgiven, in exchange for agreeing to fight with the Rudinshtein Irregulars."

"Where you formed your current partnership in crime with Dante," Rucka pointed out. "Hardly a ringing endorsement for whoever authorised your amnesty."

"What did his lordship do exactly that got him ejected from his own country?" Spatchcock asked. "I've heard how terrible it was, but nobody will ever tell me the specifics."

The inspector shook his head. "Nor will you learn them from me. I would not sully my mouth by having to speak aloud a description of what your fellow traveller did to deserve deportation. It is enough for you to know his crimes are as bad as anything you've ever done."

Spatchcock looked at Flintlock with a new admiration. "You dirty dog! I never knew you had it in you!"

Flintlock refused to meet his eye, preferring to glare at Rucka. "When the time comes for our execution, I nominate Spatchcock to go first."

"That will not be an option," Rucka replied.

"We've been given a stay of execution?" Flintlock asked hopefully.

"No, you will be executed simultaneously. I've been sent here to keep an eye on you until midday tomorrow. Then you will be transported to the place of execution to await the arrival of her royal highness, Princess Marie-Anne. She seems certain Dante will launch some sort of rescue attempt between now and the moment of your deaths, so I volunteered to maintain a vigil over you both until then. In days gone by I believe this task was known as the death watch."

"Charming," Spatchcock commented. "How long have we got left?"

"Until you die?"

"No, until the summer sales open," he replied sarcastically.

Rucka consulted a pocket watch. "You will be executed in twenty-seven hours."

Spatchcock broke wind loudly. A noxious gas wafted round the room. "Sorry," he said insincerely. "I do that when I get nervous. Expect a lot of that in the next twenty-seven hours."

"I doubt either of us will last that long," Flintlock said despairingly. "Between the biological weapon that is your arse and the fumes coming from his pipe, we'll undoubtedly suffocate first."

By the time he had reached the ambulance, Dante's wounds were already healing themselves. Tam reacted with amazement when he saw the small scars where several brutal incisions had been. "Laddie, that's impossible! You must have the devil on your side!"

"Not exactly," Dante winced, "but enhanced healing abilities can do wonders."

"I'll say!" Tam marvelled. "What was your argument with the man on that stage?"

"Better if you don't get involved." Dante took his hand off Tam's shoulder and shook the Douglas clan leader's hand. "Thank you for all your help."

"No, laddie, thank you! I don't know what we'd have done without you today – they'll be talking about that caber toss for years to come!" Tam shook his head, already marvelling at the memory of it. Beyond him the games were breaking up, the final events finished and everyone was slowly filing out of the Peebles show ground. "You did us proud, Nikolai Dante!"

"You're welcome. I…" Dante stopped, realising what Tam had said. "You know who I am?"

"Of course! I ken your face from the news, laddie. Most folk round here don't bother with what happens south of the border, but I like to know what's happening in the rest of the world."

"You weren't afraid of having the man who tried to kill the king on your team?"

"Och, no! You'd have been doing us all a favour if you'd pulled it off. The Windsor McKrays are a disgrace, no two ways about it. The sooner we restore Caledonia's own monarchy the better! The day is coming, young Nikolai, you mark my words." Tam shook Dante's hand vigorously while slapping him on the arm. "If ever you need any help, let me know. Ask anyone in the town, they'll tell you where to find me." Tam marched away, laughing to himself.

"Half the country wants to kill me for something I didn't do, the other half wants to congratulate me – bizarre." A whistle sounded in the distance, prompting a surge of movement from those queuing to get out of the show ground. "What was that?"

The Flying Scotsman, *signalling it is getting ready to leave.*

"Diavolo! How long?"

Five minutes at most.

Boyle glanced at his watch. Dobie should have been back hours ago, what was taking him so long? The bounty hunter's eyes narrowed as he glanced at Penelope on the opposite side of the vehicle. Maybe the bitch was right, maybe I did read Dante wrong and he fled the moment we got inside the ambulance. No, I don't believe that, Boyle told himself. I could see the look in his eyes, the same look I've seen in the mirror every morning since hooking up with

Dobie. Dante cares about her the way I care about my partner. He wouldn't abandon her.

Boyle's thoughts were thrown askew by the back doors of the ambulance flying open. He spun round, his pistol raised and ready to fire – but there was nobody there. "Dobie, is that you? If you're playing silly buggers out there I'll give you the thrashing of your life!"

"Promises, promises," Dante's voice replied.

"You!" Boyle said. He leaned from one side to the other, trying to catch a glimpse of his quarry, but all he could see were the citizens of Peebles walking away from the show ground. "Where's Dobie? What have you done with him?"

"Your partner had an unfortunate accident," Dante said in a sing-song voice. "He cut himself shaving and bled to death."

"You're lying!"

"Am I? How can you be sure? Your boyfriend was good, but I'm better, much better."

Boyle screamed a curse at the wind. Somehow, in his gut, he knew Dante was telling the truth: Dobie was dead and that Romanov bastard had killed him. "Damn you – come out and face me like a man!"

"I'm not sure I'm your type," Dante taunted him. "Then again, I'm not sure you were Dobie's type either. He never mentioned you when he was dying, not once."

Boyle could feel an uncontrollable rage boiling inside. He fought to control the fury, to own it, knowing his emotions had the power to destroy him. Attack is the best form of defence, he thought. Make the bastard show himself, that was the only way. Boyle lurched across the ambulance and grabbed Penelope by the hair, dragging her across to him. "I've got your girlfriend here, Dante. She's very pretty, isn't she? She wouldn't be so pretty if I blew her face off."

"I told you before, Boyle – I don't care what happens to her."

"You're lying, I can hear it in your voice. Show yourself or say goodbye to her face!"

A long, protracted silence followed.

"Well?" Boyle demanded. "I'll give you three seconds to show yourself. One!"

Still no sound or movement came from outside.

"Two!" Boyle could feel Penelope's heart pounding beneath his left hand, while his right hand pressed the pistol hard into the side of her head.

A whistle cried plaintively in the distance, followed by the sound of a train getting rolling, slowly picking up speed.

"Three!" But it wasn't Boyle who finished the countdown – it was Penelope. She flung her head back into Boyle's face, breaking the bones in his nose.

As he screamed in pain, Penelope threw herself from the ambulance, rolling away on the grass outside. At the same moment a flash of purple and silver stabbed through the wall nearest Boyle, slicing off his right hand in a single movement. Blood sprayed from the severed limb, changing the air inside the vehicle to a fine pink aerosol. Boyle sobbed in anguish, his left hand uselessly trying to staunch the bleeding from the stump where his right had been.

The bio-blade was withdrawn as quickly as it had penetrated. Within seconds Dante was inside the ambulance, picking up Boyle's discarded pistol. The bounty hunter slumped to the floor, his face a mask of pain. "You'll pay for this, you bastard," he vowed.

"I doubt it," Dante said, shooting Boyle through both kneecaps. "That should slow you down." He climbed back out of the ambulance and helped Penelope to her feet. "Are you all right?"

She nodded, rubbing the back of her head. "I'll be fine, but we've missed the train."

"I know. We'll have to find another way of getting to Orkney."

"What about me?" Boyle demanded. "Why don't you finish me off, you coward?"

Dante shrugged. "I'm not a murderer. I kill to defend myself, but I don't enjoy it – not like you." He contemplated the ambulance. "We could take this, it's got hover-capacity."

Penelope grimaced at the vehicle's blood-soaked interior. "It'll stink worse than a slaughterhouse by the time we reach the island. Let's find something else."

The two of them walked away, leaving Boyle a broken, bleeding mess in the back of the ambulance.

"Orkney is an island?" Dante asked Penelope

"Of course. Didn't you know that?"

"Local geography is not exactly my strongest area."

"There's a whole group of islands, more than seventy of them. Orkney, Hoy, Rousay–"

"Hoy!" Dante exclaimed, stopping abruptly. "That was the name I heard the bald man with the goatee say on Westminster Bridge! He was meeting someone soon and they would see with the old man at Hoy. At least, that's what it sounded like."

"He meant the Old Man of Hoy," Penelope realised. "It's a tourist attraction, quite a famous one. If that is the rendezvous point for our target, we've got to get there first, but how?"

Dante smiled. "I know someone here who owes me a favour."

THIRTEEN

"Pointless to pray when you sin without measure."
– Russian proverb

"The Old Man of Hoy is a legend among climbers. This sandstone rock stack rises more than a hundred metres from the sea, on the eastern tip of the island of Hoy, north of Britannia. To the untrained eye it best resembles a rough hewn finger of rock, pointing at the sky. The top of the stack is almost exactly level with the nearby cliffs. For centuries climbers have travelled to this remote island solely to tackle this tricky ascent. An entire tourist industry has built up around the Old Man. Weather permitting, this iconic stack is ascended almost daily during summer."
– Extract from *The Duffer's Guide to Britannia*, 2670 edition

"I never normally get sea sick," Dante whispered, apologising between retches over the side of the ferry. The old wooden vessel was bouncing about on rough water between Orkney and Hoy, pitching from side to side in the heavy swell. "I mean, I grew up onboard a pirate ship and never threw up once. But this…" He unleashed another mouthful of green bile into the churning, restless sea.

"You should have had one of my anti-nausea pills," Penelope commented.

The ferry lurched as it plunged down one side of a mighty wave, then swayed back again as the next wave rose beneath it. Dante swallowed hard but couldn't stop another surge from his unhappy stomach. He retched the results over the nearest railing, then wiped the flecks of vomit from his mouth. "This has to settle down eventually, doesn't it?"

"Let's hope so," Penelope agreed. "You'll be useless on Hoy if you can't stop throwing up."

Seventeen hours had passed since they had left Boyle bleeding to death in the ambulance at Peebles. They had headed for the nearest tavern where Dante asked for Tam Douglas. Three taverns later they found him. He was more than happy to help the saviour of the Douglas clan's honour, but could only offer them ground-based vehicles. Hover-capability was reserved for royalty, the emergency services and visiting tourists in Caledonia. "It's all part of a plot by those holding power in London to stop us reclaiming our rightful place in the sky!"

Dante and Penelope decided against going back for the ambulance, choosing to drive through the night in a borrowed school bus to the north of Caledonia, taking turns behind the wheel. They reached the docks at a desolate place called Scrabster as the sun rose on Saturday. Penelope bought anti-nausea pills from an apothecary's stall at the docks while they waited to catch the first ferry to Orkney. "I'd rather die than get on a boat without these," she admitted.

Once on Orkney, Dante and Penelope raced to the train station, but the *Flying Scotsman*'s passengers had long since disembarked to explore the surrounding islands. Penelope changed clothes in her compartment while Dante searched for Gordonstoun. The head steward was persuaded by having a bio-blade pressed against his throat. Dante described the man he had been stalking since London. "That sounds like Mr Marius Wilderhaber, a Swiss gentleman," Gordonstoun said. "He asked me for directions to Hoy, I think he is meeting friends there later today. I told him the easiest way of getting there was the hover-bus."

"What time does that leave?"

"It already has," the steward had replied with a grim smile of satisfaction. "The next one doesn't leave until Monday. Of course, you could catch the ferry to Hoy, that sails in half and hour – but the seas are very rough today. They might cancel it altogether."

Dante ran to Penelope's compartment and burst inside. "We've got to hurry. The–"

"Do you mind?" She was standing naked in the centre of the room.

"Not at all," he replied, a sly grin on his face. A torrent of obscene and abusive suggestions drove him back out into the corridor. Bojemoi, they had seen each other in far more compromising positions than that – what was her problem?

When will you learn? There is a time and a place for what you laughingly consider a romantic overture, Dante. That was neither.

Three minutes later Penelope had emerged from her compartment in a fresh black catsuit, zipping it all the way up to her throat. She had a pistol strapped to each thigh in black leather holsters and offered a similar weapon to Dante. "I'll stick with my bio-blades," he said. "I'm not much use with a gun unless it's my Huntsman 5000 rifle, and it's still at the Palace of London."

The pair had caught the ferry to Hoy with minutes to spare. Now, after an hour of being thrown about on the stormy seas, the rocky island loomed ahead of them. Bitterly cold winds sliced at the two travellers, threatening to freeze them where they stood.

Dante wished he had got changed while they were still on the train. His shirt was stained by blood, sweat and now vomit, while keeping his kilt down in these snapping breezes was proving problematic. More embarrassing was the effect of all this cold air blowing beneath his kilt, shrinking a much-loved part of his anatomy to the size of a cocktail sausage.

The ferry made its way to dock with agonising slowness, greasy black engine fumes fighting the brisk sea air for supremacy. Once the vessel was within two metres of the jetty Dante and Penelope jumped ashore, ignoring warnings from the crew. The pair ran towards dry land, searching for information. The hover-bus was parked on a landing pad nearby, some passengers from the *Flying Scotsman* still milling around. "We're lucky," Penelope said. "The pilot must have given them a sightseeing flight round the island before landing." It was Dante who spotted the elusive Wilderhaber. "There!" The bald man was ascending a vertiginous staircase up a nearby cliff. At the bottom a sign bore the words "OLD MAN OF HOY 10 KM".

As the pair watched, Wilderhaber reached the top of the cliff and disappeared inland. Dante sprinted towards the steps, Penelope close behind. "We can still catch him!"

Marius Wilderhaber was running scared. For days he had been unsettled and uneasy, as if something terrible was waiting to happen. His leisurely sightseeing trip up Britannia had passed without incident, yet Marius could not shake a feeling of impending doom, as if everything he saw and did was merely the calm before the storm. Perhaps it stemmed from his failure in London. Yes, the target he had been given was ambitious, but not unattainable. The results were disappointing. He hit his secondary target but the main one had escaped. The man from Basel was not looking forward to explaining his failure.

Marius had been haunted by his failure ever since, but that wasn't the only thing haunting him. Time and again he had felt as though someone was watching him. The first occasion had been on Westminster Bridge. Marius had been on the phone, arranging the rendezvous with his employer. For a moment the Swiss visitor thought he had seen a figure floating in the Thames. His unease had grown after boarding the *Flying Scotsman* in London the next day. Nobody knew how Marius was travelling north to the rendezvous, not even his employer, yet he felt certain someone was staring at him in the dining car that first evening on the train. The same thing happened on Thursday, when everyone got off at Nottingham for day-trips. When Marius dutifully lined up to see the castle, he could not shake the sensation of being observed, as if unseen eyes were watching him. The feeling grew in Peebles yesterday, when they disembarked to watch the Highland Games. Marius's fears had eased after the *Flying Scotsman* departed the border town for a night of feasting and festivities at Stirling Castle. He searched the other passengers' eyes but none of them paid him any attention. With the rendezvous getting ever closer, Marius had let himself relax. The train arrived at Orkney without incident and he caught the hover-bus unmolested, his confidence returning at last. He was nearly home, he was nearly safe.

Marius decided to hike across the island to see the Old Man of Hoy. There was no shortage of local hover-cabs offering to transport passengers there in a fraction of the time the journey would take on foot. But Marius wanted to savour one last trip in his own company, away from the crowds that had hampered his enjoyment of the train journey. Now he was regretting that decision, more than any other choice he had made in Britannia. Two people were stalking him along the windswept path across the island, slowly gaining on him. Every time he looked back, they were closer than before

He risked another glance over his shoulder and froze. I know those two, he realised. The woman had been one of the passengers, blending in with the others, not drawing attention to herself. But the man, that was another matter. He was dressed like one of the stewards in a kilt and white shirt, but his face was all too familiar. Marius gasped as recognition shook him to the core. It was the man he had seen floating in the Thames! The same man who had glared at him in the dining car, who had lingered at the corner of Marius's thoughts and nightmares since London. He's found me again and now he's hunting me!

Marius Wilderhaber started running.

"Bojemoi, he's running! The bastard must have realised we were following him!" Dante sprinted after Wilderhaber, Penelope close behind.

"It was inevitable," she shouted after Dante. "This path is so exposed, there's no way he could fail to see us tracking him."

The pair ran through a shallow pool of stagnant water. A cloud of tiny black insects rose from the surface, engulfing them. Dante felt a burning sensation beneath his kilt. He lifted the fabric and saw his groin was covered with minute creatures. "What are these things, Crest?"

Midges – a mosquito-like dipterous insect occurring in dancing swarms, especially near water. They are fond of feasting on human blood by piercing the skin with their mouths and sucking out the desired liquid. Each bite encourages the victim to scratch at the wound, creating irritation and swelling far greater in magnitude than the size of the midge.

Dante slapped at his crotch, trying to shift the swarm. "Fuoco, it feels as though I'm being eaten alive!"

"Leave them!" Penelope yelled, dragging him after Wilderhaber. "The more you scratch, the more they itch!"

"Easy for you to say, you're not having your life blood sucked out of your testicles!"

Wilderhaber was breathless and exhausted when he reached the eastern tip of the island. He collapsed by the edge of the cliff, his breath rasping and a metallic taste in his mouth. Close by, the Old Man of Hoy rose from the incoming tide, perhaps ten metres between it and the main part of the island. Wilderhaber peered gingerly over the edge of the cliff, but couldn't see any climbers on the sandstone stack. No witnesses who might intervene, no sign of his employer arriving to extract him. He was on his own, not even a rock nearby with which to defend himself.

The two people that had chased him across the island appeared over the brow of the nearest hill, slowing as they realised there was nowhere left to run. This was it, the end of the line. "What do you want of me?" Wilderhaber asked between gasps for breath. "Money? Do you want money?" He reached in his pocket and pulled out an Imperial Express card. "Here, take it! I'll give you my account code – just, please, don't kill me!"

The woman drew one of her pistols and took aim at Wilderhaber. "Why did you do it?"

"Do what?" he protested. "I don't know what you're asking me!"

"Tell us about the target," the other hunter demanded, one hand rubbing urgently at his groin. "Who chose the target?"

"My employer," Wilderhaber said, shrugging helplessly. "They call me, send me to a different country each time. I only find out my target after I arrive."

The woman stepped closer until she was metres away. "Who's your employer? Who paid for this job?"

"The vice president."

"Of which country?" she snarled.

Wilderhaber frowned. "H-He's vice president of a company, not a country. He works for EuroCorp, the food conglomerate."

Now it was the woman who looked confused. "Why would EuroCorp want the king dead?"

"Sorry?"

The kilted man stopped scratching his crotch and pointed a fist at Wilderhaber. A silver sword extruded from his hand, its tip nearly touching the Swiss man's face. "Why would a food company try to assassinate King Henry? What would it gain from his death?"

"I don't know what you're talking about," Wilderhaber protested. "I was sent here to buy the Britannia Food Corporation, along with its distribution network – that was my target. I secured the network but could only secure one third ownership of BFC."

The woman lowered her pistol, swearing quietly. "Nikolai, he's not the assassin."

"He must be!" her partner insisted. "I didn't chase him all this way for nothing!" The man jabbed his sword closer, the tip digging into Wilderhaber's neck, blood trickling from the wound. "Tell me the truth – otherwise I'll cut out your larynx and you'll never lie again!"

"I *am* telling you the truth!" the tourist insisted, close to tears. "I could never kill another living soul. I'm a businessman, nothing more – please, you must believe me!"

"Crest, can you analyse his heartbeat, detect whether or not he's lying?

Wilderhaber listened but heard no reply. To his amazement, the man in the kilt withdrew his sword and stepped away, cursing repeatedly.

"We came all this way for nothing," the woman sighed. "Now what, Dante? Your friends will be executed in a few hours and both of us are still wanted for a murder we didn't commit."

"Dante? Nikolai Dante?" Wilderhaber asked.

"You've heard of me?"

"Of course, you're the most wanted man in the Empire. Besides, your name has been all over the news for days. They said you tried to kill the king."

"No, I didn't!" Dante insisted angrily. "When will I find somebody who believes me?"

"I believe you," the woman replied, "for all the good it's doing us."

"I also believe you," Wilderhaber said, slowly rising from the ground.

"Why?" Dante asked.

"I heard about the assassination after my final meeting with BFC broke up on Tuesday. I was depressed, I went for a walk. I found myself on Westminster Bridge not long after dusk."

"I *knew* I'd seen you there," Dante said triumphantly.

"Let him talk," the woman replied. "What did you see, Marius?"

"Not much, to be honest. There was a mist rising from the river. As I got near the bridge I heard what sounded like a man crying out in pain, then a splash."

"The sniper's accomplice knocking me out, then probably both of them throwing me into the river," Dante said with a nod. "What next?"

"Two men were talking on the bridge. They had London accents, gruff voices. I couldn't see their faces, they were on the other side of the bridge."

"Could you hear what they said?" the woman asked. "Did either of them mention a name?"

Wilderhaber shook his head. "My employer called, wanting to know the outcome of my final meeting with BFC. When I told him what had happened, he suggested I take a few days off, see the country if I wanted. I arranged to be collected from here later today. By the time I finished my call, the two men had gone."

"Another dead end," Dante said hopelessly. But his partner had other ideas.

"Nikolai, you told me a hover-car caught Marius in its headlights – that's how you were able to recognise him as the man on the bridge." She turned to Wilderhaber. "Did you notice the car, see its identity plate?"

He nodded uncertainly. "I did see a hover-vehicle, but nothing I could identify easily."

"What about a colour? Even that would be a start," Dante urged.

"A kind of brown," Wilderhaber ventured. "It looked old but well loved."

Dante stopped talking, his head tilting to one side. "The Crest says there's something coming, a hover-capable vehicle of some sort."

The Swiss man frowned. "It could be my employer's driver come to collect me, but they are not due for another hour at least." The sound of hover-engines rose from beneath the cliff. Wilderhaber moved closer to the edge for a better look. "No, it isn't them. It looks like–"

"Marius – get down!" Dante suddenly shouted, flinging himself towards the tourist.

"An ambulance," Wilderhaber said. He felt two dull thuds in the centre of his chest, then his legs crumpled, pitching him over the edge of the cliff. He would have been terrified, but the Swiss businessman was dead before he hit the jagged rocks below.

"Diavolo!" Dante cursed, his fingers grasping at thin air where Marius had been standing. A hover-ambulance appeared from below the cliff, the same vehicle Dante and Penelope had decided against using at Peebles. Boyle was sitting in the pilot's chair, a maniacal grin stretched across his bruised and battered face. The ambulance was side-on to the cliff so the bounty hunter could fire his pistol out of the window at them. He loosed off a fusillade of shots, each bullet smacking the ground ever closer to Dante's precarious position, driving the fugitive nearer the precipice. Boyle's voice boomed at them from the vehicle's public address system. "A piece of advice for the future: if you're going to leave someone to die, don't do it in the back of an ambulance."

"Who says you have a future?" Penelope shouted, opening fire with both her pistols. The rounds smacked into the side of the ambulance, but none penetrated the pilot's door.

Boyle flew his vehicle over the fugitives and came down behind them, cutting off their only escape route. "You should have killed me when you had the chance, like I should have killed you on that bridge. Now I'll make you pay for murdering Dobie."

Dante and Penelope dived to the ground, trying to take cover amidst the rocks and moss. Dante felt naked without a gun in his hands. Bio-blades were fine for close quarters combat, but no use against other threats. What he wouldn't give to have the Huntsman 5000 in his grasp now. "Penelope! Throw me your spare pistol!"

She was trying to shoot Boyle through his windscreen, but her rounds were bouncing off. "What genius put bulletproof glass in an ambulance?" she protested, tossing her other weapon towards Dante. He reached up to grab it from the air but another hail of bullets from Boyle forced him back. The gun floated past, hit the edge of the cliff and bounced over.

Butterfingers, the Crest observed.

Boyle fired again, one of his shots hitting Penelope in her right shoulder. She gave an agonised cry, dropping her pistol. Seeing an opportunity, the bounty hunter sent the ambulance scudding towards his two targets, only centimetres above the ground. Penelope waited until the vehicle was almost on top of her, then rolled out of the way. Dante had nowhere left to go, the ambulance bearing down on him with ever increasing speed. Rather than trying to get out of its way, he began walking towards the oncoming vehicle.

Dante, are you quite insane? Evasive action! Take evasive action!

"I am," he snarled, then spun on his heels and sprinted towards the edge of the cliff. The ambulance was racing towards him, only moments from a fatal collision. Dante launched himself towards the Old Man of Hoy.

"Nikolai, no!" Penelope screamed as the ambulance swept past her.

Dante flew through the air in a gentle arc, arms and legs still pumping, trying to keep his forward momentum going. It felt as if time was slowing around him, each second stretching into an hour. Ahead, the top of the sandstone stack was almost within reach. Dante stretched out for it, his fingers clawing the cold air. He felt a hot blast of exhaust as the ambulance flew low over his head. There was a tearing sound, metal screaming in protest as it fought an unequal battle with nature, but Dante did not have time to look up for the cause. His leap of faith was fast becoming a plunge of death.

His body hit the side of the stack with a sickening thud, jagged outcrops of rock cutting through cloth and skin, slicing apart flesh and bone. His forward momentum gone, Dante could feel himself tipping over backwards, about to fall to the rocks below. Somehow he clung on to the side of the stack, despite the pain stabbing through every part of his body, despite having the breath punched from his lungs, despite the sounds of mechanical torment above.

Penelope picked herself up from the ground and walked to the edge of the cliff, grimly expecting to find Dante's body smeared across the rocks below next to Marius. What faced her instead defied both logic and belief. "Now that's something you don't see every day," she whispered.

Boyle's ambulance had collided with the Old Man of Hoy, knocking the top section of the stack off and into the sea. The space where the chunk of sandstone had stood for thousands of years was now occupied by the battered vehicle, as if the top of the stack were a natural landing pad. The ambulance had twisted sideways in the collision, Boyle's limp body impaled on the shattered remains of the windscreen. Most remarkable of all was the figure climbing the side of the stack. "You're still alive?" Penelope shouted. "You must be the luckiest bastard in the Empire!"

"Well, you're half right," Dante called over his shoulder. He tried to look at her and almost lost his grip. "Tell you what, let's save the rest of this conversation until I get to the top." Dante resumed climbing, ascending the stack with agonising slowness, hand over hand, a few centimetres at a time. Finally, he reached the top and collapsed, stretching out alongside the ambulance. "Penelope, what was it Boyle said before trying to kill us?"

"He was going to make you pay for murdering Dobie."

"Before that. He said something else before that."

"You should have killed him when you had the chance, like he should have killed you…" Her voice trailed off as she realised the significance of Boyle's words. "Like he should have killed you on that bridge! The men who attacked you on Westminster Bridge – it was Dobie and Boyle. One of them must have been the trigger man for the assassination attempt!"

Dante struggled into a sitting position, leaning back against the ambulance. "That means we've killed the real assassins and still have no proof of our innocence."

A low moan of pain drifted across from the stack. "Dante, you don't sound too good."

"That wasn't me," he replied. "It was Boyle, he's still alive!"

Ray Boyle opened his eyes to find Dante staring at him. The bounty hunter wanted to spit in the Russian bastard's face, but trying to breathe was taking all his energy. He concentrated on his hatred – that would keep him alive.

"You're dying," Dante said softly.

"Go… to hell," Boyle grimaced, the words making jagged, broken things inside him grind together. He screamed involuntarily and that made the pain worse. It was all he could do to keep from passing out. If I close my eyes I'll never open them again, he thought.

"Probably," Dante agreed, "but you'll be there before me. Besides, I doubt that either of us is much of a praying man." He moved closer, close enough for Boyle to smell the desperation on Dante's breath. "Did you shoot the king, or was it Dobie?"

"Why… why should I tell you?"

"Why not?"

Boyle tried to spit a curse at him but couldn't find the strength.

"You're right, it doesn't matter now," Dante said. "But I need to know who hired you. Was it the princess? Did Marie-Anne pay you to kill her father so she could take the throne?"

The bounty hunter laughed, despite the torture it caused. "You... you couldn't be... further from the truth..."

"Then who?" Dante demanded.

Boyle thought about it. Yes, telling Dante would be fitting revenge against the client who hired them, who set him and Dobie on this doomed path. He swallowed back a mouthful of blood and gasped a last sentence. "Follow... follow the money."

Dante laid a hand over Boyle's face, closing the dead man's eyes. Professional bounty hunters like Dobie and Boyle would have demanded a huge fee for assassinating the king of Britannia. Such a job would make them pariahs among the criminal underworld, unable to get work again. As insurance the twosome would have asked for half the fee upfront, in case anything went wrong. Follow the money. Yes, of course, Dante realised. Find the bounty hunters' bank accounts, then trace any large payments received in the past month back to the person who commissioned the hit.

Dante got to his feet, grateful for the differences his enhanced healing abilities were already making. He staggered past Boyle's body to where Penelope could see him. "How long have we got until Spatchcock and Flintlock are due to be executed?"

"About an hour, I guess. Last I heard they were scheduled for the chop at six."

He looked at the battered, broken ambulance, resting a hand against its side. "Crest, will this thing fly again?" Wires of purple and silver extended from his fingernails, becoming one with the vehicle's metalwork and circuitry. The engines spluttered, then roared back into life.

You can take that as a yes. Can you fly one of these?

"No, but I'm sure you can teach me," Dante said, before shouting across to Penelope. "Get ready to leave! We're going back to London – now!"

FOURTEEN

"Thoughts may be over the hills, but death is just over the shoulder."
– Russian proverb

"Fought in the Year of the Tsar 2669, the Battle of Britannia devastated much of the nation's capital. The country was of limited strategic importance, but the Romanovs felt obliged to defend their most vocal supporter in the fight against the Tsar. The fact that Captain Nikolai Dante and his Rudinshtein Irregulars were sent in first proved how little firepower the noble house was willing to commit to such a fight. Dante and his troops prevailed over the Tsar's Raven Corps, leaving almost as quickly as they had arrived. Britannia spent the next four years rebuilding London, particularly the area around Trafalgar Square. That same area was to suffer again when Dante returned in 2673. Nelson's Column was toppled for a second time shortly after the attempted assassination of King Henry McKray. Four days later Dante returned to the square once more in even more dramatic circumstances."

– Extract from *Britannia's Lost Landmarks*,
Carolyn Steele

Flintlock ducked to avoid being pelted by a tomato, but straightened up again in time to be hit by an airborne pineapple instead. The impact nearly knocked him out of the hover-cart in which he and Spatchcock were being paraded through the streets of London. "You'd think people would have the decency to throw rotten fruit," Flintlock complained. "That pineapple almost took my head off!" Princess Marie-Anne had purchased all the capital's fruit and vegetables, then given them away free to anyone who attended the public execution in Trafalgar Square. Since Londoners hadn't witnessed such an event for more than a century, the resultant throng had brought the city to a standstill. The Britannia Royal Constabulary was stretched to breaking point trying to control the crowds, policemen lining the route from the Tower of London.

"Stop whining," Spatchcock said between mouthfuls of tomato. "This is the first proper food I've had in days. Ripe will do me fine. Besides, I doubt they'll let you be decapitated ahead of schedule, it'd spoil everybody's fun."

By the time their hover-cart reached Trafalgar Square at a quarter to six, both men were soaked in fruit juice and covered with vegetable pulp. Two warders from the Tower had accompanied them on the journey, walking ahead of the cart. They threw buckets of cold water over the condemned pair until both men were clean. Then Spatchcock and Flintlock were marched to the empty plinth in the square's north-west corner, the shackles binding their hands and feet making each step precarious. The former aristocrat kept his eyes on the ground, but Spatchcock scanned their surroundings, taking everything in.

The square was thronged with people, all of them baying for blood. More crowds spilled out of the buildings overlooking the place of execution, chanting and howling abuse. A giant holographic screen was draped over the front of one building so everyone could witness the execution in close-up. Marksmen were stationed at every vantage point, watching the skies intently. Spatchcock nudged his friend. "See? They're still expecting Dante to rescue us. He could be here any minute."

"And dead a minute later," Flintlock said mournfully. "Face it, Spatch. We're doomed."

"Have a little faith! When has the captain ever let us down?"

"Frequently!"

Spatchcock frowned. "Come to think of it, you're right." One of the warders gave them a shove and they stumbled up a flight of stone stairs to stand on the plinth. Waiting for them was the princess in a radiant pink ensemble, and an executioner, clad from head to toe in black, a hood concealing his face.

Spatchcock sidled closer to the executioner. "How's it going, Nikolai? All set to spring your surprise rescue?"

"I don't think so," Marie-Anne snarled, lifting up the hood to show Spatchcock the dull-witted killer underneath. Last time she had been in this position was during the Battle of Britannia, when Dante disguised himself as the executioner to save King Henry from being beheaded. The princess was not making the same mistake twice. "Even if your cowardly comrade is foolish enough to try and save your worthless lives, my sharpshooters will gun him down. Nikolai Dante is as good as dead."

"Is there such a thing?" Spatchcock wondered.

Marie-Anne stroked the blade of the mighty axe held in the executioner's meaty fists. "You'll soon find out, won't you?" The princess's nose wrinkled in distaste. "What is that smell?"

Spatchcock grinned wolfishly. "A hint of things to come."

Penelope was piloting the ambulance south at maximum speed while Dante concentrated on finding out who had hired Boyle and Dobie to assassinate the king. The Crest took a sample of Boyle's DNA from the blood staining the front seat of the hover-vehicle, then created a genetic fingerprint enabling it to pose as the dead bounty hunter. The battle computer hacked its way into the Imperial Net via the ambulance's internal computer systems and ran a search for Boyle's bank accounts. *No matter where he hid his money in the Empire, I should be able to find it. Proving the money was paid by someone wanting the king dead is another matter.*

"Leave it to me," Dante replied. "A little bluffing goes a long way in my experience."

"That explains your alleged success with women," Penelope commented wryly.

He ignored the comment. "How long until we reach London?"

"Fortunately for us, this ambulance is among the faster hover-vehicles in Britannia. Unfortunately, the damage it sustained crashing into the Old Man of Hoy impaired its aerodynamics and this temporary windscreen won't hold forever."

"How long?" Dante demanded.

"Twenty minutes, tops."

"Flintlock and Spatchcock will be dead in less than fifteen."

Penelope grimaced. "I'll do what I can but miracles are beyond even me."

Found it, the Crest announced. *Boyle, Raymond. Banks with the First Imperial Bank of Vanuatu – a somewhat obscure tax haven in the South Pacific. A joint account, shared with Dobie, first name Lewis. A wire transfer for twenty million roubles was paid into the account last week.*

"Where did the money come from?" Dante asked.

Checking... Alas, whoever commissioned the hit has covered their tracks rather well. The funds were originally held in an account controlled by the Britannia civil service. Beyond that, it's impossible to say.

"King Henry's own government paid to have him murdered?"

You misunderstand. The money was embezzled from government funds. What I cannot determine is by whom and how they did it. Dante relayed what the Crest had said to Penelope.

"So Princess Marie-Anne could be behind the hit after all?" she asked.

"Or anyone else within the civil service," Dante replied. "For all we know, it could have been your old boss, F – she would have had little trouble diverting that much money."

"If F wanted someone dead, she would have used the Rippers and then launched a full investigation that conveniently covered up the truth." Penelope studied the vehicle's navigational displays. "We're passing Nottingham."

Dante, I've found something attached to Boyle's account details at the bank. It seems the bounty hunters maintained a virtual safe deposit box there.

"A what, Crest?"

The principle's the same as a normal safe deposit box in a bank vault, but this is for storing valuable digital data – computer files, important communications and documents.

"Can you get access to it?"

Already done. Boyle was meticulous in his record keeping: dates, prices – everything. There's even a file marked McKray. Yes, this is it: confirmation Boyle and Dobie were hired to make the hit on King Henry. The client wanted the assassination to take place while you were present, so you could be a scapegoat as extra insurance for the real killers.

"Who hired them?" Dante demanded. He shook his head when the Crest told him. "There must be some mistake. Check it again."

"Passing Watford," Penelope said, glancing across at Dante. "Well, who ordered the hit?"

"The Crest is confirming that now," he replied, then nodded. "Okay, okay, I believe you. Can you transmit that information to Britannia Intelligence and Scotland Yard? Well, why not?"

A proximity alarm sounded from the ambulance's controls. Penelope looked out of a window and cursed. "Somebody knows we're coming," she said. "There're six Rippers here to meet us."

"The Crest says our transmission is being jammed. It's got proof all of us are innocent, but somebody doesn't want that information getting through," Dante snarled.

"Who is it?" Penelope asked. "Who's behind all of this?"

When Dante told her, she still didn't believe him.

The crowd in Trafalgar Square was getting restless. Everyone had come to see an execution, but instead were being treated to a long, self-aggrandising speech from Princess Marie-Anne. "This woman could bore for Britannia," Flintlock muttered. "It'll almost be a relief when they chop off our heads." A sloppy sound emitted from the posterior of his fellow prisoner. "Heavens above, man! Can't you control yourself?"

Spatchcock shook his head. "I fart when I get nervous. Waiting to be executed isn't doing a lot for my intestines."

"Nor for my nasal membranes," Flintlock replied. "What a way to die! Having my head chopped off in front of millions with the stench spilling from your arse the last thing I ever smell!" A single tear spilled from Flintlock's right eye and his chin wobbled.

His malodorous comrade shuffled a little closer. "Are you crying?"

"N-No. A-absolutely not!"

"Look, since we're at the end, why don't you put me out of my misery, eh? Tell me what you did that was so bad it got you kicked out of the country."

Flintlock glared at Spatchcock. "Do you promise never to tell another living soul?"

"I'll be dead any minute, if her royal bitchiness ever shuts up – who could I tell?"

"All right." The former aristocrat leaned closer to Spatchcock and whispered in his ear. The flatulent runt's eyebrows shot upwards and his mouth dropped open in amazement. When Flintlock finished, his partner in crime looked at him with new-found respect.

"I... I..." Spatchcock spluttered, shaking his head. "I've never heard anything so disgusting, so degrading, so completely and utterly revolting in my life! I'm shocked, honestly, I am shocked! I didn't know you had it in you."

"Remember what you promised!"

"Well, I lied," Spatchcock said. "Now, all we need is Dante to save our ugly asses and then I tell the world what you just told me – you dirty dog!"

The princess finally brought her speech to a close. "Now, I shall hand proceedings over to our royal executioner." A cacophony of cheering came from the crowd as Spatchcock and Flintlock were shoved towards the twin chopping blocks at the front edge of the plinth.

Spatchcock searched the sky hopefully. "Come on, Dante, don't let me down – not now!"

The ambulance was flying less than a metre above the Thames, its hover-engines screaming in protest as Dante piloted the vehicle with reckless abandon. He had swapped places with Penelope, freeing her to shoot at the swarm of Rippers pursuing them. She leaned out of the passenger window, firing her pistols at the murderous hunters on their hover-bikes. Trying to target them was not easy with Dante flinging the ambulance about in the air. "Hold it steady!" she howled. "I can't shoot these bastards if you don't hold it steady!"

"Easier said than done!" Dante shouted back. He pulled back on the controls, sending the vehicle's nose up into the air so it skimmed above one of the bridges crossing the Thames, then flung it back down towards the water. No sooner had he straightened out again than a sailing ship floated directly into their path, forcing an abrupt swerve.

Penelope got lucky with her next shot, exploding the nearest Ripper's engine. The fireball of debris claimed two more Rippers behind it, leaving only three in pursuit, She tried to fire at them with one weapon, then the other, but both clicked repeatedly. "I'm out of ammunition!"

Dante glanced at his mirrors. "Let's see if I can't shake off the last of these bastards." He grinned at Penelope. "You might want to strap yourself in." Once she was secure, Dante wrenched the controls backwards. The ambulance shot underneath Westminster Bridge and then up into the air in a tight arc. But instead of levelling out again, Dante maintained the trajectory.

"These things aren't designed to loop the loop you maniac!" Penelope said, g-force pulling her lips back from her teeth in an involuntary grin. Around them the vehicle was threatening to shake itself apart, glass fragments flying through the air inside.

"Now she tells me!" Dante replied through gritted teeth. The ambulance was upside down but it kept going, starting to plunge towards the Thames. "Hold on, this is going to be close!" Dante snarled, keeping the controls tight to his chest. The ambulance seemed certain to smash into the river's surface but somehow righted itself, once more racing along above the water. Ahead of them the remaining Rippers were looking back, astonished by Dante's death-defying manoeuvre. They didn't notice the barge crossing the Thames in front of them until it was too late. All three flew straight into the ship, exploding in a trinity of fireballs. Dante grinned at his wide-eyed passenger. "You know, I wasn't sure that would work."

Penelope shook her head in disbelief. "I can't decide if you're the bravest man I've ever met or the biggest fool in the Empire."

Probably both, the Crest observed.

Dante slowed the ambulance to a halt, then told Penelope to swap places with him. "Are hover-vehicles required to carry parachutes in case of emergency?"

"Of course, there's one under each seat – why?"

Dante removed the parachute from beneath his position and began strapping it on his back. "You'll have to drop me off over Trafalgar Square, we'll never land this thing close enough."

"Then what?" Penelope asked.

"Knowing the person who hired Boyle and Dobie, they won't be satisfied with leaving the king alive. I'm guessing they'll use the diversion of the public execution to take matters into their own hands. You're Britannia's best secret agent – you have to stop them!"

"What about a last request?" Spatchcock asked, stalling for time. "As condemned men, don't we get a last request? We haven't eaten in days!"

"If you're worrying about losing too much weight, I believe the imminent removal of your heads is, perhaps, a more pressing issue," the princess replied. Those in the crowd who could hear what she was saying laughed a little, but the rest were growing ever more impatient. Marie-Anne nodded to the executioner, who shoved Spatchcock's head on the chopping block next to Flintlock. The prisoners' manacles were attached to a taut chain on the plinth, preventing them from squirming around or escaping the axe when it came.

"That axe isn't sharp enough," Spatchcock complained. "I don't think it's been cleaned since the last time an executioner used it. If the blade isn't sharp enough, we'll be here all night with him hacking away. I don't want him finishing me off with a pocket knife."

"The axe is sharp enough to split hairs," the princess said, "as you will soon discover!" She turned to the crowd and smiled magnanimously. "Do the condemned men have any last words they wish to say before the sentence is carried out?"

"Yes," Flintlock replied. "I'm too young and too pretty to die!"

"You wish," Spatchcock cackled.

"Anything else?" Marie-Anne demanded.

"There was one thing," Spatchcock said. "Did you know there's a madman falling out of the sky towards you?"

The princess sighed. "I didn't think there were still people alive foolish enough to believe that 'look behind you!' misdirection still worked."

"I'll take that as a no. Oh, hi, Dante!"

Marie-Anne spun round but there was nobody behind her. She turned back to face the two prisoners, her expression sour enough to curdle milk.

"Made you look," Spatchcock smirked, winking at her.

"Kill them!" the princess shouted at the executioner. "Kill them now!"

Then the sharpshooters around Trafalgar Square opened fire.

"Your majesty, you should not be exerting yourself like this," Doctor Bhamra insisted, gesturing at the chaos surrounding her. The king had demanded a holographic display for his hospital room, along with a camera crew on standby in case he wished to broadcast a proclamation.

"Nonsense, my dear! How can I be expected to rule if I don't know what's happening in my kingdom?" Henry summoned the pretty young physician closer, so he could whisper in her ear. "This is still my kingdom, isn't it?"

"Yes, your majesty, of course it is."

"Jolly good show!" The king pinched the doctor's buttocks and gave her a friendly wink. "Now, what's on today? Not one of those dreary films about the royal family – can't stand them!"

"It's the public execution," one of the camera crew chipped in, "from Trafalgar Square, Your Highness. Two of the men who tried to kill you are being beheaded."

"Really? I don't remember signing any such decree."

"Your daughter did it, while you were incapacitated," Doctor Bhamra explained.

"Did she now? The cunning little vixen! We'll see about that. Start those cameras!"

• • •

The odds that none of these sharpshooters will hit you or disable your parachute are slightly greater than seventeen thousand to one – against.

"Never tell me the odds, Crest!" Dante shouted, struggling to hear his own words above the volleys of gunfire coming at him from every possible angle. He was dropping towards the place of execution in Trafalgar Square, having jumped out of the ambulance as it passed overhead. "One more minute and I'll be safely on the ground. Those marksmen couldn't hit water if they fell out of a boat."

They may not be able to hit you, but eventually they'll realise your parachute is a considerably larger and easier target, the Crest predicted. Not sooner had it spoken than the sharpshooters shifted aim upwards. *So much for beating the odds.*

Dante's descent began accelerating with each fresh hole put through his parachute. "What I need is something soft to cushion the impact of my landing."

Like everyone else in the square, the executioner was watching the spectacle of Dante's daredevil descent. He found it all but impossible to tear his gaze from the Russian renegade's groin, fully displayed thanks to the wind tugging Dante's kilt upwards. It took a slap across the face from Princess Marie-Anne to get his attention. "Chop off the prisoners' heads now or your head will be next on the block!" Eager to please her, the executioner drew back his axe in the air, preparing to swing it down on Flintlock's scrawny neck. But the sudden arrival of Dante's feet in his face proved something of a distraction. The executioner tipped over backwards, falling on to the blade of his own axe. It sliced neatly through his spinal column, proving just as sharp as the princess had promised.

Dante dropped into a crouch, his bio-blades already extending from each fist. He sliced one sword through the air, severing the ropes and straps linking him to the parachute. The other blade cut apart the manacles holding Spatchcock and Flintlock in place. The two men scrambled to their feet, all too aware of the numerous sharpshooters nearby.

"What took you so long?" Spatchcock asked wryly.

"Traffic was a bitch," Dante replied before turning his attention to the princess. "Well, your royal highness? What have you got to say for yourself?"

Marie-Anne pointed at Dante accusingly. "This is the man who tried to murder my father!" She shouted at the crowd of thousands upon thousands gathered around them. "This is the man who butchered your beloved Queen Mother, Babs!"

"You know I had nothing to do with those attacks, princess. You know who pulled the trigger and you know who paid the assassins. You've known it all from the start, but made sure it happened far enough away from you so you could maintain deniability!"

"Will nobody rid me of these lies, these falsehoods?" the princess screamed. "Marksmen! At my signal, kill this accursed Russian dog and his accomplices where they stand! Ready!"

"Wouldn't this be a good moment to take cover?" Flintlock suggested.

"Aim!"

"I think she fancies me," Dante replied.

Marie-Anne stepped aside, giving all the sharpshooters a clean target. "Fi–"

"Hold that order!" a regal voice boomed around Trafalgar Square from the vast holographic display suspended on the northern side. The crowd dropped to one knee in homage. The familiar face of King Henry smiled down upon his subjects, a mischievous twinkle in his eye. "Hello, everybody!"

"Your Majesty," Dante said, breathing a sigh of relief before joining the others on bended knee. Only the princess remained standing, a pout on her face and both hands on her hips.

"Now, what's all this nonsense about you trying to kill me, Nicola?"

"I don't know, sire," Dante replied.

The king turned away from the camera. "I can't hear what he's saying. Can't you get a microphone pointed at him out there?" Satisfied with whatever reply he got, Henry looked at the camera again. "What were you saying, Nicola?"

"I did not try to kill you, sire – I saved you from the assassin's bullets. I only wish I had been fast enough to save your mother as well."

"Old Babs had a good innings. For what it's worth, I can confirm young Nicola had nothing to do with the attack on me, nor did her chums. I invited Nicola to Britannia to protect me from assassins and that's exactly what she did."

"But, father–" the princess tried to protest.

"Tish and pish, my girl, I'll hear nothing more from you. You've caused enough trouble while I've been laid up. Once this is all over you're going straight back to the Tower. Consider yourself well and truly grounded, my dear!"

"Your Majesty," Dante called out. "Another has been falsely accused of conspiring to assassinate you, a blameless operative from your secret service known as Agent Goodnight. But she possesses evidence that will show the identities of the true killers and the name of the person who hired them to attack you."

Marie-Anne flung herself at Dante, her fingernails flailing the air like a bird of prey's talons. "I'll kill you! I'll kill you," she vowed. But Spatchcock and Flintlock stepped in front of Dante to protect him, keeping the princess a safe distance away.

"The assassins were two bounty hunters named Boyle and Dobie," Dante continued. "Both have since died in violent circumstances, and nobody need weep for them."

"Dashed glad to hear that, Nicola," Henry said. "But who hired these bounders?"

"That was me," another voice cut in from the king's bedside. A gun appeared on the edge of the holographic display's picture aimed at Henry's head. The crowd gasped in horror. Few of them recognised the voice that was threatening the king, but Dante did.

"Why did you do it?" he demanded of the unseen voice. "Why did you hire two bounty hunters to murder the king... Inspector Rucka?"

The inspector stepped closer to the king, putting himself into the picture. He wanted to be certain everyone could see his face at the moment of triumph. "For years I worked my way up through the Britannia Royal Constabulary, proving myself over and over again. But what recognition did I receive for all my hard work? Next to nothing. And why? Because I refused to become one of the silly handshake brigade who still control so much of our life in this once great nation! Finally, I decided enough was enough. I would strike a blow for the decent people of Britannia. I would have the king murdered, so her royal highness would take her rightful place on the throne."

"So why not pull the trigger yourself?" Dante demanded from Trafalgar Square.

"Because I was ambitious and a fool," Rucka replied. "I knew this would be seen as the crime of the century. What better way to ensure my advancement by solving it, proving once and for all my genius as a detective. When the king invited you to Britannia, I knew it was the perfect opportunity. I was foolish because I entrusted the task to two bounty hunters and they let this old man escape them."

"And my daughter knew about all of this?" Henry asked.

"I gave her hints, enough for her to know her time was coming, but not enough for her to incriminate her. She is innocent, for once in her life," the inspector replied.

"Why come out of hiding now?" Dante demanded. "Why tell us all this?"

Rucka smiled. "Because after I murder the king, I will turn the gun on myself. You already have the proof of my guilt, there was no hiding place from that – but I can still rid Britannia of this old fool! He has been an embarrassment to us all for far too long. When he dies, a new era will begin." The inspector pressed the gun against the side of Henry's head. "Goodbye, your majesty – and good riddance."

A single shot rang out, a shot that was heard all across Britannia.

EPILOGUE

"Touch what hurts, admire what's pretty."
– Russian proverb

"Midge bites are painful and irritating, no more so than when they occur on sensitive parts of the anatomy. For example, a single bite to the male genitalia can cause itching, redness and unsightly swelling. In such cases, all sexual activity should be avoided until the swelling has gone and the bites have healed. Certain creams can be helpful in speeding this process, but take care during application not to cause unnecessary arousal as this only leads to further frustration."
– Extract from *The Duffer's Guide to Britannia*, 2670 edition

"I was beginning to think you wouldn't make it in time," Dante said. "I mean, could you have cut it any closer before you put a bullet through Rucka's head?"

"Probably not," Penelope conceded. "There, how does that feel?"

"Better, but now the front is starting to itch again."

"Already? I only just finished putting ointment on there."

Dante shrugged. "Can I help it if I'm extra sensitive below the waist at the moment?"

Two days had passed since the death of Inspector Rucka ended Dante's latest adventure in Britannia. The king had granted royal pardons to all those previously accused of trying to assassinate him. Princess Marie-Anne was back in the Tower of London, still vowing to have her vengeance against Dante, and the money Rucka had embezzled to pay Boyle and Dobie was back in the proper civil service accounts.

To celebrate not being a fugitive anymore, Dante had checked into the bridal suite of London's most expensive hotel. Spatchcock and Flintlock were given the room next door, but had been warned not to disturb their friend. "I've spent the past week being chased, hunted, shot at, bitten by bloodthirsty insects and generally put through the wringer," he told them. "Right now, all I want is a bath, a good meal and a bed to sleep in. Do what you like but don't disturb me! Got it?"

He waited until both men were out of the hotel before calling Penelope on her private line and inviting her over. He had hoped her acceptance signalled a thawing in relations between them at last. His hope had risen further when she arrived with a large tube of cream and a determined look on her face. "Show me your crotch," she said once they were in the bedroom.

"I thought you'd never ask," he replied, stripping off all his clothes in the time it took Penelope to remove her jacket. For once she was out of her ubiquitous catsuit, preferring a short black silk dress over matching stockings, a neat seam running down the back of each leg. She gasped upon seeing the state of his groin. "Impressive, isn't it?" he asked rhetorically.

"Have you been scratching?" she asked sternly.

"Why? Will you promise to give me a spanking if I say yes?"

"Nikolai, you've almost rubbed yourself raw! The swelling is... considerable."

"Well, I don't like to brag."

"That's not what I'm talking about," Penelope snapped. "Lie down on the bed. I'll apply some ointment to the worst

areas and you should start to feel some relief almost immediately."

"Sounds promising," he agreed.

"That's not what I meant and you know it!"

"A boy can always hope, can't he?"

Penelope settled down on the bed beside him, then quickly
stood up again. "And keep your wandering fingers to yourself!"

"Spoilsport," Dante said, sulkily removing his hands from
beneath her.

"That's better," she said, sitting down once more. Penelope turned the tube upside down above his groin and began
squeezing the thick white cream all over him. After emptying half the ointment out, she cast aside the tube and began
gently massaging the cream into his swollen areas.

"Oh, yes," Dante sighed. "I'm feeling relieved already." He
winked at her playfully. "You never told me whether you got
any midge bites while we were on Hoy."

"A few," Penelope admitted, her hands stroking the cream
back and forth on the most swollen area of his groin. "Those
bloody things always bite you in the most inconvenient
places."

"I hope you haven't been scratching."

"Maybe a little."

Dante smiled. "Let's see if I can guess where."

Spatchcock and Flintlock were returning from a hard day's
drinking in the taverns of London when they heard a terrible moaning sound from Dante's suite. "Bojemoi, it sounds
as if he's in agony!" the shorter man said, leaning closer to
the door.

"Dante told us not to disturb him under any circumstances, Spatch!"

"But what if he's dying in there?"

Flintlock shrugged. "I guess we could have a peek, see if
he's okay."

"Me first!" Spatchcock was peering through the keyhole before Flintlock could object.

"What is it? What's happening?"

"I think Dante is attempting the entrance exam for the Britannia secret service." Spatchcock muttered under his breath. "But I'm not sure he'll ever get in that way."

ABOUT THE AUTHOR

David Bishop was born and raised in New Zealand, becoming a daily newspaper journalist at eighteen years old. He emigrated to Britain in 1990 and was editor of the *Judge Dredd Megazine* and then *2000 AD*, before becoming a freelance writer. His previous novels include three starring Judge Dredd (for Virgin Books) and four featuring Doctor Who (for Virgin and the BBC). Black Flame's most prolific author, he also writes non-fiction books and articles, audio dramas, comics and has been a creative consultant on three forthcoming video games. If you see Bishop in public, do not approach him – alert the nearest editor and stand well back.